Visions of Wysteria

Tales of Wysteria: Book 1

TABLE OF CONTENTS

Content Warning:
This book has depictions of child abuse, homelessness, and
starvation.

PROLOGUE

"Princess Feather Butt!" Dezmara's tiny hand pointed toward a small dot in the distance. At first, Anazaraine wasn't sure if she was right, but it wasn't long before the indigo bird came fully into view. Relief swept through Anazaraine. She had been waiting for the latest news for several weeks now and had begun to fear the worst.

When Zinnia finally came within reach, Anazaraine stretched out her arm, and the bird, which was only the size of her fist, folded her huge indigo wings and landed softly on her forearm. While waiting to deliver her message, she groomed herself, paying special attention to the patch of light blue feathers that stood out against the deep violet of the rest of her tail.

Not wanting them to hear whatever news her messenger bird may bring, Anazaraine reminded the children to stay close to their small cabin and went inside to receive the message. Once safely inside, Zinna spoke, but it was the Queen's voice that came out. "Strichnier has taken the castle. I fear it's over for us. Whatever happens, tell my children I love them. And keep them safe."

Suddenly, the voice coming from her beloved bird changed, growing deeper. "Sent your little pet to spy on me did you? I'll find you, my love. And I will have those children." A chill ran through Anazaraine's heart at the sound of Strichnier's voice, so different from the voice of the man she had once loved; and it felt like ages ago that he had been that gentle, caring man once known as Eryk.

Anazaraine dropped to the ground, her stomachs heaving. Strichnier had defeated the Royal Army and the King and Queen were taken. Wysteria had fallen. Her best hope was gone. And he had seen the bird. For all she knew, someone had followed it to her and would be here any minute now. Breathing heavily, she picked herself up and began pacing their little cabin. She knew she didn't have much time to decide what to do. How could she possibly keep the children safe?

Briefly, Anazaraine wondered if she should go after Strichnier herself. She was once the most powerful sorceress after all. But Strichnier had become stronger. It was a long shot, but maybe if she managed to sneak up on him…

But, could she do it? Could she destroy the man she had once loved? By taking the kids to safety, instead of to him as they had planned, she had committed an unforgivable betrayal. She had known at the time there would be no going back. Eryk was long gone, but even knowing that, could she face him in battle? Her heart ached at the thought and gave credence to her fear of weakness.

Looking out the window, Anazaraine saw Kithian swinging from the trees, while little Dezmara tried her best to climb up one so she could swing too. The young Princess was a stubborn one. Although she fell several times, she kept trying to get up the tree. These children were resilient, but how long would they survive if Strichnier killed her? Their parents were taken and who knew what Strichnier planned to do with them. Or what he had already done. Anazaraine was all the Prince and Princess had left. The Queen had told her to keep them safe no matter what happened and that was what she intended to do.

Bit by bit, she pieced together a plan. It was a great risk, and she had no idea if it was even possible. But if it was, who could accomplish it if not her? She stood quickly and looked around for something, anything she could use. Glancing at the children outside again, her eyes fell on the necklace draped around Dezmara's neck. The tri-moon pendant looked ordinary to most people, but Anazaraine had been there for the Rite of Invigoration that imbued it with power. Every child received a talisman at birth. On their first birthday, this special ceremony filled them with power that could be tapped into throughout their lives. This one was a royal heirloom that had been passed down for generations, gaining more power with each new bearer. If there was anything that might work for what she needed, it was this.

After composing herself, Anazaraine walked outside where the children were playing in front of their little cabin. "Anwen, come play with us!" The children called out to her together.

When Anazaraine had first taken the children, she gave them memories of her being their mother, but after a day of hearing the word 'mommy' it became too much to bear and she changed the memory where they would still call her Anwen, the false name she had used under her husband's orders to hide while in the Queen's employment. It was safer for her heart if she didn't start to think of these children as her own. Against her own will, she had grown to love them dearly and had to admit she was enjoying their time in the little cabin, but the children had grown restless. They asked about the outside world all the time. They would beg to go with her whenever she left to get supplies, but she was afraid to let them leave.

With her mind made up, Anazaraine called Dezmara to her using the nickname she had given her after arriving at the cabin. Stooping down to look into the small child's golden eyes, she spoke gently. "I need to borrow your necklace, Mara. Kith, can you come over here too? I've decided to take you both with me when I leave the woods today!" She tried to sound excited so the children would think they were going on a fun adventure. When they immediately came running, she knew it had worked. She brought them inside to pack a quick bag for each of them, which only added to their excitement. Not only were they leaving, but they would be gone overnight. For children who had no memory of leaving this little bit of woods, that was an exciting prospect.

Once the bags were packed and she had said a silent goodbye; not just to the cabin, but to their entire world, Anazaraine gathered the children around her. Kneeling on the ground, she focused intently for several minutes. It was essential that she used exactly the right words in her incantation. When she finally thought she had put together the perfect phrase, she paused and stared at the world around her. She looked up and took in the brilliance of the red sun against the stark white sky, and realized this may be the last time she would see Wysteria.

Anazaraine took the children in her arms and, holding out

Dezmara's necklace, vocalized her spell. Giving it the enchantments required her to bind the three of them to it. Her grasp on both of the children in her arms tightened. With one last look around her, she shouted the last words of the incantation that would take them away to their new lives.

As soon as the magic manifested, Anazaraine realized it was a far more powerful spell than she had expected. The power drained from the amulet quickly, and it wasn't long before she could feel her energy being drained away. Panic struck as she began to feel weaker and weaker. Teleporting all over the world required little more than a touch of strength, but this was different, something unheard of. No one in the history of time had attempted to do what she was doing now. It would be her greatest achievement if only she could pull it off.

When the ground began to swirl around her she knew she had done it. The children squirmed and she gripped them more firmly, trying to soothe them with a few loving words before they were ripped away from the world of sanity and thrown into a frenzy of darkness and chaos.

CHAPTER ONE: AUGUST

✳   Kith   ✳

The putrid smells coming from the can made me want to turn and run, but I knew I couldn't. I took a deep breath, held it, and dug into the decaying trash. Halfway down, I came upon an unrecognizable chunk of meat that didn't smell as horrible as the rest. Shoving it into my bag, I returned to the search. There was not much left but a couple of bruised apples; grabbing them quickly, I replaced the lid. Time to move on.

Keeping my tail tucked close to my body, I followed the shadows toward the next house. If seen from a distance, hopefully, I would look like a normal child. I reached the edge, crouching deeper into the shadows while I made sure the coast was clear. Experience taught me that getting caught was not in my best interest. I sniffed the air for signs of danger, but the stench of rotting garbage, still clinging to my skin, was all I could smell.

After one last glance down the alley before preparing to sprint across the space, I saw him on the other side. There was no mistaking the menacing stance, especially his hand on the knobby, twisted cane. The dark hair that often blocked his face when he was raging was pulled back with a leather strap. The foggy crystal eye with four long scars crossing it faced my way as he turned, and I forced myself not to scream. The search party must have spread out, and it would only be a few short moments before I was caught.

Waiting until they were all out of sight, I turned my back to the town and ran as fast as I could into the woods, hoping Mara had kept hidden as I told her to. After what felt like forever, our hut came into view. It was a small enclosure set up against a tree and wasn't obvious to anyone not looking for it.

Nearing the hut, I began to whisper, "Mara." It only took her a couple of seconds to emerge, golden eyes full of fear. Grabbing our other bag from the hut before taking her hand, I knew no explanation was needed. We ran wordlessly together, sparing no thought for direction, just focused on getting as far away from them as possible.

After hours of running, we finally collapsed to the ground in exhaustion.

"Do you think we should camp in the tree?" Mara panted. "That might hide us better."

Our muscles burned, but with the help of our claws and tails, we managed to climb high into its branches before allowing ourselves to rest.

*   Mara   *

Running. All I remember was running and climbing a tree and then suddenly there was his face. He was in the tree. His men were all around me. Grabbing me. Pulling me down. The scream barely escaped my lips, then Kith was there shaking me awake and holding me until I was fully convinced Ducar was nowhere to be seen.

Darkness was all around and I knew, once again, I woke Kith long before he had time for a good night's rest. I always felt so bad waking him up like that but felt solace in knowing he was there for me.

Kith stayed on my branch until he fell asleep again. Fighting sleep, not wanting to wake him up again, I tried thinking of anything other than Ducar, but it was in vain, and my thoughts kept circling back to his hands reaching out for me. I didn't realize I had fallen asleep again until I jolted awake with Ducar's fake eye burning in my mind.

Kith asked, "Are you hungry?" Attempting to hide a yawn. He had the grace to pretend I hadn't just woken him up again.

Of course, I was. We both were.

Kith swung down to the branch holding our supplies and pulled some old meat and apples out of the pack. I watched as his fingernails extended into sharp claws an inch long to cut away bruised parts of the apple he held. He then sliced what was left of the apple into small slivers and handed it to me before raking his claws across the meat, cutting it into bite-sized pieces. By the time he started cutting up his apple, I was almost finished eating.

Something about this process always mesmerized me. I had my own claws, of course, but I had never met anyone besides Kith and me who did. It was part of what made us freaks. Everyone else looked at our abnormalities feeling fear or hatred but watching Kith do such a simple task, I just couldn't understand their worries. We survived the same way anyone did and had all the same human instincts and morals, we weren't that different. Although we looked different, we were only kids trying to survive. My brother had never used his claws to hurt anyone. Except for Ducar. Ducar was a special case, and no one could blame Kith for the things he did to get us away from him.

Finishing our food quickly, we decided to get moving again. I sensed Kith getting into one of his dark moods, so I forced myself to try to lighten things up a little. Using my claws to scramble halfway up to the next low branch before jumping, I launched toward it. Grabbing it, I wrapped my tail around the branch and then swung back and forth until gaining enough momentum to swing myself to the next tree. For a short instant, I flew.

Laughing excitedly, I called, "I bet I can swing farther than you!"

Kith's face lit up in an instant. I always knew the surest way to brighten his mood was brightening my own first. He let it get to him too much when he thought there was anything wrong with me.

"I don't know, Mara, my tail is longer!" Kith replied tauntingly, before making his way up the tree right beside mine and swinging himself to the next one. He was right, of course, his tail was longer, so he crossed long distances between trees and moved faster. It was a marvel I kept up.

Before long, we were trying new techniques to get from branch to branch. I found that curling my whole body into a ball right at the moment I swung highest in the air and then reaching out with my tail for the next branch was the best way to cross long distances. The only problem was, all the spinning made me dizzy.

After a while, I got a little too dizzy and missed the branch I was reaching for, tumbling to the ground.

"Mara!" Kith yelled, running to me. I saw the worry all over his face, but couldn't help breaking out into hysterical laughter. It hurt, of course, but it was so much fun.

Kith's expression turned to confusion and finally to humor and he began laughing as well. "You're lucky you didn't hurt yourself!" he said, thoroughly examining me to make sure his statement was, in fact, true.

"It was only a short fall, nothing to worry about. Besides, if I pulled it off that would have been the longest jump!"

"Oh, I don't think so!" We bantered back and forth while walking through the trees. My fall hurt quite a bit, so I walked slower than normal.

We spent the rest of the day moving slowly but steadily through the trees, not caring much about direction. There was enough food from Kith's trip into town the day before to last us through another day at least, so we weren't too worried about finding another town just yet.

*   Kith *

Had they not been so familiar, the screams tearing apart the air would have terrified me. The actions came so naturally to me now that I could have done them in my sleep. I could have, but Mara was too important to me not to focus on her one hundred percent.

Wiping the sleepiness from my eyes, I turned to wrap my arms around her, my tail circling the branch to hold us in place. Mara's face buried itself in my chest as I crooned to her and promised we were safe; wishing I could promise her we would remain that way, but I don't make promises I'm not positive I can keep. Somehow they kept finding us. It seemed settling down was never going to be a possibility, but as sad as that made me, it was far better than going back to the life we had.

In my tenderest voice, I asked her, "Which dream was it?" I hoped that if she talked through the dreams and memories with me enough times they would go away. Neither of us had slept a full night since we escaped several months before.

As she started out describing, in a small, scared voice, images of that night came into my mind.

We had overstayed our welcome and people in the town were getting bored of the freaks. The show that night had been almost empty, and Ducar was not happy about it. For some reason, Ducar blamed everything that went wrong on Mara and me, even though we were his big money-bringers. Mostly Mara. He seemed to enjoy hurting her.

After the people dispersed, I was locked in our cage. Watching was my punishment. Gold chains were attached to the floor outside our cage and coiled in a dangerous loop. My stomach tightened in fear at the sight of them.

Helplessly, I watched Ducar begin chaining Mara up, limiting her ability to move. He'd never chained her like this before, and they seemed to hurt her on contact. The visible pain from her bindings didn't stop him from administering his usual beatings, though.

With a sneer, he snarled, "We'll be in a new town tomorrow, and you better perform your best. You still won't be eating for a while, of course, but I haven't yet decided for how long."

He had never had her perform without food before, and I sensed a coming change for the worse. Whenever one of us was denied food, the other was forced to eat in front of us, as if it was a personal show, and if we refused, the punishments got much worse.

While Ducar was hitting her, Mara's golden eyes locked on mine and she silently cried. Brave little Mara never made any noise during the attack, she just looked into my eyes. Even without her saying anything, I could see the fear in her eyes from the changes to her punishments.

She was left there for the next day and given nothing to eat or drink. I was left in the cage and given a large meal I would normally have been glad to devour. When I tried to sneak something for Mara, Ducar threatened her with another beating. The whole time she was in the chains they seemed to cause her pain, but she didn't say much.

Finally, he released her from the chains and kicked her toward our cage. She was so weak she could barely walk, and he kicked at her with each step she took toward me. I gathered her in my arms and held her gently to not hurt her bruises. I didn't want to cause her more pain. She slumped in my arms unmoving all day while the train moved.

When we stopped, Beatrice was almost instantly at our cage with food and water. She held Mara in her lap and fed her. Once she had eaten her fill, Beatrice rocked her and sang softly, while Mara entwined her hands in her beard. Ever since she was a baby, Beatrice's beard had been a comfort to Mara. I think that's one of the reasons Beatrice doted on her as much as she did.

After several minutes, Beatrice told Mara it was time to get ready for her performance. She'd have to wow the crowd to please Ducar and prevent a repeat of the punishment.

Mara's performance that night was one of the best she had ever done, and Ducar was pleased. He even let us leave our cage and join the other freaks for the celebration. I think it was because he wanted us to notice the fresh purple bruises on Beatrice's dark brown skin, but she refused to acknowledge them.

When Mara finished talking, I held her close; my finger lightly tracing the three moons on her temple before moving to the diamond of flowers that encased them. We had no clue how we had these matching designs on our faces, but even though they had caused us many problems, Mara was comforted by the idea that they connected us. The fact that mine was at the top side of my forehead and hers was on her temple didn't change anything.

As I calmed her, I wished silently; not for the first time, that I could remove all the painful memories from her. There were too many of them for a child that wasn't even eight, yet. Knowing that was impossible, I silently vowed never to let Ducar get her back. It had taken many years to free us, and he had caught us once. It hadn't been pretty. Now he was angrier than ever since that was when I scratched out his eye.

After taking some time to rest, we set off. We had walked most of the day before we came to the outskirts of another town. With a few days of walking between us and the town I spotted

Ducar in, I figured it should be safe to scavenge some food before moving on. Knowing we probably wouldn't remain close to this town for a few days like we normally did, I decided to plan my path carefully to find as much food as possible.

The sun hadn't gone down yet, so Mara and I climbed a tree and positioned ourselves to be able to view the town without being seen. People watching could be entertaining, and getting an idea of the layout would help me find the best spots for food faster.

Mara liked to make up stories about the people she saw, and while I listened I spotted a bakery, a butcher, and several fruit trees surrounding the well. This town showed a lot of potential, it was a shame we couldn't stay nearby.

By the time sunset began, my path was plotted, so Mara and I leaned back and watched the colors play across the sky. Even though we were always outdoors, we rarely had time to enjoy the beauty of a sunset or sunrise. A part of me was still very concerned about the possibility of Ducar being close, but I let most of myself relax and watch the show. One benefit to sitting up there and resting was that I felt fairly certain Ducar was not already in the town, and I didn't see any signs of a camp nearby. Mara snuggled up against me and sighed with contentment. These small moments of peace were so rare, but incredible, especially with the high cost they had come at.

Once it was dark, I prepared myself for my job. We watched until the town's people were all indoors, and then I whispered for Mara to stay put and quiet before I silently dropped from the tree.

I found the entrance to my planned path with ease. The first cans I searched through had nothing worthwhile, but the next few had some vegetables that had been discarded. They weren't much, but I stuck them in one of the bags.

In the next few cans, I only gathered a few small chunks of unfinished meat and some partially moldy bread. The fruit trees were coming up, though, so I quickly checked my surroundings before climbing my way up to the top of the first one. Whoever had harvested the tree had done a good job, it took me several minutes to find the last two pears that were still attached. Swinging from tree to tree, I searched as quietly as I could for more fruit. By the time I dropped back to the ground to visit the well, I had added three more pears, five apples, and a handful of peaches to my pack.

The bakery had a couple of stale loaves that were wrapped in paper in the trash. Although they weren't fresh, they were cleaner than a lot of food that I had gathered in the past. With the addition of the loaves, my first pack was full. My chances of filling the other pack lay in the butcher's shop and a few more trash cans.

The next can I reached was almost empty, and the one after that only had a few partially rotten vegetables. My planned route was almost to its end, and I still had one empty bag. I fought off growing desperation and moved on to the cans outside the butcher's shop. These were the ones I was most anticipating, as stocking up on a good supply of meat would be the best thing to keep us going.

I dug through the can eagerly, but all it had were a couple of old chunks of meat and some fat that was trimmed off meat that had been sold. Disappointment hit me like a punch to the stomach. I looked to see if there was another can that I had missed, but there wasn't.

As I looked around me from the shadows, I noticed that the shop looked completely unprotected and the door easy to open. In all our time on the run, I had never broken into a building to take food. I cautiously approached the door, unsure if I was willing to open it.

When I got closer, I could smell the meat inside. My mouth watered, and I knew we would need all the meat we could carry. Before I could second guess myself, my claws were investigating the lock, figuring out how to open the door. It didn't take me long to slip inside.

The shop was completely dark, so dark that even my eyes needed a minute to adjust. There were counters where meat was displayed. On top, a scale and wrapping papers sat among other items I didn't recognize. Knowing I couldn't be in there long, I scooped up as much out of the shelves as I could, shoving it into any empty spots I could find in the already full pack. Only dried meat was on the shelves, but my nose led me to a door that opened to some steps.

The air was much cooler down there, and I found plenty of fresh meat. My first bag was already packed full, so after wrapping the meat in the papers from the counter, I filled the second bag from the cellar. Now that both bags were full and heavy, I knew it was time to return to Mara and rest for the night.

On my way out of the store, I grabbed another few slices of dried meat. Having a snack before sleeping would be nice, and we wouldn't have to break into the food we would need on the run. Retracing my steps back to the tree, I kept my eyes and ears alert to be sure I wasn't spotted. Mara looked at me silently at first, but I could tell she wanted to say something.

"Here, Mara. I figured we could eat some before settling down for the night." I handed her half of the dried meat and started chewing on mine.

"Kith, I've never seen you go inside before." Her voice was soft but full of all sorts of emotions. It was hard to tell if she was more disappointed or grateful.

"This was the first time. The trash cans were so empty, and I could smell all the meat inside." I wasn't sure which of us I was trying to reassure more, as I said, "I knew we'd need it, Mara. I don't know when we'll be able to stop again."

She let out a little sigh. "I know. I just wish we didn't have to steal it." She paused for a minute before beginning to eat. "I am glad that you were able to get a lot, though."

We finished eating in silence, then Mara snuggled against me and we drifted off to sleep.

*   Mara   *

I wasn't sure how to feel when I saw Kith breaking into one of the buildings in the town. At first, I was consumed with worry, as I had never seen him go inside before and was afraid he would be caught and killed. He had been in there for so long that I had begun to panic, thinking for sure he was in some kind of trouble. Then, when he slipped out with two full bags, the relief that flowed through me was overwhelming and my eyes began to water. I held to that feeling of relief until he was back with me in the trees. When he handed me some dried meat, though, it was hard to contain the disappointment of having stolen someone else's food.

I tried to conceal the emotion because I knew Kith was only doing this to survive. We needed the meat, and I didn't blame Kith at all for providing for us in the only way he could. Being only two years older than me, Kith was forced to take up the role of provider when we left Beatrice behind. It was obvious it hadn't been easy for him, but he tried hard to hide his struggles.

No, after everything, it was Ducar I blamed. Before this, we had always lived off of the scraps that no one wanted anymore, but because Kith spotted Ducar, we had to take what we could carry and keep moving. If Ducar would only leave us alone, we would not have to stoop to stealing other people's food.

I couldn't stop my mind from drifting back to when I had taken Ketzia's necklace.

"It was foolish to steal from a fortune teller," Beatrice said as her hand reached out.

She didn't have to tell me what she was talking about. I pulled the oval pendant out from under my dress and took it off. With a pout, I handed it over. Ketzia had the most beautiful jewelry and I didn't think she would have missed one item.

"Mara, you shouldn't take things that aren't yours. Even if you think the other person has plenty to share, you should always ask. Otherwise, you risk hurting the other person and ultimately yourself."

I looked at her in confusion. "How will taking pretty things hurt me?"

"No one trusts a thief, darling. And when people can't trust you, they eventually decide they don't want you around. Being outcast by the ones you love hurts deeply. I don't want that for you."

There was a pain in her eyes I couldn't understand. Reaching up, I ran my tiny fingers through her beard, the light purple standing out among the

Sighing inwardly, I took a bite of the meat. Despite my mixed feelings about it, the food was delicious. Far better than a lot of what we got. It would be great living off of this for a while. Kith had done well with the options he was given, and I knew he did what he did for me and I would not judge him for his actions. I didn't believe Beatrice would either. She always said his most important job was to take care of me. Sometimes, that meant hard choices had to be made.

Snuggling up against him, I was grateful for the warmth he provided. Sleep came quickly, and before I knew it, I was staring right at Ducar. He wore his typical sneer and his long thin nose was inches from mine, so close the ends of his thick oily black hair rested on my shoulders. He was yelling at me, spit flying everywhere. Inching backward, I tried to keep my face steady, knowing that Kith was close, watching, and I had to pretend I was brave for his sake. I tried to remember what it was I had done this time. Ducar was getting closer and closer to me and I just kept moving backward.

Suddenly, I woke to the sensation of falling, and Kith grabbing me by the arm. I was in the tree again, and I had leaned back enough that I was almost off the branch. Kith was staring at me, with concern all over his face.

"It was Ducar," I admitted sheepishly. "He was right there. Getting closer and closer."

Kith held me close until I was able to calm down. He then insisted we sleep on the ground for the rest of the night, just in case.

Again, Ducar was there, but this time he was standing several feet away, watching me sleep. I could sense him before I opened my eyes. He watched me for a minute with the same sneer as always before he walked away laughing menacingly. "I've got you this time," I thought I heard him whisper.

had just walked out of. Then, the room came more to light and I could see Kith in the far corner lying wide awake in our cage. Ducar walked in with Jaxon, the one they called The Lizard Man because of his green and blue scaled skin, and began shaking the bars around us.

"Get up you little devils!" he yelled. "You'll pay for what you did!"

I remembered this particular night now. There had been a show earlier that day, and one of the little boys in town had wandered into our tent, wanting to play with us. Kith and I had been telling him about life with the freaks when suddenly a woman walked in, his mother, yelling at the boy to get away from us. She found Ducar and told him all sorts of things about how to handle his child freaks and how we needed to stay away from her son before we infected him. As if just by touching us, her son would shrink, turn purple, and grow a tail.

Ducar, of course, was furious. The whole town had heard this woman yelling at him, and it was humiliating. He had shut Kith and me away in our cage and told us he would deal with us later.

He opened the door to the cage and yelled at me to get against the wall. He then brandished a long stick. This was the first time he had used a stick instead of his hands.

Kith, of course, was screaming, so Ducar pulled a handkerchief out of his pocket and shoved it in his mouth to shut him up. Then he turned to me, stick in hand, and began the torment.

The stick stung with each blow. I let out a small gasp of pain each time he struck me. After the third hit, as Ducar was rearing back for one more blow, suddenly Beatrice was there. She ran in front of me with her strong dark arms stretched out shielding me from Ducar.

"That's enough," she said in a fierce tone.

Beatrice was a large woman, but still, Ducar towered over her. He paused for a moment, seeming to debate his next move before he reared the stick back again and struck her square across the face. The blow was so hard the stick snapped in two. "You don't tell me when she's had enough!" he screamed. A few of the other freaks had poked their heads in now, curious about the commotion. Dylan, the contortionist, ran to Beatrice and pulled her out of the way. She struggled, but the strike seemed to have dazed her.

Then, Ducar turned to Jaxon and yelled at him to get him another stick. With the new stick in hand, Ducar continued the beatings with a fury. He went mad with it, just hitting and hitting so fast I barely had time to *breathe between blows. I looked into Kith's eyes and saw that they were streaming with tears. Each blow sent his body revolting as though it was him who was being hit.*

Finally, Dylan stood from where he had been tending to Beatrice, and quietly stated, "You're going to kill her if you keep this up. Then you'll have real trouble on your hands. Far worse than the mockery of one small town, I would say."

Ducar turned in a state of fury, but as he looked into Dylan's chestnut eyes he lost his steam. "Clean her up then," he spat before stalking out the door.

Dylan came to me then and lifted me. I could barely move through all the pain, my limp limbs hung loose as he brought me to my cage and set me on the ground. "I must lock you up so he thinks I've done my duty, but drink this first," he whispered, pulling a vial of strange purple liquid from his pockets. "It will help your wounds."

I didn't understand why Dylan would help me. He had always hated us, but I didn't have the strength to oppose so I drank the purple liquid and quickly drifted to sleep.

That was the first time I had heard the voice. It was a man, and he spoke to me in soothing tones telling me everything would be alright. He told me he would get me out of there as soon as he could, but I had to hold on just a little longer. I had no idea who it was. Just my imagination dreaming up a savior, most likely.

I felt my whole body shaking in urgency and was confused at first by the sensation, but I woke sharply to Kith sitting over me shaking me almost violently and yelling at me to wake up. As soon as he saw my eyes open his body drooped in relief as he grabbed me up in a hug.

"You were screaming so much and I couldn't wake you! I've been shaking you for ages! I tried everything!" His voice was a soft sob.

I was still gasping from the shock of it all as I assured him I was awake and okay. Nightmares were a constant occurrence for me, but I had never had one so vivid and Kith had never had trouble waking me before. I realized I was sweating and yet I felt cold all over. I let Kith hold me until we had both calmed and then

I laid my head in his lap as he played with my hair.

I had almost forgotten about the voice that used to speak to me. Always, after my beatings, Dylan would give me the purple liquid. He was right about it helping my wounds, but I never figured out what it was. It helped ease me to sleep, and every time I slept after having drunk it, I heard the voice. He would talk to me as I slept, telling me of the new life I would have with him just as soon as he could figure out how to get me out of there. I asked who he was, but he refused to tell me, saying it was too dangerous for me to know now, but after he saved me I would know everything.

At first, I thought it was just a dream and no man was coming to save me, but then he was always there telling me to keep holding on, and that he would come for me soon. I had asked Dylan about it once. When he gave me the purple liquid, I asked him if he knew the man who spoke through the drink he gave me. He looked at me like I had gone crazy and told me I must not give in to the craziness that was trying to break free. He said he knew my situation was hard, but I couldn't let my mind be taken over.

That was when I decided not to tell Kith. I didn't want him to think I had gone crazy like Dylan did. Kith already had a hard enough time watching the beatings, I didn't want him to think I was losing my mind too, so I had never mentioned it again. I tried to tell myself it was only a dream, but I never could fully shake it. Even after the escape, I wondered if he would realize we were alone and maybe he would come to save us.

For a while, I had watched for him, thinking that maybe he was there all along just waiting for the perfect chance to get us. But he never came, and I realized how silly I had been. I was glad then that I hadn't told Kith about him. He must have been a dream caused by whatever was in the healing purple drink that Dylan gave me. Maybe that was just how it worked; it healed your wounds and gave you comforting words to help you feel better. There had never been any sign of a man coming to save us, and I was certain now that there never would be.

There would be no more sleeping that night for either of us. The shock was too much, and the dream had left a bad omen in the air that I couldn't shake.

✳   Kith   ✳

I had never had such a hard time waking Mara up from a nightmare before. Even while stroking her hair and trying to soothe her, I couldn't quiet the panic inside me. I knew neither of us was going to sleep more any time soon.

We sat like that for several minutes, trying to dispel the foreboding feeling the night had caused. We needed to move, but I felt sluggish. When I shifted slightly, Mara lifted her head. Her eyes were wary, but alert.

"We should be moving, Mara. Maybe it'll help." I brushed a lock of hair out of her face and managed a small smile.

Mara silently got to her feet and we grabbed some meat to munch on, then shouldered our bags. I wished there was time to cook some of the fresh meat, but I wanted to get moving. Since it had lifted her spirits before, I decided we should move through the trees instead of along the ground.

We only made it a few trees before Mara suddenly halted and gripped my arm, her face a mask of complete terror. Motioning to be quiet she pointed, looking in the same direction my heart instantly sank into my stomach and began thundering ferociously. Several trees ahead of us were Ducar and his men. If we hadn't decided to move through the branches, they would have already seen us.

My first instinct was to turn and run back the way we had just traveled, but Ducar was headed that way, so he'd still be right on our tails. It would be best to go the direction he had just come from, as long as we weren't seen.

Glancing over, I saw Mara was starting to tremble and knew that staying still and letting them pass beneath us would not be a good idea.

Gently placing my hand on her shoulder I mouthed, "We need to move." while pointing to our left. If we moved out of

Ducar's line of sight, we would have a better chance to get behind them and run.

"They're close. I can feel it." Ducar motioned for his men to spread out and they all quieted their movements, almost disappearing. This wasn't going to be easy.

Moving slowly along our branch, we leaped softly to the closest tree. Once we got to the trunk we were able to hide behind it as we climbed higher. Ducar had only known us to travel on the ground, so no one was looking up, but I knew making any sound would be costly.

We continued in that direction until Ducar's men were just behind us. Every once in a while, they made a slight sound alerting us to their locations. It seemed Ducar was becoming more frustrated and desperate. When I chanced a look back, Ducar was under the tree we had just been sleeping in, holding something I couldn't identify in his hands.

I could hear him saying something about us being close, but I couldn't make out everything from that distance.

"How does he know where we were?" Mara was pale and her eyes widened.

"I don't know. He probably doesn't, he just ended up there." I didn't fully believe it, but I couldn't let her know that. "Mara, they're not going to stay over there long. We have to move away, and fast."

Moving in the direction Ducar had been coming from, our only hope was that he wouldn't think to backtrack. Scrambling through the tree branches as quickly as we could; what had been a fun race a few days ago was now a race for our lives. I heard Ducar's men getting louder, but couldn't tell if they were following us, and couldn't risk slowing down to look for them.

CHAPTER TWO: SEPTEMBER

*   Mara   *

After seeing Ducar, we ran through the trees for hours before Kith finally called for me to stop. It seemed as if we had been running for a lifetime, but I still felt like Ducar was right behind us. Panting heavily, we waited until we had caught our breath before opening the packs to get some food.

"There isn't much fresh meat left," Kith sighed. "I don't think we should make a fire to cook what we have, but it won't last much longer."

"I guess we'll just have to eat the dried meat for tonight," I said consolingly, "maybe we will be able to cook it tomorrow."

We ate the dried meat in silence, not the most exciting meal, but after running for so long, I didn't care what I ate just as long as I had food.

When it was time for bed, Kith kept insisting we sleep on the ground because of my near-fall nights before.

"He'll find us if we're on the ground! We're safer in a tree!" I insisted, but Kith would hear none of it.

"You're not safe if you fall out of a tree and hurt yourself."

I reluctantly gave in and we slept on the ground. At first, we just lay there, neither of us able to close our eyes out of fear. After struggling for some time, Kith suggested we take turns with one sleeping while the other kept watch. Of course, I knew that he meant for me to sleep while he watched, so I countered by saying I would take the first watch. Kith refused my offer and after a small argument, we came to the agreement that he would take the first watch and promise to wake me in a few hours.

We spent two nights taking turns sleeping before I accidentally dozed off during a watch. After Kith woke me up from my nightmare, I was flooded with an overwhelming sense of disappointment in myself. I knew Kith could tell, but I didn't want him trying to make me feel better about it. My irresponsibility put us in horrible danger.

"We've been running like crazy for a long time, Mara. This just shows how exhausted you were. Neither of us can keep going like this without enough sleep. We'd be too weak to do anything if Ducar did find us." Kith said soothingly.

Reluctantly agreeing that he was right, I allowed him to comfort me. After some discussion, we decided that the less time spent on the ground not moving the better, but we both needed sleep, so the taking turns stopped.

A few days after seeing Ducar, I spotted a cluster of green fist-sized balls in a tree. "Kith, what do you think those are?" I asked, pointing. "It could be food!"

Kith looked at the balls and shrugged. "Doesn't hurt to find out!" He said before scrambling up the tree with me right behind him.

Looking closer, we saw the balls were split open slightly, revealing what looked like a large nut inside. Each grabbing one we settled down on a branch to peel off the casing. Excited, I bit into the nut and quickly realized it was not edible. My teeth hurt from the effort and it didn't taste very good.

Laughing at the sour face I made, Kith tossed his away. "I guess that answers that question," he sighed. We sat in the tree for a while, deciding now was as good a time as any for a break. Several minutes later I heard rustling below us.

Tensing up, I put a finger to my lips and pointed. We sat in uneasy silence for a few moments before a squirrel shuffled out of a bush and over to the brown shell Kith had thrown on the ground. Relieved, we watched as he easily bit his way through the casing and withdrew a small lumpy nut. After nibbling on it happily, he happily scurried away again leaving Kith and I looking at each other, eyes wide.

"We have to crack this shell," Kith said, pulling apart another one of the green casings to reveal the inner shell.

"No kidding," I sighed and rolled my eyes dramatically. "How are we going to do that? It nearly broke my tooth!"

Stumped, Kith stared at the shell for a while, trying to decide what to do.

"You can't open it with your claws, can you?" I asked, but when we tried neither of us had any luck.

Finally, Kith found a couple of rocks and rested the nut on top of one while striking it with the other. It took a few tries, but the shell broke.

"My turn!" I called grabbing the rock from Kith.

We spent some time after that just collecting nuts before lining them all up to be cracked. It was nice having something other than meat to eat.

✳   Kith   ✳

I lost track of how long we had been running. We barely stopped to eat and sleep. The fear that Ducar was right behind us made resting near impossible. A part of me knew we were going to have to slow down before too much longer, but the idea frightened me.

It was after dark by the time we finally sat to eat. Too tired for conversation, we built a fire to cook some of the raw meat we had left and ate in silence. Other than when decisions needed to be made, there hadn't been much talking in a couple of days. We were both exhausted and scared.

Every night, right after we ate, I would secure our packs before making our beds. That night, however, we were too tired to even make beds.

When I woke to Mara's screams, a scurrying sound concerned me but I pushed it out of my thoughts. Calming Mara was my priority right then. Not only because of how horrible her nightmares had become but because I worried her screaming would alert Ducar to our position, though I never mentioned that fear to Mara. It would do no good and only make her stressed more. I didn't know if she was worried about it or not.

As soon as Mara fell back asleep, I rushed to check on our

bags. The first one I grabbed was still mostly full and tied shut. The other one was torn open and what little food was left had bite marks and dirt all over it. I was running us too hard and silently cursed myself for allowing an animal into our supplies. I knew we needed rest, or we risked a lot worse than damaged food.

Gathering the bad food, I moved it far away from camp so it wouldn't attract anything else close to us. Digging a hole between two large roots at the base of the tree, I buried our remaining pack and the torn bag, just in case it could be fixed. Then, I gathered large sticks and created a small shelter against the tree, covering Mara while she slept and the spot with the buried packs of our food. After making sure we were mostly hidden, I climbed in and fell asleep.

We rested for a couple of days, staying hidden in our little fort. Once we were moving again, I could tell the rest had served us well. We decided to keep moving, but not always be running. With no set place to escape to or clue what direction Ducar might come from, the best we could hope for was to keep moving and try to avoid running into him.

One morning, a couple of days later, I realized Mara and I were almost out of water. We each had only a few swallows remaining. Water was never an issue before. It was usually easy to get from a spicket in town or fill the skins whenever it rained. But we hadn't been to a town in weeks and the rain was scarce the past few days. I wasn't sure we could manage to push through a full day of walking with just the small amount of water we had left.

I cursed myself for not thinking about water sooner, and making matters worse was how much our food supply had dwindled, too. Losing one pack of meat meant the amount we had wouldn't last as long as I hoped.

All that was left now was the dried meat. It was enough to hopefully last a few more days if we were extremely careful, but I hated to think what we would do when that ran out. There was no guarantee we would find another town or come across wild food soon. Looking up, the skies showed no sign of rain, not a single cloud, and I knew then we would run out of water before lunchtime.

A little whimper from Mara pulled me from my thoughts. She seemed to be having one of her less severe nightmares so I began gently rubbing her back and humming a tune Beatrice used to sing to her when she had a hard time sleeping. After a minute, she opened her eyes and offered me a timid smile. It saddened me that a good night for Mara was one where she woke up only slightly shaken rather than screaming in terror.

"Mara, we're low on water," I said, trying to keep my voice from sounding too anxious. "Let's go easy on our water today and maybe we shouldn't push ourselves quite as hard so we don't get too worn out."

Mara, who was just reaching for her water skin, pulled her arm back and looked at the sky. "Maybe it will rain soon," she replied hopefully.

Our pace was more leisurely that day. Mara kept our spirits up by imagining what animals we might find in these woods. She, of course, talked about finding one and keeping it for a pet. I decided not to burst her bubble by pointing out that we would have no way of taking care of such a pet. It was a harmless fantasy.

"Do you think other animals see us as animals too? Because we look so different from humans, I mean? Maybe they think we're purple monkeys!" Mara giggled uncontrollably at that.

I couldn't help but laugh too. "We could be Mr. Raffles' cousins!" I burst out laughing. Mr. Raffles was Ketzia's pet monkey.

"I always thought your face looked so much like his!" Mara squealed with pleasure.

"We even swing through the trees with our tails. I'm sure that confuses them even more!"

"I bet our mother accidentally bathed us both in purple water and then she never could get us back to the right color!" Mara's laughing quickly turned to sobs and she looked away. "Maybe that's why she didn't want us anymore."

Tightly wrapping my arms around my little sister, "You don't know that she didn't want us, Mara. Maybe we just got lost." I decided not to add that something probably happened to our mother. If she looked anything like us, I can only imagine what people would do to an adult freak wandering around on her own. It would explain how we ended up in the woods by ourselves, Mara just a baby, and me barely old enough to carry her in my arms.

"Why doesn't she find us then? Or our father? Do you think they're looking for us?"

"I don't know, Mara. I wish I did." We walked in silence for a while after that.

Although we drank sparingly, our water was gone by the time we stopped for the night. There wasn't much, to begin with. I lay on the ground looking up at the stars and thinking about the conversation Mara and I had earlier that day. What if we did have parents who were out there looking for us? But how would they not have heard of the purple child freaks traveling with Ducar's famous freak show? Surely they would have heard of it. And how had we not heard of them? It wasn't exactly easy to blend in with the crowd when you looked like we did. Unless they didn't look like us at all, and that's why we were left in the woods. Maybe they hoped we would die, or be eaten by an animal and when they learned we were with the freaks they just hoped nobody would ever piece together we belonged to them.

Of course, I would never share any of these thoughts with Mara. Maybe she thought of them on her own, but if not, I wasn't going to be the one to make her think her parents hated her just because of the way she looked. I usually just tried not talking about it at all. When we were in the freak show, Beatrice was all the mother we needed. She was always kind and took care of us. I would gladly call her my mother. And with that final thought, I fell asleep and dreamed of the bearded lady whom I feared I may never see again.

The next morning, I went for my water skin before remembering we were all out. I didn't know how I could get us water. Everywhere I looked there were more and more trees. No sign of a town or a source of water. When I looked at Mara, I found her staring at me.

"I don't know what to do Mara," I confessed. "We won't get far without any water."

"Well we just have to pick a direction and start walking until the trees end," she answered. "I'm sure we'll eventually find a town or a stream, or maybe it will rain!"

That was Mara. The eternal optimist. So we picked a direction and began walking. By the time we stopped for lunch, I knew this was turning into a disaster. There were still only trees in every direction, and eating the dried meat with nothing to drink only made me feel worse. Still, we continued in the chosen direction for the rest of the day.

When we stopped that night, the situation hadn't gotten any better. The sky was clear as ever, with no chance of rain, and I felt the toll this lack of water was taking on my body. Hardly sleeping that night, I couldn't calm the sense of dread I was feeling.

Waking the next morning, a change was noticeable in Mara, too. Her pace was slower and at one point she simply sat down right in the middle of walking.

I looked at her in horror. "I just started to feel a little dizzy," she said. "I only need a minute to rest and I'll be fine."

But when she tried standing, she immediately started to fall. Lunging to catch her, I set her on the ground.

Mara looked up at me with a dazed expression. "Everything just went black. I thought I was blind."

"Can you see me now?" I asked urgently.

"Yes, I can see. But I don't think I can stand up yet. Maybe we could rest for a while."

Standing up, I realized I was feeling light-headed too, so I left Mara there on the ground while I stumbled around aimlessly looking for anything that could help us.

*   Mara   *

The world went black, as I lay on the ground wondering how long someone could last without water. When Ducar was punishing me, I often went without food or water. Back then I was caged, though, not walking all day to keep ahead of the madman hunting us who could be getting closer and closer the whole time I lay there. Looking around, I watched Kith stumble over a fallen tree branch and disappear behind some bushes. For what seemed like a very long time I lost sight of him. Sitting up in a panic, I looked all around for him.

Just as I tried standing up to go look for him, Kith came out from the bushes, hands full of something dark blue and round.

"Mara, I found some berries!" he yelled. "It's not water, but they've got juice in them. That has to help, right?"

It took a minute to understand what he was saying. Once he reached me, Kith helped me settle back down on the ground before handing over half of the juicy berries. Taking one between my fingers, I rolled it around, inspecting the tiny ball, then squished it, and watched as the juice ran down my hand.

"Eat it, Mara," Kith whispered gently.

Popping one into my mouth, I was delighted by how good it was. We didn't eat different things very often, and lately, our food was the meat Kith had taken from the butcher's shop or nuts we gathered. The sweetness of the berries was a pleasant change.

We sat for a long time slowly picking our way through the berries and just resting to get back our strength. The small amount of juice wasn't quite enough to rehydrate us, of course, but it tasted so good and was refreshing for my dry mouth. The rest of the day we took it easy and searched everywhere for more berries. Finding several bushes, we managed to get through the day and find a place to rest for the night.

Waking to Kith soothing me from one of my mild nightmares, I thought I heard a noise. At first, I told myself that I was delusional from lack of water, but then I saw Kith's long, pointy ears perk up and knew he heard it too.

"Is that water?" I asked, almost afraid to know the answer.

"I think it is, Mara." Excitement shone on his face.

Standing still, we listened carefully. The sound was coming from the direction we passed the night before, showing just how exhausted we were when we made our beds. Setting off in that direction, we walked slowly and quietly, making sure we could always hear the sound.

Half an hour later, I spotted the tiny stream just ahead of us, and despite how drained I was I broke into a run. Reaching the stream, I quickly rinsed my hands in the water then moved upstream; away from the dirt, before dipping my hands back in and taking huge gulps of water.

The water felt so refreshing and fantastic, that I almost cried. The night before I'd gone to sleep I'd gone to sleep unsure of how long we would make it, but now I drank as much as I wanted before refilling both my water skins.

While eating our breakfast right there by the small stream's edge, I repeatedly dipped my hands in for more water between bites. Kith laughed at me after several times. "You know the water will still be there when you finish eating, right?"

"It just tastes so wonderful, I can't get enough!" Squealing with pleasure, I went in for another gulp.

Staying at the stream for a while we relaxed and let our bodies take in all the water we could handle. Then, we set off walking beside it, until we got to a point where it made a small waterfall down into a little pond. Immediately, I set off climbing down the rocks to get to the bottom of the waterfall.

Not minding how cool it was, we lay in the small pond for a while. The water barely covered me lying flat, but it felt amazing to just be weightless and relaxed.

"We should probably make camp. Our clothes are going to need some time to dry." Reluctance filled Kith's voice.

"I know you're right, but I don't want to move." After lying still for just a moment longer, I rose to help him start the fire. At least we'd have plenty of water to drink with our food.

✳   Kith   ✳

Mara munched quietly on her dried meat and eyed the bag. It was obvious she was thinking about how long the meat we had left would last us but didn't want to say anything.

"Let's go a little slower today so we can spend more time looking for food."

Mara looked sheepish for a second like she thought I read her mind. "I'm usually kinda looking for food."

"Of course, but it would be best to find more before we run out completely, so let's make it our main focus. Since that animal ate so much of it, we only have enough for a few more days." I sighed, knowing I shouldn't be angry at the animal for finding food. It was my fault.

"What did the animal look like?" Mara's golden eyes lit up.

"It was small and round. I think it was a dark gray or black, and dark rings went down its tail. Everything happened so fast, though, that I barely saw it."

Mara was deep in thought trying to picture the animal I described. There was something peaceful about watching her get excited over something as simple as a cute animal. For a minute neither of us had a care in the world.

Suddenly, a deafening burst of thunder crashed above us. Mara's fantasy animal vanished as she shrieked in terror and flew into my lap; my arms instinctively wrapping around her protectively.

Looking up, I realized the sky was quickly getting dark and ugly. Rain was nothing new to us, but it had been a while since there was a thunderstorm. This one looked like it was going to be nasty. I looked around us. We were surrounded by trees and bushes, but none of them seemed to offer much shelter, especially since all the leaves were on the ground now.

"Mara, we have to find a place to wait out the storm." When she didn't move, I added, "Quickly!"

The urgency in my voice got her attention and she leaped to her feet. Her small hand found mine and we walked in the direction we saw the most trees, our feet and eyes moving quickly.

We weren't fast enough, and big drops of water landed on our heads. It came faster and faster and got colder and colder. In minutes we were completely drenched. I could feel Mara shivering beside me as I looked around for cover.

The sky showed no sign of clearing and it was getting hard to see through the rain. "We're going to need to make a fort and wait out this storm. It doesn't seem like it's going to let up any time soon."

Mara nodded, and her eyes widened. "What do you need me to do?"

"Gather thin long sticks; I'm going to need a lot of them, and stack them in a pile next to those bushes." I started packing away the food while talking, then cleared the area around the tree and started forming a dome surrounding the tree with large sticks. After making sure it was secure, I started weaving the thinner sticks into the big ones.

It had been a long time since I dealt with a storm as big as this one was going to be. It definitely would have been nice for it to hit a few days earlier, but at least our water skins wouldn't be empty for a while. Still, it wasn't something we'd want to be stuck in without decent shelter.

Once I got as many of the gaps between the sticks filled in as I could, I started piling on leaves and mud from the ground, to create a thick layer covering us so that we'd be warm and dry. I wasn't sure how I was going to cover the opening, though.

My mind drifted to another great, terrible storm that swept in and changed our once-happy lives forever.

"Kith, what are you thinking about?"

Mara's voice startled me. She was standing beside me, a look of concern on her face. "I was thinking about the first time we experienced a storm this bad."

"The one that made Ducar mean?"

"Yeah, that one."

"What happened? How does a storm make someone change like that?"

"Let me finish this and I'll tell you the story. You get on inside."

Scooping up as much mud as I could, I caked it onto the branches and covered it with a layer of leaves. My hands were getting cold, making my work clumsy, but I continued piling on leaves and mud until all of the branches were covered. Looking under them at Mara from time to time to check the effectiveness of my work, I noticed a couple of big leaks that I quickly patched up.

Eager to join Mara somewhere relatively dry and warm, I found some big leafy branches we could use to cover the entrance and went inside our fort.

Our performances in the town were going well, but it was time to move on. While packing up, however, big dark clouds came rolling in fast. We could risk traveling in the storm, or keep on the outskirts of town and wait. Ducar decided we should wait out the storm, but that there wouldn't be any shows so we didn't seriously outstay our welcome.

Before the storm hit, Ducar gave everyone instructions to keep us all safe. We were to stay in our tents and wait out the storm. No one was to wander around or go into the town. Storms have a habit of making people paranoid, and with how little people trusted freaks to begin with, Ducar didn't want anyone taking the risk.

Beatrice decided that Mara and I would stay in her tent during the storm, instead of the small one we normally stayed in together. She made us little beds next to hers, but when the thunder hit we both ended up in her bed curled up against her. That was the last moment I remember feeling truly safe, with her arms wrapped around us and her murmuring softly to comfort us.

The first night everything went fine, except for the fight that broke out between Mitch, the troublemaker strongman, and Harlon.

"Hey, short stuff, you might want to stay out of my path. I don't want to trip on you, and you're even harder to see with all this rain." Mitch's guffaw rang through the camp. He always found himself to be hysterical.

"If you're that clumsy, maybe you should stay in your tent, lumberjack." Dominic's normally grumpy face turned into a snarl. There wasn't much he hated more than his height, or lack thereof, being mentioned.

"I'm not clumsy when there aren't tripping hazards around." Putting his hand on Dominic's head, Mitch acted like he was going to steer him out of his path.

Instantly, Dominic's fists started swinging. Mitch just laughed as the punches repeatedly hit his lower legs.

When Harlon stepped up, however, Mitch's laughter went silent. "I notice how you only pick on Dominic when I'm not around." Harlon's deep voice rang clearly through the rain.

"I'm not scared of you, Fluff Ball." With all his bravado, Mitch's voice softened a bit.

"Sure." Harlon straightened his back, bringing his hairy height fully up. He towered over Mitch, and we all knew that under all his hair there was a lot of muscle.

"What are you going to do, bite me like a dog?"

Harlon grinned, showing off his oddly sharp teeth. "Don't tempt me, Mr. Muscles."

Mitch flinched at the sight, before catching himself. "Whatever. I was just teasing the little guy. No need to get worked up."

Dominic was about to say something, but Harlon held out a hand. "He's not worth the energy. Let's go eat."

A collective sigh of relief swept through the camp. Something major had been avoided.

The next day everyone kept to themselves to avoid tension. The storm was still raging, though. It was going to be a long one. That evening, while the camp chefs were preparing dinner, a loud bang rang out not too far from camp. It didn't sound like thunder or anything else I had ever heard. An odd purplish light flashed with the noise.

Everyone was scared, and Ducar was worried that the town would think we were causing trouble. He might have also been worried that they were starting trouble. It was hard to tell. Running our show was a big balancing act for him between entertaining the town, and staying too long to where they'd turn against us. We had been run out of a few towns with threats of violence when the balancing act went wrong.

Ducar knew that the strange event needed to be checked out. At first, he and Mitch argued about who should go.

"You should be here with everyone to help keep them calm," Mitch argued. "If someone else is out there, I am the best equipped to deal with them!" He boasted, flexing his arms. "They won't stand a chance against me!"

"That's why you need to be here!" Ducar countered. "If something happens in camp, you are here to help everyone."

In the end, Ducar was the one to go check it out, but he left Mitch in charge until he returned. The rain was coming down so hard we could only see his first few steps as he walked away. Then he disappeared. I thought I heard a scream, but couldn't be sure due to the thunder.

After several minutes, another weird light and sound filled the air. Grace, the trapeze artist, mentioned the idea of sending out a search party. Harlon and Jaxon were all for it, but Mitch insisted he should go alone so no *one else was hurt.*

A small argument broke out where petite Grace got as close to Mitch's face as she could and glared right at him, her small hazel eyes piercing into his pale blue ones until he looked away.

"Ducar left you to take care of all of us. How exactly do you plan to keep these children safe if you get lost out there too!?" She spoke in a quiet angry tone, pointing to Mara and me.

More discussion followed where others talked of going out in groups, but Mitch, who was now treating his duty of protecting everyone extra seriously, said we all had to stay put or more of us would be lost. They ended up deciding if Ducar didn't return by the time the storm broke, they would go out searching. No one wanted to discuss what would happen if he never returned.

After several hours, Ducar made his way back into camp. His long hair was dripping on his face, but he didn't seem to have the energy to brush it away. His normally straight stature was slumped, shoulders hunched. Mud covered his clothes and clung to clumps at the end of his hair. As he stumbled to his tent, he didn't say a word to anyone. We were relieved and concerned, all at once.

The next morning, Ducar announced we would be moving out, and that there would be changes over the next while. He didn't go into detail and got angry whenever anyone asked questions.

Over the next few weeks, anything that went wrong was blamed on us. There was always a good explanation to make it our fault. At first, the others would try to defend us, but eventually, they stopped. All except Beatrice and Grace.

It was only a few weeks later that Ducar purchased our cage.

I looked down to see Mara crying softly. "I miss Beatrice, Kith. Do you think we'll see her again?"

Kissing her head lightly, I chose my words carefully. "I'm not sure." Not completely sure, anyway.

"She always risked so much for us. Like when she threw us our birthday party, without anyone knowing."

"I remember that." I smiled. "It was a lovely night."

Mara's smile was only half there. "I only remember it a little. Would you tell me about it?"

We rarely slept deeply after the storm, a part of us was always waiting for something to happen. When Beatrice snuck into our tent late one night, she didn't even need to wake us.

Knowing better than to alert someone to her presence, we stayed quiet as she unlocked our cage and scooped us both up with one arm, using the other to secure the cage door. She wore a large shawl and used it for cover as she snuggled us close.

Peeking out before leaving to make sure we weren't seen, she hurried to her tent and set us on her big, soft bed. On the table next to the bed were two small cakes and a bunch of food. Mara eyed the food hungrily but was scared to grab any. This was one of the nights Ducar declared she was to go without food or water as punishment for some imaginary misdeed.

Beatrice looked heartbroken at our hesitance. "It's okay. Everyone is asleep. I figured we'd celebrate both your birthdays tonight." She paused, seeming to think about her next words. "I hope you two don't mind sharing your parties."

"Of course not," I whispered. The risk she was taking for one night was obvious enough. Nerves settled in my stomach, but not wanting to hurt her feelings, I started eating. The food was delicious. It had been a long time since we were allowed food this good. Once Mara saw me eating, she went for it. A long time passed since I had seen her eat so much. Beatrice was delighted to see how happy we were with the food. Before we ate the cake she sang to us softly.

Once we were satisfied, I thought we'd be going straight back to our cage. Instead, Beatrice tucked us into her bed. "You two need some good sleep. I'll watch over you, and make sure you're back before everyone is awake."

It didn't take us long to fall asleep, and we slept deeper than we had in a long time, knowing we were safe, at least for a while.

When I finished the story, I noticed Mara was looking very sad.

"I miss being safe. I just wish we knew what happened to her. She didn't deserve to be punished. She - she…"

Mara couldn't contain herself anymore, and her body shook with silent sobs. Taking her gently in my arms, I held her while she cried it out. For many nights after we escaped, I could hear Mara crying softly when we went to sleep. She begged me to go back for Beatrice at first, but I couldn't put her back at risk like that. As much as I loved Beatrice, I had to protect my sister. It was what Beatrice always told me. *"Above everything else, you must keep her safe. She is too small to survive on her own, she needs you and you need her. "*

Part of me wondered at times if Beatrice knew something was going to happen to her. She told me so often that nothing mattered but keeping Mara and myself safe. This didn't stop me from hating myself for doing nothing. For weeks I was tortured by the thought of what Ducar could be doing to Beatrice at that very moment. In the end, I knew she would never have wanted us to go back. She risked everything to get us out, and if Ducar caught us again we would only be throwing away that sacrifice.

Wiping the tears that had begun pooling in my eyes, I tried to think of a way to cheer Mara up. "Do you remember when Grace got in big trouble with Beatrice?"

Confusion filled Mara's face. "Why would Beatrice be mad at Grace?"

"Do you remember when she let us swing on the trapeze?"

"How could I forget!" Mara exclaimed. "That was the best day of my life!"

"I think Beatrice could have skinned her alive for that. She got so mad when she saw us," I started to giggle.

"Did she?" Mara asked. "I don't remember that part."

I smiled at the memory.

Grace lifted me carefully onto one of her lower swings, and of course, Mara begged to go, too. She didn't want to let her at first because she was so small, but Grace could never say no to Mara. She cherished her. So she set Mara on my lap and told me to hold her tight. I felt like such a big kid, with the huge responsibility of keeping my baby sister safe. Then she gently pushed the swing, only moving us slightly. Still, it felt exciting to kids so little.

Mara loved it, of course, squealing and laughing the whole time. I'm sure the whole camp heard us. When Beatrice walked in and saw us up there, she looked about to burst with anger. I had never seen her so mad. She told us to go to our tent, and Mara ran off crying because she had been yelled at.

I stayed at the door and heard Beatrice yelling at Grace about putting her children in danger. I think that was the first time I heard her slip and call us that. 'My children' she had said. I wasn't even mad that she stopped us swinging. I was just so happy she said I was her child.

"Of course, we were her children," Mara said when I finished. "We are her children. We just need to get her away from him, too. I bet she would take care of us forever. We could have a house somewhere far away from any villages, so no one ever has to see us." I knew Ducar would never let that happen. He would hunt us as long as he lived, but I decided not to mention that.

"I wonder how things turned out for her," I muttered after a moment of thought. "Grace, I mean."

"She was so beautiful. I want to be just like her when I grow up," Mara said wistfully. "She looked like an angel up in the air. Why did she have to leave us?"

"She got married, and her husband wanted to settle down and buy a house. That makes her the luckiest of all of us. I remember how sad she was to leave, and how shocked everyone was when Ducar told her to never come back. That was the first time I remember him being cruel."

"Part of me wishes she had stayed, though. I missed her so much. Well, I still do. I hope her husband is nice to her. They probably have babies of their own now."

I could tell the thought hurt Mara. Beatrice was like a mother to us, but Grace had been like our sister. Mara used to follow her around the tents, like a puppy dog. That seemed like a lifetime ago. I was glad she got away before Ducar got bad.

Even her sorrow couldn't stop the exhaustion from hitting, though. Mara's slight pout was interrupted by a huge yawn, and I couldn't help but smile. "Let's get some sleep. Hopefully, the storm will end during the night."

Snuggling together as best we could under our blankets, we lay in silence for a while until we finally started to nod off.

Water hitting my feet woke me suddenly, and when I moved away from the leak Mara looked up at me. "I'm going to have to go patch the fort."

The rain pouring down drenched me as soon as I stepped out of the fort. As dark as the clouds made it, there was enough light to tell me it was morning. Even so, the storm showed no sign of slowing. An icy burst of wind reminded me I didn't want to be out for long, so I hurriedly grabbed some branches to cover the spot where the leak had formed.

As I placed the new branches, lightning flashed through the sky. Except it didn't look like any lightning I had ever seen. Purple streaked through the sky, remaining a few seconds after the lightning was gone. I stood staring in confusion until a big raindrop landed right in my eye, and the cold shocked me back to my work.

After the branches were in place, I put on as much mud and leaves as I could. Even though I hoped the rain would let up soon because I could already see it wearing the mud away bit by bit, part of me wanted to see the purple lightning again. I looked around for one more sign of it before ducking back into our shelter.

*   Mara   *

While Kith worked on patching up our fort for the second time that day, I sat inside shivering. With how heavy the rain was, I was a bit surprised we hadn't been completely swept away. Of course, there were leaks, but with Kith's regular trips outside to patch them up, he managed to keep it mostly dry inside. When he came back in sopping wet and shivering, I couldn't help but feel guilty.

Kith looked around our tiny space and grinned. "Looks like it's holding up okay." Worry shone in his eyes, though, and I knew he must be thinking it couldn't hold for long.

Trying to think of something to keep his mind off the rain, I decided to get him to tell me another story. "Do you remember our first show, Kith?"

Kith looked at me for a minute, his smile growing. "Of course I do. Ducar was excited that it was finally time to reveal us to the world, so he decided to make us the stars of the night. Everyone loved us and hated us at the same time. One kid screamed when he saw us, and his mother told him not to worry because we were harmless little children. Maybe she thought it was fake like we had been painted and made to look strange. How else could there be a purple child with claws and a tail? I had so much fun doing flips and jumping through hoops, though. Of course, you were still tiny, but all you had to do was wave and everyone loved you."

"That was when Ducar was still nice. I don't remember him ever letting me just stand still and wave."

His voice growing somber, Kith spoke slowly, as if choosing his words carefully. "Ducar loved you as much as anyone. He loved us. Of course, I'm sure that was partly because we were such a hit, but he was so proud he threw a huge party in the main tent after all the guests left."

For several seconds he stared into space, silent.

"I don't remember having any parties," I said in surprise, interrupting whatever thoughts were swirling in his mind.

"He didn't throw them very often. Usually, when everyone got together, Beatrice made us go to bed, but Ducar wouldn't have that this time. We were the stars of the show, and he insisted we be there to celebrate. Everyone else was there, too. I think Dylan was the only one who wasn't happy about our success. He was glaring at me every time I looked at him." Dylan, the rubber man, had been the favorite before that night, and he was not happy to have us steal his spotlight.

"What did everyone do at the party?" I asked, trying to recreate the scene in my mind.

Kith began the story and I could see it all as if I were there again. Kith and I were doing our first performance in the main tent, where benches were set up for huge crowds of people to sit and watch all at once. Then, when our act was finished, we went to our designated smaller tents where Ducar had areas roped off for his freaks to sit and let onlookers goggle at us as much as they wanted. Our tent was packed that night. There was a line out the door that stretched through half the camp. Everyone wanted a look at the new freaks.

Ducar was ecstatic; it was the biggest crowd he'd seen in a long time. That was an easy night for us. Beatrice gave us toys to play with so we didn't get restless while all the people were staring at us. When Ducar objected, she told him people would get bored of watching two restless children try to sit still. The other freaks would talk to people and answer questions, but that was before I talked much and Kith was shy. Beatrice knew having something to play with would make it easier for him to feel comfortable around so many people. She tried to get Ducar to let us sit with her in her tent, but he put his foot down at that. Giving people three freaks for one ticket would be crazy! So, we sat there playing for hours while Kith occasionally said a few small words to the people who watched us.

Once we were closed for business, Ducar told Mitch and Harlon to bring two long tables in and set them up in the main tent. Beatrice and the conjoined twins, Helga and Heidi, brought out piles of food that they and Grace had spent days cooking. There were all types of meats and vegetables, and half of one table was covered with nothing but desserts. Cakes and pies and little tarts and much more.

Of course, Heidi and Helga argued about where their dishes should be placed. Heidi tried to head to the left end of the table, and Helga tried to go to the right end. For several seconds it looked like they might split down the middle. Finally, Heidi relented as usual, and they placed their platters down on the right end without any more trouble.

Ducar made a show of having Kith and I go first, instructing Beatrice to pile our plates as high as we wanted with whatever we asked for. People were jumping through the hoops and swinging on Grace's trapeze while waiting to eat.

After celebrating for a while; full of lots of eating and laughter, the twins climbed up to the trapeze. Everyone watched with a great deal of nervousness.

Grace stepped forward to help. "Are you two sure you should be doing stunts right now?" She kept her voice soft like she was talking to a child.

Helga glared at Grace with an anger I rarely saw. "We're fine. It's just swinging. Anyone can do it. Easy."

Grace rolled her eyes and went back to her seat. We all knew arguing with Helga was useless. Of course, we all also knew that it wasn't as simple as Helga claimed. The two managed to climb on the swing fine, but as they started swinging, Heidi began screaming and twisting. With them being *attached, her wiggling caused Helga to lose her grip and they tumbled onto the mat.*

The crowd knew better than to dare laugh. As they rose, we could see how red Helga's face was, and tears streaked down Heidi's cheeks.

"We were doing fine, Heidi! We would have made it if you would've just stayed calm. You're always bringing us down. I swear, someday soon I'm going to have you cut off!" Helga dramatically turned her head away from Heidi, as if she was pretending she had stormed off.

Heidi let out a soft sob. "I'm sorry, Helga. We can try again. I'll do better." Helga didn't respond and instead began dragging Heidi out of the big tent in silence, still refusing to look in her direction.

"Bea Bea, Helga wouldn't get Heidi cut off, would she?" I was curled in Beatrice's lap, my hands entangled in her beard.

"Of course not." She said gently, patting my head comfortingly. "Everyone knows that they'd both die if she did. Even Helga. It's just something she says when she's angry."

A loud bang roared around us, bringing a sudden stop to Kith's story. He immediately threw himself to cover me from whatever danger there could be. Of course, it was only thunder, which we realized quickly and began laughing at how scared we were.

I gave Kith a smile of encouragement, eager to return to the mystical world I could only remember as a horrid place of despair. "What else did we do at the party?"

After the twins fell, Ducar stood up and declared that he had a gift for his little stars. Mitch carried in what looked like just a plank of wood attached in the middle to a pole. Then he set it down and showed us that we were each supposed to sit on one side and use our feet to kick off the ground, sending the other straight down where they would then kick off.

Beatrice insisted that I was too small to ride this on my own, so Grace stepped in and sat me on her lap while she and Kith tried it out. Afraid that Kith might fall, Beatrice hovered right behind him.

Only one person in the whole place was seen without a smile. Dylan stood hunched in the corner the whole night glowering at us both. When Ducar made a toast to our success, Dylan's face burned red accentuating the pockmarked scars all over. When his brown eyes saw mine staring at him, he bared his crooked teeth at me and stormed out of the tent.

Even Dominic, who was always in a bad mood about something, was there eating and smiling with the rest of us. Harlon, the Wolf Man, had set up small stools all along the tables so Dominic could reach the food and fix his plate on his own. Dominic was so short, that he could never reach the food on the tables, but he got angry when other people tried to fix his plate for him like he was a child.

"That was nice of Harlon," I said, finally breaking us both out of our daydream, "I do remember Dominic being self-conscious about his height. It's what made him special, though. We all had something special about us. He should have been more proud of it."

Kith gave me a sideways glance, "I sometimes wish we weren't *special*. We could have found a home. Maybe been in an orphanage. We certainly wouldn't have to hide from everyone who came near."

Suddenly, I felt very sad. I loved the way Kith and I looked. Of course, I didn't like it when people were scared of us or when other children made fun of us, but I hadn't dealt with that as much as Kith. I was never the one who went into the towns to get food and supplies and only heard the stories about children stumbling across Kith and throwing stones at him as he ran away. It must have been worse than I imagined to make Kith hate the way he looked so much he would ever want to look like anyone other than himself.

"People are cruel, Kith. They will bring you down for any reason they can find. Looking like them won't make them any nicer, and I wouldn't want you to look any different than you do now."

Kith smiled with a tinge of sadness before pulling me in for a hug. "You're right, of course. We don't need them, anyway."

We sat there just listening to the rain until we both fell asleep.

CHAPTER THREE: SEPTEMBER

✳   Kith   ✳

Cautiously stepping out of our fort, I looked at the wreckage around me. Broken branches and fallen trees were strewn all around. After checking the perimeter of our shelter, I gently nudged Mara awake.

"Is it over?" she whispered, her voice a little hoarse.

"Yes, Mara, it's over, and now we need to get moving so we can look for more food. We're getting low."

After quickly gathering our things, we started walking. All the destruction from the storm made it hard to move. The ground was muddy, and some areas were so deep our feet sank with every step. The squishy mud felt gross between my toes, and we had to keep pulling our feet up high just to walk. Fallen trees littered the ground. Most of them were small and easy to step over, but there were a few larger ones that we had to pull ourselves up.

Stopping to look at an enormous tree spanning the area in front of us, I sighed wearily. "Maybe we should walk around this one."

Mara eyed the tree for a minute before turning to me. "Are you sure? It could be a lot of fun to climb." Sniffing softly, she stretched out her arms. "My muscles feel stiff. Using them might help since we've been so cooped up from the storm."

"Alright, but be careful. We don't need either of us getting hurt."

Having claws was helpful with climbing. The tree was only a few handholds above our heads, so it didn't take us long to get on top. The higher vantage gave us an even better view of how wet and damaged everything was.

Most trees were fine, aside from a lot of their branches being torn down. The tree we were standing on was the biggest down in the area. Now that we were on it, I could see the damage it had built up over the years that made it weak enough to be felled by the storm.

Animal bites and insect holes riddled the tree. Under the bark, though, there was a white web-like substance. It seemed to seep into the wood and stretch out. At points along the white paths colorful, rounded mounds came out of the tree. They were flat, making it almost look like the tree was decorated with shelves of varying sizes.

After a short rest, we started down the other side. Suddenly, Mara squealed and jumped down the rest of the way. I was still climbing down when a huge ball of mud splattered across my back.

Mara laughed so hard she ended up coughing. After recovering from my shock, I jumped down, landing in mud and sinking halfway to my knees.

Bending down, I scooped up a big handful of the slimy mud and hurled it at Mara. It hit her chest, splattering mud up onto her chin and neck. She laughed and coughed at the impact.

As I bent to scoop more mud, a big handful hit the top of my head, causing me to splash my handful toward Mara without looking up. Suddenly, she was sputtering and coughing and when I looked up she was trying to wipe the mud off her face with her muddy hands.

"I'm sorry, Mara! I didn't mean to get your face!" Rushing over, I tried to help her wipe off. My hands were too muddy, as well, so I gave up and used the front of my shirt to get as much off her as I could.

As soon as her face was clear, Mara shoved me playfully. After falling backward into the mud, I laughed and pulled her down beside me. Being cooped up must have had a bigger effect on Mara than I realized. She was breathing heavily after such little exertion.

After sitting in the mud for way too long, I used the tree to pull myself out. Once I was clear, I reached back to pull Mara out.

It didn't take long for me to realize that playing in the mud was a mistake. We were both shivering from being wet. Normally, we would use our blankets to warm up but didn't want to now because we were so dirty. As the mud began to dry, I started itching all over. Mud was caked into my hair and under my clothes. It hardened as it dried, making it hard to move my arms and legs. The longer we walked, the stiffer my limbs got. Not wanting Mara to feel guilty, I tried to hide my discomfort. Plus, she seemed plenty uncomfortable herself. I wasn't sure how to hide the silly way I had to walk, though.

At one point, Mara tried to make a joke about the way we were walking, but I could tell how half-hearted it was. "Sorry, I got us all covered in mud," she said feebly after her joke fell flat. "I was just trying to have fun, but it isn't fun anymore."

Attempts to reassure her that I wasn't upset were just met with silence, so we walked on miserably for hours. My skin felt stiff and brittle, but I realized it was easier to flake off the dried dirt than it was to wipe the mud away, so we both began peeling dirt off ourselves as we walked.

After a while, I wondered if I had gotten mud up Mara's nose because she kept wiping at it and sniffling. I couldn't imagine how terrible that would be.

Eventually, we decided to take a break. Digging through the packs, I tried to find what was left of the meat. Surely we had some left. After we ate earlier, I thought I had seen more in the pack. I searched for several more minutes before accepting that we were entirely out of food. My heart sank into my empty stomach. We would have to go to sleep hungry tonight and focus on finding food in the morning.

Mara hadn't reacted at all to my frantic search through the bag. She seemed to be tiring quicker than usual, even though she tried to hide it.

"We're out of food and I don't see any around. We'll have to focus on finding some tomorrow." Anger, fear, and sadness all swelled within me at once, but I fought to keep my voice even.

Mara simply nodded, her eyes downcast, and we set about making our camp in silence.

As soon as the mud that caked my body dried, I knew I made a mistake. Kith was obviously as uncomfortable as I was, but I could tell he was trying to hide it from me. He always tried to shield me from things he thought I couldn't handle. That, of course, only made me feel worse.

After we took our break, the dried mud began cracking all over my body. It felt worse than ever, and I couldn't shake the sniffles and coughing fits that developed throughout the day. Surely I must have inhaled some of the muddy water, and it would go away soon.

Knowing Kith felt bad about hitting my face, I tried to hide the coughs as much as I could. Maybe in a way, I was just as bad as he was. We were both always trying to protect each other from ever having negative feelings.

As the sun beat down on us, the mud felt worse and worse. Sweat trickled down my body now, mixing with the mud causing my whole body to itch. When the sun was just starting to set, Kith said it was probably a good time to stop for the day. The day had been miserable and draining, so we were both ready for it to end.

When Kith told me there was no food left, all I could think about was how horrible the night was going to be, hungry and trying to sleep with mud caked all over me. Suddenly, Kith called to me. "I found a puddle! We might be able to get most of the mud off. It isn't very deep, but the water is mostly clear. If we get ourselves wet enough we can use some big leaves to wipe the mud off!"

Not even realizing he wandered off, I rose to meet him, relieved at the thought of cleaning myself. I had thought about dumping one of my water skins over my body but hadn't quite decided whether the waste of water would be worth it.

Before dirtying the little water available, we used some leaves to brush off as much of the dirt as we could. Then we carefully scooped some water a little bit at a time and scrubbed ourselves down. There was no chance that we'd get our hair clean, but we were able to get the worst of it off.

"I don't think I can sleep in these clothes tonight," I told Kith and began stripping off my pants and shirt. After looking around, I started banging my shirt on a tree. Small puffs of dirt flew everywhere and Kith let out a small yelp. When I looked at him, his hands were covering his eyes. "Oh, I'm sorry, did I get it in your eye?" I asked, horrified.

"No, it's okay," he assured me as he bent back down to the water. "I think I managed to close my eyes before you attacked!" he looked up from the puddle, his freshly wet face grinning. "Banging your clothes against a tree is fine and all, but maybe make sure I'm out of the line of fire first. It does look like it got a bit of the caked mud off, though!"

We found trees spaced out a safe distance and each hit our clothes against them until all the little mud cakes cracked off. Then, Kith built a fire while I rinsed our clothes the best I could. They were still pretty dirty by the time the puddle turned into a brown sludge itself, but they were better than they had been.

As I carried the clothes back to Kith, he pointed to some sticks he had stuck together next to the fire. "It's not the best, but I made a spot to hang the clothes to dry."

"Good idea." I carefully arranged the clothes, enjoying the heat coming from the fire. We never made big fires, and usually, Kith put them out as soon as the food was done cooking. The risk of Ducar or his men seeing it was too great. Tonight, however, we decided to make an exception, hoping the clothes would be mostly dry by the time we tried to sleep.

Long after the sun went down, we reluctantly agreed that it was time to put the fire out, slid into our still-damp clothes, and curled up close to each other to share our body heat. The chill in the air left me shivering anyway, and I just wished for the sun to come out again and warm us up. Finally, long after Kith had gone to sleep, I managed to drift off myself.

Large buildings were nothing new for us, but I don't remember seeing any as enormous as the one we approached. Gray and white stone walls reached toward the sky split with a heavy, dark wooden door. The path we walked was overgrown now, but looked as if it dealt with a lot of traffic long ago. A sense of familiarity mixed with a foreboding dread, confused me.

As we walked, I realized that there was someone else with us. A woman; one who shared our light purple skin, and had a tail and claws just like us. Her mouth was moving, but I couldn't make out what she said.

Excitement was bursting through me, but it was dulled by feelings of confusion and worry. Everything was different, wasn't it? But how was it different? Should the grass under my feet be green? Wasn't it always green? Why did the blue sky and yellow sun seem so strange?

Suddenly, the woman faltered. She steadied quickly, but something seemed different about her now. It was like every step she took was harder than the last. Once we got inside the building, the excitement came back, but the concern about the woman I couldn't quite see intensified.

Crying filled the air, and the large building disintegrated. The forest swam into view, and I was with Mara again. A feeling of strangeness lingered with me, though. Images of the building and the woman lingered in my mind, and I longed for the faceless woman. Who was she? Could she be our mother? It felt like she cared about us in the dream and wouldn't have just abandoned us. Did something happen to her? I remembered the fear I felt when I saw her stumble. There was something wrong with her, but what?

I shook myself. It was a dream. The faceless woman probably didn't even exist. My mind surely conjured her from my longing for a loving adult.

As I woke Mara, I kept trying to convince myself of that. Still, I couldn't shake the feeling that I had forgotten something.

When Mara started describing the scene from her nightmare, however, my dream and the mystery woman left my mind and were replaced with the face of a woman we both had loved.

On the night Mara described, Ducar came for her again. He wasn't particularly angry, it seemed more for fun, or just to keep Mara down. This time, though, he made the mistake of coming alone while Beatrice was in our tent.

He seemed surprised to see her. Maybe he didn't realize how often she came to visit us. "Out." That was all he said to her.

Stubbornly, Beatrice planted her feet firmly between him and our cage. "No." She stared him down, completely unafraid.

Ducar shrugged, then slammed his stick into Beatrice's ribs. A thud resonated through our tent, and I knew she had to be in a lot of pain. She refused to budge, or even wince.

"Really?" Ducar snarled. "Maybe it's time for the rats to see that their beloved bearded lady isn't as strong as she seems."

Mara almost always handled her beatings quietly, refusing to let Ducar know how much it hurt, but neither of us could hold back our cries while Beatrice took the beating for her. We held each other and sobbed openly.

After a while, Ducar grew bored of Beatrice and left. It took a minute for her to collect herself and make her way to us, but then she soothed us with loving murmurs.

"My babies," she whispered, "I'll get you out of here, I promise. Be strong." She kissed us through the cage bars before slowly making her way toward her tent.

Tears streamed down my face as Mara talked about that night. It happened just a few weeks before we escaped. Beatrice spent most of that time preparing us for a life on the run. She and Dylan were both supposed to come with us, but just as we were almost out of camp we heard Ducar calling to them. Since he hadn't spotted Mara and me, Beatrice told us to run ahead into the trees and wait for them to meet us. We hid and waited for hours, but they never came.

"Kith?" Mara looked up at me, her face also streaked with tears. "Do you think Ducar hurt Beatrice for helping us escape?"

My breath caught in my chest. Dread filled me whenever Mara asked questions about what might have happened to Beatrice.

I never wanted to answer them. "Yes, Mara, I think he probably did."

Fresh tears rolled down her cheeks at my words, but she didn't add anything else. I kissed the top of her head and held her tight. "She loved us enough to accept the risk." My voice cracked and I couldn't find anything else to say. Sitting in silence, we mourned the only mother we ever knew.

*   Mara   *

"Mara?" I looked up at the sound of my name and noticed Kith had stopped walking.

"What's wrong?" I asked slowly, my brain felt fuzzy and it was hard to focus on him.

"Didn't you hear me talking to you?" Kith's expression wasn't angry but worried. I realized I had been in my own world, thinking about absolutely nothing. For most of the day, I was walking in a sort of daze.

"I'm sorry," I said sheepishly. "I didn't hear you."

Kith gave me a long piercing look before he continued. "I think I see a couple of apple trees over there. I figured we should check it out."

"Oh. Apples sound lovely." I wondered how much Kith had tried to talk to me with no response while I was walking in my dazed state.

"Are you feeling alright?" Kith asked, stepping in front of me so I was forced to make eye contact. His eyes searched mine and I could see how anxious my behavior was making him.

"I'm okay. I just didn't sleep well last night so my mind is a little foggy. I think having some food will help" I decided not to tell him that the reason I didn't sleep well was because I kept waking myself up with coughing fits. This seemed to satisfy him for the moment, but I knew he would be watching me more closely for the rest of the day.

"Once we get some food in us, you can take a short nap too." He cut my protests short by adding, "You're much better company when you talk to me," with a sly grin.

It didn't take us long to reach the trees. The only apples left on them were high up, so Kith quickly climbed the branches and grabbed them. Holding on with one hand, he swung his bag around in front of him so he could easily drop an apple inside before moving on to the next one.

Once all the apples were picked, he scrambled back down the tree and we each took an apple to eat. They were small and slightly withered but tasted fine. Kith pulled out a couple more for each of us, leaving the rest in his pack for later. As soon as I swallowed my last bite, Kith reminded me about my nap. There was no point in arguing and no point in rushing on at the moment, so I curled up on some soft leaves. It didn't take me long to fall asleep.

After I woke from my nap, Kith seemed satisfied when I told him I felt much better.

"What was your dream about?" he asked.

"It was just Ducar out in the shadows shouting my name and saying he was going to find me. He was very angry," I shuddered, remembering Ducar's voice in my mind. This hadn't been a very bad dream, compared to most, but it still left an unpleasant feeling behind.

"I had a dream last night," Kith said thoughtfully as we picked up our bags to continue walking.

Kith never talked about his dreams and I suddenly felt bad for never asking. We were both so focused on my nightmares that I never wondered if he had any himself.

"Was it a bad dream?" I asked tentatively, wondering how often he dealt with his nightmares silently.

"No. I'm not sure what it was."

This confused me. "You don't know what your dream was?"

Kith walked in silence for a moment, thinking. "Well, it was extremely vivid. It almost seemed like something I had seen before. There was a lady with us who looked like us, except I couldn't see her face. And for some reason, everything seemed weird to me. I kept looking at the sky and the trees like they were amazing and new." Kith looked sideways at me, "That probably sounds ridiculous, but it was like I had never seen them before. Like I expected it all to be different."

"You expected the trees to be different?" I asked, teasingly.

"I know it sounds crazy. The lady with us was different too. I don't know who she was, but in the dream, I could tell she wasn't acting normally. She was leading us to this huge stone building. It looked like it had been beautiful once, but hadn't been taken care of for a long time. I've never seen a building so big. Vines were growing all over the walls, and even the vines seemed weird to me."

Kith stopped talking for a while, and I walked alongside him waiting for him to continue, while trying to imagine the scene he described. I could easily assume the woman was meant to be Beatrice. She was the only woman who had ever taken care of us, but Kith said she was like us. Maybe his dream state was trying to turn Beatrice into one of us.

"I was excited about something," he said suddenly. "An adventure, I think. I was also worried about the lady who was with us. There seemed to be something wrong with her. We got inside the huge building, and I was just thinking how strange the adventure had turned out. Then I woke up."

A pang of guilt ran through me. Kith rarely just 'woke up'. He was always woken up by my nightmares. The way he was talking, sounded like he would have loved to continue his dream.

"Have you had dreams like that before?"

"I don't think so, but I don't usually remember my dreams. I'm not sure I even have one most nights. It always seems weird to me that you have nightmares every single night and I can never even remember if I dreamt at all." Kith gave me a sad look. "I wish you didn't have to deal with that. It's not fair that you've already suffered so much and now you're still the one suffering."

"It's not your fault, Kith. It's good that you don't have nightmares too. It might be selfish, but it's a huge comfort to have you there for me every time I wake up. If you were having bad dreams too, you might not wake up to mine. We would both just suffer on our own."

Kith seemed nullified by this. "I'm glad I can be there for you, too."

"If you do have more dreams, though, I'd like to hear them. It's a nice change from talking about my nightmares. Going on adventures with a mysterious lady?" I said in a mystified voice. "That sounds much better than seeing Ducar's face all the time." I grinned.

He grinned back and stopped walking. "I'm glad I have you, Mara. The world would be a terrible place without you in it."

When I woke up the next morning, I stretched my body to get ready for another day of walking and noticed I felt much more tired than normal. Once we started walking, I could feel an obvious difference in the amount of energy I had. It didn't take long for me to realize I was getting sick. Still, I tried to keep going like normal so Kith wouldn't notice.

He could tell there was something wrong, though. He always could. After we had traveled only a couple of hours, he stopped abruptly and gave me a very serious look.

"Mara, are you okay?" When I opened my mouth to protest, he cut me off. "You have been wobbling, walking slower than I've ever seen, and don't think you're fooling me when you try to hide your coughs. I'm worried. You can't push yourself too hard or it will just get worse."

He was right, of course. I thought I was hiding my coughing fits from him, but of course, I should have known better. He saw everything when it came to me.

Kith tried to talk me into taking the whole day to rest, but I wouldn't hear of it. We needed to find a town to restock our supplies. We finally settled on walking slowly for the day and taking more breaks than normal.

During one of those breaks, Kith asked if I remembered the remedy Beatrice would always make for us when we didn't feel well.

The memory brought a bad taste to my mouth. "How could I forget?" I groaned.

Kith laughed, "It was terrible, wasn't it?"

"I think it made me feel even worse than I did before taking it!" I said exasperatedly.

Kith gave me a mock stern look, "Well, if you'd rather not feel better, I can dump it out and leave you to be miserable on your own!" He said it exactly the way Beatrice always had when we complained about the medicine. We both burst into laughter.

"What I wouldn't give to have that remedy right now," Kith said, looking sideways at me. "Maybe I should try to recreate it."

"Don't you even dare!" I hollered. "I bet you would never find the ingredients out here, anyway. You don't even know what she used!"

Kith was immediately overtaken by a fit of laughter. "You should - see - your face!" he managed to spit out between laughs.

Suddenly, we were both laughing so hard we began to cry and before I knew it, I wasn't sure if I was crying with laughter or sadness.

After we had sobered up, I told Kith, "I'm not even very sick. Honestly," he was giving me a look of disbelief, "I've just got a cough. I'm sure I'll get over it in no time."

Neither of us had any idea just how wrong I was. When we went to bed that night, it took me ages to fall asleep. Even with how exhausted and desperately needing rest I was, it just wouldn't come. Coughing fits kept ravaging through me, but I tried to keep quiet.

Eventually, I drifted off, but when I woke it wasn't from a nightmare. My throat felt like it had closed up, and I could barely breathe. Intense coughing hit, and I fought even harder to draw in some air. Kith was at my side instantly, and I could vaguely feel him pounding on my back.

Suddenly, a burst of energy built in my lungs, and after a few more coughs I started to feel like I could draw in a little more air.

"I'm going to grab the water." Kith's voice felt distant, but I could still hear the worry.

Heat built in my chest, and just as Kith tried to hand me the water I coughed hard. There was a flash of light in front of me, and then my lungs filled with air. I still felt horrid, but I could breathe again. Turning to accept the water from Kith, I was surprised to see him sprawled on the ground, water all over his face.

"What just happened?" Kith looked at me as if a second head was sprouting from my neck.

"All I know is I managed to clear my lungs." I shrugged and took a swig of water.

"Yeah, by coughing out a cloud of sparks and somehow sending me flying." Kith shook his head as if he thought he must be losing his mind. "It's crazy, but I could have sworn you were glowing blue for a second."

I couldn't help but laugh. "That's all impossible. Isn't it?"

"If you asked me that yesterday, I would have said yes." He was still staring at me as if I was a stranger, and it made me uncomfortable.

"Stop looking at me like that." Suddenly, all the energy drained from me, and my legs went weak. Kith caught me just before I hit the ground.

"Are you alright?" As much as I hated seeing the fear and worry in his eyes, it was better than how he had been looking at me just moments ago.

"I'm just really tired. Sleep sounds nice." I curled up against him as my vision went dark.

Right before I fell asleep, I heard him whisper, "I knew it wasn't just a little cough."

CHAPTER FOUR: SEPTEMBER

✳   Kith   ✳

Being woken up by Mara was something I was used to. There was rarely, if ever, a night when I wasn't. In all the time we had been on the run, though, I had never been woken up by her coughing, struggling to breathe.

Normally when I was woken up by Mara, it was a simple matter of soothing her out of a nightmare. I would shake her gently and then hold and comfort her until the nightmare faded. This time, when I woke up, there was immediate fear. Mara was struggling to breathe and I had no idea how to help her.

At first, Mara did a fairly good job of hiding how poorly she was feeling. It was easy to think it really was due to wetness and mud and that she would feel better after a little time. As time went on, though, the signs of her getting sick had been pretty obvious. Long before she woke me up, it was evident that it was much more than she was letting on and I was trying to watch her carefully. It was hard to watch while I was sleeping, though.

Sleep would not be returning to me, I already knew that. I sat watching Mara's ragged breathing, a big part of me almost expecting her to just stop. It was a relief that she was able to breathe again, but I couldn't stop replaying what happened in my head. Never before had I seen anything like that. There was no logical explanation for sparks flying out of her mouth, or the blue glow that shoved me away from her so harshly.

Her shivering started getting worse, forcing me back to the present. I took my blanket and wrapped it around her. When my hand brushed her skin, I realized how extremely hot it was. A thin film of sweat coated her.

My heart started thumping and my stomach flipped and knotted. This was bad. All we had left to eat was a few of the apples I picked the day before. Moving Mara could risk her getting worse, and I had no idea how long it may take to find a town with food and medicine for her. I didn't dare leave her here while I searched, but I was now totally aware of the fact that forcing Mara to walk could be deadly.

As I watched, some small coughs would break up Mara's harsh breathing, but they didn't seem to be waking her up. No more sparks showed up, and I couldn't tell if I was relieved or disappointed. Part of me needed to see it again just to know I wasn't crazy. I knew that her sleep wasn't going to be very restful with all the coughing and ragged breathing, but I was just glad she was breathing.

The only good thing I could see in the situation was the fact that she didn't have a nightmare tonight. The coughing and restlessness weren't letting her sleep get deep enough to dream. It probably wasn't good for her recovery, but a nightmare wouldn't be either.

As the sun started to rise and the sky caught fire, I realized the only reasonable choice was to make camp. Moving would only make things worse. I wished I could find medicine for Mara, but she was right. I had no idea how Beatrice made the medicine she used to give us, so without finding a town, I had no hope of helping her. All I could do at the moment was keep Mara comfortable while she fought the sickness.

*   Mara   *

Before opening my eyes, the first thing I noticed was the chills that ran all through my body. After slowly blinking my eyes open, I saw that it was a sunny day. Confusion ran through me. Why would I be so cold on such a beautiful day? Looking down, I saw that I had not only my own blanket but Kith's as well. A shiver ran through my body. How was I still so cold? I took a deep breath, preparing to sit up, but a searing pain in my chest forced me back down. Then I was overcome with coughing.

Looking around, I saw that Kith was only a few yards away working on a fort. From the looks of it, he had been working for a while. The fort was almost done. I looked at the sun and judged that it had only been up for a short while. Kith must have gotten up early to start building.

I tried to remember what I was dreaming about. It was strange that I didn't wake up feeling scared. There was a strange creature I had never seen before. It almost seemed like one of the horses Ducar had, but it was so different. I was trying to remember what it looked like, but my mind was feeling fuzzy. With one last look at Kith, I drifted back to sleep.

"I want Mara to ride, too!" Said a tiny boy I immediately recognized as young Kith.

I was riding inside something very soft. When I looked around, I saw the brilliant white sky way above me and the pink grass underneath the wheels of whatever held me. Then I looked to the right and saw the most beautiful creature. It was the size of a horse with brilliant blue skin and dark black shapes on its body. The creature had a long round nose, again much like a horse, but there were knots of varying size down its face. The horns that sat atop its head were long and sharp.

At first glance this creature was menacing. That is until the small boy started running up to it and it bounded toward him, playfully prancing about him and stooping low to lick his face. Little Kith grabbed the horns on the creature's head and it gently raised him into the air and swayed its head slightly from side to side so Kith would swing gently about.

Somehow this creature knew the boy was his. It knew that he was small and it had to be gentle with him. The woman with us gently scooped Kith up and put him on the animal's back.

Suddenly, the woman was lifting me out of my seat. She brought me over to the creature and carefully arranged me in front of Kith. She then grabbed a rope that was tied to the animal and started walking slowly. As we moved, I could feel its back rising and falling beneath me with every step it took. Kith was laughing and whooping while I sat wide-eyed staring at the world around me.

There were men nearby working with more of these strange creatures, except they all looked different. One of them was dusty colored with large knots covering its entire body. There were ropes tied to several of these knots, and there was a cart being pulled behind it. Then I saw a man in armor race by on a dark burgundy mount with skin that looked like scales and small spikes that stuck out of its back and neck. The man rode on a metal seat that had been tied around the animal's stomach so he was not pierced by the spikes.

Of all this, however, the strangest sight I noticed was not the animals themselves, but their owners. Each and every one of them looked like Kith and me. I gawked openly as their purple skin shone in the red sunlight, and their long tails swayed. There was something more to these people, though. On each of their backs, they had large wings tucked together, so I couldn't see how large or functional they were. I wondered vaguely if they used these wings for flying.

It was only then that I realized even the woman who held the rope also shared the same purple skin. Her hair, however, was dark blue and she let it hang loose, the long waves falling down past her waist. She was beautiful. While smiling and waving at everyone we passed, she kept looking back and asking Kith if he was holding me tight. Every time she smiled at us her light pink eyes seemed to sparkle.

When we made it back to where we began, the woman lifted me off gently. The animal sank to the ground to let Kith off, and then nudged him with its nose, gently knocking him to the ground. It was obvious the care it took not to hurt him, but Kith was rolling around screaming and laughing, pretending to fight the animal off.

I was set back in my seat, then, and the woman began wheeling me away.

When I woke this time, I was smiling despite the chills that ran through my body. Looking around for Kith, I saw him sitting just outside the fort staring at me in what looked like a mixture of amazement and horror.

"What's wrong?" I asked, startled.

"You were smiling," Kith said tentatively, "while you were dreaming." He paused for a long moment and then continued, "Didn't you have a nightmare?"

"No. I dreamt about you and me when we were very small, riding on the most beautiful animal! There were people everywhere who looked just like us!" I went on to tell Kith every detail of my dream, pausing occasionally for a long round of racking coughs. Although I saw the worry on his face each time another fit hit me, Kith let me finish my story and listened with rapt attention.

"Wow, that sounds like an amazing dream," Kith mused.

He could tell the excitement and my animation in telling the story had worn me out, though, so he made me calm down and rest while he cooked some food.

My mouth watered at the smells coming from the fire. "Where did that come from? I thought we were out of food."

Kith smiled. "After working on the fort for a while, I took a break and managed to get us some meat and gathered some greens." I wondered how long I was sleeping that he had time to do all that.

When it was done, he brought me my food and water. "You need to drink plenty of water, Mara. Remember how Beatrice always said it was important for getting better?"

Drinking the water was hard because my throat hurt, and the threat of throwing the food back up made me hesitant to eat it. Eating slowly, I eventually got enough in me to satisfy Kith before curling up next to the dying fire in an attempt to warm up.

We spent a couple of hours just talking while I sat bundled in blankets. I talked about my dream a little bit, but Kith seemed to be trying to change the subject every chance he got. I wasn't sure if the idea of the dream made him sad because it was only a dream or if there was something else bothering him. Eventually, I decided to leave it alone and we talked about other things for a while before the conversation died and Kith insisted I should get more sleep. Somehow I did feel sleepy already. It felt like all I had been doing was sleeping, but I was still always so tired.

✳   Kith   ✳

Other than a few small coughing fits, Mara slept pretty peacefully. I woke on my own, instead of to the sound of Mara screaming, and realized that the sun had been up for a while. I don't think I ever slept this late before. I sat up and checked to make sure Mara was breathing. Her face looked so serene, that I couldn't bring myself to look away. Peace like this hadn't come to us in a very long time.

I'm not sure how long I watched Mara sleep, but it was a while. I wasn't sure if I was watching her more to make sure she kept breathing, or if I was waiting for more signs of sparks. After a while, she stretched and opened her eyes. She slowly looked around our fort with a slightly dazed look until she found me. "I had another dream."

"Yeah? What happened in this one?" I kept my voice even with a hint of being curious, but I was wondering if these dreams were a good sign or a sign of something bad to come.

Mara took a small sip of water before telling me her dream.

I was sitting on a pile of soft pink leafy plants and playing happily. Kith and the woman from before were nearby talking, but I couldn't really make out what they said. They didn't hold my interest, anyway.

As I was running my hands over the pink fluff under me, a big flying animal passed by. The bright colors caught my attention, and I couldn't help releasing a happy giggle.

The mouse-like animal seemed startled and flapped its big wings to bring it further away from my tiny hands as I reached out for it.

Rising on unsteady legs, I followed the blur of pinks and blues. Soon, we were in the trees. Only, these trees were different. They were many shades of pink and the leaves of some were soft and almost fluffy, while others were hard and triangular.

A small red blur rushed past, and I gave a passing thought to following that instead, but it was quickly out of sight. The flying mouse-like thing was getting further away, but I couldn't speed up without falling.

Big red flowers were off to my left. They reminded me of fluffy ball gowns and a sense of glee filled me as I rushed to smell them. Plopping down, I ran my hands over the soft, silky petals, then rubbed them against my cheek. The slight perfume and the soft petals made me feel content, and all the exploring was making me drowsy.

My eyes started to close, but a black and white bug caught my attention. After fighting my eyes back open, I saw that it wasn't a bug, but a tiny winged skeleton. Slowly, I realized it wasn't a real skeleton, but had markings that made it look like one.

It flew away, but I didn't have the energy to chase it. As my eyes started to close again, I heard my name being called. Suddenly, I was being lifted into the air and hugged tight.

"You worried me." A woman's voice said as she kissed my forehead. "Don't go running off like that!"

A feeling of peace flooded over me as I snuggled into the woman's chest and allowed my eyes to close.

Fantastical dreams should be much better than nightmares, so why did these concern me so much? For years I wished for Mara to have good dreams, but now it only seemed to be a sign of how sick she was.

Eyes full of anticipation, Mara watched me for a reaction. Not wanting to let her see how worried I was, I smiled wide. "That sounds like an amazing dream, Mara. So peaceful."

"Do you think there really could be a place where everyone looks like us?"

I paused realizing I had never given that possibility any thought. Was it possible? "I don't know, Mara. Where would a place like that be?"

She sighed with longing. "I don't know, but wouldn't it be lovely?" Her eyes were slightly glazed from sleep and illness, and her frazzled hair added a look of craziness to her.

"Let me fix your braid, Mara. That doesn't look comfortable."

She looked at me quizzically for a second but scooted over obediently and sat in front of me. Her waist-length black hair was full of huge tangles, so I carefully worked my fingers through until it was mostly smooth before braiding it and tying it off with the ribbon Grace had given her before leaving the show. It was once a pretty, silky gold, but the years and dirt had turned it a dull brown. Even so, Mara loved it. It was the only possession she had that wasn't strictly necessary.

When I was done, Mara leaned back against me, as if sitting that long had completely worn her out.

"Are you hungry?" The small amounts of food I managed to get her to eat were often thrown up during a coughing fit, but I knew she needed to try to keep fueled.

She shook her head slowly as if it weighed a ton. The heat coming off her felt as though it could burn me through my shirt. It seemed like her fever was getting worse, and it worried me even more.

"At least drink some water." I held the skin to her chapped lips and let it pour into her mouth. Wincing as she swallowed, Mara shook her head when I tried to pour some more.

Knowing I needed to keep up my own strength to continue to take care of Mara, I decided I should go ahead and eat. When I grabbed my last portion of the food, I worried about how empty our pack was. Beatrice's voice was in my head, talking about how the body couldn't restore itself without food and water to keep it fueled properly. We couldn't afford to run out of food with Mara this sick.

Sighing, I said, "I'm going to have to go looking for food. We're really low. You need to get some rest, ok?"

Fear showed in her eyes. "You're going to leave me alone?"

"I have no choice, Mara. You're in no shape to be up walking about, but we really can't afford to run out of food again."

Bravery almost always won out with Mara, so she sighed deeply and looked as determined as her very sick, young self could. "I'll be alright. Just please don't be gone long."

Settling down again to go back to sleep, she was quickly brought back up by another coughing fit. The heaving caused some of the small amounts of water I got into her to splatter on the ground.

Suddenly, a memory of watching Beatrice take care of Grace when she was sick popped into my mind. She was also having coughing fits that interrupted her sleep. Beatrice said that elevating her head would help keep her airways clear, and she'd breathe better. Pillows were piled under her to prop her up, and it was true, she did breathe a lot better after that.

"I'm going to try something," I muttered, then ran outside and gathered as many soft leaves as I could and brought them to pile under Mara. As soon as she laid back, the leaves were squished almost completely flat, which was no help at all.

I wished that I had pillows for her. It had been so long since we had pillows to sleep with. Beatrice made sure we had our packs, water skins, and blankets, but any extra stuff that she was planning to carry stayed behind with her when she got caught. Even with that stuff, pillows were never a priority, though.

My heart ached for Beatrice. She would know what to do for Mara. As gross as her medicine was, I knew we could use some now. We learned many skills while preparing to run, but not how to deal with sickness. I never thought to ask. Beatrice knew all about that, and she was coming with us.

The leaves obviously weren't going to work, so I looked around at what was available. I couldn't use the blankets, because Mara needed them. The packs would be horribly uncomfortable. There was a lot of dirt, though. Packed dirt would hold way better, so I quickly created a small mound and softened it with plenty of leaves, before helping Mara reposition so she was lying propped up.

As she settled, I could hear a slight improvement in her breathing. "This does feel better, Kith. Thank you," She offered a small smile.

Watching Mara drift back off to sleep, I wondered if she was going to have another of the crazy dreams. The world of her dreams sounded so wonderful, I wished I could be relieved she was having great dreams instead of nightmares.

Cautiously stepping out of our fort, I was blinded by the sun, which seemed so much brighter after being in the darkness for so long. Some stretching and enjoying the fresh air had me feeling almost back to normal.

Leaving Mara alone while she was sick and sleeping seemed like a terrible idea, even after she assured me she would be alright, but I didn't see any other choice. We both needed to be able to eat and keep up our strength.

First, I walked around the area close to where Mara slept so I could keep an eye on the bushes, but after a quick search, I realized there wasn't anything nearby.

Venturing out a little further, I started walking in wider

and wider circles around the hut until I could barely see it anymore. Eventually, I realized I was just going to have to go further out and hope Mara would be okay.

After picking a direction, I started walking. Wanting to make sure I wouldn't lose my way back, every now and then I used my claws to scratch arrows into the trees, facing the way I had come from.

As I went, I searched the ground and the trees for anything we could eat. Finally, I came across a bush that still had a few bunches of berries on it. There wasn't much, but it was something at least. Still, I didn't want to go back with only a few berries. I kept walking, carefully scanning every bush and tree I came across for even the smallest amount of food.

After I was gone for a little over an hour, exhaustion hit me hard. My lack of sleep must have made me tire more quickly, so I decided to take a short break. Sitting down on a grassy patch of ground, I leaned my head against a tall tree.

A sensation of falling washed over me and I jolted awake. Falling asleep so far away from the fort wasn't a good idea, so I slowly rose and started heading back, wishing I had more than a handful of berries.

Suddenly, anxiety hit me as I realized how long I had been away from Mara. I knew I had to get back to her quickly. Images of her scared and alone floated in front of my eyes and I ran like crazy toward our fort, my heart racing. It was stupid to leave her alone.

As I approached the fort, an eerie silence filled the air. No coughing or wheezing came from inside. I raced in, knocking the branches aside in my hurry. Mara's eyes were open wide, her face a dark mottled purple with thick foam surrounding her open mouth. My breath left my body as I collapsed next to her.

"Mara! Wake up, Mara!" I shook her and pounded on her back. I put my ear to her chest. Silence. Complete silence. No wheezy breathing. No heartbeat. Her limp head rolled against my arm, vacant eyes looking up at me in accusation. I left her alone. I left her alone and I wasn't here to help her. I left her alone and she couldn't breathe. I left her alone and she, she, I couldn't get my mind to wrap around the word. A scream ripped its way out of my throat and I fell forward with Mara in my arms.

My head fell forward as the scream ripped out of me. A startled bird flew away from nearby. The world swirled in front of me, but it was the forest, not our fort I saw. My chest ached and tears streamed down my face. I hadn't been breathing. Filling my lungs was painful, but sweet.

I rose to my feet unsteadily. The sun was much further across the sky than it should be. I was stuck in that nightmare for too long. My heart thumping from the memory of Mara's limp body, I raced back toward the fort, faster than I had ever run before. As I pushed the branches aside, I heard a slight cough and some ragged breathing.

*   Mara   *

"MARA!?" I woke with a start to Kith frantically crawling through the opening in the fort. "Are you okay?" He was breathing heavily and a sheen of sweat shone on his forehead.

"What's wrong? Did you see Ducar? Has he found us?" As weak as I was, I still tried to push myself up, preparing to run.

Kith's face melted into relief, and he shook his head slowly, his hands outstretched motioning for me to lay back down. "I was just afraid I had left you alone too long. I didn't want you to wake up and be worried." His eyes didn't quite meet mine and he quickly busied himself with one of the water skins as I watched him.

"Is that really all that's wrong?"

"Did you have any more of your strange dreams? With the silly animals and the people who look like us?"

This was such an obvious attempt to change the subject that I decided to lay off the questions. "I had a short one. It was just more of the horse-like creature I told you about before. I was watching you playing with it. You seemed very close to it, almost like you could understand each other without actually speaking," I laughed, "I wish I had one for myself!"

A dark look crossed Kith's face but was gone before I was sure it had even been there. *Were my dreams troubling him for some reason?* They were so lifelike, that it almost felt like a memory. *Why would that bother Kith?*

"How are you feeling?" Kith asked with concern on his face again.

"Well," I decided there was no point in hiding it, "mostly the same." I sighed. "Maybe a little worse."

A look of distress settled on Kith's face, "I'm sorry I was gone for so long. I told you I wouldn't be and then I went and fell asleep. It was very irresponsible and I'm sorry."

"You fell asleep?" This news shocked me.

"I didn't mean to. I just sat down to have a little rest and didn't even notice I had fallen asleep until I woke up again. I didn't mean to Mara, I'm so sorry."

I never knew Kith to fall asleep without meaning to, and I knew whenever we took breaks while walking it was more for me than for him so the idea of him stopping for a break and falling asleep was very unnatural.

"Are you feeling okay?" I asked tentatively. "You don't usually fall asleep during breaks."

"I said it was an accident, Mara. I really am sorry," Kith's face was dark and I could tell he was beating himself up over this already.

"It's okay, Kith, really. I slept most of the time anyway. I didn't even notice it had been so long."

Kith seemed to grudgingly accept this answer and mumbled that he needed to pee. After he left, I realized I was feeling tired even though I was in bed all day, so I laid back. I drifted in and out of sleep for a while until Kith woke me with a small shake. He was staring at me with wide eyes.

"Is something wrong?" I asked through the fogginess in my brain that never seemed to leave lately.

"Sorry, I just wanted to make sure you were okay," Kith walked back out of the fort, leaving me extremely confused.

When I emerged from the fort a minute later, Kith was at my side in an instant. "You should stay in bed until you feel better.

Are you hungry? I know it isn't much, but I did find some berries and I can keep looking."

"Why did you shake me just now?"

"You weren't making a lot of noise and I just wanted to make sure you were still breathing alright."

I supposed this might make sense. With how much coughing I was doing, maybe Kith was just so used to the noise that the quiet scared him. It was still strange for him to come and shake me though.

After we finished eating, I tried walking around a little, thinking it might be good for me to stretch my legs. I didn't get far before I started feeling a little nauseous and Kith had to help support me. I hadn't walked much in the past few days and what little food Kith managed to make me eat all came back up quickly so my body felt weak and unstable.

Kith helped me walk back to the fort, but I held us outside for a moment trying to recover from the nausea without throwing up. In the end, I lost the battle and the berries came right back up in gooey purplish clumps. Kith rinsed my face with water and helped me take a few sips so I could swish and spit the little bits of food out of my mouth.

Then, we both went back into the fort and laid down. Feeling miserable, I asked Kith to tell me a story to help me sleep.

I was so tired, though, that I barely stayed awake long enough to hear Kith finish the story he was making up for me. My sleep was so restless that I didn't have any real dreams, I just saw images pass by of Kith on his horse-like creature and a red sun shining down on me from a stark white sky. Then, the images stopped and the world went black apart from a man standing far away from me.

I knew instantly that it was Ducar. He turned and looked right at me. Suddenly, his face zoomed in close to mine and he was so close our noses were almost touching. For an agonizing moment he was staring right into my eyes and then I was awake, and there was someone else's face inches from mine staring at me. I yelped, partially from the dream and partially from the shock of my brother's face being so close to mine while I was sleeping.

"I'm sorry! I didn't mean to scare you!"

"What are you doing?" I squealed, pushing him away as I tried to calm the terror that lingered from the feeling of Ducar's face so close to mine.

Kith looked at me sheepishly. "I - I was trying to make sure you were still breathing. I woke up and I couldn't hear anything so I was listening to your breath."

It took a moment for me to register Kith's words. This was the third time in one day that I was woken up by Kith checking on me. Something was wrong.

"Why do you keep doing that?"

"What do you mean? Doing what?" His face was a mask of pure innocence.

"Earlier you ran into the fort, yelling my name and waking me up because you thought you had left me alone too long. Then you shook me awake because you were afraid I wasn't breathing and now you were just listening to my breath because again you thought I wasn't breathing. I know you're worried about me, Kith, but you're acting a little crazy."

It was quiet for a while while he stared at the ground.

"I really was afraid I left you alone for too long." His voice was so quiet I struggled to hear it.

There was a tremble in his voice that surprised me, which doubled when I looked at Kith more closely and saw that he was blinking back tears.

"Please tell me what's wrong," I whispered, my concern growing.

Kith turned away from me a little bit and began telling me about the dream he had while he was alone in the woods. It was no wonder he kept checking to make sure I was breathing.

"Do you think I'm going to die?" I asked quietly. It was something I had been trying not to think about.

"Of course not," he replied. "I'm just worried. I don't know what to do to help you feel better and I feel so helpless." he was struggling hard to fight the tears.

I scooted over to him and wrapped my arms around his waist. "I won't die, Kith. I promise." We both let out half-hearted chuckles at the idea of me promising such a thing.

Kith hugged me back, tighter than he ever had. I wanted so much to be stronger for him, but I was just so tired and weak all the time. I was sure it would pass eventually though. It had to, right?

✳   Kith   ✳

Ever since that nightmare, I hadn't been able to stop excessively worrying about Mara. At times she seemed to be breathing better; which should've reassured me, but the silence was terrifying. Telling her about the nightmare was hard, especially when she looked up at me with her innocent gold eyes and asked me if I thought she was going to die. The idea refused to leave my mind all day, but I couldn't let Mara know that.

Just sitting here worrying was wearing on me, so I stood up and surveyed the area around me. I could go looking for more to eat, but I didn't like the idea of leaving Mara by herself again. The nightmare scared me too much. It felt too real. Especially since I knew how badly she was doing. And yet, I didn't really know. Without Beatrice here to help, I had no idea how to tell what was wrong with her or how to help her. I didn't know if she would be better the next day or ever. I really didn't know anything about the situation we were in now or how to get out of it. I was in way over my head. Mara was counting on me, and all I ever did was let her down. I was barely even keeping her alive, and who knew how long that would last.

Beatrice's voice cut through the swirling fog in my brain. "Sitting around sulking isn't going to fix anything, my boy." It was something she said to me many times over the years, so of course she'd be saying it to me now.

She was right, dwelling on the terrible things that were happening wasn't going to make them any better. Determined to stop myself from thinking like that, I decided to do something to get my mind off of my failures as an older brother.

Keeping sight of our fort, I began to wander around

aimlessly. Feeling helpless, still.

After just a little bit of walking, my breathing was getting kind of heavy, and I was already worn out and cold. Realizing I needed some rest as well, I decided to go to bed.

When I turned around to walk back to the fort, I saw Mara trying to stand up. Rushing over, I put her arm around my neck.

"Don't worry about going anywhere, Mara, you just need to rest for a while," I said and gently tried to push her back into the fort.

"But, Kith, I have to pee."

"Oh. In that case, go on ahead."

Removing her arm from around my shoulder so she could walk somewhere private, I ignored the flush of embarrassment that crept up the edges of my face. When she only managed two steps before starting to fall, all thoughts of being overly concerned left my mind. She managed to hold herself up long enough for me to get to her and stabilize her. *How had she gotten that bad?*

I helped Mara sit on the edge of a fallen tree so she could do her business. I cringed at the thought of holding her while she peed but was relieved to find that she was able to hold herself up on her own.

"Don't try to get up and walk back yourself," I told her. "Just yell for me or wave when you're done, and I will come get you."

I walked a little ways away to give her some privacy, then turned around and waited for her to give me the signal. I couldn't believe how weak she was, but I should have seen it coming. Her illness caused her to throw up the small amount of food I got her to eat. Then, of course, there was the illness itself. Who knew what to expect from that?

When Mara started waving her hands, I began making my way over to her. After helping her up and back to bed, I gently tucked her in.

"You should drink some water," As I spoke, I got up to grab the water skins that were leaning against the tree.

After taking a few sips, a coughing fit caused her to stop. She handed the water back to me and laid down.

Clearing a spot next to her, I lay down and fell asleep almost instantly.

It wasn't long before I woke to more coughing, only this time it wasn't coming from Mara. A big slimy ball of mucus entered my throat, and I crawled quickly out of our fort to spit it out. I realized then how cold I was.

This cannot be happening, I thought to myself. *First Mara, now me? How will we survive?*

I laid back down and snuggled up next to Mara. She was so warm. I didn't know what else to do, so I fell back asleep.

It was a restless sleep, due to both Mara and myself waking up coughing. I woke up every time she did but managed to keep my coughing quiet enough to not wake her for most of the day. About halfway through a full day of sleeping, though, I woke to Mara watching me the same way I had been watching her.

Jerking back in surprise, I muttered, "Alright, I can see how I was being a bit creepy."

Mara looked sheepish. "Sorry. You were wheezing, and I got concerned." She looked at me closer, "You're getting sick, aren't you?"

I sighed, which led to a coughing fit. Once I could breathe again, I whispered, "I guess I'm sick. I was hoping not to worry you with it."

Mara rolled her eyes and sighed. "I'm not some delicate flower you have to protect from everything, Kith." After she finished, she looked slightly embarrassed but didn't retract the statement.

"I know, and I'm sorry I made you feel that way. You're the strongest person I know. I just don't want to put more on your shoulders than is already there."

Mara looked like she was at a loss for words, so she just leaned over and kissed my head gently. "Would you like some water?" Her tone clearly copied the doting, worried tone my own voice had carried the past few days.

After drinking some water, we went back to sleep. We woke occasionally to cough, or to drink some water, but mostly slept. Sometimes I woke up sure that my getting sick meant this was the end for us, but I was too weak to do anything about it.

It had been a while since Mara's last nightmare, and I was getting used to not waking up to her screams, which made this one extra terrifying. As I woke her up, though, I realized that it wasn't just screams. She was sobbing, as well. As I shook her, I wondered what she could be reliving this time.

It took ages for her to wake up, and the tears were only getting worse. Her face was even more pale, and the shivers came back in full force. By the time her eyes finally opened I was in a near panic.

Her golden eyes were full of confusion and sadness, but I was relieved to see them. I stroked her hair back from her wet forehead and soothed her. "I'm glad you're awake now." I was anxious to know what her nightmare was, but I wanted to give her some time to process that she was safe, first.

"What happened?"

"It was another nightmare, Mara. Do you want to talk about it?"

She paused, thinking for a minute. "Ok. Can I have some water first?"

I helped her sit and got her some water, then listened in shock and confusion as she described her nightmare.

*   Mara   *

I was standing in the courtyard of a castle overlooking the places I had seen in my previous dreams of the strange world, but as I looked around everything seemed different. Instead of being the tiny child I was in my other dreams, I was a grown woman now, and I didn't seem to have any control over what I was doing. It was as if I was in someone else's body.

The woman turned inside and walked down the hall into a child's room. We stood in the doorway for a while, just looking inside. For some reason, I got the idea it hadn't been used in quite some time. Suddenly, I was aware of the tears that trickled down her cheeks. I made an attempt to wipe them away, but her arms didn't move when I asked them to.

She slowly walked over to the child's bed and picked up a soft blanket that was decorated with all sorts of strange colorful creatures I had never seen before. She sat in an ornate rocking chair beside the bed and brought the blanket up to her face, freely sobbing into it now.

We sat like that for so long, that I thought the woman must have fallen asleep, but for some reason, I was still there in her body. Suddenly, a man's voice was yelling through the castle. The woman jumped up and ran to him, still clutching the child's blanket.

"It's happened!" The man yelled when he saw her. "He's here. We must get the children to safety."

Just then, a young boy came running down the hallway. At first, I thought he was Kith. He looked only a few years younger than me, and so much like I thought Kith must have at that age, but I realized it couldn't be him. His face was not as worn as my brother's. His skin was not as rough and calloused as Kith's had become by that time from working in the freak show, and although the tattoo on his face matched ours, it was at the top of his cheekbones while Kith's was on his upper right forehead. I suddenly realized that the man had a matching tattoo on his face as well, at the top of his forehead. I couldn't remember seeing it on any of the other faces I had seen in my dreams.

"Where are your sisters?" The man spoke to the boy, his voice full of urgency.

There was a big boom near the entrance of the castle that caused the walls to shake. It almost felt as if the rumbling tore me free from the woman's body. Feeling invincible in my dream state, I ran toward the sound.

What I saw as I walked out into the blinding light of day brought me to my knees. There were people everywhere around the castle. Running, screaming, and dying. Some lay on the ground writhing in pain, while others wept beside them or tried to drag them across the ground with them. There was a strange blue smoke in the air that seemed to be part of the cause of their pain.

Suddenly, men came riding from all directions riding on the horse-like creatures. The men coming from the castle held flags emblazoned with the same image that adorned our faces. The men charging from outside the castle waved a black flag with three purple lines swirling around each other and ending in daggers. They all wore strange masks on their faces that I could only assume were to protect them from the smoke.

As the men neared each other, they began throwing spears, shooting arrows, or tossing little balls that blew up on contact. I watched transfixed as several men stood on their steeds and unfolded the massive wings they had tucked behind their backs and soared off through the air. Their wings looked like that of a large bat, although the smooth skin that stretched across each set matched the hair color of the one who bore them. As they approached each other, each side drew their tails up, and I realized where there had once been a ball of fur, there were now sharp spikes poking out of the ends of their tails. The two groups reached each other and drew out their claws as they whipped with their tails and clawed at faces in midair.

My eyes returned to the ground, and I watched in horror as a man riding under the triple moon banner deliberately threw his spear directly at one of the animals being ridden instead of the rider. The brilliant red creature was covered in spikes and its skin looked hard as a rock. The spear caught it right in the neck where it was most vulnerable, however, and it crumpled to the ground knocking over other riders and crushing its own as it fell.

My unheard scream ripped through the night as I saw so many steeds fall on both sides. How could these men be so careless with their animals? All these people, all these animals I came to love through my dreams, were dying in front of me, and there was nothing I could do about it.

Suddenly, a small child stumbled out of a falling building just outside the castle gates. She was crawling on all fours, trying to get away from the blue smoke that wafted toward her home. Unfortunately, her escape from the smoke brought her close to the fighting. I watched as a man with the same forest green hair as she had, noticed and tried desperately to reach her. My heart lifted as I saw him reach her. He unfolded his wings and lifted off in one great swoop. They only made it halfway to the castle when an arrow struck the child right through the chest. The man stopped cold as she went limp in his arms.

A scream wrenched through the air as he fell back to the ground with the child clenched tightly in his arms. Filled with rage, he turned and found a man staring right at him laughing like a maniac, his next arrow notched and pointed directly at him. He was waiting to kill him; letting him feel all the despair of the young girl's death before putting him out of his misery. His next arrow finally flew, and the man dropped to the ground instantly.

In seconds, another man was on top of the one with the bow, wrenching him off his steed. I wondered vaguely if this man was a friend of the other because of how viciously he attacked. Screaming, he clawed at the man's *face and chest. Well after the man was dead, he continued clawing and clawing until all that was left was a bloody mass of meat at the top of a man's body. My stomach convulsed and I wanted to vomit, but the dream wouldn't allow it.*

Time seemed to speed up then, and I watched as hundreds of men and creatures fell on both sides. In the end, it was the men who waved the swirling banner who prevailed. Mourning all the death and destruction, I approached one of the creatures that lay on the ground.

It was a deep magenta, with skin that glittered in the sun and scales covering its entire body. Dried blood caked the ground around it. I lay my hand on its still-warm body, my eyes blurring as the tears rolled down my cheeks.

Then I heard a deep, gravelly voice that sounded familiar to me in a way I could not explain.

"We have lost many men, but look what we have achieved! The castle is ours for the taking! Bring me the royal family...alive."

Standing slowly, I turned and faced the crowd. There was a fierce-looking man riding on what looked like a monster. It was similar to the other creatures, but much larger with a rounder head that had foot-long spikes protruding from its face. Where every other creature had been a beauty to me, this one was only horror. Blood dripped from its teeth and glistened on its spiked head. The creature's entire body was a mass of muscle with red snake-like skin and long slender spikes covering almost every inch. It was a wonder the man could even sit on such a thing.

Then my eyes raised to the man himself. The first thing I noticed was the four long scars that ran across his cheek and down through his short-cut, red beard. His dark red hair hung loose and wild down to his chin, aside from a longer braid on the side, which reached to his shoulder. His pale blue eyes seemed to ignite as he surveyed the men around him intensely. As I continued to stare at him, I noticed what seemed like a light glow emanating from his body. It was almost like a ripple of dark light moved under his skin.

I couldn't understand why this man seemed so familiar to me, but just looking at him sent shivers down my spine. Suddenly, I became aware that his followers were gone. When I finally spotted them again, they were heading into the castle.

Running for the castle doors, I held my breath. I couldn't understand it, but these people were important to me somehow. Entering the doors, I ran down corridor after corridor trying to find any sign of them. Then the voice of the man outside rang out across the castle, sending chills down my spine.

Running back to the voice, I stopped dead at the sight of him holding the little boy who looked like Kith. He was cradling him in his arms as his mother and father were being held by his men, watching.

His mother was sobbing, begging him to spare her son. Watching in horror, I was certain the man was going to kill the boy.

And then he looked at me.

The man with the scars and the body that rippled with light looked right into my eyes. It felt like ice entered my veins.

He could see me.

His smile grew increasingly more menacing as he glared right into my eyes. I stood transfixed. For what felt like an eternity, I looked into those blue piercing eyes unable to look away, unable to even scream for all the good it would have done me. All I could do was look into his eyes as he stared into mine.

A burst of pain rippled through my entire body, and the world went black.

✳   Kith   ✳

Mara never had nightmares that weren't memories. I sat in shock for a while, not knowing what to say, just holding her as she cried for the creatures she had come to love. I didn't know if I should be more or less worried than I was after a normal nightmare. It seemed this sickness had changed things somehow.

After crying for several minutes, Mara sniffled and snuggled against me. Shivers were still running through her body. "My body hurts so bad." She paused for some coughing and moaned. "Do you think this is what Dylan felt like all the time?"

The mention of Dylan surprised me at first. "I'm not sure, Mara. It's possible."

"I understand now why he was grumpy a lot. Do you remember when Beatrice tried to convince him to leave the show?"

"I do." I thought back on the conversation we weren't meant to overhear.

Before Ducar found Mara and me, Dylan was the youngest person in the show. As soon as we showed up, he seemed afraid that we would take his place. In a way we did, in that we were doted on by the others and had a fascination with the crowds. While many people were familiar with the contortionist, no one had seen purple-skinned kids with claws and tails before. We were unique, which helped make Ducar's show more famous.

Before the storm, Dylan was nice enough, but there were some days he made it clear he didn't want anyone around. Anyone except Beatrice, that is. Dylan was the only person Beatrice would occasionally put over Mara and me. While he wasn't always fast to act in our defense after Ducar changed, he was the only one who could get him to ease up.

One day, Ducar decided to make the show longer than usual, hoping to draw in extra interest. We overheard Beatrice arguing that Dylan shouldn't do any extra, but Ducar ignored her.

During his performance, Dylan contorted himself even more than normal. He started small, showing how his thumb could be closed in his fist, but stretched out past all of his fingers. I could see people in the crowd trying to mimic him, but none were able to.

Small moves like that weren't entertaining for long, though. Dylan seemed reluctant to do his normal stunts but knew he had no choice. He stood and stretched his hands high, then bent and touched the floor with ease. Then he inched in so that his hands were behind his legs. Just as people were starting to catch on to how limber he was, he straightened, then bent backward, until his hands once again were on the floor. This time, when his hands went between his legs, his head followed. People in the crowd were unsure of what to think. Dylan put his chest to the floor, lifted his legs, and brought them around before rising to his feet once more.

Normally, he'd be done after just a few more stunts, but his part of the show lasted much longer that night, with his performance getting increasingly more difficult. As he finally left the stage, pain was written clearly on his face. He walked slowly, keeping his left arm tucked gently against his belly. Beatrice watched him, anger and sadness in her eyes.

After the show, we were given some freedom to wander around, which meant Ducar was probably in a rarely decent mood. We went looking for Beatrice, but she wasn't in her tent. On a hunch, we headed to Dylan's.

As we approached, we heard a loud popping sound followed by a low moan, and Dylan said, "Ah, I can move it again. Thanks."

Watching from the entrance, we saw Beatrice hand him a cup. "Drink your tea while your wrappings heat for a minute." Concern was evident on her face and she seemed to be contemplating her next words. "You shouldn't have pushed it so hard tonight."

Dylan's moody eyes darkened. "I didn't have much of a choice, though, did I?"

"I tried talking to him. I don't know what's been going on lately."

"I know you did." Dylan's voice held a softness that was unfamiliar. "You've always looked out for me."

Beatrice smiled and put her hand lightly on his head. "I always will, my boy."

Dylan turned away, hiding a rare show of emotion. "I'm sorry I doubted that. You deserve better."

Beatrice laughed, not a harsh one, but a gentle, loving laugh. "Jealousy is understandable. You know I love those kids as if they were my own, but many mothers have three kids they love equally." She stroked her thumb down his cheek before turning and grabbing some long strips of cloth.

Dylan was quiet as she carefully wrapped his arms from shoulder to wrist. His face displayed the pain he usually kept hidden.

When she finished, she looked at him thoughtfully before softly speaking. "Have you considered that it might be in your best interest to leave the show?"

Dylan looked like he had been slapped. "You know I can't do that. Remember what happened when Grace left?"

"Of course I do. Do you ever think that she got lucky to not have to witness this?"

"There's nothing out there for me. Grace at least had her husband and a new family to fall on when Ducar suddenly cut her off from us. What would I do out there?"

"Not have to damage your body for entertainment, that's what. I don't know how much more your body can handle before it starts breaking down for good." She paused tears in her eyes. "I'm afraid you're going to kill yourself for the entertainment of people who don't give a shit."

Dylan's eyes widened at her language, and for a second his face displayed the fear of her being right. "I'd die out there without you." His hands were fiddling with his wrappings out of nervousness, but Beatrice grabbed them in both of hers and held them until his eyes met hers.

"I never said anything about you leaving alone, my boy." She rose and kissed his forehead. "I'll give you some time to think, and we'll talk later."

Mara and I realized she was headed toward us and darted away, but I was pretty sure we had been spotted.

We sat in silence for a while. Thinking about that conversation left me feeling guilty. We spent so much time worrying about what happened to Beatrice but hadn't really considered Dylan. I almost forgot Beatrice planned to take him with us, hoping to spare him the pain his performances caused.

We were never terribly close to Dylan, but he was the one who gave Mara the drink that helped her heal faster. He was also the only one who could get Ducar to stop hurting her. He deserved more than our passing thoughts. If Ducar knew he was planning on leaving with us, he was probably punished with Beatrice, and if not, he was most likely still being forced to perform.

Mara sniffled, and I realized her tears had started again. I thought about asking why, but I knew it was probably a mix of many things. She was probably still mourning the animals from her dreams, too. With the nightmare, would those fantasy dreams end? The thought made me more sad than I expected, with how much they worried me. Talking about them made her so happy, though, and I was going to miss that.

Gently rubbing my hands on her arms, I tried to comfort and warm her at the same time. She didn't talk but curled into me a little bit more. Once she calmed down, I pulled out the water. My heart sank when I remembered that we were completely out of food.

"Mara, you need to try to get some water down." I held her water skin to her mouth. "We don't have any more food, so I'm going to have to go out again later." My throat felt like it was going to close up with the idea of leaving her alone again and the memory of what happened the last time.

Mara looked at me quietly for a minute, her eyes reflecting what I was thinking. She took several small sips of water. It seemed like she forced herself to drink more to make me feel better. "I should probably take a nap anyway. I'm pretty tired." As if to prove her point, she yawned and stretched.

Before leaving, I tucked her in on her little mound in the fort and tried to make sure she was as comfortable as possible. Leaving her again made me more nervous than I'd been in a long time, but our lack of food was urgent. She'd never get better if we were starving.

Taking a deep breath, I started walking in the opposite direction from where I went the last time. I already knew there wasn't anything that way. As much as I hated it, I knew there was no point staying close to our camp. I'd already found what little was around there. I would just have to try to be quick so I wouldn't be gone long.

Gathering my resolve, I quickened my pace. I wanted to run, but my body was telling me that wasn't a good idea. Focusing so much on getting Mara better made it easy to forget that I was also a bit sick. Somehow I wasn't feeling as poorly as she was, but I still knew I couldn't push it too much.

After I was gone for what seemed like a long time, I still had nothing to show for it. How could it be this hard to find food with plants all around? Frustration welled up in me, and I was about to yell out when I heard low voices in the distance. There were several different voices, all deep, but I couldn't hear what any of them were saying. Scrambling up the nearest tree, I looked around from my new vantage point. Using the trees as cover, I got as close to the camp as I dared, hoping I was wrong.

The men packing up their camp were quite familiar to me. Bile rose in my throat with the fear and knowledge of how close they were. As I watched, I realized something was wrong. Ducar was not with his men, nor did I see him anywhere around the camp. As I spun around and started racing through the trees in the direction I came from, I wondered how long he had been gone and how far he could have gotten. Surely he couldn't be there already, right?

Cursing myself for being stupid enough to leave Mara alone again, I pushed harder and harder to get back faster. My heart felt ready to shatter in my chest, both from fear and exhaustion. I hadn't allowed myself to acknowledge just how weak I was getting, right alongside Mara, but I refused to be weak right now.

Close to the fort, I started scanning the area, but I didn't see anyone. Maybe he wasn't here, and we'd have a chance to get away again without being spotted. I dropped to the ground as I got close to the fort so I could run in and grab Mara without being seen, but when it came into view, he was there. He was coming out of our fort, and he had Mara in his arms. I growled as I raced forward, but his sneer when he saw me froze my body.

"Oh, Kith, you should be glad. She was obviously better off with me. Let me take her home, and she'll at least live. It's pretty clear that she'll die out here with *you*." His voice dripped with venom, and his words felt like poison in my heart. Was he right? Was Mara going to die with me? Was I going to let her and Beatrice down? How could I have been failing so badly?

Breathing felt impossible, my chest was gripped with icy vices. Maybe I should just give in, and let us be taken back to where at least we'd have a shot at survival.

CHAPTER FIVE: SEPTEMBER

✳   Kith   ✳

Suddenly, flashbacks of all the nights that caused Mara's nightmares raced through my mind. The hands that held Mara so gently now were responsible for all her problems, all her pain. He still sneered at me, could tell how his words had cut, and read my hesitation. Mara looked so small and delicate, but her eyes met mine, and I knew she wasn't better off in the hands of evil. We'd make it somehow.

Ducar smiled, trying to look as nice as he could. He thought he was winning. I couldn't believe I'd almost given in to his lies. Another growl escaped as my body convulsed, trying to work its way out of whatever was holding me back. Finally, I broke free and leaped toward him, knocking him backward so Mara would fall on him and not the other way around. After giving Mara a gentle but firm shove to get her out of the way, I began clawing wildly at the closest thing to me. Due to the way he fell, that was Ducar's leg.

Feeling crazy with pent-up anger and frustration, I didn't even register what I was doing. Hands flew at me, trying to knock me away, but I kept going until a noise brought me out of my haze. Mara was vomiting again. Only then did I hear the screams coming from Ducar. He had been stupid to go out alone without his men, but they would not hang behind if they heard that screaming. Mara and I couldn't be there when they came to Ducar's aid.

I jumped up and took one look at what I'd done. Ducar's leg now barely resembled a leg at all. For a brief second, I wondered if Mara had thrown up because she was sick or because of the gore that lay in front of her, but I didn't have time to think about that.

When I picked up my little sister, I was horrified by how much lighter she had become. After quickly packing up our blankets and water skins, I raced away from the bloody mess I

created. I knew Ducar was in no shape to chase after us just yet, but I wasn't so sure about all his men. I just hoped they would be too busy tending to their master to worry about us.

I don't know how long I ran before my legs finally gave out, and I crumpled to the ground with Mara still in my arms. My whole body ached. At least a few hours had passed since we left Ducar, and I hadn't heard nor seen any sign of his men. But I was too afraid to stop. I couldn't let him get his filthy hands on Mara again. So I stood back up and set Mara on her feet.

"Can you walk?" I asked pleadingly.

"Yes," Mara whispered and then started out at a pace that was faster than I expected, but still slow.

We went for a few more hours until finally I called a break. When I sat, I realized I still had blood caked on my hands. My stomach twisted at the memory of what I had done. Anger overcame me, and I completely lost control of myself. Ducar deserved the pain, but I didn't feel right about the viciousness with which I attacked him. I couldn't waste water while we were on the run, so I used leaves and mud to scrub myself.

After resting for about an hour, we got back on our feet. I knew Ducar was wounded, but after having us right in his clutches I was sure he would stop for nothing, even recovery. That meant we couldn't either.

We moved for hours before finally taking another break. Sometimes I carried Mara when I thought she couldn't go any further on her own. Occasionally I thought about looking for food, but I was so focused on getting us away from Ducar that I could barely think of anything else.

My body ached all the time, and I don't know how I made it for so long. It seemed like every time I thought I couldn't go any further, somehow a new burst of strength would hit me. I decided it must be because of how horrified I was by the image of Ducar standing there cradling my sister and wearing the most sadistic smile I had ever seen. That smile was what kept me going. I never wanted to see it again.

As much as I tried, I couldn't get the sight of Kith shredding Ducar's leg out of my mind. It reminded me so much of the man from my dream who clawed at another man's face. It was such a gruesome scene on both counts that it made me sick. There was a different feeling while watching Kith tear Ducar apart, though. In the dream, everything was confusing with all the horrors I witnessed, and I felt sad and terrified for everyone who was a part of it.

When I watched Kith tear and tear at Ducar, however, I felt the greatest rush of relief. My whole body cringed every time I thought of how Ducar held me. I thought we were doomed, and I was preparing myself for a lifetime of torment. How could we ever escape again without Beatrice? When Ducar spoke to Kith of me dying, I wanted so much to protest, but for some reason, my voice wouldn't work. I couldn't get any words to come out, I could barely even move. As I slowly managed to turn my head and looked into Kith's eyes, I saw the doubt. I could see that he was beginning to believe Ducar was right, and for a moment I thought all hope was lost.

Once Kith jumped on Ducar and knocked me out of his arms and into safety, I felt a sudden freedom. It was as though just by touching me, Ducar had taken away my ability to control my body. I rolled over and sat up to watch as Kith let out all his pent-up anger and frustration. My initial feeling was only that of relief. Relief to be away from the monster, and that Kith hadn't given in to him.

As I watched him, though, I began to feel a mix of other emotions that at the time I could not explain. Thinking about it, I realized Kith had grown so much since we left the camp. As soon as Beatrice was gone, Kith assumed the role of my protector. I slowly came to understand the reason my emotions were so mixed. With how much Kith had grown and how strong he became, I also realized how weak I still was. I let Kith do everything for both of us with minimum contribution from me.

While we were running, my mind kept wandering back to the scenes of destruction. This helped distract me from how horrible I felt, but I wished I could think of something else. I wanted to forget Ducar holding me, and how close I was to returning to that life, but the memories haunted me. Time felt foggy, and I don't know how long we ran before my legs buckled and collapsed under me. Falling into the dirt, I barely noticed the stick that scratched my leg. My thoughts kept me distracted a little too well, judging by how completely my body was shutting down.

"Mara! Are you alright?" Kith was at my side in an instant. I hated myself for my weakness. With Ducar so close we couldn't afford to stop like this. My whole body hurt and my mind felt like it was swimming in muddy water.

"Kith. I'm so tired." My words came out distorted, and I could barely feel my mouth move. My eyes closed without my permission.

"It's alright, Mara. We should get some rest." Kith sounded like he was very far away, but I could feel him next to me. I felt him rub my back as I tried to force myself to stay alert, to stand back up and keep moving.

Everything went black.

✳   Kith   ✳

When Mara collapsed, my heart stopped beating. I knew she had to be tired but to see her completely crash from the exhaustion was just too much for me. It only took seconds for her to fall asleep, but I knew I couldn't leave her just lying there in the open.

With how sick Mara remained and how tired we both were, I didn't think sleeping in a tree would be a good idea. Quickly grabbing some branches, I made a small shelter around the tree she slept next to. By the time it was done, I was ready to pass out right next to it. Instead, I carefully climbed inside and curled up next to my sister.

When I finally woke, it was late in the day. Hunger pains were setting in and I heard Mara coughing like crazy. Lifting her onto my lap to try to help her breathe, I patted and rubbed her back. The coughing kept getting worse, though. As I continued to rub her back, I realized she was getting warmer. Suddenly, her body raised slightly away from me, surrounded by a pale blue light. Then she fell back against me. Each cough brought a small light to the shelter and repeated the lift. It was similar to what happened before when I was knocked down, but it wasn't happening as strongly. Finally, the coughing fit subsided.

As she lay back against me, I looked at her and noticed just how pale she was. Her lips were light red, and she was shivering. Her eyes seemed sunken in and she was so small. She hadn't been able to hold her food down for almost a week, and now we were out completely.

Worry settled in that I pushed Mara too hard to keep going, but I was so afraid of Ducar finding us. Even though I knew he wasn't likely to get far with how badly I hurt his leg, I couldn't depend on all of his men staying behind with him.

Mara started heaving and rolled to the side; off of my lap. Her body went through the motions of throwing up, but there was nothing inside her for it to get out. After watching in alarm as she convulsed over and over again, I grabbed the only water skin left with anything in it and held it to her lips. Most of the water dribbled down her face, and she gently pushed the skin away and lay back down.

The realization hit me like a rock. My baby sister whom I swore to protect was going to die. After all we'd been through, it hadn't been enough. I was going to lose her, and then I would be alone in this hateful world. Ducar was right, I was a failure. How did I think I could even hope to keep Mara safe? At least with him, she would have lived. Ducar always had food, even if he often withheld it for punishment. He would have known what to do to make her better. She would have lived.

But life with Ducar wasn't life at all. Mara would never have wanted to go back even if she knew she would die otherwise. It was better for her to die out here in the woods where she tasted a bit of freedom, than to live a life full of torture from that monster.

Deciding I couldn't give up, I rose. Maybe if I was able to find food and water she would live. I didn't know what else to do.

I knew Mara really needed meat, something substantial, but I didn't know how to get her any. After searching frantically for about an hour, I found a few bushes of berries. Taking off my shirt, I used it to carry every berry I could find.

As I ran back to Mara, it began to rain. It was just a slow drizzle, but it seemed that for once, nature must have heard my needs. Setting my shirt full of berries down by the shelter, I ran back to grab the water skins. Leaving them to fill, I brought the berries inside.

"Mara, wake up." I shook her gently. She was burning up, but still shivering. The fear in the pit of my stomach returned.

"Enh." Mara's eyelashes twitched, but her eyes didn't open.

"Mara, I have water and some berries." I wished I had more food for her, but knew that she needed to get something in her immediately. There was no response.

"Mara, wake up." I shook her gently. My heart started pounding. I lifted her head and her mouth fell open slightly. I lifted a water skin to her lips and poured some water inside. Again, much of it dribbled down her face, but she did swallow some. She didn't fully wake up but snuggled up against me more. I put the water skin down and wrapped my arms around her.

"I love you, Mara," I whispered against her hair. I kissed the top of her head and reached for a berry, mashing it up a bit before sticking it in her mouth.

Slowly, Mara opened her eyes. She stared up at me for a second and then ate the berry, along with all the rest that I had brought to her. After giving her some more water, I set the skin back out to refill. By the time I got back inside, she was already asleep.

Giving Mara both blankets again, I tucked her in up to her chin. The days were getting colder, bringing a whole new set of worries. We needed to find somewhere to stay for the winter, but she was in no shape to go anywhere.

It wasn't long before Mara started coughing and hacking again, and I was afraid she was going to throw up. Leaning my back against the tree, I propped Mara up on my legs again.

After a particularly rough coughing fit, her head slumped backward against my arm. Her golden eyes were rolled up, showing only the blacks.

"Mara!" I pounded her back to try to get her to breathe, but there was no reaction. "Mara!" I lightly shook her, but her head just rolled, so I stopped. "Mara!" There was some faint breath, but I was losing her fast. "Mara! Come back to me! Don't leave me! I'll do better. I'll take care of you! Please, don't leave me alone." I could barely speak through the sobs.

A tingling sensation began building up in my arms. I wrapped them around Mara and held her, rocking back and forth while my tears soaked her face. No longer able to speak, I tried to will my energy into her, silently pleading for her to wake up and get better. My arms were growing warm. The tingling was getting stronger, and they almost seemed to glow.

I don't know when I started humming. There was no melody to it, just a sound. My legs were numb, but I didn't care. I just kept rocking her, begging for her to live as my tears dripped all over her face and neck.

Her hand twitched. My heart leaped.

Nothing. My heart broke.

The tingling in my arms got too intense to ignore, but I didn't know what to do to stop it.

Suddenly, I felt a burst of energy run through me like electricity. For a second, it felt like my mind disconnected from my body, and I saw myself lay Mara on the ground and then place one hand on her chest and the other on her head.

When my mind and body reconnected, the heat coursing through me was on the edge of being painful. Slowly, the tingling went down my arms and to my hands where they were touching Mara. Just as it felt like I wasn't going to be able to stand it anymore, the heat and energy seeped out of me, and into Mara. For a minute, she shone brightly and I thought I must be going crazy.

Mara took a deep breath.

Everything started spinning.

She breathed again.

Darkness was descending on me quickly.

Mara was breathing, breathing, breathing. Without wheezing. Without coughing.

The world went black.

For days, everything was foggy, and I didn't know what was going on around me or how much time passed. I could feel myself fading away, but there was nothing I could do. My last thought was how sad I was to leave Kith all alone in a world that had been so cruel to him.

Suddenly, I heard Kith begging me to come back. Thoughts began to form again, and I wondered how I wasn't dead. It took a long time before I realized where I was. There was warmth all around me, throughout my body, and I could feel the pain ebbing away as my frail limbs seemed to strengthen. There was a light through the fog, and just as the heat through my body was becoming unbearable, it all stopped. Everything was still and quiet.

I don't know how much time passed before I began to stir. I was in a stupor of sickness for so long. I remembered Kith feeding me mashed berries. *That was recent, wasn't it?* When I turned my head, it didn't ache. Stretching my arms and legs, I marveled at the lack of pain.

Slowly it came back to me, the sensation of being rocked. There were tears. Lots of tears. *Was I dead?* I felt alive. *Where was Kith?*

Turning back to where I was lying on the ground, I saw him splayed out next to the tree as if he had been sitting up and then slumped sideways.

"Kith!" There was no response. *What happened here?* I remembered heat. A searing heat and then...and then I woke up. I don't know how, but Kith healed me. He must have. Did he die to save me? I checked. He was breathing.

A surge of responsibility filled me, and I decided to look for food. Feeling stronger than I had in years, I was determined to take part in keeping us alive from now on.

As I searched, I couldn't help thinking about Kith's attack on Ducar. There was something right at the edge of my mind that I just couldn't quite grasp. I thought back to my dream and the man who had been ripped to pieces by another's claws. The scene was revolting, but I knew my mind was trying to go past that. During the time I spent being sick, the world was such a haze that I was having a hard time remembering the dream now. I went through the whole thing in my mind, trying desperately to remember all the details. Suddenly, I grasped the thought that had been eluding me, and it hit me like an arrow to my chest.

I remembered the man whose piercing eyes stared at me as though they saw right through the dream and knew I was there. The man who appeared to be the leader caused all the destruction. The man who held the little boy who looked just like Kith with the same sort of sadistic smile Ducar showed while he held me. I remembered this man's face so clearly, and I now knew why his voice had sounded so familiar at the time. He was the man who spoke to me after Ducar's beatings.

When Dylan gave me the purple drink to help me heal, that same man was the one who spoke of saving me. He seemed wonderful; a savior who could come in and rescue us from all of this. But it turned out, he was just the same as Ducar. That horrible smile he had when watching the destruction all around him sickened me. The way his eyes dug into mine when we looked at each other made it clear he was no savior. He was only another monster waiting to snatch us up.

I never told Kith about the voice out of fear that I was going crazy. Now I knew I could never talk to him about it. It would worry him even more than the dreams seemed to. My mind felt like a mess of confusion with this new knowledge. Slouching on a stump, I considered the predicament. If only I could talk to Kith about it, he could help me sort out the mixture of emotions and feelings of betrayal I was filled with.

Sitting and dwelling on it was doing me no good, though. With a sigh, I rose from the stump and walked on. A gust of wind brought me out of my thoughts as I realized how cold it became. Wrapping my clothes tighter around me, I looked around. The wind held a faint smell that I didn't recognize.

Following the scent led me to a group of big leafy trees. Scattered all over the ground were small, round brown balls. A squirrel darted up a nearby tree as I approached, one of the round things clutched in its teeth. Bending down, I picked one up and tried biting into it. There was a loud crunch and pain in my mouth. In my hand, the outer shell had broken, and I realized it was a nut inside. After discarding the shell, I tried the nut. It was crunchy with a surprising creaminess to it.

They seemed to still be good, so I quickly gathered up as much as I could and rushed back to Kith. I didn't want him to wake up alone after all the emotion he went through just before passing out. While waiting for him to wake up, I found a rock and started smashing the nuts open, eating some as I went. Focusing all my attention on my task, I tried to keep my mind off of my dreams and in the real world.

❋   Kith   ❋

Waking to Mara staring down at me, I reached up to touch her face. "Am I dreaming?"

A sweet sound filled the air. It was a sound I didn't hear often enough, a sound that I thought I would never hear again. Mara was laughing.

"No, Kith. It's not a dream. You healed me."

"You were dying."

She smiled, and it was the most beautiful sight I have ever seen. "I didn't. I don't know how you did it, but you healed me."

"What do you mean?" I slowly sat up. My body felt extremely weak, and my arms shook when I put them down to support myself.

"I don't really remember much that happened while I was sick. It's all a bit of a blur. I do remember feeling like I was fading away until I heard your voice calling me back. Then I got really hot. When the heat left I felt all better, but you were asleep. I've been worried about you."

"How long have I been asleep?" I couldn't shake the grogginess.

"About a day."

"A whole day?"

"Maybe a little bit more." She shrugged slightly.

"Are you ok?"

"I'm great, just a little hungry. I managed to find some food, but I didn't want to leave you alone for too long."

"What did you find?" I looked at Mara. Not only did she look better, but she looked more alive than I had seen her in a long time. Whatever happened removed some of her scars, and her skin was its normal shade of purple. Looking at her, you would never guess that she had just been on her deathbed.

"Kith, you're creeping me out!" I could tell she didn't actually mean it though, because her eyes were lit up, and she was barely containing a laugh. In her hand, I noticed the food she found. Grabbing one of the nuts, I popped it into my mouth and was delighted by the crunch when I bit down.

"Have you looked for any signs of Ducar?" I asked while we continued to eat.

When Mara shook her head, the usual worry returned. For two days now, we were camped here and I slept a full day, leaving my sister to fend for herself.

Mara must have caught on to what I was thinking. "Kith, don't be so hard on yourself. You needed the rest after healing me. It took a lot out of you."

I smiled, but only partially meant it. We needed to be on our way, but I didn't want to force Mara to start moving again after being sick for so long. She kept saying I healed her, but that was impossible. I was sure she had to have some lingering effects from the sickness. When I tried to stand up to check everything out, my legs wobbled under me.

"I don't think you should get up right now." Mara looked concerned. "Whatever you did to heal me, made you really weak. You should get some rest."

"We are going to need more food. I don't think I'll recover well without it."

Mara was quiet for a moment. "Resting will help you recover, too. After you sleep, we can look for more food." With that, she tucked both blankets around me the way I always tucked her in, and snuggled in beside me.

When I opened my eyes again, Mara was sitting next to me. I wondered if she slept at all. She saw me looking at her and handed me the water, telling me to drink. My arms didn't shake as bad when I sat up, but for a minute I felt queasy. Unsure if I was going to throw up, I waited for the moment to pass.

Deciding I couldn't lay there anymore, I began trying to stand. With Mara's help, I made it out of the fort. The air felt great. Sitting on a rock at the base of a tree to rest, I was surprised at how weak I still felt.

Once I got up and really started walking, I did alright, but it was slow moving. I didn't want to stop for fear of not being able to get going again. Mara walked beside me as we searched for food. "Mara, I'm alright. Why don't you go back and rest, or look in the other direction? We can meet back at the fort with our findings."

"Are you sure?"

I nodded as I continued to walk.

Reluctantly, Mara left to look in different places, the worry still evident on her face. How had we changed roles so suddenly?

After walking for several minutes a faint smell of blood reached my nose. I looked around for Mara, but quickly realized it wasn't her blood I was smelling.

Following the smell, I found a confusing sight. A rabbit was hanging from a tree, squirming in an attempt to escape. It took me a moment to even see the rope it was hanging from.

My first instinct was to hide. I didn't know how a rope got into a tree, but all possibilities came back to a person putting it there. Looking around, all I saw was the tantalizing rabbit. My mouth began to water. After making sure no one was watching, I got closer. It must have injured itself in its struggle to get free, as there was a scratch on its hind leg.

Examining the rope, I tried to figure out how the rabbit got caught in it. Swinging the rabbit into a big branch, I hit it on the back of the head like Beatrice taught me. It didn't take long to stop moving completely. Cutting the rope from the tree with my claws, I grabbed the rabbit and headed back to Mara.

A smile spread across my face when I reached the fort and realized I wasn't the only one who found food. Mara was already back, a sizable pile of berries and more of the nuts lay on top of one of our packs for me to see. Her eyes sparkled when they saw what I was carrying, and I was surprised again to see how healthy she looked. Maybe I really did heal her. But that was impossible, wasn't it?

While the meat was cooking, I told Mara about the rope hanging. We looked at it some more and could only guess that the rabbit stepped on the rope, which somehow caused it to close around its leg and lift it into the tree. Once the meat was done cooking, all thoughts of figuring out the trap left our minds.

*   Mara   *

The day after Kith woke up, I found a row of bushes still full of small, but plump red berries that looked different from the ones we had. Calling Kith over, I eagerly began plucking the berries, excited for a new flavor.

Once we picked most of the berries, we sat leaning against a tree to eat. Dividing them up, we made sure to save some for later. Just as Kith went to stick one in his mouth, his arm convulsed and he yelped in pain dropping the berry.

"Are you okay!?" I exclaimed. "What happened?"

"I don't know. My arm hurt really bad for a second, but now I don't feel anything."

"Can you move it?" I asked, wondering if this was some late side effect of healing me. As much as Kith kept insisting it was impossible, there was no other explanation for my sudden recovery. Now I wondered if he was suffering for having done it.

He flapped his arm around out in front of him and then wiggled his fingers. "Yeah. It seems fine."

I watched him warily before grabbing a small handful of berries. When I brought them up to my mouth, my arm went through the same motions as Kith's. As soon as the berries left my hand the convulsions stopped.

"It's the berries," Kith said quietly.

Looking at him quizzically, I grabbed another handful of berries. Once again, as soon as I brought them close to my mouth, I lost complete control of my arm and the berries dropped to the ground.

"What's happening?" I could hear the fear and confusion in my voice, which annoyed me slightly.

"I don't know," Kith replied. "This doesn't make any sense."

After trying one more time and experiencing the same thing, we finally gave up and sat beside the bushes. Our bewilderment kept us frozen in place.

Every now and then, I would grab another berry and try to put it in my mouth. Each time the convulsions forced me to drop it. As a test, I ate a bite of the rabbit and nothing happened. "What is wrong with these berries?" I exclaimed.

What seemed like hours later, a small squirrel staggered out of the bushes across us. The squirrel appeared to have a broken leg, and it was making a strange sound I never heard from an animal before. It sounded like it was in a lot of pain. Noticing its ribs were easily visible, I knew it must be just as hungry as we were. The squirrel swayed as it tried to keep walking on its hurt leg.

We were so still with fatigue, that it must not have thought we were a threat. When it got close to us, I couldn't resist the urge to reach out for it.

"Stop!" Kith whispered with urgency. I looked at him in confusion. "Look at it, Mara, it could have diseases. Listen to that weird sound it's making."

"It's just hurt!" I replied, anguished by the pain it must be feeling. Sitting back down, I sadly watched the poor creature.

The squirrel approached some of the berries we dropped. I was expecting to see it go through the same trouble we experienced, but instead, it hurriedly ate them and moved along to some more. We watched in confusion as the squirrel ate the berries with no problem at all.

Suddenly, tremors started running through its tiny body. I yelped in surprise and scurried over to the animal.

"What's wrong with it?" I yelled.

Kith slowly crawled beside me to get a better look. There was foam coming from its mouth. The tremors subsided and the squirrel stopped breathing.

"It was the berries. They must have been poisonous. That's why we couldn't eat them," Kith concluded, sounding mystified.

"But that doesn't make any sense. The squirrel ate them; why wouldn't we be able to?"

We sat puzzling over that for a few moments until finally, I started digging in the dirt.

"What are you doing?" Kith asked.

"I'm going to bury it. I don't understand why we couldn't eat the berries, but the squirrel could. It feels like we cheated. The least I can do is bury it."

Kith set to work helping me dig a hole big enough for the tiny body, then watched as I gingerly lowered it into its grave. I was still confused about the berries. That was the second time in only a few short days that something had saved my life. Looking at Kith, I wondered if there was some strange power taking care of us.

Later that night, we made a fire to reheat what was left of the rabbit.

"Who do you think set the trap for the rabbit?" I asked while staring into the flames.

"I hadn't thought about it," Kith admitted, and I watched as he reached the same conclusion I had just come to. "Maybe there is a town nearby!"

Smiling wide, I nodded in excitement. "We can find the town and get more food!"

"Of course, we don't need the medicine anymore," Kith said, his face turning sour for just a moment before he perked back up. "But it wouldn't hurt to get some anyway in case we get sick again!"

"Why should we get gross medicine, when you can just heal us?" I laughed but sobered quickly at the dark look on his face.

"I'm not sure that's what happened. It doesn't make sense." He stared into the fire.

"What does make sense, then? I was dying, and suddenly woke up stronger than I was before getting sick."

"That's what I've been trying to figure out." Kith sighed. "I don't feel like someone who has mystical healing powers."

Rolling my eyes, I said, "You've always underestimated yourself, though."

"But if I could heal you, why didn't I do it sooner?"

I considered that for a moment before responding. "Maybe it's a power that you only access through extreme desperation?"

Kith looked unconvinced. With a sigh, knowing he wasn't going to change my mind, he switched the subject. "Whatever happened, we still need to find that town. And get some medicine just in case."

"Alright." I wasn't giving up, but I realized pushing the matter right now would do no good. "So, first we should go back to where you found the rabbit, right? Then we can split up and search in different directions for the town." I already knew what Kith was going to say as soon as he opened his mouth. "We'll find it faster if we split up," I argued before he could protest. "And I promise I won't go into the town. If I find it, I will meet you back here and take you there."

He was quiet for a minute until I glared at him. "Okay, okay! But stay up in the trees while you're looking. That'll make it harder for anyone to see you before you've seen them. Besides, there are probably more traps around."

"Shouldn't we be up in the trees now then?" I smirked.

"Well...I just now thought of that," Kith replied, sheepishly.

In the end, our negotiating wasn't necessary. Once we reached the spot where the trap was, Kith spotted a footprint pointing away from it, and we decided to head in that direction.

We didn't see any other tracks as we climbed through the trees, so we spread out to keep a wider search. Kith kept checking to make sure he could see me, but I pretended not to notice. I was putting all of my focus into finding the town.

After a while, the trees started to thin out. In the distance, I saw a cloud of smoke, so I quickened my pace until I could see the outlines of buildings. Calling for Kith, I made my way to where he was in the trees.

"I saw smoke that way!" I pointed, grinning. "Should we wait here until it gets a little darker?"

Once the sun disappeared, we made our way together to the last few trees before they cleared for the town. Then, we waited until there were no more lights to be seen, and Kith prepared to go in.

I watched from our tree as he stealthily entered the town. We were already so small that when Kith crouched he was barely taller than the average lurking animal, making it easy for him to hide away in the shadows. Keeping my eyes trained on him, I saw him creep around the outside of all the houses, searching through their trash cans. He stuffed some things in the bag and I knew the trip was a success. Even if it was garbage food.

While I watched, Kith circled around to the front of one of the houses and slipped inside causing my heart to stop. It was terrifying to not be able to see him. When he came out of the house, he barely shut the door before bolting back toward me. He was running so fast, I thought for sure someone saw him. I prepared myself to run when he got to me but then realized no one was following.

Kith reached the trees, instantly dropped the bags, and fell to his knees. "They had a drawing of us. Put up inside the medicine shop. Ducar must have given it to them. We can't stay here."

Disappointment flooded me. I hoped the town would be a good source of food for us for the next while.

"Let's walk for just a while," Kith said after some time, getting back to his feet. "Then we can stop for the night and figure out where to go in the morning."

We were both feeling pretty glum and not really up to talking, so we walked in silence until I finally asked if we could stop.

For the next few days, we walked along without really having a direction. All we knew was that we wanted to get far away from those drawings.

Occasionally, I tried to talk about what happened when Kith healed me. I suggested he should try to see if he could do it again and maybe I could try too. He was convinced he had nothing to do with it, though, and always changed the subject before I could get very far.

✾   Kith   ✾

I was right on the edge of drifting to sleep when a feeling like I was forgetting something important swept over me. After several minutes of attempting to ignore the feeling, I slowly rose and carefully left the camp.

Staying close, I climbed into a tree to think. A cold breeze swept over me playfully, as if it held the secret I was looking for.

As I huddled closer to the trunk of the tree, it hit me. Beatrice always celebrated Mara's birthday with us after the weather started getting colder. There would be no way to figure out what day it was actually on, so I'd just have to pick one to celebrate.

Birthday gifts while on the run would have to be practical. I wished I could find her something pretty and fun, but that would be pointless. Good food was definitely a priority when we were celebrating her birthday. I wished I thought of it before going to the town so I could get something special. Instead, I decided to try scavenging for something new. Or at least something we hadn't eaten in a while.

Closing my eyes, I turned slowly, figuring I'd just follow the direction I was facing when I opened them. As I turned quietly, my ears detected a slight rustling in the distance.

Turning in the direction the noise came from, I crept forward, being careful to make no sound. The rustle didn't last long, and I hadn't locked down where it was coming from. Hoping to relocate the noise without scaring whatever it might be away, I climbed the nearest tree and waited on the branch. Right as I was about to give up, I heard it again, followed by a soft whistling coo.

Following the movement which seemed to be coming from the ground, I climbed through the trees to avoid detection. My progress was slow since I kept stopping to listen and figure out where I needed to go. The sounds were becoming more infrequent, and I was worried I'd lose them altogether if I didn't find the animal making them soon.

Eventually, I was close enough to start looking for the hiding spot. I crept even slower through the trees, scanning the ground. Times like this made me grateful for my excellent night vision. With all our obvious differences, it had taken me a long time to realize that other people couldn't see in the dark the same way Mara and I could.

At first, I thought the animal might have gotten away, but then I noticed movement at the base of a tree close by. In a hollow under a bush, there was a small nest in which several small birds slept. We would need at least two to make a full meal for us. If I could bring back the whole bunch it would be great. Dropping from the tree, I crept up on the sleeping birds.

Surprise was my advantage, and I was hoping to use it to grab birds out one at a time, silencing them before they could alert the whole group. As I reached into the nest, my arm brushed the bush and the branches shook. Screeching filled the air as the birds scattered. Lunging, I managed to catch two of the smallest, but the rest were gone. A mix of triumph and disappointment filled me. We'd have new food for Mara's birthday, but it wasn't as much as I wanted to get. Still, I couldn't guarantee that I'd find anything better in the following days. There were even some unruffled feathers that I could give her as a gift. I decided we might as well celebrate when she woke up so the birds were still fresh.

Instead of returning immediately to camp after catching the birds, I wandered around aimlessly. My thoughts were restless. We had been on the run for several months now, and I knew that something would have to change soon. Images of Mara and I running aimlessly for years haunted me. Life had to be more than just running and struggling to find food, right?

All the emotions from the past few weeks crept up on me. Fear had kept me from having much time to process them, and now in the middle of the quiet night, they resurfaced. Sitting at the base of a tree, I let myself feel everything: the loss of Beatrice, almost losing Mara, possibly mysteriously healing Mara, and the fear of Ducar all hit me in cycles. I spent much of the rest of the night crying at the base of the tree. As I watched the sun come up, I thought again about almost losing Mara and the energy that had built up in me. She believed I somehow healed her. That was impossible, wasn't it?

It wasn't a question I could answer, but I had an odd feeling I couldn't explain. I remembered the feeling of being out of my body when I placed my hands on Mara and having no control over the energy that seeped into her. In a way, it was similar to the feeling when I couldn't eat the berries. Was someone watching us somehow? Taking control only when they could see we were about to die? Then why didn't they step in before? Why leave us out here by ourselves? None of it made any sense!

Beautiful colors washed over the sky, and I let the confusion and pain ebb away while I watched. Thinking too much about what happened always just left me feeling lost. It was easier to try and forget it.

Mara hadn't woken yet, which was good. Creeping back into our camp, I started a fire and prepped the birds. Regret tingled at the back of my mind with knowledge that I wasted so much of the night wrapped up in thoughts instead of looking for more food, but I pushed it down.

Once the smell of meat cooking hit the air, it didn't take long for Mara to wake up. She scrambled over and stared into the fire, the colors dancing in her golden eyes. "That smells delicious! I'm so hungry."

I smiled, her happiness rubbing off on me. "I was hoping to find more, but I only got the two birds." Pausing briefly, I added. "The birds did provide me with something else, though." I pulled out some of the prettiest feathers that I saved and placed them gently in her hands.

Her eyes glowed with pleasure. "They're beautiful!"

"Happy birthday, Mara." I kissed her forehead, taking pleasure in the fact that she was alive, healthy, and happy.

"It's my birthday?" She looked up at me with a mix of confusion and excitement.

"Well, I can't be completely sure, since I have no clue what day it is." I chuckled. " But, I thought today was as good a day as any to celebrate."

Staring at the feathers, she spoke, her voice quiet, "How can I keep these without ruining them?"

Struggling to hide my sadness, I sighed. "We'll figure out a way. I think we should be ok to move slower for a little bit, so maybe you can carry them until we find something better."

"I'll be super careful with them." She whispered the promise, as if speaking full volume would crumple her precious feathers.

We ate in silence, a mix of feelings flowing through us. Mostly the immense pleasure of each other's company and having food in our bellies.

CHAPTER SIX: OCTOBER

✳   Kith   ✳

We moved slowly over the next few days. Partially to protect Mara's prized feathers, and partially to look for more food. I tried returning to the birds' nest, hoping they would have resettled, but I seemed to have scared them off for good.

A gust of wind drew me out of my thoughts, sending a chill down my spine. Mara was hunched over picking some greens. As the wind swept over I saw goosebumps sprout all down her arms and she shivered. The sudden realization that we were getting closer than I realized to our first winter on our own hit me like a punch to my stomach. We were completely unprepared.

"We need to start looking for a town, and maybe a place we could camp for a while when it gets even colder."

"A camp sounds great right about now." Her hands rubbed over her arms, trying to warm them up. "It might be best if we split up to look. We could cover more ground that way."

I froze. Splitting up was something we rarely did, and it always made me worry. "I'm not sure if that's a good idea."

"I'll be fine, Kith. We can meet before the sun goes down to share if we found anything worthwhile."

The tone of her voice made it clear that she wasn't willing to back down. "Alright. But be careful." As she turned to head off, I could've sworn Mara rolled her eyes at me.

Concentrating on finding food was almost impossible. Mara's decision to split up caught me off guard, and although I knew she'd hate it, I found myself worrying about her. Agreeing to her idea had been difficult, but I knew it was important to her.

Fear stabbed at my heart, but I pushed it down. I knew I could be overbearing in my attempts to protect Mara. Protecting her had been my job for as long as I could remember. I found myself wondering what she was doing, and if she was safe. Suddenly, my vision went cloudy. As it cleared, I saw Mara. It was as if I was standing right next to her. Not only was she perfectly safe, she seemed quite content to be on her own.

I only saw her for a few seconds before my vision returned to normal.

*   Mara   *

Once I was alone, I realized with a small amount of guilt how much it was exactly what I needed. I love Kith, but his constant worrying was overwhelming sometimes and it was a bit of a relief to be out from under his care for just a little while.

At first, I walked in somewhat of a trance, just letting myself feel everything I went through without having to pretend I was okay. I thought about the dreams and let myself wonder about my sanity. I wasn't sure how much time passed before I snapped myself out of it. When I looked around, I saw that the trees had thinned out and I was nearing the end of the forest.

Stepping carefully out of the trees, I thought about how nice it was to feel the sun's full force on my skin. Ahead of me in the distance stood a large hill covered in orange and purple flowers. Without thinking, I began walking toward it.

About halfway to the hill, I remembered I was supposed to be looking for food. As guilt washed over me anew, I started looking around thinking maybe there would be animals here. Then, I realized I wouldn't know what to do even if I found one. The thought of catching a live animal and killing it with my claws revolted me, and I knew I wouldn't be able to do it. If I did find food, it would have to be some sort of plant. Berries and nuts were good options, but we hadn't seen any for a few days. I wondered what other sort of plants we could eat, and found myself staring at the grass wondering if it was edible.

Suddenly reminded of my earlier thoughts concerning my sanity, I decided grass simply could not be edible or no one would ever go hungry. When I looked up, I was almost at the top of the hill and I saw buildings at the bottom of the other side. Excitement at having found a town took over and I began to run toward it. Once I got most of the way down the hill, I could see the town completely. It wasn't huge, only a few dozen houses, but I could smell food cooking.

Getting as close as I dared, I looked down on the town for a while, thinking. At first, I considered exploring by myself but I promised Kith I wouldn't. At least I found the town, and now Kith could go in at night to find food.

As I turned to walk back, I noticed how late it was and hoped Kith wasn't already looking for me. We agreed to meet back up before the sun went down, and although there were still a couple of hours, Kith always got so worried. I thought he would likely start looking for me soon.

Thinking it would give me a better view of the town, I walked back up the hill a ways. When I turned back to look, I noticed a few little dots walking through the town. The people looked so small from up here. I watched them for a few minutes, squinting hard to see them better. Finally, I started on my way back down the hill. Just as I was reaching the bottom, my foot plummeted into a hole. I lurched forward and threw my arms out to catch myself. Pulling my leg out of the hole, I was relieved to find that although there was some pain, I didn't seem to have broken anything.

Looking into the hole, I was surprised to see how big it was. If I curled up real tight, I could probably fit my whole body inside it. Unsure how I hadn't seen it, I realized how lucky I was that I didn't really hurt myself. Bending down to stick my head in the hole, I saw a point where it veered off to the side and kept going. I wondered if there might be an animal still in there somewhere. The revolting thought of killing an animal came back to me, and I stood up to leave. An idea suddenly struck me, and I turned back to stare at the hole.

Animals sometimes go underground to stay warm in the winter. They live in little holes like these, and it keeps them warm. Why couldn't Kith and I do the same?

Excitement hit me as I knelt back down to the hole and started digging with my claws. Once I had gotten the opening just wide enough for me to fit, I wiggled my way in and started digging out the inside. I managed to make enough room for me to sit. It wasn't quite comfortable yet, but my arms were getting very tired from digging. Despite the cool air outside, I was now drenched in sweat. I crawled back out of my little cave and was shocked to see how low the sun was. I got so caught up in digging that I didn't realize how much time had passed.

Running back to the woods, I hoped Kith wasn't waiting too long. I found our meeting spot easily enough, using markings I left on a few trees just as Kith instructed. He was waiting for me, but thankfully he didn't look like he had been there for long. I stopped in front of him, clutching my side, and gasping for breath.

Kith stared at me, trying to keep the alarm out of his face. "Is everything alright? Why were you running so fast?"

"I didn't...want to...be late," I gasped.

"You ran that hard just to meet me?" Kith said, pretending to be surprised and flattered.

Glaring at him playfully, I said. "I thought you might be worried."

Kith sobered and said, "Well, I was a little worried, but I knew you would make it back."

I wasn't sure if this was the full truth or if he was just trying to make me feel responsible, but I appreciated the effort either way.

Once I finally managed to catch my breath, I told Kith all about the cave I started digging out. My excitement only grew as I saw how impressed he was. I led him back to the hill, and Kith looked inside the hole letting out a soft whistle.

"How much of this did you dig yourself? You must have been working for hours!"

I swelled with pride as Kith wiggled his way into the hole. It was a tight fit, but he managed to get his whole body inside.

"If we both dig tomorrow, we should be able to sleep in it by tomorrow night!" he exclaimed as he wiggled back out.

"Maybe I should have made the opening a little bigger," I said sheepishly, watching him struggle to get back out.

"No, it's perfect! We don't want anyone to accidentally

find it, so keeping the hole as small as possible is the best idea! Once we are able to fit in there better, we can work on digging in a little further so if someone looks inside maybe they won't even see us!"

I couldn't contain my glee. I was almost bouncing in excitement. "You like it then?"

"I love it!"

I smiled widely and gave him a big hug.

＊   Kith   ＊

My first venture into the town was largely a scouting mission, making sure it was safe and figuring out the layout. Whenever I visited a new town, I liked to make sure I knew all the escape routes just in case someone saw me and I needed to get away quickly. I did manage to get us some stale bread from the trash outside the bakery, though.

We made the bread last us a couple of days before I decided to return for more food and other supplies.

After going through most of the town and only getting a few scraps of discarded meat and vegetables, I headed back to the bakery. I hoped to bring back more food than last time, especially meat. Stale bread just wasn't as beneficial for us, but it was definitely better than starving.

When I got to the bakery, there were a couple of decent loaves thrown out as well as one that looked like it had been in the can since my last visit. I took all 3 and decided we would eat the old one first.

After that, I always ended each trip at the bakery to pick out the bread that was thrown away. It was good bread even when it was a few days old.

On my fourth visit to the town, I visited the bakery last as usual. Lifting the lid to the trash, I caught sight of the desired bread. Before I could grab it, however, I was swept up in a net. There was a trap laid out, and I missed the signs. Trying to stay as quiet as I could without panicking, I started scratching at the ropes with my claws.

Before I could get far, a voice rang out, "Aha! I got you!"

My heart thumped loudly, and I assured myself it wasn't Ducar's voice. Being caught by regular people wasn't great in my experience, either, though. "Please don't hurt me. I just needed some food."

Curly white hair was the first thing I saw as the man stepped into the light, followed by his soft, wrinkly face. Although there were laugh lines in his cheeks, he currently wore a deep frown. Eyes such a pale blue they were almost white looked in my direction but didn't seem to really see me. "Oh, my. I wasn't expecting to catch a child. I figured some pesky animal was getting into my trash."

Past experiences with being caught ran through my mind. "I'm sorry. I meant no harm, I'm just hungry."

Making a sound that seemed to be a mix of a laugh and a sigh, he wiped his large dough-covered hands on his already quite messy apron and reached up to find the knot that would release me. "I'm not going to hurt you." He paused briefly, considering something. "You must be pretty hungry to be digging around in my trash. Why don't you come inside and I'll get you some fresh food?"

Shock ran through me, making me slow to respond. "Are you sure?" was all I could muster.

"Of course. I can't let a young kid starve." He opened the door and the warmth and light from his fire poured out invitingly.

I walked to the door, eager to get out of the cold. As I was about to step in, fear crept through me. What if he was setting me up? Planning to hold me until Ducar could get to me, maybe. I hovered at the edge of the door, fear stopping me from entering.

The smell of delicious food wafted out and teased me, but I couldn't force myself to go in. Suddenly, I was pushed forward by the man and panic rose inside me. Catching myself before I fell over the doorstep, I turned ready to bolt.

"I'm sorry, I thought you were coming in." He said gently before steadying himself against the doorway, and I realized he tripped over me. Breathing slowly, I allowed myself to calm down, at least a bit.

"I don't think I can," I said, stepping away from the doorway. I didn't want to hurt his feelings, but I hadn't lied.

"Hmm." He paused for a minute in thought. "Give me a minute and I'll bring some food out to you then."

"Really?"

"Of course. Like I said, I can't let a child go hungry." He stepped into the house without another word. I could hear him moving around, and it wasn't long before he returned.

"Where are you from, child?" There was a gentleness to this man's voice that I hadn't heard in a long time. He held out a bowl of stew and waited for me to come and take it.

Staring into the bowl, I couldn't decide how I should answer his question.

"Alright. Can I at least get a name?"

I hesitated for a moment. "My name is Kith."

"Nice to meet you, Kith." He smiled, and I felt myself relaxing just a little. "My name is Isaac."

After eating in silence for a minute, I asked, "Are you really a baker?"

My question seemed to surprise him at first, but then he nodded. "I am indeed. I wasn't always blind, and by the time I was, I could've made bread in my sleep."

"Do you miss your sight?" A part of me regretted the question once it was out, but I was curious.

He tilted his head to the side like he was thinking. "Sometimes. Life was a bit easier before I lost my sight. I've adjusted, though." He paused. "And, for some reason, I feel like you wouldn't be talking to me if I wasn't blind, so right now, I'm glad for it."

His response shocked me. What he said was the truth, but I was unsure how he had gotten to that conclusion. Nothing I said had hinted so much at my differences, had it?

He seemed to sense my confusion and smiled. "I'm not wrong, am I?"

"No." I paused. "But, how did you know?"

Shrugging, he said, "Not sure. Lucky guess, maybe."

For some reason, I didn't believe that, but I decided not to say as much. Suddenly, I felt awkward. I began shoveling down the rest of the stew as quickly as I could and almost burnt my mouth. Once the bowl was empty, I held it out toward him. "Thank you for the food. I need to go now."

He held out his hand for my bowl instead of grabbing it. Once I gave it to him, he held out a small sack. "I packed up some food for you to take with you. You're welcome to come back again, but you don't have to dig through my trash. If you knock, I'll prepare you something." After a pause, he added, "And I'll keep bringing it out for you if needed." With a smile tinged with sadness, he headed back inside.

The whole experience was shocking, and I walked back to our little cave in a bit of a daze. Still unsure of exactly how I felt about the whole encounter, I told Mara everything while she ate a sandwich made from the food the baker sent with me. I felt bad that she wasn't able to have some of the stew, but she seemed plenty glad just to be eating fresh bread. It was amazing how wonderful the bread was when it didn't come from a trash can.

Watching her eat the sandwich made me even happier than I expected, and I started to wonder if I should take Isaac up on his word. With his help, we had hope of surviving, but it was hard to imagine trusting someone else after everything we had been through.

⫸   Mara   ⫷

Once the bread the baker gave us was gone, I tried to convince Kith to go back to see him. Instead, he went to town and dug from other people's trash cans. He wouldn't even go through the baker's trash anymore.

After a few days of getting nothing but scraps, I decided to talk to him about it again. "You just aren't getting much anywhere else, and going every day seems silly," I said, trying not to hurt his feelings. I knew Kith was trying, but he went to the town two times in as many days and barely had anything to show for it.

"We don't need his help, Mara. I don't mind going to the town every day if I have to. We're getting enough to eat from what's left in the cans. It just isn't smart to trust him."

When Kith returned that night, all he brought was a few half-moldy pieces of fruit. I looked at it in disdain. "Can you at least get the old bread from the baker's trash can?" I asked. "His bread is so good even when it's been covered by other garbage."

"He'll know if I come by again, and know I didn't want to see him. I don't want to offend him, I just don't think it's smart to be talking to him, either."

It was understandable that he was scared to go. Ducar was clearly looking for us in other towns, and who was to say he hadn't been here?

"Didn't you say the baker was blind? Even if there were posters, he wouldn't have been able to see them, and he couldn't see you. How will he ever know that you're one of the children Ducar is looking for?"

For a minute, Kith was stumped. "What if he just assumes and has someone else over to get a look at me?"

"If that were the case, don't you think he would have left you in that trap and called them over then? Or he would have told the others to put out their own traps so they could catch you. The fact that you haven't been caught yet means he isn't telling anyone about you."

Kith hung his head in defeat. "You're right. I'll go to see the baker tomorrow."

We ate our dinner of moldy fruit and went to bed shortly after. I could feel Kith tossing and turning. A part of me felt a little guilty at convincing him to go, but it seemed foolish not to take advantage of a good situation when one finally presented itself.

The next day, I suggested that I go with him, but Kith shot me down immediately. It wasn't a surprise, but it still hurt a little. It was only fair if I got to meet the baker, too. I told Kith I was only interested in the food, but there was also a part of me that longed for companionship. I loved Kith, but I missed Beatrice and Grace and many of the other freaks so much. It would be nice to have a friend again.

When it was time for Kith to go to the town, I could tell he was stalling. It was particularly cold that day, so we had both huddled in the cave after the sun went down to keep warm.

"Don't you think you should be going soon?" I finally prodded. Kith looked reluctant, so I said teasingly, "Unless you want me to go for you."

At that, Kith wiggled his way out of the cave. "You should stay in here where it's warm. I don't want you to get sick again."

"You act like you can't get sick," I said, rolling my eyes.

"I'll be fast!" Was all Kith said as he took off running toward the town.

I snuggled into his blanket enjoying the extra warmth, excited at the thought of more fresh bread.

When Kith returned, though, I could tell something was wrong by his reluctance to look at me. "What happened?" I asked tentatively.

"Nothing happened. I got some old meat out of a trash can."

"What about the baker?" I asked, getting irritated.

"Well...he didn't answer the door. I think he must have gone to bed already. I think I waited too long."

Of course, I knew immediately that Kith was lying. Kith rarely ever lied, so it was easy to pick up on it when he tried. I wasn't sure how to handle it, though. If I called him out on it, he would only get defensive and it wouldn't help anything. Instead, I decided I had to take the matter into my own hands.

"Oh, that's sad. I was really looking forward to another one of his sandwiches." I said and I could see the relief on his face just for a second.

A couple of days later, when we were out of food again, I decided it was my night. "When are you going to go to town again?" I asked while I sat outside basking in the sun. It was almost too cold to do anymore, but I wanted to take advantage of the little warmth the sun provided while I could.

"Probably tonight," Kith responded warily; already

knowing what I must be thinking. "Aren't you cold?"

"Nice try. Are you going to see the baker?"

"Well if he answers his door, I will. I already told you, he must have been in bed or something."

"Okay, just so long as you try again, that's fine," I said as I reached around to dig my blanket out of the cave. I saw the relief on Kith's face and smiled. He thought he got off easy.

That night, I sat in the cave wrapped up in blankets as Kith said goodbye and headed toward the town. After waiting a few minutes, I slowly crept out to see Kith nearing the edge of the town. I made my way to the same place he had entered and peeked around the building. Kith was at the house across from me, his arms already deep in the trash can. I walked out into the moonlight and saw him look up suddenly.

The shock on his face was quickly replaced with fear as I started toward the baker's house. He didn't call out to me; that could call attention to us. Instead, he quickly put the trash back in the can and set it back upright. By then I was halfway across the town, almost to the baker's. I didn't stop until I reached his back door where I stood waiting for Kith to join me.

"Mara are you insane?" he whispered, barely making a sound.

"I knew you weren't going to do it," I whispered back, and before he could respond, I knocked on the door.

The door opened little more than a crack, and I saw the baker's wrinkled face poke out. His pale blue eyes looked like they could see right through me, although I knew he didn't have any idea I was even there. "Is that you again, Kith?"

Looking at Kith, expectantly, I nodded my encouragement. "Yes, it's me," he responded after giving me a quick glare and putting his finger to his lips.

"I hoped you would come back," the baker said with a smile that took me by surprise. He looked genuinely happy that some kid he didn't even know came to visit him. "Would you like to come in or should I bring something out? I'll need a minute to prepare it."

I looked at Kith and rubbed my arms to make a show of

how cold I was. "I think I'd rather stay out here," he said, pointedly ignoring me.

The baker's smile turned a little sad, but he nodded amiably and headed back inside. I glared at Kith and he stuck his tongue out. Laughing, I peeked in one of the windows to watch as the baker heated up some stew. "I get the hot food this time," I told Kith and saw his face fall. It was my turn to stick out my tongue.

When the baker came back out with the bowl of hot stew, I grabbed it quickly and Kith thanked him. He looked to his left a little where Kith stood and his face scrunched up, his large crooked nose sniffed the air between us. "Is there someone else with you, Kith?" he asked, gently.

I looked at Kith, unsure what I should do. He met my eyes and I could see the horror. My poor big brother was so worried about protecting me that he couldn't see how kind and caring this old man was.

"It's okay, Kith. I won't hurt them, whoever they are, I just thought you might like your own bowl of stew."

Kith's horror faded as he nodded slowly. Then it was my turn to feel the horror. I coughed to catch Kith's attention and pointed to my eyes to remind him the old man couldn't see him nodding.

"Oh!" he exclaimed lamely, "yes, I would like that very much."

To my surprise, the baker broke out laughing. "You forgot I couldn't see you, didn't you?"

"I'm sorry," Kith said sheepishly.

"Not at all. I'll be right back." With that, the baker headed back inside to scoop a few more spoonfuls into another bowl.

When he came back out, he pleasantly introduced himself as Isaac. "Might I ask the name of my new visitor?"

"I'm Mara," I responded shyly. "It's nice to meet you."

As soon as I spoke, a sudden flash of pain ran across Isaac's face. It was gone in an instant, leaving me unsure if I had imagined the whole thing. "Well, it is very nice to meet you, Mara. Kith, is this your sister?"

"She is," Kith responded reluctantly, and I saw a little bit of the terror return to his eyes. I knew he was nervous about how much information we should give the man. If Ducar passed through here, who knew what he might know.

Isaac's face was troubled, and I got the idea he could tell we were trying to hide something. "Well, I'm glad you both came to see me this evening. It is chilly out, I hope you've got warm clothes on you," he said, changing the subject.

"Warm enough," Kith answered abruptly, "but we should probably be getting home so we don't get sick."

"We can't have that!" Isaac replied, "If you give me another moment, I can send more bread and meat home with you."

He went inside again, and I watched through the window as he packed a loaf of bread and some meat and cheese into a small basket. "I'll be expecting to get this basket back so I can use it next time," he said as he held the basket out for one of us to take. I knew this was his way of telling us to come see him again, and I smiled happily as I took the food.

"Thank you! We'll see you soon!" I said as Kith grabbed my arm and started gently pulling me away.

✳   Kith   ✳

Isaac's basket stared at me accusingly as I sat in the cave munching on some of the food he sent back with us. It would last us a couple of days, giving me a reason to not return too soon. I wanted to pretend I didn't know why I was hesitant to see the baker again, but I couldn't. There was too much risk involved with trusting someone.

There was definitely the fear of Ducar catching us, or being trapped in other ways. But there was also a strong fear of losing someone else. I knew we wouldn't be able to stay near this town forever. The plan was to leave once winter was over. Having an attachment would make moving on more difficult, and we didn't need that.

Determined not to become reliant on Isaac, I tried to think of what I could do to keep Mara satisfied. I could tell she was already fond of the man. Worry bubbled up in my stomach. He did seem genuinely nice, and seeing Mara well-fed and happy was such a relief, especially with winter on the way. For a second I felt my determination weaken. Having a source of food for the winter wouldn't be a bad thing, and maybe we'd be able to leave without any problems.

Images of Beatrice filled my head. Leaving her broke our hearts. Mara seemed ready to form another bond, but when it came time to leave, how much would it hurt her?

I thought about Isaac cutting me down from his trap, being careful to release me gently.

Wait. I straightened as the solution hit me. *If I can learn to make the traps, I can catch enough food for the winter. Then scraps from the trash will be enough, and we won't need to rely on the baker.*

The trap I got caught in and the trap I found the rabbit in were both made of rope. We didn't have any, so I'd have to find some. I snuck out of the cave. Mara was playing in the trees, so I may have a chance of getting to the town and back without her noticing I was gone.

I didn't want to get caught or alert any other townspeople that we were around, so I'd need to be careful. Unsure of where I could find the rope, I wandered through the shadows. After several minutes of searching with no luck, I realized I'd likely have to get a little creative. The tailor's shop might have fabric scraps I could braid into rope.

With a new plan, I headed straight to the can I needed. As I opened it, I was delighted to find it almost full of an assortment of scraps. None of them were very big, so the ropes would be a lot of work. They'd be worth it, though, if I figured out the traps.

Grabbing the whole pile, I stashed it in my bag before dashing back through the town and straight to the cave. It seemed like Mara was still in the woods. Sighing with relief, I used my claws to start cutting the fabric into the best strips I could. I knotted the end in a messy ball and started braiding. Getting the new strands to stay in was difficult. After several attempts, I started carefully knotting the new pieces into the braid. It made it clumpy and ugly, but it held.

By the time Mara entered the cave I had made a couple feet of rope. "What are you doing?" As she looked more closely, her eyes narrowed. "Kith, where did you get all that cloth?"

I felt myself avoiding Mara's gaze. "It was in a trash can."

"Right. When did you get it? I don't remember you bringing it back."

"While you were gone."

"You went to town while I was gone to get some fabric to braid?"

"I'm making a rope." I held my braided fabric up so she could see it more clearly. As she looked at it, I realized it would take me ages to make enough rope for even just one trap. I would also need to make more trips to town, as I was already most of the way through my pile. That would be a good way to draw attention. I couldn't help but sigh.

"What's going on, Kith?" There was still an accusatory tone to her voice, even though she softened it.

"I wanted to try to make a trap, and I needed rope." My voice sounded weak, even to myself.

"And?"

Sighing again, I reluctantly answered her. "I thought if I could learn to trap some food, we wouldn't have to rely on the baker."

"Why is getting help from Isaac such a bad thing?" There was a clear tone of annoyance now. My hesitancy frustrated her for some time now, I knew that. But I couldn't help it.

"How do we know if we can trust him?"

"We can't, not without giving it a try." Mara looked at me for a couple of seconds before adding, "I'd like to give it a try. Having fresh food is nice. And we could learn from him."

"I know, Mara. I do." My voice broke. "What happens when it's time to move on from the town?"

"I'm not sure what you mean." There was silence, then I

saw understanding come to her eyes. "Oh."

"I'm just not sure it's worth the risk."

"I'd rather move on with fond memories of a nice old man and really good food than memories of going hungry." There was a slight hesitation, but also a determination in her voice.

"Are you sure? I don't want to add more heartache for us."

"It's only winter. Surely we won't get that attached for it to be such a big deal. I mostly want the food." She shrugged like it was no big deal, but I didn't think she was being fully honest.

I sighed once again, realizing this wasn't an argument I was going to win. "Alright. We'll continue to visit the baker."

*   Mara   *

At first, we slept in the area of the cave that I dug out on my own. It wasn't much bigger than us, but we didn't mind. At least in the beginning.

"Ouch!" I yelped in surprise as Kith's elbow struck my cheek.

"I'm so sorry! I didn't mean to hit you, I just needed to stretch."

"I'm fine. It's not a big deal, you didn't hurt me, much." I chuckled slightly. "I think it's time to expand the cave a bit, though. Especially if we're going to stay here all winter."

Kith sighed. "You're right. It's going to be a lot of work, but we should get started soon."

After we ate, we got started with digging out the walls. Our claws weren't made for digging through dirt and rocks, so it took a long time to make any progress.

We spent most of the day working, and by the time we stopped, the sun was low in the sky. "My whole body hurts, and I'm covered in dirt." I tried to keep my voice from sounding whiny, but it was hard. I didn't expect improving the cave to be so difficult.

"Speaking of dirty..." Kith motioned to the mounds of

loose dirt we tossed out of the cave throughout the day. "We can't just leave random piles of dirt around. They might draw attention."

We dispersed the piles throughout the forest as quickly as we could before climbing back into the cave. It was harder to notice it while working, but we did have more room inside. It felt nice to be able to stretch out a little without hitting each other.

The next few days were spent expanding the cave. We decided to avoid the problem of the piles building up by scooping the dirt into one of our packs while digging. When they were full, we carried them out into the woods and scattered them on the ground.

About a week after we began, we were finally satisfied with how far our main living space had come. We were able to sleep on different sides of the cave, allowing us some space to stretch out. Of course, when I woke, Kith was always right beside me. I hoped that settling in an area and having work to focus on would ease the nightmares, but no such luck.

With Kith going to the town from time to time, we decided we would sleep during the day and work at night. This was pretty easy because the cave was dark enough to sleep no matter how sunny it was outside. I enjoyed the quiet of the night, anyway. It was nice to take a break and sit under the stars watching the night animals scurry around.

One night Kith announced that he was going to go to town. "To see Isaac?" I asked, excitedly getting ready to join him.

"No," he responded slowly, "I just thought it might be nice to have some more rope or something. It's already pretty late, we probably shouldn't bother him tonight." I knew Kith was stalling on going back to see Isaac, but he was right about it being late.

"We can see him tomorrow, then," I said. "And since you're making a trip today, he will be our only stop so we'll have plenty of time to visit." Kith didn't look too happy about that, but he didn't argue, either.

After Kith left for town, I snuggled into my blanket, enjoying the warmth, but wishing it wasn't so dark. *Maybe I should have told Kith to try to grab us some candles or something,* I thought.

Though, candles weren't usually thrown out while they were still useful. He'd have to break into a house, and that would put people on alert. They'd be looking for a thief.

If the town was looking for him, we'd both be in danger. And what if someone tracked him back here? My heart was racing as I thought about what would happen if he were followed back and someone saw him enter the cave. We'd be trapped and in some real trouble. What we needed was a second exit, a way to escape if we had to. I ran outside, trying to figure out the best spot to put an exit. We wouldn't want someone to see us running out. Once I picked a spot, I realized I'd need to dig quite the tunnel.

With a sigh, I got to work. There was no time to wait for Kith. My hands hurt too much to use my claws for digging, so I found a sturdy, but small, stick. Using it to scrape away the dirt, I was able to make progress much faster. Just as I got far enough into the wall for my whole body to fit in the tunnel, I heard a loud noise. Moving as quickly as I could, I tried to back out of the hole. I barely moved by the time I realized it was futile, and I covered my head with my hands right as the tunnel collapsed. The walls shook, and it felt like the whole ceiling came tumbling down in chunks of different sizes. Most of the rocks landed behind me, sealing the tunnel. There were several that felt like they should have fallen on me, but they tumbled around my sides.

Darkness didn't normally scare me. My eyes could see pretty well with little light. Being stuck in the rocks, though, allowed almost no light to come through. It was dark even for me. The rocks that fell to my sides made it almost impossible to move. I tried kicking at the rocks behind me, but they wouldn't budge. It would work better if I could use my hands.

I tried to turn but got stuck part way. It was so dark, I couldn't remember which way the blocked exit was. There was a part of me that was sure the small hole I was in was shrinking around me.

Just as I was about to enter a full panic, I heard a noise. Someone, or something, was in the cave. Surely it was Kith and I just hadn't heard him coming. My heart raced, and I froze. If it wasn't Kith, I didn't want to give away where I was.

"Mara?" The rocks that blocked me moved away quickly. "What are you doing in the wall?"

Relief washed over me. It was Kith, and I was free. I backed out of the start of the tunnel and brushed myself off, briefly surprised I wasn't dirtier. "I was working on a tunnel."

"A tunnel?" His face was filled with puzzlement.

"I was sitting here, and it struck me that if someone followed you or found the cave, we would be trapped. I thought having an escape option would be good."

"That's a good point. I didn't even think about that. I'll help you with it, but please don't work in the tunnel when I'm not here. I'm surprised you weren't seriously hurt."

I laughed. "No problem there. I don't want to do that again." I decided not to mention the rocks that seemed to have so narrowly avoided me.

✳   Kith   ✳

As the weather turned colder, I was increasingly glad that Mara thought of digging out the cave. After several months on the run, sleeping in the open or crudely made shelters, I almost forgot how nice it felt to go inside and feel relatively comfortable and safe.

Several weeks after we decided to stay holed up for the winter, a cold spell hit. Stepping out of the warmth of the cave felt like being stung all over.

"It sure got cold, didn't it?" Mara said as she came out of the cave behind me. "We should bring our blankets."

"That's a good idea," I said fervently as she disappeared back into the cave to grab them. "We probably shouldn't stay long either."

Mara paused and looked at me for a long moment. She was obviously debating on what to say, but I was pretty sure I knew what was coming. "Do you think we could go inside this time?" She asked, her determination winning out. We visited Isaac's house several times now, and every time he told us we were

128

welcome to go inside if we'd like. He was never forceful about it, though, and I usually just left the statement unanswered then Mara would change the subject.

Sighing, I started to shake my head, but before I could say anything she continued on. "I just feel like it's a little rude to show up just long enough to get food and then leave. He's an old man living all by himself, Kith. I bet he's lonely."

Knowing she was right didn't make the decision any easier. I did feel bad that I always ended up rushing us away from the baker's house after he was so kind to share his food for free. I was just debating her words and how cold I felt when the first snow of winter started to fall. It wasn't coming down hard, but it just seemed like the world was against me in my determination to stay outside of Isaac's house. I couldn't possibly make Mara stand outside in the snow. I was glad we at least brought our blankets.

Once we got to the baker's house, Mara knocked and Isaac came to the door, smiling as usual. "Oh!" he said, sniffing the air. "Is it snowing?"

"How do you know that?" I asked, unable to stop myself.

"I can smell it! Can't you?"

Mara and I exchanged incredulous looks before she looked back to Isaac and I braced myself for what she was about to say. "Could we come inside this time?"

"Of course!" Isaac said with a surprised smile, and I wondered what would make a man so happy about having two strange kids come into his home. "I was just cooking a large roast. Too bad I didn't know you were coming or I would have made that stew you kids like so much. Such a cold night would have been perfect for it. You can make yourselves at home while I finish." Isaac gestured toward the table, and I marveled at how well he got around even though he couldn't see.

While Mara and I watched Isaac prepare the roast, I thought about how much he had done for us. Every time we came to see him, he gave us a warm meal as well as more food to take home with us for the next few days. The cave was great for warmth and safety, but I'm not sure if I would have been able to find enough food without him. Months of repeated failures danced in my head as I wondered how well Mara and I would be doing by now without Isaac. All we would be eating is whatever trash I was able to find. And yet Isaac did not ask us for anything in return.

Suddenly, I felt a little bad for how much I distrusted him. It just seemed foolish to trust anyone too much with the way our lives had turned out. Isaac was kind, though, and he was helping me take care of Mara. I decided that he deserved my respect, at least, if not my full trust for helping us get through winter.

I was so lost in thought, that I didn't realize that Isaac finished what he was doing until he placed our plates on the table. I looked around to see Mara staring at me with a questioning look. Of course she noticed something was bothering me.

Isaac sat across from us, listening for the sounds of us eating. I dug into the meat gratefully, but with a little bit of dismay.

Isaac ate slowly, with an air of focus about him. "I'm glad you decided to join me tonight." He said, suddenly. "It is always nice to have someone to share a meal with."

"Have you always lived alone?" Mara asked, and I was so shocked by her abruptness that I dropped my fork halfway to my mouth.

Mara let out a little squeal when it crashed to the plate and the bite of roast beef fell off onto the floor. I was mortified.

"Sorry," I squeaked as I felt my cheeks turning bright blue.

To my surprise, Isaac let out a soft chuckle. "It's quite alright. The linens at the edge of the table are there for cleaning if you need one. As to your question, Mara," Isaac paused for a moment and I looked up from where I was trying to find the food that had fallen to see pain fill his face. "I have not always lived alone. I had a wife," his voice broke and I wasn't sure he would continue, but after a moment he managed to find his voice again. "And a daughter. They were both taken by an illness. My daughter was only eight years old."

Mara gasped and I was filled with shame. She was right. How lonely this poor man must be after losing his whole family. It suddenly made sense why he loved having us visit and why he always seemed both happy and sad whenever Mara spoke.

Isaac cleared his throat and dabbed gently at his right eye.

"What about you?" he asked. "Has it always been just the two of you?"

"Yes," I said curtly before Mara could even open her mouth. She glared at me but didn't say anything. I knew it was rude after he just shared a part of his life with us, but telling him about our past was too far. I couldn't allow it.

We finished the rest of our meal in an awkward silence. I could tell Mara was still angry at me, and I felt the need to make amends somehow to both her and the baker. He was so kind to us, that I wanted to do something in return.

After some hesitation, I murmured, "You've done so much for us, I was wondering if there was anything we could do to help you in return." Mara smiled encouragingly. It was a step, at least.

He paused thoughtfully. "There is a task I could use some help with, actually."

I sat up a bit higher in my chair, eager for the chance to repay some of my imagined debt. "What is it?"

Isaac smiled softly at my excitement. "I have some plants that need to be transferred inside out of the cold, which the snow makes even more urgent. I'd like to take some clippings so I can plant even more in the spring."

"What kind of plant?" Mara asked. "Can I help, too?"

"Of course you can. It's called Feverfew. I use it to make a tea that helps with aches and pains."

"Oh. That seems like a good thing to have on hand," I said.

Isaac listened carefully outside before letting us follow him out, then led us to a small plot at the side of his house. Most of the flowers died from the cold, but a few remained. Looking at the plants took my breath away for a moment, and I heard Mara's soft gasp beside me.

Beatrice kept several of the same flowers growing in pots. She was very protective of them and refused to leave them behind. I didn't know at the time why she was so attached to them, but Isaac's mention of tea reminded me of the tea she was always giving Dylan.

"Is everything okay?" Isaac asked, having heard our reactions.

"It's just that we've seen these flowers before," Mara said quietly.

"Oh?" Isaac sounded surprised. "I don't think Feverfew grows wildly near here. Perhaps further out in the forest. Do you kids do a lot of traveling?" He said that last sentence slowly, almost like he wasn't really sure if he wanted to know the answer.

"We haven't seen them out in the forest yet," Mara piped up. I looked at her sharply, but she was bent down examining a flower, not paying me any attention. "We saw them growing in pots where we used to live. She carried them with her everywhere and took very good care of them." For a moment, I think Mara forgot she was even talking to Isaac. Her eyes were misty and I knew she was lost in her memories of Beatrice.

"Our mother used to have them," I said quickly before Mara could give too much away. I saw the confusion on Isaac's face and remembered that not even an hour earlier I told him it had always been just the two of us. Why couldn't Mara keep her mouth shut? It was like she was determined to tell this man our entire life story.

Mara's face sobered as she looked at me. I knew by calling Beatrice our mother I opened up a whole new sense of sorrow in her, but she also understood that I was trying to shut that conversation down. She was dangerously close to telling him about where we were before and even she knew that was too far.

Isaac seemed to understand it was a soft spot because he didn't try to further the conversation. Instead, he went straight on to instructing us on how to gently dig the plant up without damaging the roots and place it in a pot. The ground was cold and hard, making me glad for my claws and my experience digging. We worked silently until we got inside. Once in, he showed us how to clip some of the roots off so they could be replanted.

Frozen mud caked my arms by the time we were done. I was pretty used to being dirty, though. Isaac pulled out a large bowl and started rinsing his hands and arms into it, so I did the same. The water felt wonderful running down my skin, and I splashed it a couple times playfully while rinsing. When my arms were clean, I wiped my face quickly. I didn't bother getting it completely clean, but managed to get some dirt off. I wished that I could clean all of myself, as it had been a long time since we'd been able to.

After we were done, Isaac tossed the water out back and put the bowl away. I suddenly realized we had been helping him work for a lot longer than I planned to stay. Isaac had a bakery to run, didn't he need sleep?

"I think we should be going now," I said once Isaac was back by our sides.

"I was wondering," Isaac said slowly, "if you would like to come back tomorrow for a bath?"

"Are you trying to tell us we stink?" Mara said, pretending to sound offended.

Isaac chuckled. "I just thought it might have been a while since your last proper bath."

A mix of emotions came over me. A bath sounded like heaven right now, but I was still so unsure about trusting Isaac. When I looked at Mara, though, I could see how excited she was and I knew the answer must be yes.

*   Mara   *

When I stepped outside the next day, I realized the snow from the night before was already almost completely gone. It was only a light dusting. We slept much later these days than we used to since we were usually up for most of the night. It made sense that the sun melted all the snow already. I was kind of wanting to play in it, though.

Still, nothing could sour my mood. I was so excited Isaac invited us back for the second night in a row and we were finally going to have a warm bath!

I felt a little bad knowing how uneasy Kith was about the whole thing, but it was hard to hide my joy. After only a short while, I started getting antsy.

"What do you want to do today?" I asked Kith, who was sitting in the cave with his blanket wrapped around his shoulders.

He looked at me, puzzled. It wasn't exactly a question we were used to asking each other. "I don't know. Maybe we could look for some berries or something in the forest?"

"I guess we could do that." It definitely wasn't the answer I was hoping for, but I wasn't really sure what that was either.

He laughed half-heartedly, "Are you excited about taking a bath tonight?"

"Yes!" I squealed, and this time he laughed for real.

We walked through the forest for a little while, but we both got cold before we found anything of note. After that, we just hung out in the cave for the rest of the day. It was agony to just wait around, but at the same time, it felt like a luxury I should be enjoying.

Isaac asked us to try to come a little earlier than usual because bathing would take some time. When it was just getting dark outside, we bundled up and quickly made our way to his house. I could feel the tension in Kith as his eyes kept darting around to make sure no one was watching, but it couldn't spoil my mood.

When we got to the house, Kith knocked on the door and then crouched low and beckoned for me to do the same.

Isaac opened the door and welcomed us as usual. Kith motioned for me to go in and then quickly followed.

"I just finished preparing the bath," Isaac said once the door was shut. "It may be a little too hot right now, but I'll let you test it out and decide." He walked us down the hall and into the room where a large metal tub sat full of steaming water. He showed us where the bath oil was kept and pointed to two towels he laid out. "Who's going first?"

Kith and I looked at each other. I hadn't thought of that. Kith started to open his mouth and I knew he was going to say I should go first.

"Kith can go first," I said, quickly cutting him off. He always tried to give me the better deal and I thought it was his turn. Besides, I knew how anxious he was and thought it might make him feel better the sooner he was in the bath.

Kith looked back and forth from me to Isaac, and I knew he was debating the idea of leaving me alone with him.

"Alright, Kith, if you want to leave your clothes outside the door, I can wash them for you," Isaac said before leaving the room.

Kith felt the water and pulled his hand out quickly. "It's scalding!" he said, shocked.

Laughing, I tested the water and had pretty much the same reaction.

"I told you," Kith said, rolling his eyes.

We both returned to the kitchen where Isaac just started adding ingredients to a pot. Not wanting to let the water get cold, Kith waited only a few more minutes before he went to take his bath.

A minute after Kith disappeared, his arm reappeared, dropping his clothes right outside the door before retracting back into the bathroom.

"Mara, could I ask you to watch this pot for me for a few minutes while I wash your brother's clothes?" Isaac asked. "Everything is in there, it just needs an occasional stir."

Feeling a sense of importance, I agreed immediately. Isaac grabbed a tall step stool and set it by the stove, "You can stand on here so it's easier to reach."

I watched as Isaac felt the ground in front of the bathroom to find all of Kith's clothing. Sometimes I forgot he couldn't see because of how well he managed to walk around his house and do regular tasks like cooking and gardening. It was a marvel how good he was at baking.

As I peeked into the pot, the most wonderful array of herbs and spices hit my nose. There were various vegetables and chunks of meat in a dark broth. It all looked and smelled amazing. After giving the pot a nice long stir, I set the large spoon aside and took a minute to look around Isaac's house some more. I was so nervous the night before, I barely noticed what was around me. To the left of the kitchen, down a short hall was the shop where Isaac sold his baked goods. It looked like a large room and when we picked the flowers, I saw that the front wall was made of glass. I guessed that must be so people could see the wonderful breads and desserts he made.

To the right was a longer hall that had three doors. One of those was the door to the bathroom. I was sure one of the other's must be Isaac's room and maybe the last was where his daughter had slept. Directly beside the kitchen was a small sitting room with a fire blazing. It was such a cozy room.

Realizing I had been gawking instead of stirring, I turned quickly back to the pot and grabbed the spoon. Before long, Isaac emerged with Kith's wet clothes and began hanging them up by the fire.

"How does it smell?" He asked while he hung up Kith's pants.

"What?" I asked, confused. Why would he be asking me how Kith's clothes smelled?

"The stew," Isaac said, and I could hear the amusement in his voice.

"Oh! It smells great!" I replied, feeling kind of stupid. Of course, he was asking about the stew.

After Isaac resumed tending the stew, I sat at the kitchen table. Eventually, Kith emerged from the bathroom wearing a nightgown that looked like it must have been one of Isaac's daughter's.

I laughed at the sight of Kith in a girl's nightgown and looked at Isaac to see a small grin. He must have known what I was laughing at. "I've got your clothes hanging by the fire now so they will dry quickly. You shouldn't have to wear that too long. Mara, that makes it your turn whenever you're ready. Don't forget to set your clothes out."

I went eagerly to the tub and dipped a finger into the water. It wasn't as warm as before, but wasn't cold yet. After I undressed, I set my clothes outside the door as instructed, and then climbed into the tub. I let my hair out of my usual braid and ran my fingers through it.

Dunking my entire body, I allowed myself some time to enjoy the water. Realizing Isaac must have spent a long time getting enough water to fill such a large tub, a surge of gratitude filled me. There was no reason he should be so kind to us, and yet he was anyway.

After a reasonable amount of time, I decided I should get to the actual cleaning part, so I grabbed the bath oil. I put a small drop in my hands, and beginning with my face, then moving on to the rest of my body, I rubbed off the dirt and grime.

The water was starting to get cold as I was finishing with my hair, and I was glad to be done. Grabbing the towel that was left for me, I dried off and then noticed a second nightgown. Pulling it over my head, I enjoyed the warmth of the thick fabric. Even though the nightgown was quite large on me, I loved the feeling of being clean and warm.

I left the room to find the table set and ready for us to eat. Kith was sitting awkwardly, staring at his hands. I wondered if he spoke to Isaac at all while I was gone, but the mouthwatering smell of the food quickly made the question vanish.

When I shut the bathroom door, Kith looked up, and I could see the relief on his face. He must be glad to have something to break the silence.

"Oh good," Isaac said as he grabbed the pot to carry it to the table. "Everything is ready, I was just keeping it warm for you."

"Thank you, Isaac," I said timidly. "I feel great."

Isaac just smiled and began dishing out the stew. "Careful, it's hot."

Dinner was full of awkward silences, but it didn't bother me at all. The stew was amazing and Isaac baked some delicious rolls to go along with it. After eating two rolls and a large bowl of stew, I was feeling full and sleepy.

"Your clothes are still a bit wet," Isaac said after we all finished our dinner. "Kith, yours are mostly dry, but Mara's still need some time. You are welcome to stay until they're dry if you'd like. It shouldn't be long." He rotated the clothes while he spoke to ensure each side was getting time close to the fire.

Kith's face said he wanted to leave immediately, but I knew he didn't want me wearing wet clothes out in the cold. "We can wait for a little while," he said, finally.

"In that case, I'll get to work filling your basket and you kids can make yourselves at home."

I stood from the table and Kith looked at me with wide eyes. "Where are you going?" He mouthed.

Ignoring him, I went to sit in a chair close to the fire. After a while, Kith grudgingly joined me and helped me braid my long hair.

"What are you doing?" he asked, and I realized I had started to nod off. My head jerked back up, and I looked at him sheepishly. "Were you sleeping?" he sounded half accusing and half amused.

He finished my hair and told me to rest while we waited for the clothes. "I'll wake you up when they're done."

It seemed like only a few minutes later he was shaking me gently. At first, I was worried I had a nightmare, but I didn't remember any. "Clothes are dry," Kith said gently. "Time to change and go home." I noticed that he was back in his own clothes.

We both thanked Isaac and made our way back to our cave. "I guess he isn't so bad," Kith said once we were snuggled into our own blankets. I smiled and fell asleep.

CHAPTER SEVEN: NOVEMBER

*   Mara   *

I woke up feeling the need to be moving. Even though I was sure we were fine in the cave, moving tended to help me feel like we were in control and safe. After a few attempts to shake off the energy, I rushed out of the cave.

"Are you alright?" Of course, Kith followed me.

"I don't know." I felt a buzzing in my arms and legs, followed by a prickly feeling. "I bet I can beat you to that tree." I pointed at a crazy tree, its branches twisted and mangled. It was a good distance into the woods, and we could only see parts of it from where we were.

Kith seemed confused, but I didn't wait before taking off. My body needed the movement. I was more than halfway to the tree when I saw Kith swinging from branch to branch on my right. At first, I was annoyed because we were supposed to be running. It didn't take me long to realize I didn't say that, though. Swinging did seem like fun and a better use of energy.

Quickly scrambling up a tree, I flew through the branches. By the time I made it to the tree, Kith was sitting comfortably in the branches. He smiled as I approached. "I won. Now, want to tell me what that was about?" He kept the question light, but I could sense his concern.

"I'm not sure. I just felt like I needed to be moving." I shrugged and brushed off his concern as if it was no big deal.

"I suppose that makes sense. We're so used to moving all the time, being still gets difficult." The way he spoke made me unsure if he fully accepted my answer or not. It didn't matter, though, because it was the only answer I could give.

We spent some time swinging around the curved branches of the tree before I finally felt the energy release. I curled up in a comfortable curve in the branch, and Kith snuggled in across from me.

"Swinging around like that made me feel like Grace." I smiled, maybe a bit too widely. I still felt like Kith was watching me closely.

"I can see that. I wonder if she would have taught you her tricks if things were different." I could see that Kith regretted the words as soon as they came out of his mouth, but he needn't worry. It was already something I pondered.

"I've thought about that myself. I probably would have been great at it. It doesn't matter, though, since she left us." Pain shot through my heart. "And Ducar tried to replace her with Garrett and Diana."

Kith scoffed. "Do you think they ever really became part of the group? They did seem to be trying in the little time we were there together."

"Yeah, but arrows are not as much fun as watching someone fly through the air. And they were always so wrapped up in each other." After a pause, I softened my voice. "I do feel a bit sorry for them, though. It's rough not fitting in with your group."

"That's true. We were all probably a little too harsh with them, but losing Grace hurt too much. And we were expected to accept them so soon as a replacement." Kith sighed.

"I wonder how their act has changed with time. I have to admit, it was actually kinda fun to watch. Especially the faces the crowd made when they saw Garrett holding the bow with his leg." I giggled at the memories. It was easy to see the crowd wondering how in the world an archer could shoot an arrow with only one arm.

"That was great. I was shocked at how good he was, especially with the tricks where he'd have to shoot up high. That must have required extreme balancing skills."

I nodded, my mind not completely on the conversation anymore. My stomach rumbled, interrupting the quiet that had come over us and I laughed. "I think my stomach is trying to tell me something. Should we head back and get some food?"

"Food sounds good. Maybe a nap after." Kith stretched and yawned before rising from his nook in the tree.

A large part of me was convinced Isaac would eventually tire of us coming to visit him. And even more tired of providing us with food. I couldn't deny that I looked forward to the meals he provided us, though. It was much better than anything we had eaten in a long time. Especially his rolls.

Still, even as I munched quietly on one of those rolls, I found myself wishing I was better at providing for us. As much as I didn't want to leave all we had here behind, the plan was still to move on once the weather was warmer.

"Kith?" I looked up to see that Isaac had stopped eating and seemed to be focused on me. Mara's fork hovered mid-bite as she looked up from her plate at the sound of my name.

"Yes?" Suddenly, I was nervous.

"You seem awfully lost in thought tonight. Is there something I can help you with?"

"Oh. I guess I am." I paused, unsure if I should say what was on my mind. He didn't seem like the type to drop it quickly, though, so I continued. "It's just...I don't like feeling like a burden to you." I didn't add that I also didn't want to be in his debt or any of my other feelings about the situation we found ourselves in.

A pained expression crossed his face, and he spoke with a sad frustration. "Kith, feeding a hungry child is never a burden."

"I understand. I'm not used to getting much help, is all." I wondered what he would think if he knew what I looked like and how hated I was by everyone. Realization hit me that his blindness was something I had massively been using to my advantage, and I felt a fresh wave of guilt about that.

"How long have you been on your own?" A concerned note filled his voice, and I wondered what he would do if he knew everything. Mara continued eating, but slowly. Her eyes watched the interaction carefully. She wore a slightly worried look on her face.

"I'm not sure how to answer that."

"You don't like opening up about your life, do you?"

The conversation was making me feel slightly panicked. "I think it's better that way." My eyes moved to the door, and I wondered if becoming friends with Isaac was a mistake. Was I putting him in danger? What would Ducar do if he found him?

Mara sensed my panic and was instantly at my side, her hand on my arm. Before she could say anything, though, Isaac spoke, his voice soothing. "Kith. Breathe. I won't question you anymore right now, alright? You're safe."

His words did calm me but also made me worry about how much he was picking up on. Did he know just how unsafe we were? My mind was racing, but I no longer felt a desire to flee. Mara's hand remained on my arm, her eyes on my face. She was ready to follow my lead, to leave if I felt we needed to. I silently covered her hand with mine and gave her a smile. She recognized that I was alright now, and went to finish her dinner.

We sat in silence for a moment, Isaac listening. It was obvious he was aware of at least some part of the exchange between Mara and me, but I couldn't tell how much. I put a chunk of ham onto my roll and took a big bite, hoping it would signal to Isaac that everything was fine. I wasn't sure if he was convinced, though. He seemed to be paying attention to my emotional state. His perception simultaneously terrified and fascinated me.

Mara finished her dinner and after a minute of focusing on the two of us, got bored and walked away from the table. Convinced I was alright, she curled up next to the fire.

After several minutes, Isaac spoke. "I have an idea, Kith. I get a lot of my food from traps similar to the one I snagged you in. I place them not far outside the edge of town, in spots I've become quite familiar with. Maybe if I taught you how to make some, it'll help you feel better. You can help me check the ones I have set up from time to time, as well. It would sure make my life easier."

"That would be great." We talked about the trap the rabbit was in, trying to recreate it, and my frustration when I couldn't figure it out. I left out the part about killing the rabbit before claiming it, still worried about giving him too much information about the conditions of our lives.

"Ah. I'm familiar with that type of trap, though I rarely use it." He smiled, but it seemed to be covering up his continuously growing concern about us. Maybe I already said too much. "I need to get stuff together, but if you come back in three days, it should be ready by then."

"What are these?" Mara was back, standing close beside Isaac, holding two objects out to him. My heart raced at the sight of her within his reach, but she was keeping her eyes on him.

"I'm not sure, dear." There was a smile on his face.

"Oh. Right. I'm sorry." The words tumbled out as her cheeks flushed a dark blue. "One is a book, but different from any I've seen. The words are bigger and there are more fun pictures. The other one is a small horse on wheels."

Suddenly, Isaac seemed sad. "Those were my daughter's."

Mara's eyes met mine and mirrored my shock. Unsure of what to say, we both just looked at each other. Other than the nightgowns we used after our baths we hadn't seen anything of his daughter's before.

Isaac smiled, but it lacked the joy we were familiar with. "You can keep those if you want, Mara. I have no use for them anymore." He spoke casually, but the words felt heavy.

"Thank you! I'd like that very much." Mara hugged the book and horse to her chest. Without thinking, she blurted out, "I haven't owned a toy in such a long time."

Her hand flew to her mouth in shock, as my eyes widened. I watched for Isaac's reaction, but he seemed to be hiding his emotions rather well. "I'm glad you like them." He spoke slowly, choosing his words carefully.

We sat in uncomfortable silence for a little bit longer, before Mara ran off to play. I could tell there was a lot Isaac was thinking about, but I didn't want to ask him about any of it. It might lead to him learning even more he shouldn't know.

*   Mara   *

I was growing more accustomed to our life in the cave the

longer we stayed. Kith was still anxious every time we visited Isaac, but every now and then he loosened up and enjoyed himself. Until one of us said something that revealed too much and he would tense up again. I hoped he would eventually ease up on that too. Isaac was kind, and there was no doubt in my mind that he would never do anything to hurt us.

Kith, on the other hand, needed more convincing. He tried to space out our visits as much as he could. It made me a little sad, but I knew it was important to let him take his time warming up to Isaac. He would come around.

One snowy night we made our way toward town. Our blankets were wrapped tight around us as we walked, but they did little to protect us from the bitter cold. As soon as we were inside Isaac's we headed straight to the heat of the fire. Still, the shivers took ages to subside and I was reluctant to leave the hearth to sit at the table.

After dinner, Isaac walked carefully over to a trunk in the living room and dug out two quilts. One for each of us. "These are quite old, but they're still very warm. I have more of them than I need now so you can take them home with you if you'd like."

We took the quilts gratefully and wrapped them around ourselves, snuggling into the warmth. I could see the crease on Kith's face which meant he was worried Isaac knew too much. It was almost like I could hear his thoughts. *Why would he think we need blankets unless he knows we're sleeping outside?*

While digging for the quilts, Isaac pulled out several other items. As he was putting everything back, he paused. "I don't really have much use for these either, honestly." In a small pile were several candles, a couple of pretty candlesticks, and a box of matches. Suddenly, even I was concerned that he knew more than he let on. I certainly wasn't going to tell Kith that, though.

The next day, we dug out the walls to create little shelves for the candlesticks. Each one held three candles, and once they were full we still had a few left over. We didn't light the candles often because we knew they would eventually run out, but when a storm came it was wonderful to have some light while staying inside for several days. We could see pretty well in the dark, but it wasn't altogether pleasant to live in it constantly.

On our next visit, Isaac gave me some flower petals his wife dried out to use as perfume for the house. They lost their scent by then, but when I mentioned how beautiful they were Isaac said I should have them because he couldn't enjoy their beauty anymore. The petals were now scattered along the walls of our little home.

Thinking of everything Isaac did for us, I could hardly believe how generous he was. The man had been through a lot in his life, with the deaths of his wife and daughter and his loss of sight. He could have easily become a bitter old man who would want nothing to do with us even without knowing our backgrounds. Yet he had taken us into his home and was always there with a smile each time we came back.

Whenever I thought about Isaac I ended up remembering Beatrice. She was kind and gentle just like him. I ached for her often, but knowing it hurt him to think about her, I stopped mentioning this to Kith. It was best to think of her silently and hope that one day I would see her again.

✳   Kith   ✳

After dinner one night, I sat next to the fire making more traps. I was becoming pretty good and felt pleased with my handiwork. "I appreciate you teaching me. It would have taken me forever to figure it out on my own."

"Oh, it's no problem. I forgot to tell you that dinner tonight came from a trap you made." Isaac was still, seemingly listening carefully for my response.

I beamed. "Did it really? Where did you put the trap?"

He chuckled. "I put it not too far from where I caught you. It was a pesky animal getting into my trash." He grinned playfully, and I wondered if he was telling the truth.

I couldn't help but laugh, though. "You did make sure it wasn't actually a child, right?"

His explosive laughter gave me a surprising amount of satisfaction. "Oh, shoot. I knew I was forgetting something."

Mara gave me a horrified look and slowly lowered her fork, which made me laugh just as hard.

After several moments, the laughter died down. "I'm really glad that my trap was helpful, seriously."

Isaac's eyes pierced through me in a way I hadn't experienced since Beatrice. I wondered how a blind man could stare straight into my thoughts. "You're still worried I'm going to get tired of having you around." He didn't bother making it a question. Mara glanced at me, and I knew she was thinking about all my hesitation to come, especially in the beginning.

"I guess so. I've enjoyed coming to see you a lot, but I feel we get the better side of the deal."

"Ah. But you two bring more to me than you realize." His voice was suddenly somber, and the playfulness was gone from his eyes.

"We do?" I found myself wishing I hadn't said anything, longing for the laugh to return to his face. Of course, Mara's face made it clear she knew where this was going. I just knew she was going to tell me repeatedly how right she was about Isaac being lonely and loving our company. I narrowly avoided a sigh.

"Your company brings me a joy I haven't felt in a long time. Not since my daughter and wife died."

Sorrow for his loss filled me, but I knew he wouldn't want my pity. "It must have been terrible losing them. I nearly lost Mara to sickness, and it almost killed me." I bit my tongue as the words came out, knowing it was too late to retract them. The shock on Mara's face was accompanied by a deep sorrow. She recognized the pain in both of us.

"I'm sorry you had to go through that. It must have been really hard for both of you."

"It was." My voice caught as I remembered thinking Mara was going to die, and then waking up to her completely healthy. I still didn't know how it happened, but I would forever be glad.

"I don't remember much of it." Mara shrugged. "I'm glad I got better, though."

"Me, too." Smiling, Isaac reached out as if to touch Mara's cheek. Halfway to her he seemed to think better of it and dropped his hand back to the table.

Mara watched his hand with a wariness I didn't expect. She seemed eager to trust this man, but his reaching out to her appeared to cause mixed feelings. I wondered if she was relying on his blindness just as much as I was.

As we sat in silence, I found myself wondering what normal people talked about. We couldn't talk about most of our lives, but I hated all this quietness. It made me uncomfortable to sit wondering what Isaac must be thinking about.

Mara broke the silence at last. "Do you think it will snow again soon? I really wanted to play in it, but it melted too fast." There was a slight pout on her face, and I was quite sure Isaac heard it in her voice.

"I'm sure it will." Isaac turned to pack up our usual basket. "You'll be playing in it before long."

"Do you like to play in the snow?" Mara fidgeted with her fingers as she spoke. She seemed to want to avoid the silence as much as I did.

Isaac chuckled softly. "I haven't played in snow in many years. It's not great on these old bones." He slowed down dramatically as if he was suddenly super stiff, causing Mara to giggle. I couldn't hold back a small laugh of my own but found myself wondering how much of that was true. If it was, maybe we'd end up more helpful to him over the winter than I thought.

Isaac and Mara continued their small exchanges, with Isaac doing what he could to make her laugh. Sitting back in my chair, I enjoyed the sounds of merriment and the warmth of the fire.

*   Mara   *

Every time we visited Isaac, he made hot food and gave us supplies for several meals on our own. Sometimes all he did was reheat a stew he made previously, but they were always just as good as if he made them that night. The food we took home was delicious, of course, but I missed the hot stew during those cold nights in the cave. I loved the warmth that ran through me when I ate hot food. His bread especially was a treat. Sometimes he would have some ready to go in the oven when we got there so we got to eat it fresh and hot. Those were my favorite nights.

"Isaac?" I asked timidly during one visit.

"Yes?"

"Would..would you teach me how to cook?" I stumbled through the question quickly, then stared at my feet, embarrassed.

Isaac gaped at us both. "If you don't know how to cook, how have you been living on your own?"

"Oh. We know how, or Kith does, really." I looked at Kith apologetically before continuing, "We just don't know how to cook like you do."

To my surprise, Kith laughed. I thought for sure he would be upset. "I think she's trying to say my cooking isn't any good."

"No, it's not that! Isaac's is just better," I said and looked at the floor, avoiding Kith's eyes.

"Well, Isaac has more experience, and he has more to work with. It's..um..hard sometimes to get the ingredients for stews like this."

When I looked up, there was an odd expression on Isaac's face, but he must have decided not to comment. "Of course, I will teach you how to cook, Mara. It would be delightful." He stopped to think for a moment, then added, "Kith, do you know how to properly skin an animal?"

Kith looked sheepishly at Isaac, "No. I kind of just tear it off."

"Tear?" Isaac asked slowly, quite confused. He didn't know about our claws, and you can't exactly just tear an animal's skin off with fingers. Kith looked at me desperately, trying to think of an explanation.

"Well, his knife is ancient and doesn't cut well." Kith looked at me with wide-eyed relief.

Isaac sat quietly for a moment and something that looked a lot like amusement played across his face. Kith and I looked at each other uncomfortably. "Well, I can teach you that too, if you like?" Isaac said finally, a wide smile brightening his face.

Kith beamed, "Thank you, that would be very nice."

It hit me how much more comfortable Kith was around Isaac. There were definitely moments of panic and distrust, but there were times when he was more relaxed than I'd seen him in years. I would never mention it to Kith of course for fear that would just make him panic all over again. It made me happy, though.

Over our next several visits, Isaac began teaching us. On the second visit, he had caught a squirrel in a trap Kith helped him build. I could see the excitement in Kith's eyes knowing it was his trap that caught it.

"I'll be working with Mara first, so we can all have our supper before midnight, then we'll get to work on this squirrel."

From that point forward, Isaac waited to start dinner until we arrived. I became suspicious that he somehow knew when we were coming. *Unless he waits until he's certain it's too late for us to come before he cooks for himself every night?* That thought made me sad. I didn't like the idea of Isaac sitting alone waiting for us and then, having given up, starting to cook for himself.

After some begging, I convinced Kith to go more often. Slowly, our visits moved from once every four or five days to sometimes every other day. The surprise was evident on Isaac's face the first time we returned after only one day away. Secretly, I almost hoped to catch him in the middle of his supper, but he waited for us just as I thought.

Kith and I agreed that neither of us would use our claws while Isaac was teaching us our new skills. This meant learning how to use the various knives around Isaac's kitchen. There was one for chopping vegetables, one to cut the meat that was already skinned, a small one for jobs that required more precision, and a rather large one that I decided not to ask about.

My first lesson was to cook the stew Isaac made on my first visit. He taught me how to chop the vegetables and the meat in neat little squares. He talked about which vegetables are good to add in stew and which were best left out. Then, he told me about the herbs and spices he added to his food for extra flavor.

"That's why it's so delicious!" My exclamation was met with a huge smile.

"Before we add everything together in the stew, we brown the meat." Isaac pulled his large pot out and I dropped in the meat. "I usually just wait a few minutes, stirring the meat every now and then," Isaac explained, "but you'll be able to see when the meat starts getting brown so I want you to watch it for me." Isaac let me decide when it was ready to switch from one step to the next, with his instructions on how to know when the meat and vegetables were cooked.

Once the meat was browned, and the vegetables were mostly cooked we added in the water and herbs and left the stew to finish cooking for a while. My excitement grew as we waited, and I became anxious to try our masterpiece. Once the stew was ladled into each of our bowls, Isaac and Kith waited for me to taste it first. I dipped my spoon in gingerly and blew to cool the meat and potatoes before sticking them in my mouth.

It was just as delicious as when Isaac made it all himself. After tasting it, Kith and Isaac both proclaimed it a success, making me grin. I was excited to keep learning and hoped that one day I would have a kitchen like Isaac's where I could cook all on my own.

After dinner, Isaac announced that it was time to take care of the squirrel Kith caught in his trap. Isaac was keeping the squirrel in a cage, waiting. When we were hungry and on the run, I never got a chance to appreciate how cute the fuzzy animals were. Now I found myself fighting back a squeal. I didn't want them to view me as a little girl who swooned over an animal.

Isaac swiftly grabbed the squirrel and showed Kith how to hit it on the back of the head, killing it quickly. My stomach lurched unexpectedly, but I forced myself to ignore it. Then Isaac handed Kith the big knife I didn't want to ask about and showed him where to strike to remove the head and feet. I couldn't bear to watch, however. My hands covered my eyes, even as I felt my face redden in embarrassment. If Kith and Isaac noticed, though, they didn't comment.

Once it was ready, Isaac showed Kith how to carefully separate the skin from the meat, starting near the tail and working up the belly and chest. He explained how to avoid contaminating the meat, and I realized I hadn't even known that was a risk.

The process took a lot longer than what Kith usually did, but I could tell a lot more of the meat would be saved for cooking. Thinking I would need to be able to help one day, I tried hard to watch. The sight and smell repulsed me, though, causing me to keep looking away. When they started cleaning it out, I fought the urge to vomit and stepped away.

When I was able to focus again, Isaac was explaining to Kith how the insides should be discarded far away so the animals it attracted wouldn't be brought close to us. They headed out into the woods to discard it safely, but I decided to go back inside where it was warm and smelled better.

Shame for my foolishness enveloped me, and I fought tears. I wanted to be more helpful, but I couldn't picture myself cleaning an animal like that. Knowing I was becoming more helpful in other ways, though, helped me be able to gradually calm myself.

When they returned, Isaac rubbed some of his herbs and spices on the meat after rinsing it. Then he stuck it over the fire to cook. "When that's done, you guys can take it with you for tomorrow." He smiled gently, and I could tell he knew I struggled.

Kith's excitement was almost contagious. "Mara," He whispered, "our meat will last so much longer now." He paused, his eyes scanning my face. "Since you're going to be so much better at cooking than I am, how about I take care of cleaning the animals so I'm still useful?"

That was Kith, always knowing just what to say. I smiled wide, "I like that idea!"

Isaac was listening with a smile, but there was something else in his demeanor. He was paying attention closely to how Kith and I spoke to each other, and I wondered what he was thinking.

Once Isaac started teaching Mara, every time we visited, she assisted with the cooking. She'd climb up on the counter so she could see what Isaac was doing and showing her. There was a delicate balance between wanting to be close to see everything, and needing to keep a distance. It probably would have been fine to get closer, but there was always the fear of something odd being discovered, like our tails.

I could tell Mara was fully aware of what she did with her tail, curling it up away from Isaac. The light of the flames made the gold of her eyes sparkle in a way I never noticed before. In those moments, I almost wished Isaac could actually see her. It was a pity he couldn't see how excited she was, how eager to learn.

Tonight, however, Isaac pulled up a stool and sat down. "I think you're ready to give it a try yourself tonight." His voice sounded different, but I couldn't figure out why.

"Are you sure?" Mara's sharp teeth bit her bottom lip. For a second I was afraid she was going to make herself bleed.

"I have no doubt. You'll do great. All the ingredients you'll need are laid out on the counter. You'll just be making the simple stew we've done several times." He leaned against the wall with a smile. "I'll be right here if you need me, but I don't think you will."

"Alright." Mara drew out the word slowly and then climbed up to her spot on the counter. Isaac seemed to be listening closely. I wondered suddenly what he thought when he heard her quickly scrambling up.

She started slowly, but as she went I could see her confidence build up. Since we'd started coming here to Isaac's house I'd noticed slow changes in Mara. There was an energy in her I hadn't seen in a long time. Actually having something to look forward to instead of just days of endless walking was a gigantic change for both of us.

As much as I fought it, I also looked forward to visiting. Fresh food made specifically for us was something we hadn't experienced in an extremely long time. After so many months of trash food and whatever we could find in the wild, having prepared meals that we didn't have to scrounge for was amazing.

I must admit, though, that it wasn't just about the food. Sometimes Isaac scared me with the way he seemed to understand so much even though we tried to be careful. There were times I felt like he really knew me. It was equally terrifying and incredible. With Mara, though, it was different. She thrived having the attention and care from someone other than me.

Seeing her interact with Isaac often made me wonder how things would be if Beatrice escaped with us. Would we have found a place to stay long term and been our own little family? Images of us in a cottage similar to this one filled my mind. It was Beatrice doing the cooking and teaching us and getting our baths ready, though.

A deep sense of longing filled me. Could Isaac come close to what Beatrice was to us? Would it be a good idea to let him? Weren't we still planning on moving on in the spring? The thought filled me with more sadness than I expected. The realization sunk over me that my fears were becoming actualized. We'd both become too attached to Isaac. As I watched Mara put the finishing touches on the stew, however, it was impossible to think of this as a bad thing.

Maybe we could put off moving on. For a while.

Suddenly a bowl was placed in front of me. I hadn't even realized that Mara was dishing it up. Steam wafted up as I stirred the contents. It was definitely still too hot to eat, but smelled delightful. "If this tastes as good as it smells it may be even better than when you had help." I winked at Mara, getting a small giggle in return.

"I hope it's good." she was stirring hers as well.

"I'm sure it's great." Isaac was smiling at the playfulness between us. Then, he quickly grew a bit more somber. "Are you guys aware that Christmas is coming up in a few weeks?"

"Christmas?" Mara said the word slowly, as if trying to remember what it was.

"I forgot about Christmas. It's been so long." Memories of the days when Mara and I would spend Christmas with Beatrice and the others filled my mind. All holiday celebrations stopped after Ducar changed. He didn't care about them at all, and no one had the willpower to fight him on it.

Mara's eyes were on me, full of questions. She was struggling to remember much about Christmas, but wasn't sure if she should say. I shook my head slowly and she nodded in recognition.

"I was thinking with everything going on you may have forgotten." There was a weird stress to the word forgotten, as if it wasn't what he meant at all. "I was wondering, though, if you two could help me decorate for it. I like to decorate my shop for my visitors, but it's getting harder to do it myself."

"Oh! I'd love to." Mara was practically bouncing in her seat.

"I thought you might." With a grin, Isaac picked up a colorful book. "This book has some examples of what I need. We'll probably start with the holly branches, which you'll recognize by the round red berries. With other kids finding them for their families, they're more likely to become scarce the longer we wait."

He handed me the book and I flipped through it. It seemed to be a story about Christmas, but I couldn't fully understand it. After a minute of examining the pretty pictures, I found one that showed the berries clearly. They looked quite familiar. "Oh, I'm pretty sure we've seen these before. It shouldn't be hard to collect them."

"One thing, though. Don't eat those berries. They're poisonous and will make you quite sick. If you're lucky." It was the most serious I ever heard Isaac's voice.

"We'll make sure not to eat them." Half way through the sentence I realized why they looked familiar. I handed the book to Mara and she looked at them then immediately back up at me.

"Those are the berries we couldn't eat." She only mouthed the words, so that Isaac wouldn't hear and ask more questions. I nodded. When the squirrel died I figured the berries were poisonous, but to have it told to us so seriously made it all more real.

Now the question of what stopped us from eating the

berries was back in my mind. I wondered if it was the same odd thing that brought Mara back. We may never know. For some reason, that idea was horrifying and devastatingly sad. I hoped one day we would understand.

"You two have suddenly gotten quiet. Is there a problem?"

"No. Just looking at what decorations we get to put up." Mara put a cheerful voice back on, but I could tell she was as full of questions as I was.

"I hope it's not a bother. I don't want to trouble you guys."

I couldn't help but laugh. "I think it's the least we can do, with how much you've done for us. We don't mind at all."

Isaac smiled, but it was one of the ones that didn't fully reach his eyes. "I'm glad. There will likely be a lot of other children going out into the woods to look for them, so be careful."

A shock ran through me, until I realized he meant while we were looking for the holly not at the cave. Probably. Still, he was aware that we needed to be careful around other children. My heart started racing again as I felt the fear about how much he knew building up.

My eyes darted around and landed on Mara. She made a big show of breathing deeply, her way of quietly telling me to breathe and calm down. I knew she was right. Isaac had given us no reason to worry. I allowed myself to relax and dug into the stew. "I was right, Mara. It's delicious." I said it around a large mouthful, making her giggle in disgust.

Isaac also dug in. "I was right, also. You didn't need my help at all."

Mara smiled so widely I could've sworn she was glowing, then started eating as well.

*   Mara   *

"Want to see if we can find any holly branches?" We had just finished eating, but I was too eager to get started on our task.

155

Plus, I was still quite intrigued by the poisonous berries.

"I don't know. Isaac said other kids would be looking for them, too. It felt like he was warning us." Kith's forehead creased and I knew he was getting dangerously close to panicking again. "It might be best to wait until it's darker."

"You're probably right," I sighed. "It's just going to be colder when it's darker." Pouting playfully, I hoped the change of subject would help him forget his anxiety.

Kith frowned. "True," he said slowly. "But better to be safe than sorry."

"Yeah, yeah," I said, rolling my eyes. "I know."

Kith was lost in thought and barely seemed to notice my reaction. "Do you think we should give Isaac a gift for Christmas?" he said, finally breaking his silence. "I want to do something for him, but don't know what. We don't have anything to offer."

Surprise ran through me, followed by a deep happiness. Isaac must mean a lot to Kith for him to be thinking so hard about a gift for him.

"I don't think that's true," I said comfortingly, "You've got a lot to offer." Then, after some thought I asked, "What do people usually do for Christmas?"

Kith looked at me in surprise. "You don't remember?" his face turned to a mixture of sadness and anger. "I guess you wouldn't. You were so little when we stopped celebrating. We used to have a big feast with everyone all together. Grace would make the famous apple pie her mom taught her to make. That part was always my favorite, but there was usually a huge assortment of foods and Beatrice would let us pile our plates with as much as we wanted, even though we never ate it all!" Kith was looking wistfully at his hands, lost in the memory.

"And people gave out gifts?" I asked, gently reminding him to finish explaining.

"Oh, right. Usually the gifts were some sort of treats bought in town. But we all had to give everyone else at least something. That was Beatrice's rule. Of course, she usually ended up picking ours out for us and just told everyone they were from us. She always bought or made us toys, though. There was one year that she got me a wooden bird. I loved running around with it in the air, pretending it was flying. It disappeared after Ducar started putting us in the cages. He probably sold it or something. All he cared about was money."

Kith's face started to sour, but I wasn't ready to give up on the Christmas fantasy he had been weaving.

"Well...do you think we could make something like that for Isaac?"

"I don't know, Mara," Kith looked at me like I was a little crazy. "I don't think Isaac plays with toys," he laughed and I was glad he was getting more cheerful again.

"Oh, silly me," I said, rolling my eyes in false exasperation. "Surely there's something we could do for him!"

"I don't know," Kith was thinking hard again. "Got any bright ideas?"

We sat in silence for a while. "Maybe we can find something in town?" I finally suggested.

Kith looked at me for a minute before responding. "I suppose taking something this once would be fine. Since it's for Isaac. We can start looking around and see if anything catches our eye."

I felt a little bad about the idea, but I really wanted to do something for Isaac after everything he had done for us.

We hung out around the cave after that until it started getting dark outside. Kith said we probably didn't need to wait for it to be fully dark because most parents would expect their kids back before then, so we should be able to look in peace.

Carrying empty packs, we crouched low and walked slowly just in case anyone was around. After we got into the woods, though, we eased up and decided it was okay to walk normally.

"Kith," I started tentatively, "What do you think stopped us from eating those berries before?"

Kith sighed and I could tell I wasn't the only one bothered by this. "I don't know. I've been going back and forth between wracking my brain about it and trying not to think about it at all. I might go crazy trying to figure it out."

"It seems like something or someone is working very hard

to keep us alive. First the berries, and then you healed me. It's like we're not meant to die or something. I guess that's just me going crazy like you said," Laughing, I tried to make it sound like I didn't actually believe my own words. A part of me did, though. Kith healed me somehow, and there was definitely something that stopped us from eating those berries. I wondered just how far this strange force would go to keep us alive, but quickly decided we shouldn't test it.

Kith didn't seem to want to talk about it anymore after that. I wasn't sure if my words troubled him because he did indeed think they were crazy, or because he felt the same; but decided not to press it.

It didn't take long after that for us to find some of the berry bushes, which helped to clear the awkward silence. There were a few empty bushes, but for the most part it seemed like we beat the crowd. We stayed out for a couple of hours and managed to mostly fill both our packs with clippings. I was glad Isaac let us borrow some scissors to make clipping their stems easier.

We were both so excited to have such a good haul, we decided to go see Isaac again the next night to bring them to him.

✳   Kith   ✳

One night after dinner, Mara grabbed the decorative items Isaac had set aside, and sat down on the floor in front of the fire. She held the paper showing pretty circles that were often hung up around Christmas. With a look of grim determination, she got to work.

For a moment, I thought about joining her, but it seemed like something she wanted to do herself. Since I wasn't particularly interested in making any circles, I didn't mind leaving her alone. Instead, I perched at the table looking at pictures in one of Isaac's books. He was working on some dough for the next day, as usual, and humming a lullaby. I couldn't tell if he realized he was humming, but I enjoyed it and was afraid he'd stop if I said something. Suddenly, the bowl Isaac was working with slid to the ground with a crash. I jumped in surprise, and Mara let out a squeal. Her fright made me think about how while in our forts we always worried about being snuck up on.

"Isaac?" My voice had a timidness to it that I kind of hated, but I pressed forward. "Are you alright?" In all the time we'd spent with him, I had never seen Isaac drop anything.

"Of course. It just slipped out of my hands," He moved his hand in a waving gesture, as if brushing away any concerns. "It happens from time to time." He picked the bowl up and continued with his work as if nothing had happened. I watched him for several minutes before turning back to the book in front of me.

When he was done with his dough, Isaac joined me at the table. He looked tired, but quickly perked up and smiled at me. "You're awfully quiet tonight."

"I know. I've just been thinking."

"Thinking about what?"

"Well." I wondered to myself if it was a bad idea to make the request I was about to. "Do you know any traps that would be used for… for defense?" I tried to keep my voice casual.

Isaac's eyebrow raised in question, but his voice was level. "Defense, huh? Did you have anything in mind?"

"Uhm. Maybe something that could be made quickly and easily?" I coughed nervously, while Mara watched the conversation warily, casting me questioning looks. "Like the armies use when they fear being snuck up on? I always thought those were pretty cool."

He probably saw through my lame cover, but his face remained unchanged. "Yeah, I know a few of those. The nice thing is, some of them can be used to catch food as well, so they'd be useful, not just fun." His smile seemed too gentle, and I wondered what I just gave away to him.

"Even better." I carefully kept my voice level and made it into no big deal, but the idea of traps that could possibly help protect Mara and me in the cave was reassuring. It would be even better if they managed to catch some food.

"Let me grab a couple of things and we'll get started."

Isaac disappeared outside.

Mara gave me a shocked look. "Do you think asking him that was a good idea?"

"I'm not sure, but wouldn't it be nice to have some protection? I think it would help the cave feel more safe, don't you?"

"Of course." Mara paused, biting her lip. "I hate feeling so secretive and untrusting with Isaac. He's been so kind to us."

I sighed. "I know, Mara. I don't want to put him in any danger, either, though."

Before she could respond again, Isaac returned, carrying some large sticks and a knife. He handed me a stick and sat down with his own in one hand and the knife in the other. "First I'll teach you how to make a sharp point. This has multiple different uses, and once you get the hang of it, it goes rather quickly."

He used the knife to shave large chunks off the end of the stick until it started coming to a point. The pieces that came off got smaller and smaller as the point became sharper. It seemed so simple, I was surprised I hadn't already done something like that. When he was done, he handed me the stick to look at and feel. The end was pretty sharp, and I imagined it would really hurt to be hit with, or run into.

"Ok, you try now." Isaac listened for me to begin. My claws started to come out from habit, but Mara's widened eyes stopped me. I wasn't sure if he expected me to have a knife, or if he'd be able to tell something was different if I used my claws.

"I, uhm, didn't bring my knife." I felt silly suddenly.

"Oh, right." His face seemed to display a mixture of emotions I couldn't quite explain. I could've sworn there was some disappointment and amusement both there, but that didn't make any sense. He handed me the knife, and went back to listening.

I was still not used to using a knife, and it felt bulky and weird in my hands. With some effort, I was able to shave the stick just like Isaac had shown me. As I worked, a small smile lingered on his face, a secret amusement shining in his eyes.

I was so absorbed in my task I didn't realize Mara had come over.

"I finished the circle." She held it out proudly. "I wish you could see it, Isaac. I worked really hard."

Isaac reached his hands out and felt the circle she held. "Oh, you made a wreath. I may not be able to see it, but it feels like it was done well."

"It looks really nice, Mara." I chose not to mention the scratches all over her hands from her frustrating attempts. "Where are you going to hang it?"

"Uhm. Where do they normally get put?" Mara's eyes were filled with uncertainty.

While I finished sharpening the stick, Isaac showed Mara how to hang the wreath. By the time he returned, I was finished, so I handed the stick over for approval.

"Nicely done. I'm surprised you haven't done this before." He paused, as if debating on whether or not to say the next part. "Maybe if you bring me your knife I could teach you how to sharpen it." His amusement seemed to grow even more, and my curiosity was rising.

"Did I do something funny?" I was afraid my voice came out more upset than curious. Mara returned from hanging up her decorations and watched the interaction carefully.

Isaac laughed, then sobered. "No. I'm sorry, I'm just enjoying teaching you all these things."

"It's been nice to learn it." I watched his face, wondering what he wasn't saying. I did believe he enjoyed teaching me, but I felt he was keeping something to himself, also. Judging by the look on Mara's face, she felt the same way.

"Alright, so, I'm sure you can imagine different uses for this one. If put at the right angle, someone running could be damaged on the point if they don't see it. Digging a hole and sticking a bunch of these in the bottom facing up can catch both people and animals. There are different ways to cover the hole so it's not noticeable. You'd just have to make sure not to fall in yourself."

I pictured getting stuck in one of my own traps. "That would be bad." I'd have to make sure both Mara and I were careful if I put up any traps.

Isaac showed me a few other cool ideas for defense, and I wondered if he knew how much we may come to need these.

CHAPTER EIGHT: DECEMBER

✳   Kith   ✳

One night while I sat watching him knead dough, Isaac's hand slipped and it dropped to the floor. In all our months of visiting him, I never saw him mess up dough. He simply sighed, threw it out, and started a new batch.

Once finished, he sat across from me, seeming lost in thought. "Now who is being thoughtful and quiet?" My voice was a mix of teasing and questioning, and I wondered if he also picked up on my worry.

"Kith, there's something I think I should tell you." He paused. "Maybe I should've told you a while ago, but I didn't know how you'd react." Mara was playing on the floor in front of the fireplace again, but she froze and looked up, sensing the seriousness of the conversation.

I squirmed in nervousness and could tell he was picking up on it. "Tell me what?"

"It's really something I need to tell both of you." He was silent for a moment while Mara joined us at the table, and when he spoke he used his softest, most reassuring voice. "I know who you two are, have for a while. I suspected the first night we met, Kith, but it wasn't until later that I was sure. Meeting Mara fully confirmed it."

Shock ran through me. "I don't understand." It wasn't completely true, though. His statement explained a lot that happened since we met him. Mara's hand came to my arm, slight trembles running through it. Her mouth was open as if to say something, but no words came out.

"Being in the show made you pretty famous. It was a huge deal when you disappeared without any explanation. The news spread quickly, with a lot of crazy rumors." He paused to give us time to absorb the information. "You were so scared that night in my net, I knew you must have dealt with a lot of cruelty, which made me wonder."

"Why didn't you tell us sooner?" My heart was still racing, and my thoughts were confusing.

"Do you remember the first night I met you? You only seemed to relax when you realized I was blind. I even mentioned it being the only reason we were talking, and you confirmed that." Mara's eyes widened. I hadn't told her that part of the story.

"I didn't mean that was the only reason I trusted you." I paused as memories of being caught by other people once again danced in my mind. "I figured it was the only reason you would like me."

My words didn't seem to surprise him, but confirm his suspicion. "You haven't met many nice people, have you?"

"Not many, no." Mara's voice was soft but clear. I could tell she was thinking about all the cruel people we'd run into.

"I thought not. Just so you know, I haven't said anything to anyone about you being here. I don't know what happened at the show, but I figured you wouldn't be so scared without good reason."

"Thank you." My eyes were getting all watery. "Why did you decide to tell us?"

A look of complete seriousness came to his face, then he cleared his throat. "I told you for a few reasons. A large part was because I wanted you to know that your differences didn't matter to me at all. I have enjoyed my time with you, even knowing the truth."

I had no clue how to respond to that. "What if you hadn't heard of us first, but then found out? Wouldn't you have been freaked out by me?"

He was quiet in thought for a couple of minutes. "I don't know what experiences you've had, my boy, but not everyone in this world is cruel. I hope you come to learn this for yourself."

I thought of Beatrice, and how she immediately became like a mother to us, protecting us fiercely. I longed for her protection and safety. My throat closed. "Not everyone. But most." Tears ran down my face and my eyes stung.

Isaac felt my sadness, and I could see my pain reflected in

his eyes. "I know you don't trust many people, but I hope you've come to at least partially trust me." After a pause, he continued. "Mostly, I chose now because it's almost Christmas time. This means extra people will be coming to town to visit family and buy supplies. In the next week or two it's going to get a lot more crowded."

Mara looked at me, questioning. "What does that mean?"

I shrugged, confused. "More people doesn't sound great. I guess we'll have to be more careful."

Mara looked sad. "Will that mean less visits here?"

"Actually, Mara, I'm hoping it will mean something quite different. I think you two should come to stay here."

"Stay here?" Mara's voice rang with excitement and she looked at me eagerly. "Like, overnight?"

My heart was racing, and I felt the usual panic creeping up on me. Could we really stay here? That sounded wonderful and terrifying at the same time. For a moment, I couldn't bring myself to speak.

Isaac chuckled softly. "I mean at least until the extra people leave. It would be safer for you to be here."

"Here? Where you have people coming into your shop all day?" My voice squeaked out and Mara glared at me. It felt like I was crushing her dreams with my worries.

"I understand that concern, but the shop is separate from my house. No one visits me here. You wouldn't have to be outside and at risk of being seen. We can even find places for you to hide if you feel worried."

His reasonings made sense. Would it really be safe? One look at Mara's face told me she was desperate for me to say yes. She was practically begging me to. "Are you sure it would be safer?"

"Kith, I promise I won't allow any harm to come to you while I live."

His phrasing was odd, but I could tell he was sincere. He wanted to keep us safe, and honestly believed staying in his home was the best way. "Alright," I spoke slowly. "We'll go back to the cave tonight for a final night and bring our things tomorrow."

Mara squealed and grabbed me in a big hug. "It's going to be great!"

Isaac smiled. It seemed like he wanted to comment on my mention of our cave, but decided against it. There was a part of me that was upset I let that slip, but it didn't really matter now. I sat in a daze as Mara and Isaac chatted about how she wanted to decorate everything. By the time we headed back to the cave, it felt like I was just watching myself move, instead of in control. I couldn't help it, though. A sense of happiness swept over me. We'd be staying in a house, with fresh food every day and a bed to sleep in. And we'd have someone to keep us safe. Then, the thought hit me. Could this actually be our long term home? I shoved the thought away, deciding it was best not to think about, and got ready for my last night in our cave.

*   Mara   *

When we finally made our way back to the cave, Kith was slowly dragging his feet. I was almost afraid he'd fall asleep while walking. We stayed talking with Isaac for much longer than normal. Even more than that, I knew Isaac's revelation was weighing on him. A part of me worried that when we got home he was going to tell me we were never going back. Just because he agreed when Isaac was there didn't necessarily mean he really wanted to stay with him.

It was hard to contain my excitement about the idea of staying with Isaac. Knowing how much it terrified Kith, however, I decided to approach it delicately. The entire walk home I thought about what exactly to say and still hadn't reached a good conclusion.

We were both settled under our blankets before Kith finally broke the silence that had lingered since we left Isaac's house. "I'm surprised you aren't jumping for joy right now," he said abruptly, looking over at me. There was worry and confusion etched all over his face. "Do you not want to stay?"

"I do," I said slowly, "But I wasn't sure if you did."

The confusion on his face only grew. "I said we were going to, didn't I?"

"Well… you did. It's just that I didn't know if you were only telling Isaac what he wanted to hear."

For a moment, his confusion lingered, until his face broke into a smile and he let out one loud laugh. His face sobered quickly as he considered the situation. "I'm not sure how I feel about it, to be honest. I think he has a point about it being safer for us to stay there right now, but I'm not sure how safe it would be for him."

"Because of us?" Suddenly my chest felt like it was filled with ice. "You think Ducar…" I couldn't bring myself to finish the thought.

"I don't know, Mara." Kith let out a long sigh. "I guess by inviting us; while knowing who we are, he is accepting the risk."

I grabbed Kith's hand and squeezed it hard. "He did say he would protect us." Now I just needed to force myself to believe that being hidden inside those walls would be enough.

We sat in silence for a minute before Kith responded. "You're right. It'll be okay. We can pack up tomorrow, and then we don't have to come back here again," he paused and then added, "Kind of sad to just leave after how much work we put into it."

I looked around the cave and realized he was right. It wasn't exactly a normal home, but it had become *our home*. I was excited to stay with Isaac for a while, but quite proud of the home we managed to make for ourselves here.

The next afternoon, we started getting ready. "It seems weird to say we're packing up when we don't really have that much to bring with us," I said, scanning the cave. We decided we should go ahead and empty it all out, so I started by pulling what was left of the candles out of the walls. I figured they might be nice to have at Isaac's house, too.

The excitement grew inside me as we waited for it to be dark enough to head to Isaac's. Packing had taken less than an hour, and ever since then, I couldn't sit still. Kith kept making fun of me for bouncing around. When he finally announced that we could leave, I jumped up so fast I hit my head on the cave's ceiling and crumpled to the ground laughing.

"Are you okay?" Kith was by my side in a heartbeat, but all I could do was laugh while tears filled my eyes. "Why are you laughing, I can't tell if you're hurt or not!?" This just made me laugh harder until Kith sighed in exasperation and started to walk away.

"No," I gasped, trying to get a hold of myself. Hitting my head really hurt, and I wasn't entirely sure why I was laughing either. "I'm coming!" I grabbed my bag and slowly rose to a crouch until I stepped out of the cave.

When we got to Isaac's house, he opened the door smiling wide. "I hoped you would still come," he said, happily.

"Did everyone think I was lying?" Kith asked in exasperation.

Isaac looked confused for a moment, and then he must have guessed what Kith and I talked about the night before and his smile only grew.

Isaac had dinner waiting for us, which surprised me since I usually helped make it now. "I wasn't sure how long it would take you to pack up and make your way here, so I thought it might be nice if dinner was ready for you. Did you manage to bring everything in one trip?"

Kith and I exchanged glances before I responded. "We got everything we need."

Isaac showed us to our room so we could settle in while he dished everyone up. "There's only one bed," he said apologetically, "but I thought you are both small enough, you should be able to fit if that's okay."

"This is perfect!" I said, unable to contain my excitement. After ages of sleeping on the ground, sharing a real bed felt like a dream.

I tried not to eat too quickly, but all I could think about was snuggling up in that bed. Soon after dinner was over, I announced I was going to bed and Kith and Isaac both looked surprised.

"Already?" Kith asked.

"I'm just tired from all the excitement of the day," I said defensively. "You don't have to go to bed yet."

Kith hesitated for a moment, and I got the idea that he didn't really want to stay up alone with Isaac.

"No, that's fine." He said. "I'm actually pretty tired, too."

Isaac's smile seemed a little sad, and I wondered if he understood that Kith felt too awkward to stay up with him alone.

"If you need anything, just let me know," he said, warmly. "Sleep well."

Once we settled down in the bed, I whispered to Kith. "What do you think Isaac does when he's alone and isn't running the bakery?" The thought made me sad.

"I don't know," Kith answered slowly. "He has his plants to take care of and he has to bake things to fill up the shop. I'm sure that takes a lot of his time."

"I wonder if he ever leaves. He knows his house well so it's easy for him to get around, but can he move so easily when he goes outside?"

"Well he has to leave," Kith said with a hint of laughter in his voice. "How else do you think he gets his food and the ingredients he uses for baking?"

"Oh, good point," I said, feeling silly. It always just surprised me how well he could get around without being able to see.

We talked for a while about Isaac and our new living situation, but before long I was having a hard time keeping my eyes open. Kith noticed them drooping and laughed. "Looks like it's time to sleep," he murmured and closed his own eyes.

Suddenly, Ducar's face swam into my vision, and I heard him taunting me. Then, he slapped me across the face, causing me to cry out in a mixture of surprise and pain. In the dream, I was shocked that he would hit me like that, which meant it must have been one of the first times he did it. He reared back like he was going to hit me again, and I cried out even louder and turned to run away. I felt an arm gently encircle me as I was lifted into the air. The tent in front of me disappeared as I opened my eyes and saw Isaac's face.

"Does she get nightmares often?" he was asking.

I looked over and saw Kith sitting in the bed, a mixture of emotions playing across his face. He seemed tense, and I knew Isaac holding me must be triggering some reaction in him that he was trying to fight.

"I do," I said, quietly. "But it's okay because Kith is always there to protect me when I wake up." Isaac's face turned cloudy, and I could see the worry lines crease his forehead. Kith, however, relaxed at the sound of my voice.

Isaac sat on the bed and opened his arms as if to free me. He seemed a little surprised to have me there, almost like he had come to comfort me out of instinct and now realized he might have overstepped. I wrapped my arms around his neck to let him know everything was alright. Behind me, I heard Kith's sharp intake of breath.

When I pulled away, Isaac's smile was such a mixture of sadness and joy my heart broke for him. How many times did he come into this room to comfort his little girl after she had a nightmare?

I laid down in Isaac's arms and looked at Kith. He gave me a small nod to let me know he was okay.

"Do you want to talk about your nightmare?" Isaac asked soothingly.

"There was a bad man hurting me," I said, keeping it vague.

Isaac's face crumpled, "Why would anyone ever want to hurt such a sweet girl?" Something about his tone made me ache for him even more.

"I don't know, but it was just a dream," I said. Even though Isaac knew who we were, I didn't want him to know what we had been through. He already seemed so worried. He rocked back and forth gently on the bed until I fell back asleep.

Isaac wasn't kidding about the crazy amounts of people coming into town. A few days after we brought all of our things to his house, they started pouring in. Lines of wagons carrying families passed by the windows. Mara and I couldn't help but peek around the edges of the frames. There was so much bustle and excitement going on. People greeted visitors with hugs and kisses as children ran around joyfully.

As we peeked out, I wished there was someone to greet us like that. Someone who looked forward to seeing us. It looked lovely.

"What are you two doing at the windows?" Isaac came through the door from the shop, making sure to close it tight behind him.

Mara looked up in surprise. "How did you know we were looking out the window?"

Laughter filled the air. "I didn't, but I do now."

Mara scrunched her face up in confusion. "How did you guess that?"

"Ah. You forget, Mara. I used to have a child. I know what curiosity does and how hard it is to resist." He walked over and after some patting around at the air, managed to gently pat her head. "Be careful. I brought you here so you were less likely to be spotted. Not to put yourselves on display." Regret filled his face at his choice of words.

"I don't want to be on display." Mara's voice held a deep fear, and she backed away from the window slowly.

"I'm sorry. I didn't mean to frighten you. That was a poor choice of words." Isaac sighed. "You'll be fine at the window as long as you try to stay at the edge and not draw attention."

Mara looked at the window warily. I could see the excitement of watching people come in had died down for her. Honestly, I was tired of it as well. "I think we're done for today anyway. How's it going in the shop?" I found myself wishing I could join him there.

"It's going well. I got a break from customers and figured I'd come to check on you two." After a pause, he added, "Think you guys could help me prep some dough tonight? I'll likely have a lot more people tomorrow."

"We can do that!" Excitement returned to Mara's voice.

With a grin and one last pat, Isaac turned to head back to his shop. "Great. I will appreciate having some extra help around here."

After he left, Mara turned to face me. "How many days do we have until Christmas?" Her face held her worry.

"I'm not sure." I wasn't used to looking forward to specific days. "Why?"

"We never got anything for Isaac!" There was a trace of panic in her voice.

"You're right. We should go out tonight soon after he goes to sleep and see if we can find something."

"Together?" Her eyes widened in joy, with a little bit of fear mixed in.

"Of course. Unless you don't want to come."

"I do!" It came out as a squeal, and I couldn't help but laugh.

"Great. Now we just need to wait."

With a groan, Mara slumped onto the couch dramatically.

Finally, the shop closed and the door opened. "Let me rest a bit, and then we'll start the dough." Isaac made his way to his usual chair. As he got close, he wobbled, then stabilized himself. "What was that?"

Confused, I just stared at him for a couple of seconds. Then, I glanced down and realized he had tripped on the books I was looking at earlier. I hadn't even thought about them being in his way.

"I'm sorry. I left some books on the floor." I could feel my face flush blue as I spoke, embarrassed at already causing problems.

"It's alright. I just wasn't expecting them." I could tell Isaac was being careful with his words, trying to reassure me.

"I'll try to remember to put them up from now on."

With a gentle smile, Isaac relaxed into his chair. "Mistakes happen. It's not a big deal." He seemed quite tired, so I grabbed the books and left him to rest.

Mara was in our room sitting on the bed. In her lap was the toy horse. She knew it was a toy for playing with, but didn't seem to know what to do with it. She was more lost in thought than playful, though.

"What are you thinking about?" I sat on the other end of the bed, the books still in my hands.

She looked up at me silently for a moment before speaking. "I'm sitting on our bed. Our bed is in our room. Our room is in a real house. Is this what it's like to feel almost normal?"

Her words hit me like a punch to the stomach but also caused a warm feeling in my chest. "I don't know that I'll ever understand normal, but maybe."

"Do you think we can stay here?" The words came out slowly as if she was reluctant to hear my answer.

"We are staying here. That's why it's our room."

"I know. I mean. Do you think we can stay here after winter is over? I know you didn't want us getting attached to Isaac for fear of it hurting when we moved on. But, do we have to move on? Couldn't we just stay here with someone who cares about us and will protect us?" The words started slowly, then tumbled out as if they were trying to all come out at once.

I hesitated. "I don't know. Do you think Isaac would really want to keep us here?"

"Why wouldn't he? I know he cares about us. He even knows who we are and still cares. Not because we can make him money or give him whatever Ducar is after, but because of us." Tears lined her eyes and her cheeks were so blue they were almost glowing.

"We'll have to see. I can't promise anything, but the idea of having a home and someone to keep us safe does sound nice."

As she opened her mouth to respond, Isaac called that he was ready to make the dough. "I guess we'll have to talk about it more later." She scrambled off the bed and sped out to the kitchen, and I followed along behind her.

We watched Isaac make dough many times, but this was the first night we actually helped. He showed us how to carefully measure the ingredients and add them. With a tight grip on the cup he gave her, Mara tried to copy his movements. As she turned her hand to dump some flour into the bowl, she moved wrong and half of the contents hit the side. A white cloud poofed up, and we all started coughing.

"I'm sorry!" Mara immediately started cleaning up the mess, but we were all covered in it.

Isaac laughed. "I can only imagine what everything looks like right now. Don't worry. It's a completely normal part of the process. Believe it or not, I did the same thing several times when I first started learning."

Mara's eyes went wide. "You did? But you're so good at it. Even without seeing what you're doing."

"I am now. I've been baking for many years. Longer than you've been alive. It takes time to develop your skills. Sometimes a lot of time."

"I suppose that makes sense, but I wish I could be good now." Mara pouted playfully before giggling.

"You learned cooking fast enough, you can't pick up everything that easily. You have to leave some skills for the rest of us." I elbowed her teasingly.

By the time we were done making dough, I was exhausted. With all the new people in town, we had to prepare many different loaves. No wonder Isaac wanted help. It took hours to get enough for him to be satisfied.

"I don't think I can go out tonight, Mara. I'm too tired." I mumbled the words as I joined her in our room. There was no response. "Mara?" I walked over to the bed and looked at her. Even though she had just laid down, she was already fast asleep. "I guess you can't handle going out tonight, either," I whispered the words as I climbed into bed, then swiftly fell asleep.

One night, after going to bed, Kith and I sat talking for a while until I heard a soft rumble.

"What was that?" I asked, holding up my hand to shush Kith.

We listened carefully for a while before we heard it again. It was faint and sounded like it might be coming from out in the hall. I was listening so intently when it happened a third time, that Kith's laugh made me jump and a small squeak escaped my lips.

"Isaac is snoring!" Kith whispered between giggles when I gave him a death glare.

Unconvinced, I continued to listen. This time when it happened again, I knew Kith was right. I looked at him with wide eyes and we both burst out into giggles, trying our best to keep it quiet.

For a while, each little snore sent us into another fit of laughter until we had laughed ourselves out and then we sat in silence, each of us thinking.

I was reminded of Mitch, from the freak show. He was self-conscious about his snoring, but he was much louder than Isaac's. He used to try to blame it on other people, but we all knew it was him. Eventually, Ducar made him sleep further away from everyone else so he would stop disturbing us. That was when everyone stopped making fun of it.

Surprise ran through me at the memory. I had forgotten all about the snoring until just now.

"Do you know how long it's been since we played outside?" Kith asked, suddenly, bringing me out of my thoughts. I looked over to see him staring at the covered window. This was the first night in several days that we hadn't spent hours making dough with Isaac.

It was a strange thought to realize it had been so long when before we spent every single day outside. Even when we lived with the freak show, we were always outside during the day. That's what happens when you live in a tent and move around all the time.

"I guess I hadn't thought about it," I said.

"I kind of miss it. Inside just feels so stuffy sometimes," Kith said. "It's not that I'm not grateful or anything, I know Isaac is doing us a big favor letting us stay here. I'm just not used to it, you know?" He looked a little frustrated with himself, but I understood what he meant.

"Well...why don't we go outside now?" I asked, standing up and beginning to bundle myself without even waiting for an answer.

Kith brightened up and started bundling himself as well.

We tip-toed out of the house and closed the door gently behind us so we wouldn't disturb Isaac.

Once outside, Kith stretched his arms wide and looked up at the sky. After a few minutes of walking, he looked over at me and grinned, "It's been a while since we raced to the woods," he said and took off running.

"No fair!" I whispered after him, not wanting to be too loud while we were still so close to town. I wasn't sure if he heard me or not, so I ran after him trying to catch up.

We stayed out for a couple of hours. First, we were just running around and then we swung through the trees. Before too long, we were both tired, so we sat in a tree and just enjoyed the outdoors. It didn't take long at all before I was shivering and missing the warmth of Isaac's house.

The walk back wasn't as exciting as the one out. We were huddled together, trying to stay warm. My legs were tired, and I wished we hadn't gone out so far.

When we got back to the house, we opened the door as quietly as we could.

"Is that you?" We almost jumped out of our skin at the sound of Isaac's worried voice.

"It's us," I said sheepishly, realizing we hadn't thought about what Isaac might think if he woke up and we were gone.

He let out a sigh of relief. "I was awakened by a loud noise. After checking the house, I went to make sure you were alright and you were gone. What happened?"

Looking to my right, I could see that Kith felt just as bad as I did. We weren't used to having someone care for us like this and we never considered that leaving without telling him might be a bad idea.

"We just went out to play," Kith said, miserably. "We can't go out during the day, so we were missing it."

A mix of emotions played across Isaac's face like he couldn't decide how to handle the situation. "Well, I'm glad you made it back safely," he said finally and turned to head back to his bedroom.

"I'm sorry, Isaac!" I said, desperately. "We didn't mean to scare you."

Isaac kept his back to us, but his voice was soft when he spoke, "It's okay, Mara. Completely understandable that you would be getting restless," he said. "In the future, I will assume that's where you are. This whole situation is new for all of us and will take some getting used to. I just ask that you keep track of the time and try to make sure you always get back before it starts getting light outside. And be careful if you're going to go out in those woods at night. This old man worries too much." With that, he continued down the hall, and I noticed he seemed to be having a harder time walking than normal. He was relying heavily on a walking stick he had carried out with him. He must have been tired from looking for us.

Kith and I exchanged guilty glances and then headed back to our bedroom. We decided from then on we would let Isaac know beforehand if we planned to go outside so he wouldn't be too worried.

✷   Kith   ✷

I woke up still feeling guilty. Having someone to worry about us wasn't something I was used to anymore, and I hadn't thought about it the night before. Isaac seemed almost disappointed in us, and it stung more than I expected it to.

Mara was stirring in her sleep. I hated that even with us

here in Isaac's house she still had nightmares plaguing her. Seeing Isaac comfort her that first night caused such mixed emotions. It was nice to have someone else to help ease her terror, but seeing him hold her almost hurt in a way I didn't understand.

Luckily, since the first night, her nightmares were mostly mild and I was able to take care of her without Isaac waking. There was no fighting the fact that he was now aware of the nightmares, but knowing they came every single night wasn't necessary.

I sat rubbing Mara's back, lost in thought until she slowly woke up.

"Where are we?" At first, she seemed on the verge of panic, but then she relaxed as she remembered.

"You're alright, Mara."

"I know." As she stretched with a small smile, her stomach rumbled. "I'm awfully hungry, though."

Laughing, I rose from the bed. "Let's get you some food, then."

As we opened the door, the smell of our favorite rolls wafted in. We walked eagerly to the kitchen, following the scent. Isaac stood at the table, placing the rolls onto plates. He smiled gently as he heard us approaching. "Just in time. I thought you might be."

"I don't think there's anything in the world that could keep me away from your rolls." Mara climbed up to the table excitedly as Isaac pulled out butter and honey.

"I agree. We've been spoiled completely rotten." I laughed, but felt even more guilty.

Isaac shook his head sadly. "I keep telling you two that feeding a child isn't spoiling them. It's just decency."

"It's not just food, it's the most delicious food I've ever eaten." Mara picked up half of her roll and took a big bite. "These are even better with honey."

Isaac laughed. "I'm glad you like it." After a pause, he added, "I think I should apologize for last night."

Shock ran through me. "Why would you need to apologize?"

"Having you two here is an adjustment, and I think I

overreacted last night."

Mara's chewing slowed as she looked up at Isaac. "I think it's understandable. I hated making you feel worried, but I love that there's someone that cares enough to *be* worried." She bit her lip as she finished speaking, wondering if she had gone too far. I shrugged it off, knowing that he already knew any information she would have given him.

Isaac seemed unsure of how to respond. He ate in silence for a couple of minutes. "I've got to run some errands soon. Is there anything you two need?"

"We're alright. I think there's plenty here to keep us entertained." I took another big bite of my roll, then added, "And plenty of rolls to keep us satisfied."

With a chuckle, Isaac headed to get ready for his day. We finished our rolls and went to find something to do. It wasn't long before we got tired of the toys and books and found ourselves peeking out the windows at all the people walking around. Usually, when we observed townspeople, we were far away and high up in a tree. They always looked so small. It was an interesting reminder to see how much bigger even the children were than us.

"I wonder what it's like in Isaac's shop." Mara was twirling her braid in her fingers while staring idly out the window.

"I imagine it's similar to the other shops I've been in."

With a roll of her eyes, she sighed. "That doesn't help me, though." Silently, she crept toward the door. "Do you ever think about sneaking in there?" She reached her hand tentatively toward the door.

"That's not a good idea, and you know it."

"I know." Her hand dropped down and she pouted. Right as she was about to turn away the door opened and almost hit her in the face. "Eek!" She squealed and leaped backward before dashing behind a chair.

"Mara?" Isaac's hand was on his chest, and his breath came rapidly. "What were you doing in front of the door?"

Mara's voice was timid and quiet, still trying to silence the panic. "I was daydreaming about what it was like in your shop."

"I didn't hit you, did I?"

"No. Just scared me."

"Well, we're even then, because you scared me, too."

"Sorry." Her voice was even softer than before.

"Would you like to see my shop sometime?"

"Really? Is it safe?"

I felt pride that I had taught her well enough to ask that first, but also sorrow that she had to worry about such a thing.

"Well, it's probably not the best idea during the day, but one of these nights I'll show you around."

"I wish I could see it during the day, but I understand."

Isaac started to head into the kitchen to grab some food. As he walked he almost ran into the chair I was sitting in. I forgot to push it into the table. Luckily, his hand hit it first, and he was able to move it out of the way. I reminded myself again that things needed to be put back, but Isaac didn't say anything.

As he fixed lunch, I looked around at everything else we left out. Books and toys were scattered all over the floor, put down where we got tired of them. We never had so much stuff to worry about putting away. I rushed around picking everything up, frustrated at how easy it was to forget.

Throughout the rest of the day, I tried to remember to put everything back once I was done with it. I didn't want to keep causing Isaac trouble getting around his own house. When we first visited, I hadn't realized how carefully he placed everything.

As we were getting ready for bed that night, I realized that we hadn't gotten his gift yet. Even though I was tired, I decided it would be best to get it instead of waiting longer. "I'm feeling a bit restless, so I just wanted to give you a heads up that we might end up going out again tonight." My voice felt shaky, both from the lie and from the excitement of trying to find a gift.

"Alright. Just be careful. Even more people came into town today."

Mara and I waited in our room until it was dark. I didn't need to tell her what we were doing tonight. As we waited she practically buzzed with excitement. "We'll need to be extra careful. Sneaking around town is dangerous enough on a normal night, but it's going to be super risky tonight."

I could tell she was nervous, but she nodded solemnly. "I'll be extremely careful."

We were lucky enough for it to be a dark and cloudy night. It felt like there may be rain or snow soon, but it wasn't coming yet. We crept out the back door and around the corner. Hovering in the shadows, we looked around town. It seemed completely still.

"Where do you think we should look first?" Mara's voice was so quiet I could barely hear her.

"I'm not sure. We still don't know what we're looking for."

"We could split up and try to find something."

I shook my head urgently. "Not happening. Not with how much we're already risking."

"Alright." She didn't seem surprised at all.

We crept a few houses down to a slightly bigger house. We thought we might have more luck finding something there. It would need to be something that wouldn't be missed much. The door was easy to open, and we were inside quickly. There were boxes all over, but they were all sealed. Some of them were covered in fancy paper. Slowly, we crept around all the piles of stuff.

"What about this?" Mara whispered. She held out a small carved wolf, poised in mid-howl.

Shaking my head, I pointed at my eyes. I could tell she understood my meaning by the flustered look on her face. I mouthed, "I forget, too." Then continued on through the house.

In the kitchen, I found a nice-looking mixing bowl and picked it up to show Mara. Her face scrunched in consideration, and after a few seconds, she shook her head, her braid waving with the motion. "It's nice, but I don't think he'd know the difference between the ones he has and that one."

"True." I placed it back where I found it. Finding a gift for Isaac was going to be more difficult than I thought. We looked around the house for several more minutes but found nothing that seemed right.

The next house seemed to have several guests. "I don't think we should go in there. It's too risky." I pointed at an emptier and darker-looking one further down. "That seems safer."

"Alright." I was almost surprised at how easily Mara agreed, but then I remembered that we swore to be extremely careful. Moving in unison through the shadows, neither of us made a sound.

It was just as easy getting into the darker house as it was the first. We crept in, listening carefully for anyone stirring. Other than the sounds of breathing, it was silent. This house was also filled with boxes and decorations, and we found ourselves weaving through piles again. It was difficult to avoid bumping into something.

"Kith!" Mara's whisper was full of excitement. She held an apron out toward me. It wasn't too fancy, but it seemed almost brand new, with no stains or tears like Isaac's had.

"It's perfect." I grinned. "Let's get back."

We didn't bother looking through anything else. Finding the gift took longer than we hoped, and we were both ready to be back in the safety and warmth of Isaac's house.

*   Mara   *

On Christmas morning, there was a small knock on our door. We were already awake due to another nightmare. Most of the ones I had while at Isaac's house were small enough that he wouldn't have heard them. However, there was one other one where I called out loudly enough for him to come in. He knocked then, before coming in, and just sat on the bed to talk and help calm me down. Sensing his hesitation, I crawled into his lap again, and he hummed quietly until Kith and I both fell back asleep.

Usually, in the mornings, Isaac left us alone until we came out and even then he didn't come and talk to us until he was on a break from his store.

This morning, however, he told us he would not be opening the shop because it was Christmas. When Kith opened the door, confusion all over his face, Isaac announced that breakfast was ready.

He had spent a long time at the market a few days before and when we went to the kitchen we understood why. There was a whole spread of food set out for us to enjoy. There were eggs, which was something we hadn't even seen in a long time, beans and sausages, along with some pastries and toast.

"This looks amazing!" I exclaimed, trying to decide what to put on my plate first.

We all filled our plates with food and sat together eating in a happy silence.

When we finished our breakfast, Isaac went to check the oven.

"What's in there?" Kith asked. "I'm not sure I can eat anymore right now."

Isaac laughed. "This is the turkey for dinner! I put it in last night and have been tending to it every few hours."

"Every few hours!?" I exclaimed. "Didn't you sleep?"

"A bit," Isaac said, thoughtfully. "I slept for a while and then came to check on it and went back to bed."

"That's a lot of dedication to one meal," Kith said, his wide eyes staring at Isaac like he was crazy.

"I suppose it is," Isaac said, still smiling. "But it's worth it."

Unconvinced, Kith looked at me and simply shrugged his shoulders.

Once Isaac was done, we sat together and talked for a while. Isaac told us a story about when his daughter used to refuse to sleep in her bed because she kept having nightmares.

"She was convinced her bed was haunted and in order to sleep she needed to be in our bed instead. Eventually, her mother told her she would sleep with her in her own bed in order to prove it wasn't haunted, but then she kept insisting one of us had to stay with her so the monsters wouldn't come back." Isaac smiled at the memory.

The story seemed so odd to me, but then again I never lived in a home with my parents. Beatrice was the closest thing we ever had to a parent, and while I would have loved to sleep in her bed all the time, Ducar never would have allowed it. "Did you ever get her to sleep in bed by herself?" I asked, wondering how they could have convinced her.

"Oh yes, after a while her mother would lay in bed with her until she was asleep, and then she would leave. I think waking up alone and realizing she was still safe eventually convinced her that the bed was not haunted."

"Well, that's a relief!" I said, giggling. Isaac smiled in return and Kith looked at me with a wry smile.

"What, were you afraid it might be?" He said, teasingly.

"Even if it were, she has her brother there to protect her," Isaac said, and I noticed his smile also had a sad note to it. I wondered if talking about his daughter made him miss her too much.

Deciding this was a good time to change the subject, I jumped out of my chair and clapped my hands. "We have a gift for you!" I said, unable to contain my excitement.

Kith laughed out loud. "Real subtle, Mara."

Isaac, on the other hand, looked confused. "A gift...for me?" he asked, taken aback.

"It's a Christmas present," Kith said, bashfully.

"Well, that's very sweet of you," he said, touched.

"I'll go get it!" I exclaimed, running off to our room to grab the apron. As I left, I heard them both chuckling behind me.

Coming back into the room, I held out the apron. "Tada!"

Kith looked at me in alarm, and I was horrified as I realized my mistake.

"Ah yes," Isaac said, his voice sly as he held out his hand for his gift, "It's lovely."

I could feel my cheeks burning blue. "Um, sorry," I said as I handed him the apron.

Isaac laughed until he felt the fabric in his hand and confusion filled his face. "Don't tell me," he said, holding up a hand just as I was about to tell him what it was. "Is it an apron?" he asked, feeling around the fabric.

"It is!" I said, beaming.

"But how..." Isaac's face was a mixture of emotions that were hard to read. For a moment, I started to wonder if it was a bad idea to get him a present.

"You might not be able to tell," Kith said, breaking the silence "but your old one is pretty torn up and stained, so we figured something fresh and clean would be nice to have."

At that, Isaac seemed to make a decision and set his face in a smile. It was a genuine smile, I could tell, but there was still a bit of uncertainty there. "Thank you both, very much!" he said, happily.

After a moment, he added, "I have something for each of you as well." He stood up and walked down the hall.

I looked at Kith questioningly and he shrugged. It seemed he didn't know what was coming any more than I did.

When Isaac came back he was carrying two boxes. "Who wants to go first?" he asked.

Kith, of course, looked at me and saw my newfound excitement. I hadn't even considered getting a present myself.

"Mara can go first," he said, smiling.

Isaac held out the larger box, unsure of exactly where I stood. When I opened it, I saw the most beautiful cloth doll. A small gasp escaped my lips as I pulled her out of the box to get a closer look.

"That doll used to belong to my daughter," Isaac's voice was thick with emotion. "I've kept it locked away all this time. It was her favorite toy. She would be glad for someone else to be giving it the love it needs."

Staring at Isaac in disbelief, I cradled the doll. Stepping forward, I gently wrapped my arms around Isaac and saw the surprise on his face. I never had a doll before. Some of the girls visiting the freak show would carry them around, but they seemed trivial things to a girl who rarely even had enough to eat.

"She's beautiful," I breathed. "Thank you."

Pulling away, I examined the doll and how perfect her stitches were. She wore a blue dress with white cuffs, an apron, and a bonnet. A red cape clasped delicately around her neck. Her face had been drawn in flawlessly with blue eyes and rosy cheeks. The doll was in such great condition, that I thought sadly that Isaac's daughter must not have had her for long.

I wasn't sure if Isaac knew just how much a gift like this

meant to a girl like me, but I knew what it meant to him. His daughter's favorite doll couldn't be something he would give away lightly. How was it that this man allowed strange kids to come into his home, fed them, and gave them precious gifts?

✳   Kith   ✳

A mixture of emotions washed over me as I watched Isaac take the apron. There was pride about giving him a gift, but also a bit of shame about having stolen it. I hadn't thought about the fact that he would obviously know we took it from someone else.

All those thoughts disappeared, however, when I saw Mara's gift. There were times when little girls came in carrying similar dolls with them, and I saw the longing in her eyes.

Giving her something that belonged to his daughter was a huge gesture. I realized that as much as we became attached against my better judgment, Isaac had also. He wasn't just taking care of random starving kids but actually cared about us. The realization hit me hard. Isaac had lost so much. If we moved on as planned he'd lose us, too. The other day, Mara suggested the possibility of us living like this longer. Would that be possible?

Right as I was about to start spiraling into my thoughts, Isaac's voice interrupted me. "Kith, it's your turn."

Shaking the thoughts out of my head, I took the gift from him. Inside the box was what looked like a large roll of leather. I pulled it out, slightly confused. The leather in my hand was firm but soft. There was a strap that tied it closed. Carefully releasing the tie, I rolled it open slowly. Inside the roll, several pockets spanned the length of the leather. Tucked into the pockets were several shiny knives like the ones Isaac taught me to use. They came in different sizes each with their own carvings on the handle. A larger one with a bear walking through some trees caught my eye. Slowly, I removed it from the sleeve and traced the bear with my fingertip. The knife was a bit heavier than the ones I used when helping Isaac. The blade was longer and wider, as well.

"They're wonderful. Thank you." I smiled widely, but my eyes didn't leave the bear. The details had been carefully etched into the wood and were just about perfect. These must have cost Isaac a bunch.

When I did finally look up, I noticed Isaac seemed to be focusing on listening to us carefully. Mara was playing with her new doll, pretending to read her stories and rocking her back and forth. The knife with the bear on it was still in my hand. Carefully, I slid it back into place. After another minute of looking at it, I pulled out a smaller knife with a carving of a deer. The antlers were so large they didn't fit on the knife. It was also intricately done. The eyes of the deer almost seemed alive.

"Which one had you so fascinated?" Isaac sounded almost amused at my silence.

"The big one with the bear."

"Ah." His tone implied that there was meaning behind my answer.

"What?" I searched his face for a clue, but of course there was none.

"The bear is powerful and fearsome. But, do you know what they're known for the most?"

"No."

"Their protectiveness."

"Oh." I sat silent as his words sunk in. He thought I was like a bear. Powerful, fearsome, and protective.

"What do you think, Mara? Does the bear fit Kith?"

"Yes." She giggled slightly. "My own brother bear." She winked at me before returning to her playing.

I found myself laughing as well. "I suppose so. Though, not sure about the powerful part."

"In time, you'll realize your power." Isaac's tone was light, but it felt like there was more behind those words. I decided against trying to figure it out, though. I was afraid it would just frustrate me, and I wanted to keep this warm feeling.

Mesmerized by the doll Isaac had given me, I spent hours playing with her while Kith worked with his knives. Isaac brought him some large sticks and he was practicing carving shapes into them.

Isaac was content to sit and chat with us while we enjoyed our gifts. It seemed to make him happy to know how much we liked them. Every now and then, he would get up to check the turkey. The wonderful smell of the bird roasting in the next room was starting to make me hungry again.

"You kids are quieter than my Sarah was," Isaac said suddenly. "She used to run around the house making all sorts of a racket. Her mother was beside herself, just trying to get her to act more like a lady," Isaac was smiling at the memory. "Not that her mother was the perfect lady, herself. I remember when we first met she had so much spirit. Never shied away from telling anyone what was what. That was part of what I loved so much about her."

Kith and I looked at each other awkwardly. Isaac didn't talk about his family much and we were never sure what to say when he did.

"Anyway," Isaac said, breaking the silence. "This is the first time in several years that I've had anyone to spend the holidays with. Thank you for agreeing to stay."

Standing up from where I was playing on the floor with my doll, I walked over to where Isaac sat and laid my hand on his. His eyes began to water.

"I guess celebrating without them is hard, isn't it?" I asked, quietly. "Thank you for letting us be here."

Isaac turned toward me and I saw a tear spill down his cheek. "It was a bit of selfishness, really," he said. "My home has been unbearably quiet for too many years. You have brought some life back into it."

We sat together for a while after that, until Isaac announced it was time to get started on dinner.

"I thought dinner was already in the oven!" Kith said,

flabbergasted.

"Well the turkey is, but we still need to make the vegetables and roast the potatoes," Isaac responded like it was obvious. "You don't just want meat for dinner do you?"

Kith thought about that for a moment and then shrugged. "I guess that wouldn't really fill me up, would it?" He didn't add that we had done just that many times after he took all that meat from the butcher's. There were several nights that it was all there was, and it could never fully quell the hunger pains.

Isaac laughed as he made his way to the kitchen. Standing up, I followed him and climbed onto the counter.

"Oh, you can keep playing if you like, Mara," Isaac said when he heard me. "I wouldn't want to take you away from your Christmas."

"Well it's your Christmas too, isn't it?" I asked. "I would like to help if you don't mind."

Isaac smiled brightly. "Of course."

He began pulling several vegetables out and putting them on the counter. There were some I had never seen before, and I couldn't help but grab the bag.

"What are these?" I asked, excited to try something new.

"What do they look like?" Isaac asked, confused.

"Oh, uh..kind of like tiny cabbages. They're kind of cute," I said and heard Kith laugh from behind me.

"The vegetable is cute?"

Turning, I stuck my tongue out at him as Isaac began to answer.

"Ah, the brussel sprouts. You've never eaten brussel sprouts?" he asked, confused again. His face looked a little sad, but he brushed it off quickly. "Well if you could start by cutting off their stems, then we'll roast them in the oven with some spices.

Isaac and I worked for a while preparing all the vegetables and the potatoes. After some time, Kith must have started getting impatient, because he came in and asked if he could help too. Isaac seemed to think there were too many of us in the kitchen because he went to sit on his stool and directed us from there. He insisted on being the one to check the turkey throughout our progress though.

By the time we finished, the whole house smelled wonderful, and my mouth was watering in anticipation.

Once the table was set, we all sat together and piled our plates once again. The turkey was better than I ever could have imagined.

When Kith went in for his third helping, I laughed and asked, "So do you think it was worth the trouble?" Now it was his turn to stick his tongue out at me.

Then, looking at Isaac, he said, "It's fantastic! I wish we could have meat like this every day!"

Isaac laughed, heartily. "Sadly, that's a little bit more work than I'm willing to do on a daily basis, but I am glad you like it."

✳   Kith   ✳

One night, while Isaac helped me practice with my knives, Mara played in front of the fire, pretending her doll was her own baby. She rocked it lovingly, the way Beatrice rocked Mara to sleep when she was younger before things got bad. I wondered if she remembered those nights, snuggled up against Beatrice, drifting to sleep without a care in the world.

When she murmured to the doll, "I love you, baby girl." My heart skipped a beat. I heard Beatrice say those words so many times. Isaac's face showed he was having similar mixed emotions. His thoughts clearly were torn between happiness with Mara being near, and mourning his daughter. I wondered if his daughter said those same words to the doll.

Isaac got up suddenly and walked to his room. Mara looked up at me, curiosity and worry written all over her face. "Did I upset him?"

"I don't think so."

"I hope not." She pouted slightly.

In a couple of minutes, Isaac returned, holding something in his hands. "Here, Mara, you can use this as a blanket for your doll." He held out a small baby blanket. It was purple with pink and green flowers all over it.

She looked up eagerly. "Oh, she'll love that. Thank you!" Her hands reached up gingerly for the blanket, realizing the importance of it. "It's so soft."

Isaac smiled. "It is. My wife made that for our daughter when she was still pregnant with her. She'd be happy to see how much you like it."

Mara rubbed the blanket on her cheek, delighting in the feel of it. "It feels like pure love."

Isaac turned away slightly, but his voice remained light. "That's what it was made from."

We sat at a loss for words for a long while. In a need to break the silence, I asked Mara, "What are you going to name her?"

Biting her lip, Mara looked down at the doll she held in her hands. "I was thinking about naming her Gracie."

"I think Grace would love that." I smiled.

"Who's Grace?"

Mara spoke slowly, thinking over the words. "Grace was an acrobat in the show we were in. She was so pretty and flexible and strong."

"Sounds like you must've been close."

"She was like a big sister to us. We had a lot of fun together. She used to always do my hair before our shows. The ribbon I use in it now was hers." She toyed with the ribbon at the end of her braid, lost in thought. "There were times she would put us up on her swings. It was so much fun. Beatrice would get so mad." She giggled at the memories before realizing she had dropped another name.

"Beatrice?"

This time I answered. "Beatrice was the bearded lady. She took care of us most of the time."

"She was essentially our mother," Mara added, giving me a stubborn look.

"I see. Where are these two now?" Isaac spoke slowly, afraid of asking too much.

"Grace left the show several years ago when she got

married." Mara's voice was soft and her fingers returned to playing with the end of her braid.

"We're. Uhm. We're not positive what happened to Beatrice." My voice broke with the answer.

"Ah." Isaac paused for a moment. "Would you tell me something about Beatrice?"

We sat in silence for a second to collect our thoughts, and then Mara burst out, "She was the best. I used to curl up in her lap and play with her beard. It was so soothing. I'd fall asleep that way sometimes, with a fist full of her beard."

"She made us these cakes sometimes. They were one of the best things I've ever eaten." I added, the memories bringing a faint reminder of the taste to my mouth.

"No one wanted to make Beatrice mad. Everyone; even the big, tough men, was scared of her. She was fierce and never backed down." Mara's voice was filled with awe and sadness.

Isaac chuckled at how quickly the words tumbled out. "I think I understand why you both care about her. She sounds amazing."

"I miss her." Mara's bottom lip started to tremble and she hugged Gracie close.

"I can tell." Isaac's voice was soft. "Grief is hard to deal with. It never truly ends. Not knowing what happened to her has to be hard."

"It is." The words barely came out with how tight my throat felt.

Silence fell between us. There was much more we could say about both Grace and Beatrice, but it felt like it was enough for tonight. Suddenly, I was quite tired. It wasn't hard to see that Mara was also.

Ever the one to pick up on how we were feeling, Isaac said softly. "I think it may be time for bed."

"Stop it, you're hurting her!" Kith's voice sounded far away.

I raised my head to see Ducar looming over me. He was holding my arm, twisting it just enough to make me want to cry out.

This wasn't a normal beating. Ducar was walking past our tent when he tripped on a root. We didn't know he was nearby or else we wouldn't have made any noise at all. As luck would have it, though, Kith had just told me something that made me giggle. He was always trying to cheer me up, to help me forget where we were. But this time, he happened to tell me a joke at the wrong time, and just after I laughed, Ducar came storming into our tent.

"Oh you think that's funny, do you?" He bellowed, and before I knew it he had reached into our cage and dragged me out by the arm, twisting it as he went.

He slammed the door shut behind him and locked it so Kith couldn't get out. Then he turned his sneer to me and lifted me into the air by the arm he was twisting. Intense pain shot through my shoulder as my arm felt like it was being pulled off, and I couldn't help the scream that escaped.

Ducar looked at me and must have realized he caused real damage because instead of hitting me he flung me back to the ground. The fall was excruciating as Ducar was much taller than I was and my limp arm could do nothing to try and catch me. I thought for sure he had torn my arm out and I would never be able to use it again. After shoving me back into the cage, he left with the same sneer on his face. I just lay there and sobbed.

It was in the middle of my sobbing that I realized there were arms around me, lifting me into the air. Opening my eyes, I saw Isaac's concerned face.

"Sarah, honey, it's okay," he said soothingly. "There are no monsters under the bed, I promise."

Still dazed by my nightmare, I stared at Isaac like he had gone mad until my eye caught the look of sadness on Kith's face as he looked from me to Isaac. It was then that I realized he thought it was his daughter he was comforting in the middle of the night.

Involuntarily, my tail twitched and brushed against Isaac's side. The concern on his face turned to confusion, and then I saw realization and what might have been an embarrassment.

"Mara…" he said so softly I barely heard him. "I'm sorry, I lost myself there for a minute."

"It's alright," I squeaked, unsure what else to say. Isaac seemed to be getting a little absent-minded lately, and I wondered if something was bothering him. I was thinking about asking when he started talking again.

"You screamed, and it must have reminded me…" he trailed off before seeming to come back to himself again. "Was it another bad dream? You were inconsolable when I picked you up."

Suddenly feeling bashful about the fact that Isaac was woken up by my nightmare, I tried to nod before remembering to speak. "Yes," I said simply.

"Do you want to tell me about your nightmare?"

I looked at Kith, not sure if I should, and he simply shrugged, unsure himself.

"It was a bad memory," I said, and Isaac stayed silent waiting for me to continue. "From before we left."

Recognition hit Isaac and I wondered if he would ask more. We sat in silence for a while, and then Isaac came to a conclusion. "Why did you leave?" He asked gently.

"He was mean to us," I said, leaving it vague, and saw Kith nod in approval.

"Ducar?" Shock ran through us both when Isaac said his name. "I'm sorry," he said, quickly. "I told you there was talk of the show. He was the manager, right?" Isaac avoided saying the name again, as if he thought it would upset us more.

"Yes," Kith said, calmly. "He got mean after a while and we didn't want to deal with it anymore, so we left."

I was surprised to see the anger creeping up in Isaac's face and fascinated by the way he tried to hold it back. "Did he hurt you?" he asked, his voice strained. Kith and I locked eyes again and neither of us said a word.

I looked back at Isaac just in time to see the red hot fury burn across his face for a split second before it was replaced by a deep sadness. He hugged me close to him and then opened up his other arm for Kith to join. Tentatively, Kith made his way into

Isaac's arm and he held us both tightly.

As I looked at my big brother, I watched him crumble into those arms and was surprised to see a tear streak down his face. No words were necessary. We both knew what Isaac was trying to tell us.

CHAPTER NINE: JANUARY

✳   Kith   ✳

After Christmas was over, it didn't take long for the extra visitors to start leaving town. The excitement the flurry of incoming guests brought was missing this time, replaced by heartache from seeing loved ones go away again.

Mara and I avoided looking out the windows. We could feel the sorrow hanging in the air even without watching it. There wasn't a lot of talking during the days, either. Isaac was kept extra busy by travelers needing to stock up before their departures.

I sat with some wood and my knives, trying hard to make something take shape. Mara was playing quietly with her new doll.

"Kith?" Her voice was quiet, but it still startled me enough that I jumped slightly and feared cutting myself.

"Yes?"

Her eyes stayed down, refusing to meet mine. "Do you think Isaac will still want us here once all the new people are gone?"

"I don't see why he wouldn't. He admitted to using that as an excuse to get us to come stay here because he was lonely." I couldn't imagine him telling us we needed to leave after we'd been here for a few weeks now, but the thought made my heart race.

"I know. But what if he changes his mind? It would be safe enough for us to leave now, right?"

"Do you really think he'd tell us to go?"

"No. At least, I hope not." After a pause, she added. "What if we told him too much about Ducar and made him worry about keeping us here?"

"If anything he'd want us here even more after that. You know how protective he is. Even knowing we were hungry and homeless upset him enough."

"You're right. I just feel so off ever since the nightmares got worse."

"I know. I feel it, too." I had gotten used to how tame her nightmares were for so long. Now they were getting worse again, and a deep fear settled in my stomach. As much as I was trying to ignore it, it wouldn't go away. "Anyway, even if we did leave, at least we still have the cave."

"I loved the cave, but I think it would be really hard to go back to it after being here."

"That's true." I looked at the knife still clasped in my hand. Sighing softly, I slid it back into its spot and rolled the pouch up.

"What happens now, though?" Finally, she looked up at me, her eyes wet.

"What do you mean?"

"Are we going to stay here once it becomes spring? Will it be safe to stay here for a long time?"

I knew what she really meant. We kept moving for food oftentimes, but also to avoid being caught by Ducar. Somehow he was always able to get close to us, or even catch us.

Before I could answer, Isaac came in from the shop, locking the door behind him. Somehow it was already evening. "Would you two mind helping me with a project tonight?"

"Not at all." I was relieved for something to ease our minds for a little bit.

"Remember when you helped me move the feverfew inside?"

"Of course. It reminded us of Beatrice." Mara's voice had a hint of eagerness in it.

"Yes, I remember you mentioning your mother at the time." He smiled knowingly at us and I felt a small spike of guilt for all the secrets we used to keep from him.

"What are we going to be doing with the feverfew?" I rose as I spoke, making sure to put my knives away.

"I'm almost out of the tea I use it for, so I need to make some more."

"You make tea out of flowers?" Mara's nose crinkled, likely remembering the various teas Ketzia always made. She used all sorts of ingredients for them, especially bark and roots.

"Yes. It's great for pain relief."

"Is that why you drink it?" Worry coursed through me. Was he in pain?

"Yes. Getting old comes with plenty of aches and pains." Isaac laughed softly, but it didn't sound like his normal laugh.

"Do you think that's why Beatrice kept the plants with her?" Mara's face was scrunched up in thought. "She was often giving Dylan tea that he didn't always want to drink"

As she spoke, Isaac pulled down a book and flipped through the pages, stopping when he felt a petal stuck on a specific page.

"That's true." I nodded. "He did always seem to feel better after he drank it, even the times he argued about it."

"I'm guessing Dylan was another member of your show?" Isaac's voice was light as if he was trying to avoid pressuring us for more information. It didn't really matter now, though, did it? He already knew so much.

"Yes. He was 'The Rubber Man' as they called him. He was amazingly flexible and could twist his body into all sorts of crazy positions." I remember watching the audience freak out when they saw the way he could move.

"And doing this caused him pain?" There was a bit of confusion on his face, but he didn't say anything else.

"I don't think it always did, but he was often in a lot of pain. Beatrice took care of him a lot." Mara smiled sadly.

"So, he was pretty much your brother?" As he spoke he showed us the page that was marked in his book. There were pictures of what the flowers that were ready to harvest looked like.

"I guess you could say that. He wasn't always too fond of us, though. I think he was jealous that we stole the attention from him." Carefully checking each flower, I gently broke off the ones that matched the picture.

"That's understandable, I suppose." Isaac braced himself against the nearby counter as we worked.

After a few more minutes of working in silence, we were confident we got all the flowers. Isaac pulled out a flat metal sheet. "Now we're going to dry the flowers so they can be used to make tea later."

We arranged the flowers carefully over the sheet, spreading them out so they weren't touching too much. Once they were ready, Isaac set them in the top of the oven. "I have the oven warm, but not as hot as usual. This way it will dry the flowers without cooking them."

"That was easy." Mara seemed restless like she wanted more work.

"Yes. It's a fairly easy process. Having you around does make it easier, though, so I don't need to rely on touching the flowers or end up picking some that aren't ready. Maybe I'll let you guys taste the tea the next time I make it." He said with a chuckle.

"Do you make it a lot?" Concern filled Mara's face.

Isaac's pause was slight but noticeable. "Not that often, no. Besides, if you drink it too close together it eventually stops working as well."

His answer was not as comforting as he was hoping it would be, but I tried not to focus on that.

When Isaac turned to walk from the oven back to his chair, he tripped over another toy that was discarded by one of us. He sighed. "Alright, you two, come here."

We were doing better with keeping things picked up, but it was harder to remember lately. "We're sorry, Isaac." Mara's voice was timid. "We'll do better."

"I'm not mad. I just think it might be a good idea to focus on something else for a bit."

"Like what?" Focusing on anything other than fear sounded good to me.

"Well, you seemed eager to help with the feverfew, so maybe it would be a good idea to start teaching you more useful skills. You can work on them during your own time and that will give you something to do while I am in the shop."

"What kind of things?" The idea of learning something new was enough to get my attention.

"Let me think." He paused for a couple of seconds. "I taught you how to properly skin animals, but what would you think about learning how to use the skins?"

"You know how to do that?" For the first time in several days, excitement coursed through me.

"I do. Would you like to learn?"

"Yes, please." I tried not to sound too eager, but it was hard.

"Great. We'll start tomorrow. Try to think of other skills you might like to learn or think would be useful, and we'll see what we can do about those, also."

The way he spoke made me feel like something was wrong, but I couldn't figure out why. All he was doing was trying to give us something to do so we weren't restless all day, right? Dismissing the feelings, I decided it was just my natural tendency to worry about everything.

When Mara and I were alone in our room, she whispered, "What kind of skills do you think we should ask about? What would help us if we do end up leaving?"

"So, you still don't think we'll be staying here?"

"I hope we can, but we've been on the run for so long it's hard to think of any life skills that would be important unless they would help us in the wild. Learning how to make that tea would be good. It can help if one of us gets sick again, and Isaac did say it grows further out in the forest."

I nodded, remembering the sickness Mara went through only a few short months ago. At the time, I was desperate for some medicine. "We did start out without much experience. If we do have to go out on our own again, it would definitely be good to know more."

Nodding, Mara snuggled into bed. I followed suit, eager to start learning new things.

*   Mara   *

Isaac admitting he made tea for his pain alarmed me, but I tried hard to ignore it. I couldn't help but notice every time he made it, though. He said it wasn't often, but he was making it every few days. I was already nervous that he would decide we should leave. Kith seemed sure he wouldn't make us go, and I wanted to be, too. Even if he didn't, though, could we really be safe here for a long time? We had never stayed in one place for long. As much as I hated moving around all the time, it made me feel more secure in a way.

I spent most of the days that Isaac was in the bakery taking care of Gracie and thinking about the new things we were going to learn. Isaac started by teaching Kith how to use the skins of animals they trapped. Although I was glad that less of the animal was wasted, I didn't want to participate in those lessons.

It wasn't long before we moved on to lessons for both of us, though. We thought the skills may really come in handy one day, so we were determined to learn as much as we could. Besides it was a good way to give us something to do while he tended the shop, and also help ease our worry.

During the evenings, Isaac would check in on how much we were learning and; once he thought we were ready, begin teaching us something new. I was beginning to think he knew everything! There was a book on poisonous plant life that we were particularly fascinated with. He told us how to tell if something was harmful and that if we were ever unsure we should simply leave it where it was. Sometimes, the way he talked made me feel like he was reading our minds.

One night, while we were starting dinner, Isaac started digging through the cabinets and drawers. "Are you looking for something? Maybe I could help?"

With a sharp inhale, Isaac turned toward my voice. "I didn't hear you coming at all. You startled me."

"I've been here this whole time so we could cook dinner together." I tried to keep my voice level and lighthearted, but it stung a bit that he forgot I was there.

"Oh, right. I'm sorry, I got distracted looking for my pot."

"Do you need a different pot?"

"What do you mean? I need my usual pot, but I must have misplaced it."

Confusion coursed through me. "Isaac, you just got the

pot out a minute ago. It's on the stove."

"Oh. Right, right. I must have gotten distracted." He pursed his lips and we silently started working on dinner together. I couldn't help but watch him carefully. He wasn't one to normally forget things so quickly. And using the same excuse twice? Something odd was going on, I could feel it like a stone in my stomach.

Partway through cooking, I noticed Kith and was surprised to see how sadly he was looking at Isaac. He must have noticed the same things, but I hated seeing the worry there. It made it feel too justified. I wanted to pretend he really was preoccupied with worrying for us or thinking of new things to teach us.

Dinner was silent, with Kith and I avoiding looking at each other or Isaac. I tried to avoid thinking about the weirdness earlier, but it kept floating into my mind.

"What's gotten into you two? I can't remember the last time you were this quiet?" Isaac's voice held a teasing tone, but I could tell that it was forced.

"I think we're both just a little concerned." My voice cracked and I cringed.

"Concerned? What about?"

"You've been acting a bit odd, Isaac. Forgetting things a lot. And you've made your tea a lot more often than you said you did." Kith clamped his mouth closed to avoid saying anything more. I hadn't realized he was also paying extra attention to the tea.

"I guess I've just been rather tired lately. Still recovering from the Christmas rush and all the excitement." As if to make a point, Isaac yawned.

It made sense to me that Isaac would be tired. Lately I heard him coming out of his room a lot during the night. I wasn't sure what he was doing, but he would walk down the hallway and then a short time later go back to his room. Was he checking around the house to make sure we were still safe?

Kith and I looked at each other at last. We were wondering if we should believe his excuse. Both hoping we could, but also knowing we didn't.

A few days later we were all working together in the living

room and Isaac announced it was dinner time. He got up to go to the kitchen while Kith and I finished up our projects. Suddenly, we heard a crash and a heavy thud. Jumping up, Kith and I ran into the kitchen.

Isaac was sprawled out on the floor with his large pot laying beside him. He looked dazed, and when Kith knelt beside him and touched his arm asking him if he was okay, he jumped. "Where am I? How did I get on the floor?"

When the understanding hit his face, I knew something was terribly wrong. Holding back tears, I helped Kith lift Isaac to his feet and bring him back over to the couch.

"Isaac," Kith's voice was a soft, almost scared whisper. "What's wrong?"

"I must have tripped…"

"No." I was surprised by how stern Kith's voice was now. "What's wrong?"

"Really, I just need some sleep. Haven't been sleeping well lately. Must have caught up to me."

Kith looked on the verge of either hitting something or breaking down into tears out of frustration, so I grabbed Isaac's hand gently and whispered, "Please tell us, Isaac. We know something is wrong. You haven't been yourself. It'll only make it worse if you don't tell us."

Isaac's face broke and I was surprised at how quickly the tears streamed down his face. He took a moment to compose himself and then squeezed my hand.

"I'm sick," he started, unsure of himself. "Very sick. I was getting treatments and hoped they would help me hold out longer for you, but right before Christmas when I went in they told me the treatment had stopped working. There's nothing more they can do for me."

"Nothing?" Kith asked, in a strangled voice.

"Nothing," Isaac replied, flatly. "I don't know how much longer I have left."

Realization suddenly hit me. "That's why you've been teaching us so many things."

Isaac hung his head. "I want you to have a good life. It

hurts me to think of you living out there on your own again. So if there is anything I can do to make it easier for you, I want to try."

Kith and I looked at each other and it was all I could do not to break down and sob. I wanted to be strong for Isaac, wanted him to believe we were going to be okay. But I just wasn't sure anymore.

✳   Kith   ✳

Isaac's revelation hit me like a cannonball. "I'm sick," kept bombarding my head all day. I knew Mara was feeling it, too, but we didn't talk about it. The whole day while Isaac worked, we drifted around the house in silence, almost as if we were ghosts haunting the place, not children who lived there.

How long would this be our home? I never intended to end up here, but we did. Now the thought of leaving was painful. How much longer would we be able to hide in the house? The townspeople would find us if we stayed on our own, which would lead us straight back to Ducar.

These thoughts circulated in my head, never revealing a solution, but refusing to leave me alone. I longed for something to distract me, but nothing seemed remotely interesting.

Finally, the shop closed and Isaac entered. He looked exhausted as he made his way to his favorite chair. "How did you two spend your day?"

Neither of us answered quickly, and I could see concern grow on Isaac's face. "We didn't really do much interesting." I tried to keep my voice level as I spoke, but it cracked a bit as if not being used all day weakened it.

"I guess with staying cooped up all the time, you may be running out of things to do."

"It depends on the day." Mara's voice sounded almost far away, even though she wasn't even on the other side of the room. "Sometimes it's easier to entertain ourselves than others."

"That makes sense." After a pause, he added, "My day was

pretty uneventful as well. Not much interesting goes on in the shop most days."

"You don't talk to your customers?" Mara sounded surprised.

"Well, I do, but not about much that's important or interesting. Mostly about the bread."

"I guess that makes sense." Suddenly, I felt incredibly awkward. I wanted to run and hide, but there was nowhere to go. It seemed Mara and Isaac were feeling similar to me, as both of them fell silent.

Even though the awkwardness lingered in the air, it was better than the emptiness that filled it earlier. For a while, I was able to escape into the pictures in one of the books I'd looked at so many times already.

I heard the familiar sounds coming from the kitchen, but when I looked up, it was Mara cooking, not Isaac. Even though she was quite skilled now, she rarely cooked alone. As I watched her, I heard the faint snores coming from Isaac's chair. He had fallen asleep, and rather than wake him, Mara decided to fix dinner for us.

"Do you need any help?"

Mara jumped and looked up at me in shock. "I didn't hear you come over." After she calmed down, she added, "I could use some help, actually. Would you chop these vegetables?" She handed me some potatoes and carrots and went back to work.

"Sure." I had only practiced cutting the vegetables a couple of times but managed to get the job done all right.

As we were setting the table, Isaac walked over. "I think I fell asleep. Something smells good, though. Thank you for taking care of dinner."

We sat down and ate, trying to pretend it was like the old days. Those days felt so long ago, even though it was only yesterday that everything changed.

After we ate, Isaac got started on prepping for the next day. Although he only prepped a couple of loaves, I could see how tired he was.

"Isaac, why don't you take a break, and we'll continue the

bread later?"

With a sigh, he went and sat down. "A rest does sound nice. Do you want to practice some of what we've been working on?"

"Sure. We haven't finished our baskets, yet." I grabbed the basket I was weaving and handed Mara hers.

"How are you doing with the weaving?" Isaac was leaning his head back but seemed to still be listening intently.

"It's similar to the way I used to make our forts, so it's not terribly hard for me." I felt a sharp pain in my chest as I realized that one day, maybe soon, I'd have to resort to throwing up a quick fort again.

"Ah. Where did you learn how to make forts?"

"Through a lot of making them wrong and having to rebuild them, mostly." I laughed, but I could tell Isaac wasn't as amused.

"I'd add that to the list of things to work on learning, but it seems you probably know more about making forts than I do." This time Isaac chuckled, and I smiled. I had been missing his laughter. Ever since he had told us he was sick he was a lot more serious.

It wasn't long before the seriousness returned, and I could tell he was wrangling his thoughts. Turning my attention back to my work, I tried not to worry about what he was thinking. It was almost working, until he startled me back to attention. "How well do they keep you warm and dry?"

"What?" My mouth suddenly felt dry. It was a simple question on the surface, but I knew there was a much deeper meaning underlying it.

"The forts. Are they enough to keep you warm and dry?" His voice was soft, and I thought I detected a tremor.

"Well, we usually move around a lot. This is the longest we've stayed in one place since we left." I paused to give myself a second to think. "Normally we would make a small fort under a tree or something. The trees would help with keeping us dry most of the time. Sometimes we'd be able to stay in the same spot for a few days and make it a bit warmer and more comfortable, though."

Isaac was silent for a moment. Mara was concentrating intensely on her work, refusing to look up at me or join the conversation.

"Maybe the practice of weaving will help." He sighed sadly. "I wish…" His voice trailed to silence.

Unsure how to respond, I waited silently for him to continue. After a while, I figured he decided against finishing the thought and went back to focusing on my basket.

We sat in silence for quite some time, concentrating on our work. When I set it down to take a break, I noticed Isaac was asleep again. "Mara, do you think we should get everything ready for the shop so he can rest?"

"Maybe. I'm afraid of messing up, though."

"We've done it with him so many times, I think we can handle it."

"Alright."

We carefully got everything together. Right as we were about to start working, Mara sprang up. "Wait. We forgot the salt."

"That would have been bad." I laughed nervously.

"Seriously."

We worked in batches, using all of Isaac's mixing bowls at once. While we were waiting for something with one loaf, we were usually able to work on another. It surprised me how easily we fell into a decent system with each other, and the work flowed quickly.

Just as we were finishing up, Isaac's voice right behind us startled us almost out of our skins. "What are you two up to?"

"Uh. Well, we thought you might like some help with your dough." Mara squeaked.

"How much have you made?"

"As much as we usually do when we help you." It surprised me how nervous I sounded.

"You've done it all? How long was I asleep?"

"A while. You seemed like you needed it." Mara sounded more sure of herself now.

"I suppose I did."

"I think I could use some rest now." I chuckled softly, and then yawned.

"Me, too." Mara half spoke half yawned.

Isaac laughed. "I'm sure you two are tired. Go on to bed. Goodnight."

"Goodnight." We spoke together as we headed for our bed.

*   Mara   *

"It would probably be safe for you to play outside at night again," Isaac said one evening when he came in from closing the shop to find us lounging around the living room. I felt a little guilty, realizing it must have been obvious how bored we were getting. "Most of the visitors have gone now, so the shop is getting back to its steady pace. I'll still need help with some of the baking, but we won't need to make nearly as much."

"A trip outside would be nice," I said, "I've been dying to play in all that snow!"

Isaac laughed, "Well you better do that soon while you still have the chance. It's starting to get a little warmer and the snow may not last too much longer."

Turning to Kith in urgency, I said, "I guess that means we'll have to go tonight!"

Kith nodded fervently and turned to Isaac. "Should we get started on baking?"

Isaac laughed so hard it brought on a coughing fit and I saw worry fill Kith's eyes, but it was over quickly. "Are we skipping dinner then?" Isaac said when he finished coughing, a smile still on his face.

"Oh!" It was Kith's turn to laugh. "I guess I forgot about that part."

Isaac crossed the room to his stool and gingerly lowered himself onto it, wincing slightly. Regular movements seemed harder for him sometimes. "I just need to rest for a bit, if you don't mind getting started. There's still some stew we can heat up and there are rolls left from what we baked yesterday for the store."

That worried look crossed Kith's face again, but I couldn't understand why. Isaac worked a long day in a busy store, of course he was going to be tired. I started heating up the stew, and getting everything ready for us to eat.

Once we were finished, I realized Isaac did seem more tired than normal when we were all baking. After only a short while, he went back to the stool and gave us instructions on how many of which items to make. Working the extra hours over the holiday season must have gotten to him, but I was sure he would perk back up after a few days of rest.

Isaac announced he was going to bed shortly after we finished making everything for the store the next day. Usually we would all stay up and spend a little bit of time together after we finished, but I understood he needed rest. Besides, I was eager to finally get out and play in the snow.

After bundling ourselves up, we headed out Isaac's back door and took our usual path out of the town. It felt great to be outside, but I immediately missed the heat.

"You know what will help us stay warm?" Kith asked, mischievously.

I was opening my mouth to respond when he pulled his arm from around his back and flung a snowball at me, hitting my left side.

Letting out a yelp of displeasure, I quickly scooped up my own snow, but of course he ran away the second his snowball made contact.

"How is hitting me with snow supposed to keep me warmer?" I yelled at him, after my snowball missed by a long shot. Grabbing another one, I took off running after him.

Kith reached the trees and abruptly slowed down. Mistaking it for him getting tired, I yelled triumphantly and threw my snowball directly at his back.

Stopping dead in his tracks, he crouched low and turned to look at me, motioning wildly. Fear gripped me immediately and I dropped to the ground. A small part of me hoped he was playing some sort of trick and in seconds he would be pelting me with more snowballs, but I knew him better than that.

Crawling to where Kith crouched, I heard noises and understood why he originally slowed. It sounded like people moving through the trees, not animals.

When I looked at Kith, I could see him searching the area. He was barely breathing, sitting stone still and watching. The moon reflecting on his face made him look white as a ghost. He almost glowed as he sat there looking for him.

I tried to hold on to a hope that maybe this was just a random group of people hanging out, but we had never seen or heard anyone out this late before.

Finally, I glimpsed a torch in the distance as a man walked out from behind a tree. Dread filled me when I saw the fire dancing in his crystal eye and lighting the scratch that ran across it. Kith seemed frozen in place. Crouching even lower, I grabbed his arm and pulled. He dropped to the ground almost instantly and we made our way back the way we had come.

We were practically crawling until the cover of the trees was gone. Then, feeling very vulnerable in the open clearing that was between the woods and the town, we ran like our lives depended on it.

✳︎   Kith   ✳︎

It felt like we were running for hours by the time Isaac's house came into view. Rushing through the door, we closed it tight behind us. Without a word, we both looked around for something to use to block it.

We settled on the heavy table next to the door. It had three drawers full of random things Isaac stuffed in them, and was taller than us. As we started dragging it to block the door, the feet let out a loud screech of protest.

Moving the cumbersome table was slow work. When we got it partially in front of the door, a voice from behind made us jump out of our skins. Without even thinking about it, I shoved Mara behind me.

"Kith? Mara?"

It took a few seconds for us to register that the voice came from Isaac and was actually speaking to us.

"Yes, it's us." My voice felt like a croak and my throat was still tight from my heart hammering in it.

"What is going on?" Tiredness mixed with worry and a tinge of anger at being woken filled his voice.

"He… He's here." The words came out of Mara as a gasp, barely escaping before the tears came.

"Who is here?" All anger was gone, replaced by a deep concern.

I hesitated for several seconds. The look on his face made it obvious Isaac was trying hard to be patient. "Ducar. Ducar is here. We saw him in the woods with his men. They've found us again."

"Did they see you?"

"I don't think we would have made it back if they did." Mara's voice was a soft whisper, but held the weight of experience in it.

"They haven't found you, then. And now it's our job to make sure they don't." He felt his way over to us, finding the table we were trying to move. Without saying anything further, he helped us push it the rest of the way in front of the door. "I know you've been feeling cooped up in here and were looking forward to enjoying your nights roaming outside again, but I don't think either of you should go out any more."

As much as I loved being outside, there would be no arguing about that. "We won't."

Surprise filled Isaac's face for a second before vanishing. He didn't expect us to agree that easily. "I know you don't like to talk about what happened much. I won't press. But I'm beginning to think it's worse than I imagined. I'll do everything I can to make sure you're not found."

"Thank you." We spoke in unison, neither of us denying his fears. I wasn't ready to tell him just how bad it was. Talking about the beatings I was forced to watch, or the days without food or water, being forced to perform, it all felt like too much. Other than the nightmares, it was beginning to feel like we really escaped. Like it was all behind us. Until tonight.

"Do you think you'll be able to get any sleep?"

"I think we could both use some time to try to calm down first. If you need to go back to bed, we'll be alright. You do have to get up early." I fought hard to keep my voice from shaking, and was proud that it only did a little.

"I could use some time, as well." Carefully, he guided himself to his chair and sat down. I could tell he was deep in thought, but I didn't want to ask what about this time.

Mara and I curled up on pillows next to the fireplace. The fire was long out, but the spot still held some comfort for us. We all sat together in silence, trying hard to convince ourselves we were safe. For the first time since coming to stay in the house, I didn't actually feel it.

I'm not sure how long we all sat there before Isaac decided everyone should try to get some sleep. Reluctantly, we headed to bed. It did seem like we were still hidden from Ducar, for now.

It didn't take as long to sleep as I feared, but it also didn't take long before I was being jolted awake by Mara's screams. She woke easily when I got to her side, but quickly started sobbing against me. As I stroked her hair, my usual comforting words failed me. Ducar was somewhere nearby, and as long as that was true I couldn't promise to keep her safe.

"What if he finds us?" The words came out in spurts between sniffles.

"I don't know. But I do know I'm going to do everything I can to keep that from happening."

"I know, but I'm scared."

"Me too."

After being silent for a couple of minutes, she added solemnly, "We should prepare to be on the run again."

Her words startled me, even as I recognized the truth in them. "Why would we go on the run again? Don't you think we're safe here?"

"Do you really think Isaac can protect us against Ducar and his men? We're only safe if he doesn't figure out we're here. If he does, then Isaac is in danger and so are we."

"Are you saying we should leave?"

"No, of course not. Not yet, anyway. I don't want Isaac to get hurt, though."

"He won't." I tried hard to reassure myself of that.

Mara's eyes met mine, more serious than I had seen them in a long time. "We thought that about Beatrice, too, didn't we?"

No response came. I desperately wanted to make her feel better, but I knew she was right. "We'll focus on learning what we can and staying safe for now. I don't think going on the run now is a good idea. We don't know where he's camping out, so we don't know which direction to go."

"I know. It's not like I want to go, but I don't want anyone else getting hurt, either."

Nodding, I found myself too tired to continue the conversation. Sleep hadn't been coming easily. Once I laid back down, Mara put her head on my chest. My fingers instinctively traced the moons at the side of her forehead until she fell asleep. Even as her breathing settled, I knew sleep wouldn't return for me quickly.

Whenever I closed my eyes, images of Mara in chains floated in front of me. Digging into my determination, I promised myself that would never happen again. We'd do everything in our power to keep Mara away from Ducar. After some time, I was able to banish the images and drift off to sleep.

⁎   Mara   ⁎

From the moment Isaac told us he was sick, panic started forming inside me. We all tried to distract ourselves, and for a while it seemed like it might work. Until the night we saw Ducar. Now I was living fully inside that panic and it constantly threatened to overwhelm me. The smallest tasks became too much for me, and I regularly dismissed myself to the bathroom so Kith wouldn't see me breaking down.

Kith was feeling all of it, too, but I wanted him to think I was strong. I wanted to be strong. For Kith and for Isaac. So anytime I felt like exploding, I pretended I suddenly couldn't hold it any longer and dashed for the bathroom. Most likely, it wasn't fooling anyone, but it made me feel just the slightest bit better not to be breaking down in front of them.

Meanwhile, Isaac continued to decline. Cooking while he napped became a more regular occasion, and after a while, Kith and I started making dinner before Isaac closed up for the day so that it would be almost ready by the time he finished. This way Isaac could come in from work and relax by the fire for just a few minutes before we all sat down together to eat.

One night, Kith and I lay in the bed not speaking. Our nights were so quiet now, neither of us able to think of anything worth talking about.

Finally, after I thought he was already asleep, he whispered into the darkness. "Are you awake?"

Jumping a little, I calmed myself before responding. "I thought you were asleep."

"I'm sorry," the sadness in Kith's voice was evident, and I wondered if he was crying. I had spent many nights crying silently in the cover of the darkness. "I think we should stay and take care of Isaac. I know you thought leaving might be the best idea to keep him safe, but I can see how tired he is all the time. I think he needs us, Mara."

Months ago, these words would have thrilled me. All I wanted was to settle down here with Isaac. He had become such an important part of our lives, and I was truly beginning to see a future for us here, with him. I let myself believe we were safe and that as long as Isaac was here, nothing would happen to us.

Now, the clock was ticking on our time with Isaac and we were anything but safe with Ducar so close by. All those ideas of growing up in this house, continuously learning things from Isaac, eating his wonderful food, having a bed to sleep in, and a warm fire to curl up beside. It was all going to end.

I lay in silence, wallowing in my own self pity for so long that Kith asked again, "Are you awake?"

"What are we going to do after…?" I couldn't bring myself to say it, but I knew he understood.

He sighed heavily, "I guess that's something we have to start preparing for. We can't stay here without him."

"I don't want to leave," I sobbed and turned into Kith, allowing my tears to flow freely. "I don't want him to go. Why does this keep happening to us? I just wanted to be a family."

Kith squeezed me tightly and I could feel his body shudder as he sobbed along with me. After some time, once our breathing returned to normal, Kith spoke again.

"He is our family now, Mara. No matter how much time he has left. That means we have to take care of him." I knew he was right.

I was selfishly thinking of everything we were going to lose instead of how Isaac must feel. This whole experience must be terrifying and devastating for him. Finally pulling myself together, I decided to think of him from now on. I would make his time left something special instead of pulling myself away from him. He deserved that much. And when it was all over, Kith and I would find a way. We always did.

✳   Kith   ✳

Screams. For a long time it was whimpers, mostly quiet and easy to comfort. Tonight, however, the screams returned and ripped through the night. Ducar was near, and the terror he brought seemed to be making the nightmares worse again.

As I moved to comfort Mara, an ache spread through my muscles. Suddenly, I realized how weak our stay here made us. Now, with needing to help Isaac more, my body wasn't as up to the task as it would have been before.

Even as I comforted Mara, fear spread through me. One day we would have to leave our new home. If Ducar stayed nearby, we'd need to do so quickly and quietly. Without being able to go outside, how would we regain our strength for a run like that?

"Kith?"

"Yes?" I didn't realize she was awake, so her voice startled me.

"What are you thinking about? You look so serious."

"Do I normally look silly after your nightmares?"

"No, but you had a faraway look on your face, like you were deep in thought."

"Oh. I wasn't really thinking about much. It's still the middle of the night. We should try to get some more sleep."

Without argument, she snuggled back down. I traced her marking until she was asleep once more. I tried for a while to settle back down, but all I could think about was needing to go on the run after several months of staying still. We were completely unprepared.

Part of me wanted to jump up and start running in place right that instant, but I knew that would wake Mara up. Then she'd know for sure what I was thinking about and would never get back to sleep.

As I lay there, I thought about why my muscles were sore. We were doing a lot to help Isaac for the past few days. Maybe that would be enough to help prepare us? If we kept helping him, or even took over more of the work, it would at least make us stronger, right?

Light slowly filled the room as I lay there thinking. Lack of sleep was something I'd have to get used to again, anyway. Climbing out of the bed, I wandered out to find breakfast. Sometimes Isaac still prepared something for us, but not as often as before.

I was almost done eating when Mara joined me in the kitchen. "Did you even go back to sleep at all?"

"I tried. It didn't work." I shrugged.

"You must be tired. I'm sorry I woke you."

"I feel fine right now. Plus, I can always take a nap later if I need to."

"True." As she busied herself with finding food, she asked, "So, are you going to tell me what kept you awake all night?"

"I was thinking it might be time for us to take over even

more around here."

"Did something new happen?" All thoughts of food faded for a minute, and she just stood looking at me.

"No. I just think he could use a bit more help. Plus, it might be our only way to increase our energy for being on the run again." I found myself avoiding looking directly at her.

"Alright, I suppose that's a good point. We've already been doing a lot, though. I'm not sure how much more we can really take on."

"I know. I wish we could run the store for him. That seems to be what wears him out the most."

"Me too, but that's just not possible."

"I know."

"Could you imagine us running a shop together, though? Wouldn't that be something?" Her voice held a wistful longing.

"I didn't know you wanted to run a shop."

"Well, I'm not certain I do. I have no clue what it's like in one." She chuckled dismissively. "It was just a random thought."

There was something that told me it wasn't so random, but I let it go. We went back to our food without continuing the conversation.

The day passed much the same as others, but as soon as Isaac came through the door I knew it was different. He was always fairly tired after working in his shop all day, but the way his body slumped into his chair showed an even deeper exhaustion.

Mara watched him with wide eyes, but didn't make a sound. Instead, she busied herself with serving up the dinner we prepared. After a while, Isaac made his way to join us at the table. Each step looked as if it took all his energy.

"I think you need someone to help you in the shop." I tried hard not to let my voice shake as I spoke. Mara focused intently on her food, but didn't seem to feel like eating.

Isaac sighed. "You may be right. I've been trying to put it off, but it's likely time. I'll see if anyone may be considering an apprenticeship."

Expecting a fight, or even just a slight argument, I wasn't sure what to say when he agreed so easily. It was clear, however, that my fears were true.

"I would help you in the shop, if I could." Mara's voice came out so quiet it sounded like she was mostly talking to herself.

"I know you would." Isaac smiled sadly.

Once again, we found ourselves finishing a meal in silence. Once we were done, we pulled out our baskets again. It wasn't long before Isaac was asleep in his chair. He seemed to be getting worse a lot faster than I expected him to.

Glancing up at Mara, I found myself thinking back to when she was sick. She got worse quickly, too. I almost lost her, but somehow seemed to have healed her. The memories were still strong enough I could almost feel the heat that had coursed through me.

After a moment of doubt, I crept over to Isaac. Did it matter where I put my hands? I wished, not for the first time, that I had some sort of understanding of what happened that day with Mara. In the end, I decided to place one hand on his chest and one on his head, like before. Closing my eyes, I willed the heat to come, but nothing happened.

Breathing deeply, I brought back up all the feelings I went through when I thought I was losing Mara. Then I added in all my fears of losing Isaac. For several minutes, I waited for the heat to come, but there was no change.

When I could no longer bear the disappointment that was building up inside me, I dropped my hands to my sides and sighed. As I turned, I noticed that Mara was watching me, a mixture of hope and sadness in her eyes. I couldn't bring myself to speak, so I just shook my head and headed into the kitchen to get ready to prep for the next day.

*   Mara   *

The ground was cold and hard. Although I got used to sleeping on it during the warmer months, winter was just setting in and the nights were becoming too cold to bear. Kith and I huddled together to keep warm under the thin blanket we were given, but I could feel my teeth chattering.

It was hard to perform with the lack of sleep building up and Ducar got increasingly angry each time. This, of course, only made it harder to sleep as we stressed over what might happen the next time we slipped up.

During rehearsal one morning, Kith tripped over his foot and fell sprawled out on the ground. He recovered quickly and jumped back to his feet, returning to the routine. It was impressive because the fall looked like it really hurt, but Ducar didn't care. The moment Kith fell I saw his face twitch with what looked like a mixture of anger and delight. Then it turned to me, and he looked crazed as he stared at me not even seeing Kith return to his act.

"STOP!" He yelled and within seconds he was holding me by the hair and dragging me off the side of the stage. "Look what you're doing to your sister! You make her look stupid when you mess up like that. You make ME look stupid." Ducar's lip curled as he watched Kith's anguish, daring him to try and stop him.

"What are you doing? Drop her right now!" Beatrice's voice rang out from the front of the tent. Turning as much as Ducar's grip would allow, I saw her standing in the doorway with Ketzia. Wondering if Ketzia told her what was going to happen, I shook my head vigorously. Beatrice interfered before, and I didn't want her to get hurt again.

By the time I realized my mistake it was too late. When Ducar felt me shaking my head he pulled harder on my hair and turned me to look at him. "Oh, are you worried about your ugly friend over there?"

By the time Ducar threw me to the ground, Beatrice was there scooping me up. She glared at him, daring him to challenge her, but for a moment all he did was smile.

Then, out of nowhere he reeled back and punched Beatrice square in the face. I could tell it was all she could do not to drop me as she stumbled back and fell to the ground.

"Ducar!" Ketzia gasped from the front of the tent.

He glared up at her with an evil glint in his eyes, "Oh are you next?" Ketzia went silent.

Ducar wrenched me out of Beatrice's arms and flung me to the ground behind him. Then he started wailing on her. A purple blur ran past me, and I watched as Kith tried to pull on Ducar's arms to get him to stop.

Finally, Ducar stood up and turned on Kith. With one quick punch to the gut he sent him to the ground, wheezing. Then, he turned and walked

When I woke up, the face I expected to see wasn't the old man with the kind blue eyes and crooked nose. Vaguely aware that I was screaming, I slowly began to realize Isaac must have been awake and heard me before Kith. Turning, I saw that Kith was watching sleepily as Isaac lifted me from the bed. "I've got her," he whispered to Kith who seemed to be only half awake. Isaac must have come in quickly.

He carried me out of the bedroom; gently shutting the door behind him, and to the living room. It was still dark outside, only the moonlight showed slightly from behind the curtained windows. Isaac sat on the couch and cradled me in his arms. "Your nightmares," he whispered. "Are they about the past?"

"Yes," I wasn't sure if I was ready to tell Isaac what I just relived. I wanted the memory to go away, but all I could see was Beatrice's bloody face and Ducar's smile. After he left, Ketzia rushed to bandage Beatrice's face, apologizing over and over again for not stepping in, but Beatrice wouldn't have any of it. She knew all it would have done was make Ducar's wrath even worse if someone else defied him, too.

She let Ketzia clean her up and apply bandages to some of the more severe cuts, but then she insisted on attending to Kith and me. After checking if we were hurt, she held us close and said everything would be alright. Beatrice was always telling us that. I wished she was there now to tell me one more time.

Tears leaked down my face as I buried it in Isaac's chest. He stroked my temple and started humming a soothing tune. After a while, I felt him reach one hand over to the stand beside the couch and grab a mug. He sipped on his tea, and I realized it must be the feverfew. He must have been awake because he was in pain, and that was why he heard me so quickly. This only made me feel worse.

After setting his tea down, he started singing softly. I didn't catch all the words, but his voice was soothing, and after a while, I was finally able to calm down enough to drift back to sleep.

CHAPTER TEN: MARCH

✳   Kith   ✳

It only took Isaac a couple of days to find someone to help him in his shop. While sitting at dinner the first night after the helper joined him, Isaac was fairly quiet. He didn't seem to be as worn out as usual, though, which was a relief.

"How was it having someone help you today?" Mara sounded like she was trying to mask concern with curiosity.

"It was nice having some help." He took a bite and chewed slowly, as if thinking. "The problem is, though, he doesn't know much about making bread or running a shop."

"Isn't that the point of being an apprentice? To learn these things?" I felt like I wasn't going to like where Isaac was going with this.

"Yes. But we're not sure what time frame we're working with, and it would be helpful during the day if he was able to do more."

"That makes sense, but what aren't you saying?" I was trying not to get frustrated.

"We decided he'll need to come for some extra one-on-one learning time. Starting tomorrow he's going to be coming to help me prepare for the next day and I'll be teaching him about running the shop."

"He's going to be coming here?" Mara squeaked. "But he'll see us!"

"It isn't ideal, but you two will need to stay in your room while he's here. He will be learning about bread, not snooping through the rooms."

"We'll have to be quiet, too." Fear crept into my stomach. This was an incredibly risky move, but I understood why it was essential.

"Yes. I know it won't be fun, and I'm sorry. It wasn't what I wanted to have to do, but there's no getting around it." Isaac sighed, and I could see the weariness that came with the decision.

"We've been through worse. We'll make do." I shrugged, more for Mara's benefit than anything else.

"That's true. I mean, we spent several days in the cave barely able to even stretch out. At least we'll have a full room with toys and books." Mara's voice had a fake chipper tone to it.

"What cave?" Isaac looked confused.

"Oh. Uhm. When we first came to this area we found a small cave outside the town. After some opening up it was kinda cozy. I definitely enjoy our room here more, though." The words tumbled out of Mara as if she couldn't hold them back.

"You lived in a cave?" Surprise crossed Isaac's face. "I thought you said you made forts to stay in. How long were you here before I caught you in my trap?"

"Not very long," I spoke up. "Mara found the cave. It was warmer than the forts so we decided to stay for the winter."

Isaac smiled and I was surprised to see relief fill the creases in his face. "Here I was this whole time thinking you were out there living in a stick fort while it was freezing outside. I feel much better knowing you had something at least a little warmer. Still, I'm glad you're here instead." His face clouded. "You're safer here."

The next day, when it came time for Isaac to close the shop for the night, Mara and I moved into our room with our books and toys. Just as the door was closing behind us, we heard Isaac and his new assistant come in. Isaac entered first, and I could picture him listening intently to make sure we were hidden.

As we settled ourselves with what we brought in, I thought about our conversation the previous night. Mara had talked about the cave and how it didn't compare to living in the house. We both enjoyed having a room with a real bed and a feeling of safety. It wouldn't last forever, though. In fact, it probably wouldn't last much longer.

We were going to be back on the run, making quick forts that barely did anything more than hide us a little bit. Or maybe we'd get lucky and find some caves here and there. But we'd be going back to always being on the run, sleeping on the ground and never feeling safe. We did it before, but I felt completely unprepared for doing it again.

I would have to, though. Mara would be relying on me to take care of us, and I couldn't let her down.

With Ducar nearby, as soon as we weren't protected, we'd have to move quickly and avoid stops as much as we could. Having enough food for a few days would be a good idea. I would need to ask Isaac about teaching me to preserve meat so it would last longer. Then maybe I could try to get us some food stored away before we needed to go.

There was a large part of me that wanted to discuss all this with Mara, but talking right now seemed like a really bad idea. We both waited quietly until Isaac came to tell us the assistant was gone.

*　　Mara　　*

After a few evenings of staying cooped up in our room, it was becoming almost impossible not to dwell on everything that happened to us. The days were getting worse and worse and by the time Isaac was done with his apprentice, Kith and I were sick of each other and both wanted all of his attention.

One day after Isaac told us we were free to roam the house again, I started asking him all about his day. Mine was so miserable, I wanted to live through him a little bit.

"Is the new guy getting better?" I asked, thinking of the pastries we sampled the other night. They were okay enough, but nothing compared to Isaac's. If he was going to be a successful baker, he would have to learn to do better.

"He's doing fine," Isaac replied, sighing tiredly.

I was not deterred, though. "He has a lot of practicing to do to be anywhere near the baker you are. But I guess you have been doing it for a long time. How long do you think it will take him to master it?"

Isaac grinned. "You always have been a little blunt, Sarah.

The boy is doing fine, and like you said, he just needs more practice."

I gaped at Isaac, unsure what to say. The first and only time he had called me Sarah, he was half asleep and noticed his mistake quickly. This time, he didn't seem to have a clue. I looked at Kith unsure what to say.

"Sarah? Would you mind making me some of my tea? It was a long day, and teaching isn't as easy with everyone as it is with you," he sighed as he sat in his chair.

Tears began to form as I watched him sitting there perfectly content. "I'm Mara," I whispered.

Isaac blinked. "What?"

"You called me Sarah. I'm Mara," my voice broke at the end. It was all I could do not to run back to our room, but I reminded myself that I promised to be strong for him.

Isaac breathed in slowly and took a long exhale before he hung his head and replied, "I'm sorry, Mara. I lost myself for a minute there. I still know who you are." His face looked pained.

Taking a deep breath, I composed myself. "Of course you do! I'll have your tea right up!"

Isaac smiled in relief. Wiping my eyes, I quickly headed to get the tea started. Once the water was heating, I started pulling out everything I needed to make dinner. Kith asked if I wanted any help, but for the first time I told him no. I wanted to be alone in the kitchen for a while.

By the time we were eating dinner, Isaac seemed to have forgotten anything happened. He was telling us all about his day and how much work his apprentice needed.

"It is nice having him around, though. He has started taking care of most of the customers and I just sit and listen and answer any questions he doesn't know yet. I think he will make a fine baker after a while, he just needs to learn to be more patient. He gets antsy waiting for the bread to rise and always puts it in the oven too soon. Sometimes it makes me wish you could run the store, Mara. You learned so quickly."

Pride swelled in me, and I tried to squash my feelings from earlier. I would have loved to be Isaac's apprentice, and even though I knew it wasn't something worth thinking about, it was hard not to imagine myself behind the counter telling customers all about the breads, pastries and pies. I thought I would be pretty good at it if only I didn't look the way I do. No one would ever come to a shop I ran.

Later that night, when it was dark and I was sure Kith wouldn't notice, I let the tears fall.

✳   Kith   ✳

"What are you doing?" Mara jumped at the sound of my voice and guilt immediately filled her face.

"I just want to watch them. Just for a minute." She fought to keep the whine out of her voice, but couldn't stop from pouting.

"I know, but you know we can't be seen."

"I'd be sneaky. You know I can."

"That's true, but is it worth the risk?"

Mara's hand dropped from the door. "No." She curled her legs under her and sat staring at the door.

"Watching the door won't make it invisible." I tried to sound playful, but failed.

"Obviously. Plus, it being invisible wouldn't help, since we'd be seen." Her voice held a bitterness I wasn't used to.

"What's really bugging you?" I dropped down next to her.

"Nothing."

"Right."

"It's true."

"I agreed with you."

"Ugh. Fine. It's just that we'll always be the secret children."

"The what?"

"We'll always be a secret. Even if all of our dreams of staying here with Isaac came true, we'd always be kept away from everyone else. A secret."

I thought about her words. It was true. We'd still only have

Isaac and would have to hide if he ever had company. He never would've been able to talk about us to anyone, and we'd never be able to see anyone but him. Staying with Isaac seemed like the most wonderful thing, but it still would've been lonely. "Oh. I hadn't thought about that."

"I love Isaac and I'd love to stay here forever. But I don't want to always be hidden away. Do you think we'll ever find a place where we're truly welcomed?"

"I really hope so."

Without saying anything else, she put her head on my shoulder. We stayed there sitting by the door until Isaac came.

"Are you two ready for dinner?"

"Yes." We rose slowly and followed Isaac out to the dining area. There was no sign of his apprentice, but also no real signs of us. All the things we used were to be kept up so they didn't cause suspicion.

Mara hopped up on her stool to help Isaac cook dinner while I set the table; trying not to think too much about what Mara said.

We tried to act cheerful during dinner, but I got the feeling Isaac knew we were upset about something. He always had a way of picking up on these things, but he was fairly quiet himself. While I fought my own thoughts, I also found myself worrying about him.

Once we were all finished eating, Mara and I wandered off to play for a bit. Usually Isaac rested before our evenings together. He wasn't always able to teach us things or work with us much anymore. Instead, we would tell stories about when we were younger, and he told us things about his wife and daughter.

While putting away the books I was looking at I saw Mara near the window, peeking out at the last few people out and about. I realized with sadness that there was nothing I could say or do to make anything better.

Just when I was about to go over to talk to her, a loud crash from the kitchen drew my attention. Turning toward the sound, I saw Isaac's chair lying on its side. The chair next to it was pushed out. After a second of looking, I realized Isaac was on the ground between the two chairs. The next second I was by his side. His chin caught his fall, which left the rest of his face pushed back at a sharp angle. It looked horribly uncomfortable, and I worried about his ability to breathe, so I rolled him gently onto his back.

"Isaac?" I shook him slightly as I spoke.

A feeble moan was my only answer. Even so, it was enough for me to breathe a little. His chin was bleeding, but other than that he didn't seem to have gotten hurt. Mara handed me a clean cloth and a small bowl of water so I could clean his face.

"Kith?" Isaac's voice was slurred and quiet, but I was relieved to hear it.

"Yes. You're alright. You just fell. There's a little bit of blood on your face. You hit your chin."

"Ah. It does sting a bit." He pushed up with his arms and carefully moved to sit. "I'm just going to make my way to my chair."

"I think maybe you should go to bed and get some sleep."

"No, I want to hear you two tell your stories." His voice sounded odd, but I couldn't quite tell how.

"Are you sure you're up for that?"

"Yes, yes." He felt around until he found the chair next to him and braced against it to begin to rise up. Just as he was about all the way up he started to fall again. I was able to carefully guide him to sitting in the chair so that he didn't end back up on the floor.

"I think you need to go to bed. You don't seem to be feeling great."

"I'm fine, I'm fine." He waved a hand at me dismissively. "Where's Mara?"

"I'm right here, Isaac."

"Ah, great." He smiled wide. "Tell your brother I'm fine and don't need to go to bed."

"Isaac…" Mara's voice trailed off and tears rolled silently down her face. "I think Kith might be right."

Her voice seemed to bring him back to himself for a second. "Are you alright, Mara?" Concern covered his face.

"I'll be fine, Isaac. You should get some rest, though."

"Rest does sound good, to be honest. I feel like I hardly spend time with you two, though." He frowned.

"It's alright. We'll spend time together tomorrow."

With a sigh, he pushed himself to his feet. He wobbled for a second, but then steadied. I walked beside him as he made his way to his bed, even though I knew I was too small to stabilize him if needed.

Once he laid down, I pulled his blanket up over him. "Get some rest, Isaac." I closed the door behind me, fairly certain that he was already asleep.

"Maybe we should get some rest, too." Mara was in the small hallway, twisting her fingers.

"Do you think you could sleep right now?"

"No. I don't know that I want to stay up, though."

"I feel the same. It would be a great night to go play in the woods if we could."

"I miss the outdoors so much. Why is Ducar here? Do you think he'll leave any time soon?"

"Well, it's obvious he's looking for us. I hope he leaves really soon. I'm not sure, though." These were all thoughts I didn't want to be having right now. There was never a good time for them, though.

"I don't want to have to leave here with him still so close."

"Me neither. We may not have a choice, though."

"I know." She looked toward Isaac's door sadly, then back at me. "I need a distraction. Do you want to look at books and make up stories to go with the pictures?"

"A distraction does sound nice right now." We got the books and curled up on our bed to pretend to read until we fell asleep.

*   Mara   *

One evening, Isaac came to our door and let us out much earlier than normal. At first, I was excited that he finished early and

228

immediately started asking him questions. Until I noticed the way his lips were pursed and the crease lines between his eyebrows. He quickly walked away from the door and into the kitchen.

Kith and I exchanged worried looks before following him. When we got to the kitchen, we saw that dinner was already prepared and the table was set. This worried us even more. Why would Isaac keep us locked in the room while he made dinner, and how did he have time to work with Ralph and cook?

"I sent Ralph home after work today," Isaac said as if answering my inner questions. "I told him I needed to get other things done and didn't have time for a lesson," Isaac paused and wrung his hands. I got the idea that he was nervous about something.

"What's wrong?" Kith asked as I just gaped at Isaac, imagining what terrible news he could have for us now. I was completely unprepared for what came out of his mouth.

"Ducar came into the shop today," Isaac said slowly, and I felt my world begin to spin.

He hadn't left like we hoped he would. He was still here, weeks later. How could he possibly know where we were?

"But…" Kith began, unsure of himself. "How do you know it was him?" I hadn't thought of that. Isaac can't have seen Ducar. Did he ask for us outright? Did he know we were here? We had to leave. We had to get away before he came back.

"Ralph saw him." Isaac was calm now that the news was out and his voice returned to its regular soothing tones. "He seems to stand out quite a bit from our regular customers, and Ralph was very excited to tell me all about the man with the crystal eye and a scar across half his face. He apparently also has quite the limp and walks crouched over a cane. Ralph seemed to think he looked like a villain from some story book, which I thought fit the bill," at that Isaac's voice lost just a little bit of its composure and I could hear the slight anger in his tone. I knew how much Isaac hated Ducar for what he had done to us. And he didn't even know most of it. "I can't imagine there are many people around who fit that description," he concluded.

"A limp?" Kith asked, a little awed. "I must have done real

damage."

"What's that?" Isaac asked, confused.

"Uh… you're right, that has to be him," Kith looked at me and I could see his terror building, but when he spoke it was to both of us. "What do we do now?"

I hadn't been able to form one coherent thought since Isaac finished talking, aside from *run*. Yet, it felt impossible to move. Somehow I found my way to a chair and I sat there with my mouth gaping open, just staring at Kith. Maybe that was why his terror seemed to rise when he looked at me.

"You stay inside. I know you've been doing it for a while now and it has to be getting tiresome, but you stay, and you wait. He.."

"Did he ask about us?" I blurted out, suddenly aware of myself again. "Does he know we're here?" Once I began talking, I couldn't stop. "Did Ralph tell him anything? Was he alone? Is he coming back?"

The hand on my shoulder touched me before I even realized anyone moved. I looked at Kith in confusion at first, wondering who was touching me.

"Mara, it's okay," came Isaac's soft, calm voice. He was almost whispering. "Ralph doesn't know you're here, that's why you've been hiding, remember? He couldn't have told him anything even if he asked, and he didn't. I heard their whole conversation and I couldn't even tell he was anything other than a new customer until after he was gone and Ralph told me what he looked like," Isaac hesitated for only a second before continuing. "Yes, I'm sure he is looking for you, but he has probably gone all over town searching. Just because he was here doesn't mean he knows."

"But why is he *still* here?" Kith asked, and I was surprised that instead of helping Isaac comfort me, he was asking the tough questions right along with me.

"That I can't tell you. Maybe he doesn't know where else to go and outside a town is a good place for him to regroup?"

"No, he's always moving. He knows we're here somehow. If not here with you, he knows we're close."

A gasp escaped my lips, "Do you think he found the

cave?" If he went inside, it would be obvious someone was there, and who other than us.

Kith's forehead creased in thought. "Maybe, but then he would see we aren't there anymore and think we moved on, wouldn't he? Why would he stay?"

"Maybe he did see us before and we just outran him. If he's limping, he would be moving pretty slowly." Kith looked unconvinced, but couldn't seem to think of another argument.

"Whatever the case may be, he doesn't know you're in my home and I plan to keep it that way," Isaac said from beside me. "I want you two to feel safe here and I will do whatever is necessary to make that happen. If I need to stop having Ralph stay, I will. He has learned a lot already. If I need to close the store entirely, I will."

The seriousness in Isaac's voice made me sad. I could tell he really would do whatever we asked him to. "No," I said softly and touched Isaac's cheek. "You don't have to give anything up for us. Ralph needs to learn and the store has to be open for him to do that," Isaac's face melted when I touched it and now he grabbed my little hand in his comparatively huge one. "But maybe we could set up some traps or something to make sure no one can get in?"

"I think we can do that," Isaac replied. "We can move heavy furniture in front of the doors to make sure no one can get through them. First, let's eat."

After dinner, we moved the table in front of the main door to the house and Isaac's chair went in front of the door to the store. "Just wake us up in the morning to help you move it. I don't want you trying to do it by yourself," Kith said, wagging his finger at Isaac even though he couldn't see him. I giggled and Isaac faked an exasperated sigh before agreeing.

Later that night, once we were alone, Kith reluctantly told me we needed to plan for when we had to leave. "We'll have to pack lightly," he said. "We aren't used to carrying things around anymore, and we need to be able to move quickly if Ducar is still here."

"We'll need food for several days, though," I chimed in, thinking of what usually slowed us down. "We won't have time to stop and find anything."

"I think we can carry enough food for several days along with some supplies. We'll still need the blankets Isaac gave us, too."

The whole conversation was too sad to handle, and yet we knew it was something we had to talk about and plan. "I guess I'll have to leave Gracie here," I said, hugging the doll tightly. "She'll take up too much space." I held back the tears that threatened to fall.

"No, Mara, I'm sure we can fit Gracie," Kith's face was kind and I knew he understood my feelings. "She's part of the group now, we can't possibly leave her here to fend for herself. Isaac would want you to keep her."

Jumping up off the floor, I hugged Kith tightly. "Thank you! She won't get in the way!" It was a small consolation for everything I knew we were about to lose.

✳   Kith   ✳

"Careful." My voice was as quiet as I could get it, and I was practically holding my breath.

"I'm being careful." Mara's irritated words came through gritted teeth, as if she was trying to contain them. Her hand was steady as she moved the triangular block to the top of our tower, which was almost level with her eyes. "Got it!"

We stepped back to admire our handiwork, the tallest tower we'd managed to build. The once brightly colored blocks were faded from time, but that didn't matter at all as we viewed our masterpiece. As we stood admiring it, I was suddenly filled with the desire to knock it down. Grabbing one of the horse toys we often played with, I acted like it was charging the tower.

"Kith, what are you doing?" Mara squealed in horror.

"It has to come down somehow." I shrugged. Mara thought about it for a second before grabbing the other horse and joining my charge. Both horses slammed into the bottom of the tower and the wooden pieces fell with a clatter. Laughter erupted from both of us as the blocks scattered across the room.

"Will you two keep it down?!" It took a couple of seconds to realize the yell ringing out through the house came from Isaac. The same Isaac who never even raised his voice at us. We looked over in shock. He sat leaning forward in his chair, his hands at his temples, his face reddened.

"We're sorry, Isaac." We whispered in unison. In complete quiet, we picked up the scattered blocks and put them away. Without a word, we headed to our room and sat on the bed. As soon as we were alone, Mara burst into the tears she was holding back.

"Why is Isaac mad at us?"

"I don't think he really is. Must be that the sickness making him angry. I think his head hurts, too."

"Did we make it worse?"

"It seems we got too loud at a bad time." I rubbed her back as she released her emotions. My heart ached, and I wondered what this new development meant. Would Isaac become cranky with us a lot? Was this a sign his health was getting even worse? A stone dropped in my stomach at the thought.

"I guess we need to be as quiet in the evenings as we are during the day." She wiped at her face in frustration. "Soon we'll become secret even to Isaac." I could see the regret in her face as soon as she said it.

"I don't think we'll ever become secret to Isaac, and I don't think we always have to be quiet. Maybe we'll just check in with him to see how he's feeling and decide what to play after."

"Do you think that will work?"

"Hopefully."

She let out a small sigh. "Building and destroying that tower was the most fun I've had in such a long time. I'm scared of what that means."

"Why?"

"I love Isaac. So much. You warned me against it and I tried to fight it, but I couldn't help it. And you were right. We're losing him, and it hurts so bad." She looked at her hands and clenched them together before continuing, "I saw you trying to heal him and I really thought it was going to work. You healed me.

I know you did. Why wouldn't it work with him?"

Gesturing around the room, she continued, "I hate all of this. I hate being cooped up without being able to go out. I hate hiding in our room all the time. I hate that all these things I hate are about to go away completely. I should be glad just to have the time with Isaac that we do, but I want more."

It took me a minute to gather my thoughts before answering, "I hate it, too, Mara. I feel much the same way as you. I don't think it makes us bad. It's normal. The whole situation is horrible, and it's fine to say and feel that." Taking a deep breath, I added, "I wanted you to be right. I wanted to heal Isaac. I did everything exactly the same, but it didn't work. I'm not special. I don't have magical healing powers. I'm useless."

Mara leaned over and put her head on my shoulder. "You're not useless. I don't understand what happened when I got better," she seemed to be avoiding saying I healed her now, "but you not being able to heal Isaac doesn't make you useless. The doctors couldn't even heal him."

With no energy left to argue, I squeezed her hand gently to let her know I understood what she was saying. We sat there without another word, until we both eventually curled up and fell asleep.

We woke the next morning to the smell of our favorite rolls. It had been quite a while since Isaac made them last. The memory of the morning after we snuck out and worried Isaac popped into my head. He made a big spread of rolls as an apology.

Slowly, we crept out of our room and made our way to the table. Isaac was waiting for us with a spread similar to before, but this time there was the addition of eggs and our favorite strips of meat. He really went all out.

We sat down in silence, but both of us were reluctant to reach for the food. "Are you two actually here or did I imagine hearing you come out?" Isaac's voice was gently teasing, but also held a note of concern.

"We're here." Even though I tried to speak up, my voice came out soft.

Isaac's head lowered and he sank into a chair. "I'm terribly sorry. I don't know what came over me last night. I never should have raised my voice at you."

Mara was climbing into Isaac's lap before I even noticed she moved. She wrapped her arms around his neck. As he comforted her, she whispered my fears. "Are you getting worse?"

"I don't know. I'll try to do better at controlling the crazy anger, though. I promise."

We ate together, not talking much. As delicious as the food was, it was also a reminder that this would all come to an end, and probably a lot sooner than we hoped.

*   Mara   *

Isaac sat on the floor with Kith and I while we all played with some of the toys he gave us. He awkwardly attempted to play along with whatever games Kith and I made up. He was getting more and more quiet lately and his moods would swing without much notice, but he seemed to enjoy sitting there with us.

After he snapped at us, Kith and I were sure to play quietly, but sometimes it didn't really seem to matter what we did. Usually, Isaac was still the kind, calm, happy man we knew, but occasionally he would snap again for little things. I knew it wasn't the real Isaac who yelled at us, so I wasn't angry at him for losing his temper. I was only sad.

"Isaac, Gracie wants to visit the bakery to buy 4 pieces of cherry pie! One for each of us! How much will that cost her?"

Isaac laughed, but his voice sounded different. "For Gracie..." he trailed off and I looked up quickly. His face had gone completely blank.

"Isaac?" Kith asked.

Suddenly, Isaac started jerking. I screamed and bounded to my feet. "What's wrong with him?" I sobbed.

Kith sat on the floor dumbfounded.

Isaac fell to the ground and began convulsing even harder. His arms and legs flailed wildly, scattering the toys we were playing with.

Kith began picking things up and moving them out of the way, but all I could do was stand there and sob.

Isaac was slowly inching toward the table as he went, and Kith was frantic.

"Mara! Don't let him run into anything, he'll hurt himself!"

I gaped, "How are we supposed to stop him!?"

Kith threw all of the toys he picked up out of the way and began running around, putting himself in between Isaac and anything hard he might come into contact with.

Isaac's leg involuntarily kicked Kith hard in the shin, but he didn't cry out. His face was stony and he was determined not to let Isaac come to any more pain than he was already in.

After what seemed like ages, Isaac's limbs calmed and he lay still on the floor.

Tentatively, Kith and I walked over to him.

"Isaac..?" I asked.

Isaac propped himself up on his left arm and took a deep labored breath. "What happened?" he asked.

"I...I don't know. You were shaking and your arms and legs were just...all over the place," Kith said.

Isaac's brows creased as he took another long breath, then laid back down on the floor.

Kith and I looked at each other in concern. "Isaac...would you like me to make some of your tea?"

"Yes, Sarah dear, that sounds nice."

Kith looked at me, but I refused to let any emotion show as I got up and made my way to the kitchen to make Isaac's tea.

By the time I was done, Kith had coaxed Isaac off the floor and onto his chair. He sipped his tea slowly and continued his long deep breaths. His eyebrows were creased in pain.

We sat there in silence for a long time before Isaac announced he was going to go to bed. He stood up and wobbled a little. Kith and I ran to his side, but he managed to stabilize himself. We both walked with him down the hallway and to his bedroom, where Kith followed him in and made sure he was comfortable before joining me again.

Neither of us had words to talk about what just happened, so we went to bed and just laid there in silence. After a while, Kith reached over and squeezed my hand. I wasn't sure if this was for my own benefit or for his. Probably both. I squeezed back, and let the tears fall.

✳   Kith   ✳

I lay in bed, staring at the ceiling. It was still dark out, and eerily silent. Sleep was becoming increasingly more difficult for me as time went on. When I did drift off, I found myself waking soon after. I focused on the silence, as if it held an important message for me. If there was something to be heard or learned, though, I wasn't getting it.

Sighing, I sat up. Sleep wasn't going to be coming back. Restlessness swept through me. If I wasn't going to be sleeping, I should be doing something else. Creeping out of bed, I grabbed my knives from their shelf and went to grab some wood. I thought about curling up in front of the dark fireplace, but I knew Mara would be stirring at some point. I wanted to get to her before Isaac woke.

Sitting in the corner of our room, close to the bed, I unrolled my knives. There was a selection of small ones that were made for carving more detailed items. My interest was usually in the ones that would allow me to defend us, so I hadn't really used the small ones, much. The wood piece I found was small, but mostly flat. It was perfect for trying some carving for fun.

As I turned the wood in my hands, I let an idea formulate for what I wanted to create on it. Pulling out one of the small knives, I pushed it against the wood. I expected to just slice through it easily like it did when I made spears, but this took a lot more effort. Especially to control how much I was removing. Right when I was trying to carefully remove a small chunk of wood Mara thrashed and yelped in her sleep. It startled me, and I took a huge chunk out of the wood. Sighing, I set aside the ruined work. I supposed I should be glad it wasn't my hand.

It didn't take me long to get Mara awake and calmed down. We decided it was bright enough outside to give up on sleep and went to find some food. It wasn't too much longer before Isaac joined us. He walked slowly to the table, moving as if his whole body was stiff.

The crazy shaking happened a few more times since that first awful night, and each time seemed to leave him weaker and in more pain than before. Without a word, Mara started making him some tea. I watched her work, her hands familiar with the movements. There was such a seriousness to the task, and to Mara in general.

"Here's some breakfast, Isaac." I set his plate in front of him and handed him a fork. He took it with a wobbly hand.

"Thank you." His voice was soft, and almost hard to hear.

As I was eating, I looked up to notice Isaac's food kept falling off his fork. His hand would shake on the way to his mouth and it would fall. Mara looked up and saw it at the same time I did. She looked over at me in worry, but I didn't have any idea how to respond.

"Let me help you." I gently put my hand on Isaac's and grabbed the fork. After a slight hesitation, he let me take it.

Cutting his food up smaller than I probably should have, I fed him bite by bite. He didn't say anything, but I knew he hated having to be fed. Once he was done, I decided it was time for the conversation I was dreading.

"Isaac, I think we should talk. Are you in a state where we can?"

"Yes. I'm afraid I know what you're going to say, too." His face looked weary and sad.

"I think it's time for you to let Ralph take over the shop. Fully."

"I thought that's what you were going to say. I know you're right, but I love my shop. I planned on running her for a long time to come."

"I know. I didn't want to have to say it."

Isaac covered my hand with his own. "Sometimes it's hard

to believe you're only a child, Kith. You've really grown up way too fast."

I chuckled slightly. "It's funny you say that. I often think the same way about Mara." I looked up to see her watching us, her eyes full of the sadness I didn't want to let encompass me. It was everywhere these days.

"It's true for both of you. Way more grown up than you should be. But you're both so incredible. I hope you realize that."

I didn't have any clue how to respond, and a lump in my throat would've prevented me from speaking even if I did.

"We think you're incredible, too." Mara's voice was soft. I hadn't realized she came closer until she put her hand on Isaac's arm. We sat in silence for a while, knowing all too well that we were getting close to the end of our time together.

*   Mara   *

With Isaac no longer working, we spent all day every day with him now. A few months ago, I would have been excited about this. Now, it just made everything seem more real.

As the days dragged on, Isaac slept more and more. I started making him tea as soon as I woke up, knowing he would be in pain. Sometimes, he played with us, and Kith and I reveled in it, trying to make the whole thing last as long as we could. More often, he sat in his chair and we all just talked.

He told us about his family and his life growing up. Kith and I were both surprised to find out that his nose had been broken in a fight when he was a teenager and that was why it was crooked. Try as I might, I couldn't imagine Isaac fighting with anyone.

"I was a rowdy young man," Isaac said, sleepily.

Lately, it was hard to get him to finish a story. He would sip his tea and begin talking, but trail off somewhere around the middle as he began to doze. This was better than the times that he sat holding his head and moaning. I was horrified the first time he did this, but like everything else, we became accustomed to it now that he was with us all day. It made me wonder if he ever did it in front of Ralph and how Ralph reacted. Had he taken care of him at all during their days together?

This is why I had tea on hand at all times now. If Isaac started that moan, I would pour him some tea and Kith and I would sit with him quietly.

After the first week, Isaac barely got out of his chair. He brought his blankets to the living room and started sleeping there at night.

Later, when Kith and I talked about it, he said he thought Isaac couldn't handle walking back and forth anymore, but he wanted to be near us, so in the chair he stayed. This idea made me sad. I thought his bed would be more comfortable for him, but whenever we suggested he move there, Isaac insisted he wanted to stay where he was.

Kith and I talked about sleeping in the living room with him, but I was still having nightmares and I didn't want to disturb Isaac with them. Instead, we would stay up late into the night watching over him. Eventually we would go to our room for a troubled sleep where my dreams were haunted by a different problem entirely.

As the days went on, it became consistently clearer how much Isaac was declining. He no longer had the strength to mask how much pain he was constantly in. Peace only came when he was sleeping, and even then it was sometimes a restless sleep.

One night, I watched Isaac's head bob as he tried to keep himself awake. Kith was telling him a story, and Isaac was trying so hard to listen. That was when it hit me.

Isaac was ready to leave, but he didn't want to leave us. We were his unfinished business, holding him back from his endless sleep.

Even though I knew Kith was still speaking, all I could focus on was Isaac. Pain was written all over his face and in his entire body. Although I knew he was hurting all this time, I still kept hoping he would hold on. Stay just a little longer with us. I wanted us to keep him all to ourselves for as long as we could. But

Isaac was in pain. He was tired. He was ready.

I'm not sure how long I sat there before I finally forced myself to stand up. Kith had finished talking and was in the kitchen getting Isaac his tea.

Walking over slowly, I climbed, gently, into Isaac's lap. His face lit up in surprise and I almost lost all my resolve. He wrapped his arms around me and all I wanted to do was crumple into him. But I had promised to be strong.

"Isaac?" I whispered as Kith walked over with the tea.

He smiled softly. "Yes, Mara?" His hand played with my braid.

"We... " I paused, almost losing my nerve. "We, Kith and I, that is. We'll be alright."

His eyes were shining. "You're strong kids."

I locked eyes with Kith, found my courage again, and nodded. "We are. We're strong and you've helped us so much. We'll be alright."

My eyes couldn't leave Kith's. I saw the pain there and I knew he understood what I was doing. Isaac needed to know we would be alright before he would ever let himself be at peace, and I had to give that to him. I couldn't let him continue to struggle like this for our sake. It was time for him to move on.

Isaac's hand had gone still on my braid as he listened. "I worry about you two."

The pools that had begun forming in my eyes threatened to fall, but I held them in just a moment longer. "I know. We both love you for it." I brushed his cheek softly and noticed how the purple of my skin contrasted with his increased paleness. "I know you're tired, and I want you to know that we'll be alright."

I laid my head down on Isaac's chest and listened to his heart beating while the tears fell.

✳   Kith   ✳

None of us wanted to go to bed, but eventually,

exhaustion led us to give in. As we curled up next to each other, a cold lump of dread sat in my chest. I was sure I'd never sleep, but the tiredness won.

I woke suddenly, not sure what pulled me from sleep. It was still the middle of the night, though I knew it had been at least a few hours since we went to bed. Then I heard it. Shuffling sounds from the kitchen, accompanied by some heavy breathing. Isaac. What was he doing?

I crept out of our room slowly, trying hard not to wake Mara. Our packs, once stored and unneeded, were on the table. Carefully wrapped foods lay all around it. Knives and spices and everything else we may need surrounded the table. I hated that my first thought was immediately that it was too much for us to carry.

"Isaac?" I kept my voice soft to avoid startling him since I was unsure if he had heard me come out.

"I should have guessed you'd wake up." There was a chuckle followed by a rattling cough, but there didn't seem to be any joy in his laugh.

"Did you not want me to?" The hurt I felt surprised me.

"No, that's not what I meant. I just wanted more time to prepare your things, so you wouldn't have to."

"You've done enough." I took his hand gently. "You've taken such good care of us."

"My boy." His shoulders slumped and he let me lead him to his favorite chair. "I would have loved to continue taking care of you. There are bigger things in your future, though, than being hidden away in an old man's home."

"What do you mean?" I couldn't tell if he was still with me.

"I don't know how to explain it, it's just a feeling. You two were meant for something amazing. You'll find it in time. I just wish I was able to prepare you more."

"We're a lot more prepared than we were." It was all I could think to say. What he said confused me, but also made all the sense in the world. As I sat holding his hand I could hear his breathing change. "I'm going to go wake Mara."

"Yes. That's probably for the best." There was a small

sigh.

I walked slowly back to our room and shook Mara awake. There was no grogginess, and no questions. She needed no explanation as she looked up at me. She gave him permission, and she knew what would follow. Her eyes were deep golden wells of sadness, but she was calm.

My throat closed and my heart stopped beating as we approached Isaac together. In the short time I was gone his breathing changed even more. There wasn't much time. The cottage seemed to swirl around me as we walked. His head raised and his eyes fluttered when we got close. He tried to lift his arm, but it was too heavy for him.

We were at his side in a second. "Isaac. We're here."

"I'm glad. I love you both more than you'll ever know. I hope that what I was able to teach you helps. It's not as much as I wanted to, but keep practicing, alright?"

"We will.." Mara reached out and kissed his pale hand. "I love you, Isaac. Beatrice would've liked you. She'd be glad we had you to care for us, even just for a while."

A small tear escaped Isaac's eye and trailed down his cheek. "Thank you." He reached out and brushed Mara's face with his fingertips before dropping his hand again.

I felt a strong urge to beg him not to leave us. As if explaining that we still needed him would enable him to stay a while longer. Mara was right, though. We had to let him find rest, so instead, I reached out and grabbed his hand again. "I still don't understand why you were so good to us, but I'll always love you."

A small sad smile curved his mouth. "Find kindness, Kith. There's more of it in this world than you realize."

Using as much strength as he could, he held out his arms. We leaned in and let him hold us for a final few moments before he couldn't hold his arms around us anymore. Stepping back, we interlocked our hands without even thinking about it.

There were a few more ragged shallow breaths, and then they stopped. I wanted to yell for him to come back, but if Mara could be selfless, so could I. Instead, I sat holding his limp hand in one hand and Mara's warm one in the other. We sat that way for several minutes. He was gone, and Mara and I were alone in the world again. One more spark of goodness was gone and the world got that much darker.

Crawling over to Mara, I put my arm around her. She curled into me and we cried together.

At last, she looked up at me. "I had to let him go, Kith. It hurts so bad, but I had to do it." She sobbed into my shoulder.

I stroked her hair gently. "I know, Mara. And you were right. We'll be alright." After a pause, I added, "In time."

*   Mara   *

We sat like that for what seemed like hours. I didn't want to move, didn't want to think about what just happened and what must happen now. He was gone and it seemed like the rest of the world should stop moving forward. How could we continue on now? First Beatrice, now Isaac. Would everyone we ever loved leave us in the end?

Too soon, Kith broke the silence. "Mara...I think we should leave now."

I jerked upright to look at him, ignoring the pain that shot through my now stiff limbs. "Already?"

"If Ducar is still close, we need the cover of darkness when we leave," his eyes were bloodshot and watery and I could see the streaks on his cheeks where tears had fallen unhindered. He was pointedly looking anywhere but at the chair where Isaac's stiffening body now lay. "I don't know about you, but I can't handle being here with him all day. It's too much. We have to leave." I was surprised by the pleading tone his voice now took. I promised myself I would be strong for Isaac and for Kith. It was time to hold up to the second part of that promise.

Standing on wobbly legs, I held my hand out for Kith. He took my hand and it was all I could do not to crumble back to the floor. Looking around, I realized our presence here would be obvious. "We have to make it look like we were never here," I said,

244

trying to sound brave, but hearing the weakness in my own voice. Kith looked at me questioningly, so I explained. "Isaac was supposed to have been living by himself this whole time. What will everyone think when they come to get him and there are toys around the place and the second bed has clearly been slept in? Ducar will know exactly what it means. We need to make it look like it did the first time we came. Maybe then he won't know to come after us."

Kith was looking at me with his mouth slightly open in surprise. I almost laughed. "I hadn't even thought of that," he whispered and then got straight to work taking all of the toys down from their new homes we had given them around the house and putting them safely back in Isaac's trunk. We took the bedding off the bed and attempted to fold it the way other things inside the trunk were folded. They didn't look quite right, but we put them on the bottom and decided people probably wouldn't notice.

We packed our few possessions into the packs Isaac set out on the table. Then it was time to decide what we could actually take with us. Isaac set out way more food than we could carry, but we stuffed as much of it in as we could along with his smallest cooking pot, a small cloth bag we decided could be used to separate things like berries and nuts from the other food, a few knives, some spices, one small bowl for each of us and a cup. We decided we could share the cup to save space.

Throughout all of this, we were both studiously avoiding even looking at the chair. The cabin now looked like we were never there, aside from our bulging packs that were piled at the door. As I took it all in, sadness overwhelmed me again at the thought that we would never see this place again. Or the man who lay on the chair.

✳   Kith   ✳

"I think that's all we'll be able to take." I lifted the packs. They were as full as we could get them while still keeping them light enough to move quickly.

"You're probably right. I hate to waste all this food, though." Mara sighed as we both looked at the table covered in so much of the delicious food Isaac always fed us.

"Let's grab a couple of rolls to eat as we head out. It's been a while since dinner and I could use a snack."

After putting away the food we couldn't take, we grabbed some of the rolls and turned for one last look at our home. It looked so empty now. Almost unrecognizable. With a sigh, I shouldered my pack and headed to the door. We couldn't waste any more time here. The sun would rise soon and we needed to be far away from Ducar's camp.

Mara followed me silently. We knew where we were headed, for now at least. The horrible conversations we had over the past few weeks prepared us with a plan. We discussed it many times so we'd be able to move together quickly and silently.

Hunching over to make ourselves smaller, we crept carefully to the tree line. Once under their cover, we ran through the trees until they were thicker and closer together. As soon as we could see the branches were close enough together to move through, we used our claws to climb a tree. We were faster through the branches, and being above the heads of any men possibly waiting below made us feel more secure.

It didn't take long for me to feel the effects of us having been still for so long. My breath became ragged and my lungs burned. My whole body was screaming in pain, but I pushed on. We needed to get further away.

"Kith." Mara's voice was soft between heavy breaths. "I need a break. Just a short one."

"Alright. A rest sounds good." We found a larger tree that we could sit in together and pulled out our water.

"I wish we managed to stay more active while at Isaac's." Mara was rubbing her legs as she spoke.

"Me, too. It would've been easier if we were able to go play in the forest."

"That's true. If only it was safe. But, then, if it was, we wouldn't be in the hurry we are now, either."

"You're right." I cursed Ducar in my mind as I rose from my seat. "We should continue on our way."

With a sigh, Mara rose, wincing as she moved. "Are we going to be moving all day?"

"We'll have to. I don't think it will be long before Ducar somehow figures out we're gone. Even if he doesn't suspect we were at Isaac's."

"But how? I don't understand how he knew we were there."

"I don't either. He seems to have some way of knowing, though." The thought had been lingering in my mind since he showed up. He shouldn't have been able to find us. We were hidden and as far as I knew we weren't spotted. Isaac never heard any rumors of us being around.

"Is he going to keep finding us forever?" I could see the exhaustion in her eyes. Not just from being back on the move, but from the worry of being chased. And the sadness from all we had lost.

"I wish I could tell you he won't, but I can't."

We fell silent again, focusing on moving and breathing. I fought to keep all the fears out of my mind. No thoughts of Ducar or Isaac, just focusing on what may be ahead of us. Once again, we were directionless and adrift. Wandering with no set course. As I thought it, it felt like it should have been freeing, but I just felt empty and lost.

CHAPTER ELEVEN: MAY

Trying not to show how weak I became, I pushed myself as hard as I could, but I could tell Kith was getting worn out faster too. Our bodies just weren't used to being on the run all day anymore. It didn't help that we didn't get much sleep before leaving. Not to mention why we were leaving in the first place, but every time I started to think about that, I forced it back down. I needed to stay focused on putting as much distance between us and Ducar as possible. If I thought about Isaac, I might not be able to continue.

"Alright, Mara, I have to stop. We need sleep," Kith was panting and looked as tired as I felt.

"Should we cook some of the raw meat Isaac packed?" I asked, trying to decide if I had the strength to make a fire.

Kith had plopped down right where he was standing and looked up at me in exasperation. "Probably. It won't last long if we don't," he sighed. "Maybe we should have left it."

I sat on the ground, deciding we could use a break at least before building the fire. Once I was resting, I couldn't keep everything that happened from seeping into my thoughts.

"We just left him there," I said miserably.

"I know. But what else could we do? It's not like we could have buried him."

"How long do you think it will be before someone finds him?" I didn't want to think about the state his body would be in if it took months to find it.

"I'm sure Ralph will go looking for him soon. He is still in the shop every day, it's not like he won't notice Isaac never checks in on him anymore."

"That's true." The thought comforted me a little. At least he would be found soon. "But what will they do for him? The town, I mean? Do you think they'll have a big service? I wish we could do something for him." My mind wouldn't stop. Now that I had opened the gate, all I could think about was Isaac.

"I do too," Kith answered after a while, and it took me a second to remember which thought he was responding to.

"Maybe we can," I said slowly. "Just a little service of our own," I said, standing up. Suddenly, the energy that seemed to have left my body for good was back and I was ready to make that fire.

Kith followed me around, confused at first, until I started collecting and stacking firewood. He helped, without asking any questions.

When we lit the fire, we stood staring into the flames for a long time. Then, while Kith got the meat started, I rummaged through our bags and pulled out the small cloth bag we took. Inside it I had packed some of the flower petals Isaac gave us in the beginning to decorate the cave. I didn't want to part with them, but I thought they would do alright for our little service.

Kith never asked me what I was doing, he just stood by my side ready to do his part. Squeezing his hand, I began the only thing I could think of to celebrate the one friend we made on our miserable journey.

"Isaac... you were the best thing that could have happened to us." My voice shook but I continued on. "I don't know how we would have made it through the winter without you." I began dropping the petals into the fire one at a time, then held the hand with them piled in it out to Kith so he could join me.

"You gave us so many precious things that I never would have dreamt of. Most importantly you were our friend. You were the most generous man I've ever met, and I am so glad to have met you. Your wife dried these flowers and spread them around your home, just like Kith and I spread them in our little cave. Take them back with you now so you can give them to her when you see her again. Kith and I will look after each other now. We will never forget you or what you taught us." My voice was barely a whisper now, "I love you."

Kith whispered a gentle, "I love you" and let the last flower slip from his fingers. We hugged each other close and stood there staring into the flames until there were none left.

After Mara's goodbye ceremony, I didn't know what to do. Everything seemed pointless. I'm not sure how many days passed while we walked in a haze. We would spend our days walking aimlessly, occasionally stopping to munch a little on the food Isaac packed up for us, but we often forgot about meals altogether. Even when we did remember to eat, I had to force the food down. Nothing seemed appetizing and the only reason I ate at all was because I knew I needed it to keep my strength.

One morning, after crawling out from under her blanket, Mara sniffed the air and then began to sniff herself. Her nose scrunched up, "I think I stink."

I couldn't help a small laugh, but when I smelled myself, I realized she was right. "I don't smell so great, either." I yawned and stretched. "Maybe we should try to find a place to clean up."

"I suppose a puddle or something will have to do for now until we find some more water," Mara said, as she chose a direction and started walking. I trailed along behind her, my feet shuffling through the grass.

Laughter and yelling filled the air, and we came to a sudden halt. Mara's eyes widened with fear, as I felt myself freeze. We crouched down while we figured out where the sounds were coming from. Kids were playing off in the distance, not too far from where we were heading. One of the kids held a ball while the others seemed to be getting into a predetermined place, forming a circle. Then the one who held the ball dropped it and kicked it hard in the direction of the girl who was straight in front of him. Some of the boys in the group jeered at her until she kicked the ball hard and it went soaring past all of them. Even though I didn't really understand it, their game looked like fun, and I felt envious of their carefree playing.

Isaac tried to get me to believe that there were more nice people out there than just him and Beatrice, but I wasn't sure that was possible. Maybe I should approach the kids and test his theory. Turning in their direction, I tried to make my feet move forward, but I couldn't. Fear coursed through me, and I stepped back.

"Maybe we should come back later, Mara."

Mara nodded silently and put her hand in mine. We walked all the way back without speaking, but I felt ashamed for being too scared of some kids. Was I going to let Isaac down? His last wish was for me to discover the kindness people had to offer, wasn't it?

At least the fact that the kids were here meant there was a town nearby and Mara and I could use the chance to stock up on more food. What we brought lasted us a long time with how little we were thinking to eat, but it was still beginning to run out.

"Let's just sit for a bit." Mara's voice was soft, as if she felt I needed to be handled gently. "We can scope out the town later after the kids have gone home."

It wasn't long before the sound of the kids hit us again, and we realized they were getting closer. "We have to go, Mara, or they'll spot us soon." Fear was creeping up on me again, and I despised the feeling.

"Let's climb a tree then." Mara strapped her backpack on as she spoke. "We don't want to go too far away or we may lose the town. We can keep away from them if we're up in the trees and then we can follow them home."

"That's a good idea," I said and was surprised when I saw Mara slightly roll her eyes. "What was that for?"

She was abashed for a moment and then looked me straight in the eyes. "You don't have to sound so surprised that I would have a good idea."

Shock ran through me as I processed what she said. I hadn't realized my voice sounded surprised, if it really even did. "Mara, I wasn't...that's not what I was trying to say."

"It doesn't matter, let's just get moving so they don't find us."

Confusion filled me, but I ignored it for the moment deciding she must just be feeling out of sorts with everything that had happened. I was sure having to hide from the kids didn't help any, either. It still bothered me, though, that she would suggest I seemed to think she wasn't smart.

Staying in the trees, we moved around whenever the kids

got close to us. Eventually, the game wound down and they got ready to head home. I longed to play games with them, and laugh and yell. Mara and I used to play that way. We were happy and carefree once. Mara could barely remember it, but I could. Running together, for fun, instead of for our lives, and giggling as we caused havoc in the camp. Beatrice was often sent to wrangle us up after the others got tired of our mischief. She'd laugh while scolding us, then let us play in her tent until we fell asleep.

When the kids headed home, we followed from a distance until their town was in sight. Knowing it would be a while before everyone went to bed, we decided to take a nap while we waited. My heart was heavy as I allowed myself to drift into sleep. It wasn't restful, however, with images of a disappointed Isaac still lingering in my mind when I awoke to Mara's crying. I shook her gently, and let her rest her head in my lap while I played with her hair to calm her until she fell back asleep.

Mara's hand on my arm startled me, and I realized I must have drifted off again. I had planned to wait until she was fully asleep and then make my way into the town, but now the sun was almost up and it was too late for that. I must have been more tired than I realized.

We decided I would go into the town that night instead and we would just hang out around the area until then. It was weird sitting still after walking so much. There wasn't much time to just sit and think about everything ever since we left Isaac, and I could tell Mara was becoming as uncomfortable with the thoughts as I was.

We spent several hours trying to figure out something to do. First, we sat in silence for a while, each lost in thought until I felt like I would burst from all the emotions I didn't want to feel right then. Then, we tried talking, but it was clear we were both avoiding particular subjects and that quickly became even worse than the silence. After that, we got down from the tree and roamed around looking for any food that may be in the area.

It wasn't much after noon when we heard the kids starting to play nearby again. My heart sank. This was going to be a common thing, with the weather warming up. It hit me suddenly that we had three options, and I wasn't sure any of them sounded good. Meeting the kids terrified me, but the idea of hiding in the trees again or going back on the move without visiting the town didn't sound any more appealing.

Sighing, I jumped down from the tree where we had finished eating a quiet lunch. "Mara, stay here for now."

Her eyes widened. "Where are you going?"

"Isaac wanted me to meet more nice people, so I'm going to give that a shot. I want you to stay here while I decide if it's safe."

"I'm scared."

"Me too, but it's what Isaac wanted us to do, isn't it? I have to try.

"Be careful, Kith. Don't get too close to them unless you know it's safe."

Gathering up all my courage, I smiled at Mara before turning toward the sounds of laughter, my heart thumping loudly in my ears. As far as I could remember, I had never introduced myself to other people on purpose.

Once the kids were in view, I crouched behind a tree to watch them for a minute. They had a few balls made from cloth that they were throwing around. They'd switch between catching the balls and throwing them to hit each other. There was a lot of yelling and name calling, but they all seemed to be having fun.

Slowly, I stepped out from my cover. I was hoping to approach slowly, but I stumbled and stepped on a stick. The sound brought lots of heads swiveling in my direction. They all froze as they saw me, and I smiled through my fear and rose my hand to wave a greeting.

"It's a monster!" One of the larger boys shrieked and pointed at me.

"I'm not a monster!" Hurt and anger flooded me, but I was desperate to make this work.

"You sure look like a monster." One of the smaller boys spoke up, his lip curled in disgust as he looked at me.

"I'm just a boy." I fought the shaking that was trying to overcome me.

They ignored me, as they all started chanting "monster" repeatedly. The one who first spoke picked up a large clod of dirt and threw it at me, hitting me in the chest.

"Get out of here, monster, before we get our parents to run you out." The rest of the children copied the first boy, and I was pelted with a stream of dirt and rocks.

Turning, I ran. They followed close behind, and I suddenly knew that I couldn't return to the tree Mara was in. I hoped she was still hidden as I ran in the other direction, leading them away. I ran as hard as I could, but their longer legs carried them faster than my small ones. Knowing I had to lose them, I scrambled up to the next low branch I saw and used my tail to swing up further into the tree. Climbing higher, I put some distance between us before jumping to the next tree, then the next.

"He really is a monster!" I heard one of the boys yell.

"He's part monkey!" Another called out.

I heard more dirt raining in the branches behind me, but they were no longer so close. It didn't take me long to lose them once I was up high. I stayed perched in a tree until it started getting dark and I figured the kids were probably headed inside for the night.

That was it. We'd have to leave. Our safety here was compromised, and we couldn't stay. News of the monster would spread, and there was a large risk that Ducar would hear of us soon. Clinging to the tree, I let the anger and sadness overwhelm me. The feeling that I failed Isaac sunk deep in my chest.

As soon as I was sure it was safe, I headed back to find Mara, knowing she'd be extremely worried about me.

*   Mara   *

Unable to help myself, I followed well behind as Kith went to talk to the kids. I was far enough away that I could see what was happening, but didn't hear anything until the kids started shouting "monster" and chasing Kith away. My heart broke as I watched him run and I prepared myself to console him. I quickly made my way back to the tree where Kith left me so he wouldn't know I saw, but somehow I was suddenly aware that he changed course and started running in the opposite direction. I couldn't explain how I knew this, but the faint yells of the children told me I was right. How stupid I was to assume they would chase him away and then be done with it.

Darting back through the trees, I tried to find the children who were chasing Kith. When I finally caught up to them, they had stopped running and seemed to have lost track of Kith. I should have known he would get away from them, with how fast he was in the trees.

Turning, I started heading back to the tree still hoping I could make it there before Kith did. Once I started getting close, though, I realized something was wrong. Stopping to listen closely, I couldn't hear Kith at all even though I was sure he should be close by now. Turning around in a circle, I felt something pulling me in a certain direction. I couldn't explain it, it was like I was being guided to Kith.

At first I moved slowly, half expecting Kith to pop up suddenly. Before long I started to feel a sense of urgency and suddenly I was running full out, a panic overcoming me. *Not him too,* my mind kept saying, but I couldn't make sense of why. Kith was safe, the kids had left him. A noise ahead caught my attention and I slowed on instinct, crouching low.

Three grown men were in the distance, crowded around something I didn't need to see to know was Kith. I could hear the taunting tone in their voices. Rage flared inside me as I crept slowly around to get a better view.

Kith was on the ground, trembling, his hands over his head. It was clear the men had been hitting him. One jerked him up and tossed him roughly into a small cage meant for holding an animal. It was then that I noticed the assortment of bows and large knives around them. They must be hunters.

"Just think how much money we'll get for turning him in," one of the men said, grinning.

"If only the girl…" I jumped out of the tree and landed directly on top of the man who was speaking. Not knowing what I was doing, I ripped at his face before kicking off of him and landing on the man nearest him. I scratched at him as I fell toward the ground, tearing a large gash that went down his entire body. Then I turned to the man who held my caged brother and the snarl that escaped my lips would have shocked me if I wasn't blind with rage.

The man looked at his comrades who now lay on the ground, one of them moaning, and grabbed his knife. Behind him, I was vaguely aware of Kith gawking at me.

"Let him out," I said in a voice that sounded much calmer than I felt.

The man looked at Kith in the cage behind him, and that was the last mistake he ever made. Before his head could turn back around, I was on top of him slashing at every piece of him I could reach. His failed attempts to cut me with his knife got increasingly more feeble as I went, until finally the only thing that brought me to my senses was the small voice that came from the cage.

"Mara?" Kith asked, as if he could no longer recognize me.

Standing, I turned slowly to the cage and felt all the rage suddenly leave my body. Exhaustion overwhelmed me as I grabbed the keys from the man's pocket and let Kith out of the cage.

The first man moaned but as I started to turn toward him, Kith caught my arm and led me the other way. "They won't be getting up anytime soon, Mara," he said softly, almost as if he was slightly scared of me. "We're safe now. You saved me."

Looking down, I was confused to find that I was covered in blood.

✳   Kith   ✳

After the beating I had taken, I was too sore to climb into and move through the trees. We were stuck on the ground again, which made the drudgery of walking all day, every day even worse.

Staying put all winter, and having more to do than just walk aimlessly had spoiled us. The grief we were both struggling with only made it all worse, and we found ourselves falling into a slump.

If that wasn't bad enough, I kept having images of Mara covered in blood flash through my head, accompanied by the chants of the children. When they called me a monster, I said I was just a boy. But we weren't ordinary children. Deep down, I was acutely aware of our potential for harm. Mara was just protecting me, though. She was still the gentle Mara of a few days ago. In fact, it was almost as if she didn't even realize how much damage she did. She returned to normal as soon as we left the men laying there, only one of them still making a sound.

As soon as the light started to fade, we decided it was time to make camp. We often pressed on until it was too dark, or we were too tired, but I didn't think that we could go much further without some decent rest.

"Do you want to sleep in the trees or on the ground tonight?"

"Let's sleep on the ground under a tree this time. I don't feel like climbing."

I found a tree that had a nice groove in the bottom between the roots, cleared the leaves and tried to create a level surface for us to curl up on. Right before Mara laid one of the blankets down for us to lay on, my hand hit something that didn't feel like the rest of the roots.

"Hold on, Mara. There's something here." I cleared more dirt and saw some round, light brown clumps. When I pulled a group of the clumps up out of the ground, I stared at it for a minute, unsure what I was holding. I had never seen anything like this before.

"What is that?" Mara looked curious, but doubtful. "Can we eat it?"

"I don't know what it is, but we could give it a try. I don't think it would hurt us." I scraped off as much of the dirt as I could and handed half the bundle to Mara.

Tentatively, she took a bite. She didn't seem to mind the taste much, but then again, we weren't eating a lot since leaving Isaac's. Suddenly, I realized just how hungry I was.

Biting off a slightly bigger chunk, I chewed slowly, unsure what to expect. The lack of real taste surprised me. Most of what I did taste was the dirt I pulled the thing out of. I was too hungry to care, but found myself wondering if this was something normal people actually ate.

"Maybe these will taste better if we cook them?" Mara was moving the mystery food between her fingers.

"You may be right. I was thinking about starting a fire to heat up some of the food in our packs anyway."

"While you start the fire, I'll see if I can find any more of these odd little things." She scrambled around the tree and started digging behind it. After a couple of minutes she pulled out another small bundle. It was only about half the size of the first one, but it was more food. It also meant there might be more under other trees. It wasn't anything like we were now used to, but it was something we'd be able to keep in mind once our packs started running low.

Pulling myself to my feet, I looked at the tree we were under. The leaves were straight and as thin as the needles used to sew our costumes at the freak show. Looking around, I saw a lot of trees that looked just like it. I figured trees that looked the same would have the highest chance of having more of these tasteless balls of food.

I built the fire and started cooking food from the pack along with what we had already harvested. Mara ran around searching all the trees in the area, and came back with another five bundles. One of them was bigger than the first group I found, but the others were all pretty small.

"I think they're done cooking." I pulled our newly found foods out of the fire with a stick and put them in a bowl before pulling the meat off the fire, as well.

"Ouch!" Mara quickly dropped the food she was holding and waved her hand around quickly. "That's hot."

I couldn't help but laugh. "It just came out of the fire."

After sticking her tongue out at me, Mara laughed. "I know. It still hurt, though." She tentatively picked it back up using her claws and blew on it before taking a tiny bite. "It honestly doesn't taste much different, but the softness is more enjoyable." She slowly ate the rest before moving on to some meat.

We went to bed right after eating. Both of us were exhausted. I knew we'd need to take a longer break soon, but the idea of Ducar being close behind us worried me too much.

Walking the next day wasn't quite as dreary as the previous days. While we still weren't exactly having fun, we fell into a decent rhythm and had new food we knew how to find. Having more options always made us feel better.

"I think I'd like to camp up in a tree tonight. Is that alright?"

Mara shrugged. "Yeah, that works. Can we make camp early so we have time to look for more food before it gets dark?"

Looking up at the sky, I realized we'd need to stop soon. We didn't have much daylight left. "That sounds good. Let's start finding a good tree."

It was several minutes before Mara pointed to a tree with a thick trunk and low, large branches. "That one looks good for climbing. If you want to sleep low, those bottom branches would be good."

"They would, but I'd like to go a bit higher since the branches seem pretty sturdy most of the way up." It wasn't the tallest tree around, but was high enough with space around it to be able to look at the stars while trying to sleep, which we hadn't done in so long.

"If you want to go ahead and make the bed up there, I'll start looking for the food." Mara walked off searching without even waiting for an answer.

It didn't take me long to find enough long, stringy plants to weave a support out of. The knots Isaac taught me came in handy with securing it even better than the ones I made in the past. By the time I put the blankets in place it was starting to get darker. I looked around, but didn't see Mara.

Quickly climbing down the tree, I started calling out. I had no clue what direction she walked off in. After a minute of calling, and listening carefully for her, my vision went cloudy then I saw Mara running toward me as if she was right in front of me. In an instant the vision cleared. I didn't see Mara anymore, but I heard her coming. She stopped beside me a minute later, her breath heaving in and out.

"I'm so sorry!" Her words were coming out between puffs. She must have gone pretty far to be that out of breath. "I wasn't finding anything in the area, so I kept going and going. Didn't realize just how far away I was until I heard you calling. It sounded like a whisper."

"I'm glad you heard me." Noticing how dirty she was, I couldn't help but smile. She looked like she was rolling around in a huge pile of dirt. Shoving the weird vision of Mara out of my head, I focused on getting food ready.

"Oh, I did finally find a couple of groups of the stuff. I also found some berries that are just barely ripe enough to eat." She pulled her findings out of her bag as she spoke. There wasn't much, but it could be added to some of the food from our packs to create a fairly nice meal.

After we ate, we secured our packs well, and climbed the tree. The woven bed I made was big enough for us to lay together comfortably.

"The stars are lovely tonight." Mara's voice came out as a mumble, her tiredness slurring her words a bit. It wasn't long before she was asleep, snuggled up against me. I watched the sky for a while, the twinkling of the stars calming my overactive mind.

Eventually, I must have fallen asleep because suddenly I was being woken up by Mara tossing and turning, a quiet cry escaping her lips. It definitely wasn't her worst nightmare, but I pulled her into my arms to calm her. Her eyes fluttered open, and I could see her adjusting to reality as her arms wrapped around me. She put her head on my chest and sighed.

"I'm glad you're here, Kith."

"Where else would I be?" As I spoke, I thought of the cage I was thrown in not too long before. If it weren't for her quick acting, I wouldn't be here with her at all. I kept my thoughts to myself, though.

"I don't know." Her voice had a slight hesitance, as if she was thinking similar things as me. Unsure about whether or not I imagined it, I pushed all thoughts of the men with the cage out of my mind.

Instead, I kissed her forehead. "I'm not going anywhere."

We lay like that for a while and watched the sun rise over the trees. The beauty of the moment seemed so out of place in our lives. How were there moments like this that were so peaceful and beautiful with all the pain and heartache we had known?

Instead of appreciating the moment, my mind wandered to everyone we lost. Our unknown parents, a loss we couldn't remember, but still felt strongly in longing. Beatrice was the only real mother we knew, and we didn't even know what happened to her for sure. All the other freaks were family in some way. We didn't always get along, but did any family? In a way, Ducar even fit into that count. The Ducar before the storm.

And now Isaac. He tried to prepare us for his loss, but it was still devastating. We were alone again. At least we had some new skills from the months we spent not moving.

I knew soon we would need to eat and be on our way, but I was reluctant to leave the tree. I almost felt like we could forget our pain here.

"I'm so tired." Mara looked up at me and I could see dark circles marring the soft skin under her eyes. She laid her head back on my chest and I could feel her exhaustion. Adjusting back to being on the run was hard for us, especially with the weight of grief making us want to sleep more. When we did get sleep, it was usually broken by her nightmares.

"I'm tired, too. Let's stay here for a bit and rest." I stroked her hair with my fingers. "I'm pretty sure we're safe here for now, maybe we should just take a while to get some extra sleep."

Mara nodded wordlessly into my chest, her eyes already closing. Extra rest was definitely what we needed. Allowing my eyes to close, I drifted off into a deep sleep.

Every night, I found my thoughts drifting to our evenings with Isaac and the reminder that we'd never see him again hit all over. To make it worse, we had lost much of our endurance and we were running out of the food Isaac left for us. Not for the first time, anger rushed through me as I remembered those kids who ran Kith off. I wished we could have stayed by that town to get some more supplies. At least we were now more skilled with finding food for ourselves.

What would Isaac think of the way I saved Kith? I knew I likely could have found a way to get him free without hurting anyone, but it was hard to feel bad about hurting those people. They hurt him first, and he didn't do anything to them. Why should I feel bad about making sure they wouldn't be hurting him any more?

Pushing all the thoughts down, I decided not to dwell on it any longer. Maybe some stew would help us feel better. Rising up, I started getting out everything I'd need. We were out of potatoes, but I thought the roots might make a good substitution for them.

Kith and I built a fire together, and as I filled the pot with water from our skins, I realized we were also running out of water. When I pointed this out to Kith, I could see the alarm pass through his face.

"How much do you need for the stew?"

"Well, I can try to use less. We just need enough to cook everything, really." I poured just enough water to cover everything into the pot and set it on the fire.

Once everything was cooking, I went to our packs and grabbed out Gracie. After leaving, I packed her away and hadn't even looked at her. It hurt to look at all the things Isaac gave me, and it hurt most of all to look at her. I hugged her close and let the tears stream down my face.

Shame filled me for neglecting Gracie for so long. Isaac would have been sad to know that I abandoned her. I sat on the ground and began playing with her, occasionally wiping away the tears that wouldn't stop coming.

While I was rocking Gracie, a smell started tickling my nose, hinting at something. At first, I ignored it, absorbed in my thoughts. The smell only got stronger, though, and suddenly I realized it was the smell of something burning. Panicking, I rushed to the pot and yanked up the lid. All the water I put into the pot was gone, and the vegetables were spotted black.

Just after opening the lid, I heard Kith coming back from his attempt to find food or water, and I knew I must have been playing for a long time. I couldn't believe I let our food burn, when we were already running low on both food and water. My eyes were blurring with more tears as Kith stepped up beside me and looked into the pot.

"Maybe we shouldn't have put in less water," he said as he wrapped his arm around me and pulled me toward him. "It's alright Mara, I'm sure we can eat it anyway. Not everything is burnt."

Pulling myself away from him, I wiped at the tears now streaming fiercely down my face. "It's all my fault! You should have the parts that aren't burnt and I'll eat the black stuff. You shouldn't have to eat that just because I can't make it right without Isaac telling me what to do! We're almost out of food and water, and I burnt the little we did have left. What are we going to do now?" Panic rose inside me as I thought about our situation. It was as though my emotions were numbed since we left and now everything was coming out all at once. I couldn't stop the tears flooding my cheeks.

Kith looked taken aback by my outburst, and I watched as his face crumbled. "Mara, it has nothing to do with you needing someone to tell you what to do. I haven't tried hard enough to find us supplies. It's been hard to focus on anything. Isaac worked so hard to make sure we were ready to come back out on our own, and I haven't done a single thing he taught me. I'm sorry, Mara."

I knew Kith went through as much of a slump as me. Isaac became such an important part of our lives, and losing him was hard for both of us. I stepped up to Kith and wrapped my arms around him.

"We have to do better. We both do. For Isaac."

Kith's arms tightened around me and I felt his body shake a little as he whispered, "For Isaac."

*   Kith   *

Thinking about food, or anything really, was difficult. Whenever we were walking, it felt like we were going through a thick fog. The world seemed different, and being out in it again felt empty. I remembered missing the outdoors, but now I wondered why. Maybe we failed to see how lucky we really were.

After stumbling upon the lumpy, tasteless roots under the tree, I realized just how hungry we actually were. Isaac worried we would struggle after he died, but none of us thought about us not even trying.

Embarrassment and shame flooded through me. All of Isaac's care and lessons would be wasted if we just gave up. Not just his, but Beatrice's as well. I was letting them down on top of letting Mara down.

Was Mara hungry all this time, but not saying anything to spare my feelings? My heart hurt at the thought.

When we set up camp that night, I told Mara I was going for a walk. After wandering a short distance from our small fort, I set some traps. There was only enough material from what Isaac gave me to make four, but it was better than nothing. Maybe using what I learned from him would help us cope with losing Isaac. Even if not, I needed to try. I promised Mara I would.

When I got back to camp, Mara was inside snuggled up in her blanket. "Did you enjoy your walk?"

"It was alright." I wasn't sure why I didn't want to mention that I was setting up traps, but I couldn't bring myself to tell her. "We should try to get some sleep."

She didn't argue. We were still adjusting to our changing schedule and were exhausted at most times, so sleep came quickly for both of us.

I woke in the middle of the night, my body confused and fighting sleep again. After laying in my quilt for a few minutes, I gave up and crept out of the fort. The night was cool and it felt nice outside. It was getting warmer during the days.

Sitting next to the spot where we cooked the last of the clumps, I listened to the sounds of night. Animals were moving around, and I heard some birds flying above me. Night was familiar, and it felt peaceful. For the first time in weeks, I breathed deep and allowed myself to feel calm.

Mara emerged from the fort just before the sun started to rise and came to sit next to me. "How long have you been up?" Her voice had a tinge of worry to it.

"I'm not sure. Maybe a couple of hours." The passing of time surprised me. I didn't realize I was here that long until she asked.

She put her head on my shoulder and I wrapped my arm around her. "I miss him, Kith. Sometimes I wish I hadn't promised him we'd be alright."

The sight of Mara in Isaac's lap giving him permission to rest filled my mind. "You were right to, Mara. It's hard, but he deserved to find peace."

"I know." Her voice sounded so small, and I was reminded again of how my baby sister was more grown up than she should have to be.

After a few minutes of quiet, I whispered, "I put out some traps last night. I'll go check them in a few minutes. Maybe we'll have some meat for today."

Mara nodded, but remained silent. I had a feeling she was remembering the same conversation that prompted me to set them. Either that, or she just didn't want to get too hopeful about the prospect of fresh meat and full bellies.

I sat for a little longer, reluctant to break the calm. I knew I couldn't put off facing the day any longer, though, especially with the light spreading quickly across the sky. As I rose slowly to my feet, I realized that I suddenly wanted to go back to sleep. Pushing the tiredness away, I walked to where I left the first trap. It had been set off, but hadn't managed to snag whatever triggered it.

Sighing, I collected the materials and bundled them back up before moving on. The next trap seemed completely untouched. I tried to shove my disappointment and worry down as I realized I was half way through my traps and had nothing.

I approached the next trap cautiously, not wanting to scare away any potential catches. As I drew close, I spotted movement. A large badger was swinging in the net, angrily chewing at the ropes. If I waited much longer, it probably would have escaped.

Using the techniques Isaac taught me, I quickly put the animal down, carrying it by the tail as I went to check the last trap. I could smell the blood before I approached. While I mostly used nets for simplicity, I was curious about the log drop trap that I learned. That was what I used here.

Once the trap was in sight, the first thing I saw was a clump of brown fur. As I lifted the log, I realized I never spotted an animal like this one before. It was long and brown, with white running down it's belly. It's legs were short, but I was surprised to see six of them. I knew that there were animals with six legs, but they were more rare. It looked like the type of animal Mara would adore, which made me remember the night that I learned about skinning animals.

Poor Mara looked so sick at the sight. She never really watched me prepare our food before, and it seemed quite a shock to her. I vowed to keep her from as much as I could, to try and preserve what little childhood she had left. Briefly, I wondered if it would be different now, but decided it was best not to find out. Since I was a decent distance from our camp, I decided to go ahead and deal with the skinning where I was and only bring back the meat.

It didn't take me long, and I headed back feeling accomplished. Isaac would be proud to see me use what he taught. When I approached the camp I was almost smiling. Mara's eyes met mine, and she offered a timid smile. "That's a lot of meat." She didn't say it, but her eyes were glowing with the reflection of my thoughts.

I handed the meat over to Mara since it was now her job to cook more. As she walked over to the fire with it I realized there wasn't a fire when I left. She must have started it out of a show of belief in me. I was even more glad I didn't come back empty handed.

We cooked up all the meat, using as little of the spices from Isaac as we could. I knew getting more would probably not be easy, and I didn't want to run out too soon. The delicious meals we shared with him had slightly spoiled us, and I didn't want to go back to completely unseasoned meat any time soon.

After our meal, we packed up the extra meat and all of our stuff to head out once again. "I guess I was right, huh, Kith?"

I looked down at her with questions in my eyes, but then it hit me. "Oh. I told you that you were."

"I know." She put her hand in mine, but didn't say anything else.

Lightly squeezing her hand, I whispered, "We'll be alright."

CHAPTER TWELVE: JUNE

✳   Kith   ✳

As Mara started pulling out the things to fix our dinner, I looked at how low our stores were. I already knew I needed to head to the town tonight. We passed it a while back, and I didn't know when we'd run into another one.

The first time going back into a town was difficult. My traps were helpful, but not nearly as much as I hoped. If we felt safe staying still for a few days at a time, they would've been better, but I felt an extreme need to stay on the move after being still all winter.

I tried to avoid raiding shops as much as possible, and when I did go into one, I only took a few things. Attention was the last thing we wanted. Everything I brought back was portioned out to last us several days at a time so that my trips could be pretty infrequent.

Even so, I wasn't thrilled with how empty our food and water always seemed to be lately. The increasing heat made rationing out the water more difficult, though. Hopefully, the well wasn't overly exposed and no one was out wandering around.

Shouldering my pack, I said farewell to Mara with my usual cautions and moved toward the town as fast as I could. Scouting wouldn't be possible, as there were no good vantage points. I would just have to be careful.

Cautiously moving through the shadows, I crept as low and close to buildings as I could. Hearing anything past the thundering of my heart was difficult. Even though I had done this many times, it still terrified me. Pausing at the edge of a building, I took some time to look around.

The night was still, much to my relief. No one seemed to be out, and the moon was thin, giving off very little light. With my exceptional night vision, this was the perfect scenario. Spotting the well didn't take long. Since filling the skins would be the biggest risk, I decided to get it over with first.

Cranking up the bucket took a lot longer than I wanted, and my arms grew tired. Luckily, one bucketful was enough to fill two of the skins, so I only had to pull it up twice. Once they were full, I gulped down the bit that was left. Having completely full water skins was a huge relief. I headed back to cover quickly, breathing deep once I was secure. I hadn't realized I was holding my breath most of the time I was getting the water.

Once I was breathing regularly again, I began digging through the trash close to the house I was hiding beside. For trash, it didn't smell nearly as horrid as I came to expect. Right on top sat a mostly untouched roast. I had no clue what type of meat it was, but we weren't very picky. It was big enough to last us a couple of meals. Shoving it in the pack, I went back to digging. There were some scraps of bread and vegetables, but not a lot more. Even so, I was off to a much better start than I hoped.

Sneaking around the rest of the buildings, I was able to stock up on enough to not need to go into any shops. Several smaller pieces of cooked meats and a couple full loaves of stale bread made for a decent haul. The abundance of vegetable scraps was a great addition, even though I wasn't sure how long they would last us. Maybe Mara could make a stew from them and some of the meat. It would help with the taste that always accompanies eating food from the trash. Stale bread would probably be better dipped into stew, as well.

Taking one last look around, I quickly ducked out of town and started running back the way I came. Excitement for the large amount I was bringing back fueled me, enabling me to push past the growing exhaustion.

Suddenly, I heard a loud sound. I couldn't quite identify it at first, but then I recognized it as a low snarl. It came from my right, so I veered left and sped up, not even taking the time to spot what was lurking nearby.

Movement up ahead made me falter. I realized, too late, that I was being herded into a trap. Judging by the sounds behind me, there were several animals completely surrounding me. They looked similar to wild dogs, but their skin was black and smooth with no fur. And they were hungry. Gleaming red eyes stared right at me as they closed in, baring fangs as long as my fingers.

*   Mara   *

After Kith left for the town, I began preparing our meal. Ever since I burned the stew, I was careful to keep a close watch whenever I was cooking. I cut up one of Kith's most recent catches and put the biggest parts in the pot. The meat was small and I guessed it was probably a squirrel, but I didn't ask Kith. He always skinned the meat before bringing it back to spare me from seeing the process, and I was happy not to know what poor animal he caught. I set aside some of our last vegetables to add once the meat was cooked, and wondered if I should use any of our spices. I loved the extra flavor, but we were almost out of all of them. In the end, I decided to save them for something else.

While the food cooked, I thought about how much our situation changed since before we lived in our little cave. When I realized how far Kith had come with his trust in me, I couldn't help but smile. I remembered the frustration I once felt with how little I could contribute and how much of a burden I was. Now, I made all of our meals, helped build the fires and occasionally even helped Kith build his traps. Of course, I never went with him to check the traps, I couldn't stand the idea of seeing a poor animal struggling to get away. I was happy with my new role, and every day I was more aware of how much Isaac helped us both grow.

After a while, the scent of the meat started to change and I knew it was getting close to being done. Using a small knife, I checked the meat to make sure it was cooked through. The first time I cooked after burning the stew, Kith took a big bite of meat only to find that it was still red and bloody in the middle. I was so worried about burning the food that I didn't let it cook long enough.

The memory made me smile a little. I was so anxious about the food that when I saw blood dripping down Kith's face

270

after that first bite, I felt ready to cry again.

Kith reassured me that the food could always be cooked more, but it was hard to cook it less. It became a bit of a joke between us now, where Kith would ask how I cooked his food today.

All the same, I was careful now to make sure the food was cooked, but not over-cooked. Once the vegetables were also done, I put it all into the pot and set the lid on top to keep it warm. I usually finished cooking before Kith made it back from the town, but it never took him long.

While waiting, I decided to play with my doll. I had taken to carrying her with me daily. The sight of her caused me so much pain at first, but I knew that was something I needed to work through. I couldn't stop the memories from coming, so I decided to embrace them. Now, every time I looked at Gracie, it brought a smile as I remembered the man who gave her to me.

After I played for what seemed like a much longer time than usual, I began to wonder what was taking Kith so long. The food in the pot was still slightly warm when I checked but it had cooled a lot. Thinking surely Kith would be back soon and would want his food hot, I set the pot back on the fire to warm it back up.

After a few minutes, I stirred the food and set the pot back out of the fire with the lid still on it. I was beginning to worry about Kith. It shouldn't take him this long to make it back.

✳   Kith   ✳

Running for the closest tree, I tried to scramble up into it. My claws caught the bark, but fangs closed in on my left leg and dug deep. Pain seared through me as the dog-like animal shook its head wildly, and my hands released in reaction. Slamming into the ground knocked the air out of me and spilled my bag. I could feel the blood running down the leg that was still encased in teeth. Wildly thrashing, I kicked the head that was attached to me, causing it to open enough for me to yank my leg free.

The meat that fell out of my pack stole the attention of the other animals, leaving just the dazed one I kicked focused on me. Leaping toward me again, its foot landed on a water skin, squirting the contents over its own legs. Startled by the water, it paused, giving me a chance to recover some of my senses.

Thirsty animals moved in, lapping at the water that sprayed out, and when that wasn't enough, the skin was quickly shredded before the glinting eyes turned back in my direction. I had to move, but my leg wouldn't hold my weight. Looking at it would be hazardous, though, so I had no clue how bad the damage was. Grabbing my pack, I threw one of the smaller pieces of meat out to distract the beasts again, and crawled on my good leg to the base of the tree.

Claws digging into the bark, I shoved myself upward as fast as I could. Intense pain shooting through me caused my vision to go white and red. Unable to see much of what I was doing, I felt around and secured my claws higher up, using my tail to give myself a boost. As I was lifting myself higher, teeth grabbed at my leg again, ripping some of the already shredded skin. If my claws hadn't been embedded deep, I would have fallen again, probably not getting up this time.

Kicking and thrashing, I managed to rip myself free. Pulling myself up was becoming increasingly difficult. Strength was failing me. My tail found a branch above me and wrapped around. After a deep breath, I pushed off against the trunk and swung myself up, the impact sending another shock of pain through me.

Resting didn't seem like a good idea, not with several animals moving below me. I could feel them jumping against the tree, and the night was filled with their growls. Steadying on my better leg, I reached for the next branches and scrambled up. Bark scratched at my wound and I bit my lip to keep from screaming.

Going further up would be best, but I knew I couldn't. Visibility was fading fast as the pain overwhelmed my body. Pulling my shirt off, I did my best to wrap my leg, but I knew it wasn't going to do much good. It was badly damaged. Walking back to camp wasn't going to happen any time soon.

Mara would be extremely worried. Images of her terrified

and alone floated through my head as the world went black.

*   Mara   *

Once the food was again cold, I began to panic. Kith never took this long in the town. My first thought was *maybe he got lost*, but I dismissed that quickly. Kith's sense of direction was the best, and of all the times he went out into the woods with no plan on how to get back, he always found his way easily.

I knew Kith wouldn't have taken this long to get supplies. He was always so cautious and his trips into the town were as brief as he could make them. The only option left was that something bad happened to him.

What if someone in the town found him?

It worked out well for us when Isaac accidentally caught Kith in a trap, but what were the odds of another person being as understanding as Isaac? After extinguishing the fire, I made a small hole to bury the pot that held our now cold food. I hoped the hole would keep animals away so when we got back we could eat it. Then, I rolled up our blankets and hid them under a pile of leaves. Kith would want me to be careful to hide our camp, even with the panic I was feeling.

My hands shook as I finished hiding everything. I couldn't imagine what was happening to Kith right now. At first, I set off in the direction of the town at a brisk walk. Then, when I couldn't stand it anymore I broke out into a full run.

What am I going to do if someone has caught him? I wondered as my panic continued to spiral. I was imagining scenarios where Kith was being tortured by town members, maybe even being stuffed into a cage to wait for Ducar to retrieve the "monster." Images of my claws thrashing at skin filled my mind. I pushed them away, but even as I did, I realized that I'd do whatever it took to make sure he was safe.

Every now and then, I would quietly call out Kith's name. I didn't want to alert anyone to my coming, but I knew our hearing was better than most. If he was nearby he would hear me before anyone else would.

Once I got to the clearing that made way for the town Kith left to visit, I stopped so abruptly I teetered on my toes before landing back on my feet. Although I had never been to a town without Kith, I knew I would have to approach this more carefully than to just run right in calling his name. How would I know where he was?

Squinting hard at all the buildings and the lights in the town, I tried to make out any disturbances that could have been caused by someone finding a strange looking child. There weren't many lights even on and I couldn't see anything or anyone moving around. Slowly creeping toward the town, I was getting close to the first house, when I saw a footprint leading right where I was going. Kith stepped in a soft spot of earth that showed me this was where he entered the town. I began searching the area for any more footprints.

I reached a shop a few doors down from where the first set of footprints were, and spotted one heading in the opposite direction.

So Kith was leaving. Did someone catch him before he made it out?

Following the direction of that print, I found another one just outside the town. Now confusion hit me. The footprints suggested Kith made it out of the town alright. Why didn't he come back? I continued in the direction of the footprint, scanning the ground for another clue. I was back inside the cover of the trees before I saw a new footprint. This one looked like a paw and as I squinted at the ground around me, I saw several large paw prints.

Deciding to continue my search from tree branches in case these animals were still nearby, I scrambled up and grabbed with my tail, swinging my body forward. At each new branch, I scanned the ground until I finally saw another one of Kith's footprints. This print was headed off to the side rather than in the direction of our camp. I soon saw several other footprints leading in the same direction. I also saw many paw prints.

Understanding trickled through my brain and my insides

turned to ice. I threw all caution to the wind and began yelling Kith's name in hysteria. In the distance, I caught sight of one of our packs ripped up and strewn across the ground. As I approached it, I saw dark splotches all over the ground. The smell of blood filled my nose and tears began to pool in my eyes. I was now screaming Kith's name with no response.

Suddenly, my vision faded and a warm sensation passed over my body. It felt like Kith was sitting right next to me. As strange as it sounded, I was completely sure he was alive. When my vision cleared, I dropped to the ground and ran to the bloody scene. I saw smears of blood all over the tree trunk and my eyes followed it up, all the way to the mass that lay in one of the branches.

"KITH!" I jumped with all my might, claws digging into the tree then swung myself upward from branch to branch until I reached my brother. Gently, I rolled him over, terrified of what I was about to discover. His eyes were closed, and he didn't stir as I moved him. His shirt was tied around his leg, and soaked through with blood. I began unraveling the shirt to get a look at the wound. I had to keep myself busy, I couldn't focus on the lack of response I was getting. I unwrapped his leg quickly and saw the bloody mess that was once a leg.

A scream of pain tore through the night, and relief flooded my body.

"Mara!?" Kith's eyes were fogged over and confusion was all over his face.

"Did you manage to get any water? I need to clean your leg." Now that he was awake, my senses were cleared and I knew that I needed to act fast to take care of him. He slowly began to reach for the pack that was still strapped to his back. Motioning for him to stop, I grabbed one of the skins I now saw tied to the pack. Pouring water on the leg, I tried to keep my face neutral even with the sight of all the torn skin. Kith sat rigid with his eyes clenched shut and his jaw set tight. I knew he must be in excruciating pain.

Looking at the mess before me, I felt the sinking realization that there was only one thing I could do. "I have to go to the town."

Kith's eyes flew open, "Mara, what…"

"You need bandages and medicine. More than what we've got at camp. I have to go now. If we wait too long, it will only get worse."

Quickly, I wrapped the bloody shirt back around Kith's leg that was still fresh with blood. It needed to be covered with something, but I knew his dirty shirt could not be good for an open wound. Kith tried to stop me, but he was in no shape to do much, and I wasted no time in wrapping him up and quickly heading off with the now empty water skin and what was left of the torn pack that lay on the ground.

Sprinting through the trees, I was vaguely aware of the dim light that announced morning was fast approaching. I would have to be quick if I was going to get all the things we needed before anyone woke up. This time, I did not stop at the edge of the clearing. I plowed straight through to the town, running past all the buildings, taking just a quick peek inside. Finally, I spotted a house with several plants growing in a little garden, and as I approached I recognized a large stock of feverfew. I peeked inside and knew immediately that this was the medicine man's house. Approaching the door, I tried to open it. It was locked. I looked around in panic. I had to get into that house.

My eyes fell on a large stone, and I only hesitated for a second before grabbing it and plunging it into a window. The noise it made was loud, and I knew I must move even faster now. Squeezing through the broken glass, I felt the sharp edges scraping my skin in a few places. Once inside, I yanked bandages off shelves and spotted jars of clear liquid that looked like water. I remembered times when Beatrice poured a clear liquid over a cut Kith or I got. The stuff always stung, but she explained it was the only way to keep the cut clean and make sure we never got an infection.

Grabbing two of the bottles, I shoved them into my pack. Knowing it was risky, I ran to the kitchen to look for a pot and cup. I knew Kith was going to be in a lot of pain and feverfew tea was the best way to help that, but our pot was back at camp full of food and I needed a way to make the tea. Picking up a small pot, I thought about how little space we already had for carrying things. We would probably have to leave this behind when we moved on.

If we could move on.

Shaking that thought from my head, I ran to the door just as I heard someone coming.

While sprinting back toward the trees, I spotted laundry hanging on a line. Dashing to it, I grabbed the first shirt I saw. Kith would need something new to wear after getting blood all over his. As I continued running, I heard someone yelling. They must be waking up to find their broken window. A sting of guilt hit me, but the only thing that mattered at that moment was getting back to Kith.

✻   Kith   ✻

Mara's insistence on returning to the town I just left terrified me. Good luck didn't seem to last for us, and until the animals, I was having great luck at that town. Mara had never even gone into one aside from our time with Isaac. Now, she was suddenly going in alone, when the sun was only a couple of hours away from rising.

Unable to do anything but lie in the tree, I listened as hard as I could. My vision kept fading and slowly returning, but I refused to lose myself to the darkness again until Mara was back safely. Blood was seeping through the shirt wrapped around my leg. Looking at it turned my stomach, but I knew I couldn't remove it without the bandages Mara went to retrieve.

Waves of darkness kept hitting me, and I was hit with images of Mara fading while in my arms. At the time, I felt a weird heat and energy, and she came back from the brink of death. Maybe, if I focused hard enough, I could do whatever I did to her and heal my leg. If only I knew what exactly I did.

Bending carefully over my leg, I gingerly placed my hands on the bloody shirt. Trying to ignore the twist in my stomach and the pain in my leg, I focused on my hands. Willing energy to spring forth and heal me, I squinted and glared at my hands. Nothing was happening. I tried to remember what happened before the burst of energy, but it was all fuzzy.

It was fuzzy even when I wasn't on the edge of passing back out from an injury, but all my focus was gone. I could barely even see straight, much less summon some mystical energy. Shaking my head, I tried again. I couldn't give up that easily. My arms raised up and came down quickly, as if I could force the healing power out of them with quick movements.

"Heal! Please heal!" It started as a yell, but ended as a cry. It was useless. Even if I did know how to do what I did, I probably wasn't strong enough.

Irritated at my own uselessness, I thrashed at the tree with my claws. The bark crumbled off and I saw the stringy threads of wood that lay under the top layer of bark. I grabbed and yanked big handfuls of it out, laying them on the branch next to me. Soon, my hands and claws were covered in a sticky goo. The more I tried to rub it off, the more annoying it got, and slowly, it started to turn black.

Giving up, I looked at the pile next to me. The long strips brought back memories of sitting in Isaac's house looking at books. There were pictures that fit this tree. Mara was curious about what the pictures meant. After some confusion, Isaac was able to explain that we were looking at an Eochee tree, which was known for the ability to create sturdy rope from the flesh right under its bark.

Desperate for something to occupy my mind, I straightened all the strands and started braiding them together, adding in new strands when the ones I was using started getting short, and twisting them together. I tried to make it look like it did in the pictures, but it wasn't easy.

As I was ripping out more strands, being extra careful this time to get longer ones, I heard Mara approaching cautiously. She looked at my new spot and the ripped bark in silence, obviously trying to sort me out and figure out what she could say. The worry in her eyes was evident.

"Look, Mara. It's that tree we learned about with the stringy stuff under the bark that can be braided into rope. I thought it might be helpful." I shrugged, avoiding her eyes, uncomfortable with her concern.

Mara was silent for a moment longer. "Rope would probably be useful." I could see the exhaustion and wariness all over her face, but she ignored it. "Kith, I need to clean and bandage you now. It might hurt, but we can't let your leg get infected."

Grimacing, she slowly removed the bloody shirt. Not a spot on it was free of blood anymore. She threw it gently onto a nearby branch before squirting some water on my leg. Biting down hard, I didn't even realize the hole I made in my cheek due to the intense pain coursing through my leg. Once she cleaned off most of the blood, she eyed the damage, trying; and failing, to mask the extreme worry.

"How bad is it? I haven't had a chance to really look." Keeping the pain out of my voice was difficult.

Slowly, Mara spoke. "We're going to have to secure a spot where you can rest for a while." After a short pause, she added, "A long while."

Grabbing a different bottle she got from town, she poured some of the liquid over the wound. Incredibly intense pain shot through me, and I couldn't hold back the groan that was almost a scream. Mara winced at my pain, but continued cleaning my torn leg. When she was satisfied, she pulled out a large bandage and carefully wrapped it tightly.

"The good news is there isn't much bleeding right now." A small sigh escaped before she could stop it. "Oh. I got this for you, too." She handed me a shirt that was a bit larger than the one now hanging from a neighboring tree, but at least it was blood free.

"Thank you." I decided not to ask how she managed to get all this, my stomach already knotted enough without knowing the details. At least she came back safely.

Jumping down from the tree, she began gathering wood.

"What are you doing?" I asked, struggling to speak loud enough for her to hear.

"I need to make you some feverfew tea for the pain. It should help you sleep."

The sun was starting to rise. I realized that Mara must have been up all night; first worried about me, then looking for me, then raiding a town. Guilt ripped through me. I should have been more careful coming back. At least we were both relatively safe, for now.

"Mara, I'm fine really. You should get some sleep." Without even responding, she continued making a fire and didn't pay me any attention until she was handing me a cup of tea. I tried to hide my disdain while drinking it, not wanting to complain after all her hard work, but the extreme bitterness made it difficult to finish.

"Alright, you've got me all patched up. Now can we get some sleep?"

Nodding slowly, Mara curled up against me. Neither of us had the energy to try to build a bed, we just fell asleep leaning against the trunk of the tree, my arm wrapped around her protectively.

*   Mara   *

When I woke up, the sun was well on its way across the sky telling me that Kith and I slept much later than we normally did. Looking over at him, I saw that he was already awake, watching me. I knew I must have woken him up with my stirring. The nightmare hadn't been a bad one, but Kith was always on the alert when it came to me and my nightmares.

Not wanting him to dwell on it, I sat up and looked at his leg.

"How do you feel?"

He looked at me and I could see his quick debate on whether to answer truthfully. "It's not too bad," he replied, but I knew he was in a lot of pain. I wondered then if he actually got any sleep.

"I'm going to go get our stuff and bring it here. You're in no shape to go anywhere so we'll have to camp here for a while." I stretched as I spoke, waking my body up for the journey ahead.

Kith sat up abruptly, beginning to argue, but a flash of pain flew across his face and he changed his mind. "I guess it might be good to stay here for a day or two, but I should be fine after that."

Even though I was sure Kith wasn't going to be walking on that mess of a leg any time soon, I didn't argue.

"Stay in the trees while you travel, Mara. Just in case those animals are still around. They might have found our stuff, if there's anything wrong just come back here and leave it for later," Kith's voice was close to hysterics.

"Kith," I said soothingly, "I'll be fine. I buried our things before I left, so I don't think they would have found them. I will check the area and make sure they're all gone before I set foot on the ground. Okay?"

He looked at me sheepishly, aware that he was being over protective again. "I'm sorry, Mara. I just want you to stay safe."

After assuring him that I would take every precaution, I grabbed our remaining bag and set off back to our campsite. Try as I might not to think too much about the situation we were in, I couldn't stop the sense of dread that shrouded me. I wasn't sure how long Kith's leg would take to heal, or if it ever would completely. It was so mangled and bloody, I couldn't believe he thought he would be walking on it in only a couple of days. I was only grateful we were close enough to the town for me to get the right supplies to clean it. Without them, I was sure he would never use the leg again. Not with that dirty cloth on there.

Dragging myself out of my thoughts, I realized I was almost to our campsite and hadn't been paying any attention to my surroundings. Feeling guilty after promising Kith I would be cautious, I doubled back a little and looked around just to make sure there were no signs of the paw prints nearby. I finally got back to our camp and was surprised by how long it took. With how worried I was the night before, I hadn't realized how far I traveled. After surveying the area closely, I jumped out of the trees and quickly packed up the bag.

My stomach growling reminded me of the untouched pot of meat and vegetables. We never got a chance to eat with everything that happened. It didn't take long to dig our things up. I'd have to arrange them carefully in the pack to carry it all. I placed the pot at the bottom and padded it with our blankets so it wasn't banging into my back the whole time. Once I finally had everything ready to go, I realized that it had taken me longer than I expected. I needed to get back to Kith. Looking up at the sky, I couldn't help but sigh. By the time I got back with our things most of the day would be gone, and I still needed to build us a shelter.

The trip back was slow. Even with my careful packing, my bag was quite heavy and I hadn't built up enough strength to run with extra weight. Until that moment, I didn't realize how much extra Kith carried. My muscles ached with exhaustion by the time I reached him, and it took all of my strength not to collapse on the ground.

When I approached the tree Kith was laying in, he sat up and I could see the worry all over his face.

"I'm alright," I sighed, "It just took a while to pack everything up so the food wouldn't spill while I was walking."

Kith relaxed and I began dishing up some food for each of us. Of course it was cold by now, but I was so hungry I barely noticed. After wolfing down my portion, I got ready to work on our fort.

"Maybe we should just make something small for now and we can work on something better later. Surely my leg won't take long to heal enough for us to build a nice fort together."

My lips tightened into a thin line as I considered what to say next. "Have you looked at your leg?" I asked softly.

He shrugged. It was hard to tell if he was pretending for my sake or if he truly didn't understand how bad his leg was. With everything going on, he probably hadn't taken the time to really look at the injury.

"My vision wasn't great when I wrapped it." He said as if he read my mind.

"It's not good." I sighed. "You need time to heal." After a short pause, I added, "Probably a lot of time."

Shock filled his face, and I knew he wasn't pretending. He really hadn't understood just how bad the situation was. Unable to take the conversation any longer, I started busying myself with clearing an area to make our fort.

Never having built our shelter before, I wasn't really sure how to do it. Still, I wanted to try it on my own before asking Kith, so I gathered long sticks and set them all around a large tree. I thought it might be useful to use the tree as one of our walls. This way if something or someone came near us while we were in the shelter, we could climb it. That would be the only way of escape for Kith for quite some time until his leg healed.

Jamming the long sticks in the ground around the tree, I tried to make a circle. When I stepped back to look at it, though, it became obvious we wouldn't have anything covering our heads. After some thought, I remembered how Kith always angled the sticks a little so I pulled them all back out of the ground. It was too late for me to start over, though, so I decided to wait to try again.

Once the sticks were back in their pile, Kith called me to him. "I hate that you're doing everything. I can't move very well on my own, but if you can help me get down, I can build a fire while you gather the sticks." Seeing how much it pained him to watch me doing everything, I swung up to the tree and tried to figure out how we could get him down without damaging his leg.

We decided the rope Kith made from the tree would be the only way to lower him down gently, but he hadn't made enough of it to get him all the way to the ground. He tried to argue that he could claw his way down the same way he got up, but I wasn't sure that was a good idea either. Eventually, we decided we would stay in the tree for at least another night. He could make more rope while I worked on the fort. I knew he was unhappy with the decision, but at least there was something useful for him to do.

After we finished eating the next morning, Kith immediately asked me to help him out of the tree, showing me how much rope he made while I was fast asleep. Desperation filled his face and voice, and my heart ached for him.

"I don't think it's a good idea yet. Let's see how the day goes and maybe we can try later." Swinging down out of the tree, I picked up where I left off the night before with our shelter.

Again, I jammed the sticks into the ground, but this time I tried to angle them so they would rest against the tree in the middle. After repositioning some sticks a few times to make them actually reach the tree, I stepped back to look at it again. This time, I stepped inside only to find that having the tree in the middle gave us very little space inside.

I was beginning to get frustrated now at how long the process was taking me. Kith always made our shelters so easily. Pulling all the sticks back out of the ground, I decided to simply build the fort right beside the tree. It was getting late, though, so I decided to break and bring some lunch up to Kith, trying my best to hide my frustration from him.

His feelings weren't as easy to hide. "I wish you'd let me help." His pout reminded me of a young child like the ones we had seen comforted by their parents at the show.

"I know. I understand the feeling well." I tried not to take his request as a slight against my struggles, but it was difficult.

"I'm sorry you've felt this way for so long." Kith looked like he wanted to say more, but he was obviously exhausted.

"I know. Get some rest. I'm going to get back to work."

By the time I managed to get the biggest sticks to stay in place it was quite dark and I realized there was no way I'd be able to finish without some rest. I climbed back up the tree, my body aching from the work and dropped to sleep beside my snoring brother.

✳   Kith   ✳

Mara having to do everything on her own was draining on her. I could tell how exhausted she was, even though she tried hard to hide it. She also made it clear that me complaining about not helping with the fort wasn't going to get me anywhere.

As a wave of pain went through my leg, Mara's words echoed in my mind. Was it really that bad? I looked down at her, working so hard on making the fort just right. Would she be working so hard, letting herself get so exhausted, if she didn't think we needed to stay here for a long time?

Staring at my carefully wrapped leg, I debated on

284

unwrapping it and taking a look, but I felt frozen. Once I looked at it, I'd know for sure how bad it was, but I wondered if I was truly ready to face that information.

Apparently, I sat frozen in debate for a lot longer than I thought, as suddenly Mara was next to me, offering food. Her eyes showed her worry at the fact that I hadn't responded yet but she didn't say much, or maybe she did and I didn't hear it.

Seeing her exhausted, but still making sure I got food, broke me out of my trance. Desperation filled my voice as I spoke, "Can we try getting me out of the tree again? I'd like to be on the ground. Maybe I could find a way to help finish the fort without causing my leg more problems." Hearing the whine in my voice was embarrassing, but I couldn't stop it.

Mara's eyes were full of emotions as she spoke carefully. "I don't think it's a good idea for you to be on the ground before I have a safe spot for you to sleep. I know the fort is taking me longer than it always takes you, and I'm sorry. I don't think you're going to be able to help with this one."

As she made her way back down to the fort, shame overwhelmed me. While trying to be helpful I hurt Mara. Insulting her progress with the fort wasn't my intention at all. My frustration getting the better of me, I ripped at a new area of bark. Suddenly, I realized I tore deeper into the tree than I meant to, causing real damage; not just to the tree, but to the inner bark I was using for the rope. The one chance to be useful I was given, and I messed it up badly.

My hands curled in fists seemingly on their own and my eyes stung as I fought back tears. "Get a grip, Kith," I muttered to myself, struggling to catch my breath and calm down. After several minutes, I forced myself to find a new spot and start gathering strands for the rope. My hands didn't take long to get extremely sticky, but I ignored it. The only thing I allowed myself to focus on was the rope I was creating.

"Looks like you've got about enough for us to get you down once the fort is finished." Mara's voice right next to me caught me off guard, and I jumped, wincing as pain shot through me. The worry was still evident on her face, "Sorry. I didn't mean to startle you."

"You're fine. I guess I was just really focused." I smiled sheepishly, and avoided her eyes. Her perceptiveness was not something I wanted to deal with at the moment.

"Well, it got you good results..." Her voice trailed off as she noticed the spot of the tree I destroyed, but she handed me my food and tea without saying anything else.

Famished from my work and healing, I dug in with a greater enthusiasm than I expected.

Mara seemed pleased to see me eating well, but she looked at my still full tea cup with disdain. "Kith, drink your tea. It will help."

Scoffing, I looked into the murky liquid. "It's gross, Mara. I hate it." A childish pout formed before I could stop it.

Coughing in a terrible attempt to hide her snort, she spoke sternly. "I don't care. You need to drink it." Her tone was serious, but there was a hint of a smile she couldn't hide.

Grumbling under my breath, I swallowed the bitter drink as quickly as I could, shuddering as I finished it off. She held back a giggle at my reaction. "If it helps you feel better, I've finished the fort. We should be able to move you down tomorrow."

Unsure of how to react, I smiled. "That's good to hear."

We were both completely worn out, so we curled up for sleep without much more talking. Getting comfortable wasn't easy, moving hurt and it was hard to get my leg in a spot that didn't cause more pain. Eventually, the tea started easing the pain and I drifted off into an uneasy sleep.

I woke up to Mara whimpering. Her exhaustion seemed to be lowering the intensity of her nightmare, or at least her reaction to it. If I wasn't so trained in reacting to her, I probably wouldn't have even been woken up by it. Guilt ripped through me. She shouldn't be working so hard to take care of me. That was my job.

Gently brushing the hair off her face, I murmured a lullaby, hoping to ease her into a more peaceful sleep without her waking. As she calmed, I lay back down beside her. Excruciating pain ripped through my leg with every movement that I made, and I bit my lip to keep from yelling out from it. Knowing that sleep would not return through the blinding pain, I stared at my surroundings. What was I supposed to do now?

No answers seemed to be coming. My mind was a swirl of frustration and pain, making thinking difficult. Restlessness overcame me. All I wanted was to be moving and I couldn't. Walking would be impossible with how much just shifting hurt.

Shoving the question of whether or not I'd walk again to the side, I tried to think of anything useful I could do while recovering. Traps wouldn't work, as I wouldn't have the strength to set them. None of the stuff that was usually my responsibility was going to be possible for an unknown length of time.

Mara's hand on my arm let me know she was awake. "It'll be alright, Kith. You just need to give yourself some time to rest and heal." She paused, her thoughts hidden behind careful eyes. "Let's get you out of the tree. You'll feel better."

As much as I wanted out of the tree, nerves suddenly overtook me. The slightest movement was extremely painful, so I wasn't sure how this would go. "Getting out of the tree sounds great." My voice wavered even as I fought to keep it steady.

Looking at me in silence for a moment, Mara seemed to be having second thoughts. "Alright, but let's take this slow."

Tying the rope under and around me to make sure I was secure, she then wrapped the ends of the rope around the branches I sat on. Once they were secure, she helped me lower off the branch. I swung free for a second, almost crashing into the trunk, before she stabilized me with the rope.

It felt like hours before I reached the next level of branches. Once I did, I used my arms to gently arrange myself on them, ready for a break. Mara untied the rope and climbed down to join me. I found myself envying her agility.

We only rested for a few minutes before moving on. As I swung down from this set of branches, my leg scraped against the trunk. A scream burst out of me before I could attempt to stop it. Fire spread through my entire body, leaving me shaking uncontrollably. I knew Mara was saying something, but my ears were ringing from the pain and my vision went dark.

I felt her grab me and move me onto the next row of

branches. "We're almost there. Can you continue?" She waited quietly for me to respond. "Kith?"

Slowly, my vision and sense returned. "I'm alright." I realized I was cradled in her arms the way Beatrice used to hold us when we were hurt or upset. I looked up at her tear stained face, wishing I could reassure her. "Can we rest for a little bit before we go down the rest of the way?"

"Of course." She smiled gently and moved my hair out of my face. "We'll wait until you're ready."

Her fingers traced my face gently and I felt my body relaxing. I knew the trick, Beatrice had often used it to lure us into sleep, but I didn't fight it.

I don't know how long I slept, but when I woke I felt ready to finish my journey to the ground. Mara moved more slowly this time, careful to keep me far away from the trunk as I made my way down. When I was close to the ground, she moved down and tied another length of rope around my good leg, pulling me into a lying position.

"Hold your leg up so it doesn't touch the ground when you do." When I was ready, she inched me slowly down the rest of the way.

Once I was down, she told me she was going to work on making the fort more comfortable before we tried to move me in there. Again, I was helpless just watching her work. Anger at everything suddenly welled up inside me, needing to escape somehow. Grabbing the closest thing to me, I started ripping at it. Before long, the stick was completely destroyed, but I didn't feel any better. I grabbed another stick, a sturdy, straight one. This time I focused my frustration, ripping off chunks at the end of the stick in careful amounts. Before long, the end was a sharp point. Refining it took a lot more attention, and I let myself get fully absorbed. This felt much better than braiding sticky rope.

Once I was happy with the sharpness of the end, I held up my new spear and thrust it around, focusing on only moving my upper body to not disturb my leg. It felt like it would be a decent weapon. Hunting might be in my future, if walking would be.

While carefully cleaning up the rest of the stick, I looked

around for the shredded leather from the bag that was destroyed. Spotting it only a few feet away, I stretched out my arm to try and grab it. Frustration hit again as my fingers came only inches from the bag. Looking around to make sure Mara wouldn't see me, I drug myself across the ground. The pain that filled my leg was excruciating and I tasted blood as I bit my tongue to hold back a scream.

After breathing heavily for several minutes to calm myself down, I focused my attention back onto the scraps of leather. I could easily reach it now, so I grabbed it hastily and wrapped it around the base of my new spear. Now holding it wouldn't hurt my hands as much.

Satisfaction washed through me, and I let it linger, pushing down all the negativity for now. Creating a weapon was something I could be proud of, even if I couldn't do much else right now.

*   Mara   *

Over the next several weeks Kith's restlessness only grew. There were a pile of spears and long strands of bark rope to prove it. Conversations between us were diminished to me forcing him to drink feverfew tea and allow me to change his bandages. Most of the responses I got were in grunts. I knew he was trying not to take his frustration out on me, but the silence was draining.

After a particularly bad night with neither of us sleeping much, I made a fire to make some more tea. When it was done, Kith took it begrudgingly. He didn't complain, but his face displayed his reluctance to drink it.

"How are you feeling?" My voice wavered despite my best efforts.

With an extremely fake smile plastered on his face, Kith used a sickeningly chipper voice. "I feel great. So much better. I'll be running in no time." His voice cracked and he turned away from me.

My chest constricted and breathing felt painful. There had

never been such a gap between us, and I hated it. I wished I could heal him like he did for me, but I couldn't figure out how to get it to work. Of course, I only tried while he was asleep so as to not get his hopes up or make him feel worse.

Moving away from him, I went to smother the fire. I sat and watched the last of the smoke fade away. The heat and lack of sleep worked against me, and I felt my eyes closing. I'm not sure how long I slept next to the fire, but I woke a while later to a crash followed quickly by a stifled groan. Surely Kith wasn't trying to walk. It was much too soon for that, but when I opened my eyes I saw him dragging himself to his feet. Not even a full second passed before he was back on the ground, his fist pressed into his mouth to hold back a scream. The urge to go to him and convince him to stop overcame me, but I knew it would only make him feel worse.

I watched in agonizing helplessness as he tried again and again only to slump down in frustration. Eventually, he crawled over to a tree, dug in his claws, and began lifting himself up. Wincing in pain through the entire process, he gradually made his way to a standing position. He looked around in triumph, only for his face to fall when he realized he still wouldn't get anywhere on that leg. Anger flew across his face as he lowered himself back to the ground, a small yelp escaping as his leg made contact with the ground.

This whole situation must have been terrible for him, and we both feared the consequences of staying still too long with me looting the town. Isaac had made us feel protected. Safe. I wondered if we'd ever feel that way again. Shaking the thoughts out of my head, I turned back to Kith's struggle.

As I watched, an idea formed in my mind: *What if I could make him a sturdy stick that he could take with him to carry part of his weight when he couldn't put it all on his leg?* I wasn't exactly sure how I was going to do this, and I knew it may still be some time before he could even do that much, but it was worth a shot.

Pretending I wasn't watching him, I rose and stretched. Kith didn't even look up at me as I started wandering around, looking for a large branch that I could claw into the size I would need. While making the fire for our dinner that night, I found the perfect one. Wanting to surprise Kith with his walking stick, I set it aside out of sight and continued on with dinner.

When I was going through the packs, getting our food, I sighed, "I think I'm going to have to go into town tonight. We're really low on food and we could use more water too. Besides," I added, looking mournfully at Kith's leg, "I think it's time to rewrap your leg again." Kith's leg required constant attention. I had already rewrapped it so many times that we were almost out of bandages and the cleaning liquid was gone completely. We were also low on feverfew, as I made Kith drink it on a regular basis.

"I can go into the town tomorrow. I'm starting to feel much better." Kith had tried this the last few times I went to town and each time he found he wasn't strong enough to walk.

"Kith, you're being stubborn. I can go into town myself. I've been fine so far haven't I? I'll be careful. Can you watch the food for me while I go?" I hoped giving him a task would at least ease the pain of having me perform his usual job. He looked at me for a long moment and I expected to hear more protests.

"Okay, I'll watch the food. Don't stay too long and don't let anyone see you."

I tried to hide my excitement as I emptied the packs to make space. Only having gone into town by myself a few times now, I loved having the chance to look around. Once I reached the edge of the trees; however, the typical nerves set in. Going to town was exciting, but I was fully aware that there was always a risk. That was part of what made my visits so exhilarating. It felt like a great achievement each time I made it back with bags full of supplies.

When I came here the first time, I didn't even stop to think about what I was doing. Kith needed supplies immediately, so I came to get them without a second thought. Now that he was no longer in immediate danger, I had time to think about all the things that could go wrong while I was in town. For a moment, I stood at the edge of the clearing, preparing myself. I caught sight of the well in the middle of the town and decided to get the water first.

With a deep breath, I darted out toward the well. Grabbing the rope, I began pulling up the bucket of water. Twice, my hands slipped and the rope fell. Cursing myself for shaking so badly, I took a deep breath and kept going. Finally, I managed to get the bucket all the way up and dumped it into our remaining water skins.

With our skins full, I set off to the house where I was getting Kith's bandages. My heart was nearly beating out of my chest with worry that they would be ready for me by now. On my first visit to this house, I just grabbed supplies without thinking. When I came back, I realized the part of the window I broke was stuffed with towels inside the hole, making me realize how much more careful I needed to be. Now, whenever I came, I tried to spread out what shelves I took from and never took as much as I did that first time. I hoped this would keep them from noticing, but I was still scared each time.

Tiptoeing up to the house, I peered inside the window. It seemed empty. Guilt washed over me as I removed the towels and crawled slowly back in through the same gap. Creeping through the house, I collected the same clear liquid, bandages, and more of the feverfew. I tried not to disturb anything in the house except what I needed, but as I was grabbing the last of the bandages my eyes caught on a pair of sticks. They were a little taller than me with a Y shaped curve at the top and a handle about halfway down. Looking at them, I remembered a young crippled boy at one of our shows who was using something similar to help himself walk.

They were under his armpits and he was using them to support his weight, keeping some of it off of his legs. These were much taller than what Kith would need, but they could be trimmed off at the bottom. Staring at them for a long time, I debated with myself. On the one hand, I was already taking so much from these people, did I really dare take more? On the other hand, Kith's leg was in really bad shape. The stick I found would work for him, with a lot of work, but modifying one of these would go a lot faster. Kith was eager to walk again, but he would need something to help him if he was going to get moving any time soon. He could even end up needing it forever. Trying not to let that thought overcome me, I finally decided the need was too great. Hating myself for doing it, I grabbed one of the sticks and started shoving it through the window before crawling through myself. Once I was sure I had everything, I carefully stuffed the towels back in place.

Having completed the hardest of my tasks, I was starting to feel more calm. The thought of giving Kith his new walking stick helped boost my mood as I set the stick in a hidden spot close to my path out of town. It would be too difficult to carry the whole time. Although I still tried to make as little sound as possible, my heart no longer felt like it was going to explode and I was moving more confidently. Approaching the butcher's shop, I turned the handle cautiously. The door opened with ease. Peering all around the room, I made sure the coast was clear before stepping in.

Still eyeing every inch of the space, I quickly grabbed some dried meat, wanting to spend as little time in there as possible. While dashing back toward the door, I noticed a calendar posted on the wall. Curiosity hit me, and I stepped up to examine the days. Just from looking at it, I couldn't quite be sure what day it was. I needed to look at the moon for better judgment, but I realized with a jolt that Kith's birthday was coming up in just a few days.

How perfect it would be to give him the walking stick for his birthday! I paused for a moment, debating, and then worked the calendar off the wall and shoved it into my bag. Being out on our own made it hard to know the days. With this to go off of, I thought I could probably make another one for the following year so we could continue tracking the days.

Heading out of the house, I felt slightly guilty for the extra things I took, but also pleased with what I found. Then, I went around to a few trash cans searching for any other scraps I could find. Once it seemed like I had a pretty good load, I headed out of the town, grabbing the stick on my way.

After walking most of the way through the clearing, I noticed a ball laying in the grass. Walking over to it, I picked it up and rolled it around in my hands. It was a little flat, but seemed like it would still be fun to kick around. The grass underneath it had all died and I realized it must have been sitting there for quite some time. Deciding that the kids who once played with this ball must have rejected it, I took it with me thinking it would make another great gift for Kith.

Before I walked back into the trees, I pulled out the calendar and examined the moon to find that there were three days until Kith's birthday. It seemed like fate that I saw the walking stick and the ball so close to his birthday! I knew his leg would hinder the fun he could have with the ball right now, but if my idea worked, the stick should help him get on his feet a little more. All in all, I thought it was a successful trip and I couldn't help but grin the entire way back to camp.

＊　Kith　＊

Being stationary for weeks was driving me insane. Knowing Mara wouldn't want me walking so soon, I started attempting to while she slept. At first, I tried standing still and putting little bits of weight on my leg. The first few times were so painful I couldn't even count to five with my foot touching the ground fully, but after a few days I could stand for about half a minute before giving in to the pain.

Whenever Mara announced that she would be going to town my heart skipped a beat. Her first trip worried me enough, but I never expected it to be a regular thing. I honestly thought my leg would be healed before we'd need to make another run. Going this long without walking, or even standing, never even occurred to me in the beginning.

As soon as Mara crept off, I practiced standing again. Slowly, steadying myself against a tree, I took a step with my good leg. It was painful, but I breathed in deeply and braced myself to move the wounded leg. Pain ripped through my body again, but I pushed forward. Sweat coated my body and I was breathing heavily. My heart felt like it was pounding hard enough to burst through my chest.

Two steps was going to have to be enough for a first try. Prying my hand loose from its grip on the tree, I slid to the ground. Feeling completely drained, I put my head back on the tree and allowed myself to rest.

My thoughts drifted to Mara. For so long she pestered me to give her a chance to prove herself and I tried to shelter her. When it came down to it, though, she had proven to be quite capable. Teaching her the things when she asked would've made this all easier on her, though. Instead, she had to learn the hard way while I was unable to do much to help her.

After resting for long enough, I rose to my feet again. This time my legs started off wobbly, but I ignored it. I repeated the two steps, but again my strength failed before I could take another. Sliding down the tree, I wiped the sweat off my face before putting my head in my hands. Frustration teased at the corners of my mind, but I pushed it back with reminders that I was making some progress.

When Mara returned, I was still at the base of the tree. She stashed all her finds and came to stand in front of me, a fresh batch of tea in her hands.

Sitting next to me, she spoke softly. "How are you feeling?"

I knew she noticed the sweat that still covered my body. "Tired." I sighed.

"I'm sure. We'll get some rest soon." She handed me the tea with a look that let me know I better drink it. "I got some clean bandages. Time to tend to your leg again."

I winced, knowing that the process was going to hurt my already throbbing leg. Maybe I shouldn't have tried walking. "Do you think it needs it tonight? Maybe we can wait."

The grim line returned to Mara's mouth and her eyes spoke even more than her mouth. "I think we should do it now, Kith. It's probably been longer than it should have been already."

While she gathered her supplies, I braced myself. Hopefully, it would hurt less this time than the other times, but I couldn't count on that.

"Take a deep breath." She waited for a second, then carefully started pulling back the wrapping. She had been wrapping the leg pretty tight, just on the edge of painfully tight, and it being unwrapped was a weird mix of relieving and painful. As she cleaned it, I ignored the pain and leaned forward. All the other times it got cleaned, I was in too much pain; and maybe too scared, to look at it.

The cuts were starting to close, but I could see the thick red marks covering most of my lower leg. Before it started to heal, it must have looked like a big piece of raw meat like the ones I pulled out of trash cans. My stomach lurched. No wonder it was taking so long to heal. By the look of it, I came close to losing my leg altogether. Mara hadn't been joking with how concerned she was.

Feeling queasy, I leaned back against the tree again as the fresh wrappings were put on. I was still determined to recover, but I finally understood the seriousness with which Mara spoke. Recovery would mean learning to allow myself to take it slower, as hard as that would be.

Weariness overcame me, and I asked Mara to help me into the fort. Surprise shone in her eyes as I willingly allowed her to help, instead of fighting all her efforts. Curling up, I allowed my mind to go blank and drifted to sleep.

CHAPTER THIRTEEN: JUNE

With only a few days to work, I knew I couldn't delay. The handled stick I grabbed was much too tall for Kith. Carrying it back from town was difficult with everything else I was holding. Keeping it steady with its length wore my arms out and dumping it at my working spot was a relief.

While lying next to Kith that night, I looked him up and down to see how much taller than me he was. I never realized it before, but he had grown a lot in the time since we arrived at Isaac's house.

He was much taller than I was now, and without getting too close, it looked like his armpit was even with my forehead! Using this information, I cut the stick I found for him with my claws. After testing the stick on myself, I decided I needed something to wrap over the part that would go under his arm to pad it so that putting pressure on the stick wouldn't hurt Kith's armpits.

After puzzling over what to use for padding, I remembered passing a shop in town that had heaps of materials in the windows. There was a pretty dress that caught my eye, but there was no place for fancy items like that in our lives so I ignored it. Some of that cloth would be great for padding, though. Going back to town two nights in a row seemed risky, so I decided to wait until the next night.

I was jittery with anticipation the whole next day, and as soon as Kith's breathing changed that night, I slipped carefully out of the fort. He couldn't know I was doing something as stupid as going back to the town. Especially since he didn't know I took as much as I did. I tried listening for sounds in the night, but all I could hear was the pounding of my heart. Still, I needed that cloth. It was the only thing I could do to help Kith.

Clouds drifted in front of the moon as I approached the

town, giving me an extra advantage. It almost felt like the clouds were helping me, encouraging me that this was the right choice. Creeping carefully to the shop, I ignored all the other usual stops in town. This needed to be a super quick trip. Luck continued to be on my side. The shop had discarded some damaged clothes, and heaps of material lay in the bins. Digging through, I found some soft, thick scraps that would be perfect for what I needed. There were many other colorful and soft scraps, and I pictured making Gracie all sorts of new dresses. Quickly scooping up as much as I could easily carry, I ran back the way I came.

My heart didn't return to normal until after I stashed all the fabric with the stick. It might have been foolish to grab as much as I did. I pictured Kith's worry when he discovered how risky I behaved, but I brushed it off. There was nothing I could do about it now. Once I calmed down, I carefully climbed back into the fort. Sleep wasn't going to come easy.

The next day, as I was wrapping the fabric I stole around the curved part of the stick, I made a mental note to look for a new bag the next time I went into town. It would be hard to continue on with all of our things plus any food we find without at least one more pack. Maybe I could even find something bigger to fit more supplies.

With the size and padding correct, it was time to work on the handle. With the size adjustment, it was almost at the bottom of the stick, and wouldn't be helpful at all. Removing it and making a new hole to wedge it into didn't take as long as I thought it would, though.

I was growing more excited about giving Kith his walking stick, but when I looked at it it seemed like it needed something more. Unsure about what kinds of decorations Kith would appreciate, I sat and stared at the dark wood in front of me. Something simple would probably suit him, but I wanted so desperately for it to be perfect. I began carefully etching tiny leaves and vines all along the edges with my claws.

Usually, it would've been hard for me to get a lot of time to work on the stick without Kith knowing what I was doing. His distance was finally proving useful, as much as it still stung. On the night before his birthday, I waited until I was sure Kith was asleep and got up from bed. There were just a few finishing touches left before I was satisfied with his gift.

Just before I reached the tree where everything was stashed, I heard Kith's sleepy voice mumble, "Mara, what are you doing?" I hoped the tea would help to make him a heavier sleeper, but with all the conditioning of waking up to my nightmares, I supposed I should have known better.

Pausing for only a moment, I answered, "I have to pee. I'll be right back."

I waited several minutes and when I heard Kith's heavy breathing again, I pulled out the stick and sank to the ground. After a little over an hour, when I held the stick up in the moonlight, I finally decided it was done. I set the stick back in the tree, laying against two branches and placed the ball over it to keep it in place. Then, I slowly crept back into our fort, excited for the next morning.

Waking early the next morning, I could barely contain my excitement. I bustled through breakfast and when Kith asked what I was in such a hurry for, I just smiled and said, "It's a surprise."

Kith barely waited until we were done eating to start pestering me. "Alright, Mara, you have to tell me what's going on." There was a sense of anticipation about him as if my mysterious excitement was rubbing off on him.

"I don't know what you're talking about." Smiling sweetly, I blinked at him a couple of times before breaking out into giggles.

"Come on, Mara." His pleading felt more desperate than I expected and I realized just how much he needed something different than just sitting around all day.

"Alright. Guess what today is!"

He looked at me with raised eyebrows and answered slowly, "How do you know what day it is?" I walked to my hiding place and grabbed just the calendar I found. "Mara, did you take that from someone?"

"Well, I did, but only because I thought it was important to keep up with the dates."

Handing Kith the calendar, I watched as he scrutinized it,

"Is it...my birthday?"

Beaming, I raced up the tree where his walking stick and the ball were hiding. Once I climbed back down, I hid them awkwardly behind my back, while walking to Kith slowly.

First, I pulled the ball from behind my back and tossed it to Kith where he sat on the ground. His eyes lit up with excitement. "Don't you think the children will notice it's missing and come looking for it?" He asked, and I could see him struggling between his excitement and worry for our safety.

"It's been sitting in the same place since we stopped here and the grass under it was all dead. I don't think they play with it anymore."

Kith's smile widened as I spoke and he tossed the ball back to me. I tried to catch it with my one free hand, but it tumbled to the ground.

"What's behind your back?"

"Well, I thought this might help you while you're trying to start walking again," I explained as I pulled the walking stick from behind my back and handed it to him.

The expression on Kith's face was hard to read. There was a look of longing mingled with fear and sadness all at once. Grabbing the stick gingerly, he looked at me with a serious face. "Mara, where did you get this?" he asked in a small voice

Suddenly, I felt the guilt filling me again. "I took it from the medicine house," I responded sheepishly, but before Kith could respond, I continued, "Kith, I had to! I know you've been trying to walk and I think this could really help you!"

Kith's expression became even more hard to read as he stared at the stick. Seeming to come to some sort of conclusion, he said "Thank you. I don't know how soon I can use it, but I know it will help," he noticed my etchings and began examining each one. "Wow," I couldn't help but feel pride rush through me, "Mara, this is beautiful!" I knew he was trying to make me feel better. He couldn't undo me taking the walking stick, so there was no point in arguing now, but I was sure he would be more wary of me going into the town after this.

We spent the rest of the day tossing the ball back and

forth. I could see how it bothered Kith when I was the one chasing it every time one of us didn't catch it, but he seemed to enjoy it all the same. Seeing him smiling again made everything feel worth it.

✳   Kith   ✳

Mara's behavior confused me, and when she showed me the calendar she stole, a wave of disappointment hit me. I hated how much we stole, but her excitement was such a rare thing. Not wanting to ruin it by scolding her, I bit my tongue.

Looking at the calendar, it took a long time for me to realize that it was my birthday. I barely even remembered that I had a birthday, much less exactly when it was. Things like that weren't important when you were running for your life from a deranged man.

When the realization did hit, my mind went reeling. Memories of our few happy birthdays drifted through my mind. Just another part of normal life that was stolen from us. As I felt my mind spiraling, Mara whipped a ball out from behind her back and tossed it to me. Pulled out of my mental distraction, I caught the ball. My ball.

Isaac gave Mara his daughter's doll, and she had played with it lovingly. Happiness filled me while watching her finally have a toy of her own, but; until that slightly flat ball landed in my hands, I hadn't realized how much I longed for one also. Normal childhood things, even in small doses, were most of what I longed for.

When I tossed the ball back to Mara and she dropped it, I realized she was still hiding something behind her back. I was too absorbed in my ball to notice before.

"What's behind your back, Mara?" Curiosity spiked, edged with a rare feeling of anticipation.

"Well, I thought this might help you while you're trying to start walking again," her voice was soft but full of pride.

I wasn't sure what to expect, but it certainly wasn't the

stolen walking stick she pulled out. Emotions overwhelmed me, and I barely managed to force myself to respond through them. When I looked at my wound for the first time, I finally realized how bad it really was. Mara's cautions and concern sank in with full force, and I was wondering if I was ever going to regain full use of my leg. With this walking stick, there was more hope of me walking again, but at what cost? It was dangerous to take such an important item from the store and I was sure someone would have noticed it was gone.

If I was ever going to walk again, though, it would take time and work. The walking stick would help a lot. When I held it in my hands, I realized the amount of work she put into it, the intricate carvings that covered the whole thing must have taken her a lot of time. Realizing how much Mara put into the extra details meant more to me than I was able to express. I could tell from her voice that Mara was already feeling the guilt of having stolen the items, so I decided not to push the matter further.

"Let's play catch for a bit." The words felt strange, but I relished them.

Throwing the ball around was even more fun than I expected, but watching Mara run to fetch it made me wish I could chase after it. Looking at my new walking stick, I reminded myself that I would be working on that.

We played until the sun started drifting down and the sky darkened. As Mara started prepping dinner, her thoughts seemed to turn serious again, but she didn't say much. I noticed that there weren't many feverfew flowers left, which seemed to be what was worrying Mara.

"Hey, before I drink that nasty tea, how about I try out this stick?" A smile played at Mara's lips when I mentioned the nasty tea. At first, I drove her crazy with how much I hated it, but eventually she saw the humor in my complaints. Once it was there, anyway.

"That sounds good." There was a brightness in her eyes that I never wanted to leave.

Offering me her hand, Mara steadied me as I got stable with the stick. It took some adjusting to get used to putting my weight on it, instead of my leg, but I got it. The difference was noticeable immediately. While standing was still uncomfortable, the pain wasn't shooting through my whole body. Tentatively, I took a step forward with my good leg. So far, so good. The first step with my injured leg was painful, but I managed. Mara's eyebrows furrowed in concern as I winced, but I assured her I was alright.

After walking around our camp in a circle, I was completely worn out, but the pain wasn't as bad as before. "Mara! I walked way further than I have before!"

My excitement curbed when I realized I was practicing walking behind Mara's back. She laughed at the look on my face. "It's alright, Kith. I saw you taking some steps one night."

"Oh. I'm sorry. I shouldn't have snuck around like that."

"I understand why you did. Seems you came to understand a bit of how I've felt for years." Her voice was teasing, but I knew her words were the truth.

Instead of responding, I drank down the bitter feverfew tea. Mara chuckled softly and began dividing our food. Dinner tasted fantastic after all the playing and walking. Usually after eating, we stayed up and talked or relaxed, but I was exhausted.

"I hope we have a lot more days like today," I mumbled as I drifted off into sleep.

*   Mara   *

Risking going back to the town after all I had taken seemed too scary, so we carefully stretched all of our supplies out as far as we could. Anger at myself burned deep in my stomach, even though I knew the items were desperately needed. Still, I hated the constant hunger and fear. It made me miss the safety Isaac offered even more.

Eventually, even our careful rationing couldn't stop us from running out of food, and with a sick feeling, I knew I had to go back to town. As I made my preparations, Kith asked in a tone that sounded like forced calm, "Why don't you just try taking things from the trash cans for a while? Give it some more time before you go back into any houses and let any suspicion ease up."

We already had this conversation many times over the course of my town visits, and it always bothered me that Kith didn't trust my judgment. "I already told you, I don't take from the same place two visits in a row. The medicine man is the only one who has noticed anything and I don't need to go back there this time. And I don't like eating the food out of trash cans anymore. It's better for you to have fresh food while you're healing." I wasn't entirely sure if that last part was true, but it sounded like the best way to help my argument.

Kith looked skeptical but stopped arguing anyway. I gave him a small smile, trying to be reassuring before I headed to the town. As confident as I tried to appear, I was more nervous than ever about entering the town. However, when I made it back to the camp later that night with a full bag of food and no problems I felt reassured that things were going to be alright.

After that night, I noticed Kith was practicing increasingly more with his walking stick. It hurt to watch as he took a few steps only to sink back to the ground looking exhausted. It was clear from his face that every step was excruciating, and each time he stopped the look of defeat was hard for me to bear. Even after several weeks his leg still pained him so much.

At first, I tried to convince him to let me help him until one day he snapped and yelled at me about how he was never going to get better if he relied on me all the time. It hurt and he apologized for it later, but I stopped offering after that. I was beginning to wonder if he would ever walk again.

My next visit to the town became an ordeal as Kith tried to make me promise before leaving that I would only go into houses if there was no food in the trash cans. "I don't want to eat trash can food, Kith. It tastes horrible," seeing the slightly hurt look on his face, I changed my tone. "It was okay before when that was all we could get, but ever since we were with Isaac, it's just so hard to eat that stuff anymore."

Kith's face softened, and to my surprise, he agreed. "I know, we got spoiled by Isaac's cooking. Stale bread is nothing compared to what he used to make us." His voice held a longing I knew all too well.

"Do you remember that sweet bread he made?" I asked wistfully.

"Oh yes! I wish we could make it ourselves."

We continued reminiscing for a while until I got the sneaking suspicion that Kith was stalling my trip to the town. After I finally got away, I was still thinking of all the great things Isaac used to make for us. Once I got there, I began my usual rounds. Each time I went, I picked a section of houses to go into. There were three separate sections so that visits to each one were widespread.

At the third home, I realized it was the baker's residence. Tiptoeing inside, I looked around remembering all the wonderful breads and pastries Isaac made for us. As I walked past the rows of bread, I saw a loaf of sweet bread like the kind Kith and I were just talking about. Throwing caution to the wind, I grabbed the whole loaf and stuffed it in my pack, thinking how excited Kith would be when I showed it to him. Then, I grabbed a loaf from the very back of a different shelf and put it in the pack as well.

From the next few houses, I grabbed meat and some vegetables. I was able to find a few spare bandages, but the supply was pretty low and I couldn't find any feverfew. Knowing that Kith would freak out if he knew I went back to the medicine house, I decided to check a few of the houses that weren't on the original agenda for this visit. Eventually, I was able to find a little bit of the plant, and I took it all for the sake of time.

Heading back to our camp, I was very excited to show Kith the bread I found, but when I got close, I saw him on his walking stick trying to come toward me.

"Mara! Where have you been, I've been so worried!"

I ran to him and helped him settle back down to the ground, surprised by his lack of complaint at my helping him. "I'm sorry. I couldn't find any feverfew and I didn't want to try the medicine man's house yet so I had to go into some other houses to find some."

Once Kith had settled down, I began showing him

everything I found. I pulled the sweet bread out last and held it to him, beaming.

"I thought it would make a nice treat for us tonight."

Kith smiled feebly, and I could see that he was biting back a scolding.

"Well, if you don't want any, that's fine." I snapped, speaking a little more harshly than I meant to.

Looking taken aback, Kith quickly insisted that he wanted some of the bread. Feeling bad for snapping at him, I tried to be reassuring that everything was alright and I was being careful.

"I'll wait a little extra time before I go back this time, okay?"

That seemed to cheer him up a bit, and after some time we were again reminiscing about Isaac and the time we shared with him. When we went to bed that night, I was both happy and sad. I felt a growing pride each time I made a successful trip to the town, but Kith still seemed to doubt my abilities and it was frustrating. For several weeks now, I had been taking care of him, and he still acted as though I were a helpless child.

My next visit to the town was, as promised, over a week after the last. For a few nights in a row, I tried to tell Kith it was time for me to go and he kept telling me to wait, reminding me of my promise. When I finally opened our pack and saw that we had only a day or two worth of supplies left, I insisted on going that night. "We can't let our supplies get too low. If something happens and I can't go to town for a while, we would end up going without food. It's best for me to go now."

Kith, looking surprised that he didn't think of that fact himself, agreed but insisted on walking part of the way there with me. It was slow going, and after only a short while, he finally decided I would have to continue without him. Promising him I would be careful, I continued on my familiar route.

When I got to the town, I noticed something was strange. There were candles lit inside many of the homes. It seemed odd for anyone to still be awake at this time. It was even later than I normally came, after having to make part of the journey with Kith. Deciding to avoid any houses that had candles lit, I tiptoed toward the well. After filling up all of our water skins, I made my way to the first house which was all dark.

Creeping inside carefully, I went straight to the kitchen. There wasn't a lot of food to be found, but as I headed back toward the door I saw a large pack, bigger than ours and much more sturdy. It seemed to have been packed with storage items and stashed out of the way. It surely wouldn't be missed any time soon, but I didn't have time to take any of the items out. I would have to take it as it was, without even going through it.

I got out the door and turned to walk toward the next house. Not even two steps in that direction and I stepped on a piece of rope. Instantly, I knew that I was in trouble.

Ropes enveloped me and I was raised up high in a huge trap just like the ones Isaac taught Kith to make. Only this one was bigger. This one was made for a person, not an animal. Panic coursed through me as I hung in the air. I saw a candle being lit inside the house and I began fighting frantically to get out of the net. Finally, I realized I could cut the rope with my claws so I sawed as quickly as I could. Just as the front door was opening, I managed to make a hole large enough to squeeze through. There was a scream and the candle fell to the ground, returning the world to darkness. Taking my chance, I sprinted away as quickly as I could. Just as I was reaching the edge of the town, I heard more doors opening and people yelling.

The woman who saw me was frantically trying to tell the others about the monster inside her net. Pausing for only an instant, I listened as the others told her she had gone mad. There were accusations being made, and I realized everyone was trying to blame anyone they could for things that went missing in the town over the past weeks.

Turning again, I ran as fast as I could out of the town. When I reached Kith, my whole body trembled, and the tears streamed down my face as I told him what happened.

The whole time Mara was in the town, I sat where we split up trying to convince myself she would be okay. Each of her visits worried me, but they were especially worrisome since she stole my walking stick. When I heard Mara's rushed footsteps approaching, I felt relief at first, followed immediately by panic when I realized the speed at which she was approaching.

Grabbing my walking stick, I slowly rose in an attempt to meet her, but before I took more than one step, she was close enough for me to see. Fear enveloped me as I saw the tears streaming down her face.

"What happened?" I gasped, trying to keep myself steady.

"You were right," Mara was nearly sobbing at this point and we almost fell over as she rushed into my arms.

Carefully guiding us toward the ground, I stroked Mara's hair until she calmed down enough to tell me what happened.

Icy tendrils of fear gripped my stomach as I listened to Mara speak. Images of her caught in nets with townspeople leering at her caused bile to rise in my throat. "You can't go back." My throat was tight, the words barely squeaked out.

"We can't go without supplies."

"I can't stand for it. It's too much of a risk."

"What are we supposed to do, then?" Tears lined her eyes and her voice trembled. Her sense of failure was so strong I could feel it.

Brushing her cheek gently, I softened my voice. "It's not your fault, Mara. It's not. I know you think it is, but the truth is, I knew this day would come. You've had to steal valuable supplies to take care of me. People were bound to notice."

Shaking her head, she whispered, "What are we going to do?"

"We'll have to move on."

Her head rose sharply. "Kith…"

"Before you argue, listen. We don't have a choice. We'll have to move slowly, for sure, but you know I'm healing. I have been walking with the stick."

"I've only seen you take maybe ten steps at a time." The skeptical tone in her voice was lightened by the fact that she knew what I said was the truth.

"I said it would be slow, didn't I?" I smiled teasingly and a giggle escaped her. "Besides, I made it more than ten steps tonight, didn't I? I just needed a little help to do it. We'll rest up tomorrow, and then head out the next day, how about that?"

She sighed. "I don't see any other choice, but I'm scared."

"I know." I wrapped my arms around her and she rested her head on my chest. "We'll be alright. We have to. You promised."

She shook against me, her sobs occasionally disrupted by uncontrollable giggles, which she seemed to be fighting to suppress. I rubbed her back and sang what I could remember of the lullabies we fell asleep to when we were little. The laughter scared me, but I wasn't sure if mentioning it would make things worse.

Eventually, Mara quieted and then drifted off to sleep. As confident as I pretended to be for her sake, I was terrified. Walking was still extremely painful, and I wasn't really joking when I said it would be slow going. Moving on was not something I was looking forward to at all, but I knew we had to. Getting caught wouldn't mean anything good. At the very least, there would be torment from the townsfolk, but there was also a very high chance that it would put Ducar back on our trail. We hadn't talked about him much in a long time, and Mara's nightmares had been so mild we allowed ourselves to relax a bit. If we got spotted, though, we'd be in huge amounts of trouble.

Regret for trying to meet the kids from the other town filled me suddenly. It was to honor Isaac's memory, but it was foolish. "Too late now. No sense dwelling on it." I muttered quietly to myself. Then, I remembered the men Mara attacked to save me. Yet another cause of my foolishness. She never would have been put in that situation if I hadn't gotten myself caught while running away from a group of cruel kids.

Pushing all the other thoughts out of my mind, I looked

down at my sleeping sister. She worked so hard to take care of me, and I refused to waste her efforts. We would rest and then continue on and I would do my best to make it. With a sigh, I gently woke her so we could make our way back to the fort.

After the day of rest, we were up with the sun. If we were going to make any decent progress, we'd have to leave as early as possible. We munched on some bread as we packed up the last of our things and chose a direction. The random choice was always hard. Being directionless and drifting was exhausting. For what must have been the hundredth time, I wished we had a set destination.

Hiding how much pain I was in wasn't easy, but Mara was having a hard enough time with leaving. Unable to stand the idea of adding to her struggle even more, I grit my teeth and put as little weight on my bad leg as I could. As hard as I tried, though, it wasn't long before I was desperate for a break.

Mara didn't miss a thing. "I'm getting tired. I guess I'm not used to walking so much anymore. Do you mind if we take a break?"

Having my own tricks used against me was both funny and frustrating. It also made me realize that Mara was obviously aware of what I was doing. "A break sounds nice."

Breaking was a relief, but I knew we couldn't rest long. We needed to make enough progress to have hope of finding another town we could camp nearby for a while. Mara seemed about to argue when I said we should move on, but she knew I was right.

By the time we stopped to make camp, my leg was throbbing so much it was almost numb. We didn't have much of the feverfew left, but Mara made me some tea. I never expected to be so glad to drink the gross stuff. Even with the aid of the tea, it was hard to sleep.

Getting started the next morning was even more difficult. The throbbing from the day before hadn't subsided much, and I was exhausted. Even so, I tried my best to keep a steady pace. Allowing my mind to drift, I entered full autopilot mode. Mara's sharp voice shook me out of it, and stunned, I looked at her.

"I think we should take a break." Her voice quivered

slightly.

"We need to make more progress." My voice sounded distant and weird.

"Not right now, we don't." Stubbornly dropping her pack and sitting, she stared at me until I eased myself to the ground.

"Alright, settle down."

Glaring, she grumbled, "Did you even hear a word I was saying?"

"When?" Confusion and guilt swirled around me.

"For several minutes while walking. I was talking to you and you wouldn't respond. Just kept that glazed look on your face and kept stumbling forward." She didn't say it, but I knew I worried her.

"I'm sorry. I didn't sleep well last night, and I zoned out for a bit."

The unhappy look stayed on her face for a minute before she relaxed. "Maybe you should try to take a nap before we move on."

Even though she said "maybe" her tone didn't leave much room for argument. Even though I didn't think that I would be able to sleep, it didn't take long for me to drift off into blackness.

*   Mara   *

When Kith said we had to leave, I knew he was right. I jeopardized us too much by taking so many things from the homes of the townspeople instead of searching the trash cans. Although I knew it was my fault we had to leave, I wanted to argue and make him stay.

Each wobbly step Kith took sent guilt coursing through me. His leg was not healed enough for him to be walking on it so much. As I watched him leaning so heavily on his walking stick, I was glad I took it for him, even if it did cause us to leave. We might not have been able to move at all if he was trying to walk without it.

While the first day was slow and obviously painful, the second day terrified me. Never had I seen Kith with such a blank look on his face. When he didn't respond to me for several minutes I almost panicked.

After he woke up from his nap, I spoke using a voice I knew he would take seriously. "I've decided we're going to rest every other day. We go a bit further today to find a good stopping spot, but we're resting tomorrow."

"Mara…"

Holding up a hand before he could continue, I said sternly. "It's useless to argue with me, Kith. I've made up my mind."

With a sigh, Kith agreed to my new plan. "Let's get moving then, so we can at least cover some ground today."

As we got moving, I suggested we try swinging from the trees instead, thinking having the weight off his leg would be better. Nodding, he tried jumping to grab a low branch, but instead cried out in pain. Taking some deep breaths, he decided to climb his way up the trunk of the tree. Once he reached the first branch, he let his legs dangle and I saw the familiar wince of pain. He swung himself back and arched forward, but a small yelp of pain escaped just before his hands grasped the next branch. He hung there in defeat for a while before hoisting himself onto the branch.

"That hurts more than walking on it does," he said quietly, avoiding my gaze. I knew he felt ashamed for what he thought was weakness.

After helping him crawl back down the branch, I managed to convince him to take a break. While we sat there, I changed his bandages. The wound was beginning to look better, but the area around it reddened with agitation. As I cleaned and rewrapped his leg, I hoped it would heal soon.

The days dragged on as Kith insisted he was fine to walk and struggled for hours before relenting to take a break. Taking rest days in between walking was helping, but I still hated how much pain he was in. The extra time was hurting our supplies as well. Each time I got food out of our packs, I was reminded of how low our supplies were getting. Since I was unable to get much that last night before I was caught, we were quickly going through what was left. I hoped there might be some small scraps of food in the pack I swiped, but luck wasn't on our side this time.

One resting day, I went for a walk to look around. We were camped in a small peaceful clearing, and there were flowers of all colors growing in abundance. My worry for Kith lately kept me from noticing how beautiful the forest was becoming. On the far side of the clearing was a cluster of trees with small red fruit hanging from them. It had been years since I last saw cherries, but I could remember Beatrice sneaking us some as a special treat. Smiling at the memory, I rushed to the trees, plucked a cherry and stuck it straight in my mouth. The juice was sour, nothing like the sweet cherries I remembered. Still, it was definitely food. Gathering as many as I could, I brought them back to Kith.

"We still need to find a town for supplies, but we need to get back to finding food out here, away from towns. Maybe stealing less food and gathering more will keep the next townsfolk from catching on so fast and we could stay still longer." As I said this, I realized I should have been looking for food this whole time. I hadn't even been looking for the trees those potato-like roots were usually under. Kith was in no shape to spend his time foraging after a full day of walking. Kicking myself for the time wasted, I decided I would start spending our off days searching for as much food as I could while Kith rested.

"You're right. I am going to miss all the delicious bread, though." Cherry juice ran down his chin as he grinned.

After several days passed, I began to realize Kith was improving. While watching him, standing close as always just in case he fell, I realized he wasn't putting quite as much pressure on the stick as he normally did. Allowing myself to fall a few more steps behind him, I watched critically as he walked on. He was definitely favoring his injured leg and still relied on the stick, but he was moving faster than before. Even more importantly, I realized with pleasure that he wasn't wincing at every step anymore.

Once Kith realized I was falling behind, he turned to look back and I saw his balance slip a little. "Is everything okay?" He asked and I heard the worry in his voice.

"I was just checking your progress. It looks like you're

starting to get the hang of walking again!"

He grinned and I could tell he noticed it too. "It's a little sad when you're so excited that your big brother has learned to walk," he said in a teasing voice that I hadn't heard since he got hurt.

"Well, I won't be really impressed until you can beat me in a race. Of course, you couldn't do that before you hurt your leg either."

It felt good to be joking around with Kith. He was so out of it lately with all the stress of trying to walk on his injured leg. Reality came crashing down on me again, though, when I opened our packs that night and saw that we were almost completely out of food. Even with carefully portioning out our next few meals, it didn't look like it would last more than a day unless we really stretched it.

Although I tried to hide this fact from Kith, he knew me too well. When I started cooking, he could tell something was wrong. He checked the packs, and I could see his mind working, trying to think of how he could fix the situation. I hoped I could find more food soon.

*   Kith   *

Pain became my normal state during our walking days, and going into auto-pilot mode was easier than dealing with it. We were careful to take a lot of breaks, at Mara's insistence, even on the days we were walking. While I was reluctant to admit it out loud, her idea of break days in between was a good one because I gradually felt my leg getting stronger.

Luckily, my wound didn't need much cleaning anymore. Our water was also getting really low, even with us trying not to use it much. When Mara's face scrunched up with concern while she was making dinner, I knew things were getting bad.

Looking into our last water skin, my stomach twisted into knots. Even with how carefully we were rationing out our water, there was only enough for another day or two.

We ate without really speaking, both of us lost in thought. As we were getting ready to sleep, I caught sight of the hopelessness that filled Mara's eyes. She still blamed herself for us having to leave the town.

"Mara," I paused, trying to decide how to convince her, "We'll be alright."

She looked at me warily. "Of course. That's what we keep saying, but saying it doesn't make it happen."

The despair in her voice surprised me. We had been in sticky situations before, and always got out of them alright. "No, just saying it doesn't, but we'll figure something out."

She nodded but didn't say anything else as she snuggled down into her blanket. Sleep didn't come to me that night. Something was going to have to change. Taking these rest days for my leg was slowing us down, and we needed to keep moving if we were going to find water. I just needed to figure out how.

When I pulled Mara out of her nightmare the next morning, I wondered if the tears on her face were just from the dream that haunted her. Holding her, I wished I could make everything better.

She pulled away after a minute and stood. "I'm going to keep walking for a while to see if I can find anything. I'll come back for you tonight."

"Mara," She looked at me and I could feel her daring me to argue. "I'm going to take my spear and try to get us some food," I said, switching tactics.

Her face twisted with surprise and fear. "I don't know if that's a good idea. You're just starting to walk without completely relying on your stick. How are you going to handle hunting?"

"I'm not sure," I paused, thinking as I went, "but I have to try. I think we could both use some meat." As I said it, I realized how much I really wanted to go hunting.

A look of understanding came to her face. "Meat would be nice. Are you sure you can handle it?"

"I'll be fine. And if I don't get anything, we won't really be any worse off than we are now, will we?"

After thinking about it, she shook her head. "I guess not. Just don't stay out too long. You're supposed to be resting, remember?"

I mumbled an agreement then gave her a quick kiss on her forehead as I headed out with my spear in the opposite direction of the one she chose. That way we could cover more ground and maybe one of us would find a town. Careful not to hurt my leg, I walked for several minutes trying to be as quiet as I could. The further I walked, the more I kept an eye out for any movement. Quiet wasn't something that Mara and I usually bothered with, since we were just focusing on moving on. With all the noise we made, seeing a bunch of animals wasn't really common.

Once I was a fair distance away from the camp, I crouched down and stayed still, watching for any signs of what direction I should go. Some prints caught my eye, and I slowly approached them. They were tiny paw prints, each about the size of my fingertip, but there were a lot in the area. It seemed like there were several of the little animals, all headed in the same direction. Looking around, I hoped I'd be lucky enough to see them hiding in some of the brush around me.

All I saw were more prints a few trees away where the ground was soft and clear. They were the same type of prints, so I slowly crept in that direction. After following the tracks for several more minutes, I found a tree with a hole. Small squeaks came from the hole, and I knew I had my mark. Judging from the size of the tracks, the animals were small. We'd need at least two, but hopefully more.

Looking around, I tried to figure out how to best catch as many of the animals as possible. It didn't take me too long to figure out a plan. Taking some larger sticks, I created a direct path away from the tree, blocking other escape routes. Then, partway down the path, I dug a hole. I wasn't sure how deep to make it to trap the animals, so I went down until most of my arm could fit into the hole.

When I felt that I was ready, I pushed my spear into the tree slowly, scaring the animals. Five of them ran out. They were just bigger than my hands. Black, brown, and gray fur went scurrying everywhere, trailed by long hairless tails, as they tried to get away from my spear. One started climbing the branches I used to block the paths. While it was slowed down, I grabbed it.

One more escaped, and I didn't manage to get it fast enough, but the others ran down the path I made and ended up in my hole. Relief filled me as I prepared the animals to be brought back to camp. It wasn't as much as I was hoping to get, but I agreed not to stay out too long, and I was already tired and anxious to start cooking.

Scooping up the parts I wasn't going to be bringing back to camp, I walked a bit further to discard them where animals could make use of them. As I turned to head back to camp, the smell of wet earth hit me, but it hadn't rained in days. Standing still, I tried to figure out where the smell was coming from. Gradually, I picked up on the sounds of moving water. A stream.

Moving toward the sound, I felt my heart start to race. We hadn't seen a stream in ages. A clearing opened up and water flowed right through the middle of it. The clear water was moving quickly, but not fast enough to turn white. It was easy to tell it got deep in parts. Bushes, with berries large and juicy, mingled with flowers around the stream and into the clearing. Shadows and light danced across the ground, making the whole clearing appear to sparkle.

Awestruck, I decided I must have stumbled upon paradise. My breath caught at the beauty of the area. The grass under my feet felt soft and welcoming. As tempted as I was to sit and stay, enjoying the comfort, I forced myself to turn around. Mara needed to see this.

Walking as quickly as my leg would allow, I returned to camp. Mara got back shortly after I did, looking downcast.

"Did you get some meat?" She asked, sounding only half interested.

"Better. Help me pack everything up. We need to go." I couldn't find the words to tell Mara how wonderful the area was, so I rushed to get everything packed so I could show her. Her curiosity was brimming over, but she didn't press.

It didn't take us long to get back to the clearing since we

weren't worried about scaring off animals. Mara's eyes lit up as she scanned the area. All hopelessness disappeared as she rushed forward with the water skins.

Refilling them, she then scooped up some water in her hands and drank it down, repeating this several times. Rationing out our water meant we were always thirsty, so I joined her for a long drink. The water was cool and refreshing.

Once we had our fill, I showed her the meat I got. "It's not as much as I was hoping for, but it should last us a couple of meals, especially with the berries," I said pointing to a nearby berry bush.

Mara grinned. "Those berries look so delicious, too."

We went to work setting up a camp, knowing we'd be spending the night here. My hunting and then our moving here had taken most of the day. Once we were all set up, we sat on the soft grass at the edge of the stream. Stretching out, I dipped my toes in, letting the water swirl around them.

Dirt swirled away with the water, and I was suddenly aware of how grimy I was. "Mara, let's take a bath. It's been so long since we've been clean."

Mara's face changed at the word "bath." There was the expected anticipation, but also the pain of remembering where we were the last time we took real baths. The memory was as painful as it was lovely.

Sadness overcame us both as we were washed away with memories, but we pushed them aside and focused on the moment. Stripping down to our underclothes, we slowly waded into the stream. The water felt wonderful. Sinking into the coolness, I began to scrub away the dirt with some leaves I picked up at the edge of the stream. Then I dipped my head under and scrubbed at my face and my hair, where dirt was really building up.

As I came up, I looked around for Mara. She was sitting on a rock she found in the stream, slowly combing through the knots in her hair. Seeing her looking so content brought a sense of calm. There were still deep shadows under her eyes from all the restless nights, but she seemed peaceful. Catching my eye, Mara grinned and slid back into the water.

Disappearing under it, she popped up at my side and splashed me. Giggles filled the air as I splashed her back. We swam around chasing each other for several minutes, but soon the exertion of the day started to catch up to me. Flipping onto my back, I stared up at the clouds, allowing myself to float. Mara followed suit, and we floated in silence for several minutes.

When I finally looked around, I realized we had been carried downstream a ways. Laughing, we swam back and climbed up to the grass to dry. After a break, we washed out our clothes the best we could and hung them in the trees to dry.

"It would be nice if we could dry the clothes closer to the fire. They'd probably dry faster." Mara was staring at our dripping clothes, her head tilted in thought.

"We could probably make a drying rack, but I'm not sure it would be worth the effort."

A look of mild annoyance crossed Mara's face but was gone before there was time to guess what it could be about. "It would still be nice to have." Without further comment, she headed to start a fire.

We decided we could each have a full animal since it had been a while since we ate any meat. After our bellies were full, we lay back and watched the sky darken.

"It's so beautiful here." Mara sighed and yawned.

"It really is." Drowsiness overcame me, and I allowed myself to drift off.

*   Mara   *

The morning after we found the stream, I woke up feeling better than I had in a long time. Looking around, I saw Kith's eyes drowsily watching me. I couldn't remember much of my dream, but I knew it must not have been a bad one if Kith wasn't fully alert.

"Are you alright?" he whispered.

"I'm great, actually. We should try to get more sleep. We

don't need to do any walking today so there's no rush to get up." Kith eyed me for a moment, thinking, then deciding to take my advice, he closed his eyes again and was back asleep in moments.

Laying still for several minutes, I tried half-heartedly to sleep again, but knew I was already too awake. Rising as quietly as I could, I grabbed Gracie and walked far enough away to not disturb Kith's sleeping, but still close enough that he would see me when he woke up.

Careful not to get the doll dirty, I played with Gracie by the stream for a while, as I dipped my feet in the cool water. Looking around at Kith, I was happy to see how peaceful he looked. His leg was getting much stronger, but I knew it still pained him a lot. It felt good to give him an extra break to sleep after so long spent walking.

Still, I felt all the guilt of the past weeks weighing on me, and wished we didn't have to push so hard. Staring down into the water, thinking, I didn't notice the huge fish swimming around until it was right under my feet. I yelped a little, in surprise, and heard Kith stir behind me.

"Mara?" The alarm on his face subsided slightly when he saw me sitting by the water, unharmed. "What happened?"

"A really big fish swam right under my feet. It just surprised me. I'm sorry I woke you up." I said, cursing myself for waking him, and the fish for startling me.

With Kith awake, we got our meager breakfast from our packs. While he heated some water, I collected some berries to add to our meal, feeling glad for the supplement to what little we had left. After we started cooking, I looked down into the water again and thought of the huge fish.

"Do you think you could catch one with your spear?"

Kith looked at me oddly and I realized I hadn't been listening to what he was telling me. "Catch one what?"

"A fish!"

Kith's face lit up a little at the idea. Another idea hit me, "Maybe we should also try putting up some traps. We could really use the meat."

Looking anguished, he said, "I can't believe I never set up

a single trap while we were stuck in those woods. Isaac would be so disappointed."

"You were in a lot of pain. You probably couldn't have strung them up very well, much less taken an animal out of them, and we both know I wouldn't have been able to do it." I felt a little silly at the knowledge that I would probably never be able to kill an animal, but it was the truth all the same. Even with how badly we needed food, I couldn't have made myself do it. I even thought about it a few times while we were stuck there. The thought made me feel squeamish, though, and I knew it would never work. Sometimes I thought about the men I hurt and wondered if maybe I could attack an animal after all if I really needed to. I just didn't think I could kill one if it wasn't hurting us.

Kith looked at me seriously, "Okay, I'll try to catch a fish first and then we can set up the traps later today. If you can just help me string them up, I'm pretty sure I can do the rest myself now."

Excitement filled me. If this worked, I was sure I could convince Kith to stay a while at the stream. The exercise had helped strengthen him, but I wanted him to have a chance to rest too.

Of course, without a town, we'd have no access to medical supplies, but I felt certain we could figure that out. Kith's leg didn't need to be bandaged all the time anymore, though having it wrapped did seem to help with the pain. Without it bleeding, though, the bandages that were on it were able to be washed and reused. Feverfew would be nice to have, though.

Laying back, I watched Kith struggle for a long time, trying to catch a fish, and my spirits began to sink. He was still not very stable on his leg, and he couldn't very well use his walking stick while trying to spear a fish. Several times, when he went to lunge for a fish, he fell over into the water and I had to help him out. He was determined to catch one, though, and each time I convinced him to take a break, he got back to it after only a few minutes.

Finally, after what seemed like ages, I watched Kith lunge once again and prepared myself to help him up out of the water. Before I could even get up, he rose out of the water holding up his spear triumphantly, shaking a skewered fish.

We were both so excited, we decided to cook the fish right then for an early dinner. While it was cooking, we worked together to make the traps. I never really got the hang of making the traps since Kith was always the one who set them, but I was able to help with his instructions. By the time the fish was done cooking, there were two traps all ready to go.

Feeling very accomplished, we halved the fish and decided we would only set one half aside for later, hoping that we would have more meat soon. We hadn't had a chance to find any other food growing around, since the whole day was focused around the fish. Still, it was nice to have something meaty again, and there were always berries nearby that were a great snack.

"Do you think we could stay here for a while? It would be great to have a chance to rest, and the traps will work better if we give it some time to actually catch something." I stole a glance at Kith's face and it didn't look promising, "We could set more traps tonight and give them a few days." I rushed on, "Maybe try fishing again?"

Kith laughed, "Are you going to let me say anything?"

I looked at him sheepishly, and he laughed again.

"We can stay for another night since we took the trouble to set the traps. Let's try to get up two more before we go to bed."

Although that wasn't exactly the answer I hoped for, I was confident that I could get him to extend the time if we managed to catch anything in the traps, so I worked hard and we got up two more just as it was getting dark.

The next morning, when I woke up, Kith was already out of bed. Wiping the sleepiness from my eyes, I looked at him again to find that he was working with his knife. I jumped up in excitement "We caught something!"

I started to walk toward him, then stopped when I saw the dead rabbit in his hands. Turning away, I breathed deeply, calming myself.

"I'm sorry, Mara, I was trying to finish skinning it before you woke up!"

Feeling silly again, I allowed Kith to finish skinning the

rabbit as I went to the stream to dip my feet in the water. I wasn't sure why it bothered me so much to see him skinning the animals we ate. When I was cooking the meat, I knew that it came from an animal and that Kith killed that animal for us to eat it. Still, something about seeing the meat still intact just caused knots in my stomach.

"What do you think about finishing off that fish, since we'll have other meat for later?" Kith's obvious choice of not mentioning the rabbit directly made me smile.

"That sounds good. After we eat, I'll go looking for some fruit or something to accompany the meat later." I took it as a good sign that he didn't bother objecting to me going out by myself to look for food.

That evening, as the rabbit cooked, I tried again to ask Kith if we could stay at the stream for a while. I found a big bunch of small purple berries to accompany the meal, increasing my certainty that staying would be a good idea.

"Maybe one more day since we caught something in one trap. We might be able to catch more and that would be good to have when we move on."

I didn't like that Kith kept talking about moving on. It made sense to me to stay here where there was plenty of water running right beside us and so far we had good luck with catching food. If Kith wasn't sure by now that this place was perfect for us to stay for a while, I would have to convince him. Showing him we could be safe here would be essential. As I got ready for sleep, plans started forming in my mind.

The next day, while Kith checked the traps, I began looking for the perfect spot to build us a shelter. After a while, I found an area that was full of tall bushes all bunched up together. I looked at it for a while, thinking. Getting on my hands and knees, I used my claws to clear a small path into the middle of the bushes. Then I cut away an entire bush from the center of the area and began laying leafy branches across the top of the open space. There were scratches all over my body from the process, but once I was finished I crawled back out to examine my work.

Anyone looking at it closely could tell the middle of the

bunch looked different than the rest, but no one just walking by should notice anything. Taking some more leafy branches I weaved them together to make a door that would cover the crawl space I cleared.

Then, walking back to the fire, I decided having a place to sit by the fire would be nice too. Along with the drying rack I planned to make. I searched the area for a log big enough for us to sit on and then began dragging it over to the fire. It was heavier than I expected, but I got it to the fire and placed a large rock behind it so it wouldn't roll. Right as I finished, I heard Kith quietly calling my name. Excited, I went to find him.

"Two of our traps caught something!" He grinned. "One of them is big enough to feed us for several days." He knew by now not to tell me what animals he caught, and I was happy to know we would have meat for quite some time.

"I told you they'd be a good idea." I smiled teasingly at him. This only strengthened my position that we should stay put.

"Where did you go?" Kith asked while we sat on the log I put by the fire, working together to cook the meat. He had stopped to look at me, "You have scratches all over you!"

"I was making us a shelter," I said in excitement. It wasn't how I had planned to tell him, but I couldn't resist answering.

Kith looked a little worried, "I don't know if it's a good idea for us to stay in one place for too long. If any word from that town gets out, Ducar will know to look for us in this area."

Determined to change his mind, I walked Kith near the spot where I made our fort in the bushes. He looked around confused, "What am I supposed to be looking at?" he said finally.

I laughed triumphantly, and then removed the door from our new fort and crawled inside. I heard Kith gasp.

"Wow. This is really hidden. You must have worked hard on it."

His acknowledgment sent pride shooting through me. "We can't stand up at all, and the inside is pretty tight, but no one would see us if they happened to pass by."

Kith stared at the fort and looked all around for a long time, then sighed. "Okay, Mara, I can tell you aren't going to give

up on staying here. Let's try it out for a few more days and see if
we can keep catching food like we have been."

CHAPTER FOURTEEN: AUGUST

✳   Kith   ✳

As much as I fought Mara's requests to stay at the stream for long, I was glad when she found a way to force me to give in to her. The area was calming, and the opportunity to rest was a relief.

While my leg was definitely getting stronger, it was still painful to walk on it for long. The pain was more bearable, but with us being out of feverfew, it was nice not to worry about overworking it. I didn't want to admit to Mara how right she was, though. Part of me knew I should, but the stubbornness overshadowed that part.

Lounging in the grass; massaging another cramp out of my leg, I breathed in the scents of the area. The sound of the water moving over the rocks was almost musical. Sunlight sparkled across the top of the water enticingly, and I realized it had been a few days since I last bathed.

Once the cramp was gone, I slipped out of my clothes and dipped my feet into the cool water. Mara was already splashing around further down the stream, her face displaying pure bliss. My heart warmed at the sight of her having fun, with no traces of fear.

Walking deeper into the stream to wash, I realized it was much less painful than walking on land. I felt lighter, so it didn't feel like I was putting as much pressure on the injury. Rising up on the balls of my feet, I let the muscles stretch. Without having to support so much weight, the pain wasn't as searing as it normally was.

After washing, I returned to walking around. There was definitely still pain from the muscle getting worked, but I was able to tolerate it much more. Walking around was exhilarating, even though I knew it wasn't much. As I got more confident, I decided to take a risk: I jumped slightly. Most of my body still remained in the water, allowing me to drift back down slowly. The impact of my foot returning to the bottom of the stream sent a shiver of pain up my leg, and I inhaled sharply.

"What are you doing?" I didn't notice Mara watching me, but she was clearly able to see the pain the jump caused.

"The water makes me lighter and walking doesn't hurt as bad. I think it could help my leg."

Eyeing me suspiciously, she spoke slowly, like she was thinking about her words carefully. "You seemed to be in a lot of pain with that jump."

It was obvious there was more she wanted to say but chose not to. "Jumping so soon probably wasn't my best idea. Still need to work up to it. I can bounce and stretch a bit, though, and it doesn't hurt much."

"I'm glad it doesn't hurt much." There was a slight hesitation with the 'much' and she paused before continuing. "Just make sure not to overdo it. If you hurt it too badly, I don't have a way to treat it anymore." For a second, I could see the guilt and worry she had been dealing with return, but she shook her head as if to force the thoughts away.

"I'll be careful, Mara. I promise."

Grinning, she splashed me. "Good." Then she turned and ran through the water. Her running was slowed, but even so, I struggled to catch her. Even though I wasn't used to moving quickly, I managed to close in and splash her back before losing balance, causing me to tumble fully underwater.

Laughing, I popped up just in time to get splashed in the face. Sputtering out the water, I looked around, but Mara was hidden. As I turned, she leaped up from behind a rock and splashed me again, a burst of giggles ringing through the clearing.

Chuckling, I raised my hands. "I surrender. Need to rest."

Pulling myself onto a nearby rock, I sat and kicked my legs slowly through the moving water. Mara spotted a butterfly resting on a flower, and crept as close to it as she could, moving in complete silence. Watching in awe, I realized how stealthy she had become, and how much control she had over her body. When she got close to the butterfly, she crouched next to it and stayed perfectly still, examining its beauty. It was several minutes before she got tired of looking at the creature and moved away.

Feeling rested, I dropped back into the water and continued walking around. Every once in a while I would bounce a bit, but I didn't try jumping again. By the time we went to bed, I was exhausted. Even so, the pain in my leg was mild, especially compared to how it felt while we were traveling.

Most of the next several days were spent in the water. I still had to take several breaks, but they gradually decreased. Bouncing became less difficult, as my muscles readjusted to the movement.

While not the main goal, I wanted to get back to being able to jump around. I missed leaping into the trees and swinging with Mara. Landing was much too painful at first to make that a good idea, but I kept working on it every day.

One night, Mara and I stretched out next to the fire. She smiled in contentment, and I couldn't help but smile back. "Alright, Mara. You were right."

She raised her eyebrows as she glanced over at me. "About?" I could tell by the gleam in her eyes that she knew what I meant, but I said it anyway.

"Staying here. It's been great."

We stayed there in silence for a while longer, watching the stars sparkle in the sky. As often as we stared at those same stars, it was never as relaxing as it was here.

One day, about a month after I started working my leg in the water, I noticed that bouncing barely bothered it, even when I moved quickly. Crouching down, I felt the muscle. The scars were still large and bumpy, but other than that it felt close to normal. Squeezing didn't hurt like it used to.

Looking around to make sure Mara wasn't watching me, I took a small jump. Landing was uncomfortable, but didn't really hurt. I jumped a bit higher. There was a small spark of pain, but it faded quickly. Jumping even higher, I allowed myself to land with almost full force. This time the pain hit hard for several seconds, but I breathed deep and allowed it to subside. Grinning, I sat on my resting rock. It would still take some time and work, but I'd be able to jump again.

Kith's leg had gotten so much better that I was beginning to think he would be able to walk on it like normal soon. He was gaining more strength all the time and I watched as he started doing more without his walking stick.

The stream proved to be a great place for us. Kith was able to swim without hurting too much, we always had water right by us, and between the fish and our traps, we were able to keep ourselves well fed.

It felt good to be on our own and not relying on the town to supply everything for us. I was finally beginning to feel like all of Beatrice and Isaac's hard work with us was paying off, and I knew they would be proud.

One day, after Kith speared a rather large fish, he was cleaning it over beside the stream while I worked on our lunch. Right as I was finishing up, he called me over.

"I know you don't like to see the insides but look! I was cleaning the fish out and some of his guts fell into the water and three more fish came over to eat it!"

"They eat the insides of other fish?" I yelped in disgust.

"Don't you understand? We can use the insides of the fish I spear to lure more fish to us and catch them!"

"That would be a good way to stock up!" I said, trying not to think about how disgusting the whole thing was. "I've been thinking about how we're going to last this winter without Isaac helping us. If we can catch a lot of fish, maybe we can smoke them."

Kith looked at me thoughtfully, then looked back down at the fish who were now swimming away, having finished what they came for. He stared for a while, and I knew he was thinking hard.

"Do you think we could find some way to trap the fish without killing them and keep them in the water?" he asked.

Not sure what he was trying to accomplish, I thought for a moment before responding, "If we had some sort of net we could catch them."

"I'm thinking if we can trap the fish then we don't have to kill them right away. We can keep them in the water and just have them easily available when we need the meat. Then, when it gets close to winter, we can stock up on the fish we've already got trapped so we're less likely to run out."

I stared at Kith for a moment, thinking through his idea. It was brilliant if we just knew how to make it work. We sat by the stream and dipped our feet in the water as we ate, watching the fish swim by.

Suddenly, a thought came to me. "We could dig a little pond for them to stay in so they can't continue downstream."

Kith's face lit up, "That's brilliant! We can use rocks to block it off and dig it just to the side where the current can carry the fish in, and then they can't get back out!"

We started digging the pond that evening. I didn't know if the fish would really fall for our little pond very easily with it being off to the side of the stream, but it felt good to be working toward something again. We spent the next several days digging out the pond and setting large rocks all around so the fish couldn't get back out once they were caught.

Moving the rocks around several times, we tried to find the best way to catch the current. After watching a fish escape when the pond overflowed, we rearranged the rocks again to leave tiny gaps to allow the water to continue to flow out of our pond and back into the stream.

Once we finally finished digging, we started putting the fish guts into the pond. At first, it seemed like it wasn't going to work. We stood there watching for a long time. Finally, Kith suggested we go for a swim and check on it later. When we came back a few hours later, there were two fish in our pond. One was so small, I didn't think it was worth keeping it, but Kith said it could grow over time so we decided to let it stay. The other was a good medium-sized fish.

After building the pond, we started throwing all of the guts from the fish and the animals we caught in our other traps into it. It seemed to be working quite well. Before long, there were several fish trapped, and I began to wonder if we made it big enough.

By now, Kith's leg was well enough that he started trying more short hunting trips. I argued at first that it was unnecessary because we were already getting plenty of food between the traps and the pond. Kith pointed out; however, that if we needed to leave the stream it would be good for him to have more practice with hunting.

At first, I insisted he stay close by so if anything happened I was within ear shot. Annoyance flicked across his face at my insistence, but I knew that he was remembering all of his own worrying over me. Trying to hide my amusement, I watched him battle with his own pride, and in the end he agreed to stay within earshot.

When Kith came back with the meat from an animal I didn't care to know about, he looked thoughtful. "Between the traps, the pond, and my hunting, we might be able to save up enough meat for the winter, but we'll need somewhere to store it."

Seeing the light in Kith's eyes, I could tell he already had an idea. "What did you have in mind?" I asked.

"Well, I figured we could just dig out a little cellar for the food, kind of like how you dug out our cave. We could cover it to keep animals out."

Over the next few days, we each worked on digging out the cellar. We dug down a ways and then over, making a space where we could stand up. Then we collected long sticks and pushed them into the dirt, putting several side-by-side to make shelves for storing the meat.

Stretching out on the grass, I sighed. "I'm seriously looking forward to some rest."

Kith's smile looked like it was half grimace. "About that..."

Propping myself up on my elbow, I scowled at him. "What?"

"Do you remember what Isaac said about making food last longer?"

It took me a minute of thinking to recall what he was talking about. "You're saying we need to build a smoker like he showed us."

"Yes. We can use all the mud we pulled out of the ground from the cellar and the cave. It shouldn't be too difficult since he explained how to do it."

Flopping back down, I covered my eyes with my arm. "I understand that we need it, but can we at least wait until tomorrow to start?"

With a chuckle, he joined me on the ground. "Starting tomorrow sounds good."

Luckily, the work for the smoker was easier than digging out and building a cellar. We used sticks to build four frames for the sides, with one a little shorter than the other three. The sides of the longer frames extended a few inches past the rest to give us room to dig them into the ground to make them more secure.

Before encasing the frames in the mud, we crisscrossed some sticks between the walls to create a bunch of shelves to hold the meat. The fourth side was encased in the mud but only tied in place so we could remove it to empty and restock the shelves.

Once the sides were complete, we made a lid. Isaac said the lid would need to allow some of the smoke to escape, so we left small holes close to the corners. The finished smoker wasn't as pretty as the ones in the books Isaac let us look through, but; after some testing and fine-tuning it worked well enough.

This time, I waited until our first batch of meat was smoking away before I allowed myself to relax on the grass. "Now I'm seriously looking forward to a break. And don't tell me we have some new project to do."

Laughing, Kith crouched to add another stick into the fire at the bottom of the smoker. "I do believe we've earned some rest."

One day, while Kith was out hunting, I started the smoker and then went to wash off in the stream. As I splashed around, I heard a bird whistling. The sounds of all the animals were so serene out here so far from the towns. I listened for a while, and soon heard a different tone whistling in reply to the bird. I lay back in the water and floated, just listening to the birds whistling back and forth to each other.

I started to wonder what they could be talking about. Birds

had so many different tones, I wondered if they had a different tone for every type of conversation. My mind wandered to thinking of birds giving each other warning through a whistle. Maybe when they saw a scary animal, they would whistle a warning tone to let all the other birds know they needed to stay away.

This gave me an idea. When Kith got back from hunting, I told him my thoughts about the birds. As my story progressed, Kith's lips twitched up into a grin. "Are you about to tell me we're going to come up with a secret code through whistling?"

Smiling sheepishly, I admitted, "I've already been practicing."

Throughout the next weeks, we came up with a warning whistle, a whistle to say the coast was clear, and one simply to let us know where each other were. Whenever Kith left to go hunting, we would practice our whistles, occasionally trying them out to see how far apart we could get and still hear each other. It became a little game, but also something we took quite seriously.

✳   Kith   ✳

Time passed quickly at the stream. It was like we were living in a dream, spending so much time relaxing and having fun. For several days in a row, I even forgot to worry about anything. For some reason, this slightly bothered me.

It wasn't that I enjoyed worrying, but I was afraid that I was becoming lax in my precautions. Mara's nightmares still came every night, however, her reactions were calmer, and she didn't take long to forget about them.

After one of her slightly worse nightmares, I sat and watched her drift back to sleep. In my mind, I saw the frail little girl with sunken eyes and pale sickly skin that I escaped the freak show with. The young girl lying beside me was completely different. Although it had only been somewhere around a year and a half since we ran away, she had grown so much.

My mind froze as I realized how long we had been on the

run. We survived for quite some time, which was amazing, but I knew at that moment that I was forgetting something huge. Without waking Mara, I carefully searched around for where she stashed the calendar she stole. She was still marking off the days, so it wasn't hard to find what date it was.

Quickly confirming my suspicions, I counted the days until Mara's birthday. She made mine so special, I couldn't forget hers or she would be devastated. Returning the calendar to her hiding place, I made sure it wasn't noticeable that I took it, and crept outside.

There were no nearby towns I could sneak into to find her a gift. Whatever I gave her would have to be something I made. She made several changes to my walking stick, which made it much more special, but I couldn't think of anything I could make that she needed as much as I needed that.

A special meal could be done, but I wanted her to have something to keep with her. I'm not sure how long I sat staring at the water, lost deep in my thoughts before Mara emerged from the fort. She smiled wide and gave me a little wave, Gracie grasped tight in her arms. There was a time when me being out of the fort before she was up would have worried her, but now it was normal for us to rise at different times. I was always there to calm her nightmares, but I often let her go back to sleep and got up.

Since it was still early, Mara decided to play with Gracie for a bit before we made breakfast. She really loved that doll. It was the first toy she ever remembered, and I knew how much it meant to her. Dirt and leaves clung to the doll's hair and clothes, but Mara didn't pay much attention to that.

While watching her, inspiration struck. Without drawing any attention, I looked around for some decent-sized branches. With how many trees we were surrounded by, it shouldn't be too hard to find, but I wanted it to be perfect. Finding time to work on my idea might prove to be difficult, though. Even with all our free time, Mara and I still spent most of it close to each other.

While I was getting out the food to fix breakfast, I looked through and located the knives and chisels that Isaac left us. They would be needed for my gift. Tucking them away for later, I made breakfast in a distracted state. Suddenly, the smell of burning meat brought me out of my fantasies. Groaning, I pulled the food off the fire and set it down.

Sniffing, Mara came over and gave me a questioning look. "Did you fall asleep?"

"No." I pushed some dirt around with my toe, avoiding looking at her. "I was just distracted watching the light on the stream."

With a quick shrug, my answer was accepted and we ate. Luckily, the burning wasn't too bad. Mara gave me a strange look as I shoveled the food into my mouth, hardly tasting it at all. Remembering how oddly she behaved before my birthday, I forced myself to slow down. I didn't want her to know I realized her special day was coming up.

"Since the water distracted you enough to burn our food, do you want to go swimming again today?" Mara's tone was light, gently teasing.

"Swimming does sound nice. I've really come to love the water." I was hesitant to waste time, especially since my project would likely take a lot of work, but I didn't think I could get much done with her up and about, anyway.

While floating on my back, just letting the stream carry me, I spotted a branch that would be perfect. It was almost as thick around as my leg, and straight. Looking at the shore, I tried to remember as much about the area as possible so I could return to chop off the branch.

After lunch, I decided to take a risk. "I've been thinking it might be a good idea to build some more traps and other fortifications. Think I'll work on that. You can play or swim if you want."

"Alright. Let me know if you need some help." Grabbing Gracie, she wandered off and found a tree to climb to play in. It wasn't long before I heard her giggling as she swung around on the branch.

Racing back to the tree I saw earlier, I started cutting at the base of the branch. The thickness would be perfect for her gift, but cutting it down was more difficult than I thought it would be.

Once I finally got it down, I trimmed it to where it would be just barely longer than the doll was tall. It was rough and ugly at this point, and I was exhausted from all the cutting. I knew I needed to have something to show Mara, so I quickly made some spears to place in hidden spots around the edge of the clearing.

Although I intended to stay up after Mara fell asleep to work on her gift again, I fell asleep quickly. Waking with a start, I realized it was more than half way through the night, and I hadn't done any work. Grabbing the chisels and sneaking out of the fort as quietly as possible, I grabbed the branch from its hiding place. The bark needed to come off before I could do anything else, so I ripped it off in huge chunks. The wood underneath was smooth and pale.

Taking a chisel, I carefully made a line going down the middle of the wood. I hadn't used the chisels much at all, but I figured they couldn't be too difficult to get used to. Digging into the wood all around the line, I slowly made it deeper. By the time I split it, the sun was rising, and I needed to go back into the fort.

Over the next few days, I hollowed out the wood carefully. The bottom was scratchy, so I used the chisel to slowly try to even it out. Just as I was almost satisfied, the chisel caught on a bump and twisted. I almost screamed as a chunk of wood came out with it, leaving a hole as big as my thumb going all the way through. Mara's birthday was in just a couple of days, I didn't have time to start over.

Sighing in frustration, I decided to finish it as it was and try to find a way to patch the hole. I continued hollowing out both sides and made sure they'd close together well. Once it was usable, I added some flowers on the top as a special decoration. It wouldn't stay closed, though.

There was still some leather left from the destroyed pack, but not much. As I searched through the bags to find it, I came across a bundle of scraps. Some of the fabric matched the cushion that Mara made for my walking stick. She didn't mention taking more cloth than she used, and I didn't often go through the pack she carried. Deciding not to let that bother me, I grabbed the scrap leather and one particularly soft scrap of cloth. Hopefully, Mara wouldn't get upset about me using it. I placed the soft scrap in the bottom for a mattress, and then used a thin strip of the leather to tie the box closed.

The night before Mara's birthday, I went to bed eager for the next day. She was silent most of the day, and I wondered if I succeeded in making her think I forgot her birthday was coming up.

*   Mara   *

Ever since taking the calendar from town, I kept track of the days. It seemed important to me for us to know what time of year it was. So when it started getting close to my birthday, I wondered if Kith would know. I didn't want to point it out and make him feel like he must do something for me, but I silently wished for a birthday like most people would get.

For a while, I was certain Kith didn't have a clue. It wasn't until a couple of days before my birthday that I realized he was acting a little strange. At first, I didn't think anything of it, until I remembered how strange I acted leading up to his birthday. Paying more attention, I started to watch him, but either I misread something or he was very good at hiding.

The day before my birthday came, and a part of me was certain Kith was up to something, while another part still wasn't quite sure. I tried to decide if I would bring it up the next day, but I didn't want to make him feel bad if he didn't do anything. Going to bed, I decided to just wait and see what he did before figuring out whether or not to mention it.

When I woke up the next morning, I instantly knew Kith was planning something. He wasn't in our little bush fort anymore, which wasn't altogether strange. He used to refuse to leave my side while I was sleeping, but since my nightmares had gotten calmer, he began leaving the fort when he awoke. Still, he was never far away in case I needed him.

I wasn't really sure what tipped me off; I just woke up and

knew. Laying still and listening, I heard Kith whistling a tune we hadn't practiced before. When I listened closely, I realized he was whistling the same tune Beatrice used to sing to us on our birthdays. I couldn't remember the words, and maybe he couldn't either, but the sound was definitely the same.

A huge smile spread across my face as I sat up and crawled outside. Kith was standing not far from the entrance, holding a bunch of berries and still whistling the tune. When he saw me emerge, he smiled broadly.

"Happy Birthday!" He said happily, handing me the bouquet of berries. I plopped a few berries in my mouth gratefully. One sniff told me he already cooked our breakfast as well.

We ate the fish Kith prepared and then went for a swim in the stream. The water was getting a little cold now, so we didn't stay for too long. Once we were out, Kith gave me a mischievous smile.

"Did you know I knew it was your birthday?" he asked.

"I thought you might, but I wasn't really sure until I woke up this morning."

Kith's smile broadened and he asked excitedly, "Did you know I was making you something?"

Bouncing excitedly, I asked, "What did you make?"

He laughed and ran off to the trees. A few seconds later, he came trotting back with his blanket wrapped around something. "Did you even notice Gracie wasn't in your bag?" he asked.

Confusion crossed my face, "No. Is Gracie in your blanket?"

Kith laughed again and handed me the blanket. It was heavy, and I felt something hard inside it. Pulling the blanket off, I revealed a hand-crafted box. It was beautiful, with flowers carved into the top and some of the leather from our old pack used to tie it shut.

Thinking of what Kith said about Gracie, I untied the leather carefully and opened it. Gracie lay neatly inside. She looked like Kith cleaned her, too. The twigs and leaves that were stuck to her were gone, and a stain where I dropped some of my food on her, had been almost completely scrubbed away. She looked almost new, and I couldn't help but be reminded of the man who gave her to me.

Looking at Kith, I tried to keep the tear that was forming in my eye from falling, and I could tell he knew what I was thinking. He hugged me close. "Now you can carry her safely so she won't get so dirty from riding in the packs."

Wrapping my arms around my brother, I squeezed him tightly. Isaac wouldn't want us to be sad today, so I bounded back out of Kith's arms and gave him a big smile. "Thank you! I can already tell Gracie loves it!"

We spent the rest of the day playing with Kith's ball, and swinging through the trees while Gracie watched from safely inside her new case. Kith was much slower than me after his injury, so we didn't race, but I couldn't help noticing how much better he was getting. He seemed to be favoring the injured leg less, and I knew before long he would be back to normal again.

✳   Kith   ✳

One of my favorite things about staying near the stream was the ability to wash often. We had spent so much time covered in grime, that being able to keep clean was such a relief. The dirt that covered me often disguised the fact that there was blood mixed in. Some of it was my own, small scrapes and cuts gotten during our travels, but often it was from preparing the meat.

We did our best to get the worst off during our travels. Rainy days were often used for getting as clean as we could since we didn't want to waste the water in our skins. Even so, being able to actually dunk underwater and scrub off the grime was much better. Our bathing area of the stream was further away from camp, downstream so we didn't make our drinking water gross.

After one particularly nasty day, I headed for the bathing spot. I had slipped in mud while checking the traps, and leaves were stuck all over me. Mara looked alarmed when I approached to drop off the meat, but as I wordlessly headed for the water I heard her giggles trailing behind me.

Once I scrubbed myself clean, I lay back on the water to listen to the birds like I often did. It was several minutes before I realized there was no music coming from the trees. Looking into the red and yellow branches, I realized most of the colored leaves had drifted to the ground. It happens every year, so it shouldn't be a surprise. We had been so separated from the world here I almost forgot about the passage of time.

I tried to keep drifting, but my mind felt bogged down with the realization of all the changes. As I walked back to camp, the smell of the meat Mara was cooking hit me, and I reveled in the familiarness of it. My stomach rumbled, letting me know how hungry I was. Berries would make a good snack while I waited to eat.

Looking around at the bushes, I realized they were all empty of berries. Most had lost their leaves as well. As my eyes wandered the clearing, I noticed that a lot of the flowers were gone, as well. Everything looked completely different, and I didn't recognize the oasis that we had come to love.

Sitting next to the fire and trying not to pout, I said. "All the berries are gone."

"I noticed that earlier. Too bad we can't cook them and store them in the cellar for winter, isn't it?"

"Yes." Suddenly not feeling talkative, I sat quietly and watched the fire. We were working on preparing for the cold and the lack of food, but I hadn't even thought about how the oncoming winter would change the whole clearing. The beauty of the area drew me here, but now it just looked dreary.

"Are you alright?" I could feel the concern directed my way.

"I'm fine." Sighing, I added. "The birds are all gone, too. Everything is changing."

"It's almost winter. This happens every year."

"I know, but it feels different." I paused to find the right words to explain how I felt, but I barely understood it. "Time almost seemed to stop here. But now I'm seeing all these reminders that it hasn't."

"I understand." When I looked at her face, I realized that there was an underlying restlessness to us both. An uneasiness, one that wasn't just explained by the oncoming cold. The reminder of time passing brought up emotions and thoughts we were pretending weren't always right under the surface.

We fell into silence, the understanding that passed between us enough for the moment. The rest of the day was subdued and quiet as we processed our realizations.

*　　Mara　　*

While I was playing with Gracie one day, I heard Kith's whistle announcing he was coming home from hunting. We had started a ritual of announcing our return any time we left camp. This way, if we heard someone or something coming unannounced, we would know to be on guard. So far, this only happened once, but it turned out to be a large animal. It didn't come through our camp, but when I heard it passing by I climbed a tree; waiting until it was gone to come back down.

Our time at the stream had been pretty peaceful and sometimes I was surprised by how few dangerous animals we saw. We didn't see any more of the animals that attacked Kith. I often wondered where they were now and why they happened to come by us just the one time.

Even still, we were both serious about our safety. Sometimes I felt like it was too much, but I knew how much better it made Kith feel about staying at the stream.

Whistling my reply to let him know I was safe, I waited for him to join me by the stream. When he walked up, the bag he carried was full of meat and I knew it was a successful hunting trip.

"Sorry it took so long. I needed to go out a little further this time to find anything, but I did manage to catch something. I found another berry bush, so I stocked up on those too."

At that, I smiled up at him. "Berries sound great! Could I have a few now for a snack?"

We sat for a while, munching on berries and dipping our toes in the stream. The water was getting colder as the months went on and I wondered how long it would be before we couldn't stand to get in it at all.

Life at the stream was comfortable and an unexpected calm had come over both of us. Sometimes, I wondered how long the calm would last. I wished we could stay here forever, but I wondered if the little fort I built would be warm enough to last through the winter. We would have to leave eventually, but where would we go? I didn't know what we would do to stay warm without having the cave.

"What are you thinking about so intently?" Kith asked, pulling me out of my thoughts.

"Oh. I was just wondering where we will go when we leave the stream."

Kith's face suddenly got serious. "I've wondered the same thing. Maybe if we cover the bushes a little more to keep out the wind, it won't be too cold inside the fort. Then we could stay here and wait out the winter. Of course we'd still have to do our cooking outside this time, but the fire should help to keep us warm."

Although I wasn't fully convinced this would work, I wasn't ready to give up on the stream either. Besides, there were no other options. So we spent the next several days building up around our fort. We decided that being careful with keeping it hidden wasn't as important as adding warmth so we started piling branches and mud around the bushes to block the wind from entering. Kith fashioned a new door out of some branches. While he worked on that, I used a large, flat stick to dig into the small indentation I originally made, until our tiny fort was closer to a small cave.

It was exhausting work, and after several days of digging I decided it would have to do. I longed for a bed to crawl into for rest. There was enough space now, but it still wasn't going to be comfortable. Deciding to do what I could to fix that, I wandered outside for ideas, and saw some of the plants Isaac taught us to weave with. If I were to weave us some mats we could use leaves to soften the ground of the cave and still keep from getting extremely dirty every night. Once Kith finished, he joined me, and I could tell he was missing having an actual bed as well.

With it still being slightly warm outside, it was hard to tell whether the work we did would be enough. It felt warmer on the inside now, though, so we decided to wait and see.

My concern was eased enough that I decided not to worry about the cold until it got here. Surely once it got colder, we would be able to figure out warmth. Even if it meant staying huddled in the fort most of the time. At least we'd be better off inside than roaming around the forest.

✳   Kith   ✳

Cool air hit me as I crawled outside. The sun wasn't fully risen yet; the sky still a swirling piece of art. Mara was as unprepared for the chill as I was.

"I guess the additions to the bushes are helping." She smiled playfully as she rubbed the chill off her arms.

"That seems to be true." I smiled back, but felt a building reservation. The time we spent in our cave last winter was uncomfortable, even with Isaac's help. I felt horribly unprepared for the one we were facing, especially since we were in his house by the time the worst hit.

At least we were able to preserve quite a bit of meat. We filled both our old packs, then stored a lot in the cellar, but I wished there was something other than meat. I already missed the juicy berries we had an abundance of during the summer.

It was tempting to go back inside and wait for the day to get warmer, but I knew there were several things that needed to get done before it got cold for real. As Mara started the fire, I took the pot and went to the stream for water.

The water that ran over my hands as I dipped the pot under was ice cold, sending shivers up my arms. I doubted we'd be doing much more swimming for the next while. The water was getting colder every day, and it took a lot longer to warm up than the rest of the clearing. We had still been getting in during mid-day when it was the warmest, but I wasn't sure how warm it would be getting now.

My hands were still freezing when I put down the pot, so I held them out over the newly blazing fire. The morning seemed so quiet. I thought about talking just to break the silence, but decided against it.

Our morning meals were usually the smallest, since we weren't as hungry as we would be after a full day. It didn't take us long to finish eating, but we stayed next to the fire sipping our warmed water for several minutes. I wished we had tea leaves or something flavorful, but it was still nice drinking something warm with the chill in the air.

I tried to savor the heat from my small metal cup, but it faded quickly once my water was gone. This was a sign that it was time to get up and busy, but I had no desire to go anywhere. Sighing, I stood slowly. "I guess I ought to go check the traps."

Mara nodded. "That's probably a good idea. I think I'll do some more work on our fort, maybe expand it just a little bit."

"More space would be nice, but don't open it up too much. We want to keep it warm."

"I know. But being able to stretch out a bit more would be nice." I knew she was thinking about the cave we were in last winter. It was barely warm enough, but we had a lot of space inside. Without being able to spend a lot of the winter inside a house with a fire, though, it would have quickly gotten too cold for us.

It was nice and warm as I headed out to check the traps, and I enjoyed the feeling of the sun through the trees. Jumping up, I grabbed a branch. My leg still felt tight when jumping, but there wasn't any actual pain anymore. Even swinging and landing didn't hurt much. Every once in a while, I would land at an odd angle and a small twinge would go up my leg, but it faded quickly.

Checking the traps was much faster now that I had healed most of the way. As I got to the last trap, I realized that I would be bringing back a lot less meat than normal. Only two of the traps caught animals, and they were both on the small side.

Not for the first time that day, worry filled me. Winter was going to be extremely rough without Isaac. The rest of the year was hard enough, but cold and snow would make everything more difficult.

As usual, I skinned the animals before taking the meat back to Mara. Caught up in trying to figure out how we were going to survive winter, I almost forgot to greet Mara with my whistle to let her know I was approaching. By the time I whistled, I was a lot closer than normal.

"Sorry, Mara." I could tell my delayed whistle put her at alert. "I wasn't paying attention to how close I was."

She glanced at the meat I was carrying. "Caught up worrying about winter?"

I nodded. She knew me too well for me to try to hide it.

"I worked on the fort some. It should do better at keeping us warm, but we'll also have a bit more room for stretching out."

We smoked the meat without discussing the oncoming winter anymore, but it was reassuring to know I wasn't alone in my concerns.

As we went to store it with the rest before bed, Mara started counting what was in the cellar. "If we divide this out carefully, we could probably make it last all winter."

"We'll be back to being hungry all the time, but I suppose it's doable." I held back a sigh.

She gave me a smile full of worry. "Hungry all the time is better than starving. And we still have some time to prepare."

"There's also the fish in the pond. I don't think we'll be catching many more than we have, but it's something."

"Oh! The fish!" Mara's eyes lit up with excitement. "Do you think we'd be able to lure animals to the traps the same way we lured the fish into the pond?"

Surprise washed over me. How had we not been using the animals we caught as bait? Occasionally, I'd put some small pieces of meat in there, but I tried to avoid using too much so we'd have enough for us.

"That's genius, Mara. I don't know why I didn't already

think of that." I couldn't help but grin. We'd make it through this.

*   Mara   *

As the world got colder, Kith's anxiety worsened. He spent much of his time making sure I was warm enough and insisting we take breaks throughout the day to warm up inside the fort.

The fish we caught in our pond were all stored by now. We already counted up all the food we had, and using the calendar, judged how much food we could spare for each day until winter was over. Our daily servings were usually split in three with the hopes that spacing out our measly portions would make it easier to bear having so little to eat. Still, it was better knowing that we wouldn't starve all winter.

The water was so cold, we couldn't dip in it anymore. Now, when we wanted to bathe, we took a large pot and warmed the water by the fire before splashing it on our faces and bodies. Then we sat by the fire to stay warm while we dried.

One morning, after sitting together in the fort, trying to stay as warm as we could, I finally emerged to get the day started, and found the world covered in white.

"Kith! It's snowing!" I exclaimed and moved faster to get outside, barely noticing the cold through my excitement.

Kith emerged shortly after me, and I was waiting for him with a ball of snow clutched in my hands. I pelted it at him and ran, knowing he would be scooping up a snowball of his own.

Hiding behind a tree with another snowball in my hands, I waited for Kith to come near me. Knowing his senses would tell him where to come to find me, as soon as he was close, I jumped out and pelted my other snowball at him yelling "Gotcha!"

Kith yelped and dropped the snowball he had clutched in his hand, and I took the opportunity to put more distance between us. This time, I grabbed a snowball and climbed a tree, waiting to see Kith again. I crouched down and held the snowball, ready to throw it.

As I stared all around the ground, I suddenly felt a ball of cold snow hit my back. Yelping in surprise, I turned to see Kith howling with laughter three trees over. "How did you find me!?"

"Well, when I'm up here and you're only looking down, it isn't hard to sneak up on you!" he snickered.

We continued our snowball fight until we were both wet with snow and shivering from the cold. As Kith started building a fire, I grabbed our blankets so we could snuggle up around it while having breakfast.

"I had a hard time finding dry sticks for the fire. They were all covered with snow." Kith's voice sounded strained.

"I didn't think about that being a problem." We stood in silence for a few seconds before a solution occurred to me. "We should start keeping some wood in the bottom of the cellar. It will keep it dry for us. We don't keep the meat on the ground anyway."

Kith smiled at me. "Right. We should get to work on that later today." After another long silence, he added solemnly, "I hope the fort is going to be warm enough in the snow. It already seems to let in a bit of the cold."

He was right. It was getting even colder at night. We talked for a while about how we might keep warmer over winter, but neither of us had any grand ideas. With a sigh, Kith rose. "I've put off doing the rounds long enough."

I watched as he left to go check the traps, then finished my water. A feeling of restlessness overcame me, like I should be doing something while Kith was away, but all the work we were doing on the clearing seemed to be done. In an attempt to feel like I was doing something, I took the wide stick I used to dig the cave out and used it to brush the snow to the edge of the clearing. It would be nice to walk around our usual spaces without the cold wetness under foot.

Kith's returning whistle sounded when I was about halfway done. He came into view soon after, and I eagerly checked to see how much food he brought back. There was a lot of red, and at first I thought there must be a lot of meat to go with it. As he got closer, though, I realized there was no meat in his hands.

Instead, there was blood pouring out of several gashes in his arm.

CHAPTER FIFTEEN: DECEMBER

✳   Kith   ✳

Even though I hadn't found anything in them for a couple of weeks, I kept my routine of checking the traps quickly each morning while the water heated. As I approached each time, my heart fluttered with anticipation, just to sink when they were empty.

This time was no different. As I got close, I listened carefully, hoping for something, even one small rabbit. Suddenly, a snarl roared through the air. It came from up ahead. Freezing in terror, I was transported back to the night my leg was shredded. Before I knew it, I was up the nearest tree. Once the shaking subsided, I inched along slowly toward the sound.

Continuing through the trees, I made my way to the first trap. It remained empty. The snarling was getting louder as I moved on, and I had to force myself to keep going. As I neared the next trap, I thought for sure there was a beast waiting to jump out at me. My heart felt like it was in my throat.

When the trap came into view, it took me several seconds to understand what I saw. The beast I heard was caught in the trap. Being trapped was obviously making it furious. It wasn't just trapped, though. There was blood matted in its fur and splattered all over the ground.

It was bigger than the large dog-beasts that tore apart my leg, but it looked similar. Unsure of how to continue, I watched the animal for several more minutes. To give myself time to think, I went and checked the other traps before returning. It wasn't much of a surprise that they were empty.

Usually, the animals I caught were small and I didn't need anything but my claws and knives to take care of them. This one presented a challenge, though. Briefly, I considered going back for my spear, but I was already starting to freeze and didn't want to waste time.

As I approached the trap, I found a large rock. Climbing

back into the trees, I moved over the animal as quietly as I could before leaping down with the rock at the ready.

It took me a while to get the meat ready to take back, and I was covered in blood and scratches from the struggle. Mara was going to be worried when I showed up like this, but there wasn't much I could do about it.

The gasp as I entered the clearing told me I was right. At least the whistle signal let her know I was alright. "Kith! What happened?"

"There was an animal in one of the traps. A big one. Probably bigger than anything I've brought back before." I couldn't hold back the grin as I pulled it out from behind me.

Eyes wide, she stared in silence for a couple of seconds, "I'm glad my idea worked so well." She grinned. "Come drink some of the hot water and warm up. Let's get that cooking, then I'll bandage you… again." I could've sworn I heard her laughing softly as she turned away.

*   Mara   *

The snow continued on and off for weeks so that the blanket of white covering the ground thickened and the air got even colder. Nights in our dirt and tree covered fort were getting harder to bear. We started sleeping closer together to share body heat and piling both blankets on top of us.

Kith was obviously beating himself up over our situation, so in an attempt to keep his mind off of things, I tried to keep our days light and fun. Random snowball fights were a staple and good for getting our blood pumping, but they could get old quickly so I was forced to think of other ways to get our minds off of how cold we were. We started wrapping leftover cloth straps around our feet to keep them warm. Not having shoes wasn't too much of an issue for us before, but the cold snow changed that. Wrapping them up made a huge difference, and each night we would unwrap them and hang the wraps up by the fire to dry for the next day.

We spent our days racing through the trees, trying to see who could swing the furthest using their tail, playing catch, kicking Kith's ball to each other, and making an entire family of snowpeople. The snow made for a lot of great games, we just wished it wasn't so cold.

Once the snow came, we noticed the stream beginning to freeze over. At first, we were able to hit the ice with a rock in order to break it and get to the water underneath. When we wanted to bathe, we would fill our pot with the icy water and heat it for a while before using it to rinse ourselves off. After a while, though, it was frozen over and we were now setting long sticks on fire and using them to melt the top layer of ice in order to get our drinking and cooking water. We gave up on bathing for the time being.

One day while we were melting the ice, I looked out at the stream and realized just how thick the ice was.

"Do you think the ice is thick enough to hold us?" I asked, a new idea springing to life.

Kith gave me an expression that clearly told me I was not to try such a crazy idea. Grinning at him mischievously, I tenderly set one foot on the ice. Grabbing a thick branch nearby, I stepped forward with my second foot. Kith was holding his breath, his eyes bulged as he watched me let go of the branch and slide my feet across the stream.

Letting out a shrill of excitement, I called for Kith to join me, my hand outstretched.

"Mara, you're crazy! What if it breaks!?"

Laughing, I continued to glide across the ice. Finally, I turned in time to see Kith adjusting himself on the ice and slowly letting go of the same branch. His eyes were huge, locked on mine, as he moved one foot and then the next. His face broke out in a grin and he let out a small "*whoop*" and slid over to where I was. He tried to stop about a foot from me and there was barely enough time to notice the look of terror return to his face before he crashed into me, sending us both falling to the ice.

"I'm so sorry! I couldn't stop! Are you...laughing?"

The fall was painful, but I recovered quickly and couldn't help but laugh. I tried to hide it at first by burying my head in my hands, but then I realized that just made Kith think I was hurt.

"You should...have seen... YOUR FACE!" I finally managed to say between bursts of laughter.

Glaring, he tried to stand up only to slip again causing another fit of laughter.

"Are you okay?" I asked, trying to calm down and make myself sound more serious.

"It's so slippery!" He exclaimed.

Deciding to try it myself, I put my hands firmly on the ice and pushed my legs up. Then, slowly, I lifted the top half of my body to standing. My arms flailed for a few seconds in an attempt to stabilize myself. Once I felt stable, I looked at Kith triumphantly.

"Show off!" He yelled and then mimicked my technique. "Well, how do we stop then since you're already such a pro?"

"I guess we just don't run into things and we'll stop eventually on our own!" I smirked.

Kith glared again, but I could see that he wasn't really upset. There was a tiny hint of a smile on his face that he was trying to hide.

We spent a while sliding around on the ice, until we were both cold, tired, hungry, and sore from falling a few more times. Ice skating was added into our regular list of things to do. I was changing it up regularly so we wouldn't get too bored with any one thing, but skating on the ice soon became a favorite and we were getting pretty good at it. It was a way for us to enjoy the stream again even when we couldn't swim in it.

One morning, after eating our breakfast, Kith went to the stream without saying a word and tenderly set his feet on it to test the ice. We knew that eventually the ice would melt, and even though the world was still frozen, we were careful to test it each time before we put on our full weight.

Once Kith was in the middle of the stream sliding with ease, I joined him. We slid up and down the stream for a while until he asked if I wanted to play ice ball again. It was a game we made up ourselves with different variations. Some days we kicked the ball down the stream, racing after it to get in the next kick while others we grabbed large sturdy sticks and hit the ball with them. Sometimes we awarded points for how far the ball went and other times we aimed for certain places and allotted a number of points to hit the ball there. Many sticks were broken in the process, but it was still a fun game.

"Let's just kick the ball today. I'm tired of you constantly breaking all the sticks." Kith said with a grin.

"That sounds good, except it's you that always breaks the sticks." I stuck my tongue out as I kicked the ball past him, making him run down stream to get it.

"That was just mean, Mara." Kith huffed his way over to the ball and kicked it even further down the stream.

"No fair!" I dashed across the ice to try to catch up with him and the ball. "You're supposed to kick it back to me."

"Oops." Kith laughed as he kicked the ball to me.

"Oh, I'm sure it was an accident." I rolled my eyes and kicked the ball toward him. He barely missed it and it continued on downstream.

We both took off running after it, but Kith got there first. He kicked the ball a little too hard and sent it flying into a tree. Laughing, I ran full out for the ball and had almost made it when I heard a cracking sound that made me stop dead in my tracks. Before I had time to think, a large branch dropped from the tree toward my head. I managed to dodge the branch, but the ice under me broke open. With just enough time to scream, I was plunged into the icy stream.

✳   Kith   ✳

The first time Mara went out on the frozen water, I felt an intense panic go through me. When she got to the center, though, and seemed to be having so much fun, I decided to put the worry aside and enjoy it with her.

Winter was bleak and cold, but Mara was always good at

353

finding ways to make things enjoyable. Once it was frozen over, the stream stopped providing me with the enjoyment I experienced for the past few months. It was as if the last of the hope the area promised disappeared.

Running around on the ice brought some of that back, though. It was a reminder that the stream wasn't gone, just covered for a while. More and more, I found myself drawn to our games on the ice, even knowing the risk.

When Mara ran for the ball laughing, I couldn't help but smile. Then I saw the crack, and heard the sound of ice ripping apart. It happened so fast I couldn't react, yet time seemed to move slowly as Mara's laugh turned into a scream and she sank out of view.

I ran to the hole, hoping to see her just below. When I didn't, I jumped in without hesitation. Frozen water surrounded me and the stabbing pain of the cold made my body stiffen immediately. Against my instincts, I opened my eyes and looked around. Instantly, the iciness of the water stabbed at them. While they were great in darkness, my eyes weren't used to darkness under water. Still, it didn't take me long to find Mara. As soon as my hand grabbed her arm, I pushed myself up and we rose to the hole together.

By the time we got to the top, a small layer of ice already covered the hole, and I had to break it to climb out. My lungs burned when the cold air hit them, but I ignored that. Mara was coughing and sputtering, but I found myself glad she was still breathing. Feeling useless as she struggled to clear all the water, I rubbed her arms and patted her back. Her shivering kept getting worse, though.

Once her coughing slowed, I picked her up and carefully worked my way off the ice. Snow started coming down again as I made my way back to camp with Mara. I expected her to fight me at some point, argue that she could walk on her own, but she didn't. Our wet clothes clung to us, the water starting to freeze at the edges. Even walking normally, it would have taken several minutes to make it back to camp at the distance we went, but each step was agony. Forcing myself to keep going took all of my determination.

Eventually we made it back. Setting Mara on one of the logs next to the fire pit, I built a fire as quickly as I could. Once it was up and roaring, I grabbed the blankets out of our fort. "Mara, we need to get the wet clothes off of you."

Her eyes looked glazed from the cold, and her shivering was so intense her whole body was shaking. I helped her out of her wet clothes and bundled her in the blankets. She huddled up quietly.

I took my clothes off as well, struggling with how frozen and heavy they were, and laid both sets on the drying rack Mara had made next to the fire. Huddling under my blanket, I let the warmth cover me. The numbness in my body started to ebb away, replaced by stabbing pains and dull aches. My leg throbbed where the scars were. The cold made it ache often, but with the cold, walking, and stress the pain was more intense.

Once I thawed, I went and sat next to Mara. She felt warmer, but was still shaking quite a bit. Exhaustion overcame me and sitting felt like a lot of work. "Let's go get some sleep, Mara. I think we both could use it."

Nodding, she followed me into the fort. Our clothes dried and warmed next to the fire, so I helped her bundle back up before bundling myself. We curled up together and tried to stay warm.

After some rest, I hoped we'd both feel better, but I woke to Mara coughing. It wasn't the worst cough I'd heard from her, but it worried me. At first I was relieved to notice how much warmer she felt, until I realized she felt too warm. Instantly, I found myself transported back to the moment I almost lost her. Breathing became difficult as my chest tightened. I couldn't allow her to get back to that point.

The ache in my leg remained intense and hard to ignore as I built a fire and started heating water. Mara came to sit next to the fire wrapped in her blanket. She didn't seem as out of it as the night before, which I hoped was a good sign. With my experience taking care of her while sick before, I figured Mara might not be hungry, but knew she needed something in her. Adding some dried meat into the water, I hoped to create a decent broth that she'd be willing to drink.

When I handed her a small bowl of the warmed liquid, she sat staring into it for several minutes before tentatively taking a couple of sips. She winced as it went down, but didn't say anything.

"How are you feeling?" I was concerned by her silence.

When Mara's eyes met mine, there seemed to be a lot of conflicting emotions swirling around in her. "I'm… " Her voice trailed as she thought about her next words. "I'm not sure."

Unsure how to respond to her apparent confusion, I remained silent and waited for her to work out what she was thinking.

"I'm getting sick, but I think I'll be better after a couple days of rest. Is your leg alright after carrying me so far? That couldn't have been easy."

That was just like Mara to be more concerned about me than herself. "I'll be alright. I'm just glad I was able to get to you in time."

She smiled at me before going serious again. "Anyway, it's not being sick that has me feeling so odd. I had a crazy dream last night. It felt so familiar, yet not. I'm not sure what to think of it."

"Tell me about it, and maybe we can figure it out together."

*   Mara   *

Gathering my thoughts, I tried to remember all the details of the odd dream.

The dark walls around me felt like they were closing in. Looking around, I wondered how I got here. I was standing in a narrow hallway leading me down to a room filled with darkness. Whispers were coming from down there, and curiosity got the better of me as I slowly creeped forward.

When I got to the opening of the dark room, I peered around the walls and shock and terror coursed through me, followed quite suddenly by confusion. Ducar was there, but he was different than Ducar was now. For one, he was sitting on the floor of a small square cell not more than four feet across and a single tear lingered on his cheek. The idea that Ducar would ever cry was astounding. As I studied him, I saw that he was losing much of his hair, and his face was far more lined than I ever saw it. This Ducar looked much older, and I wondered if little more than a year could really age someone so much.

I blinked and suddenly I was looking at Ducar from behind the bars of a cell. That was when I realized he didn't have his fake eye or the scratch Kith gave him. Startled, I tried to look around, but I couldn't control my body. Tears streaked my cheeks, and I noticed I was holding someone else's hand between the bars of another cell. My eyes moved without my consent and briefly looked at the man who held my hand before drifting back to Ducar. I could see others in the room out of the corner of my eye. They all had purple skin and dark hair just like mine, and each of them was watching Ducar intently. They looked familiar somehow, but I couldn't quite remember how I knew them.

"I couldn't believe the little devil had done it! I ran out of the tent, just in time to see Kith shoving the last bits of cake in his mouth. Licking his fingers, he actually laughed at me before he turned tail and ran! At least I knew my cake wasn't a complete disaster if he liked it so much to take off with the whole thing!" I stared dumbfounded as Ducar and everyone else laughed heartily.

"I knew my Kithian would be a troublemaker. Such a prankster he was, even when he was so small. Anwen was always telling me…" the words felt insane coming through my mouth, even though I guessed the woman was actually the one speaking. Her voice was soft and I could hear both joy and pain in her words as they trailed off. It seemed she was unable to finish. The man in the cell beside ours squeezed the hand we somehow shared gently.

"And what about Dezmara?" he asked Ducar, his face lighting up.

Ducar smiled and his eyes lit up in a way I had never seen. "The most gentle child, she was. She was still quite small when I was taken, but I could already see how kind her heart was. She would run along behind her brother all the time, I couldn't get her to leave his side. She always admired him so much. He loved it too, I could tell. When she got too far behind, he would slow down just slightly so she would never lose sight of him."

I felt sobs run through my body, the pain of them building up in my chest. The man in the next cage was holding me as well as he could, trying unsuccessfully to soothe me. My eyes remained locked on Ducar, though.

"Thank you," she whispered so quietly I barely realized we had

spoken. "It brings such joy to my heart to hear you talking about Kithian and Dezmara like this. It's hard to think of the years I've already missed with them. They will be grown when I see them again, I am sure." Again, I wondered if she could be talking about us. The names were similar, yet so different.

A boy, a little younger than Kith, sat in the other cell next to the woman. Throwing a dark look our way, he asked "Does everyone on your planet look as weird as you do?"

"Alsandyyr!" We hissed reproachfully. "That is a rude thing to say."

Ducar only laughed and repeated the question back to the boy, teasingly.

Everyone chuckled at that, and the boy seemed to get his courage from the banter, "Do you think we could ever see your world? What does it look like?"

Ducar began explaining the green grass and blue skies that were known to me. The boy gasped at silly things like trees with brown trunks, and laughed out loud when Ducar told him the sun was yellow, and the clouds were white. This all seemed strange to me. What color ought the sun to be?

As I watched, the conversation continued to play out, but the voices got quieter, fuzzy sounding, until they were gone and I was laying dazed in our fort, where I could look outside and clearly see the blue sky and brown trees.

✳   Kith   ✳

Mara's dream brought back all the weird dreams she had the last time she was sick. Once she recovered, I forgot about them. Was she more sick than I thought, or was this her becoming more normal with her nightmares not being as bad as before?

I was lost in thought when I realized Mara was looking at me expectantly. It took me a minute to realize she didn't remember the dreams from before. After some internal debating, I decided to tell her about them as best I could remember. As I spoke, her confusion only deepened.

"I think I remember those a bit, now that you've brought

them up." She paused, as if deep in thought. "What if they're real?"

"You said something similar at the time. I mostly just brushed them off as fever dreams and a sign of how sick you were. You're sick again, but not as sick as then. I don't know what to think of it. Especially of Ducar being there. That makes no sense, especially him being nice."

"I know. The weird thing is, all the stories he told were from us as babies. Or maybe he didn't want to tell them any of the ones after the storm so he could stay on their good side?" I knew she could spend the whole day trying to delve into the meaning of the dream, but I wasn't sure if that was a good thing or not.

"Maybe we shouldn't give the dreams too much thought. There's no way for us to know right now what they mean."

"I know, but it's fun to think about." She smiled again, and I realized that even if they were crazy, the dreams were at least a great break from nightmares.

"It is fun to wonder. As long as it doesn't consume you."

Rolling her eyes and giggling, she said, "Of course, Kith. You worry too much." Shaking her head, she rose from the log next to the fire and disappeared into the fort. I heard her rustling around for a minute before she reemerged with Gracie tucked under her arm.

Seeing her return to playing even while sick was comforting. I knew she wasn't in danger of becoming as bad as she did before if she was feeling up to walking around. Allowing the relief to spread through me, I relaxed next to the fire. The heat was soothing to my leg, and I gently massaged it to try and work out some of the pain.

After some time, I stretched out on the log and let myself relax. Just as I was about to drift off, I heard a voice say, "Kithian! Come look at this!" The addition to my name was weird but held a familiarity to it. I looked around, confused. Then I heard Mara laughing.

Of course. In her dreams, I was referred to as Kithian. Rolling my eyes, I went over to see what she was holding. It was a triangular black rock with a sparkling white line running through it. Partway through the rock it split into two lines, creating an interesting design.

"That's a cool rock." I held it and turned it around in my hands, letting the light glimmer on the white parts. Mara was beaming at me, amusement still showing on her face.

"I really like it. I think I'll keep it." She grabbed the rock out of my hands and moved it around, watching the light play on the sparkles. Chuckling and shaking my head, I wandered back to the fire. I was halfway back when a coughing fit hit Mara.

Having almost forgotten she was sick, I was back at her side in an instant. The coughing didn't take long to subside. Mara must have been putting on a bit of a show to cover how she was feeling, but that slipped while she was coughing.

"I think it's time for a nap."

At first, it looked like there was going to be an argument, but with a slight nod of her head, she followed me inside. I found an old scrap of cloth in our packs that could be used to wipe her nose, and then we settled down.

Even though I was mostly lying down to convince Mara to nap, it was several hours later when I woke up. Mara was still sleeping, her breath making little wheezes with her stuffy nose. My stomach grumbled angrily, so I decided to let Mara rest and get some food started.

Cold blasted through me as soon as I was out of the fort. The fire was dead, so I'd have to wait for it to warm up. If I wasn't so hungry I would've gone and curled back up in the fort. Besides, Mara would get better faster with some food in her.

I grabbed the allotted amount of meat out of our storage area. After I caught the beast in my trap, we spent a lot of time reportioning everything because of how much meat it added. Looking at how much I pulled out, I was glad for the addition. It still wasn't a lot, but it was enough to mostly fill us up.

Shredding the meat and dropping it into the heating water, I found myself thinking about all the fun stuff we did when the weather was warmer and the clearing was full of life. I didn't realize how much I'd miss the chirping of birds and the sounds of small animals running around. Even the stream was silent, the gentle movement stilled in the ice.

"I wish there was more to add to the soup." Mara's voice startled me out of my thoughts and I jumped. Her eyes fixed themselves on me, full of curiosity. "Did I scare you?"

"I guess I was distracted and didn't hear you," I mumbled, embarrassed. "I wish we had more for the soup, too, though."

"Maybe I can find something?" The hope written all over her face made my heart ache.

"I'm not sure what you'd find, but I guess it doesn't hurt to try."

"I'll be back." She dashed off, kicking snow up and looking around.

Several minutes later, I wondered if I should go find her and convince her to give up, but she came running back to me with her fists full of slightly wilted, long, green plants. The long jagged leaves were staggered up the stem. At the top of each stem was a bundle of small white flowers.

Holding them up triumphantly, she exclaimed in a panting breath, "These don't smell great, but they might be good in the soup."

Hesitantly, I grabbed a small chunk of a leaf and stuck it in my mouth. It had a bitter taste to it, but it wasn't horrible. Plus, judging from past experiences, if it was harmful I wouldn't have been able to get it in my mouth.

"It can't hurt to try, right?" I was unsure about the stems, so I just tore off the leaves and dropped them into the pot. It wasn't much of an addition, but it was better than a thing.

The leaves tasted a lot better once cooked. The green floating in the soup was a nice change, and we ate in silence for several minutes before Mara spoke. "I had another dream." She sat stirring her soup with her spoon, seemingly deep in thought.

"About the people that look like us?"

"Yes." Something seemed different this time. Usually, her dreams made her excited and eager to talk about them, but she seemed reluctant this time.

"What happened?"

Mara's eyes were watery when she finally looked up at me.

*   Mara   *

My previous dreams were fun to talk and ponder about, but the dream I just woke up from left me feeling sad and confused. I wasn't even sure if I wanted to tell Kith this one, but I felt almost as if I had to. Sighing, I started at the beginning.

I was in the same hallway as before, but the happy sounds were gone. In their place I heard crying and what sounded like begging. My heart was racing, and I wanted to run away. Instead, I felt myself moving forward as if I wasn't in control anymore.

The room looked much the same as before, with the individual cages full of people who seemed so familiar, yet not at the same time. Instead of telling happy stories from his cage, Ducar was chained to the wall. His head drooped to the side, his long hair hiding his face.

Suddenly, I realized there was another figure in the room. He was in the shadows, and I didn't notice him at first. As I looked at him, dread filled me and my stomach lurched. The images from my nightmare long ago filled my mind. I had forgotten those dreams, but they were back.

This being was the one I saw attack the castle I came to know through my dreams. He led the assault that caused all the death and pain I was forced to watch. Anguish filled me as I realized that he now held these people.

The woman who begged Ducar for stories in my last dream was crying, pleading for Ducar not to be hurt. She cared about him in a way I couldn't understand. As I got closer, I felt myself connect to her again and looked at the man as if from her eyes.

The laugh that came from him made shivers run down my spine. "What is he to you? Your one connection to the two who escaped?"

"He's innocent." The words seemed to come from me, but I didn't choose them. I never would have referred to Ducar as innocent.

"What do I care about innocence? He is useful." The spiked end of his tail lifted Ducar's chin so he was facing the man. "You have been so incredibly helpful."

Ducar's eyes were filled with deep despair. "You'll never find those kids. They're smarter than you know." His voice was a whisper, but didn't waver, even as the man narrowed his eyes and dug the spike deeper into his flesh.

Those kids. Was Ducar talking about us? Confusion overwhelmed me, and I started to lose focus on the room. A scream brought it back into focus, however. Chains wrapped around the man who previously comforted the woman whose body I shared. They seemed to be hurting him, or weakening him somehow. It took me a second to realize they looked similar to the chains I was bound in not so long ago. The ones that caused so much pain.

I fought dizziness as the memories flooded back. Much of my time was spent trying to forget everything that happened, but it was all so fresh. As the memories flew through my mind, I felt a deep sorrow fill me. As upset as I was, it didn't feel like my sorrow.

When he spoke again, the man's voice shook through me. "They may be smart, but they can't hide forever."

Shock ran through me as his eyes swept to us. They locked onto her eyes, which I looked through, and he smiled. "That's right, child. You can't hide forever."

The woman's body shivered slightly with his words. Suddenly, I was forced out and woke up with a start.

✳   Kith   ✳

When Mara finished, I didn't know what to say. She seemed to feel a connection with these people, but they couldn't be real, could they?

"Kith, what if these aren't dreams, but something else?"

"What do you mean?"

"What if they're real? These people that look like us, what if they're really imprisoned and we're supposed to help them?"

"How would we help them, when we don't even know where they could be, or if they're real?"

"I don't know." Her head drooped. "That's what hurts so bad. If I could believe it was just a dream, I could move on."

"You don't think it is, though, do you?" She talked about

these dreams possibly being real before, but I always thought she was playing.

She shook her head in frustration. "I'm not sure. I just wish I could find out."

"I know it's not what you want to hear, but maybe you should pretend you know they're dreams. Even if they were real, there's nothing we can do right now."

"Maybe you're right. I just need to clear my mind." Before I could respond, Mara's bowl was in her place and she was gone, walking slowly through the trees. I watched her until she was out of view, a pain I couldn't describe building up in my chest.

As I sat thinking about the dreams, I remembered something I wasn't supposed to hear.

I heard someone whispering as I passed the door to Ketzia's tent. Her tent was always kept dim with extra drapes she placed around to block out more of the sun. I didn't really understand, then, what it was that she did. People lined up outside her tent, and she only allowed one in at a time to hear whatever it was she had to tell them.

I asked Ketzia once why she didn't let more people in to see her show, it seemed like such a waste of time. She responded about how her customers deserved something called privacy. She then asked if I wanted her to read my hand, which I didn't understand at all, but agreed to excitedly. Beatrice, however, forbade it, saying she wouldn't have Ketzia filling my head with her "nonsense."

It was hard to say whether people liked Ketzia or not. Sometimes they came out of her tent looking so happy and squealing about their great luck. Other times, they came out in tears, or yelling at Ketzia about how wrong she was. It all seemed strange to me.

So, when I heard the whispering, I thought it was finally my chance to get an idea of what it was she actually did. Slowly, I crept to the opening of the tent and peeked inside.

Surprise, and even more intrigue, hit me when I saw Beatrice staring stone-faced across a table as Ketzia looked at a strange ball she held delicately in her hands.

Ketzia's long black hair was decorated with her typical variety of colorful beads. I couldn't see her face as she looked into the ball, but the distaste in Beatrice's normally soft brown eyes held me transfixed.

"You have to see that they are different!" Ketzia was whispering, urgently. "Why is this so hard to believe?"

"Are you not different?" Beatrice asked, coldly. "Am I not? Does every woman you know grow a beard faster than you can cook a birthday cake?"

"Don't be ridiculous, Beatrice…"

*"Ridiculous?" Beatrice's voice rose just a hair as she tried to keep her composure. "The things you say are **impossible** and I'm the one who is ridiculous?"*

"I saw it, Bea, you must believe me. The first time I touched that sweet boy's hand. He is special. And this is not where he belongs."

At this point, Beatrice stood straight up out of her chair, nearly toppling over the table. "He belongs with the people who love him. Who takes care of him? How dare you suggest otherwise."

"Bea, I…"

"Hey, Ketzia!" A new voice from outside the tent called. Alarm rose inside me as I turned to see Jaxon's pale green eyes boring into me. "Careful what you say in there, you've got a peeping Tom!" He turned away, laughing, his green-blue skin glinting in the sunlight.

As I started to run, I heard shuffling just inside the tent and Beatrice yelled "Kith! What are you doing, child?" I continued to run as tears streamed down my face.

Why would Ketzia say I don't belong here?

Had Ketzia known something? Was this really not where we belonged? Was there by some chance a place where people looked like us?

Shaking the memories and thoughts out of my head, I decided not to say anything to Mara about that memory. It would only make her feel worse.

It was crazy, I knew that. How could I be dreaming about real people I had never seen before? And how could Ducar be with them when he was trying to find us? It didn't make any sense. It must be my mind trying to come up with explanations for who we were and everything that happened to us.

But it didn't feel crazy. Something inside me kept telling me these people were real, and I was really seeing what was happening to them right now. They needed my help. How could I help them when I didn't know where they were, though? Or even who they were?

Worse still, I was in no position to help anyone. It was hard enough just trying to survive. As if on cue, I was hit by a coughing fit. I was glad Kith wasn't near enough to hear. The look in his eyes every time it happened was almost impossible to bear. It was clear that he was reminded of the last time I got sick every time I coughed. It must have been terrible for him to think the one person he had in this world was dying.

I couldn't imagine how I would handle losing Kith. The closest I experienced was when he was attacked by the animals in the woods. Remembering the fear I felt as I was searching for him, I couldn't stop myself from thinking about how much worse it could've been. But, I found him quickly. The fear for me was short-lived, while Kith felt it for days. Although he was badly injured and there was the worry he would never walk again, I knew he was going to live. The thought of going weeks with the worry of his death constantly in the air brought tears to my eyes.

After that, I decided I had to take good care of myself and try to get better as quickly as I could so Kith wouldn't have to worry anymore. It was the best way I could help him. A coughing fit ran through me, and I cursed myself for staying out in the cold for so long. If I was going to get better, I needed to keep warm.

Even though I wandered far away from Kith and the warmth of the fire, I found my way back easily. Kith was sitting right where I left him, his face creased with concern. When he heard me approaching, he jumped.

"Mara, you look frozen! Come sit at the fire, you need to stay warm."

Remembering all my recent thoughts, I smiled at him warmly and walked to the fire. "I'm sorry I was gone for so long. I was just thinking and lost track of time. I'm going to get my blanket so I can warm up by the fire for a while."

For the next few days, I stayed bundled up in my blanket most of the time. Whenever I was outside, I walked with it draped around me trying to stay as warm as I could. Kith insisted I take his blanket during the day as well, and with minimal argument, I agreed. It wasn't long before I was feeling much better. I still had a cough, but I was able to function almost completely normally.

Expecting Kith to be delighted by my quick recovery, I tried to play more snow games with him. At first, when I suggested making snow angels, he told me he didn't think it was a good idea for me to be in the snow. A few days later, when I pegged him with a snowball, he only laughed half-heartedly and sat down next to the fire.

Kith seemed to be handling winter even worse than I expected. Sometimes I noticed him heavily favoring his injured leg. When I asked him about this, he told me the cold was bothering the injury.

One day as I watched Kith limping around, I realized he didn't have this big of a problem with it until I fell into the stream. Sure the cold was bothering him before, but he didn't let it slow him down. Now it seemed like he couldn't take more than a few steps without it hurting.

The weather continued to get colder, and a part of me knew this was likely much of the cause for his pain, but there was also a big part that told me this was my fault. If I wasn't so careless out on the ice, he wouldn't have gone in after me. I tried to erase these thoughts from my mind, knowing that the cold was bound to get to him anyway, but as Kith grew more distant, it was hard not to think about it.

Determined not to give up, I continued trying to get Kith to play with me in whatever way I could. Once, I managed to get him to kick the ball around with me for a little while, but it wasn't long before his leg was bothering him and we quit. Of course, I knew ice skating was never going to happen again, but there were lots of other things for us to do. I tried swinging through the trees, and all of our favorite games. Nothing seemed to hold his interest for long.

When I tried to talk to Kith about it, all I could get out of him was, "I'm fine, I'm just worried about getting us through the winter." Most days I resorted to playing with Gracie.

It didn't help Kith's mood that all we had was meat, though the thin soups we made helped a little. Especially when I could find more wilted plants to add to the pot. Somehow, even with the extra meat from his large catch, we never seemed to feel quite full without our usual variety.

I found myself wishing winter would end, more because I wanted the old Kith back than because of the cold. He wasn't normally so gloomy for such a long period, and it worried me. All I could do now was hope that when the weather got warmer it would get him out of this slump.

✳   Kith   ✳

Thin streaks of light lit the edges of the cave. Normally, such little amounts of light wouldn't wake me, but I was restless. Wrapping my blanket tighter around me, I tried to go back to sleep, but it was useless. Cold seeped into my bones, and warming up felt impossible.

Hoping to not wake Mara, I grabbed my blanket and left the cave. Everything was coated in white fluff. It should be beautiful, I knew that, but to me, it signified my loss of hope. It wasn't long before I got a fire going and started to feel the deep chill leave. Lost in thought, I was staring into the embers when Mara sat next to me. I didn't even hear her get up.

She was silent for several seconds, then in a worried voice whispered, "Are you alright, Kith?"

Shrugging, I mumbled that I was fine. We both knew it wasn't true, though. Something about the winter was making functioning feel almost impossible.

After another moment of silence, she spoke, her voice more firm this time. "I know you've been restless and not feeling like yourself. Maybe it would make you feel better if you went hunting?" Her smile was gentle, almost like she was afraid I would break.

"You're probably right. Even if I don't get anything, it might be good just to stretch my legs a bit." As I said it, I realized that was probably her real motivation. Keeping me moving might keep me from becoming a complete shell of myself.

The woods next to the stream were darker than the clearing, but the light hitting the snow gave the air a soft glow. My eyes didn't need long to adjust, and soon I could see all the small movements around me. Making myself as small as possible, I crept through the trees, my steps so light I didn't even sink into the snow.

After several minutes, I saw holes in the snow. Every few steps, one of the holes extended, making a line. It seemed the deer that left the tracks was limping. If my luck held, I might bring back a good amount of meat.

Trying not to get my hopes too far up, I followed the trail. I was almost able to forget how little color there was in the woods, but the empty berry bushes caused a pang in my stomach every time I glimpsed them.

The sun moved across the sky as I followed the tracks, making the snow sparkle wherever the shadows ended. The tracks led to a small section of the stream. It was mostly frozen still, and I could see skids on the ice that showed where the deer walked, but there were no tracks on the other side. I tried following the marks on the ice, but they seemed to go in circles.

Eventually, I admitted defeat. There were no signs of where the deer headed. I let the disappointment sink in for a few minutes. The thrill of hunting bolstered my mood for the time I was tracking the deer, but it all came crashing down around me.

Allowing myself a few minutes to grieve my hunt, I stood

and looked around. Not ready to give up just yet, I would have to continue my search while heading back in the direction of the camp. It would take me a while to get back as it was, and I was feeling eager for the warmth of the fire.

Halfway back to camp, I stood still and swept my eyes across the dense trees in front of me trying to see some movement. All seemed still. As I turned to my left to inspect the trees in that direction something in the distance caught my eye. Glancing around to make sure I was alone, I quickly climbed the nearest tree.

Scrambling through the treetops as fast as I could, I found myself hanging above another clearing. Directly in front of me stood a small cabin. It looked old and worn down, and almost all of the windows were broken or missing. The door hung open, the lowest connection was the only thing holding it in place. It looked about to fall off completely.

Gaping, I looked around the rest of the large clearing. To the left of the cabin, there was a smaller building that I guessed was some sort of shed for storing things. There were no windows, and it looked a little weather-worn, but sturdy. Between the two structures, was an outhouse.

Slowly moving further left, I saw a large barn in the corner of the clearing, back behind and to the left of the shed. Like the others, it looked a little worse for wear, but it seemed fairly sturdy. The cabin was the worst off with its broken windows and the door having come off.

Watching carefully for any signs of movement, I decided to check it out. Dropping from the tree, I crept carefully to the door. The inside was dark and covered in dust. It didn't seem like anyone had been here for a long time. It was all one room, with a fireplace on one end and a bed in the middle of the wall across from me. Cupboards lined the wall next to the fireplace and a small table was in the middle of the room.

After clearing away some of the spider webs, I realized that the cabin held a lot of potential. It was close to the stream, so we would be able to get water, and the clearing could easily be filled with the traps I learned from Isaac to protect against intrusion.

While we were camped at a nice little spot at the stream, I

couldn't stop my mind from producing images of us living in a real home again. I saw us at the fireplace cooking, eating together at the table, and a chance for us to sleep in another real bed.

We obviously wouldn't be able to stay here forever, but I knew this was what I needed. Having a cabin instead of a cave would make winter more manageable. It would need work, and I was tempted to start fixing it up before getting Mara. Knowing she'd want to be here to help, I resisted.

Making my way back to the camp, I paid extra attention to where I was going so I'd know how to get back. With my sense of direction, I didn't figure I'd have much difficulty.

Too excited to keep a slow pace, I found myself running back. Mara must have sensed me coming because she was standing next to the camp holding our bag, her eyes wide with fear.

Cursing myself for forgetting the cause of the only other time I ran back to camp like this; especially since I forgot our special whistle in my hurry, I slowed and came to a stop in front of her. She relaxed a bit when I stopped, knowing that if there was danger I wouldn't have.

"I found something wonderful." I was breathless from the run and the excitement coursing through my veins.

"What is it?" Her voice was soft, she was still calming herself from the panic my run induced.

"Come and see." I stopped only to take a long drink from the water above the fire and refill our water skins. Then I grabbed her hand and led her toward the woods.

"Where are we going?"

"You'll see. Trust me, it is wonderful. I don't want to ruin it for you." Smiling down at her, I squeezed her hand.

She returned my smile and the nervousness changed to excitement. "Can we run? I can't wait."

I laughed. It was good to be running alongside her playfully again. With my injury and moodiness, it had been a long time since we ran carefree.

As we got close, Kith slowed and told me to close my eyes. Grabbing my hand, he slowly led me forward. My excitement was building, and it took all my willpower to keep my eyes closed.

"Open," Kith said quietly, and I slowly opened my eyes. Immediately, I knew he found us a home. A real one this time, not something we dug in the dirt to build.

"Is it safe?" I asked, trying to contain my excitement only long enough to know for sure.

"It's been abandoned for years, and we can set up traps for safety." Kith, still holding my hand, pulled me gently toward the door. "There's a bed."

"A real bed?" He let go of my hand as I stepped forward and pushed open the door.

My eyes swept over the room as I walked toward the bed. "It's dirty, but we can clean it." I spoke with relish, thinking of how beautiful this place could be.

Stepping to the cabinets, I looked through them carefully. There were plates, cups, forks, knives, and a pot. There was even a half-full box of matches. My mind raced with the possibilities.

"Why don't you get started settling in, and I'll find some wood for the fireplace."

As Kith left the cabin, I continued to stare, taking in everything around me. We would have to fix the broken windows, of course, to keep the warmth of the fire in. The door at least stayed shut once we pulled it up and in. It took a lot of effort with the top not being attached, so fixing that would be nice too. I opened the rest of the cabinets until I eventually found a broom with half the bristles missing, and began sweeping out the dust and grime.

A dirty rag sat on the counter, right next to a barrel of water. The barrel had obviously been sitting for a long time, as there seemed to be almost as much dust and grime as there was water. Still, it would work for cleaning the cabin. For now, at least. Before rinsing the rag, I took it outside and pounded it against the outside of the cabin to get as much of the dust off as I could, then I scooped some of the water into a bowl and rinsed it. Once it was clean, I began wiping down the table and counters. It was far from clean, but after rinsing the rag and returning to work several times, I was able to cut back on the layers of grime that covered everything.

Despite the cold that was seeping in through the windows, I realized I was sweating from the exertion. I let out a small laugh and before I knew it, I couldn't stop laughing. Looking around at everything and how much work I did, I saw how much was still left. Instead of being discouraged, this made me happier than ever.

A few moments later, Kith came in with some firewood, looking much more cheerful than he had since I fell into the stream. He surveyed the room with a surprised face.

"Wow, you got a lot done! It looks great!"

I beamed at him. "We just need to cover the windows somehow before we go to bed so we don't freeze tonight." We both searched the cabin for towels and sheets and anything we could find to shove in the holes of the windows. It wasn't a permanent fix, but it would work until we could find a better way.

✳   Kith   ✳

As I stepped outside and looked around, I fought to ignore the ever-growing ache in my leg. Everything was still covered in snow. Finding wood for a fire had been tricky lately, but I was hoping to gather enough to last us a few days at least. Even though I wanted to hurry so I could return inside where it was at least a little warmer, I realized quickly that heading out without my walking stick would be a horrible idea.

The snow crunched under my feet as I walked along. At first, the walking stick kept dragging and I continually fought with it. After I accidentally pushed up a large chunk of wood with it, however, I started using it to find all the wood I could. Some of it was almost dry; I grabbed those and kept going. As I rounded the corner behind the cabin, I saw the small shed. I had forgotten about it in my excitement. Behind it, closer to the other side of the clearing, was the large barn. It looked dark and foreboding, so I decided to check out the shed first. It was way smaller than the cabin, but looked like it was still fairly sturdy, and not at all scary.

Carefully, I creaked open the door. It was completely dark inside. Even my eyes took a second to adjust. A shovel and some other tools I didn't recognize lined the wall, but in the center of the shed was a small pile of logs. It would only be enough to last us a couple of days, but they were completely dry.

Putting down the wet logs, I grabbed a few of the dry ones. They could dry in here while we used what I took. The size of my pile would need to be increased, though. Moving as quickly as my leg would allow, I gathered as much wood as I could and added it to the shed. I left some space between them and then recollected the dry ones.

By the time I went back inside to start the fire, Mara had the place cleaned up quite a bit. It was still going to need a lot of work, but we could fix it up into a decent home.

As I started the fire, Mara reminded me how much cold air was flowing in through the broken windows, so we stuffed what we could find in them to try to stop it. It was still chilly, but already warmer than our fort.

Tiredness was quickly overcoming us, and we were both fighting to get anything accomplished. "What do you say we see what condition the bed is in?"

Mara grinned at the word bed and raced over to it. The thin blanket left on it was full of small holes, but after cleaning off most of the dirt and grime outside, we decided it would still be worth keeping. It could use some more cleaning, but now we could add it to our blankets.

Pale wood made up the frame of the bed. It rose at the top and bottom of the mattress and was engraved with a cool swirling pattern. Someone put a lot of work into building it, so why would they just leave it behind?

The question was quickly pushed out of my mind as Mara climbed on the mattress. "It smells really funny, but it feels better than the ground."

"The whole cabin smells funny." I paused as the smell from the mattress hit me. "No, you're right. It smells weird."

Laughter rang through the cabin, and I smiled. Even with the smell that was deeply embedded in everything, I felt like we'd do well here.

The cabin was getting increasingly chilly, so I went to get our blankets out of the pack Mara brought, but they weren't there.

"Oh, no."

"What?"

"We left everything but our water and the food you managed to pack at the stream."

"Oh." Mara thought for a moment. "Maybe we'll be alright with just the blanket that was left here? I mean, it's gross and has holes everywhere, but it's better than nothing, right?"

"It is. I'll have to go back for our supplies first thing in the morning." Climbing into bed, we snuggled under the blanket. I wasn't sure if I'd be able to sleep, but before I knew it, the sun was hitting my eyes through the windows. As I stretched, Mara whined. Her nightmares were light enough that they rarely woke me anymore, but I knew she still had them every night. Well, except for the times she had crazy dreams.

Rubbing her back, I whispered to Mara that she was safe. After a couple of minutes, she settled back into a deep sleep. The sun hadn't been up long, and the chill in the air was heavy. My leg felt knotted and angry, but I wanted to get our stuff from the stream early. Grabbing a water skin, I crept out as quietly as I could. Mara would know where I went and that I'd be back soon.

Running back to our clearing at the stream was a lot harder without the excitement. I didn't notice the icy air stabbing my lungs or the searing pain in my leg when running with Mara, but keeping myself moving now was almost impossible. I couldn't run the whole way this time. Slowing to a quick walk, I continued.

After what felt like hours, I saw our little clearing. My heart felt a pang as all our good memories here ran through my mind, yet the place felt distant and unfamiliar. Looking around, all I wanted was to be back at the cabin.

As my eyes wandered, I saw the pot hanging above the fire pit. My heart sank as I realized it was likely still full of water. Water that was now frozen. Looking down at it, I could tell that it wasn't quite solid, yet. Still, it was going to take time to clear out. I went ahead and started a fire with what little wood was left in the pit. It could melt as I gathered everything else.

The fort was still considerably warmer than outside. It didn't take long to pack our stuff up, but I wasn't quite ready to face the cold again. My hands still felt half-frozen, and I couldn't feel parts of my face. Rubbing my hands together to generate a little heat, I let my mind wander. So much had changed over the years, and it seemed clear that more was changing. Picturing our future always used to be a bleak venture, but things were looking up now, in ways I hardly dared imagine.

Once I warmed a bit, it didn't take long for my desire to get back to the cabin to overshadow my dread of the cold. I held my breath as I stepped out, hoping it would help me handle the sting better, but it didn't.

Before heading into the cellar to grab the meat, I ran over to the fire; both to check on the pot and for a little extra warmth. While there was still a lot of ice, the outer parts were melted enough that I thought it would be fine. Carefully grabbing the pot, I dumped it over the fire. The ice slid out slowly in a large chunk and crashed into the embers, sending them flying. Smoke flew into my face, causing an extreme coughing fit. Once I could breathe again, I finished smothering the fire and headed to grab our food.

After filling our second pack as full as I possibly could, I was forced to admit defeat. We were going to have to make at least one more trip to get the rest of our food. What I managed to pack would last us quite some time, though, so at least there would be no rush to get back.

Noticing I took longer than expected, I decided to try running again. As I picked up speed, the extra pack slipped, slamming into my bad leg. Excruciating pain shot through my body and I fell forward, sinking into the snow. Several seconds passed before I could fill my lungs and several more before I was able to pick myself up out of the snow.

Running didn't seem to be a good idea. My trip back wasn't going to be easy or short. Sighing, I rose and started walking, being careful to keep the pack up and away from my legs.

Numbness spread through my entire body part way through the trip. One step in front of the other, over and over. My mind became blank other than focusing on moving. Forcing my legs to keep going was becoming increasingly difficult as they got increasingly stiffer.

Just as I was beginning to think I might not be able to make it back, a smell hit my nose. It was faint at first, but as I continued I recognized it as the smell of smoke. I could smell the heat up ahead. Mara started a fire! Thoughts of the warmth welcoming me into its embrace quickened my steps.

Relief rushed through me as I whistled my return and heard Mara's response, the notes ringing in my ears and filling me with energy. As I entered the clearing, Mara opened the door and rushed to help me with the packs, wrapping the dirty blanket around my shoulders and pulling me to the fire.

"You're frozen. I knew you would be with how long you've been gone. Sit here and warm up, I'll fix some soup." She bustled around that cabin like she had been there for years, throwing together a quick soup. It wasn't super flavorful, but I eagerly devoured it, relishing the warmth that spread through me.

*   Mara   *

When I woke up and found Kith gone, I was sure he went to get our things. Wishing he waited for me so I could help, I decided to make a fire so he could at least warm up when he got home.

Once the fire was roaring, I began looking around the cabin and found an intricately decorated sewing box. I opened it to find needles of several different sizes and many spools of thread. My eyes were immediately drawn to a small spool, almost empty, but holding the most beautiful blue thread.

The color reminded me of a time Beatrice took me into the town for ice cream and I saw a dress almost the same color as this thread. I remember begging Beatrice to buy it for me because it was so beautiful. She explained to me later that the colors used to turn the dress into such a vibrant shade of blue were expensive and she could not afford to buy something so impractical. At such a young age, I didn't understand what she meant by this, but the dress left my thoughts easily and I didn't think of it again until this moment.

Not for the first time, I wondered who lived in this cabin before, and why they left so many things behind. The day before, I opened an old trunk to find several fabrics, neatly folded. Like most things in the cabin, they smelled musty and old. I planned to return to them once it warmed up enough to wash things in the stream again, but as I stared at the many spools of thread, my mind reeled.

What if I could teach myself how to sew? I knew it couldn't be easy work, but we could both use new clothes. The ones we wore were getting so small, they barely fit anymore, and they were full of holes from our travels. I didn't think we could continue wearing them for much longer. As I continued sifting through the sewing box, I also found a pair of small scissors and something that looked like a tiny silver cup.

After looking through the entire contents of the box, I pulled out some of the smelly fabric. I knew that I needed to put the thread through the tiny hole on the end of a needle to start, but I did not know how difficult just this beginning step would be. The hole was so small, it took all my concentration to get the thread through it. Once I finally did, as soon as I started pushing the needle through the fabric, the thread pulled back out. I attempted a few times to get the thread through the fabric, but it kept falling out of the needle. For some time, I stared at it wondering how anyone ever got it to stay.

Finally, after some frustration, I realized that by tying knots at the end of the thread, I could keep it from slipping through. Pulling on the thread, I made sure it was secured on the needle, then began running it back and forth through the fabric.

Just as I was getting the hang of it, I heard Kith's whistle announcing his approach. Stuffing the fabric, needle, and all, back into the trunk, I rushed outside to help him.

For the next few days, I was so busy with cleaning and settling into the cabin that I didn't have time to try sewing again. When I finally got a chance to try it out, I realized how much it hurt my fingers to push the needle through the fabric over and over again. I ended my practice earlier than planned because it hurt too much to keep going.

As we sat at the table eating that night, Kith looked at my hands in shock, "What in the world have you done to your hands!"

Sheepishly, I showed him the sheet of fabric I was practicing on.

His eyes lit up as he took the fabric and inspected the stitches. "You did these?" he asked, amazed, "You're teaching yourself to sew!? That's incredible!"

I decided not to point out how terrible my stitches were. They were loose, and way too far apart in some places but too close together in others. Not to mention the short line I made was completely crooked.

Showing Kith the sewing box, I watched as he pulled out the small scissors and the tiny silver cup. He scooped it up with the end of his pinky and it now sat on his finger as he examined it. With a small squeak of excitement, I held out my hand for the object. Setting it on my finger, I grabbed the fabric and used the small cup to push the needle through. It was clumsily done, but I was sure this was what it was for! Kith starred as the excitement rushed through me.

"I'm assuming you weren't using that before?" he laughed.

"No, I didn't know what it was! This should help my hands!" I tested it out and found that it was quite helpful for pushing the needle through the fabric. After that, I began practicing sewing regularly. I still poked myself sometimes with the needle.

Over the next few days, I also started looking around the cabin trying to think of ways to dress it up a little. During a trip to the stream to collect water, I found a rock lined with varying shades of gray and black.

"This is pretty," I said more to myself than Kith.

"You could probably find some good rocks further down where it's closer to the cabin, too," Kith pointed out. "We'll want to get our water from there so we don't have to come way over here every time."

"I didn't think about the stream getting closer to the cabin." I twisted the rock in my hands, watching the sun make the gray parts sparkle.

"Me neither, but I was following the stream when I found it. It will be nice not to have to come all this way."

"Not having to always carry it all the way back from here will be nice." Wandering off, I looked at more rocks, choosing a few to bring home with me, determined to find a place for them.

CHAPTER SIXTEEN: JANUARY

✳   Kith   ✳

Leaving a fire going all night didn't seem like a good idea, so we let it burn down before going to bed. I woke to Mara shivering in her sleep, the cold seeping in enough to cause her discomfort, but not enough to wake her from her nightmare.

Before getting up, I wrapped all three blankets around her. I was surprised at how cold the cabin got overnight, until I remembered the broken windows. Our fill in from a couple of nights ago probably wasn't doing much good.

While going out to get more wood for a fire, I looked at the windows from the outside to try to figure out how to go about filling them in to help hold in the heat. I had filled in a lot of forts, but never with logs this big, or windows.

After I fixed a small breakfast, I headed outside to get to work. Using my walking stick, I brushed aside some snow at the edge of the clearing. My claws extended as I reached down to gather some dirt. Instead, the impact against the ground sent a pang of pain through my whole arm.

How did I forget that the ground would be frozen? Sighing, I rose to find a large stick and something to collect the dirt. A small bucket sat behind the cabin. It was full of frozen water, its sides bulging out with the strain. It was still in good enough shape for my purposes, though.

Before I could use it, I would need to thaw the water, so I brought the bucket inside and set it next to the fire. While waiting, I went back out and started scraping at the hard ground. It was tedious work, but after almost an hour there was a big enough pile to get started with. Luckily, the water was melted enough for me to mix it with the dirt.

Once the mud was lining the bottom of the window, I needed a break. My hands were numb from the cold and stiff from the mud coating them. It didn't take me long to realize that fixing these holes was going to take a long time. I'd be lucky to get one even mostly done by the end of the day.

The branches I pushed down into the mud kept falling out. After a few times of digging them back in, I decided to make my base a bit taller and started securing them at the top as I placed them instead of waiting until they were all up. It was a lot slower but held better.

I decided to eat some lunch before I wove in the smaller sticks and started the mud cover. Part of me wanted to keep working, but I knew I needed some food and warmth.

Mara was already heating up some food for us when I headed in. She seemed distracted while we ate, but I figured she had just been working around the cabin, especially when I saw that her hands were a bit red. We didn't talk much, our thoughts were elsewhere.

When we were done, I headed back out with a mixture of reluctance and desire. Weaving the smaller branches into the ones already in place proved to be a bad idea before the mud fully dried. The mud kept falling on me, and it was refrozen. The stinging where I was hit convinced me it was time to move to the other window while this one set.

Collecting more mud was draining me quickly. My arms were burning and my hands were freezing. Looking around to make sure I wasn't being watched, I focused hard on the ground. Even though I felt silly, I was desperate enough to try using any power I may or may not have to make the mud for me. Unsure of how it might work, I tried laying a hand on the ground and focusing my intention through it. There was no sign of anything happening, however, and I was only getting colder. As the sky started to get dark I decided to call it a night and continue the next day.

Finishing the outside of the windows took me another couple of days, but I got it. Once it was all dry and I was satisfied with it, I headed inside and carefully removed our temporary stuffing. A feeling of pride and accomplishment welled up in me. It felt great to be working toward a future for us. Something real, something I could see and touch.

Until my eyes started to water with emotion, I didn't realize how much it all meant to me. At that moment, however, a cold breeze drifted by. My cover kept most of it out, but plenty of chill still crept in and glided across me, causing a shiver.

Unsure if I was more disappointed or glad to have more work, I looked around to build a plan. Grabbing some straw from the end of the bed, I packed it into the holes where the windows had been. It kept falling out, but once I had more sticks in place it would hold.

The next couple of days were spent closing up the inside of the holes. When they dried, I stood next to each for several minutes, waiting for a draft to come in. Barely anything was coming in from the windows. I did, however, realize that there were many holes in the material that was used to bind the logs together. Large chunks of it were missing, letting in quite a bit of cold air. With the windows being such a large concern, I didn't notice.

With no clue what was used for that, or how to make it, I decided I would again be using mud. I found myself wishing we found the cabin before everything was frozen. This work would have been much easier in the summer.

Complaining was not an option, however. Ever since we got here, I caught Mara watching me multiple times, and I started to realize just how gloomy I was lately. Guilt overcame me often for that, and I strived to only show her how glad I was for the cabin, even, or maybe especially, with all the work.

Once it was patched up it would be quite cozy, and next winter we wouldn't need to go through all of this. I paused as the thought brushed through my mind. Would we still be here next winter? Could we spend that long in one place? We spent months stationary before, but never a full year. The idea of it made a warmth spread through my body, and I couldn't stop images of what our future might look like from flying past my eyes.

Curling up in bed later that night, I wrinkled my nose. "With all the other work being done, the smell of the bed is becoming more obvious."

Mara giggled sleepily. "I know."

"We may have to figure out something to do about that," I whispered. She was already asleep, however, and didn't respond. At least, not before I drifted off.

*   Mara   *

While Kith worked on patching up the windows, I was either practicing my sewing or cleaning the cabin. It was hard work; the cabin clearly had not been lived in for a long time, but I loved every minute of it. It was nice having our own place again, and this one held the potential to be even better than any cave.

Looking around the cabin, I was trying to decide what to do with all the rocks I collected from the stream. While the walls weren't exactly pretty, they weren't too bad. The filled-in windows, however, were ugly. A few pretty rocks could be just what they needed. Wetting the mud just a little, I pressed the rocks into it. Once the mud dried, they stayed in place nicely. Many more rocks would be needed to line all of the windows. This was something that would keep my attention for a long time because it took a lot of rocks to line just one window, and we didn't go to the stream often with how cold it was. I was also a bit picky about the rocks I took home with me, meaning I could spend an hour looking around just to bring home a small handful of rocks.

We no longer needed to leave our shelter to build a fire, and now that the windows were patched, the cabin stayed warmer even after the fire was gone. The best thing about the cabin, though, was how much it changed Kith's mood. It was becoming unbearable watching him suffer through the cold before. His leg still bothered him a lot, but with something to do, he was able to push past it. I often needed to remind him to take breaks, especially when I noticed him wincing in pain.

One afternoon, when I told Kith he needed to take a break, he insisted I take one as well. While we sat together, he asked if I had taken Gracie out at all to see the cabin.

"She doesn't have to stay shut in her box all the time now

we have a place for her."

With all the excitement, I hadn't even thought about getting Gracie out of the box Kith made for her. I opened it up, and pulled her out, looking around.

"I could fix her a bed. Right next to ours. There's plenty of fabric for her blankets. I think she would like to sleep beside me."

Smiling, Kith nodded, and I immediately began looking around for something I could place the box on. There wasn't anything close enough to the bed, and I refused to leave her on the floor.

After a few minutes of looking through the cabin, we realized there wasn't anything inside that would work. Bundling up quickly, we dashed outside. The barn might have the perfect thing inside, but it still scared me too much.

We ran around looking for the perfect item until we were too cold to stay out any longer. In the end, we decided to put it on the edge of the bed, carefully surrounded by scraps of cloth to hold it in place. I trimmed up some fabric to add a little more cushioning for her and even stuffed a small bit of straw from the bed underneath her sheets. Leaving the box open, I lay Gracie down so she could test out her new bed.

"It's perfect!" I said gleefully. "I can leave it open for her so she isn't shut away from us while we're inside!"

"You may still want to close it while you clean though," Kith said thoughtfully, "so none of the dust and grime gets on her by accident."

After that, Gracie always slept beside me with her case opened. Some nights, I would grab her and fall asleep holding her. Doing this before was an issue because if I slept with her she would fall in the dirt or the leaves and get dirty. In the cabin, however, the floor was swept enough by now that falling down wouldn't cause her any harm. During the day, when I was cleaning, I closed her lid as Kith suggested.

It didn't take long for me to think of the cabin as home. With the windows patched, and the fire burning, the place was so warm I could forget it was freezing outside. Nights still got chilly, without the fire, but it was warmer than our fort was and when we snuggled up in our blankets, it was warm enough for a good night's sleep.

✳   Kith   ✳

With the holes all filled in, it was time to focus on our safety. Reluctantly, I headed outside to devise a plan. It didn't take me long to realize that the pit traps I was thinking about would have to wait. There was no way I'd be able to dig the holes needed for those with the ground as frozen as it was. I could, however, get started on making the spikes for the bottom.

As much as I wanted to get back inside quickly, I decided it would be better to make a good plan early, so I could work on implementing it. At each spot I decided a trap should go, I made a little mark on a nearby tree to keep track.

Once I figured out that part, I started gathering the wood to make the spikes out of. I had to wander a lot farther from the cabin than I would've liked to find usable pieces of wood, but I managed to gather a large bundle before returning to the cabin for lunch.

After eating, I went through my collection to find the best ones to use. Mara watched me for a minute before coming and sitting next to me. "I want to try."

Handing her one of the sticks from my pile, I showed her how to make the end sharp. It didn't take her long at all to pick it up, and the work went faster with her help. We talked about ideas for the cabin and how to make it even better.

"I wish we had some seeds or something." Mara sighed. "Remember Beatrice's plants? The only thing she never let us touch. I wanted to play in them so badly, but I didn't want to make her angry."

"It didn't make sense at the time, but I understand why she had them now. No wonder Dylan was reluctant to drink the tea she gave him. It's gross." I made a face and Mara giggled.

"Be glad you had it." She nudged me gently with her

elbow. "Even if you did act like a baby every time I made you drink it."

"I did not!" I swiped at her playfully with the unfinished spike in my hand, but she dodged it, swiftly leaping to her feet.

"Yes, you did. I've never heard you complain like that." A spike came at me from the side. I hadn't even seen her pick it up and barely managed to roll out of the way, jumping up to my feet after.

Without saying anything, I lunged after her. She was too quick again, and darted out the door, her giggles trailing after her. They cut off short, however. Racing out after her, I saw why. A dog, smaller than the ones that attacked me, but still big, was standing just a couple feet in front of her, teeth bared.

Mara backed slowly toward me, and the dog crept forward. As it approached, I moved around her and lunged at it with my spike. It wasn't quite as sharp as I wanted, but it managed to pierce it. The door banged behind Mara as she rushed back inside.

I followed her inside a while later, meat and cleaned hide in hand. Mara looked shocked to see the meat, but decided against commenting.

"We can have fresh food for dinner." I smiled, hoping to ease her emotions.

After a second, she smiled back. "At least it won't go to waste, right?"

"Yes. And neither of us were hurt." My leg twinged with the memory of the last time I faced an animal like that, not in a trap.

"True." Her eyes followed my thoughts.

"I'll start cooking this up."

Mara set the table with plates and cups that were in the cupboard. We'd been mostly eating soups made from the dried meat to try to extend it, so we hadn't touched the plates yet. I got the food from the fire and served it.

We sat in silence as we ate, savoring the moment too much to speak. The food was delicious, and we had a home. Neither of us wanted to mention that the last time we had eaten off plates at a table was with Isaac.

Kith was looking into each of the water skins as if he was searching for something and I knew what this meant. We put off going back to the stream for more water, not wanting to leave the warmth of our home for too long, but it seemed we couldn't put it off anymore.

"I think we'll really have to go to the stream today. We're practically out. It was probably careless for us to let it get so low," he sighed. "We may as well go back to the clearing so we can get the rest of the meat too."

We began bundling up as much as we could, wrapping our blankets around us for extra warmth. Kith told me how his walk back to get our supplies seemed so much longer than it had before, and now I understood how he felt. When he took me to the cabin, it seemed like a small run because I was so excited to see what Kith wanted to show me. Now, however, we were walking away from the place we wanted to be, and this made the walk long and tiring.

Kith had the foresight to bring one of the sticks we sharpened with us for breaking up the ice. Once we finally made it there, he got to work on the ice while I sat by with the skins, ready to scoop up the water that lay underneath. The ice was thick, and a part of me yearned to skate around on top of it, but I knew that was a bad idea. So instead, I grabbed the biggest stick I saw and tried to help break up the ice.

After only a few jabs at the ice, my stick crumbled into several pieces causing Kith to snicker. I glared at him, "Well I'll just let you do it yourself then!" Now he was laughing outright and shaking his head. Concealing the smile that was playing with my lips, I stood up pretending to stalk off. Of course, I didn't go far, I simply walked to our old fort and peeked inside. It was strange how quickly I came to think of the cabin as home, and how foreign this tiny hole in the bushes now seemed to me.

Suddenly, Kith was beside me holding our full water skins and I realized I must have stood there staring for longer than I intended.

"Oh, I'm sorry! I didn't really mean for you to do it all yourself!"

Kith grinned and handed me some of the skins to put in my bag. "Ready for lunch?" he asked.

We gathered the meat quickly and munched on some quietly while we walked, both of us eager to get back to the warm cabin. "Since it looks like we'll be home in time for dinner, what do you say we cook up some more of that fresh meat?" Kith smiled at the thought.

"That sounds good. I just wish there was something to cook up alongside it."

When we finally got back to the cabin, we started a new fire and huddled by it warming back up. Glancing at each other, both smiling broadly, we relished the feeling of having a home to come back to after a long day. Jumping up, Kith dashed to the bed. For a moment, I thought he was going to lie down, but instead he grabbed his ball and tossed it to me.

He threw it to the side a little to make sure it avoided the fire and I barely caught it. Standing up, I threw it back to him, but veered it a little to his left.

"Hey!" he called as he caught the ball with ease. "I did that so it wouldn't land in the fire!"

We threw the ball back and forth, each time throwing a little further from the other, laughing as we lunged this way and that. Kith threw a particularly high throw, that barely slipped through my fingers, and slammed with a hard thud into the wall directly beside a window. The laughter died as we both realized how close we came to breaking one of our few windows that was still completely intact.

We made eye contact and immediately burst into giggles, happy that our little game hadn't gone as badly as it might have. All the same, the ball was put away, and we decided not to play with it inside anymore.

The cupboard door closed a lot faster than I intended, making a loud bang. Mara jumped and an involuntary shriek slipped out. "I'm sorry! I didn't mean for it to close so loudly."

Peeking at me through her fingers, she said, "It's alright. I just got startled." Giggling to relieve the tension in the air, she rose. "What are you doing, anyway?"

I shrugged. "Nothing, really. Just looking around at the stuff we haven't gone through, yet."

"Oh, I keep forgetting that there's more hidden in the cabinets. I guess I'm still not used to a lot of stuff, or places to keep it."

"It is taking some getting used to, isn't it?" I bent and looked in the next cupboard as I spoke. We were keeping all the visible areas clean, and the shelves with our pots and dishes, but we hadn't bothered with these unused spaces. Cobwebs clung to my hands and arms as I reached in and pulled things out.

Grabbing the items from me, Mara used a damp cloth to gently remove all the dust and cobwebs. Two small books with pictures on the pages were the first things I pulled out. The dust covered a lot.

"I'll set these aside to clean more. I don't want to tear the pages."

"That makes sense." I handed her a wooden box next. As she wiped it down, we saw a checkered pattern on the top. A drawer in the side slid out, and inside were a bunch of wooden figures in slots. Some of the slots were empty, though.

"This looks like it's missing pieces. I don't know how to play, anyway, though, so I guess it doesn't matter much, right?" Mara took one of the pieces out and examined it. "I'm guessing it's for two players. One takes black and one takes white. Maybe we could make up some fun things to do with these."

After putting the little horse piece back, Mara set the box aside and reached for the next box I handed her. This one wasn't closed, and was full of little wooden pieces of all sorts of different shapes. On the side there was a dirty, peeling painting of a little house built from the pieces.

"These look like the ones we used at Isaac's. We could have a lot of fun with them." Mara carefully cleaned each piece with the cloth, her attention and care exposing her underlying feelings.

"What's wrong?"

Mara's hands stilled on the triangular shape she held. She was silent for a moment, sorting her thoughts. "I'm happy to find new things to do, but they make me wonder about who was here before us. What happened to them?"

"I have no idea." I shook my head and let the question linger. What had happened to them? It was obvious that a lot of things were removed from the cabin, but not everything. And it was left clean, but in such disrepair.

"Let's look through the cupboard more later and play now."

Pushing aside the unanswerable questions, I rose. "I need to clean up first. I'm a mess." As if my nose agreed, a sneeze hit me. "Ugh. So much dust."

Once I was clean, we pulled out the blocks. I put down one of the biggest ones, and Mara added to it. Soon we had a tower almost as tall as Mara. With a fit of giggles, Mara pushed the middle of the tower and watched as it came tumbling down.

"Let's play with this board." I pulled out the drawer and let her look at the pieces. "Which color do you want?"

"I like the black ones." She picked up the horse piece she looked at earlier and placed it on the board before carefully picking up the rest.

We put all our pieces on the board randomly and took turns moving the pieces around. Mara made up a story for them to be acting out, and I went along with what she said. Her voices for each piece made me laugh.

"Castles don't talk." I couldn't hold back the smile as I said it, though.

"Oh, but what if they did? What kinds of stories do you think they'd tell?" She smiled wistfully.

"That's a good question. I imagine they'd have all sorts of stories to tell."

"I bet they'd have a lot of stories of secret love." Mara's face was all lit up with excitement, and our game was forgotten as she got lost in thought about talking castles.

*   Mara   *

It was strange being in the cabin. The last time we had something this close to a home was with Isaac. It was hard not to feel his absence in everything we did. Sometimes when I was cooking, I would turn around and almost expect Isaac to be there listening to the sounds of me working. It hit like a punch to the stomach the first time, and I couldn't even think of a lie quick enough when Kith asked about it.

After finally adjusting to life on the run again, this kind of simplicity felt almost wrong. There were days when we didn't even leave the house. Days when we just sat and talked and played with the random toys and games we found in the cabinets. The fireplace made it easy to keep a fire going, with no wind to blow it out. We already portioned out enough food for the winter. The once meager portions had increased a fair amount since we first divided them, and it left little room to stress about starvation.

Even Ducar seemed to be taking up less time in our minds, which was the scariest part of it all, when I thought about it. My nightmares were less severe again. It was almost like being in the cabin was driving them away. I knew Kith sometimes still woke up to them, though. It made me feel bad that even though we were in a real bed, in a home of our own, he still wasn't always getting good sleep.

The strangest thing about life in the cabin was when the boredom set in. The only time I remembered being bored ever before, was when we were with Isaac and we couldn't go outside because it wasn't safe. Now we didn't go outside simply because we chose not to when it was too cold. It was odd to be bored almost by choice. Occasionally we bundled up and went out into the cold to play. With the warmth of the cabin being a regular thing now, the snow turned back into a source of fun. However, there were days that we didn't want to go out. We just wanted to enjoy being comfortable.

We had carved a pile of spears by now that sat in the corner waiting for it to warm up enough that we could set them up around us. Sometimes I found myself cleaning surfaces that weren't dirty just for something to do. Neither of us complained. After the life we lived for so long, it was wonderful to have the time to just lounge around a warm home, playing games, and talking about nothing in particular.

I continued trying to decorate the cabin, partially for something to do. Kith was appreciative of the rock idea. He helped me search for rocks every time we went to the stream, both of us freezing our fingers to dig into the snow or grab a rock from under the water. Once one window was mostly completed, Kith commented on how it made the window look nicer to have something lining it instead of just looking at the rough ugly mud. This gave me another idea.

Taking scraps of cloth, I began cutting shapes into them. Kith, after watching as I cut out a flower and then stuck it into the mud of a window, decided he wanted to help as well. I began attempting to sew bits of cloth together to make flowers that were more lifelike rather than simple cut-outs. It took several tries before I had one that was passable. For weeks, whenever we got stuck in a slump of boredom, we would work on making cut-outs or sewing things together in an attempt to dress up the muddy windows.

Deciding to fold a long sheet of fabric in half, I practiced stitching the two ends together. Once I stitched all the way down the line, I looked at the stitches in despair. They were all over the place, barely holding the two sides of the fabric together. Taking the thread off of the needle, I slowly began pulling it all back out of the fabric, careful not to break the thread. There was no sense wasting it on those terrible stitches.

Although I had the cup to protect my finger, it only went

on one. This helped a lot with the pain of pushing the needle through the fabric but did nothing for the many pokes I endured from the other end of the needle. I decided that once I managed to get through this sheet of fabric with a decent line of stitches, I would begin working on clothes for Kith. It would take a long time, but as I examined the calendar, I was confident I could finish by his birthday.

One evening, while I was working on my sewing, a storm raged outside. Immersing myself in my work, I tried to ignore it for as long as I could. When a huge bolt of lightning streaked across our window, lighting up the whole cabin, I put my needles down. Kith and I rushed to the window to look outside.

"I'm glad we're in here," I said, shivering. "It looks dreadful out there!"

"Yeah, I think…" At that moment, lightning struck a tree directly in front of the cabin, and we both screamed. The tree cracked and splintered all down the center until one half broke away, and I watched in horror as it started falling right toward us. The world slowed down around me as I stared out the window. Energy burned inside me and my whole body started to tingle. I focused hard on the tree and the half that was now slowly falling toward us. It was strange how slowly it was falling now, but I knew I must stop it from hitting the cabin.

The energy inside me grew until it felt like it was bursting. Breathing in deep, I tried to calm my senses which were now on fire. When I exhaled, I felt it all release from me in a rush. What looked like a large blue shimmery bubble grew outward from where we stood, encompassing the entire clearing. The world suddenly accelerated, and I watched in wonder as the tree, now falling quickly, seemed to bounce off of the bubble, which pushed it up and away from us with a blue burst of shimmers.

A deafening crack rang through the clearing. The top of the tree was now breaking off and a huge pile of branches came falling toward the ground. Except they stopped only a few feet above the height of the cabin and tumbled away as if they were rolling down a hill. Each time they bounced away there was another burst of shimmers, so the sky almost looked like a light show. Silence fell between us as we stared out the window unable to comprehend what we just saw.

"What…just happened?" Kith asked slowly, his voice trembling.

Whatever it was, it left me feeling dizzy and weak. My legs couldn't support me anymore and I crashed to the floor.

✳   Kith   ✳

I woke up with a start. Something was different. There was something missing from my usual morning routine, but I couldn't quite place it. For one, the position of the sun seeping through the window told me that it was much later than when I was used to waking up. But there was something else. Something I didn't do. I sat up to look around and then it hit me. Mara. I didn't hear her scream or groan or mumble once all night. This worried me. Ever since we managed to escape Ducar, the only time Mara ever went a single night without having nightmares was when she was sick and had strange dreams.

As much as it hurt me every time I saw her writhing in her sleep or held her while she cried, it became something I was used to. Something I thought would never end. And although it seemed like I should be rejoicing, I dared not give myself the pleasure without being certain that everything was alright.

Although I hated to wake her, the anticipation was growing, and I needed to know that she was okay, especially after she collapsed the day before when she released that barrier around the clearing.

"Mara," I whispered quietly, "Are you alright?"

Her eyes opened sleepily and tried to focus on my face. "What's wrong, Kith? Do we have to leave?"

Relief swept over me as I looked at her confused face. "No, nothing is wrong. You didn't wake me, so I was concerned."

She blinked while what I said registered. "I… I didn't have a nightmare."

"That's great!" I grinned. That never happened without her being sick. A full night without nightmares. As I snuggled back down, my dreams from the night came back.

While I was still debating on whether or not I should tell Mara about it, she realized my change in mood. "What are you thinking about, Kith?"

"I did have a dream last night." I paused, unsure if telling her was a good idea.

"Tell me about it." Eagerness filled her face as she curled up to listen.

"Alright."

We were playing outside a cabin in an area that didn't look like anything I had ever seen. Everything looked all wrong, but I can't remember how. We were both quite a bit younger, and there was a woman standing at the door of the cabin calling to us. She seemed so familiar, but I surely hadn't seen her before.

I would have remembered seeing a woman who looked so much like us. The woman seemed worried about something but was trying hard to hide that from me. I could hear her muttering something under her breath while she started packing our bags, but I couldn't understand it.

Suddenly, she stopped and looked around. After a minute, she picked Mara up and gently took off her necklace. My attention tried to focus on the necklace since I had never known Mara to wear one, but I couldn't see it.

Kneeling on the floor, she held us to her while she said something I couldn't quite make out. Suddenly, everything was spinning out of control. The spinning made my stomach turn, and I heard Mara crying. As soon as it stopped, I reached out to comfort her. She was in my arms before I realized everything looked different. The vibrant greens surrounding us confused me.

The woman who was with us didn't seem to be feeling well, but I tried not to worry. Excitement filled me with a desire to go exploring, and I ran off to look around. We seemed to have found a castle. As I explored, I found comfy stuff to bring back to the woman to lie in. She didn't feel up to any more walking, and I figured she could use a nap.

It was hard not to go far away from the castle, but worry for the woman and taking care of Mara kept me going back.

Mara was silent for a minute after I finished telling her about the dream. I knew she'd struggle with it after her troubles with her own dreams.

"Can you remember what the other place looked like?"

"No, I can't. Just that it was so different. It's odd, though. The whole thing seemed so familiar."

"I understand that feeling." Mara sighed softly.

"I guess you do." I played with her hair for a minute. "I'm sorry I didn't take your feelings about your dreams seriously. It was wrong to just dismiss them."

Mara's eyes were slightly watery when she looked at me. "Does that mean you think they're real?"

"I'm not sure what to think, honestly."

*　　Mara　　*

Kith's dream and his new receptiveness to the possibility that this other place was real, scared me more than I expected. I tried to convince him before of how real it all seemed to me, but his insistence that it was impossible was somehow a comfort. Never fully able to put the imprisoned people out of my mind, I was at least able to suspend my worry for them because of how impossible it really seemed.

As Kith told me about his dream, I felt the elation that filled me when I realized I didn't have a nightmare ebbing away. I tried desperately to grab it back. Since we left Ducar, the only time I didn't have a nightmare was when I was sick and dreamt about that other world. It would have been a nice escape if those dreams hadn't turned into nightmares as well.

"Are you okay?" Kith asked quietly. "I know how much your dreams bothered you before."

"I just don't know what to do," I replied feeling torn. "When I had my dreams, I was sick. It was easier to dismiss them because you were so sure they were just fever dreams. But now you're dreaming about similar things and it doesn't seem like a coincidence. But if these people and that place are real...how is it even possible that we're seeing what's happening?"

"I'm not," Kith responded and when I opened my mouth to retort, he continued, "We were in my dream. It can't be what's happening because we're here now. And we were younger. It felt more like," Kith hesitated, looking at me like he wasn't sure if he should continue. "A memory."

I let his words sink in. "You mean, maybe that woman you saw," My breath caught, "was our mother?" Then a realization hit me. "And she was bringing us here to give us away." I finished bitterly.

"I don't know, Mara. She was sick or something. The whole situation seemed strange."

"Well, of course, it was strange," I managed a small chuckle.

Kith looked at me, questioning. "You didn't have any nightmares last night. Did you dream at all?"

I thought about that for a minute, trying to remember. "I don't think I did. I can't remember anything."

Kith grinned, "We should be celebrating a night without bad dreams instead of worrying about people who may or may not exist." When he saw my face, he added, "I'm not saying I don't believe they exist. I really don't know. I'm just saying, there's nothing we can possibly do when we don't know who or where they even are. But we do know you didn't have any nightmares last night, and that is a big deal."

Watching Kith while he talked, I realized he really was more worried than he was telling me. He was just trying to get both our minds off of the situation with the happy occasion.

Deciding he was right, I forced a grin. There was no point dwelling on the dreams when we couldn't do anything about them.

Even though I knew Kith could tell it wasn't fully sincere, he said, "That's more like it!"

In an attempt to get my mind off of the dreams, I jumped out of bed and announced I was going to make breakfast. Kith cut in quickly, telling me to lay back down because he was making me breakfast in bed to celebrate. I half-heartedly argued against this while Kith gently forced me to sit back on the bed.

"Oh, alright!" I exclaimed, quickly bundling myself back up in the blankets and leaning against the headboard.

"Well that was difficult," Kith joked, rolling his eyes.

Already beginning to feel better, I lay in bed talking to Kith while he made a fire and fixed our breakfast. It didn't take long with dried meat being the only thing we really had, but Kith heated up some water for us as well. Since we put the fire out at night, it still got pretty chilly in the cabin so we continued our habit of drinking hot water in the mornings to warm up.

Kith brought me my breakfast, and we sat in bed talking about all the terrible dreams from the past. As depressing as that sounds, it was actually a cheerful conversation.

"Do you remember when I almost fell out of the tree because I was thrashing around so much?" I asked, eyes wide at the memory.

"Oh, man. Of course, I do! I was terrified!"

Suddenly, I had a thought. "Do you usually have dreams? We're always so busy talking about my nightmares that I never think to ask." I asked apologetically.

Kith thought about that for a moment. "I think I do, sometimes. I can't remember any of them though. When I wake up, I can remember pieces of them but it goes away so quickly. My mind gets occupied with other things I guess."

"You mean you forget them because you wake up and immediately have to help me get through a nightmare," I said simply, guilt washing over me.

"That's not necessarily a bad thing. There's no point in dwelling on dreams. I mean look at how bad yours are. It's probably a good thing I don't have to remember mine."

Again, I knew he was just trying to make me feel better. I also didn't miss his not-so-subtle comment about not dwelling on dreams. Even though I knew he was right about that, it was hard not to think about all those people caged up.

We spent the rest of the day in the cabin, occasionally talking about dreams, but mostly avoiding the subject of the people who looked like us. Whenever I looked like I was getting too thoughtful, Kith would begin talking about anything he could think of to distract me. He kept proposing activities, like our game with the funny pieces we found or rolling his ball across the floor to each other. He even suggested I sew for a while. By the time the day was over, I was beginning to feel trapped inside. I longed to have something; anything, new, to do.

CHAPTER SEVENTEEN: FEBRUARY

✳   Kith   ✳

Stretching out in front of the fire, Mara let out a soft sigh. I knew she didn't want to complain about being bored. Neither of us did. The chance to feel boredom was a great relief, but it left us feeling at a loss. We weren't used to having to find things to fill weeks or months of stillness. At least at Isaac's, we got to talk to him and learn new skills. Without him here, it seemed like there was an empty space that the two of us could never fill.

"Wanna play with the little wood pieces?" The board stayed at the end of the table since we found it. Nothing else was going there, so it made no sense to put it away.

"We've played with those a million times," Mara grumbled, but she rose up and joined me at the table.

As we placed the small figures around the board, I could tell her heart wasn't really in it. Mine wasn't either, honestly. A deep restlessness consumed me. My body hadn't adapted to being so still, so contained. Some days I thought the silence would make my head explode.

For years we longed for this peace. Why were we having such a hard time with it? Frustration welled through me as I tried to answer the question.

"Kith? What are you thinking about?"

"What?" I was confused by Mara's voice for a second. "Oh. Not much. Just distracted, I guess."

"Oh. Ok." Mara's voice held a slight angst.

Looking down, I tried again to focus on our game. They were always different, with no set rules. We mostly just goofed off. Sometimes I wished we actually knew the real game. I wondered what it was like.

"Are you hungry?" My stomach was rumbling.

"Of course I am. But it's not time to eat yet."

"Why do you get to decide when we eat?" The words

slipped out without any thought, and I immediately wished I could take them back.

Shock and pain were evident on Mara's face. "I never said I do, but we have to be careful not to run out of food before we can get more. You can eat now if you want, it just means you will have less later."

"I'm tired of always being afraid of running out of food." It felt ridiculous to be pouting like I was, but I couldn't help it. "If Beatrice or Isaac were here we wouldn't be struggling so much all the time."

Mara quickly rose up from the table, grabbed Gracie, and headed outside. My stupidity stared me in the face as she sat out in the snow shivering. Guilt flooded me. Grabbing her blanket, I followed her out. She turned her face away from me and swiped it with her arm.

Putting the blanket around her shoulders, I dropped down next to her. "I'm sorry, Mara. I shouldn't have said that. I'm restless and miserable." After a look at her face, I corrected myself again. "Not the right word. I'm having trouble saying what I mean. I just feel out of sorts being still this long."

She sniffed and looked up at me. "I know. I thought winter would be easier in the cabin. I mean, it is, because at least we're warmer, but it didn't solve the food problem. I'm tired of just eating meat. I still feel hungry all the time. And I miss Beatrice and Isaac so much." She paused and wiped away some more tears. "I had a dream last night. Not a nightmare, or a memory, or with people who look like us."

"What was it then?"

Tears streamed down her face as her eyes met mine. "We were in this cabin. But it wasn't all old and run down. All the windows were there and everything. And…" Her voice trailed off and she looked away.

"And what?"

"Beatrice was here with us. We were a real family in a real home." Leaning into my chest, she let the sobs overwhelm her.

One of the only good things about being on the run so

much was the inability to focus on our losses. Even at the stream during the warmer months, we were able to find enough to fill our days and not think about it too much.

With our current struggles, though, it was harder to ignore the longing for the only mother we ever knew. I held Mara and stroked her hair until we cried all our tears.

*   Mara   *

A few weeks passed since my first night without any nightmares and I continued to go without them. Some nights I simply didn't dream at all. Or if I did, I couldn't remember when I woke up. Other nights were filled with dreams like the one with Beatrice. Dreams of things I wished could be true. The strangest one was a dream of Kith and me when we were little and in the freak show.

"We were playing with Grace in the big tent and her fiance came in and said he wanted to play too. We all started chasing each other around. Grace grabbed me, swung me in the air, and said we needed to quit to get some lunch. It was just the four of us still. Grace and her fiance were making lunch and they sat with us in her tent to eat."

Kith was watching me with deep interest the whole time I was telling him about my dream. "When we were all eating, Grace said she had an announcement. She said we were going to go live with them after they got married. Her fiance looked so happy. He said he hoped we would accept."

I paused to watch Kith take this in. "Then, all of a sudden, it was dark outside and I heard Grace and Ducar yelling in Ducar's tent. I woke you up, and we snuck around the back of his tent to listen in. Ducar was yelling at Grace for trying to take away his star act. She tried to tell him the freak show was no place for kids and that we deserved a normal life, with her, but Ducar laughed at her and told her we weren't normal. He said we were freaks and with the freaks was where we belonged. He threatened her, too. Told her if she took us he would hunt her down."

Silence filled the cabin for a while before I asked what was on my mind since I woke. "Kith...do you think that was a memory? Do you think Grace really did want to take us with her?"

Kith looked startled by the question. I had been watching his expression the whole time to see if he remembered anything I said, and he looked so wrapped up in the dream that I thought surely it was real.

"Mara," he started, pausing to think, "I'm sure Grace would have loved to take us with her," his voice was so careful like he thought I couldn't handle what he was going to tell me, "But I don't think that was a memory. I don't remember any of it."

"Well just because you don't remember it, doesn't mean it didn't happen," I tried to keep the venom out of my voice.

"Ducar didn't know Grace was leaving the show, remember? He was so upset when she announced it, I'm sure she can't have told him about it before."

"Maybe he thought when he told her she couldn't bring us that she would stay behind with us. So he was surprised and angry when she decided to leave anyway."

"What about Beatrice? Do you really think she would have let Grace take us away from her?"

"Maybe she didn't know! Ducar obviously didn't know until after Grace told us! I bet someone was spying and heard her tell us so then they went to Ducar. It was probably Dylan!"

"I think you just want this to be true, but it really doesn't seem likely that it happened. I mean none of your other dreams lately have been memories, why do you think this one has to be?"

"Why don't you think it was possible that Grace wanted us!" My voice shook with anger, and I barely noticed that I was on the verge of yelling. Kith looked shocked.

"I..I mean..I never said she didn't want us. I just don't think she tried to steal us away without telling anyone is all."

Turning away from Kith, I breathed heavily and tried to stop the tears that were pooling in my eyes.

"Mara, Grace loved the freak show. She wasn't there for any of the bad things that Ducar did to us. We were treated well by everyone when Grace was there so she had no reason to think she needed to take us away from that. She would have thought she was taking us away from our family. Don't you remember how sad she was to leave everyone?"

Sniffing involuntarily, I nodded. "I'm sorry I yelled at you," was all I could manage. Wiping my eyes, I turned to face Kith. "I think I'm going to do some sewing,"

Sitting on the bed, I faced away from Kith and got to work on my sewing. For a moment, I thought he was going to try to continue the conversation, but he seemed to think better of it. I could tell he was hurt, but I was done talking. He always talked to me like I was a child, and I couldn't take it anymore.

For a long time, I sat there working in silence. My fingers soon ached from how many times I distractedly poked myself, but I kept going. Once I made a long line of stitches, I looked down to see that it was crooked. Angrily, I began pulling out all the stitches and yanked so hard that I broke the thread. Letting out a grunt of frustration, I threw the fabric, needle and all, on the ground.

Turning away from my mess, I saw Kith walking over to me with a cup of hot water and some food. Pausing only a few steps from me, he stared at the fabric on the floor. He must have decided it was best not to comment.

"It's lunchtime, I thought you may want something to eat." He said, setting the food a foot away from me on the table and stepping back a little.

Guilt washed over me, and my eyes began welling up with tears again. Feeling like a child, I tried to hold back the tears as I thanked Kith for the food.

"I am sorry," I said as Kith turned to get his own plate. I put away my sewing stuff and joined him at the small table. "It wasn't fair for me to get upset at you just because my dream wasn't real. I mean, it wouldn't matter if it was real anyway. She didn't take us with her whether she wanted to or not."

"It's okay. All of your nightmares were memories, so it makes sense for you to assume your other dreams might be memories too."

"No, it wasn't that," I said quietly. "There was something

else to it that made me want it to be real," a realization hit me. "Grace isn't with the freak show anymore."

Kith laughed, "Are you just now figuring this out?"

I glared at him for a second then continued, "Of all the people we've known, Grace would be the only one we could live with freely because she already left the freak show a long time ago. I just think my mind came up with this fantasy because it was the most realistic," Kith was staring at me, "Is that stupid?"

"No, it's not stupid. I just don't know how realistic living with Grace even is," Kith began, sounding worried.

"Of course, I know that!" I interrupted. "I was just trying to figure out my dream. I'm happy in the cabin. I don't think we should leave."

Kith nodded, relaxing. "I'm happy here too. As soon as it gets warmer, we'll put up our defenses and then I think we could really stay here for a long time."

✳   Kith   ✳

I woke with a start. Usually, at this point, I'd be waking Mara up, but her nightmares stopped several weeks ago. It still took some getting used to, but it was a great adjustment to make. This time, however, it was my own dream that woke me. Laying in bed, I tried hard to recall what happened. It felt important.

After several minutes, I got up and started heating our water and warming the dried meat. I couldn't shake the feeling that there was something I needed to remember, something the dream tried to remind me of.

Mara rose when I set the hot water on the table. I could feel her watching me as we warmed up, but she didn't say anything. With the arguments that happened over the last couple of weeks, we were both becoming more hesitant to speak.

Staring down into my cup, I swirled my water around, my eyes following the movement. Suddenly an image of Ketzia staring into her tea leaves filled my mind, and the memory that alluded me returned.

"I had a dream last night…" I hesitated, remembering our last big argument, and the fact that I still didn't remember the dream. "Well. I can't remember the dream exactly, but it made me remember something from a while back. Before we left the show."

Mara tensed as I mentioned the show, but she tried to brush it off. "What was it?" Her voice cracked and she cleared her throat.

We were supposed to be taking naps. Beatrice got rare permission to let us into her tent and tucked us into her bed. Mara fell asleep almost instantly, but I remember pretending to sleep while relishing the feeling of Mara being peaceful next to me.

While we were in bed, Ketzia came to visit Beatrice. They huddled together away from the
bed and whispered.

"This is where you must take them when you leave. It's important." She handed
something to Beatrice as she spoke.

"Are you sure about this? It doesn't make sense."

"Do they make sense to you? BeBe, they're special, and you must help them realize that."

"I know they're special." Her voice was full of worry. "If I take them there, will I lose them?"

Ketzia hesitated. "I don't know exactly…"

"That's a yes. You're asking me to give them up to someone or thing that's so unknown. I don't
know if I can."

"It's hard. I know. But they're not yours, not really."

Beatrice's face turned red in instant anger. "Don't you dare tell me they aren't mine. They're as mine as if I birthed them myself. I love them as much."

Apology was written all over Ketzia's face. "I know. I misspoke. I'm extremely sorry. We should talk more about this later." With that, she looked over at us and swiftly left the tent.

Beatrice sat at her table and put her head in her hands. I wanted to curl up in her lap, but I was supposed to be asleep and knew I shouldn't have heard the conversation.

Mara didn't say anything for a couple of minutes after I finished. When she did speak, her words came slowly. "I don't think that actually happened."

Confusion filled me. "That was a memory, Mara. Not a dream."

She shook her head as red splotches built around her neck. "No. I don't think so."

"Mara.."

"No. Just, no, Kith! You don't get to go having dreams that are real about us being *special*. Because we aren't. We aren't special, we're freaks. We're freaks and that's it!"

My mouth was open, but no words could come out. I reached out toward her, but she yanked away. "Mara, I didn't mean to upset you."

She gulped back a sob. "How dare you tell me that. Why?" Her hand swiped out as if to hit me, but she pulled it back.

"I don't understand." What did I say that was so wrong?

"Why did you have to tell me we're special and how much Beatrice loved us? It doesn't change anything!" She turned and grabbed Gracie, holding her to her chest.

"But she did love us."

"DID! You speak about her as if you know for sure she's gone. Do you? You never answer me when I ask." Her voice was a whisper at the end.

"I don't know for sure, but I can only guess that she is."

She dropped to her knees and curled into herself. When I reached for her she flinched away. "I hate you." She spat the words at me. "Why did you let me hold on to hope, only to take it away while telling me how *special* we are?"

"Mara." My mind was blank. "I'm sorry."

"Grace is still out there somewhere. She's safe. But you made sure I knew we could never be with her. You shouldn't have told me this."

"You're right. I wasn't thinking about any of that. I was thinking about the place we were supposed to go. We were supposed to go to a certain place, Mara." All of a sudden, my selfishness hit me. For so long I dreamed of a destination, a goal, that I didn't think of how much this revelation would hurt Mara. "Mara, I'm so sorry. I didn't mean to hurt you."

My heart was heavy as I reached for my spear. "I'm going to go hunting. I don't know that I'll catch anything, but I think we could both use some space."

Mara slowly nodded. "Space sounds good." Her voice sounded blank; empty, and I caused that. Cursing myself, I headed out into the snow.

When I got close to the edge of the clearing, something odd caught my eye. The sunlight was catching something just inside the tree line that shimmered a light blue. When I reached it, I held out my hand to touch it and for just a second there was a small resistance as if I were pushing my hand through water and then it was gone. Stepping forward, I passed through the barrier with the same slight resistance. So small it was barely noticeable.

Awestruck, I looked back at the cabin, wishing I could go and tell Mara, but remembering how angry she was at me I decided it better wait. Sadly, I turned back toward the trees and kept on moving.

At first, I was so caught up in my thoughts that I barely noticed the cold. When it finally started to seep through my thoughts, I realized I had forgotten to take anything for warmth. Knowing I still couldn't go back yet, I moved on, trying hard to ignore my entire body shivering.

There was no way I was going to be able to focus on hunting, so I just walked aimlessly with my spear. I heard Mara leave the cabin and head in the opposite direction, and I hoped she would be alright. Would she forgive me for this one? What if I had hurt her too badly with this, after our last argument?

The cabin was supposed to be great, but winter was dragging on and we were losing control. We needed to find a way to get a grip. I vowed to spend all the warm weather preparing for next winter. We couldn't let it be this bad again. I wasn't sure if we'd survive it.

After some time, the coldness finally overcame me, and I headed back, swiftly realizing I walked farther than I intended.

Wondering if Mara was still angry, I rushed back to the cabin. My apology would need to be grand for this one, and I'd be careful. No more fighting. We had to stay together.

Eventually, maybe we'd make it to wherever we were supposed to be going, but I buried that. I'd not speak to Mara about it again.

*   Mara   *

A mixture of emotions swirled through me, making me feel like I might explode. I needed air and was relieved when Kith chose to leave first. The air was still cold. At first, I thought about going out immediately anyway but decided it would be smart to bundle up. As I did so, I thought about how Kith hadn't bundled himself up enough. At first, a sense of satisfaction hit me and I hoped he was miserable out there. Then, a small feeling of guilt as I wondered if there was any chance he would catch something. At least that would give us something else to talk about.

As I walked through the snow-covered trees, I thought about Grace. She was safe somewhere, with a home and a family. Was hoping to be reunited with her so bad? Why did Kith have to squash that without even a second thought? I knew it wasn't possible, but it was nice to fantasize about it and he just couldn't let me have that.

His words echoed through my mind as I walked. All this time he was sure Beatrice was gone, and he kept that from me. To protect me, I'm sure. Without realizing it, a growl escaped me. I was incredibly tired of being protected all the time like I was too fragile to trust with the truth.

Knowing why Kith lied about the possibility of Beatrice being alive didn't make me feel any better about it. I hated being treated like a child all the time. He was my age when we left the show, and even then he acted like he was in charge of everything.

Anger and pain surged through me. Rushing at the nearest tree, I slashed at it with my claws. Bark flew everywhere as I continued my flurried attack. A scream built up and then released as I struck the tree harder. Suddenly, the energy drained out of me and I collapsed at the base of the tree. Images of everyone we lost floated through my mind as I curled into a ball and let the sobs come.

Once I cried myself out, I stood and continued walking, not really going anywhere. After a while, I jumped up into a tree and slipped a little when my hand caught mostly snow. Cursing myself quietly, I repositioned my hands on the branch and then began slowly swinging from branch to branch with the help of my tail. My muscles were stiff after so much time inside and it felt good to work them.

The cold air stung as it hit my face, but I continued anyway, grateful for the distraction. It had been days since I was outside and even longer since I was in the trees. The realization hit me that I needed to come out by myself more often. Being stuck in the cabin with Kith all the time was making me feel suffocated and I needed more time away from him. Sadness crept in through my anger at the thought. We never fought like this before. Then again, I used to let him tell me what to do without question. Maybe this was just part of growing up.

Remembering my harsh words to Kith, I wished I hadn't told him I hated him even though I felt he deserved all of my anger. Surely he knew I could never hate him, but it must hurt all the same.

Dropping back to the ground, I realized how late it was and decided it was probably time to go home. I wasn't sure if I was ready to face Kith yet, but my muscles were sore and I was cold.

When I got close to the cabin, I grudgingly whistled the tune that would tell him I was coming. Safety couldn't be compromised just because I was still angry.

As I reached the cabin, Kith came walking outside. When I met his eyes, I could tell he had been crying. Good. Maybe this would finally help him understand. "I'm sorry, Mara!" he said, reaching for a hug. I let him hug me for a moment before pulling away, noticing the hurt on his face

"I don't hate you," I said stupidly, before walking past him and into the cabin.

When I got back to the cabin and it was still empty, I figured Mara still needed some space. Still, I was surprised and hurt by how long it took her to return. It was a sign that I messed up, and I got the feeling she wasn't going to forgive me easily for this one.

The rest of our night was spent in silence and she went to sleep shortly after we ate. She must have exhausted herself while out because she fell asleep quickly. Or at least, she pretended to. Late into the night, I sat next to the fire watching the flames. A part of me was hoping the solution to everything would appear there, but of course, nothing changed.

Eventually, I started struggling to stay awake and put out the fire. With how badly I hurt Mara, I didn't feel comfortable curling up on the bed next to her, so I curled up on the floor in front of the fireplace. It was chilly without the fire or blankets, but I refused to take one from the bed.

Sleep didn't come easily, and I woke the next morning feeling stiff and cold. Mara wasn't in bed anymore, and it took a couple of minutes to spot her outside playing with Gracie. I was blocking the fireplace, so she had been unable to heat any water.

I brought a cup of steaming water to where she sat. She accepted it without looking at me. "Thank you."

Watching her take some small sips, I tried to think of something to say. After a couple of minutes, I gave up and walked away. Figuring she'd probably be wanting to go inside to warm up before long, I headed to the shed. It needed to be cleaned out and organized before summer so I could build up a good-sized wood pile.

A crash resounded through the shed when I moved a large cart, causing my thoughts to come to a sudden halt. Cautiously, I crept around to investigate. Laying on the floor was an old bow, covered in multiple layers of dust and grime.

Picking it up carefully, I moved it between my hands. It needed a lot of cleaning, but it seemed sturdy enough. Pulling back the string, I moved it into a position similar to the one I saw in our show. The performers were new when we left, so I didn't have time to learn much from them, but I had some memories of the way they held their bows.

There was a small rag on the floor, which I used to start scrubbing off some of the grime. It wasn't very useful, though since it was also dirty. "Mara!" Her name caught in my throat as I remembered I was giving her space.

With some work, I could make this into a nice gift for her birthday. It wasn't for quite some time, but I could make a quiver and arrows to go with it. It's not like it would be very useful without at least arrows. My thoughts lingered on her birthday, wondering if she'd have forgiven me by then.

Where would I hide the bow, though? Looking around the shed some more, I found a small nook in the back corner that I could slide the bow into. Cleaning out the shed was a lot more exciting as I planned all the cool things I could do with the bow.

*   Mara   *

At first, when I woke up, I was confused. Kith wasn't in bed and when I looked around, I didn't see him. It took a while for me to notice the lump on the floor next to the fireplace. He must have decided sleeping on the floor was better than being in bed with me. Part of me was offended by this, but another part felt just a little bit of satisfaction. It couldn't have been comfortable on the floor, and maybe he deserved to be uncomfortable.

Grabbing Gracie from where she lay on the bed beside me, I tip-toed out the door. Not ready to deal with Kith yet, I decided I could forgo the fire for now.

Sitting outside, I let the cold sink in while I stared at Gracie. The same thoughts that swirled inside my mind since my fight with Kith, continued to cycle through. Why was Kith so quick to dismiss the idea of Grace? She loved us, she could take care of us. It was selfish of him not to even think about it. Just like it was selfish of him to hide his true feelings about Beatrice from me. And how did he know, anyway? He didn't see any more than I did while we sat there terrified, waiting for her to come back. He couldn't possibly know what happened. He was only guessing.

Even as I thought that, though, I knew it was wishful thinking. I was almost certain now that Kith was right. I allowed myself to hope for so long, and in a single moment, he took all of that hope away. What gave him the right to do that to me? What gave him the right to decide where we would and would not go? Just because he had some stupid dream, he thinks we have a true destination, but my dreams mean nothing.

After a while, I realized I was shivering. Unsure how long I was sitting still, I decided I should probably move around. Stretching out my legs in front of me, I lifted Gracie and gave her a big hug. That was when I heard Kith coming. Deciding against standing, as I had planned, I waited to see what he was doing. My back was to him and I refused to look as I heard him walking toward me.

When he gave me the cup of hot water, I was incredibly grateful. It got so cold just sitting still out there. Aside from a thank you, I couldn't bring myself to talk to him, though. Sipping the hot water to buy myself some time, I tried to think of what else to say. My mind reeled with angry words, but there were apologies mixed in there too. I hated the distance there was between us and I wanted to make it right again. But I was still full of anger and I just didn't know which part of me would come out if I opened my mouth so I kept it closed.

As soon as I heard Kith rummaging in the shed, I made my way inside to warm up by the fire he left going. I was sure he knew I would be cold and want to come inside. Even while I wasn't speaking to him, he was trying to take care of me. Because to him all I would ever be was someone who needed taking care of. Someone he couldn't be honest and straightforward with. Someone fragile.

Realization hit that all I did was trade staring blankly in the cold to staring blankly into the fire while the same thoughts ran through my mind. Sighing deeply, I stood and walked over to the bed to lay Gracie down in her box. Looking around the cabin, I decided I could use some food. For a moment, I wondered if Kith had eaten, but immediately was sure he didn't. He would have brought me food too.

After heating some of the dried meat, I debated on whether I wanted to bring Kith his. Instead, I decided to walk out to the shed and simply said, "I heated some food if you want it," and then turned and quickly walked back inside.

I finished my food by the time Kith came in, but I was still sitting at the small table, staring at my plate. When he opened the door, I stood and busied myself with my dishes so he wouldn't know I had just been sitting there. Then I sat on the bed and grabbed Gracie again. Feeling awkward, I started bouncing her on my knee as if she were a real toddler. After a while, I noticed Kith watching me and stopped abruptly. His eyes quickly went down to his plate and guilt surged through me.

"What were you doing in the shed?" I asked, tentatively.

Kith's eyes slowly rose back to my face, and I looked back down at Gracie to avoid eye contact. "Just trying to clean it out," Kith said, quietly. He sounded sad. "It would be nice to have more space in there for wood, and I was curious what was in there."

"What is in there?" I asked, my curiosity piquing.

Kith paused for a second, and I looked up to see he was thinking about something. "Mostly junk so far. But there was a cart we could use to collect the wood."

With no idea why, I felt like Kith was keeping something from me. Again. Annoyance spread through me and I stood up and walked out the door, leaving Kith gaping.

Once I was outside, I realized how ridiculous I just behaved. Poor Kith probably thought I was trying to patch things up and then I just walked out like I cared nothing about what he had to say. *A cart would be very helpful with the wood. Why did I get so annoyed all of a sudden?*

Although I knew I should go back and apologize, I just

couldn't bring myself to do it yet, and then Kith walked outside. He took a glance at me and offered a half smile before continuing around the cabin to get to the shed.

For the rest of that day, I mostly wandered outside. I attempted to do some sewing, but after poking myself so hard I started bleeding, I decided maybe it wasn't a good day for it. Kith seemed to be having the same problem. There were several times I saw him just standing in the doorway of the shed staring into it.

At the end of the day, we actually sat together at the table to eat. There was mostly silence between us. Kith seemed determined not to talk to me unless I spoke to him first.

"Does the cart work?" I finally spat out, after spending ages telling myself I should say something.

"What?" Kith asked, utterly confused and surprised by my sudden outburst.

"Never mind." Just like that, I was annoyed again. More at myself than him, but it was hard to differentiate the two at that moment. Getting up, I walked over to the bed. "I'm tired," I said, even though I didn't feel tired at all. I was just ready for this day to end. Laying down, I squeezed Gracie close to me and hoped the next day would be better.

✳   Kith   ✳

Sitting at the table, I watched in confusion as Mara curled up in the bed. Did I say something wrong again? Her emotions seemed to be all over the place and I couldn't figure them out. One second she'd seem to be reaching out and the next she'd be pushing me away again.

Not that I could blame her though. It was obvious I really messed up and it would take her some time to get over it. If she did. I glanced over at her, lying curled up in the bed. Even though I was pretty sure she wasn't asleep, I knew saying something was a bad idea.

Instead, I grabbed my knives and went outside. I planned

to try carving something, but I ended up just staring at the bear on the handle. As I moved it around, I thought about the day Isaac gave it to me. He thought there was a reason I was drawn to the bear, but maybe his judgment was wrong. I didn't feel at all like the protector he thought I was.

Cold crept through me, and I wondered if Mara was asleep. Even if not, I knew I couldn't stay outside any longer. Without even looking at the bed, I curled up in front of the fire. It was low, but still burning. I thought about putting it out, but the warmth was welcome after my time outside. Especially since I'd be sleeping without a blanket again.

After a fitful night of tossing and turning, I woke when the sun came up. For a while, I tried to go back to sleep, but I knew it wasn't going to happen. I looked over at Mara curled up with Gracie in the bed. She seemed to be sleeping peacefully.

It was still a little early for making a fire and starting to warm our breakfasts, so I went out to the shed and decided to move some more wood into the cabin, instead. Once I moved enough for a few days the shed looked rather empty. Frowning around at the clearing covered in wet snow, I decided it would be best not to wait to fill it up again.

By the time I gathered enough to feel satisfied, my stomach was growling. Creeping back into the cabin, I relished the feeling of the warmth washing over me. I didn't even realize how cold I got while working.

"You look like you could use some food." Mara handed me a bowl with some meat that had been heated in a bit of water to make it softer and a cup of water.

I accepted it gratefully. "I meant to get back in time to start all this before you got up." My fingers wrapped around the cup, absorbing the heat from it.

She eyed me warily. "How long were you out?"

Shrugging, I avoided her gaze. "I got up a bit after the sun. I figured it would be a good idea to have more wood in here, and then the shed seemed too empty so I decided to refill it."

"The extra wood was a good call. It's nice to have it close and ready to use instead of always having to gather it."

"It really is. It might be one of my favorite things about the cabin." But at least when we had all the small tasks to do I didn't mess up all the time. I was much too busy for that. Staring down into my cup, I let the water swirl.

"There's a lot to like about the cabin." Her voice was soft, and I wondered if she was thinking the same thing. There's a lot to like about the cabin, but our fights weren't one of them.

I wanted to respond, to keep the conversation going, but I felt my throat tighten. It was as if I was forgetting how to talk to her. There was a deep fear of making everything worse, so instead I just continued to stare into my cup.

"Are you going to eat?"

"Oh. Uhm. Yes." I had forgotten about the meat and how hungry I was. Setting my cup down, I gobbled up the meat so fast I barely tasted it.

After several moments, Mara broke the silence. "Kith, I think we should talk. A serious talk."

Raising my eyes to her face, I locked eyes with her for the first time in days. "Alright."

"I don't want everything to be bad between us."

"I don't, either."

"But there are things that need to change. For one, I think we need more time apart. Too much time together with too much time to think is a bad thing. For both of us."

"You're probably right."

"Another thing. I need you to realize that I'm not a fragile little girl anymore. I'm capable and strong. And you need to ease up." Her voice was firm, but there was also a tenderness there.

"You're right. I know you're strong. You're probably stronger than I am. But if anything happened to you it would kill me. I don't know if I can be less protective, but I will stop treating you as if you can't do things yourself." She nodded as if my answer was exactly what she imagined it would be.

"My emotions have been all over the place. I'm still struggling with everything from the past few days, but I don't want this weirdness and silence."

"I don't either." My heart ached thinking about all the pain from the past few days. "I am sorry, Mara. I know I was wrong."

Her face fell. "I know. I don't want to talk about that, though. I'm not sure I'll ever be ready for that."

"I understand." A wave of frustration with myself rolled through me. For over a year now, one of the main things I wanted was a set destination. A place to head toward every time we were forced to start moving. Maybe that would be the one place we'd be safe. But my desire for that led to me hurting Mara. It didn't matter anyway, right? We had the cabin now, with no intention of leaving.

"Good. Now, how about we go for a walk? I could use some air." She grabbed her blanket and wrapped her feet without waiting for me to answer, so I did the same.

We walked in silence for a while, just enjoying being in each other's company without any tension between us. After some time, though, I realized we needed a bit more.

"Bet you can't catch me!" I jumped into a tree and started swinging away as fast as I could. Without looking back, I could tell Mara wasn't far behind me. Laughing, I swung higher and farther. Even so, it wasn't long before she tackled me mid-swing and we tumbled into a big pile of snow and leaves.

"I think I got you." She dropped a snowball in my face and quickly climbed into the nearest tree. Before I could even pull myself up she was several trees away.

We raced around in the trees until we got tired and cold, then headed home. Things weren't perfect between us, but we were headed back to normalcy, which was enough for me.

*   Mara   *

"What are you looking at?"

The sudden break in silence startled me and I jumped a little before turning from the one good window that was just low enough to see out of to look at Kith.

"I was just thinking it looks like there's less snow on the ground. It must be getting warmer!" I replied brightly.

Kith looked skeptical as he walked over to the window, and I felt a stab of annoyance. My anger was flaring a lot lately and I knew it was time to get out of the cabin again.

"I guess it looks a little lighter, maybe."

"Well it's not like I said it was gone," I replied, rolling my eyes. Before Kith could respond, I changed the subject. "I think we should make a trip to the stream. We haven't been out in a while"

After packing up quickly, we headed out. When we got to the shimmery blue wall, I realized that I must have walked through it a few times already, but had never paid enough attention. This time, I noticed the slight tingle that brushed my skin as I stepped through. I was about to ask Kith if he felt it, but he spoke first.

"You walked right through without slowing down." His surprise intrigued me.

"I did. All I felt was a slight tingling sensation." I paused to look at the shimmering air behind us. "Why? What's it like for you?"

"There's a slight resistance in the air right there. Like it's deciding whether or not to let me pass." He shrugged. "I wonder if we'll ever truly understand this. Or ourselves." There was a hint of sadness in his eyes as he turned around and continued toward the stream.

We walked in silence for a while. Finally, without looking at Kith, I said, "I'm sorry I've been getting annoyed so easily lately."

Kith was silent for a moment. "You've been fine." His voice was quiet and reserved.

"Either way, getting out for a bit seemed like a good idea."

"I agree. It feels good to be moving."

"Seriously. You were starting to get so lazy." I kept a gentle teasing note to my voice. Things were improved between us, but sometimes when I wasn't careful I could see Kith sinking back into his guilt.

"You're one to talk. Always just sitting around with some cloth in your lap."

I couldn't help but laugh, partly in relief that we were teasing each other in a normal way again.

We bantered back and forth for a while before Kith changed the subject. "It does seem a little warmer."

"Oh, you think so?" I said, in what I hoped sounded like fake irritation. "Well, if you say it is, it must be."

Kith glanced at me and relaxed when he saw I was grinning. "It's still cold though!"

"I think we've been spoiled by the cabin," I responded. "Remember last winter? We walked to Isaac's house in the cold all the time before we ended up staying with him."

Kith looked thoughtful, "That's true," he said finally, "but when we got to his house we stayed inside where it was warm. Then when we got back, we stayed in the cave and that was pretty warm, too. Plus, that walk wasn't all that far."

"I guess we got a little spoiled with Isaac, too," I said sadly.

We finished the walk to the stream talking about Isaac and the things we did with him the winter before. We only talked about the positive things. We both knew that was what was needed right then.

Once we got to the stream, we went to where our dug-out cave was. It looked so small and strange now.

"I'm glad we didn't have to stay here all winter," I said.

"Yeah," Kith responded, "just imagine how terrible the fighting would be if we were stuck in *there,*" he laughed lightly.

"No, thanks." I giggled, but imagining it for real was sobering.

After we were there for a while, I decided it was time to fill our water skins, so we started working to break the ice. As we did so, I noticed that it cracked much more easily than usual.

I smiled broadly, "I told you it was getting warmer! There's barely any ice left!" Our small fish-catching pond caught my eye. It was still empty, but I had a feeling we'd be able to catch fish in it again soon.

Sipping the freezing water sent pangs through my stomach. "Did we bring any food? I'm hungry."

"I grabbed a little before we left. Thought we might want something to munch on." He pulled out some meat and handed me my half with a smile.

"Great thinking." I took a big bite and grinned at him.

While we ate, we did our usual stroll around the stream, collecting any pretty rocks we found for the windows. Each time we came, we found less and less good ones. We did manage to find a few passable rocks, though. We packed them up and did one last fill of the water skin we used during lunch before heading back.

✳   Kith   ✳

"Kith! I can see the ground!" Mara was staring out the window and jumping up and down.

Peeking out, I could see one mound where the tip of it wasn't covered with snow. It was a small circle of dirt, but it symbolized so much more to two kids who had been stuck inside for what felt like endless days of cold.

I couldn't contain my smile. "Once it's warm enough, we should start preparing for next winter. We don't want it to be like this one was."

Mara's glance told me I was ruining her excitement, "True. It would be nice to have a little more variety in our food." Her stomach grumbled as if on command, and I chuckled.

"It would for sure." With our careful rationing, there was enough food to last the winter, but it was all meat and a few random greens we were able to find. We both missed the variety from before the ground turned too cold for things to grow. Without it, I never seemed to feel full. We avoided discussing the matter much, as there wasn't much we could do about it.

"Let's go outside and play for a bit." Mara's excitement returned, and I could tell she needed to let out some energy.

"Alright. Let's get bundled up." We put all our clothes on, wrapped our feet in our makeshift shoes, and headed out. The cold was still biting, but I closed the door securely behind us and stepped into the snow.

"Watch this!" Mara jumped through the snow, making holes where she sank. Then she fell onto her back and started moving her arms and feet. "Look at the cool picture I made."

As I watched her, I thought of how that request should have been made to our parents. How many times had we heard, "Mom, watch this!" while other kids ran and played? We would watch from our places in the show and pretend that we weren't longing for that experience. Of course, Beatrice was there. Maybe that shouldn't have been so different, but it was.

Mara didn't need to know these thoughts, and I knew if she paid any attention to me, she'd see them written on my face. Shaking my head, I forced my attention elsewhere. Running and taking a large jump, I fell into a pile of snow. Freezing wetness surrounded me, shocking all other thoughts out of my head.

Whooping loudly, Mara sprang up onto a low branch. I watched as her hand almost slipped, but she adjusted quickly and held her grasp as she pulled herself up. She did get quite strong somewhere along the way. She moved along the branch in a crouch, her movements thought out and careful, while still being swift. I half expected her to drop on some poor prey, but instead, she grabbed the branch and allowed her body to swing.

With all the time we spent swinging, I had never seen her gain that much height. When she released and let herself soar, my heart leaped into my throat. She landed close to me, in the large pile of snow, her laughter echoing through the clearing.

"You have got to try that!" Her face was flushed from the cold and excitement, and I couldn't say no.

Following her up into the tree, I felt my body releasing tension I hadn't realized it was holding. I felt a sense of awareness and life I hadn't felt in way too long. The wind moved the tree beneath me, but I moved with it and paid hardly any attention. My focus zoned in on the biggest pile of snow, and I propelled my body forward, releasing the branch. For a second, I flew, and then I was again engulfed in the snow.

Mara landed shortly after I did. We rose, laughing and out of breath. Without saying anything, we headed back toward the tree. I was halfway there when I heard some loud cracking sounds coming up from my side. Turning, I saw a large, brown bear approaching the clearing. It seemed focused, heading straight at us.

"Mara! I think we should get inside," My voice was low, but I knew she'd hear me. She turned to ask me why, but all that came out was a small gasp. Without me having to repeat myself, she started carefully heading for the door. I did the same, thinking about how we'd keep the bear from entering the cabin. Our door wasn't exactly sturdy.

As I was deciding we'd have to move the bed in front of the door, the bear reached the glowing edge of the clearing and stopped suddenly. It moved its head around and sniffed the air. A frustrated huff came out, and the bear seemed like it was going to move toward us again. It moved its legs but didn't come any closer. Blue sparkles lit the air where the bear made contact with the shimmering air.

The growl it released sent a shiver down my spine, but I was frozen in place with confusion and fascination. Mara was close to the door but had also frozen. Snow was piling up around the angry bear's feet, but still, it didn't come closer. After what felt like ages, it released one more angry growl and turned away.

Air rushed into my lungs, and I realized I had been holding my breath. "What just happened?"

Mara's eyes were wide in fear and shock. She shook her head at me. "I have no idea. I thought we were goners for sure."

"Me too," I was glad for whatever had turned the bear away but was ready to not be in the snow anymore. "Let's go get warm."

Mara didn't argue. We soberly went inside and heated some water to drink while we stood around the fire.

"With it starting to get warmer, I think I'll start trying to collect more wood to store in the shed. It will have to dry, so I'll only be able to collect a bit at a time. I want to have a lot saved up before next winter, though."

"Good idea," Mara was distracted, and I wasn't sure she knew what I was saying.

"I'll start tomorrow."

"Alright," Mara stared at the fire for a few seconds and then looked at me. "What happened out there, Kith? With the bear?"

"I wish I knew."

Her hands rubbed her arms as she thought. "Do you think that shimmering in the air is some sort of barrier to keep danger out? Rain and leaves come through it fine, and obviously, we can. But it stopped the tree, and now the bear."

"I guess it's possible. I just don't understand how. Not that I'm complaining."

"We're not normal, are we?" Questions much bigger than that one lay unspoken.

"What is normal, though?"

"Not us."

"That's good, though, isn't it?"

"I… I guess so."

"Whatever this… weirdness… is, it's the only reason we're still alive."

For several seconds there was no response. "I hadn't thought about it like that, but you're right."

I reached out and moved some loose hair out of her face. "I think you're pretty cool just the way you are."

"I think you are, too," Her smile was genuine, which made me feel better.

We finished our water in silence. We may never know what caused the strange things that happened to us, but I was coming to accept that. I wasn't lying when I said we would be dead without them.

*　Mara　*

"Wow, Mara, your stitches are getting better!" Kith exclaimed, peeking at the bit of material I was sewing.

His attention made me wonder how I would be able to make his clothes without him knowing what I was doing. He was always admiring my progress, which was nice, of course, but also frustrating. It was supposed to be a surprise when I presented him with a full set of new clothes. That was assuming I was even able to make them. So far, all I had to show for my work was a very lumpy and lopsided bag that I made from several bits of animal skins. More than once, I pulled the thread out and redid several places, and when it was finally finished, I stared at it in frustration. Looking at it again, I resisted the temptation to tear it apart and start over.

The cloth I would use for Kith's clothes was picked out, and I had already been using myself to try to measure how much I would need for the shirt and pants. I decided to try it out on making clothes for Gracie first, though, so I didn't use up a bunch of fabric just for the clothes to be all wrong. Gracie was small, so I thought it should go faster and hopefully help me figure out my technique without wasting too much.

After a while of puzzling over what I would do, I decided to just get started. First, I worked on a pair of pants for Gracie. The excitement I felt at the idea of making clothes was quickly squashed by how difficult it proved to be. My first attempt at a pair of pants turned out to be something I couldn't even pull up to cover any more than her legs, and I was very confused about how on earth to get the pants to go up and over her bottom.

Eventually, I decided to take off my pants and examine them whenever I was working on the ones for Gracie. After a few attempts at copying my pants, I was able to make something passable for Gracie. They looked a little odd around her stomach and bottom, but at least they covered her. They also ended up quite a bit too short by the time I was done, so I made a mental note to add on a bit of extra cloth at both the crotch and the end of Kith's to make sure he didn't experience the same issues.

Once Gracie had a decent pair of pants, I moved on to a shirt. Again, I took off my own to examine and copy during the process. The shirt proved to be easier than the pants were, although it still didn't look quite right in the end.

After some inner debate, I decided the clothes were at least wearable and therefore it was worth making some for Kith. A part of me wanted to try more outfits for Gracie first to get the technique a little better, but I knew I didn't have a lot of time to spare if I was going to have a full outfit made for Kith by his birthday. With how long it took just to make clothes for a tiny doll, I had to assume I needed a lot of time for Kith's.

Once I started on Kith's outfit, my progress was slow because I could only work on them when we were not together. On a few occasions, I used our bickering as an excuse to get away and once I saw him leave the cabin as well, I would come back and work on the gifts. The problem was that I wasn't always in the mood to sew after an argument. I usually just wanted to go walk outside to clear my mind. Sewing wasn't exactly relaxing for me, and sometimes it put me in a worse mood than I was in to begin with.

"What are you making now?" Kith asked one day as I sat sewing, managing a mostly straight line.

I looked at the two pieces of fabric I was sewing together. "Well...I actually don't know," I said and saw the amusement dance across Kith's face. "I guess I'm just practicing right now," I said, feeling a little irritated. He was the one I was doing all of this for and he was laughing at me.

Kith seemed to sense the start of an argument and led the conversation differently, "Well," he said optimistically, "if you need a break or anything, I wouldn't mind stretching my legs a bit. It's a nice day out, maybe we could go for a walk?"

His deflection of my mood made me feel a little guilty. I smiled at him, "It does look pretty out. I hope it will be nice enough to swim soon!"

Kith's face brightened at the thought. "You know it's not very cold right now. I bet if we give it just a few more days it would be warm enough," When I looked at Kith skeptically, he added, "I'm sure once we got in we would get used to the cold. I mean we did wash in it before when it was pretty chilly!"

I laughed out loud. "That was washing, not swimming! And we sat by a fire after!"

"Well then let's make a fire and it will be fine!"

"Why don't we start with a bath first and see how that

goes before we decide to go swimming?" I asked, still chuckling.

"Okay," Kith said, dragging out the word. Then he exclaimed, "Let's do it next time we go for more water!"

It was a relief to see Kith genuinely excited about something again, and I couldn't stop myself from laughing. "Alright. We could both use a bath anyway. Maybe we could even wash the blankets." I crinkled my nose thinking about how the bed was starting to smell.

"That's probably a good idea." Kith glanced at the bed as we headed out the door. "It's too bad we don't have a way to get fresh straw, too."

CHAPTER EIGHTEEN: APRIL

Even with all the water I had been drinking, we were still a couple of days at least away from a water run. Staring at the water bucket, I contemplated just dumping it. I could make it look like an accident. Then we'd have to go to the stream.

Sighing, I realized how irrational that idea was. Water runs were hard, and I appreciated that we didn't have to make them constantly. Although I should have been glad that the bucket lasted us for so long, I felt an eager anticipation to be back in the water. Even if it was freezing cold.

"I need to do something," I muttered to myself and pushed off the wall I was leaning against. Playing felt useless right now. Only something productive would take my mind off of how stifled I still felt.

My eyes drifted around the cabin, avoiding Mara's gaze. I could tell she was pretty sure where my thoughts had been. She tried to hide that she was watching me, but it wasn't working. It didn't take long for me to see the pile of spikes we had made.

With the weather getting warmer, the ground might have thawed out enough to start our planned defenses of the clearing. For a second I wondered if it was still even worth it to put them up. There hadn't been any problems, and everything was so calm.

Even so, it wouldn't hurt anything to take some extra precautions. Plus, I really needed something to do. I headed outside to check the ground.

After grabbing the shovel from the woodshed, I went to the very edge of the clearing. Stepping on the shovel, I pushed it into the dirt. The shovel was originally way too long for me, so I used my knives to cut away some of the handle in order to make it the perfect length. I was hoping that with the slightly warmer temperature digging would be easy, but the ground was still hard. It wasn't hard enough to stop me, though.

The holes didn't need to be deep for the spears I planned to line the clearing with, so I decided I would start with those. The deeper, more difficult, traps would wait.

By the time Mara joined me, I had three spikes in the ground. "You've gotten a lot done. Want to take a water break and I'll dig some?" She held out a freshly filled water skin.

Glancing at her suspiciously, I took the skin. I was actually thirsty this time, so it wasn't hard to gulp a bunch down. Mara was already almost through a hole by the time I stopped. She stuck the shovel into the ground one more time and jumped onto it with both feet, sending it down a fair amount into the packed dirt.

As she was scooping it out, she noticed I was watching and grinned up at me. "This one is ready for a spike."

She moved a few feet over to start digging the next hole as I put in the spike and secured it. Watching her dig the hole was fascinating. The shovel was still a little taller than she was, and with the dirt packed and still partially frozen she had to put all her effort into getting it to go into the ground. Her braided hair flailed out behind her with each jump.

As much work as it was, she seemed to be having fun. We got about a fourth of the way around the clearing before deciding to quit and head inside. It was cold and we managed to get ourselves pretty dirty.

Of course, the good side to that was using water from our bucket to clean off the best we could. Maybe I didn't have to solely rely on drinking extra water to empty it. Getting work done would be helpful as well.

*   Mara   *

Holding in my laughter every time I saw Kith chugging water was becoming increasingly difficult. He was obviously trying to be sneaky about it, but I saw him several times. What was really funny was how often he was now having to go outside for the bathroom. Once, I saw him bouncing in his seat, trying to hold it in as long as he could.

Unable to control it, I burst out laughing. Kith looked up at me in complete confusion. "What's so funny?"

"Just..go..to the..bathroom already!" I said between gasps of laughter. His confusion quickly switched to embarrassed amusement.

"It's just so annoying having to bundle up to go."

"Well maybe if you drank less water…" I watched him through the corner of my eye as I spoke.

Kith beamed, "I don't know what you mean. Water is good for you. Maybe you should be drinking *more* water!"

I laughed harder, unable to stop. Kith started laughing too. "Stop! You're going to make me pee my pants!"

"Oh, and wouldn't that be great for you because then we would have to go to the stream to clean them!"

We laughed harder and Kith crossed his legs, still bouncing in his chair.

"Just go to the bathroom!" I yelled.

Kith suddenly jumped up and ran outside without even bundling up. When he came back in, I was still laughing, clutching my sides.

"Feel better?" I managed to say between giggles. Kith just glared at me and sat by the fire.

A few days later, I used up the last of the water from the bucket to fill up our skins. I decided this was close enough to finally put Kith out of his misery.

"Hey guess what!" I called to Kith, who was outside working on defenses again.

He didn't miss a beat, "It's time to go to the stream?" he asked excitedly, putting down his shovel.

No longer able to contain myself, I finally pointed out what was so obvious to me this whole time. "You do realize we could have gone to the stream any time right? The new spot is close enough that we really don't have to be getting water to make the trip."

Kith walked to where I stood and stared at me as I laughed. "But you're the one who said to wait until our next water run!”

After several minutes, I got my laughter under control. "Well yeah, I didn't know you would be so ridiculous about it! I just wanted to give it some more time to warm up." More giggles escaped as I remembered his behavior over the last while."

Once we got to the stream, we filled the bucket first, and then we each pulled out a blanket to wash.

"It might be kind of hard to bathe in such a small area," Kith said as he started walking out into the stream. Suddenly, he swayed as he stepped on an unsteady rock and the current pulled his feet out from under him. Just as I was getting ready to rush in after him, he resurfaced, gasping for a deep breath of air.

As Kith left the stream, the blanket was haphazardly wrapped around him and he looked very cold. Once I knew he was okay, I got busy building a fire to warm him up.

He sulked a bit as he dried off. "This spot isn't as good as our old place! There's no way we're going to be able to swim here. I don't think bathing is a good idea either."

"We could fill the bucket and dump it over ourselves to bathe," I suggested, and Kith's face told me he was not going to settle for that. At least not when he had been so excited for a swim. The disappointment on his face was too much for me. "We could still go to the other spot too."

"Are you sure?"

"Of course. We can bathe and stay in our old fort for the night. Like a vacation." I grinned. "We can wash our clothes there too."

"That sounds great! Let's get this water back and then we can make the trip there tonight and spend the day tomorrow!" Before I could think about responding, he packed up the still-dirty blanket, walked over to the bucket, and stood holding one side, waiting for me to grab the other.

It was almost dark by the time we reached the stream. The setting of the sun made it colder, so we headed to our fort to make our beds for the night. Kith went out to test the temperature of the water.

When he came back, he was smiling, "It's still cold, but

I'm pretty sure we can handle it long enough to bathe. Maybe even swim around a little."

We ate our dinner inside the fort and sat talking. "It's weird how small it seems here now. I didn't remember it being so small."

I thought about that, "Well, the cabin gives us quite a bit of space to ourselves so it makes sense our old fort would seem small. Plus, I definitely remember you rolling over on top of me a few times."

"Look at us turning into spoiled snobs," Kith grinned. I laughed and began settling down in bed.

"I'm pretty tired," I yawned as if to prove this was true, and Kith snickered.

Suddenly, Kith was shaking me gently. The nightmare faded quickly but left me feeling out of sorts. I was just starting to get used to not having them. Groaning, I sat up and rubbed my eyes. "I haven't missed the nightmares."

Kith didn't bother hiding the concern etched on his face. "It's been a while since you've had one, I wonder what caused it."

Pausing, I thought back to my first night without a nightmare. What was different then? I gasped softly as the realization hit me. "That first night without a nightmare was the night after that blue light saved us from the tree. Do you think the barrier also keeps out the nightmares?"

After thinking for a second, Kith spoke carefully. "Maybe since the light seems to have come from you, it considers the nightmares dangerous and somehow blocks them?" He laughed nervously before adding, "That's not possible, though, is it?"

Was it? I had no answer for that, so I just shrugged. "I've become aware of the fact that I have no clue what's possible anymore. I guess there's no point dwelling on it right now, though. I'm just happy not to have nightmares every night anymore."

Snuggling back down, I drifted slowly back to sleep.

After we finished eating the next morning, we went for a walk around the area, waiting for the sun to reach its peak.

"I can't wait for everything to turn green and colorful

again," I sighed. "Once the flowers start growing, I want to take some to decorate the cabin with."

"That will be nice." We continued walking, reminiscing on how beautiful the place was when it was in full bloom.

Finally, when the sun was high in the air, we headed to the water to take our baths. Dipping my big toe in the water, I shivered. "I think I'm going to have my blanket waiting for me when I get out," I rushed back to the fort and grabbed both our blankets.

We washed our clothes first. They were grimy from all the heavy cleaning we did during the winter. After setting the clothes out on the old drying rack to dry in the sun, we finally dipped ourselves into the water. My body reacted to the cold, but it was not unbearable. Wanting to get the worst of it over with quickly, I dunked my entire body in and came up shivering.

"Move around more, it will help you stay warmer," Kith called. He was downstream and seemed to be immune to the cold. He took off swimming as I attempted to follow his directions.

After a few minutes, I started raking my fingers through my hair to get out all the dirt. I took a few more dunks before calling it a day and heading back to my blanket, shivering uncontrollably.

Kith was still in the water, having a blast. "Are you done already?" he called, disappointed.

"It's s-so c-c-cold in there!" I called back. My wet hair draped around me, keeping the cold close.

Kith laughed and continued to swim around for a few more minutes. By the time he got out, I had mostly warmed up but continued to sit still under my blanket, with the sun mercifully beating down on me.

"That wasn't too bad," Kith said as he grabbed his blanket. He was shivering now too, but didn't seem to be too bothered by it. Except, as he walked toward me, I realized he was limping more than usual. I decided not to ruin his excitement by commenting on it.

We ate our lunch and sat around the fire, covered in our blankets, waiting for our clothes to dry. It took a few hours, during which we washed the blankets, but eventually, we decided our clothes were dry enough to be worn. They were still damp, but the sun had at least warmed them up a lot.

Happy to finally be clean, we headed back to the cabin. Knowing that Kith's leg was bugging him, I walked slowly, pointing out all the interesting sites on the way. If he caught on to what I was doing, he didn't say anything.

When we went to bed that night, I was scared to fall asleep, certain I was going to have another nightmare. Knowing Kith needed his rest, I tried to act normal. He was asleep long before me. When I finally did fall asleep, it was peaceful, completely uninterrupted by dreams.

* Kith *

Spending some time at the stream was great. I felt refreshed and renewed. It had been a challenging winter, but knowing that we were reaching spring made me feel like I could breathe again.

With the weather warming up, the cabin started feeling even more stuffy. I wished we could open windows and let in a breeze. Sometimes we opened the door for a while, but we didn't like leaving it open for long.

We were building a town with blocks when I noticed a sound coming from outside. It was faint, but I paused and listened as a shrill whistle sailed through the air.

"Birds!" The word felt like magic, and Mara's excitement was the fulfillment of my spell.

"I have missed the music of the birds so much." her voice was almost a whisper as if she feared scaring Spring away for good.

"Me, too." It surprised me how hard it was when all the sounds of the birds were gone. "I wonder if this means my leg will feel alright enough to go hunting again soon."

"That would be great." Mara sighed, now uninterested in our town.

"Let's go for a walk. We can spend some time looking around at what wildlife is active now." It was a good reason for a walk, even if it felt like an excuse to get outdoors.

"A walk sounds fantastic." Mara reached for her blanket out of habit but grinned as she put it down.

Green was starting to cover the ground again, and a few early flowers were peaking through. I took a deep breath as we walked into the woods, letting the clean air and smells of spring fill me. Mara's arm wrapped around mine as we walked.

While we walked, I realized how unfamiliar we were with the area around the cabin. It was all covered in white the whole time we had been here, and the times we ventured out, we weren't focused on the sites. "I think we should circle around the cabin, and get to know the area nearby now that it's clear."

"Good idea." A slight humming came from her as we walked, and I couldn't help but smile.

"Look, Mara, tracks!" It wasn't until I saw them that I remembered that was the supposed reason for our walk, but I didn't tell her that.

"There's a lot of them!" She carefully followed different trails for a few minutes before returning to me so we could resume our walk.

As we walked on, I kept an eye out for more tracks. Several different birds chirped, mixing their songs. I saw some tracks that looked to be a bigger animal. Without moving, I followed them with my eyes. They faded away into a little mini clearing that I never noticed before. It wasn't far from the cabin, but I didn't go there at all.

"Look. There's something in that clearing."

We crept closer, not sure what we were approaching. There was a small fence around the clearing, but the gate was hanging open. In the middle were two white stones, about as tall as my hips. Mara ran her hand over the front of the smaller one, clearing away dirt and grime that covered words and a picture of a small person with wings.

"Are these… graves?" Her whisper contained a mixture of emotions.

"I believe they are."

"Is that why the cabin is empty? The people who used to live here died?"

"I don't think all of them did. Otherwise, they wouldn't be buried."

"Oh. Yeah, I didn't think about that." Her nose crinkled at the image that was brought.

I ran my hand over the top of the stones. They felt heavy. How did they get here? Had the person who put them here needed to bring them a long way? Did they make them themselves? I was so absorbed in the questions springing to my mind that I didn't notice Mara's tears until she sniffed.

"Mara?"

"Do you think Isaac has a grave?"

"I would imagine he does."

"And Beatrice?" I hated the question that hung there. The question I couldn't answer.

"That's possible." The words caught in my throat.

"Graves that we'll never be able to visit." Her hands were busy cleaning off the stones the best she could.

"No, I guess we won't." I wanted to touch her and comfort her somehow, but it felt futile. I couldn't make anything better. I couldn't even answer her questions about Beatrice.

"With it being spring we should be able to visit his grave."

"Well, we could visit these graves," I spoke hesitantly.

"True. They need to be tended to, anyway."

"Yes. But I think we've tended enough today. We should go home before it gets dark."

Our walk home was a lot more somber, and as soon as we were inside Mara curled up on the bed with Gracie grasped tightly in her arms.

*   Mara   *

After finishing a leg of Kith's pants, I held them out to

look. It wasn't great. The stitches were a little crooked and some segments became skinnier than others, but when I slipped my leg through them it seemed like they would work nicely.

Knowing I had to move on to the shirt if there was any hope of finishing in time for his birthday, I couldn't keep taking out every stitch I made. I could see that I was getting better though, and the stitches looked sturdy enough, at least.

Kith was out collecting more wood. A little pang of guilt plagued me for not helping, but I really wanted to get his clothes finished. Listening carefully for Kith to come back so I could pack it up before he got inside, I started on the second pant leg.

When Kith finally did come back inside he looked excited. "I think I found some berry bushes!"

Bounding up, I followed Kith outside. It was warm enough now that bundling wasn't necessary. It still got chilly, but bundling just made me hot instead. Following Kith into the trees, I looked around at all the green that replaced the white.

We walked for quite a while and I started to wonder why Kith was out so far. "You came all this way just for wood?" I asked, skeptically.

"Well, no," he admitted. "I kind of just started walking. It feels so nice out."

While looking around, I spotted a bush that looked familiar. "Kith, wait!" I knelt to examine the bush and found several tiny balls growing on it. I stood up to see Kith smiling at me.

"I told you! There's tons of them just over there." He pointed and I saw several more bushes just like the one in front of me.

For a moment I looked at the bush, thinking hard. "Do you think we could move some of the bushes closer to the cabin?"

He looked startled. "What do you mean, move them?"

"Well, Beatrice and Isaac both had plants they moved from somewhere else. Isaac's whole garden behind his house and Beatrice traveled with her potted plants. I think if we dug around underneath the bushes, we could replant them closer."

Kith's eyes were wide, "Mara, you're a genius!"

I walked around the forest some more, looking at the other bushes. Then, I saw a different plant I recognized. Creeping close to look at the plant, I bent down to examine the leaves.

"What are you..oh no," Kith groaned, and I burst out laughing.

"I guess you recognize it too, then?"

"Please don't tell me you're going to start making more tea," Kith grumbled as he stared at the feverfew.

I laughed again. "It will come in handy if anything happens to us. You know it helped, no matter how bad it tastes. I think we should try moving some of this closer too. We shouldn't take all of it though. Just in case moving it doesn't work."

We rushed back to the cabin to get the shovel and started with one of the berry bushes. Kith dug wide around the bush to make sure we didn't hit any of its roots. Once he got deep enough, I began scooping up the bush as he dug it out. Finally, I was standing with the entire bush in my arms.

Kith stood up and started laughing. "That bush is as big as you are! Do you want me to carry it?"

Making a show of sighing deeply, I thrust my chin up indignantly, "I can carry the bush just fine, thanks! Maybe you should start on the feverfew. And if you destroy it on purpose, I'll know!"

As I wobbled my way back to the cabin, I could hear Kith grumbling. The bush made it difficult for me to walk, especially since I couldn't really see around it. It was a good thing I had a great sense of direction. Once I got back to the cabin, I realized I didn't have a way to dig a new hole for it because Kith had the shovel.

I walked all the way back to find Kith struggling to carefully pile several feverfew plants in his arms without smushing or dropping any of them.

"Hold still with your arms out and I'll pile them on top so you don't keep dropping them when you bend over," I laughed. After piling all the plants he dug out into Kith's arms, I grabbed the shovel and led the way.

Once we got back, we took turns digging out holes for the

berry bush and the feverfew. We made a little plot just off to the side of the front door for the feverfew and put the berry bush on the other side of the door. "Maybe we could bring one more berry bush, and I think that would be good for now," I said standing back to admire the effect.

We went back and Kith worked at digging out the bush, while I held it again. Once we got it up, I carried it back to the cabin. Relying mostly on my sense of direction to walk, I didn't notice a large root that stuck out from a nearby tree, and I tripped on it, falling on top of the bush.

"Are you okay?" Kith knelt down to help me up.

"Oh no!" I cried, looking at the bush that still lay on the ground. "I smashed it!"

"Oh, it's fine," Kith replied soothingly, "I'm sure it will still grow berries. It's only a little smashed."

I wasn't so sure about that, but I didn't want to spend any more time digging another one out right then. After we finished, we were both worn out.

"Who knew moving plants around could be such hard work?" Kith mused after a long drink of water.

"It's going to be worth it though!" I sighed happily, thinking of how great it would be to have something to eat other than dried meat.

✳   Kith   ✳

While I finished putting the last berry bush in the ground, Mara went to use the bathroom. After patting the dirt all around the bush, I looked at it and noticed a few branches snapped when Mara fell onto it. Staring at the branches, I imagined putting them back together. It would be impossible to do, right?

Looking around to make sure Mara wasn't watching, I took a deep breath and put one hand over the snap in the branches and the other at the tip. I felt crazy. There was no way this was going to work, but after seeing Mara create that barrier, I just wanted to try one last time.

I focused on what I wanted to do. *Stitch the broken branches back together.* Focusing all my energy on the bush, I was shocked when I started to feel the warmth building. *I'm imagining it,* I told myself, while still focusing on the bush. The heat inside me rushed to my hands and suddenly it burst out. The bush started to glow for just a moment and I watched in amazement as the broken branches were mended. The light subsided and the bush was left looking as good as new.

"I thought you would be done by now," Mara's voice made me jump out of my skin and I hurriedly stepped away from the bush. "Is something wrong?" The worry on her face was evident.

"You just startled me is all," I tried to keep my voice even. "All done here, I'll go put the shovel away now." Grabbing the shovel, I noticed her eyes follow me, the concern still there.

Once I made it into the shed, I closed the door and slid down to sit at the foot of it. I was feeling weak after healing the bush. It was like it took all the energy out of me to heal it.

Alone in the shed, I began to process what I just did. All this time, I doubted when Mara told me I healed her, but she was right. Healing the bush felt the same, except that it didn't take as much out of me. The heat building, the burst of energy, and the glow. It was all there.

*But **why**. Why now? Why for a stupid bush? Such an inconsequential thing. Where were these so-called 'powers' when I was trying to heal Isaac?*

Before I knew it, the tears were streaming down my face. *Why couldn't I save Isaac? I must not have tried hard enough. Maybe I could have saved him if I just would have tried. I healed a bush! I healed Mara when she was on the brink of death! Did I just not care enough about Isaac? Why didn't I keep trying? I gave up so easily. I could have done it! I could have saved him if I just would have tried harder!*

All this time I just told myself Mara was wrong. I couldn't have saved her because I couldn't save Isaac. I couldn't heal myself when I was attacked by those dogs. It was impossible. She was wrong. But now I couldn't deny it anymore. I did heal her. But I couldn't do the same for Isaac. Because I gave up after one measly little try. *I really am useless.*

"Kith? Did you get lost while putting the shovel away?"

Clearing my throat, I tried to keep the emotion out of my voice. "No, I'm just checking the situation with firewood." Knowing she would see right through me if she saw my face, I tried to buy myself some more time. "It's mostly dry, but I think I need to stack it differently so it will dry better."

"Okay." The silence hung for a moment and I held my breath wondering if she would offer to help. "I'll just get started on dinner then."

It took a few moments before I heard her footsteps back toward the cabin, so I made sure to start moving around some wood so it sounded like I was telling the truth. As I did, the bow hidden in the corner of the shed caught my eye. I was holding onto it for Mara's birthday, but as I looked over it, I realized neither of us knew how to use a bow. What would be the point of giving it to her if I couldn't teach her how to use it?

Deciding I needed the distraction from my other thoughts, I let myself ponder on what to do about Mara's gift. There were only two old arrows in the shed. She'd need more. Sitting and studying the arrows, I tried to figure out how they were made. Every time my mind would wander back to that moment with Isaac, I forced it back to the arrows I held in my hands.

The tips were different. One was what seemed to be bone, and was smaller and slightly blunt, while the other was a very sharp stone. The straight part looked like some branches on a lot of the trees in the area, which shouldn't be too hard to find. I could heal the branches if I had to. No, I wasn't supposed to be thinking about that. Focusing back on the arrows. Feathers for the ends were a problem. I caught birds in the past, but not with feathers as large as these.

"Dinner's ready," Mara called tentatively from just outside the shed. I didn't even hear her coming and definitely didn't realize it had already been that long.

"Coming!" I quickly stashed the bow and arrows and

headed out of the shed.

Mara gave me a suspicious look but didn't say anything as we headed inside. I cleaned off quickly, then we sat down to eat. When we were finished, at Mara's suggestion, we started pulling out games. After everything that happened that day, I was ready for some resting time. Mara seemed to be in agreement, especially since she had insisted on doing a lot of the work with the bushes.

Isaac and the bow were still on my mind, though. Every time I thought of Isaac, I tried to redirect my thoughts to the bow. It seemed like a much safer thing to think about, especially with Mara nearby. I wouldn't be able to explain myself if I suddenly burst into tears again.

Thinking about the bow and the arrows, I didn't know how long it would take to get everything ready. I needed to start soon. Shortly before we escaped the show, a new act joined us. They did stunts with throwing knives and bows. At the time, I didn't see a reason to pay much attention to them, though. They were aloof and kept to themselves. Now, I wished I tried to pick at least something up from them.

I was deep in thought trying to remember how they held their bows when Mara's voice interrupted me. "Everything alright?"

"Of course. Why?"

"This is the third time you've knocked your stack over."

Looking at the blocks in front of me, I saw that they were spread out after having fallen down again. "Oops. I guess I wasn't paying much attention."

"Seems that way. What were you thinking about?"

Rolling onto my back, I sighed. "I was just thinking about how delicious the berries are going to be. I do believe I've almost forgotten what they tasted like." I put my hand to my forehead for dramatic effect.

She laughed. "I have missed berries so much. Or anything fresh, for that matter."

We were both glad for our stores, but dry meat took a long time to chew and could make your mouth tired after a while. It didn't taste as good as fresh meat, either.

The next day, Mara took off on her own so I decided to use my free time to practice with the bow. Grabbing it and the arrows, I headed away from the direction she went. After going what I thought would be far enough, I picked a small mound to aim at. I thought about aiming at a tree but didn't want to risk damaging the arrows.

Holding the bow was uncomfortable. I spent several minutes trying to figure out a decent grip. Eventually, I felt ready to pull the string back. It was a lot harder than I expected, but I did alright. As I released it, the string snapped forward and hit the base of my thumb. A thick red line appeared, followed by a searing pain.

"I'm going to assume that means I'm holding the bow wrong," I muttered to myself as I held my throbbing hand. When the pain subsided a bit, I tried again. This time I arranged my hand to be out of the way of the string. I put an arrow notch on the string, but the end kept wiggling around. It was impossible to aim.

After way too many attempts, I got it balanced on my hand. When I pulled the string back this time, I was able to aim at the small mound. Holding the string back for too long was tiring, so I released it. The arrow sailed right over the mound and landed several feet away. My fingers tingled slightly.

Even though I knew it would take a while to get it right, I was already feeling frustrated. I hoped Mara would be too distracted to ask about my hand. The color was fading, so maybe she wouldn't notice.

After what felt like hours of practicing, I was starting to get a little closer to the mound. My hands and arms ached from the bow, though, so I decided to call it a day and head back. I stashed the items in the hole in the shed and headed into the cabin to carefully wash up.

Working on the cabin over the next few days was hard. My mind was on the bow, and my hands hurt. Collecting wood was especially painful, so I was really slow with it and didn't get much. In my spare time, I was still practicing with the bow. My hands needed time to rest, but I wanted to get better with it. Eventually, my hands started to toughen up some, which made using the bow easier. They definitely weren't very pretty, though.

* Mara *

With the warmer weather, Kith and I started spending most of our time outside. A lot of it was spent together, working on the traps, visiting the stream, tending our plants, and playing; but we also started spending a good amount of time apart.

After being stuck in the cabin for so many months, we each needed some time by ourselves. It wasn't because we didn't want to be around each other at all, it was just nice to be alone, too. A lot of this time was spent working on Kith's clothes. I took the sewing box and a small basket with the material I was using out in the woods and hid them so that I could work outside without Kith seeing me carrying the supplies to and from the cabin.

One afternoon, I sat up in a tree, sewing one of the sleeves together for Kith's shirt. My mind started to wander and I found myself thinking about the graves we found. I wondered again what had happened to the people who lived in the cabin before us. Soon my thoughts drifted to all the people we lost, and I began to feel sorry for whoever was left behind to set those gravestones in place.

Although I knew the people in his town must have buried Isaac; and made a stone for him, I wished I could have done something more. He did so much for us in the short time that he knew us, I just wanted to repay him, however silly it may be. Losing all focus on my work, I found myself scanning the area. My eyes landed on a cluster of lovely purple flowers growing nearby.

Jumping down from the tree, I carefully put my sewing things away. Plucking a few of the purple flowers, I walked through the trees for a while, swooping to pick up as many different colored flowers as I could find.

While walking along, I relished all the colors of the forest. The trees were green again, and many of them had little blooms of their own growing. The white blanket of winter was gone, and the forest seemed even more beautiful than it was before. I wasn't sure how long I walked before deciding I gathered enough flowers. I was in no hurry.

When my hands were full, I stopped and thought for only

a second before my instincts told me where to go. I realized that I was subconsciously walking in the right direction the whole time.

It only took a little while longer before I came to the little graveyard. Arranging the flowers neatly, I began decorating the areas in front of both gravestones with them. Before I knew it, tears were pooling in my eyes as I imagined these graves were for Isaac and Beatrice. Something deep inside told me Kith was right when he said he believed Beatrice to be dead. For so long, I held on to hope, but somehow I knew now. Beatrice died to help us escape from Ducar.

"I'm sorry," I whispered to her while I let the tears roll freely down my face, "I'm so sorry."

"Mara?" Kith's voice sounded far away.

Wiping my eyes, I tried to compose myself before turning around. Kith was standing just outside the gate, watching me. He seemed unsure if he should come inside.

"I just..well I wanted to bring them flowers. I mean, I don't know how long it's been since they've gotten any. Who knows how long they've even been.." I couldn't finish the sentence with my thoughts still on Beatrice. To let Kith know I wanted his company, I held out my hand with a few flowers still clutched inside. The flowers were a little crushed, but Kith took them and gently placed one across the top of each gravestone. He then sprinkled the rest on the ground with the ones I had already laid.

"They both knew we loved them." Kith whispered, reverently. "And they both loved us. Very much." Kith's voice cracked as he spoke. I reached out my hand again and took one of his, squeezing hard.

"They would want us to be happy," I said, "but I think they would also like for us not to forget them. We should keep these graves clean. These people don't deserve to be forgotten either."

After staying at the graves for a while, Mara and I walked back to the cabin together. We had started the day with our need for separation, but now all I wanted was to spend some time together. There was hardly a word between us on the way back to the cabin. There hadn't been a whole lot of talking at the graves, either, though.

Once back, we tried playing some of our games, but neither of us was interested in keeping them going long. My mind kept replaying the image of Mara at the graves when I showed up. She looked so sad, it broke my heart.

"I feel the need to do something." Mara rose from the floor and looked around.

"Like what?"

"Work, I guess."

"Well, what work needs to be done?"

"I'm not sure. How are we on firewood? We need to get enough to last the winter, even while we're using it to cook."

"We've got a big enough pile at the moment, but we can always look for more if you want."

Mara looked around thoughtfully. I understood the need to be doing some work. It was a great distraction from all the thoughts that became overwhelming. "We haven't done anything with the barn yet."

"True." I had been putting off dealing with the barn. It was huge and a little bit scary. It seemed like it would be hard to get it lit. The cabin was easy since it was small. With the windows and door, we had enough light, and the fire brightened it a lot.

We gathered candles and cleaning supplies and made our way outside. I could tell Mara was also a little hesitant to go in the barn, but her determination was winning.

I tried hard to hide my apprehension as we approached the building together. It was way taller than the cabin, due to the other level. Two or three if not more cabins would fit inside it. The overhangs kept the windows dark, so not much light was coming in.

Mara lit a candle and held it out. The light didn't reach the walls, but it was nice to have some. Before getting started, we walked around to get familiar with the space. There were six animal stalls lining a hall-like area. They were obviously empty.

"One day we should fill those with animals." I pictured big horses like we had in the show, but I hadn't seen any horses in a long time. Plus, they ate a lot and wouldn't really be all that useful. They were beautiful creatures, though.

"That would be great. What would we put there, though?"

"Good question. Think we could get birds to stay so we could get their eggs?" I chuckled at the thought of birds in our barn, but the idea lingered in the back of my mind.

"Kith! Look!" Mara had walked away from me but came running back as she yelled. In her hands, she carefully held a lamp. It was only half full of oil, but that would last a while if we were careful.

"A lamp!"

"I think there might be a bit more oil in the boxes over there." Mara was grinning from ear to ear, and I couldn't help but grin back.

"Let's go look."

There were several boxes piled against the wall. It seemed like they were packed but left behind. Maybe the person who left ran out of room and decided they didn't need them. I pulled the top one down and put it on the floor.

Removing the lid, I pulled out the top item, a round metal box. It looked like it once held important things, but it was empty now. I guess whoever left it behind decided the items inside were worth keeping. Quickly looking through the bigger box, I found turtle, bear, and deer figurines. They were covered in dust, but with cleaning, I was sure they'd look great in the cabin. There were also a few paintings I thought would be good decorations. "This box should come back with us. They must have planned to use it all again to decorate and then decided they just didn't have the space for it all."

As I moved it to the side, Mara started pulling out the

figures and wiping them off as well as she could. "These are really cool. It's sad they got left behind."

I pulled down the next box and opened it before responding. "I know. It seems they didn't have much room to carry things. So much got left." The box in front of me had a spare blanket as well as what looked like a coat for a child. When I pulled out the coat and held it up to me, it was just a little bigger than what I would typically need, but considering our circumstances that made it almost perfect. There was another coat, this one had a more feminine cut and was longer. It was taller than Mara, but I held it up to her anyway.

"I bet you could cut off some of the bottom and it would be great! It's big, of course, but better too big than too small." Looking back at the smaller one, I reconsidered. "Or you can take this one. It's at least a little closer to your size."

Mara laughed, "I don't mind taking the bigger one. I like it!" She snatched it from me and held it up. "I'll just have a lot of extra fabric once I make it short enough for me to walk without tripping on it," she lowered the coat again and grinned.

After neatly placing the coats and extra blanket back in the box, we moved on. In the rest of the boxes, we found an assortment of things. There were a few more paintings, which we added to the box that was going inside with us. We also found some more fabrics. Mara was excited to see that some of them were of higher quality than what she had been working with. She pulled one out and eyed it with awe. Then, a look that looked almost like regret crossed her face.

"What's wrong?" I asked.

Mara jolted and looked sheepishly at me. "Oh...I was just thinking it would have been nice to have this fabric sooner."

"Well you got to learn on the other stuff and now that you're a pro you can use this!" I said, winning myself both a cheerful grin and an eye roll.

When I pulled the next box down, I saw that shoved behind the pile of boxes were a hoe and a rake. Thinking these might be useful for cleaning up the graves, I wasn't entirely sure what else to use them for until I pulled a small box from the bottom of the larger one I just set down.

There were divisions running down the box, making long separate boxes inside. Each one was filled with a different type of seed. There were pictures on the lid, but most of them had faded.

"Mara." I found myself whispering in excitement, like an explorer discovering a hidden treasure. "Seeds. It's full of seeds."

She instantly set aside the trinkets she was cleaning and moved to my side, her eyes wide with excitement. "We can grow our own food. More than just the berries." I could tell she wanted to be jumping around celebrating, but she joined me in whispering and moved slowly as if she was afraid they'd all blow away.

"I guess we know what our next task is going to be." It was hard to contain the excited energy coursing through me. I almost didn't even want to continue looking through the rest of the boxes, I was ready to start planning a garden right then. But when I opened one of the several boxes that were left half full, I was glad I continued. Inside these boxes was a variety of canned goods that we were both excited to see.

"Wouldn't this have been nice to have all winter while we were eating dried meat!" I exclaimed, exasperated.

"We'll have them for next winter now!" Mara grinned, "We might have enough for years..."

Confused, I looked at Mara to tell her how I didn't think these cans would be enough for more than a winter. Then I saw the look in her eyes and followed them across the room. On the side of the barn were several shelves housing lots more cans like the ones in these boxes.

Unable to contain our excitement, we walked over to the shelves to investigate the cans. We saw pickles, peaches, jams, honey, and other fruits and vegetables. Each new find brought on a whole wave of excitement and ideas of what we could do with it.

Once we had worn ourselves out with conversation, we began taking trips to the cabin to bring some of the canned goods in there now, as well as the box filled with trinkets and paintings.

It took several trips to get everything, and the cabin was suddenly quite cluttered. I didn't worry about it, though. It would just give us more to occupy ourselves with.

After deciding to get started with planting the following day, we allowed ourselves to release our excitement by running around the clearing and planning out where to plant. The garden beds were an obvious starting point, but we also wondered if something might start growing there on its own, and didn't want to disturb anything.

Grabbing some fallen branches, we marked off the areas we thought would be great for growing. Mara twirled as she ran around, copying some moves Grace did in her performances. For so long, Mara avoided any moves that reminded her of performing, but they flowed from her without thought as she floated around. Her feet barely brushed the ground.

I got so caught up watching her, that I forgot my own celebrations. Seeing how happy and free she was made my chest feel light and warm. For many minutes, I just stood and observed. Suddenly, Mara turned and looked at me.

"Kithian? What are you thinking?" Her voice took on the teasing tone it always did when she used the name from her dreams, but her eyes showed a mix of emotions.

Smiling, I replied, "I was just thinking about how much I love seeing you happy." I left off the 'free', not wanting to bring dampening memories to the moment.

A grin spread across her face and she returned to her dancing, brushing a quick kiss against my cheek as she whirled past. I knew she understood my deeper thoughts, the unspoken well of emotions that her dancing freely caused.

Tumbling into a heap of giggles several minutes later, Mara breathlessly murmured, "It felt so good to be dancing again. Because I wanted to." She didn't say any more, and I didn't add to it. We lay in the grass watching clouds in silence.

*   Mara   *

Over the next few weeks, we made a lot of progress with the traps. As I stood at the door of the cabin and looked around our clearing, I could barely see where they were. Anyone who didn't know to look for them would easily fall right into the holes we dug. I knew Kith had several other plans for them, but I was impressed by what we already accomplished.

Turning to see the berry bushes, I bent to check them. Excitement ran through me as I realized a few berries looked almost ready to eat. I was sure within the next day or two, we would have several berries ready for us. Which was good because aside from the cans we found, our food supply was almost at its end.

We only planned enough food up through the end of May, and that was quickly approaching. There was enough to last a little longer after the wild animal that almost attacked us, but it was still a rather small supply. I was eager for fresh meat and berries again. My mind wandered to the seeds we planted, and I wondered how long it would take them to grow. It would be great to have fresh vegetables again, too.

"Kith!" I called. He was inside, getting ready to go collect wood. "We've almost got some berries ready to eat!"

Kith poked out his head, "That's great!" He stepped over and looked at the berries. Then, he plucked the ripest one off the bush and plopped it in his mouth. His face contorted, making me giggle, "Okay, you're right they aren't quite ready yet," he laughed. "Not too bad though," he reasoned and grabbed another berry.

I whacked his hand away as he went for a third. "I want some of them to last long enough to get ripe!"

He walked away smiling, "I'm going to go collect wood."

Walking back into the cabin, I looked around, thinking about what to do. The cabin was a mess with all of the dirt we had been tracking in, so I grabbed the broom and started sweeping the best I could. Once I got all of the loose dirt swept outside, I wetted some rags and started scrubbing the floors. It was a lot easier to clean now that it wasn't so cold outside. I left the door open the whole time and wrung out my cloth outside before pouring more water on it and going back to scrubbing.

As I cleaned, Kith walked past the cabin a few times with his arms full of wood. It made me smile to think how we were doing such normal things as cleaning a cabin and piling wood in the shed.

While stopped for a water break, I heard Kith howl out in pain. Dashing out of the cabin, I ran toward the sound. He was standing outside the shed, holding his right pointer finger in his left hand and jumping up and down in pain. The sight might have been funny if I wasn't so worried.

"What happened?"

"The wood!" He gasped, "A piece of it is stuck in my finger!"

Walking over to him, I forced him to release his finger so I could take a look. It was all red, and a small piece of wood was barely sticking out enough to see. At first, I tried to use my fingernails to dig the piece of wood out, but there wasn't enough for me to get a grip on. Looking at Kith's hand, I wondered why it looked so beat up. Sure, he had been collecting a lot of wood, but I didn't think that was enough to cause all the calluses or blisters I saw.

"I know this isn't going to sound pleasant," I said, deciding now was not the time to question him, "but I might have to use my claw to dig it out," I finished apologetically.

Kith groaned, "You can't get it with your regular nails? Try squeezing around it, maybe you can push it out."

Looking at my nails, I had a thought. "Actually, it might be easier if I used my sewing needle. I think I could get a better handle on it!" Seeing the look on his face, I conceded, "I'll try squeezing it out first, though!"

Determined to try it the easy way, I held his finger gingerly and tried squeezing. When it didn't work, I squeezed harder until Kith yelped in pain and yanked his hand away from me. "Well, it was your idea! Either you let me try that again or I'm bringing out the needle!" Just then, I remembered that my sewing box was not in the cabin. It was hidden by the tree I liked to sew in.

Kith consented to let me try squeezing the strip of wood out of his finger again, but it wouldn't budge. His eyes watering in pain, Kith told me to go get the needle. I ran, not wanting to make him wait too long, but the box was a good way out in the woods.

By the time I got back, Kith was pacing back and forth around the shed and looking rather sour.

"What took you so long?" He yelled when he saw me.

"Well, the last time I was sewing, I wanted to do it outside and accidentally left my box out there. I needed to go and find it," I said, hoping he wouldn't get too curious about exactly what I had been sewing.

Kith grumbled a response while I opened the box and pulled out one of the sewing needles. "Okay, you're going to need to stay very still," I told him pointedly. "I don't want to stab you with the needle."

Glaring, he said, "You're about to stab me with the needle anyway."

Rolling my eyes, I held out my hand, "Do you want me to get it out or not?" Kith placed his finger in my hand and gritted his teeth. "I need you to pinch the skin around it so it will poke out a little more," I instructed.

While he pinched the skin, I stuck the needle barely into his skin just beside the piece of wood and pushed it upward. I could hear Kith grinding his teeth, but he didn't move. "Aha!" I yelled as the wood slid out.

Kith sighed in relief and stared at his finger. "Thanks, Mara!"

Once he was calm again, I decided it was a reasonable time to ask. "What have you been doing to get so many blisters on your hands? They look terrible."

"Oh gee, thanks!" he responded, mockingly.

"Oh, come on! You know what I mean. What did you do to your hands?"

"I don't know, Mara, I've carried a lot of wood today. Look in the shed, we've got a great pile going."

Peeking in the shed, I was impressed to see how much wood Kith collected so far. I could tell he was hiding something with the way he deflected me from talking about his hands. With my own secret sitting not too far away, however, I thought it might be good to let it go. The thought even occurred to me that our secrets may be for similar reasons. Was Kith making me something for my birthday again? I tried not to think about it too much at the risk of ruining my own surprise.

CHAPTER NINETEEN: JUNE

✳   Kith   ✳

"I think I'll go out and try to do some more hunting tomorrow." Our dinner soup looked especially thin as I let it run off my spoon back into my bowl. I'd only gone hunting a couple of times since the weather got warmer. We were trying to make the meat from each trip last as long as we could so we could focus on progress around the cabin.

"That's probably a good idea. I don't like being back to making soup to make the meat last longer. At least we have the food we found in the barn."

"True. It's so good, though, that I'm afraid of running out too fast. It's nice to have something other than dried meat and thin soups, however." My stomach rumbled as if in agreement, which made Mara laugh.

The next morning, I was up before the sun. Anxious anticipation kept me up all night, readying myself to be on the hunt again. Even though my last trip was only a few weeks ago, it felt like it had been ages. My dreams were full of feasts of fresh meat, alternating with empty tables and hunger.

Brushing Mara's hair out of her face, I whispered a quick goodbye before grabbing my spear and heading out. The morning was cool and still. Breathing in deep, I quietly headed into the woods. For a long time, I walked slowly, keeping an eye on everything around me.

After getting farther away from the cabin, I leaped into some low tree branches and continued on my way, stopping occasionally to look for tracks or other signs of an animal. Usually, when I hunted, I'd pick a spot and wait for a while if I didn't find tracks to follow. None of the spots I stopped at felt right, though, so I kept moving on.

Suddenly, I heard a familiar sound coming from up ahead. Without realizing it, I had been heading to our clearing at the stream, as if something was drawing me there. The beauty that originally drew me to the place returned with full force, and I found myself wishing the cabin was right in this clearing.

Shaking my head to fight the desire to lay in the grass and enjoy the area, I pulled the small basket from the bag and collected all the berries that looked ready to eat. There were bushes at the cabin now, but it didn't make sense to ignore the ones here. I popped a couple in my mouth as I headed to rinse my hands in the stream.

Our enclosure for catching fish was still mostly standing, and three decent-sized fish were doing lazy circles inside. It didn't take me long to get them all with my spear. It wasn't the meat I hoped to bring back, but I knew I'd be heading back with enough for a few days.

As I was getting ready to leave the stream, the plants Mara and I used to add to our soups caught my eye. I had forgotten about them, but there were many of them all over the clearing. Grabbing several bunches, I added them to the basket with the berries.

The stream was lower than usual due to a recent lack of rain, so I crossed over it and decided to continue on. Somehow I never got around to exploring this direction, and I hoped that I'd find something good to bring back home with me. The woods on the other side looked much the same. It shouldn't have surprised me, but it did a bit. It wasn't long, however, before I saw a difference.

In the distance, there was a large hill, with a straight wall facing me. It wasn't extremely high, but looked like it might be fun for a climb. After securing my pack, I climbed into a tree at the base of the cliff. The bottom portion seemed too flat to get good handholds, but from the tree, I could get started. Up above, I saw a ledge. I was a bit more than halfway up, but I'd been higher while climbing trees. Perching up there for a bit could help me decide where I should be hunting from.

As I got close, a large bird swooped down toward the ledge. Seeing me didn't make it happy, and a low whistling screech came out as it swirled overhead. Ignoring it, I kept climbing. It landed on the ledge and I heard a rustling. Pulling myself onto the flat area shortly after, I saw the reason for the distress.

A large nest was secured onto the ledge. Four eggs about half the length of my hand were being sat on by a bird that looked very similar to the one that just landed. The bird that was in the air released something from its talons and flew at my face. Reflexively, I batted it to the side, but it swooped and came at me again. This time, I released my claws and struck at its head. It landed in a heap next to the edge of the cliff. A whistled shriek similar to the first, only louder, came from the other bird. Rather than wait for it to attack me, I raced to it and swiftly broke its neck.

The birds were too big to carry in my bag. In fact, they were almost as big as me. Deciding I would have to pull them behind me, I tied them together with a length of rope before attaching it to my waist. Then I turned my attention to the nest. I couldn't remember the last time we ate eggs. Scooping them up carefully, I nestled them in the plants I picked earlier. Another shrieking filled my ears, but it wasn't the same as the one from the birds. It was accompanied by a scurrying sound.

Creeping carefully over to the other side of the nest, I saw what the bird dropped. It's intended dinner was a little baby bunny. With the blood that covered it, I couldn't really tell what color it was. One of the talons had punctured it somewhere.

Indecision struck me. I thought about putting the bunny out of its misery and adding it to my bag, but it was so small it wouldn't even provide much food. Images of how sad Mara would be to see the even smaller bones and sections of meat flashed through my mind.

For a moment, I thought about healing it. As I approached the bunny, the image of Isaac lying in his chair sprang into my mind. *I couldn't save him.*

My vision started to swim and my breathing got heavy. Looking around, I tried to find something else to focus on. The bunny's squeals pierced the air again and I shook my head trying to focus.

Looking down at the bunny, I took a deep breath to steady myself and made a decision. Pulling a scrap of old blanket from the pack, I used it to gently pick up the animal. Most of the blood seemed to be from a gash in its hind leg. With some care, it might make it. Carefully wrapping the bunny and tying it to my shirt, I started my descent.

Either the small rabbit knew I was trying to help, or it was in too much pain to struggle.

Unsure which it was, I was relieved not to be getting scratched to pieces. More hunting would have to wait. There was enough to last us a while, and I had a long distance to cover before the bunny could get cleaned up and treated.

With the birds tied behind me, my trip back to the cabin was much slower, but I went as quickly as I could manage. Crossing over the stream was a bit tricky with the extra weight throwing my balance off, but I managed. Whistling as I ran into the clearing, I stopped right outside the door out of breath. Mara must have heard my deep breaths because the door swept open.

"Kithian! You worried me." Her glare was shortened as she looked at me. "Whatever happened to you?"

"I got food." Laughing, I told Mara the whole story as I handed her the small animal. She took it gently and stroked its head as we entered the cabin. "I think you can save her, Mara."

Her eyes were full of shock and wariness as she looked up at me. "I'm not sure I know how to."

"You saved me." I knew I didn't have to say anything else.

A small smile played at her mouth. "I will try."

"A pet, Mara. How many times did we beg Beatrice for a pet?"

This time a full laugh escaped. "Way too many, probably."

Leaving her to get familiar with the bunny, I got started with cleaning up the meat I brought home.

*   Mara   *

Cradling the rabbit in my arms, I stroked her fur softly. "I think I'll call her Fluffy," I announced to Kith who was sweeping the floor after having tracked dirt everywhere. "What do you think she eats?" I realized I had no idea what to feed a rabbit.

"Fluffy is a great name," Kith smiled, "and I would guess she eats some sort of plant. Rabbits aren't really hunters, so I doubt she eats meat."

Kith dipped a cloth in the water that was heating over the fire and carried it over to me. I gently scrubbed the dirt and blood from Fluffy's fur. She wiggled a little, and let out a small squeak when I cleaned her injured leg. "Shhh," I said soothingly, "it's okay Fluffy, I just want to help you feel better. Are you hungry?" Looking up, I realized Kith was gone. The cloth he gave me was now dirtier than Fluffy, so it needed to be rinsed before I could use it anymore. I started to stand, still cradling Fluffy, just as Kith walked back in carrying a variety of green plants.

"What are you doing with those?"

"I thought we could try them out and see which one Fluffy eats," he said brightly. "You should stay sitting, though, she looks a little freaked out right now," Kith set down the plants and grabbed the dirty cloth from me.

Plucking a leaf from a vine that Kith carried in, I held it up to Fluffy's nose. She sniffed at it a few times and turned away. Kith chuckled, "Well not that one, I guess."

He brought the cloth back to me after having wrung it out, and I finished cleaning and bandaging Fluffy while Kith tried holding various plants up to her to see if she would eat them. Finally, he held up a clover, and after some hesitation, Fluffy scarfed it down.

"You found a winner!" I cheered, startling Fluffy enough that she attempted to hop out of my lap. Luckily, my hold on her was firm. With how bad her leg looked, I was sure she should be resting and not hopping about.

"Mara," Kith began quietly once I got Fluffy calmed back down, "Do you still want to have the service today?"

"Of course! I'm sorry, I got distracted with Fluffy. I think if I pile up some blankets for her to lay in she should be okay to rest while we go."

I made the bed up for Fluffy while Kith found her some

more clovers to eat. We made sure to set them close to her so she wouldn't have to move around to get them. Then I put a small plate of water down next to her. She didn't seem big enough to get her head into a bowl.

Before going to the grave sites, we stopped at a few places where we noticed an abundance of flowers. We each gathered several flowers of different types and set off together. The silence was mutual between us. We both took this task seriously, and I knew Kith was remembering the people we were about to honor, just like I was.

Once we made it to the grave stones, Kith and I each picked a site to place our flowers around. We cleaned the stones and the areas around them in preparation earlier in the week, and now we took care to decorate each of them. Placing each flower, one at a time, I remembered the petals Isaac gave us to decorate our cave.

Glancing over, I saw that Kith was tenderly placing his flowers to make the shape of a heart. "That's beautiful," my breath caught.

"Do you remember how much Beatrice loved hearts? Her jewelry box was covered in them."

"And she used to make our birthday cakes in the shape of hearts. I had forgotten about that."

Looking down at my own flowers, I began carefully rearranging them. I noticed Kith watching me.

"A flower for Isaac," Kith smiled, "a flower made of flowers. He would have liked that."

Once all our flowers were placed, we stood up and I beckoned for Kith to go first. "Beatrice and Isaac were the best people I knew. Beatrice helped us even when she got in trouble for it. She loved us when everyone else was afraid to come near us. She...died to save us."

My breath caught in my throat. After our huge fight, we hadn't talked about Kith's assumptions that Beatrice was dead. For so long he let me hold onto hope even though at the back of my mind, I knew there was none. We were finally coming to terms with what we both knew must be the truth.

Tears were pooling in Kith's eyes and I knew it was my turn to continue. "Isaac took us into his home and cared for us. We were strangers, but his kindness knew no end when it came to helping us. Who knows where we would be, or if we would have survived that winter without him. Isaac and Beatrice both saved our lives and we will never forget either of them. We will make the best of these lives they helped us have," I grabbed Kith's hand and squeezed.

"We will never forget their sacrifices, or their love." We whispered the words together.

Standing silently there for a long time, we thought of the two people who made such a huge difference in our lives.

✳   Kith   ✳

The heart and flower on the graves stood out against the sparse grass that grew in the little fenced area. The symbols for the two people we loved most. Standing still, I let the memories and emotions wash over me. Much of our time was spent avoiding feeling the anguish of our losses, but I opened myself to it all.

Mara's hand trembled in mine, and I knew she was having a similar experience. We didn't talk anymore, we just felt. Standing there, lost to time, we let the world around us melt away.

A howl pulled us out of our memories suddenly. It was then that we realized the sun was lowering in the sky. "We should get back to the cabin."

Mara nodded and we set off. The walk wasn't a long one, but it was almost dark by the time we made it back. Since we didn't know how long we'd be gone, Mara cooked our stew that morning while I was out hunting, so we were able to just warm it up and put it in our bowls. It wasn't exactly like the stews we had with Isaac, but it was close enough.

At first we ate in silence, letting our emotions rest. "Do you remember all the times Beatrice snuck us food?" I barely heard the words, they came out almost as a whisper.

"Yes. She always risked herself for us."

"Isaac did, too, right? Because who knows what the other people in the town would've done if they'd caught us there. Or if we'd been found."

She didn't need to say any more. "That's true. I didn't think about that as much. It was just nice to have food and feel safe for a bit."

"It didn't hurt that he made the most tasty food." Mara grinned past her tears.

I chuckled. "Can't argue with you there."

After we finished eating, we curled up on the bed with a couple of books, Fluffy tucked carefully into Mara's arms. It felt like Beatrice was there reading to us again as we took turns making up stories to go with the faded pictures. Gradually, Mara's head moved to my leg. I continued making up stories and stroked her hair the same way Beatrice always used to. It wasn't long before she was asleep.

Fluffy wiggled in her arms restlessly, so I gently removed her. I didn't want Mara to wake up. With Fluffy in my arms, I crept silently out the door. The moon lit the clearing enough that I could have seen even without the help of my increased night vision.

"Ouch!" The sudden pain in my arm surprised me. I had forgotten about the restless rabbit in my arms. "Sorry, Fluffy." I patted her head and released her to relax in the grass. As I watched her sniff around one of the bushes we moved into the clearing, I thought back to the night Isaac asked me to help him with a similar task. He could have easily done it himself, but he knew how much I needed to help him somehow. Now, with what I learned enabling us to bring more food into the clearing, I was extra glad he showed me how to do the work.

"Thank you, Isaac. Surviving is a lot easier because of you. I'm sorry I couldn't save you." My voice broke as I spoke out into the sky, wishing for a reply that I knew would never come.

During the weeks following our ceremony, I spent most of my time finishing Kith's clothes for his birthday. Every time I looked at the calendar, I couldn't help but panic a little. Whenever I held up my work to look at it, I would get very frustrated with myself and begin taking out stitches and redoing them. Finally, I realized I needed to accept less than perfect work if I ever hoped to finish.

Several times, I held up the shirt and started to take out stitches before reminding myself it was good enough and I needed to force myself to continue. The pants were definitely more simple. It was difficult to get the sleeves to hang properly, so the shirt took more time.

Finally, two days before Kith's birthday, I tried the shirt on myself and inspected the sleeves. It still looked a little funny, but I was confident it would at least fit Kith. The clothes certainly weren't pretty, but they were better than the rags he had been wearing that were getting much too small for him.

After examining the outfit for a long time, obsessing over some of my mistakes in the stitching, I finally forced myself to set it down. When I got back to the cabin, Kith wasn't there. This was no surprise with how little time we spent together the last few days. I realized I had become so obsessed with finishing Kith's clothes that I was gone all the time.

Fluffy was in the cabin, hopping around happily. Her leg was looking much better now, but I wanted her to be fully recovered before she took a long trip outside. She looked healthier, though, and I thought it wouldn't be long before I could bring her out with me.

Stepping carefully, I looked at the floor as I went. One problem with keeping her inside was the mess. Each time I came home, Fluffy left more little poops around the cabin floor. Grabbing the cloth that we designated to the task of cleaning up after her, I went around picking up the pellets.

Gathering some of the clovers and other plants we found

that Fluffy would eat, I sat with her while she ate out of my hands. Each time we left, on our way back to the cabin, we would pick up more food for Fluffy, to make sure she never ran out. Once she was done eating, I refilled her water from the bucket outside. One of the plates from the kitchen served as her water dish.

Now that I was finished with Kith's present, I was antsy for his birthday to get here. I spent the next day cleaning the cabin just to keep myself occupied.

"Didn't you just scrub there? I don't think it's getting any cleaner than it already is," Kith sounded quite amused.

"Oh." Sitting back on my heels, I examined the floor of the cabin. "I guess I'm pretty much done. I just wanted to make sure it was clean since Fluffy has been pooping everywhere." This was partly true. I didn't think there was a single bit of the floor Fluffy hadn't pooped on at least once.

Kith laughed, "Who knew bringing her home was going to be such a mess?" He looked back down at the stick he was carving. "I'd say that's pretty sharp," he said, gently pressing his finger on the tip. He was making more spears to put around the cabin for our defenses. "Can we go to the old stream spot tomorrow? I would love to go swimming."

Looking sideways at Kith, I scrutinized his face. Something told me he knew tomorrow was his birthday, and he was testing if I remembered. "Sure, that would be fun. I know how much you like swimming. Should we make a whole day of it again? Fluffy might be well enough to tag along. I'd worry about leaving her alone overnight. Who knows what kind of mess we would come home to!"

Kith grinned. "That sounds great!"

The next morning, I was happy to find I woke up before Kith. Quietly slipping out of the cabin, I headed to the tree where the gifts were hidden. When I got back, Kith was up and starting on some breakfast. "Is your stomach upset?"

"What?" I asked, confused.

"Well, you slipped out so quickly and you were gone for a while so I thought maybe you were in the bathroom?" Kith continued staring at me, but I could see the smile forming. "I guess not?"

By now, I was sure he knew I was up to something. Putting my hands on my hips, I glared at him, "Why would I discuss my visits to the bathroom with you?"

Kith burst out laughing. "So you aren't going to tell me then?"

"Oh, fine!" I stepped back outside and grabbed the clothes. Holding them behind my back, I walked back inside. Kith grinned wider. Of course, he must have guessed there was a reason I was gone so much in the days leading to his birthday.

"Happy Birthday!" I said, proudly handing him the shirt and pants. To my surprise, his mouth dropped open in a look of complete shock.

"Mara..what?"

"Oh come on, you clearly knew I was making something."

Kith continued to stare at the clothes, not saying a word.

"Is something wrong? If you don't want to wear them it's okay. I know I'm not very good at it yet, but I can try again. I've definitely gotten be..." Before I could finish, Kith grabbed the clothes from my hand and pulled me into a huge hug.

"You're right, I knew you were planning something, but I never guessed you were making me new clothes. Mara, this is amazing! I didn't realize you were so good." He was back to staring at his gifts. "They're perfect!"

"Well, yours are so small on you now and they're all dirty and torn up." I could feel how blue my face became at his praise, "I just thought they would be useful."

Kith hugged me again and then hurried into his new clothes.

"Oh no! They don't fit you right at all! The sleeves are all wrong, and the pants are too long! I was just trying to make it longer than me, but I must have misjudged it."

"Mara, stop! They're wonderful! It's good the pants are long, I can roll them up now and then they'll still fit when I get taller! I will need some string to hold them up though so they don't fall down when I run."

My feelings of utter failure must have been clear on my

face because Kith hurried on, "It's good they're loose too. Now when I get fat, they'll still fit." He was grinning ear to ear, and even though I was a little disappointed with parts of my work, it was hard not to feel proud too.

"Maybe I could cut a long strip from one of the animal hides for you to tie around your waist? Might work better than string."

"That's a great idea!"

Kith finished breakfast while I found a long piece of hide to cut. I wrapped it around his waist to make sure it would be long enough and then cut off a long thin strip.

"Perfect!" Kith announced, tying it around his waist. "Now you just need to make yourself some new clothes too." Kith grinned.

"But, first, let's go swimming!" We packed up and headed to the stream, with Fluffy cradled gently in my arms.

*   Kith   *

Whistling my return, I ran into the clearing. It was taking all my strength not to scratch all my skin off.

"Kithian! What did you do?"

Stinging pain and intense itchiness clouded my mind too much to react to the name or the scolding. "I was going after these eggs." Somehow they survived my frantic run, and I released them into her hands. "They were under these clumps of plants with pointy leaves. There was a bunch, and I got stuck in them."

Swatting my hands as I tried to scratch, Mara sighed. "At least your clothes are just dirty, not torn."

"That's good. I was too frantic to check." Relief flooded through me. The new clothes didn't fit perfectly, but they were more comfortable than my old ones and left plenty of room for me to grow.

"Take those off and I'll get them clean. You should try scrubbing down with some water and see if that helps." After grabbing my discarded clothes she walked off, the shake of her head so slight I almost didn't notice it.

White bumps covered my arms and legs where I touched the plants. Wondering if the eggs were worth the trouble, I poured cool water over my bumpy skin. After a few times of running water over the red area, the stinging and itching started to subside. It was still bugging me, but at least I wasn't feeling a need to remove my skin anymore.

My clothes were hanging by the time I was done rinsing. "Feeling better?" Mara was coming out of the cabin with a bowl in her hands.

"Yes. Some, anyway." I reached to scratch but stopped myself.

"That's good." She grabbed a cloth from the bowl and grabbed my hand.

"What is that? Wait. I recognize that smell." I couldn't stop the groan that came out.

Laughing, Mara started gently rubbing the cloth over the angry skin. "Don't worry. I won't make you drink it." After I sighed, she added, "Unless it doesn't help this way."

"It's helping." The words tumbled out quickly, causing Mara to laugh harder. "Alright, I rushed a bit because I don't want to drink it, but it really is helping."

"I'm glad." For a brief moment, she looked almost serious.

"At least we have eggs for dinner."

"True." Returning the cloth to the bowl, she looked up at me. "I don't think you need to go digging through those plants anymore."

"I wasn't planning on it."

"Not even for eggs?" She held back another laugh.

"It's not funny, Mara."

"You didn't see your face when you came running into the clearing." She snickered.

"I saw yours, though." This time I laughed as Mara slapped at my arm.

"Those eggs you worked so hard to get won't wait forever. Let's get cooking." Her eyes twinkled at me.

Still laughing, we headed into the cabin.

*　　Mara　　*

"What in the world have you been doing to your hands!?"

Kith looked down at his hands in confusion. "Oh. Um. I guess it's from putting the spears in the ground or something. The shovel kind of hurts my hands sometimes. Hey, I had an idea today." He announced, changing the subject away from his blistered hands.

"Nice change of subject," I scowled, "what was your idea?"

"Well, it's not exactly a change of subject. I was wondering if you would mind making us some gloves..for winter...to keep our hands warm. But now that you've mentioned my hands, they could be helpful for using the shovel too!"

"Oh! That's a great idea!" I started thinking about the supplies I had on hand, "I would want to use the hides. Which means I need some more," I was now rifling through the box I was keeping all the leftover scraps of fabric and leather in. "We have a few good pieces and some scraps. I think it would make it a lot easier if I could use one long piece for each glove, though. So I will start working with what I have, and you can go hunting and try to get me some more good leather!" I beamed up at him.

"How close are you with your clothes? I mean, you need those too. You can finish those before you start on the gloves."

I thought about that for a minute. "I think gloves are more important to finish sooner. Especially if you need them for digging. Your hands really look awful. And I want to make sure I have them done by winter."

Kith grinned, "Thanks, Mara!"

After lunch, I grabbed the supplies I would need and went to my normal sewing spot, with Fluffy trailing along behind me. Her leg was mostly healed now and she started following me around everywhere. I didn't mind this at all. Getting her out of the

469

cabin meant less of a mess to clean up, and I loved having the company. Wanting to be down close to Fluffy, I started sitting on the ground at the base of a tree for sewing. Taking her up into the tree with me seemed like a terrible idea.

Once I got situated, Fluffy snuggled up beside me on the ground. Taking out my long strip of leather, I stared at it blankly, not altogether sure how to get started. When Kith asked me to make gloves, I was completely confident, but now that it came time to do it, I wasn't really sure how. I needed to make the leather go around each finger separately so that we could still use our hands like normal.

Setting my hand on the leather, I spread out my fingers. If I cut out around my hand, leaving space around the outside, I should be able to sew the two pieces of leather together and still fit my fingers inside. I would have to use Kith's hand for the outline of his gloves to make sure they were the right size, which meant for today, I would have to start on my own gloves first.

Using the pins that were in the sewing box, I marked the outline of my hand, making sure to leave plenty of space around it. Then, I cut around the outside of the pins. The leather was much more difficult to cut than the fabric I used for our clothes. Once I finally finished cutting out the first outline, I used it to make another one exactly like it.

Finally, I pinned the two sides together and got started with the sewing. The leather was much thicker than my typical fabric, and it was difficult to get the needle through both pieces. While using the small cup on my finger to try to force the needle through, it bent almost in half and jabbed into my hand. I let out a yell that sent Fluffy flying in terror and grabbed the hand the needle pricked. It was bleeding, but not too much.

Once the pain subsided, I inspected the needle and grabbed the others from the sewing box to compare. The one I was using was the second smallest of the bunch. There were four more needles, each getting thicker than the last.

Grabbing the thickest needle, I practiced pushing it through the two pieces of leather. Thankfully, it worked much better, and the needle seemed sturdy enough to survive the task. By now, there was blood trickling down my hand. Sighing, I got up and headed back to the cabin. I didn't want to get blood all over the gloves, and I hadn't brought any extra scraps of cloth with me that could be used to wrap up my hand. As I went, I searched for Fluffy and found her nibbling on a patch of greens.

Approaching slowly, so I wouldn't startle her, I gently patted Fluffy on the head. She ignored me and continued chewing happily. Deciding she was probably fine where she was, I went on to the cabin to clean up my hand.

Kith was gone, which was a relief. If he saw the blood he would freak out and feel bad for asking me to make the gloves. Scooping up some water from the bucket, I rinsed the blood off my hand. Then, I grabbed a long scrap of cloth and tied it tightly around the cut. It wasn't bleeding heavily so I was sure the tie wouldn't be needed for long. Maybe I could even get away without Kith realizing I cut myself at all.

After I finished, I headed back to my sewing area, checking that Fluffy was still nearby before settling down to try another round of sewing the gloves. It still wasn't an easy task, but the new needle worked much better. I could tell this was going to be a much longer process than I originally thought.

✻   Kith   ✻

Mara was outside playing with Fluffy when I returned from hunting. At the stump at the edge of the clearing, where I normally skinned my catches and treated the hides, I started laying out my tools to prepare. As I pulled out the first of the three rabbits I brought back, a screech rang out, freezing me where I stood. After a couple of seconds, I turned to see Mara glowering at me.

"Kithian! Not in front of Fluffy!" Mara scooped up the rabbit and stomped into the cabin. She was still glaring at me when she came back out.

"What?" I was thoroughly confused.

"Fluffy is a rabbit." Mara's voice dripped venom as her face clearly told me I was being dumb.

"I'm aware of that. So?"

"So, we EAT rabbits!" She was completely annoyed with me.

"And?"

With a sigh, Mara explained, "I don't want Fluffy to know we eat animals like her. She'll be afraid of us."

"I'm sorry, Mara. I wasn't even thinking about that. I won't let Fluffy see the meat before it is prepared anymore."

My apology seemed to appease her and she came to look at my spoils and help prepare the hides.

"These are so soft." Her hands were running over the fur still attached to the hides. "Almost as soft as... " Her voice trailed off and her hand faltered.

"Mara?"

"I love Fluffy. Is it terrible to still eat other rabbits?" Her eyes remained on the hides she was working on.

"No. We need to eat to survive. And you take really good care of Fluffy."

"True."

"Fluffy was going to be eaten by a bird if I hadn't happened to hunt that bird. I'd say she's a pretty lucky little fuzzball."

Even without her looking at me, I could tell she was smiling. "You're right. And we keep her well fed. I supposed we deserve to eat well, too."

"Of course we do. Fluffy needs us healthy so we can continue to keep her safe."

This time she actually laughed. "That's just odd. Eating rabbits to stay alive to keep another rabbit safe."

Holding back my own laughter, I shrugged. "I guess that's life."

I was glad she reached a state of peace with our odd situation, but from then on I waited until Fluffy was in the cabin before opening my sack. Usually, Mara would grab her up when she heard my whistle and come back out without her by the time I stopped at the stump. The times I came back to see her rushing inside always caused a smile, as I remembered Mara scolding me so forcefully.

CHAPTER TWENTY: JULY

The sun beat down on me as I sat with my back to a tree in our clearing, sewing. Fluffy was playing in some bushes nearby, and Gracie was sitting beside me. A few days earlier, I got the idea to sew a new dress for her. The one she was in when Isaac gave her to me had gotten pretty dirty, and I didn't think it would take long to make her a new one since she was so small.

It was also easier to make clothes for Gracie because I could put them on her and sew some of the more difficult parts while she was already wearing the dress. It made it easier to make sure it fit properly. Lace lined the bottom of the old dress, and I always thought it was pretty. There wasn't any lace in the trunk of fabric, but there was a small amount of blue ribbon. I decided to line the bottom of my homemade dress with that instead.

"That looks great, Mara! I'm sure Gracie will love it!" Kith stood right outside the door of the cabin, holding the pair of gloves I made for him.

"Oh, are you going to be working?" I asked, thinking I should probably help.

Kith moved like he was attempting to hide the gloves, then stopped and said, "No, I just thought I would try the gloves out."

Suspicion crept up, as I asked, "Well, where are you going then?"

"Nowhere really, just exploring. I may get some wood while I'm out. I think the gloves will be helpful to make sure I don't get any more little pieces stuck in my hands."

Thinking this wasn't the entire truth, I said, "That is a good idea! Mind if I join you?"

"Oh, that's okay, Mara, you're so close to finishing the dress."

"Okay, then. Have fun." I smirked, knowing Kith was definitely hiding something.

I went back to my sewing, and soon the ribbon was nicely placed at the bottom of the dress, with another loop around the waist. Slipping the dress onto Gracie, I admired how nice she looked. For a brief moment, I imagined making a dress for myself. Maybe I could even make one to match Gracie's. But I decided this would be a silly waste of both time and fabric. I hadn't worn a dress since we left the freak show. They just weren't practical to wear on the run.

When Beatrice was preparing us to leave, she gave me an old pair of Kith's clothes and told me I would have to dress like a boy for a while. This didn't bother me since I preferred pants anyway. Ducar always made me dress pretty for the show, and I hated it. The dresses I wore between shows were in rags, probably clothes that were handed down for years. They were usually too big and looked terrible on me. Then, whenever there was a show, Ducar would take out the same horrible dress for me to wear. It was heavy with way too much fabric and made me itch all over. It was difficult to perform in, but Ducar expected my best all the same.

Once the dress started getting too small for me to wear, Ducar got angry. He said a dress like that was too expensive for me to get another one. One night, after Beatrice couldn't even get the dress to zip up anymore, Ducar beat me, claiming I did it on purpose, and then put me in an old outfit Grace used to wear. It was huge on me, but with all the flips and everything Grace always did, she couldn't wear a dress while doing it. Instead, she wore a pair of tight pants with a ruffled top that buttoned between her legs. Even though the outfit was so big on me, I loved wearing it. My movements were easier, and I didn't feel so ridiculous performing our act. After that, I hated putting my old dresses back on even more.

Suddenly, I realized I had been sitting there staring at the dress I made for Gracie for a long time, lost in thought. Pulling myself together, I picked up Gracie and carried her over to one of the tree stumps in the clearing to play. Once again, I wondered where Grace was now. She was the only other person who really cared for us. The only one left. As I played, I tried to put her out of

my mind, but it was difficult not to imagine what life could be like
if we found her again.

❋   Kith   ❋

Rippling as my fingers ran over it, the feather seemed
ready for flight. Once used to soar through the skies as part of a
bird, it would soon be flying through the air on the end of an
arrow. Hopefully.

Sighing, I looked down at the growing pile of failed
arrows. Foolishly, I once expected this process to be simple.
Instead, frustration and panic were mounting as Mara's birthday
drew closer. Turning away from the arrows, I picked up the bow
and looked at it. The string was old and about to break. It would
need to be replaced, but I wasn't sure what to do about that, yet.
Cleaning the wood of the bow itself had been a pain, but it was
nice and clean now. Clean, but plain.

My mind started to wander as I rotated the bow in my
hands. As it moved, a pattern started to appear as clearly as if it was
actually carved into the wood. Flowers and vines wrapping around
the wood in a flowing swirl. Carefully, I got to work bringing the
image to life. I was afraid of damaging the wood, but it was sturdy
and the etching didn't harm it.

Suddenly, I realized that it was nearly dark. While I was so
focused on bringing the image in my mind to life, I hadn't noticed
the passage of time. I had been sitting in my nook under the tree
for hours. Rising stiffly, I stashed my work before heading home.

"I was about to go looking for you." Mara looked relaxed,
but her tone held a sharp scolding edge.

"I'm sorry. I lost track of time."

A small sigh escaped. "It's alright. My mind just went back
to…" Her voice trailed off as her eyes drifted down to my leg.
Guilt coursed through me.

"I'll be more careful with the time."

"Are you hungry?" Her stomach rumbled, and I realized

she was waiting for me to join her for dinner.

"Famished."

We were finishing off a deer I brought home a couple of days before. Mara had cooked a large chunk of the meat and pulled out one of the cans of vegetables from the barn for us to split.

We dug into the meal with gusto, eating in silence, both of us lost in our thoughts. Images of the unfinished bow kept floating in my mind. I had hoped to finish the carving all at once, but I was only about halfway through. And I didn't have any clue what to do about the string. It would probably last for a while still, but I wanted to put a new one on before giving it to Mara.

My distraction for the rest of the evening caught Mara's notice, but she didn't say much about it. Just kept looking at me from time to time and waiting for me to realize she was talking to me.

Early the next morning, I started for the woods.

"Going out again?" Mara was perched on a stump playing with Gracie, holding her carefully to keep her new dress clean.

"Yes. I..." Pausing, I scrambled to think of an excuse to tell Mara that would keep her from knowing what I was up to. "I was thinking I might try to gather some more underbark and make some more rope. Never know when it might come in handy."

Her head tilted slightly to the side as if in question, but then she shrugged. "I guess more rope might come in handy. Maybe we could do something fun with it. You might as well bring some meat with you, though, in case you don't make it back before dinner time."

"Good idea. I'll be home before it gets dark, though."

With a smile and a nod, Mara turned back to Gracie.

Not wanting Mara to stumble upon me while I was working, I kept my nook a fair distance from the cabin. Impatience to get working overcame me, so I took off running at full speed. Running had all new meanings now, but sometimes it brought back unwanted memories. There was a time when our speed meant the difference between freedom and captivity, life and death. As much as I wanted to forget these things, I knew keeping all those memories just under the surface was important.

Once I settled into my spot, I shook all the thoughts of dangerous times out of my head and focused on the bow, willing the image from before to come back. Nothing came. Sighing, I decided to try to carve it by memory, the knives I got from Isaac ready at my side. There was a vine that I didn't finish, so I started there.

The knife slid easily through the vine, widening it to match the rest. I knew it needed to branch out to connect to the flowers that would be coming, but my hand froze. Where should the branches go?

Fear of messing up the design kept me frozen, and I felt a small sense of panic rise through me. Putting down the knife and bow, I took a deep breath. My wandering thoughts during my run caused an unease that I needed to shake before I could continue.

Jumping up, I climbed into the tree. Might as well start with the rope. Mara would be suspicious if I returned without any. By the time I made a long length of rope, my mind was clear but my hands were sticky. Getting rid of the stickiness was difficult, but soon I was settled with the bow in my, only slightly sticky, hands.

This time it didn't take long for the image to appear again. Without hesitation I got to work, removing small slivers of wood at a time. I thought the knives would be awkward to use, but they enabled me to remove smaller areas and get a more clean image. Carving with my claws always left the item rough-looking, but the bow was looking great. It was too bad I didn't have anything to smooth it out with.

Even with working slowly, and my delay in making the rope, I finished the bow just after lunchtime. There was plenty of time to make it back before it got dark. My eyes landed on the pile of arrow attempts, and I sighed. Hopefully, I will have plenty of time to make it back. Picking up one of the arrows from the shed, I examined it yet again. Willing the frustration and annoyance out of my mind and letting it go blank, I focused on all the small details.

As it moved around, I could feel the connections forming in my mind. If I tried to focus on them, they'd float away. Keeping my mind as blank as I could, I switched that arrow out for one I was currently working on. The differences seemed to almost light up, allowing me to tweak them until they matched as closely as I could manage. My focus remained steady as I worked through three more arrows, then started to fade. Six arrows still wasn't a lot, but it was better than only two.

With the remaining light, I gathered my work and hid it again. Running back as fast as I could, I was determined to keep my promise to be back before it got dark. As I raced into the clearing holding the rope, Mara looked up from where she was playing with Fluffy, a smile on her face.

"Told you I'd be back before dark." I was almost out of breath from pushing myself harder than I had in a long time.

"You sure did." Mara giggled at my heavy breathing. "Dinner is ready, I left it to warm."

*   Mara   *

"Do you think it might be time to harvest some of the things in the garden?" Kith was peering out the window while sipping on his morning water. Now that the weather was warmer, we skipped heating it but still enjoyed the routine of the morning drink.

"That's possible. The squashes that I saw yesterday, the ones that weren't eaten up, anyway, looked close. We should check on at least the potatoes and carrots. If we can get enough, I'll make stew tonight."

Kith smiled widely. "That sounds wonderful." After a small pause, he added, "We may want to put some sort of fence around the gardens. Maybe it would stop some of the animals from eating our crops."

"True. Oh." My eyes widened in excitement. "What if we put traps around them? We know animals are coming, so we could use that to our advantage!"

"That's a great idea!"

Grinning, I rinsed out my cup and headed out the door with him. The anticipation grew as we walked to the garden, both of us hoping for good news. Kith walked over to the first potato plant and looked at me questioningly. "Should I just pull it all the way out and see what we've got?"

"I don't know any other way to tell if it's ready," I gestured for him to go ahead.

As he pulled, I realized that it was more than just one potato coming up attached to the stalk. A group of five good-sized potatoes dangled from his hand once he got it up.

After helping him pull out several clumps of potatoes, with varying sizes, we switched to the carrots, assuming that if the potatoes and squash were ready, then the carrots must be too.

The first carrot we yanked up was small, but not tiny. Unfortunately, the next ones were quite a bit smaller. After pulling another sad carrot out of the ground, I looked up at Kith. "Do you think we should try the carrots again in a week? They're so small!"

He looked sadly at the small, withered carrot I held in my hand. "Yeah, that may be a good idea. Hopefully it helps. The potatoes are doing so well, I just thought it must be time!"

"Maybe carrots take longer to grow," I shrugged and tossed the carrot into our pile of food to bring back to the cabin.

"Either way, I'm excited for our stew tonight! I bet the carrots will still taste great in it." I could hear the longing in Kith's voice. It had been a long time since there were fresh vegetables for a stew.

Once we finished in the garden for the day, we headed back to the cabin to wash our crops and begin the stew.

"Hey, maybe we should get some more berries too. They could be our dessert!" Kith said as we walked past the berry bushes in front of the cabin. Those bushes were plucked on a regular basis so we knew there wouldn't be much that was ready on them. We both were in the habit of plucking berries as we walked by, usually sticking a few of them in our mouths.

"Why don't you go check the other bushes while I get started on the stew?"

Setting down his spoils from the garden, Kith headed off into the trees. There were several places outside our clearing that were full of berry bushes. He was sure to find a few with good berries on them.

Once inside, I began washing the vegetables. As I worked on the familiar recipe, I couldn't help but smile and hum a little. Cooking like this always reminded me of Isaac. I chopped up the vegetables and the stew was bubbling nicely by the time Kith arrived.

"Sorry I was gone for so long," he said sheepishly. "I..got distracted," he finished, not meeting my eyes. I fought to hold in my laughter. It was amusing how bad Kith was at hiding things.

"That's okay, dinner should be ready any minute."

Kith breathed a sigh of relief, and I couldn't suppress my giggles any longer. He must have thought I would question him.

"What?" He asked, suspiciously.

Pausing only for a second to look at him, I said, "You're all covered in dirt!" Then I looked down at myself, "We both are! We should wash up before we eat."

Once we were both cleaned up, we dug into the stew, too hungry and excited to wait for it to cool.

✳   Kith   ✳

Hard work wasn't anything new to either of us, but all the harvesting and working on the clearing was a whole new level of difficulty. "Think the garden will be alright if we don't do anything with it today?"

Mara rose partway from where she was lying on the floor playing with Gracie. "I think one day would be fine. What were you thinking?"

"I need a stream day." I stretched, my sore muscles fighting the movement.

"We could each use a bath, anyway." Her nose crinkled as she giggled.

The anticipation of a stream day gave me an energy boost and I hopped up. While I gathered our stream supplies, Mara secured Fluffy with enough of her food to last the day. As we were headed out the door, the coil of rope I made caught my eye.

"What are you doing with the rope?"

"I'm not sure. We might be able to figure out a use for it." Shrugging, I shoved it in my bag and closed the door behind me.

Usually, we ran all the way to the stream, but today we switched between running and walking. Sounds of rushing water and birds singing filled the air before we saw the sparkling stream. Scents of flowers and berries and water swirled around us as we put our supplies down. We'd visited the stream many times, but it still felt magical every time.

"I'm going swimming." I was already halfway to the stream.

"I figured you would." Mara chuckled. "I'll join you in a few minutes."

Gracie was out of her carrying case, and Mara was wandering the clearing smelling all the flowers with her. Cool water enveloped me as I dunked my head under and pushed myself out to the middle of the stream. My body relaxed with the weightlessness that came with being in the water. Floating up, I lay on my back and looked up at the sky. The trees that lined the stream were at the edge of my vision.

Suddenly, I realized what the rope would be perfect for. Rushing out of the stream, water splashing in my hurry, I grabbed the rope out of my sack.

"Kithian! You startled me." Mara's eyes were still wide, but her anger seemed exaggerated.

"Sorry! I was struck with inspiration." Grinning, I headed toward one of the bigger trees on a higher part of the embankment and started climbing. When I got to the branch that hung out in just the right position, I tied the rope tightly around it, making sure it was secure.

"What are you... oh. I see." Excitement filled Mara's face as she watched me finish securing the rope.

Once I was back on the ground, I grabbed the rope and yanked. Nothing happened. Satisfaction spread through me. "I'm going to test it out." Backing up slowly, I ran forward and leaped, flying through the air over the stream. Letting go when I was over the deepest part, I braced for impact with the water. As I burst up through the water, I felt a surge of energy race through me with the instant desire to do it again.

"My turn!" Mara was jumping up and down at the side of the river, impatient for me to get out of the way. I couldn't blame her, as I was already feeling impatient myself.

Squeals filled the air as the swing brought her far out over the stream. I didn't realize just how high I went until my chest tightened in instant fear seeing Mara looking so small up in the air. When she released the rope and started dropping I fought hard to hold myself together.

I was unaware that I was holding my breath until Mara's head popped up above the water. "Kith, you're a genius. That was so much fun!" Laughter flowed from her as she rushed to where I stood, but she stopped suddenly when she saw me up close. "Are you alright?"

Shaking my head to clear it, I spoke carefully to keep my voice steady. "Yeah. I'm fine."

Her head tilted slightly to the side as she looked up at me. "I scared you, didn't I?" She was fighting to hold back a giggle.

Grabbing the rope, I backed away from her. "Not at all." My denial only made the laughter escape, though.

"Oh, Kithian, ever my protector." I was relieved that she was joking and grinning about my fears instead of being annoyed with me.

Pushing all thoughts out of my head, I ran out and jumped over the river again, letting the exhilaration run through me.

We took turns swinging out, and eventually, I was able to watch Mara without any fear. Of course, something like this would come naturally to us.

"I'm tired." Mara pulled herself up the little hill and lay down.

Joining her in the grass, I sighed contentedly. "Me too."

We lay there for a long time, watching the clouds go by.

"Should we head home? I'm starting to get hungry." Even as she spoke, she showed no sign of wanting to move.

"We still need to gather food from the clearing. I imagine

we can eat some berries as we go, and then we'll head back." It took all my strength to raise myself up off the ground, and I reached a hand down to help her up. She took it begrudgingly and stood next to me.

There were several bushes still full of perfectly ripe berries, and we started from opposite ends of the clearing to get through them faster. I popped the first one I picked in my mouth. Suddenly, I was aware of just how empty my stomach was.

It was hard not to eat every berry I picked. My stomach kept growling angrily at me. After we gathered all the berries and other plants from the clearing, I headed to our trap in the stream. It was empty more often than not since we moved to the cabin. We weren't putting anything in there to lure fish in. This time, however, there was one big fish swimming around. It didn't take long to catch it.

"You caught some dinner!" Mara grinned as she approached me, her face and hands red from berries.

"Yep. We can cook it up when we get home."

"We should come back soon. The swing was so much fun!" Mara still had a skip in her step.

"I agree. It's too bad we didn't think of it earlier in the summer."

"I know. But at least we'll have it the whole summer next year."

The thought of spending a whole summer taking break days to swing at the stream gave me a boost of energy. "You're right. That'll be great."

"Maybe next summer we should start trying to use the stream trap more again."

"Good idea. I like the idea of more traps in general."

"With more traps up, and the garden doing well, we shouldn't have any trouble having enough food." There was a satisfaction in her voice, one that I understood deep in my bones.

We walked in silence for several minutes, not wanting to break our happiness by delving deeper into the topic of food. It seemed like a weird sign when I saw antlers out of the corner of my eye. There was a deer not too far away, one that would feed us for a long time. There was still meat from the last one, but the idea of storing some didn't hurt.

"Mara. You go ahead. I'll catch up." I kept my voice low, so only she could hear. When she nodded, knowing instantly what I was up to, I quietly set down my pack and climbed the tree. I waited until she walked far enough out of view, then crept through the branches until I was above the deer.

It didn't take me long to be ready to follow Mara home. It was a slow process with the large deer dragging behind me, but all my tools were at home so I would have to finish preparing the meat when I got there.

Fluffy was out in the clearing as I approached, Mara standing over her watching her run around and stretch her legs. She looked up as I pushed my catch next to the stump, careful to place it in a spot where it wouldn't be visible.

A smile played at her mouth. "The cabin is a huge mess. We should get a box or something to train Fluffy to go in when we're gone."

"Do you think you can train her?"

"Maybe?"

"Well, good luck." I turned to the deer. "I need to get started on this. Is that alright?"

"Yeah. It will be fine." She gently guided Fluffy further away from the stump.

While I was working on the deer, I realized the strong cords in its legs felt similar to the cord on the bow. They'd need to dry, but I felt confident I could figure out how to make the replacement. Working carefully, I set all four aside to be cleaned and dried later.

The day had been one of the best days, but I was exhausted and glad when the work was done. We didn't even play after dinner like usual, just collapsed into the bed and slept.

Once summer started getting further along, we began to think seriously about all the preparations we should be doing for winter. Neither of us was looking forward to months without fruits and vegetables again, and we didn't want to use up the canned ones too quickly, so we decided we needed to learn to preserve as much as we could to add to our stash.

"Now that we have an oven, I was thinking that might make it easier to dry out the vegetables," I was saying to a distracted Kith.

After a pause, he replied, "Yeah, that makes sense. Do you think we should chop the vegetables, or put them in there whole?"

At least I knew he was really listening to me, even though he kept glancing off into the trees. I studied the area he was looking at but didn't see anything that should be causing such a distraction.

"Mara?" Kith was looking at me expectantly now. I thought for a second before remembering his question. It appeared he wasn't the only one who was distracted.

"I think the bigger things like potatoes would probably do better if we sliced them. The carrots are so small, though, that we might be able to just put them in there whole. Oh, and I bet we could try it with the berries too!"

Kith smiled, "Sounds reasonable,"

"We'll have to be careful though, and watch it the whole time. I don't want to accidentally burn anything. The oven should be at a pretty low heat. We just want it to dry them out, not cook them."

We were working in the garden, pulling up the rest of the crops that came through. Sadly, most of our carrots were still pretty small. There were a couple of good-sized ones, but most were kind of disappointing. The rest of the crops seemed to have come along fairly well, so I wasn't sure what the problem was.

Pulling out a particularly tiny carrot, I scowled down at the ground. Then a thought hit me. Kith and I seemed to have some rather strange abilities that we didn't fully understand. Maybe we could do more than we even realized. Thinking about it carefully, I remembered what happened with the tree. The air began to shine when I released my breath.

Unsure of why it mattered, I checked to make sure Kith wasn't paying attention to me. Then I focused on where the rest of the carrots were growing. Staring intently at the little plants, I breathed in deep and slow, then released the breath in one big whoosh. It was so slight I might have imagined it, but it seemed like the plants shivered and grew just the tiniest little bit.

Repeating the process a few more times didn't seem to have any effect, so I went ahead and pulled up the bigger plants. They weren't exactly big carrots, but they were some of the largest we picked. As I placed them in the pile, I wondered if I actually made a difference or if it was just a coincidence. Either way, it was exciting to see how much we had that we could dry out now and save for the winter. As much as I loved meat, it was nice to eat something else with it.

After we finished harvesting everything that was ready, Kith washed the vegetables while I chopped and prepared them to go in the oven. It was a small oven, so we couldn't do too much at a time. Chopping the potatoes and squash in thick circles, I arranged them in the oven to make as many fit as I could, then added one full carrot in to test out how well it worked without chopping it at all. Setting the oven to low, I picked up my sewing kit and prepared to head outside.

"Aren't we going to chop the rest of the vegetables?" Kith asked in surprise.

"Well, we don't want to chop them all now. What if it takes days to get them all dried out? The other stuff would go bad waiting for its turn to go into the oven."

"Oh," Kith smiled sheepishly, "that makes sense."

Laughing, I continued outside. "I was just going to sew right out here and let Fluffy run around. I can check on the oven pretty easily, so you don't have to stay here."

"Well, it's already getting pretty late," Kith said, stepping outside and looking at the sky.

Looking up, I realized the placement of the sun. He was right. It was almost time to start working on dinner. "Wow, I guess time flies when you're having fun!"

Kith laughed, "I think you're the only nine-year-old girl who would call working hard in a garden 'fun'."

I smiled, "Probably the only nine-year-old girl who runs a household side by side with her twelve-year-old brother, too."

Laughing again, Kith said, "You're probably right." Then, turning serious he added, "You are pretty amazing, Mara. I couldn't do any of this without you."

The sudden change in him surprised me. I knew Kith appreciated what I did, and he knew I felt the same, but it was usually unspoken. "You're amazing too," I said quietly. "I'm lucky to have a big brother who always takes such good care of me."

Kith's face got a little dark, and I knew what he was thinking. "Kith," I started slowly, "I know there have been some rough times, but you have always done the best you can. It's a miracle I'm alive and that's all because of you."

He was quiet for a while, and I continued my sewing.

"Do you want me to start on dinner?" he finally asked awkwardly. I could tell he was still thinking about what I said and wasn't sure whether I was right or not. It made me sad to see him thinking of himself as a failure when he did so much for me.

"We can do it together," I responded happily, ready for the mood to lighten.

Over the next few days, we dried out the majority of the vegetables from our garden. We even tested out a few, making sure we knew how to cook with them. Watching our food stores grow gave me an incredible sense of satisfaction. It was always reassuring to have meat on hand, but having vegetables that we grew ourselves ready to last us through the winter was a completely different level.

After we got through most of the vegetables, we spent a day out in the woods collecting as many berries as we could.

"Those smell great." Kith hovered over the oven like a kitten getting ready to pounce. "Can you imagine having berries to snack on through the winter?" He grinned and eyed the pile waiting to be dried.

"It really would be lovely. This winter is going to be way better than last." I wondered briefly if that was the wrong thing to say, but Kith seemed unaffected.

"How long is this going to take?" Kith groaned as he checked the oven again. "I can't wait to try them out."

"It might take a while. They're really juicy. Let's play while we wait."

"Alright." Kith stuck a partially fake pout on his face and joined me at the table with some of our toys. He was still distracted during our games, but it did seem to help the time pass faster.

"I think they're finally done." I pulled the pan of hardened berries out of the oven.

"Ouch!" Kith quickly stuck his finger in his mouth. "That's hot."

Not even bothering to respond, I laughed and scraped the berries onto a plate to cool. Kith gingerly picked one up with his claws and blew on it before popping it into his mouth.

"Whoa. It's so chewy. Almost like leather. It tastes a bit different, but not too bad."

I couldn't resist trying one as well, and he was right. They definitely weren't like the berries we were used to, but were still a delightful little treat. They would be great during the winter for when we needed a quick pop of tastiness.

As I sat chewing, I wondered if there was a way to change them up a bit. Looking at the berry pile, I let my mind run wild. A flash of inspiration hit and I grabbed our pot. Kith watched me in silence as I tossed in some berries, honey, and a tiny bit of water. As it heated, I mashed the berries until the honey and berries were all mixed together in a thick paste.

Carefully, I spread the paste out over our pan and put it in the oven. Kith's eyes followed all my movements, but he still didn't speak.

"Hopefully that doesn't take too long. I'm eager to try it." I smiled at Kith and headed back to the table to distract myself with our games. He joined me and jumped right in, seemingly wanting to make the time pass as much as I did.

After what seemed like ages, the paste seemed dry enough. I cut a couple of strips and handed one to Kith. It was still leathery like before, but the honey added a delightful sweetness to it.

"Mara, you're a genius. This is wonderful. It will make winter a million times easier to deal with." He grinned widely before taking another bite.

I couldn't hold back my own smile. It was nice to have ways to plan for winter and make it easier, especially after how hard the last one was. It wasn't an experience I wanted to repeat.

After a few days of working our way through drying the food for preservation, Kith came running in from the garden.

"Hey, Mara," his voice held a mixture of excitement and hesitance, making me instantly curious. "As much as I hate to say it, do you think we should try drying out some of the feverfew too? It could be useful over the winter."

Laughing, I followed him outside to our plants. "That's a great idea! Let's pick some now and run them through next."

As much as the barn scared us, we decided it was the best place to store the extra food. We wanted to use the shed, but it was full of wood. Plus, the food we found that had been left behind was already out there.

✳   Kith   ✳

The night before Mara's birthday I laid in the bed pretending to sleep until I heard her breathing change. Quietly, I snuck out the door, hoping she wouldn't wake while I was gone. Her gifts were still stashed a distance away from the cabin, and I didn't want to have to retrieve them in the morning.

The air was cool as I ran toward my hiding spot. With the heat during the day, it was almost hard to remember that winter was closing in. Only a couple more months, and we had so much work to do.

Shaking my head, I refocused on Mara's birthday. Winter could wait another day. The gifts were right where I left them, wrapped up and ready to be brought home. Crouching down, I opened the wrap and looked at everything again. Even without having much knowledge of these things, I thought I did a pretty good job.

Shouldering my pack with the gifts inside it, I turned around and headed back to the cabin. I knew I should be hurrying, but I found myself keeping a slow pace and appreciating the stillness of the night.

The shed was getting filled up with all our supplies for winter, but there was a spot behind the wood that I was easily able to slide the bow and arrows into. They wouldn't have to hide there long, anyway.

With all the time I spent on Mara's bow, I was only able to make two targets with some plants I wove together. It was a long and difficult process to make them thick enough to have any hopes of holding together. Still, they were better than nothing. I dragged them out of the barn where they were hidden. They were too big to stash with the other items, and Mara usually stayed away from the barn.

At the edge of the forest behind the cabin, there were a couple of trees with lower-hanging branches. They were perfect for hanging the targets from, as Mara wouldn't be able to see them until we came around back.

Holding on to one of the targets, I jumped up to grab a branch. Pulling myself up with one hand wasn't working, so without thinking about it, I reached up with my other hand. Suddenly the air was being forced out of my lungs as I landed on my back. It took me a few seconds to realize I was on the ground. The target must have hit the tree and knocked me loose. This was going to be harder than I thought.

Once I got my breath back, I brushed myself off and stood up, ignoring the pain in my back and bad leg. Using the strap for tying, I secured the target onto my back. Jumping up, I grabbed the branch with both hands. As I pulled myself up, a sudden jerk sent me back to the ground, and I landed hard on my leg. A searing pain I was almost unfamiliar with ripped through my leg, and I bit my lip to keep from calling out.

Giving up on jumping into the tree, I quickly climbed up the trunk. As I moved to climb out on the branch the target snared in the branches. I could feel the strap begin to tear. In frustration, I shrugged the target off and yanked it out of the entanglement. Feeling myself starting to wobble, I dropped and grabbed the branch, almost losing the target in the process. Relief rushed through me as I managed to keep it from falling.

Tying it to the branch was way easier than getting it up. Having learned my lesson, I was a lot more careful with the second one. I slipped once, but was able to catch myself before getting hurt. Once that was done, I stood back and admired my handiwork. They were horribly crooked and hanging weirdly, but I didn't care. I was tired and in too much pain to do anything about it.

Briefly wondering if there was a way to make tea without waking Mara, I decided against it and crawled back into bed. Even with the pain that coursed through me, I managed to fall into a deep sleep.

"Kithian!" Mara's voice held the sharpness of irritation mixed with concern.

"Mmm. What?" I felt like my brain was swimming in fog as I tried to wake fully.

"Are you feeling alright?" My eyes opened to Mara's face very close to mine.

"Mara!" I was suddenly a lot more awake.

Her hand covered her mouth to stifle a giggle. "I'm sorry. You weren't waking up. It's been a long time since you've slept this late." She eyed me suspiciously.

The ache in my body reminded me why I slept so late. As I looked down at myself I realized I was still covered in dirt and leaves. "Uh. It was difficult to sleep, so I spent some time outside last night."

"Right." Mara smiled. "I made breakfast. Are you hungry?"

"Famished, actually." I moved slowly, trying to hide my stiffness from Mara. She was already handing me a cup of tea, though. I looked at it disdainfully. "What's this for?"

"Drinking, silly." She laughed as she turned back to putting some sliced potatoes and veggies onto my plate. "Once you're done with that you can have some of the juice I made with berries and fruit from the trees. It's quite good. And warm."

Making a face, I gulped the tea down quickly. The stuff was gross, but it helped. Mara watched with an odd look on her face, as if by drinking it without too much complaint I was affirming something for her. Handing her back the cup, I made a grab for my plate.

My fingers brushed it as she pulled it back slightly. "What were you really doing last night, Kithian?"

"Food. Mara, I need food." I grabbed the plate and shoveled food into my mouth before she could question me again.

"How long are you going to make me wait?" A fake pout formed on her face, her golden eyes full of humor.

"Wait?"

A slight growl was the only response as she handed me my cup back with my tasty drink. There were still some chunks from the berries in it, but it was delicious. I restrained myself from drinking it all at once so it wasn't gone too quickly.

Once I was finished eating, I decided to oblige Mara and put her out of her waiting misery. "Alright. I guess it's your birthday today, right?"

She looked at me, but didn't respond.

"I might have something for you. I'll be right back." Without waiting for a response, I headed out to the shed to get the bow and arrows.

*   Mara   *

In the middle of the night I woke up to find the other side of the bed empty. At first, I just thought it was a little strange, but then I decided Kith probably went to the bathroom. After I quickly drifted back to sleep, I wasn't sure how much time passed before I woke up again and found he was still gone.

This time, I sat up in bed quickly, suddenly alert. This was a long bathroom break if that was what he was doing. Sitting there for a while, I listened hard. After several minutes passed, I got up from the bed and went to the door to peek outside.

There was no sign of Kith anywhere in sight. I told myself he must have just gone for a walk, but I couldn't help the worry that creeped in. Closing the door, I sat at the table looking around the cabin. My eyes fell on the calendar, and suddenly I remembered what the next day was.

Laughing out loud, I realized what Kith must be doing. It was a good thing I didn't go after him. I could only imagine the look on his face when I caught him with whatever my gift was going to be. He would be so upset if I ruined the surprise.

For just a second, I contemplated peeking outside again, just to see if I could get a glimpse of what I was getting. In the end, I decided I may as well wait just a few more hours. Climbing back into bed, I lay wide awake, too excited to see what Kith made for me. His previous gifts were so thoughtful, I was sure it would be something wonderful. I laid in the bed for quite some time thinking about what it could be.

Just as I was finally drifting back off to sleep, I heard Kith approaching the back of the cabin. No wonder I didn't see him when I looked outside. It was smart of him to work on it back there. I closed my eyes and pretended to be asleep as Kith came inside. His breathing was heavy, which confused me. *Did he run back?* Then, I realized his foot falls sounded different. He was favoring his bad leg again, so he must have hurt it somehow.

A tinge of guilt hit me. Maybe I should have gone to look for him. What if he hurt himself and he could have used my help getting back? He seemed to be making his way around the cabin well enough though, so I decided he probably still would have been upset if I found him.

Once Kith got into bed, his breathing changed almost immediately. I opened my eyes just a little to look at him and realized he was already asleep. He must have been exhausted.

After laying there for a few more minutes, I was finally able to drift back to sleep. When I woke only a few hours later, I looked over at Kith who was still dead asleep. Closing my eyes, I tried to fall back asleep. I was tired too, but the excitement for the day wasn't letting me sleep anymore.

Finally, I got out of bed and let Fluffy outside. She, of course, used the bathroom on the floor overnight so I cleaned that up quickly and then stepped outside with her. It was later in the day than I thought, and I wondered how long we were both up the night before. Fighting the temptation to walk around the back of the cabin and investigate, I decided to start on breakfast.

Remembering how Kith was favoring his leg last night, I figured he could probably use some feverfew tea. He wouldn't be happy about it. Maybe if I made some juice it would make him feel better about having to drink the tea. Juice took a little longer than tea, and I figured I could use the distraction anyway while Kith slept. After I mashed the berries and fruit and they were in a pot with some water, I began cooking breakfast.

Every few minutes, I would check on Kith, but he still seemed to be dead to the world. I wondered how long he could possibly sleep. Once I got the tea started, I sat at the table, waiting for everything to finish. Every once in a while, I glanced over at Kith. Once, I even put my ear close to his face to make sure he was still breathing. I wondered just how long he was gone.

Once everything was done cooking, I decided I couldn't stand it anymore.

"Alright sleepyhead," I called loudly, "it's time to wake up now." Nothing happened. "Kith!" He didn't even stir.

Walking over, I laid a hand on his shoulder. "Hey, get up." Still nothing. "Kithian!" I yelled in frustration and felt fear creeping in. How could he sleep through me yelling at him? I bent down just in time for him to finally respond and open his eyes. Served him right for the scare he got when he saw my face right up in his.

While Kith drank his tea and ate his breakfast, I tried to be patient, but he already made me wait so long. The juice I made turned out really good, and I sipped it while waiting for Kith to grab whatever it was he was giving me. Luckily, it didn't take him long, and I heard him call from outside, "Okay, Mara, you can come out!"

Springing out of my chair in excitement, I dashed to the door. When I opened it, Kith was standing in the clearing holding a bow and a bag full of arrows. Stopping dead in my tracks, I stared at him for a moment.

"Kith, how did you make these!?" I asked while walking over and taking the bow from my brother. I ran my finger over the design he carved into the wood. It was rough, but beautiful.

"Well, there was an old bow in the shed when I was cleaning it out. It wasn't in great shape, so I fixed it up a little."

Grabbing the bag of arrows next, I examined the feathers on the top. "Did you make these? The feathers look familiar," I peered at him questioningly.

"Yes, they're from the birds I brought home when I got Fluffy. That actually turned out perfectly. I wasn't sure how I was going to make them!"

"Kith, they're amazing! I knew my gift was going to be great, but I never expected this. Have you tried shooting with them?"

"I have," Kith looked a little sheepish, "I put up some targets last night for you to practice on. That's why I slept so late. I was gone almost all night. Took longer than I thought it would."

I laughed and hugged Kith tight. "Can we go try it out now!?"

✳   Kith   ✳

Mara's eagerness to use her new bow caused a deep sense of pleasure to build inside me. I didn't realize how nervous I was about her gift until it all faded with her excitement.

"Of course, we can go try it out." I paused. "Grab the gloves you made, first, though."

"My gloves?"

"Yes. Trust me."

Shrugging, she pulled out her gloves while I got mine. Then, grabbing the bow and arrows, we headed around to the targets. Daylight showed how truly lopsided they were, but Mara didn't even seem to notice. Her eyes lit up with excitement as she lifted the bow as if to aim, but didn't pull out an arrow.

Her stance was all wrong, but I could tell she knew that. Scrunching up her face, she seemed to be trying to recall the same memories I used to teach myself. She had been much younger, though, and the images didn't seem to be coming easily.

"Do you mind if I show you what I've learned?" I knew offering help could upset her, but it was the reason I spent months in pain learning.

"You know how to shoot it?" Surprise filled her face. "I was thinking it would take forever for me to figure it out." Her faint laughter floated through the air.

"It took me plenty of time, and I think my memories of Garrett and Diana are a bit more clear than yours."

"Show me." She thrust the bow at me insistently.

"Alright." I felt strangely relieved as I took her spot.

Placing my legs carefully, I lifted the bow as I practiced. Mara copied my stance, her hands held up as if she were holding an invisible bow.

"Here, I'm going to adjust you just a little bit, alright?" After she nodded, I dropped my stance and shifted her position to better suit her size difference.

Once I was satisfied with her stance, I pulled an arrow out of the quiver. "Getting the arrow into position and correctly shooting it took me the longest to learn. Don't be surprised if we spend most of today working on it."

"Really?" Her voice was tinged with disappointment.

"Yes. But I spent months learning how to shoot so that I'd be able to help it go faster for you."

Reassured, she smiled. "I bet I'll learn it really fast."

She took the bow and followed my directions for loading the arrow, but it kept slipping or her hand would be in the wrong spot. After several tries, she paused and took a deep breath, muttering a reminder of what I said.

It didn't take her long to be ready to try again. Learning something new was a great area for her stubbornness to shine through. After a bunch more tries, she looked up proudly, the arrow was nocked and held carefully in place.

"Nice! Now you have to work on pulling back the string while keeping the arrow in place."

With a huff, Mara pulled the string back. She wasn't expecting to need to use as much strength as was required, however, so it didn't go back very far. The arrow slid off and dangled.

Muscles in her arms twitched as if she was considering throwing the bow down in frustration. Instead, she tried again with more determination but with similar results.

Without commenting, I watched as she worked on getting the string back. After several tries, I could tell she was getting tired. "I'm hungry. Let's go get some lunch."

At first, Mara just glared at me, making it obvious she knew what I was doing. After a few seconds, however, her shoulders sank and she relented. "Food does sound good."

We ate slowly, Mara was distracted with frustration, but trying to be happy because it was her birthday and she didn't want to seem ungrateful for her gift.

"It's alright to be frustrated, Mara."

She was silent for a moment. "Were you frustrated?"

"Of course. I didn't have any clue what I was doing."

"Or anyone to help you."

"You're getting it much faster than I did."

Even as she rolled her eyes, there was a glint of pride in them. She started eating faster, her determination renewed.

"I'm going to take care of Fluffy for a little bit before I get back to practicing." The rabbit was hopping around her feet, vying for attention. Scooping her up, Mara headed outside toward a patch of greens.

"Good idea. Do you mind if I shoot some while you tend to her?"

"Go ahead. Maybe I'll pick it up faster watching you."

Not wanting to shoot the targets before Mara had a chance to, I aimed at the dirt between the roots of the trees they were hanging from. Mara didn't say anything, but I could tell she was paying close attention to everything I did.

After Fluffy ate her fill and spent plenty of energy running around, Mara scooped her up and brought her back inside where she'd be safe. "I want to try again."

Ready for a break, I handed over the bow willingly and sat down on a nearby stump to watch.

Watching me definitely helped her get a better idea of what she was supposed to be doing. She carefully aligned herself and pulled back the string. The arrow slid, but not as much, and Mara was able to get the string back almost the full way before slowly releasing it.

We spent the rest of the day until dinner time working on her getting the motions right. As we headed in, Mara seemed to be torn between feeling pouty and excited. "I was really hoping to actually get to shoot something today."

"I'm sure you can shoot at the targets in the morning. It might help you improve your technique as you get feedback from the shots."

Grinning, Mara set out the plates for her birthday feast. "Great. But now I just want dinner." After a pause, she added. "Thank you, Kith. I really do love the bow."

*   Mara   *

After only having learned the basics of how to hold and shoot the bow, I was excited to finally practice for real on the targets Kith set up. In the midst of wolfing down my breakfast, I looked up to see Kith smirking at me. When I lowered my fork, he burst out laughing.

"I guess you're a little excited, aren't you?"

Smiling sheepishly, I grabbed my fork back up and made a show of taking a long time to bring my food to my mouth. Kith laughed harder.

Once we finished breakfast, I pulled on my gloves, grinning at how smart it was of Kith to suggest them. I didn't have a clue that I was making something to go along with my own birthday present. Kith had asked the day before if he could still tag along for my practice. Even though he said he would like to practice too, I knew it was because he was worried about me practicing with the bow alone. I decided not to let that bother me. He was the one who fixed it up for me after all, so he must have some confidence in my ability to use it.

Once we got to where Kith set up the targets, I opened the bag that held my arrows. Kith really outdid himself with them. They were perfect. I was grateful to see that Kith was standing back to let me practice without his instruction. Maybe he had more faith in me than I originally thought. Or maybe he just knew it would annoy me if he hovered and told me what to do the whole time.

Holding the bow the way he showed me, I notched my arrow and pulled the string back. I went for the closest target first, holding the bow steady. When I released the arrow, it nicked the edge of the target and kept on going. I looked back to see Kith watching me with a straight face, he looked tense like he thought I may be upset.

"Well it was only the first time," I laughed, "I'll get better!" Kith relaxed and smiled. I wasn't sure why he was so tense about it. Was it just because he really wanted me to like his gift?

After a few more tries, I was getting the hang of aiming the bow. By the time I was beginning to feel worn out, I had progressed to the next target which was a few feet further away. Kith whooped loudly when I managed to hit the target exactly where I wanted.

"You got the hang of it way faster than I did!" He cheered, sounding impressed.

"Well of course I did," I said, grinning. "I think you just waited until my birthday so that you could practice before I got to use it."

Kith's mouth dropped open in false horror. "How did you know!?"

We bantered back and forth until I relinquished the bow, ready for a break.

The next day, Kith added a few more targets. He didn't want to hang them for some reason, so he left them leaning against a couple of trees a short distance into the woods. He was pretty good with it already, but still had a hard time hitting the furthest targets exactly where he wanted. At least he wasn't sending my arrows soaring into the trees like I did on a few occasions.

"I figured out that if you aim a little higher, it will go further." Kith explained as he continued trying to hit the center of the furthest target. "The arrow kept falling way closer than where I wanted it. It's hard to aim, though, when you raise it up higher." I watched as Kith struggled, trying to hit the center of his target. I was eager to try hitting the further ones too.

When Kith decided he was done, I got up quickly, ready to try out the same target he was aiming for. I stood, facing the stump, and pulled back hard on the string. Remembering what Kith said, I pointed my aim above the edge of the target, breathed in deep, and released.

My arrow soared well above the target and kept going until it sank right into a tree. Kith burst out laughing. "I said to aim a little higher, not to aim for the sky!"

Sticking my tongue out at him, I said "Okay so maybe I aimed a little too high."

"That was a powerful shot though!" Kith said, impressed. "Did you see how far it went? You've got the strength for it, for sure. You just need to work on the aim."

I grinned. After putting so much strength into that one shot, I was already tired again. Stretching my arms, I said, "I think I'm going to be sore tomorrow."

"Oh, I'm sure you will be. It takes a lot more muscle than I realized. I'm surprised you didn't notice how sluggish I was after my first few days of practicing. It was rough!"

"Oh great," I rolled my eyes. "Nice of you to tell me what I have to look forward to."

"Would it have stopped you from trying so hard?" Kith asked, matter-of-factly.

Ignoring the question, I went out to retrieve my arrow. It really did go pretty far. Even though I was way off from hitting my target, I was proud of the progress I already made in just a few days.

CHAPTER TWENTY-ONE: OCTOBER

✳   Kith   ✳

Mara stretched and yawned. She lay in the grass, taking a break from another practice session with her bow. We still had a lot of work to do, but almost every spare moment was spent perfecting her aim.

"You've been improving a lot with that bow."

A grin flashed across her face. "Thanks! I'd probably improve faster if it didn't make my arms so sore." She ran her hands over her arms as she spoke, and an exaggerated pout fixed itself on her face.

"I'm sure you would. You are getting stronger, though."

"I know." She flexed her muscles the way Mitch used to during his shows and giggled.

Laughing, I rose to my feet. "Alright, Strong Girl, I'm heading out to work on putting up more traps. Want to help?"

"Sure." Hopping up, she quickly got her things put away and met me at the edge of the clearing.

"Do you remember where everything is supposed to go?" She stood beside me, looking into the trees.

"Yes." My eyes scanned the area, and the spots where we planned to put traps looked like they had a faint glow. It must have just been the fact that I was focusing on them, though. "Where do you want to start?"

"What do we need?" There was already a shovel in her hand, held absentmindedly like she didn't even realize she picked it up.

Knowing how much she enjoyed using the shovel, I smiled. "You can start with digging. I'll mark the spots where we need holes."

Grinning, she followed me to the first spot. As soon as I marked the outline for the hole, she got started. I marked several more for her, clearing the leaves from the area and using a stick to draw a big square with a cross through it.

While she worked on the ground, I got started with the traps in the trees. These were mostly for trying to catch meat. I developed a routine of checking them every morning. Sometimes we were lucky enough to have a couple of days' worth of food caught inside. It helped a lot with building up our stores. I still hunted occasionally, though, because the traps mostly caught smaller animals. Hopefully having more traps would help us make it through the winter.

"I'm done with the holes you marked." Mara was standing under the tree I was working in, her head on her hand at the top of the shovel.

"You've gotten faster."

"It's a lot easier now than it used to be." She brushed some of the dirt off her arms and shrugged.

"Let me finish this trap and I'll mark some more spots for you."

"Alright." She nestled down into a groove between two roots. "I'll just take a little break."

It didn't take me long to finish my work. When I hopped out of the tree, I went to mark the next few areas for Mara to dig. We made a fair amount of progress already, and it wasn't even halfway through the day.

"I marked four more for you. That should be good for the day."

"We've gotten a lot done so far. Do you think we'll make it all the way around the clearing before winter?"

"Maybe. Why don't we check the perimeter before we get back to work? We can check how much we have left to go."

"That sounds like fun. Race you!" Before I could react Mara scrambled up a tree and leapt to the branches in the next one.

"Wait!" I jumped up into the tree and took off after her.

Giggling, Mara sped up when she realized I was coming after her. She was flying through the trees, but I was gaining on her. I propelled myself faster until we were racing side by side.

It had been a while since we moved so quickly through the trees. The wind rushing past felt amazing, and the feel of the bark under my hands and feet was strangely comforting. Years of moving this way toughened our skin, so the abrasiveness of the bark was barely noticeable.

Suddenly, Mara laughed and dropped from the branch, her tail catching as she fell. Hanging from her tail, she swung lazily. "We're back where we started. I guess we tied, but we didn't figure out how much work we have left."

"Guess we'll have to go around again." Laughing, I left her behind as I raced off. It didn't take her long to swing back up into the tree and start chasing me.

"Kithian! You cheated!" Her words came out between bursts of laughter and sharp breathing.

"You cheated first." My breathing was getting heavier, too. Laughing while running made it a lot more difficult. When we were spending all our time on the run there was almost no laughter.

It didn't take long for me to see the spots I just marked for digging, which brought me to a halt. "Alright, it's time to get serious." I couldn't hold back my laughter, even as I spoke.

"I'm serious." Mara grinned. "Serious about beating you this time." The words trailed behind her as she dashed off again.

"Mara!" I feigned frustration as I pushed myself through the trees. Launching myself off one of the branches, I realized too late that I was positioned poorly. Pain shot through my bad leg as I flew through the air. Coughing back a yelp, I tried to keep moving.

Looking around, I realized I couldn't see Mara anymore. She wasn't that far ahead of me, so the pain in my leg shouldn't have slowed me down enough to lose sight of her. Listening carefully, I kept following our circle around the clearing.

A flash of movement off to my side caught my eye, but too late. My tail caught me and stopped my fall, Mara clinging to my side.

"I got you!" She was laughing hard and her grip loosened, so she let herself drop to the ground.

"You sure did." I followed her down, trying to be careful with my leg.

Nothing escaped Mara's notice, though. "Is your leg bugging you?"

"I twisted it during a jump a minute ago. It's not too bad, though, just a little sore."

"I'm sorry. I didn't mean for you to get hurt." Her thoughts seemed to be deeper than just a little pain in my leg, but I couldn't read them.

"Mara, I'm fine. And it was a lot of fun." She didn't seem fully convinced. "If it will make you feel better, you can make the gross tea for me later, and I'll only complain a little."

She couldn't hold back the laugh. "You promise?"

"Promise. Now, we really should get back to work."

*   Mara   *

"I think we should work on the walls tomorrow," I said after dinner one night, while inspecting the mud fillings in our walls. "We want to have them done before it gets really cold."

Kith hopped up from where he sat examining one of the little horses from our game and walked to where I was looking. "You're right," he sighed while peeping through a hole in the wall. "Just when we think we're close to being ready, we always find more things to be done."

"I think that's just how it goes when you're running a home. Our work will never be done!" As strange as it was, I took comfort in that. It was hard work keeping up with a garden, working on the cabin, making winter clothes and gloves for Kith and me, and of course taking care of Fluffy. All while still finding time to relax and play. But it felt good to have a home to work for.

The next morning, we dug up a good amount of dirt and poured some water into it until we came up with what seemed like a good consistency. I worked inside the cabin, slowly checking all the spaces we patched before and packing on more mud wherever it was needed. Kith was working outside, doing the same.

Once I got through the repairs on our previous work, I started working my way around the rest of the cabin, checking for gaps and holes in the wood. After a while, I decided it was time for a break. Heading outside, I found Kith; almost completely covered in mud, with a muddy Fluffy resting in his lap. "I sat down to take a break, and she jumped in my lap. I guess she's been hopping around in the mud this whole time because now I have it all over me!"

Laughter bubbled out of me, and Kith gave me a dirty look before laughing as well. Soon we were both laughing hard. Fluffy looked back and forth between us innocently, before hopping off Kith's lap and coming to my feet.

"Geez Kith," I sputtered between laughs, "if you wanted to bathe in the mud, you could have just said so! I'm sure we could dig up enough for you to roll around in!" I laughed even harder as Kith playfully glared at me. As I bent down to pat Fluffy's head, a big ball of mud splattered on my back.

"Hey!" I turned to see Kith retreating around the corner of the cabin. Scooping up a handful of mud, I yelled, "I'll get you for that!" and took off after him. We ran in circles around the cabin, until I got the idea to turn and run the other way. Kith, who had been expecting me to be behind him, yelled in shock when I suddenly appeared in front of him and pelted him with my own mud ball.

Laughing hysterically, he picked up more mud and rubbed some on my cheek.

While trying to turn away from his hands, I ended up with mud in my mouth instead. Kith let out a gasp and started backing away as I glared at him. Quickly grabbing up another mud ball, I threw it without aiming. He was too fast, though, and my ball fell just short of him. We chased each other around our little clearing for several minutes, smearing mud all over the place. By the end of it, we were both completely covered and exhausted.

We finally collapsed in a fit of giggles, too tired to continue the fight. "You know...what this...means?" Kith asked between breaths. I looked at him questioningly and noticed how his face was lit up. I knew what was coming before he said it. "We're going to have to go to the stream now to wash all the mud off!"

Laughing, I relaxed back onto the ground. "You're right. I don't know how I'm going to get it all out of my hair!" I said, exasperated. "Let's rest for a minute, though. I don't know if I can take another step."

It was Kith's turn to laugh. He got up from the ground and announced that he would pack some food while I rested. "All that running around made me hungry," he said. "I'm sure we're going to be home late with how late it is already."

"Make sure Fluffy has food, too!" I called after him while contemplating if I ought to get up and help. In the end, I decided to give myself another few minutes.

It wasn't easy getting all the mud off of us and our clothes, especially with how shallow the stream was closer to the cabin. The water was going to be too cold to really enjoy soon, and I knew how sad that was for Kith. "We should probably make a trip to our old spot tomorrow so we can wash off better," I said casually, knowing how excited he would be. "Plus, we have to get some more use out of that swing!" I decided not to add that it could be one of our last chances before winter.

✳   Kith   ✳

"I haven't missed having to make runs for wood on cold, dark nights." Mara set down her armful of wood next to the fireplace and fed a few pieces to the fire. She sat, her hands extended toward the heat for a minute.

"Me neither." The days were still warm, but the nights were already starting to get pretty chilly. With all our preparations, the cabin was nice and warm, though. "Tomorrow, we should stack a bunch in a corner and work on filling the shed back up."

"Good idea. Not having to run out every day would be nice." Her eyes swept around the cabin, and I could see her thoughts returning to endless days cooped up inside. We'd need plenty to do to keep us occupied.

"Right. Though, with the warm stuff you've made and the coats we found in the barn, we should be able to go out more often."

Her eyes stopped wandering the cabin and landed on mine. "Of course. We should go back to the stream and slide around on the ice again." The grin that spread across her face seemed a little forced, but I didn't push it.

"Definitely." Remembering our fun on the frozen water almost made me anticipate the cold dreary months ahead. I struggled not to think about Mara falling in. We'd be more careful this time.

The next morning, I woke to the sounds of Mara moving things around. Once my eyes focused, I could see the big pile of boxes from the barn had moved out of the space between the fireplace and the stove. They seemed to take up a lot more space out in the middle of the cabin.

"What are you doing?"

"Oh, good, you're awake. I've cleared a spot to pile the wood." She handed me my plate with breakfast and went back to moving things around.

"I see that." Realizing that she was eager to get to work, I ate my breakfast quickly and got ready for the day.

Chill from the night was still hanging in the air when we went out, but it was warming up. We had filled the shed most of the way with wood and kept up with stocking it pretty well, so there was plenty to carry in. I loaded Mara's arms first, then carefully piled a bunch on my own and followed her to the cabin.

"That was fast." Her wood was stacked neatly against the wall before I even got there.

"I didn't have that much." She shrugged and started grabbing the wood from my arms, adding it to her stacks.

We repeated this several times, gradually filling the space most of the way up. Once there was a fair amount of empty space in the shed, we decided it would be best to switch to filling it back in.

During good weather, we liked to go out further away from the cabin while gathering anything so we'd have resources closer to home. As we wandered, Mara started humming softly. I was glad she was more relaxed now.

"Ow! What was that for?" The stick that flew into my arm

now lay at my feet.

"You were supposed to catch it." Fake frustration filled her voice. In front of her, she held a stick similar to the one she threw at me. A sly smile flashed across her face before she lunged at me.

Rolling to the side, I picked up the stick and managed to block her attack. As soon as I rose she came at me again, striking at my leg. Again, I managed to move out of the way just in time.

"Mara! What are you doing?"

For a second, a look of horror appeared in her widened eyes. "That was your good leg, right?"

"What? Uh. Yes."

"Whew. That's good. Fight back, Kithian. I'm just playing, I won't really hurt you." The laugh that followed wasn't as reassuring as her words, but I made myself relax.

This time she circled me before coming in to strike. Moving my stick, I blocked hers and went to strike in return, but was also blocked. Our sticks whizzed through the air, smacking against each other as we raced through the woods, circling around each other as we went.

SNAP

Ducking down, I barely managed to dodge Mara's stick as mine broke in half and dangled uselessly from my hand. With a chuckle, I threw the still connected pieces at Mara's feet.

"You win."

"Great. I'm tired." She sat down with a small giggle. "Let's take a break for a bit before we collect the wood."

*　　Mara　　*

As I was making breakfast one morning, I caught myself staring at the box of things we brought in from the barn months ago. Some of the things, like the figurines and of course the seeds, had been used, but there were still several things sitting in the box waiting to be unpacked. With everything else that needed to be done to prepare for winter, unpacking the boxes was not high on our list of priorities. Now, though, with our preparations done and a long winter ahead of us, there was plenty of time.

"I think it's getting cold enough we could probably use that blanket we found in the barn," I said as I handed Kith his plate. I let him sleep in a little bit that morning, in the interest of improving his mood. The day before, he was quick to argue, and I sensed it had something to do with the weather.

"Yeah, probably so," was his response as he began picking at his food.

Poking around in the box, I found the paintings we planned to put up in the cabin. "Hey, remember these? They're beautiful. They would be a great way to liven this place up a little."

Kith must have realized the point I was making because he composed himself and walked over to the box to look through it again.

"Where do you think we should put them?" he asked with genuine interest, scanning the cabin walls. "Where do you think they used to be?" this time his voice was almost reverent. He was thinking about the people who lived here before.

Scanning the walls, I looked for some indication and found a few small holes in the wall above the bed that looked like nails were once there. "I think one of them went here! See!"

Kith smiled and pulled out the three paintings. "Which one do you think would look best?"

I ended up choosing the painting with a field of flowers and one huge tree in the middle. It was my favorite of the three. Kith found the next set of holes, in the kitchen area, where the table was, and we decided to put the painting of a couple enjoying a feast together there. The last one, a herd of wild horses running through a field went beside the door.

We both stepped back to admire the effect. "It looks nice," Kith said, happily. "I guess we should empty out the rest of the box too."

We took out the coats and set them aside. Under the coats, we found before were another three we didn't notice. Two of them were sized for adults, and there was another child-sized one. The smaller ones brought on a sadness that I wasn't expecting.

The smaller two were a little bit too big on us, but we could wear them, and they were warm. The larger ones all looked like they were made for a woman like the one we found before, and were way too big for both of us.

"They're warm," he said, trying one on.

"Kith? Where'd you go?"

"What are you talking about? I'm right here."

"All I see is a coat." I stifled a laugh.

"It's not THAT big on me." I could hear the eye roll in his voice, even without looking at his face.

"I suppose."

"You're just jealous because it looks so good on me." He grinned and spun around like he was one of the ladies who would show off the new coats at the shops in towns we'd stop in.

"You're right. I could never look good in a gorgeous green coat." I sniffed as if saddened by the fact, using it to hide more laughter. "Even if I don't look as good as you, though, winter shouldn't be so bad this time." I said while unfolding the extra blankets, "It will definitely be warmer at least." I looked at Kith, expecting this to make him happy, but instead his face had gone dark. "Are you okay?"

Kith's face changed immediately, and he looked at me with confusion, "Yeah, I'm great! What else is in the box?"

I knew Kith was putting on a fake smile so I wouldn't worry, but surely he knew that wouldn't work. After how bad our moods got last winter, I hoped all the preparations we made would make it better this time. Maybe he just needed time to see that it wouldn't be so bad. We wouldn't be cooped up inside all the time with proper clothes and coats for the winter. I was even working on new socks for us, as well. None of the fabric was really thick, so I planned to make a few for each of us so that we could layer them up. There were also a good amount of vegetables and dried berries to tide us over as long as we were sparing with them.

"I made stew." Mara greeted me with a bowl, tendrils of steam still drifting off of it. "Did you find anything good?"

Dropping my bag, I took my dinner. "Thank you. It smells amazing." After I shoveled a few spoonfuls into my mouth, I continued. "I found quite a lot. But with the way that bunny is eating, she's going to need way more than I can gather in one day to make it through the winter."

"Did you forget lunch again?" Sternness and amusement both displayed at once in her face and voice. As she spoke, she pulled the greens out of my bag and started laying them out to dry. We had experimented with drying out the leaves and flowers that Fluffy liked. It took some figuring out to get it just right, but she ate them willingly.

"Maybe." There was only a small laugh in response, and I didn't bother saying anything else as I gobbled down the rest of the stew. It wasn't quite the same as what Isaac taught her to make, but we'd found plenty of plants that helped with the flavor.

After gulping down a second bowlful, I went to wash my dishes. "Hmm. Think we're going to need to do a water run soon."

"Oh, I was going to tell you that I noticed we were low while making the stew." She didn't look up from where she lay on the floor feeding her rabbit. "A bath day is probably a good idea, too."

"A bath does sound pretty nice. I was thinking about going hunting tomorrow, but we can do a stream day instead and I'll hunt the next day."

Silence filled the cabin, and I could tell Mara was thinking about something. "I was actually thinking that I'd go hunting with you." There was a slight waver to her voice, but she quickly strengthened it. "I've been getting quite good with my bow, and I think it's time to put it to use."

"Are you sure?"

"Yes."

"Alright. We can leave in the morning and make a day of

it; hunting, gathering more plant life, and getting more water. We'll need to empty out all the packs so we have room."

As I looked at the packs, I realized how much time passed since we'd dealt with moving while carrying so much weight. It would probably be a good idea for us to practice. It was just one more way we were getting soft from life in the cabin. For a few seconds, I felt myself drifting down the abyss of worry that accompanied realizing how relaxed we got over time.

"Kithian." Apparently, my face betrayed my thoughts.

"I'm alright." I gave my head a shake to rid it of the sinking feeling.

Her eyes stayed on my face for another few seconds before she turned back to emptying the packs. I must have sunk further into my fears than I realized since I didn't even see her rise off the floor. Once the packs were empty, she put them next to the door.

"We should probably go to bed early since it's going to be a hard day tomorrow." Her voice held a heaviness I couldn't fully read.

"Alright. I'm pretty tired, anyway."

We headed out right after eating the next morning. It was chilly enough that we put on our gloves. We didn't bother with the extra clothes because we figured we would warm as we walked and didn't want to have to store them.

Even without anything in the packs, it was difficult to get into a steady pace together. Hunting and gathering were our first tasks, then we planned to stop back at the cabin for the bucket and run to rinse off in the stream before making the trips to refill the barrel.

"Kith!" We were taking a break, sitting in the grooves at the base of a tree and munching quietly on some dried meat. I almost didn't hear her say my name, her voice was so quiet, but her hand motioning toward the ground close by caught my attention.

Deer tracks went across our path, faded where we were walking, but more visible where the undergrowth got thicker. Without waiting, she slid into the growth, soundlessly following the tracks. Her movements were mesmerizing, and she almost disappeared from view by the time I shook myself and followed her.

We wove through the trees carefully, losing track of time completely. Mara was focused on the tracks, and I was focused on watching her. These skills must have come in handy when she tracked me down after I was attacked. Only, she was likely frantic then and now she seemed completely calm.

Suddenly, she froze. I stopped where I was and waited before slowly moving up to meet her. The deer stood near a thicket in a small clearing. He was a smaller deer, his antlers only slightly bigger than his head.

Still frozen, Mara stared. After several seconds, she seemed to remember what she came for. Without making a sound, an arrow slid into place as she aimed her bow. Her movements seemed slow and forced as she pulled the string back, and I wondered for a brief second if she'd actually be able to release it.

She did, though. A shriek tore through the air as her arrow met with the deer's leg, sticking out the other side, and the deer took off running, a trail of blood in its wake. This time I was the one to take off without remark, trailing after the wounded animal. It wasn't until I silenced the screaming and got the deer ready to be packed in the bags that I realized Mara wasn't with me anymore. I loaded up my packs and headed back to find her.

She stood where I left her, her face white and her eyes wide. "Mara?" Her eyelids flickered, but she didn't acknowledge me. I moved closer. "Mara?"

"Did you…?" Her voice trailed off.

"He's not in pain anymore."

"That's good." Her eyes met mine, and I could see her anguish in them. "I didn't mean to get his leg."

"I know. You did extremely well for a first hunt, though."

Her head tilted slightly. "It doesn't feel like it."

I almost laughed, but knew that would be a terrible idea, so I didn't. "I know it doesn't. You'll get better, though. If you still want to."

"I'm." She took a shuddering breath. "I'm not sure."

"Just let me know."

"I will." She was silent as we continued on, gathering more food for Fluffy and ourselves while heading to start refilling our water supplies. The journey was even more difficult with the extra weight in my pack, but I refused to mention it.

After I filled the bucket and skins, I looked at Mara. She was washing her face and hands in the stream, silent tears falling down her face. I crouched down beside her.

"Mara?"

"I'm alright, Kith."

I brushed her hair out of her face. "You don't have to pretend with me, you know that."

"I didn't expect it to be so hard. I love meat, but the deer was so beautiful. I mean, I never liked it with Isaac and stayed inside, but it was so much worse this time." She stared at her hands as if they were stained with the deer's blood.

"We only do it to survive. It's the way of things." I paused, thinking. "How about if from now on we thank the animals we eat for providing us with food? Maybe a little ritual? Do you think that would help?"

"Yes, I think that would." She gave me a small smile. "Do you think I'm weak?"

"Weak? Mara, no. You have been strong your whole life. Stronger than any child should have to be."

"What do you know of what a child should be?" Her voice held a teasing scoff to it.

"I know many things." I straightened up as tall as I could while kneeling and mimicked the high-class people who occasionally sneered at us through our cages.

Mara's serious face broke into a laugh. "You sure do, Kithian, you sure do."

*   Mara   *

The night after our hunting trip, I dreamed about the deer. When I woke up, my cheeks were wet with tears. Relief flooded me when I realized Kith was still sleeping and hadn't noticed.

Wiping my eyes, I got out of bed and began preparing for our trip to our old spot at the stream. The night before, we decided to go for one last swim before the water got too cold. By the time Kith was awake, our lunches were already packed and breakfast was ready for him.

"Why didn't you wake me up? I would have helped." he protested as I handed him his plate and told him I was ready to go whenever he was.

"You just looked like you were sleeping so well," I said with a smile, hoping he wouldn't see through it.

Kith hurried through his breakfast and before long we were on our way to our swimming hole.

I tried not to let our time at the stream be tainted by my feelings about the deer. It was difficult, however, since I kept hearing its shriek of pain, and seeing it run away, limping. Knowing Kith's eyes were on me, I ran into the water and dove under for a swim.

It was several minutes before I realized how cold the water was. Shivering, I turned to see Kith tentatively walking into the water, staring at me like I was a crazy person. The laugh that escaped was real, despite what I just experienced.

"You just have to dive in, and get it over with quickly!"

"Oh, because I can't see how violently you're shaking right now!" Kith retorted.

Giggling, I lowered the back of my head into the water and ran my fingers through my ratted hair, working out the dirt. Again, I fought back the sounds of the deer.

We didn't last long in the water. I got out before Kith was even able to get his hair wet.

Wrapping in a blanket, I started building a fire for us to warm off next to.

"I'm sorry, Mara. I never meant to put you through something like that," Kith's words caught me by surprise. Lost in thought, I hadn't even noticed him get out of the water. He was sitting a few feet away from me now, wrapped in his own blanket.

"I asked you to let me come, Kithian." My voice was stern.

"You can't blame yourself for everything."

Kith sighed and nodded. He knew I was right. We finished drying off by the fire before putting our clothes back on and continuing on to look for more food for Fluffy. Most of the evening was spent in silence. We gathered until it got too dark, and then camped for the night.

The next morning, I woke suddenly to the remnants of my nightmare hovering in my mind. After so long of not having them, I was finally used to peaceful sleep. It made it harder to shake off this one, but I didn't want to make a big deal of it.

Once I assured Kith I was fine, we headed home. He obviously wanted to keep me distracted from thoughts of the deer and my nightmare, as he kept up a string of small talk while we walked. All I really wanted was time to be alone and process everything that had happened, but I forced myself to stay in the conversation anyway.

Finally, when we made it home, I took Gracie out of her box. "I think I'm just going to play with Gracie for a while," I said as I headed for the door.

"That's a good idea!" Kith said with a smile that told me he knew exactly what I was doing. "You haven't played with her that much lately."

Nodding absent-mindedly, I headed outside.

Later, I found myself sitting on the ground propped against a tree, Gracie held tightly against my chest. I positioned myself to face away from the cabin, so Kith couldn't see me unless he came looking.

Staring at Gracie, I thought of the woman who was her namesake. Grace had always loved animals. She used to talk about how she wished she could be a bird. She would fly away from those who ridiculed her, and see all the places she ever wanted to see. She used to leave pieces of bread outside her tent, just in case an animal passed by who needed some food.

I wondered what she would say if she knew I shot a deer. Peering down at Gracie, I began speaking to her. "I'm sorry, Grace," my breathing was getting harder. "You should have seen the way that poor deer ran after I shot him." My eyes were pooling with water. "He never knew what was coming, and then my terrible aim left him in agony until Kith could finish the job for me." A single tear rolled down my cheek as I realized this was a huge part of what really bothered me.

"I shot him, Grace. I shot him, and then I couldn't even put him out of his misery. I just let him limp away in pain. If Kith wasn't there, who knows how long that poor thing would have run around on his hurt leg just wishing the pain could end." More tears began streaming down as I talked freely now.

"You should have heard him yell. I've never heard an animal make such a terrible sound. And I'm the one who caused it. Then, what did I do? I stood there. I just stood there! Staring at the blood he left behind." My words were beginning to slur, but I knew it didn't matter. Grace could understand everything I needed to say.

"I'm weak," I said, finally. "Kith won't tell me, but I know he thinks I am. How could he not? He's been providing for us both this whole time. He knows he has to take care of me because he knows how weak I am. He…"

Suddenly, I could hear Grace's voice. A small part of me knew how insane it was, but I stopped everything and looked down at the doll I held in my arms.

"You are the bravest girl I know, little dove." I had forgotten that she used to call me that. Grace loved birds so much, that I remember feeling honored.

"I can't do anything without Kith!" I said, remembering another time I had said those exact words to her.

"Mara, don't you realize? You and Kith are what give *each other* strength. He depends on you as much as you do on him. There are things that he's better at, sure, but there are things you excel at too, that he could never pull off. Just because there's something you can't do, or something he's better at when you have to try so much harder doesn't make him better than you. You are both brilliant."

Stuck in the memory now, I thought of what was so troubling to me as a young child. There was a move Ducar wanted us to do, that I just couldn't seem to get the hang of. Kith got it right on the first try, and for several of our performances, he had to make up for my mistakes. One night, after the crowd laughed at my attempt, Kith turned his move into a blunder as well to make it look like it was part of the act. He then started doing other moves and messing up here and there. While I knew he was trying to make me feel better, it had the opposite effect. In my mind, I messed up so badly that Kith had to pretend to be bad too, just to make me look better.

After the show, I ran to Grace crying. Her words helped me understand that I had to use my own strengths to my advantage and realize that there were going to be things that took longer for me to do. After that, I stopped trying to do the other moves during our performances and came up with my own way of adding to the show while Kith performed it.

When we weren't performing, I continued to practice and eventually got it right. I remembered how happy I was the first time we performed it together in front of an audience.

Then, a gasp escaped my lips as I realized this memory was from before Ducar changed. The Ducar I remembered would have beat me for my failed attempts, but suddenly I had strange glimpses of him attempting to console me. I remembered a sad, disappointed smile, that he tried to hide behind words that told me it was okay, and I would get it next time. Confusion fell around me as I felt a strange connection to the man who turned our lives into a nightmare for so long.

Pushing away the thoughts of Ducar, I wiped my eyes with my sleeves and stood up. Grace was as right now as she was then. Kith was a better hunter than me. It came more easily to him. But that didn't mean that I couldn't do it.

Remembering his suggestion to thank the animals made me smile. Of course, he knew that I needed my own way.

❋   Kith   ❋

"It's snowing!" Mara was peering out the foggy window

with delight. I wasn't entirely sure why this was such a good thing, but I didn't want to spoil her mood.

"Really?" I asked in what I hoped was an excited tone. Peering out, I saw a blanket of white covering the ground. It must have snowed all night

Mara was halfway through dressing herself to go outside before I realized she must want to play in the snow.

Looking outside once more, I sighed inwardly and began bundling myself up.

"You don't have to come out if you don't want to," Mara said, looking at me sideways while wrapping her feet in cloth. I should have known she could see right through me.

"I want to play with you, Mara!" I said, truthfully.

Mara smiled and stood up all ready to leave. "I'll meet you out there!" she said and dashed out the door.

Forcing myself to get excited, I slowly opened the door and snuck outside. Mara's back was turned, so I took the opportunity to scoop up a small ball of snow. Just as she turned back around, I released the ball and almost hit her square in the face. Luckily, she lifted her hands just in time, and the powdery snow showered down her front.

"KITHIAN!" she exclaimed, half screaming, half laughing.

Before she had a chance to scoop up any snow, I turned and ran back into the cabin, yanking the door closed behind me. I heard a scandalized yell from outside, and then Mara came bursting through the door.

"No fair! You can't start a snowball fight and then come back inside!" Mara's eyes twinkled, and I knew she found my little stunt amusing, even if she wasn't going to admit it.

"How about a truce, then?" I asked, timidly. "Since I won?"

"You cheated!"

Laughing, I snuggled up under the covers and yawned loudly. "Guess I'll just be here, staying warm."

Mara rolled her eyes dramatically and walked back outside. Reluctantly, I got back out of bed and waited a moment before slowly opening the door again.

"Ha!" Mara yelled as she pelted me in the side with a snowball. "Now we can have a truce!" she said, sticking out her tongue.

We both laughed, and I swung my tail forward with a smile. "Truce?" I asked.

"Truce," Mara replied, and shook my tail with her own, laughing.

For a while, we ran around in the snow, making snow angels and looking at the various animal prints. When Mara stooped down and started to roll up some snow, I panicked and gasped, "We have a truce!"

"What?" Mara looked at me in confusion and then giggled. "Oh no, I was just going to make a snowman!"

Joining her in gathering snow, I helped carefully shape it into a ball. Once the area we started in was getting low on snow, we rolled further away, continuing to collect as we went.

"Our circle is a little lopsided," I observed.

We started padding on more snow, in an attempt to make the base more of a circle. Eventually, we managed a rather lumpy ball that was mostly circular and decided that would do.

After we repeated the process twice, making each circle slightly smaller than the last, we stood back to admire our work.

"He needs a face." Mara mused. "What could we use as his eyes?"

Looking at the snowman, I wondered what would make a good set of eyes. At first, I thought of rocks, but we would have to dig around looking for two that were roughly the same size. "Oh. What about some of the buttons that were in that sewing kit?"

Mara's eyes brightened. "That's a great idea!" She ran back toward the cabin, and returned a few minutes later with two black buttons.

We ended up having to scrape small holes out of the snowman's face to get the buttons to stay in place, but managed.

"Now you get to pick his nose!" I said to Mara, decisively.

Grabbing a long rock, Mara forcefully pushed it into the middle of the snowman's face.

"Huh," I mused. "I thought of rocks first for the eyes, but

didn't think about it for the nose at all."

Mara smiled, "Now what about his mouth?" she asked, sounding troubled.

We both stared at the snowman for a while. "We could break up some sticks and push them in to make the shape of a mouth?" I asked, unsure. Mara shrugged in agreement, and we began breaking sticks into small pieces and making them into the snowman's smile.

Standing back, we admired our creation. "I feel like he's missing something," Mara stared at the snowman, thinking.

"That's because he doesn't have any arms!" I laughed.

Mara shrieked. "How could we forget to give him arms? I'm sorry, Mr. Snowman."

We looked around for some sticks and managed to find two long ones that were similar enough to work as his arms.

"That's better!" Mara exclaimed. "Now, what should we call him?"

"Uh..well Mr. Snowman sounded pretty good to me," I responded, thinking of Mara's earlier words.

Mara burst out laughing. "Mr. Snowman it is!"

I laughed too, "Great! Mr. Snowman can be our new friend for winter. Look, Fluffy is already ready to meet him, too!"

Mara turned to see Fluffy hopping over, looking warily at the snowman. Scooping Fluffy up, Mara snuggled the bunny against her chest. "She is probably cold, we should bring her back inside." she said as she turned on her heel and headed back to the cabin.

"Bye, Mr. Snowman," I said, waving. "See you tomorrow!" I heard Mara giggle ahead of me and smiled.

*   Mara   *

"Kith, is your leg okay?" He had been sitting at the table massaging it for several minutes. "Should I make you some tea?"

"No, it's fine!" The words tumbled out quickly and his leg

dropped to the floor.

I rolled my eyes. "You've been favoring it a lot today. More than you normally do when it's cold."

"I'm okay, Mara, promise." I watched as his face twinged a little when he stood up, but he attempted to walk on the leg like normal anyway.

"You are so ridiculous, I'm making the tea."

Kith stepped over to the only good window and looked outside. "It's snowing pretty hard out there. The sky looks bleak, too. I think a storm might be coming."

"You're not distracting me from making the tea."

"No, Mara look. It looks terrible out there!"

Looking out the window, I saw what he meant. The sky was filled with dark clouds.

I sighed. "I guess that means we won't be going outside today. Maybe it will pass quickly."

As the day went on, I could tell Kith's leg was hurting him more and more. He winced every time he moved. I knew it was bad when he finally broke down and asked me to make the feverfew tea.

"I wonder if it's the storm that's making it hurt so bad," I thought out loud.

"I think it is," Kith's eyes got dark. "It usually gets a little sore during storms, but I think the cold is making it even worse," he moaned as he stretched out his leg and took the cup of hot tea. "I hate winter."

Kith drank his tea with barely any complaint about the taste. I wished it wouldn't bother him so much in the winter. He already got grumpy during the cold, he didn't need another reason to be in a bad mood. Trying to think of something we could do to pass the time, I pulled out some of the games.

"Do you want to play?"

"Actually, I was thinking about taking a nap. I think the tea may be helping, but it made me kind of sleepy too."

A rumble shook the cabin, and I knew the storm had reached us. I heard what sounded like tiny pebbles falling on the roof, and looked at Kith in surprise. "What is that?"

We both walked over to the window and peered outside. The snow was hardening in midair and falling like little pellets onto the ground.

"Still think you can sleep?" I asked.

Kith sighed and sat on the floor beside where I pulled out the toys. He grabbed the extra blanket off the top of the bed and draped it around himself. "Good thing we have a fire. Just looking out there was making me cold."

We played for a few hours while the snow pellets continued to fall on our roof and the sky growled at us. Luckily; since we spent most of our summer outside, the toys we had were a little more enjoyable now that we weren't tired of them. Yet. Kith kept rubbing his leg every now and then and he still winced a bit when he moved, but I could tell there was a difference in his pain level.

After a while, I grabbed the other blanket off the bed and draped it around me too. "Do you think those things are doing damage to the roof?"

Kith looked up, horrified. "If they are, I don't know how we would fix it!" Suddenly, I wished I hadn't said anything.

The storm dragged on all day, and Kith's mood got increasingly worse. I couldn't blame him because of how much pain he was in, but it wasn't fun to deal with. When it got close to time for us to go to bed, I asked if he wanted more tea, fully expecting him to reject the idea.

"Yes, please."

Turning to him, I let my mouth fall wide open in exaggerated shock. "What did you say?"

Kith burst out laughing and stuck his tongue out at me. "It helps, okay?"

"This storm is changing you," I said in a high-pitched, worried voice. "What has happened to my brother?"

It was Kith's turn to roll his eyes. "If you don't want to make the tea, just say so. I can make it myself."

Laughing, I put the water on to heat and sat back down on the floor, just as another rumble sounded in the distance. "It sounds like it's finally getting further away," I said cheerfully.

"Well, it's about time. The rocks stopped falling, too." I hadn't even noticed that one. I looked out the window and saw what looked like a mixture of snow and rain falling. At least it wasn't the snowy rocks anymore. A shiver ran through me and I quickly finished Kith's tea before sitting back down to bundle up in my blanket.

We were both bored with the toys and were just sitting on the floor in silence when I noticed Kith nodding off. "Maybe we should go ahead and go to bed," I said and took one last peek outside. It was still rain-snowing pretty heavily, but the thunder had at least stopped.

✳   Kith   ✳

Scooping the dried food into Fluffy's food dish, Mara seemed to be concentrating hard on keeping her face neutral.

"Is her food running low?"

"No. It's fine. It should last a while." Quickly closing the bag, she gave the bunny her food and turned to wash the breakfast dishes.

"I was thinking I'd go out and check everything, make sure the storm didn't do too much damage. I'll try to find some good plants we can bulk her food up with."

"Are you sure you should be going out? Your leg was pretty bad last night."

"It's feeling better. You can brew up some tea for me if you'd like."

"Alright. Make sure to wear your warm clothes." It came out as a sigh.

"I will. Don't worry." I could tell there was a part of her that wanted to come with me, but she held back. With how bad the storm made me feel, I knew she worried a lot. Even though she seemed to be sleeping every time I woke up throughout the night, I couldn't help but feel she was pretending. I felt guilty for being so moody and making her worry.

Getting everything together didn't take long. Snow tumbled into the cabin as I opened the door. Mara followed me outside to take a look around. My knees were barely above the snow, and the wet cold sent a shock of pain through my leg. This was going to be a miserable outing, and I was glad Mara wasn't coming to see it.

"That tree looks damaged. Do you think we need to do anything about it?" The tree she was pointing to was just a little way out of the clearing. It was leaning at more of an angle than before, and a big strip of bark was gone, the flesh under where it was had a splintery look to it. The snow seemed to weigh heavily on the branches.

"It doesn't look great. If I get back early enough I'll see what I can do. Otherwise, we might have to see about taking care of it tomorrow."

"Alright." She looked uneasy but didn't say anything else.

"It should be fine until at least tomorrow." I headed around the cabin to look at the rest of the clearing before going out into the trees. Everything was covered in deep layers of snow, but I didn't see any serious damage. The roofs on all the buildings looked a little shabby, but I didn't see any holes. Even so, we'd need to work on fixing or replacing them soon. Once I figured out how in the world I was going to do that.

Grabbing the shovel from the shed, I cleared a path to the outhouse before leaving the clearing. Having that path clear would make trips a lot easier, especially on my bad leg.

Finding food for Fluffy wasn't going to be easy. She could eat some of the vegetables we had grown, but she didn't seem to like the jarred ones too much.

Trees and branches were strewn all over the ground in the woods. With how undamaged the clearing was, I didn't expect to see so much chaos in the woods. Not too far from home, I came across a larger tree that was down. It took me only a second to decide to drop down and go under, rather than attempt to climb over with all the snow piled up on top.

My hands on the ground, I shrunk down to ease under it, trying to avoid crawling in the snow while not scraping my back on the bark of the tree. As I started to straighten back up, small green spots caught my eye. The tree caught most of the snow, leaving the area right under it mostly bare.

There were a few bundles of wide-leaf plants that Fluffy liked, which I quickly yanked up. The hard ground offered more resistance than I was expecting, and the stems left my fingers with a sharp pang of pain. I was once again glad for the gloves Mara made.

Each fallen tree I could see was likely covering greens. Looking around, I saw enough large branches and downed trees that I should be able to make it back with a fair amount of food for the fluff ball. Moving further into the woods, I followed the destruction of the storm and filled my packs with all the plant matter I could stuff into them.

As I rose from under the shadow of one particularly large tree, I was greeted by swirls of pink entering the sky. Somehow sunset was beginning. I had been gone all afternoon. Mara must be so concerned.

Guilt swept over me. Securing my packs, I oriented myself toward the cabin and took off running at full speed. Unfortunately, full speed wasn't very fast while running through deep snow with pain shooting through my leg at every step. Still, I refused to stop until I saw the clearing.

"Oof." Mara and I both sprawled on the ground.

"Kithian! I was about to go looking for you." Mara scowled as she stood and brushed herself off. "You were supposed to be back a long time ago."

"I'm sorry, Mara. I managed to find a lot of good food for Fluffy. I got caught up gathering it all and lost track of time." As I pulled myself out of the snow, a wave of exhaustion and pain washed over me.

Mara sighed. "Well, I'm glad you at least found her a lot of food."

As she reached to take one of the packs a loud crackling sound filled the air. We looked up in horror as the leaning tree shook violently and started to fall toward our cabin.

"Fluffy!" Mara screamed and dashed toward the cabin

before I could grab her.

"Don't go in!"

The cracks and groans coming from the tree were so loud I couldn't even tell if she could hear me. The tree dangled dangerously close to the roof before dropping fast, heading straight down toward the cabin Mara was right next to. I stood frozen as time slowed. Mara looked up in terror and raised her hands instinctively to shield her face, but seemed almost as frozen as I was.

My throat closed around my scream. Breathing was impossible. Everything was completely still. For several seconds the tree hovered, blue sparks filling the air around it, then started to straighten back up before rolling and tumbling down to the side, just outside the clearing. A bright blue light flashed as the tree fell, accompanied by a loud shattering boom. Snow and debris flew everywhere as it crashed to the ground, sending out a shockwave that seemed like it must've followed an explosive crash. Birds protested their territory being disturbed, flying around angrily. I'm sure there was a lot of clatter coming from them, but I couldn't hear a thing, my ears ached from the sound the tree caused.

After several minutes, everything went still. Without my hearing, it was eerily calm. Mara's hand grabbed my arm, making me jump. I hadn't even noticed her coming toward me. When my eyes landed on her face, she pointed toward her ears, shaking her head. I shook mine in return. Neither of us could hear.

Somehow we were in the cabin. Mara must have pulled me in. It was familiar and new at the same time. A cup of tea was pushed into my hand, and the exhaustion and pain decided to remind me that they were present in full force. Gulping down the tea, I did my best not to make a face, but that only seemed to worry Mara more. I could tell she was watching me as she emptied my packs and fed Fluffy a big handful of fresh food.

Once the packs were dealt with, a gentle hand lay on my arm. Looking down at her small purple hand, I thought about the way she raised it to protect herself from the falling tree. Had she somehow pushed it away? It was a crazy thought, but it wasn't the first time she seemed to have done something like this. We had experienced so much insanity in our lives. My fingers absently traced the veins in her hands as my mind drifted off.

Mara let me sit like that for several minutes before she grabbed my hand and pointed to the bed. We climbed in and settled down. As Mara's breathing deepened, I noticed my hearing starting to return. With the hope that things would return to normal soon, I allowed myself to drift into the darkness.

*   Mara   *

After the storm, Kith's mood swings became something I had to watch for regularly. His leg seemed like it was in almost constant pain, and I could tell he was trying his best not to let it get to him. It didn't help that my nightmares started coming back. They weren't very bad, but after the third night in a row, I was afraid that with the barrier gone, they were back for good. During the few times I was outside without Kith, I tried desperately to put the barrier back, but I couldn't get as much as a slight glimmer to come out no matter how hard I focused. Looking for something else to occupy both our minds, I suggested we play outside for a while.

The snowman we made was torn apart by the storm. All that was left were two balls of snow stacked on top of each other, covered with craters caused by the rock-like snowfall. His head had fallen off completely, and all that was left was one of his button eyes lying in the snow a few feet away from him. His arms were still intact, at least. We must have dug them in deeply enough for them to stay put.

When I saw how Kith's face fell when he looked at Mr. Snowman, I knew we had to fix him.

"Oh no!" I called. "We have to put him back together!" Kith looked at me in confusion for a second before he understood. His face turned sheepish as he realized I must have seen how sad he was.

Then, as if he decided not to be sad anymore, he smiled.

"Yeah, let's fix him!"

We spent a lot of time taking handfuls of snow and patching up the holes that were made during the storm.

I stepped back to admire our work, "Oh no...I'm not sure if it looks better or worse!" We managed to make the circles incredibly lopsided and lumpy during our patching job.

Kith started laughing, and I couldn't help but join in. "Maybe instead of just patching holes, we should re-cover the whole circle, and" he pointed to the left side of the bottom circle where a huge lump protruded from Mr. Snowman's hip, "we should probably just slice that part off!" We both burst into laughter.

Pulling out his arms for safekeeping, I started trying to tear off the big lump on his body with my fingers, but Kith held up a hand for me to stop, "I have an idea!"

He walked over to the shed and a minute later came back with the shovel. I laughed again as he dug into our snowman, swerving and taking off much more of his hip than was necessary.

Kith yelled out in exasperation and flung himself dramatically backward into the snow.

"I think you made it worse!" I said, looking at our poor snowman. Suddenly, a huge ball of snow hit me square in the back.

"I want to see you do better!" Kith had stood up and was now running away at full speed. I dashed after him, collecting snow in my hands as I went.

My first attempt missed him completely because he jumped up and caught a tree branch, but as he was pulling himself up, I quickly collected a smaller ball of snow and managed to catch him in the arm.

Thinking I could find a better place to hide, I turned and ran back toward the cabin. I did a quick lap around the cabin, hoping this would throw Kith off and then darted into the shed. Outside, Kith started yelling my name in fake menacing tones.

"Oh Mara!" he said in a sing-song voice. "I'm going to get you, Mara!"

The door to the shed opened, and Kith stood there holding the entire chunk of snowman he dug off with the shovel.

I screamed and jumped as he threw it toward my feet. Kith started laughing so hard he was clutching his sides. "You didn't really think I would hit you with such hard-packed snow, did you? That would have hurt!"

Sticking out my tongue, I insisted we get back to work on fixing Mr. Snowman.

"You just don't want to play anymore because I won," Kith said, smirking.

Rolling my eyes, I walked past him back out into the snow. It took us a few hours to get Mr. Snowman back into the right shape, but we managed..mostly. A few more random snowballs were thrown throughout the process, which slowed us down a bit.

Once we finally got the three pieces of Mr. Snowman put back together, we dug his arms back deep into his body and went in search of his other eye.

"I think I found his nose!" Kith yelled after a few minutes. "I can't tell for sure. It looks like it." he said, shrugging while he held up the rock for me to see.

Walking over to him, I grabbed the rock for closer inspection. "It's close enough," I said. "I might have to get him a new eye, I don't see the other one anywhere."

"Poor Mr. Snowman," Kith said in a sad tone. "So young and he's already lost an eye."

Wiping an invisible tear from my eye, I turned to make one last sweep of the area. After another few minutes, we decided it was a lost cause and I got another button from the sewing box.

"You have to take better care of this eye, Mr. Snowman," I chastised him as we dug his eyes into his face. "We only have one more that looks like this one. Next time you're getting a rock!"

Kith laughed and started breaking up more sticks that we could poke into Mr. Snowman's mouth.

When we were finally finished, we both sat down beside the snowman, for a rest.

"Well, Mr. Snowman, are you happy to have your body back?" Kith asked, in a very serious tone.

* Kith *

The screams were familiar, but it had been so long since they interrupted our sleep that they terrified me. I rushed to the bed where Mara lay tossing and turning, her face a mask of terror.

"Mara, wake up!" I pulled her gently into my arms, rocked her, and smoothed her hair until her golden eyes looked fearfully up at me.

"Kith?" She looked confused, almost disoriented. "Where are we?"

Her confusion surprised me. Mara had woken terrified before, but never so lost.

"We are in the cabin, remember?"

"But Ducar..." Her voice trailed off fearfully.

"We haven't seen Ducar in over a year."

"But, he was here. He tied me up. They had a trap laid out for you. I screamed, but they gagged me. They were talking about killing you and taking me back to the show. He kept calling me 'the witch.'"

"It was just a dream, Mara." I found myself wondering if we should leave, but I couldn't stand the idea of leaving our home. We'd been safe here for such a long time, and I didn't see why that would change now.

"My nightmares have always been from memories before. Well. Except..." Her voice trailed off, but I knew where her thoughts were headed. After a moment she shook her head as if to clear it. "What do you think this means?"

"It's probably from where we've been still for so long. Maybe you're just getting nervous."

"What if I'm dreaming of the future?" Her voice shook as she asked the question.

"I don't know if that is possible." My blood chilled at the thought, not just of her having dreams of the future, but of that being our future. Mentally shaking myself, I forced those thoughts away.

"Kith, maybe we should leave. What if we aren't safe here anymore?"

"Do you want to leave?"

"No. I love it here. But are you sure we're safe?"

"It was just a dream, Mara. I haven't seen any sign of Ducar or his men."

She took a deep breath to steady herself. "Alright."

After a couple of minutes, she climbed out of the bed.

"What are you doing?"

"I'm hungry. Going to start some breakfast." With that, she turned and started bustling around the kitchen, putting way more focus into cooking our meal than was needed.

As I watched her, there was so much I wanted to say, but I recognized the clear signals she was giving that she was done talking about it. As she cooked, I headed outside. Her dream showed a future that sounded impossible. We escaped Ducar, didn't we? There had been no sign of him, and no nightmares. We were safe.

Weren't we? Were we? I looked around the clearing. The sky was mostly clear, with just a few fluffy clouds floating by. Everything seemed so peaceful, how could we be in danger?

Deep down, I knew that peaceful surroundings weren't an actual promise of safety. We had witnessed that truth too many times. I wanted so badly for it to be true now, though, even as I knew I should be planning the departure from our home.

*   Mara   *

No matter what Kith said, I couldn't get the dream out of my mind. I was terrified that something bad was coming. It was obvious Kith wasn't as calm as he was trying to be, either. Now and then I caught a glimpse of fear on his face as he stared out the window before he saw me looking and masked it.

Two days after the dream, I was completely stir-crazy and

knew that I had to get out of the cabin and be on my own for a while.

"I need some time outside," I said cautiously, not wanting to hurt his feelings.

Kith looked at me with a puzzled expression that only lasted a second. "What should we do?"

Looking at my feet, I tried to think of the best way to respond, but Kith must have read my mind.

"You want to be alone." He looked a little sad, but I thought it was probably because he knew why I needed space more than the fact that I wanted to be away from him. Still, I was reluctant to respond.

"It's okay, Mara. I have some things to do around here, anyway. Plus, I can watch Fluffy while you go." He hesitated as if deciding whether to say the next part. "Just..be careful, okay?"

Kith helped me pack a snack for my trip, and soon I was walking slowly through the trees, lost in thought.

What could have caused me to see the things I saw? Was it a premonition of some kind? How could it be, those weren't real..were they? Was I somehow seeing the future? It didn't make any sense though. A ball of fire had hit Kith, and Ducar wasn't even standing by the fireplace. Where would it have come from? Ducar can't just make fire out of thin air. Can he?

Now I knew I was crazy. Wondering if a man could conjure up a ball of fire with his bare hands and throw it at someone. It all seemed so real, though. Everything about the dream set me on edge. Even though I knew it was insane, I couldn't shake the fear that enveloped me.

Trudging through the snow, I couldn't stop myself from remembering the horror almost like it was all happening again. When I closed my eyes, I saw Ducar hitting Kith, while I sat helplessly tied up. Crying out, I wrenched my eyes open and stared around at the trees. For one heart-stopping second, everything looked like it was on fire. Then, the image cleared, and I stumbled forward panting.

A large part of me wanted to turn and run back to Kith to make sure he was okay. The image of him hitting the cabin floor was still burning in my eyes, but I knew if I went back now it wouldn't make anything better. It would only make Kith think I couldn't handle myself anymore, even though it was him I was trying to protect.

Slowly lifting one foot after the other, I forced myself to continue walking. "Kith will be okay" I found myself muttering under my breath. Picking up the pace, I continued saying those words every time my mind wanted to go back to the dream.

How could I survive without Kith? What would be the point? Would a hit like that have killed him? He looked so lifeless lying there on the ground.

"STOP IT!" I was breathing as though I'd just run a mile. "Kith...will..be..okay!" I told myself angrily.

"I'll make sure of it." This promise hung in the air as determination filled me. Soon I was lightly jogging, feeling ready to take on anything. This time I would keep Kith safe.

Or so I told myself.

CHAPTER TWENTY-TWO: DECEMBER

✳   Kith   ✳

Silence filled more of our time than usual, laying heavily over the cabin. "Mara?" She jumped at the sound of my voice, her eyes widening for a slight fraction of a second. "Would you like to play with the board and pieces?"

"Sure." She rose in short, jerky movements, so very different from her normal fluidity of motion.

Still, I pretended not to notice all these differences in her mannerisms and how quickly she put her guard up. The one time I tried to bring it up she snapped at me and was gone the whole day.

It wasn't so different for me, but I also refused to acknowledge how fearful I had become. Sleep did not come easy, however, and I spent many of the past few nights on guard, waiting for something sinister.

Pieces danced around the board in pretend merriment. "You've moved that same piece four times in a row now." Mara's eyes were filled with a mix of emotions as she looked at me accusingly.

"Oh. I guess I did." I dropped the piece in my hand and moved to grab another. We changed the rules of this game often, and I couldn't quite remember which rules we were playing by, but I could feel her eyes digging into me.

"Kith."

Her whisper was so soft I almost didn't hear it, and she was quiet for a length of time afterward like she was deciding whether or not to continue. "Yes?"

"Do you, do you really think we're still safe here?"

Pain shot through me, deep to my core. In truth, I wasn't sure we were safe, but I didn't want to panic her. "I haven't seen any signs otherwise."

There seemed to be something extremely interesting going on on the floor, and whatever it was, she couldn't take her eyes off it. "Me neither. I wish I could forget that dream."

"I know." Thousands of thoughts rushed through my mind, but nothing seemed suitable to say to her at that moment.

"I'm going to go to bed."

It was barely dark out. Usually, we would stay up much later, but she seemed so drained, that I decided it would be best not to argue. "Alright. I'm going to go outside for a bit, but I won't leave the clearing. Promise"

The night was cool and inviting, the kind of night that typically creates a sense of calm and rightness in the world. My feet led me to the barn, its hulking shadowy interior calling to me, even as it terrified me. Boxes lined the wall still, filled with extra stuff we hadn't needed to bring into the cabin.

Extra. There was a point in our lives when the word extra felt like fantasy, but we were living it here. Living the fantasy, and it had to end. Mara's nightmare was unlike anything we had experienced, but I knew that it meant we weren't safe anymore. I'm not sure how I knew, but I did, with a positivity I couldn't ignore.

As I sat pondering what clues her nightmare hid, I felt as if puzzle pieces were drifting together in my mind. Flashes of Mara's bad nightmares, followed by Ducar finding us, or getting close, shortly after ran through my mind. It seemed so obvious as I recalled all the times it happened. That time she had her really bad nightmare when we were at Isaac's. Didn't we see Ducar only a short time later? We thought we were safe, but then she had that nightmare and suddenly he was there. How did we miss something this big?

My stomach retched and my heart shattered as I realized we definitely needed to leave. How would I tell Mara?

Running this time would take some planning and some care. I wished, again, that I had a destination I could plan for, but there was nothing. We'd be going back to running randomly, hoping to find towns and avoid capture.

I sat on a nearby box and sighed. We had so many plans for this place, and put in so much hard work. Saying goodbye was going to be one of the hardest things we'd have to do. Hiding my plans from Mara seemed to be the worst and the best way to go about it.

As the darkness closed in around me, I turned and opened the box I was sitting on. The packs I started weaving from bark rope lay inside. I couldn't pack things in our bags without making Mara suspicious, and these seemed to be a suitable replacement. We might even be able to find a way to bring all of them if we were careful.

The weaving pattern had taken some time to figure out, but I worked on it so much that as I sat in the dark, I didn't even need to look down as my fingers moved. Weaving our packs was the only thing to help me relax over the past few days. Collecting and cleaning the strips of bark was time-consuming, but I made decent progress.

My hands were raw and sore by the time I decided to try to sleep. Even as I thought of what I needed to do to prepare for us to depart, I hoped things would return to normal soon.

*   Mara   *

When I looked up from my sewing, I noticed Kith staring out our one good window like he was waiting for something. He always tried to pretend my nightmare didn't bother him, but I knew better than that.

Deciding to attempt to brighten the mood, I called "I'm almost done with all of our extra clothes!" and instantly regretted it when I saw how Kith jumped.

He turned to me and smiled almost too wide. Trying to return the smile, I held up a pair of pants that was the last thing on my list of things to sew. We decided that having two whole outfits each would be nice for when we needed to do laundry. Our old clothes were small and torn up enough that they were slowly set aside each time a replacement was made.

It was a satisfying feeling each time we got to set aside an old article of clothing for a new one.

Before the nightmare, we were both so happy about our new clothes. Now it just seemed inconsequential.

"That's great!" Kith took the pants and examined their seams. "Wow, Mara, you've gotten really good at this! Your stitches are perfect!"

Looking at the pants in his hand, I could have pointed to a million places where they were not so perfect. "I don't know about perfect, but I am getting better at least," I said, grateful for the compliment. Kith's excitement at the whole situation was obviously forced, but I knew he meant what he was saying.

He was still examining the pants when his face suddenly turned sour.

"What's wrong? Did you decide they aren't so perfect after all?" I joked, trying again to lighten the mood.

Kith started and looked at me. "Oh. I'm sorry, Mara, I was just thinking these look so good, I bet you could sell them!"

My eyes scrunched together as I glared at my brother. "But?" I asked pointedly.

Kith sighed. "But...I don't know how you would get anyone to look at what you made. No one would ever want to buy something from either of us."

He was right, of course. No one would buy clothes from the purple freak. "That doesn't matter," I said slowly, ignoring Kith's skepticism. "We don't need anyone to buy things from us when we don't need to buy things ourselves." I pushed down the thoughts of my nightmare, and forced a smile that I hoped looked sincere. "We have everything we need right here."

Kith was suddenly unable to look me in the eye, and I got the feeling he was hiding something.

"I'm going to go check some of the traps," he mumbled as he headed for the door.

Wanting a break from sitting inside, I stood up and started putting away my sewing. "I'll come with you."

Kith's dark face turned into a half smile. "That would be great. You can check the traps out back, and I'll get the ones in the front. We'll be done in no time!"

"Bet I can finish before you!" I chimed and darted off in the direction of the first trap.

Kith yelled, "You cheated!" before hurrying to check his traps.

As I ran, I couldn't help but laugh. We were two kids making a game out of checking traps for dead animals that we could eat. If only life could always be this way.

After seeing that the first few traps were empty, I began to lose my momentum. When I realized I couldn't remember where two of the traps were, I slowed to a walk, almost losing interest completely. I wandered around for a while only half paying attention to what I was looking for. My mind returned to the nightmare, and I was trying to keep myself from running to find Kith. *He's okay,* I kept telling myself.

After about an hour, I heard Kith calling for me. "Did you get lost?" he asked when I finally came back into view, empty-handed. Guilt washed over me when I noticed the worry on his face. I should have known I wouldn't be the only one who was worried.

"Not exactly," I said sheepishly. "I just lost some of the traps."

Kith laughed half-heartedly and held up his empty hands. "Well, it looks like neither of us was successful. But at least I won," he grinned.

✳   Kith   ✳

Once more the night was torn with screams; screams that shook me to the core. Usually, it was at least the middle of the night before the nightmares woke me, but we had only been asleep for a little while. Her screams sounded so much louder than they did in the past, and so much more painful. At first, I thought I was imagining how much worse they sounded since I had gotten used to peaceful nights, but it wasn't long before I discovered that was wrong.

"Mara, wake up!" I tried to soothe her, but the screams continued. I shook her lightly, but she only got louder.

I tried to resist shaking her harder, but it was difficult. Rubbing her arm, I allowed the soothing phrases I normally used to tumble out in hopes she would hear them somehow. Suddenly, pain shot through my face and my head jerked to the side. While focusing on trying to wake her, I failed to notice her arms starting to thrash and strike out, hitting my cheek quite forcefully. Rubbing my face, I resumed my efforts to end the torment.

As the thrashing got worse, I grabbed desperately at her arms and tried to hold them to her sides, but she twisted and turned so strongly it was starting to hurt. If I gripped her tighter, there was a risk of hurting her, so I let her go and laid her down on the bed. Even through all that, she slept. In a fit of fear, I lightly slapped her face to try to shock her awake. Still, she screamed.

Eventually, I gave up. Nothing seemed to help. After pacing the cabin, I lit a fire so that it didn't seem so dark and desolate. Mara's voice began to crack from the strain of screaming, but still, she wailed, with no sign of waking.

Helplessness seized me as I watched the moon move across the sky. Again, I went to her and tried to wake her, to calm her. Still, nothing helped.

"Mara, please wake up." I was shaking; I had never been so frightened. Even when I thought she was dying, there was the solace of her being free from all the torments our lives held. Now, however, it seemed she might be forever trapped in those torments, trapped in her own mind as I was doomed to watch her suffer.

When watching her became too much to handle, I rose again and walked to the fireplace. Her blankets were on the floor, pushed there from all her thrashing. At least the fire was keeping the cabin decently warm, she wouldn't be cold. Then I thought that maybe being cold would wake her. I filled a bowl with water and used it to dab her face, cleaning off the sweat and tears. As I wiped, I could see how shrunken her cheeks looked, and the dark bags that formed under her eyes stood out strongly against her pale purple cheeks.

Finally, Mara started to slow down, and I hoped it meant she was waking up. Instead, it became clear that her body was becoming weaker; her flailing limbs slowed, her breathing grew ragged, and her voice was strained to little more than a whisper. My hand hovered above her cheeks with the cloth. Surely it was my imagination, but they looked like they had sunk in even more since I started. Heaviness gripped me as I realized if she didn't regain consciousness soon, she likely never would. I had to wake her quickly, or I might not get her back.

"Mara! I need you to wake up. I love you, Mara. Come back to me." I held her and shook her gently. Images of her dying from illness flashed through my mind. That heat that had moved through me, was that what brought her back? Searching deep, I focused all my strength on the memory of that heat.

For several seconds, I felt a warmth building in my arms, but it flickered away again. How did I make it happen? Or did I do it at all? Maybe I imagined the heat.

"Kith?" With my focus, I barely heard her tiny, whispering voice.

"I'm here, Mara." Had the warmth actually worked? It didn't matter, I didn't have time to dwell on that. Mara's breathing was raspy, so I rose from under her and grabbed some clean water. She drank as if she hadn't in weeks. "Small sips. You don't want to make yourself sick." After she handed me back the cup, I finally asked, "What happened?"

"Everything."

"What do you mean?" My voice shook as I asked, but I was afraid I already knew the answer.

"All the beatings, all the terrible things he did." She began to cry. "Everything. I relived it all. I feel it all. I hurt so much." She wrapped her arms around herself, and I could see how weak she had become.

"I'll get you some tea. It'll help you feel better so you can sleep."

"I'm scared to sleep. What if the dreams come back?"

"I'm here, Mara. You need to get some sleep. I'll grab you some food, and then you sleep, alright?"

"Alright." I laid her back down and went to make her some tea. As I brought her cup, it was hard not to relish the fact that I was the one bringing the tea, not the one drinking it.

*   Mara   *

The first thing I saw when I woke up was Kith's frantic face inches from mine. His cheeks looked wet, and his eyes were red and splotchy. I tried to sit up, but my entire body ached, and I was drenched in sweat.

Suddenly, Kith was hugging me and saying something I couldn't understand. Everything sounded so far away like I was still dreaming. A shiver ran through me as I thought about the night I just had. Kith pulled away and looked at me again, his face etched with worry.

"Mara?" He asked. His words were getting clearer.

Looking at my brother, I couldn't think of anything to say. It was like my mind had been emptied. When he asked me questions, I answered automatically without really knowing what I was saying. I was in so much pain.

When I moved, I winced from the pain and closed my eyes. Kith mumbled something about tea, and then I was alone on the bed.

A face popped into my mind, and I almost screamed. Ducar sneered at me and raised his hand as if for one more beating. My eyes flew open to see Kith busy at the stove. Looking around the cabin, I finally let it sink in that everything I experienced that night was a dream. It was hard to understand though, since everything in the dream was something that happened before.

Every beating Ducar ever gave me had been flashed before me in order. Another shiver shook my body as I thought about each incident. I could feel the pain through my whole body as if it all just happened to me.

The light in the room told me it was late morning. Did my nightmare last all night? Judging from the look on Kith's face when I finally woke up, he must have been trying to wake me for ages.

Without me noticing he moved at all, Kith was by my side handing me a cup. Gingerly, I took a sip of the scalding tea. I must have made a face because Kith smiled knowingly at me.

When I reached out to set the tea on the floor, Kith blocked me with his arm. "Drink your tea, Dezmara!"

Shock ran through me at the name. Kith rarely called me that. Staring at him, I felt my eyes begin to water. Kith moved beside me on the bed and wrapped an arm around my shoulders as I slowly sipped some more tea.

Blinking hard to let loose the water pooling in my eyes, I finally brought myself to tell Kith about the string of nightmares I just had. I decided to skip going into a lot of detail, as I felt it would just make the memories worse.

"It almost feels like it really happened," I whimpered when I finished. "My whole body hurts."

Kith, who was quiet throughout my entire explanation, finally said softly. "You were thrashing all night. It can't have been easy on your muscles. I tried to calm you down, but you kept swinging your arms and legs. Eventually, I had to give you space. I tried holding you still, but I was afraid you were going to hurt yourself."

For the first time, I noticed how ragged Kith looked. His eyes were bloodshot with bags underneath, and it looked like a bruise was forming on his left cheek. He looked like he hadn't slept in days.

Touching his cheek softly, I asked, "I hit you, didn't I?"

Kith's eyes went to the floor, "I'm just glad you're okay. I was starting to wonder if you would ever wake up. It was terrifying to see you like that. I mean, I was right here, but I still couldn't help you. Every time he hurt you, I couldn't help you, and now I still couldn't even though he wasn't even here!" His voice broke, and I could tell he was holding back tears of his own.

Trying to imagine what the night was like for Kith was heartbreaking. I didn't know what I would do if the roles were reversed and I was forced to watch him struggle like that all night.

"Please drink your tea, Dezmara," he said, using the name again. "It really helps. Besides, it's only fair that I get to make you drink it occasionally."

We both laughed at that, and I slowly continued with my tea. I fully understood why Kith hated drinking it. It really didn't taste good. Once I finished, I lay back down, exhausted.

Kith looked worried, and I knew he was wondering if I would have more nightmares. Somehow I knew I wouldn't, though. I already went through everything. There was nothing left. Ducar was done, and now I could sleep.

✳   Kith   ✳

With my realization about the nightmares' connections to Ducar, I knew this meant we needed to get going soon. We shouldn't have delayed it. Now we'd be moving with Mara needing to recover instead of us both strong and healthy.

Some tasks still needed to be taken care of before we headed out, though. Refilling our water and gathering as much wild food as I could were the most immediate. Luckily, I managed to finish our new packs and set the extra coats and some of our dried meat in them. More food could be grabbed from the barn when it was time to go.

Mara gained some of her strength back after finally getting some real sleep, but her recovery was going to take time. I was torn between being glad Mara could recover in the cabin and feeling like we should have left earlier. On the one hand, I was glad that Mara wasn't out in the wild in the state she was in now. On the other, maybe the all-night nightmare wouldn't have happened if we were gone.

Heading out early in the morning, I hoped I would be done by afternoon. When I checked the traps, I wasn't surprised I didn't find anything. With us being stuck in the cabin, I checked them regularly just to have something to do.

Snow had fallen deeply the night before, so I climbed a tree to avoid walking through it. Climbing along through the low branches of trees, I made sure to pay attention and keep an eye out for any sign of movement. Hunting wasn't my goal, but I would be a fool to ignore an animal if it happened to come close.

Jumping from the lowest branch, I began filling each of our water skins before starting on the bucket. Not for the first time, I was grateful for the gloves Mara made for me. Normally by now, my hands would be so cold, I would have to build a fire so they could function.

It always took several trips to fill the barrel. When I reached the stream the third time, my stomach growled loudly as hunger pangs hit. Pulling out the food Mara packed for me, I ate my lunch before refilling the bucket. The full water supply added too much to my burden for me to take the trees, so I had to trudge through the snow for each return trip. I was almost halfway home when my foot hit a large root. Pain shot up my leg and I fell, the bucket landing on the ground next to me. All the water was gone.

Once the pain subsided, I turned back toward the stream, cursing my clumsiness. This time, I walked back even slower than before due to pain and fear of falling again. Even though the barrel wouldn't be full, I decided this would have to be my last trip for the day. Our water skins were the main thing that mattered, anyway.

As I got closer to the clearing, I realized that it was getting dark. Thinking there was no way I was gone so long, I looked up and noticed that a storm seemed to be rolling in. Picking up my pace, I hoped I could make it back before it started.

The temperature began steadily dropping as I clambered back toward the cabin. By the time I was in the trees at the edge of our clearing, I was frozen. There was smoke coming from the chimney and it looked warm and inviting, so why was my body trembling uncontrollably? The warning signals in my head were sounding.

That was when I saw the blood trailing away from the trap

nearest to me.

That wasn't there earlier.

My heart was pounding in my ears as I dropped all the supplies except my spear and slowly went to investigate the other traps.

There was a pit trap near me that I went to first. It was empty. Unsure what to think of this, I continued to a stake trap. There was blood. Blood and cloth. A person had been cut on this.

When I checked the next pit trap, I found the mangled body of a familiar man. It was one of Ducar's minions. Looking down at the man stuck in the trap, my blood ran cold.

It took all of my willpower not to scream. Slowly creeping up to the cabin, I looked inside the window.

Mara was sitting at the table, tied down and gagged. Cuts covered her arms and her face was bruised. Agony pierced me as I wondered how long she had been like that.

Then, I heard Ducar's voice. Fear filled me as I backed away from the window, trying to control my breathing.

Knowing I must save Mara, I crept back to the window for a closer look. Mara's eyes rose to my face, but she gave no sign of seeing me other than that. Scanning the cabin, I saw two men by the door and another two by the fireplace. Only one man guarded the window I was at. Ducar was still out of sight.

As my eyes lingered on Mara, my fear turned to anger. Anger at myself for not getting us out of the cabin when I should have, and anger at Ducar for everything he had done. I tried to think of a plan, but I couldn't get my thoughts to clear.

After moving away from the window, I sat in the snow for a minute and looked around.
My eyes fell on the spike that snagged one of the minions. I knew what to do.

When I returned to the window, I held two spikes in my hands like spears. I knew that would be all I had time for before it came down to using my actual spear.

Before stepping back up to the window, I grabbed a large rock and threw it as hard as I could. The window shattered, sending glass everywhere. Without stopping to look at the shards of glass that pierced my skin, I took careful aim with the first spike. The man closest to the fireplace crumpled in a heap with the spike through his stomach. There were yells inside as the rest of the men realized what happened and came for me. I quickly threw the other spike, but this time it only grazed the man's arm before landing in the fire.

Grabbing my spear, I slammed the end of it into the head of the man next to the window as he reached for me. As I landed on the floor, I kept low and swept the side of my spear into the knee of the closest man. When he fell next to me, I finished him off with a blow that went right through his head.

The men were getting smarter and started trying to attack me from a distance. A knife grazed my side, and I stifled the yell that threatened to rip from my throat. Picking up the knife, I returned it to the sender, burying it in his chest. Only one minion remained. As I approached, he panicked and ran out the door. I didn't stop him.

I still didn't see Ducar, so I rushed to the table and began untying Mara. She fell into my arms.

"I'm so sorry, Mara. I should have gotten us out of here a long time ago."

"Kith!" Mara screamed, but it was too late. Ducar came out of nowhere and smashed something on the back of my head. While I was dazed, he grabbed Mara. I heard something about her being the only one he needed as he headed for the door with her. Climbing to my feet, I tried to follow, but Ducar flicked his wrist and a bolt of heat exploded against my chest.

Everything went black.

*   Mara   *

Ducar dragged me, kicking and screaming, out of the cabin. A raging panic coursed through me, as I tried everything to get away. Teeth meeting flesh, I bit down hard, the taste of blood filling my mouth. There was a curse as Ducar flung me down.

Before I could get up, he was forcing a rag into my mouth, screaming something at me.

I could hear men's voices all around, but everything sounded so far away. Ducar smacked the side of my head and kept yelling, spit flying from his mouth. Looking down, I saw a chunk of his left hand hanging loose where I bit him. Ready to take advantage of his pain, I lunged at him, but someone grabbed me from behind.

My body continued to thrash as I watched a tall slender man bandage Ducar's hand. Trying to take advantage of the distraction, I landed a kick to my captor's shin and then slammed my head backward into his chest, hoping to dislodge the arms that held me.

"Feisty little monster!" The man said loudly as his grip on me loosened, and I heard someone laugh.

Another man with scraggly brown hair and a jagged face grabbed me and suddenly ropes were being wrapped around my arms and legs. Punching and kicking any direction my arms and legs would go, I tried to keep them from tying me up. Before long, four men were looking down on me; two holding me still while the others tied the knots.

Once I was tied up, a stocky man with red hair picked me up and slung me over his shoulder. I continued to wiggle as much as I could, but it was no use. For almost an hour, he walked with me slung across his shoulder, trying to wiggle my way out of his arms before I finally hung limp.

The man tightened his grip as if he expected me to make a sudden break for it, but I already knew there was no point. Despair washed over me as I finally allowed myself a breath to think about what happened.

Why didn't we leave? I thought to myself. *I should have forced him to go. I was supposed to make sure the nightmare didn't come true. I was supposed to protect him! This is all my fault...*

Suddenly, I got an idea. Kith and I could sense each other. It was always there, like a part of us that we didn't quite understand. It was how we always managed to find each other. All I had to do was call out to him, and he would come and find me.

Closing my eyes tight, I thought of Kith. I called to him in my mind, expecting to feel his presence somewhere nearby, but all I found was a vast emptiness where Kith was supposed to be. It was like losing one of my basic senses.

Squeezing my eyes tighter, I focused all the energy I had left on finding Kith. He had to be out there. I was sure he would be on his way to finding me by now.

Nothing.

Dread filled my mind as I thought about Kith lying limp on the cabin floor. His wound was bad, but could it kill him? *NO!* I told myself he couldn't be dead. Kith was a survivor and he would make it through this. One last time I called out to him. This time I tried to yell his name around the dirty rag in my mouth. I waited for ages, pleading.

Nothing...

TO BE CONTINUED....